HIGH BLOODS

BY JOHN FARRIS FROM TOM DOHERTY ASSOCIATES

All Heads Turn When the Hunt Goes By
Avenging Fury
The Axeman Cometh
The Captors
Catacombs
Dragonfly
Fiends
The Fury
The Fury and the Power
The Fury and the Terror
High Bloods
King Windom
Minotaur
Nightfall
Phantom Nights
Sacrifice
Scare Tactics
Sharp Practice
Shatter
Solar Eclipse
Son of the Endless Night
Soon She Will Be Gone
The Uninvited
When Michael Calls
Wildwood
You Don't Scare Me

JOHN FARRIS

HIGH BLOODS

A TOM DOHERTY ASSOCIATES BOOK

NEW YORK

OCT 2 8 2009

416 3685

This is a work of fiction. All of the characters, organizations, and events portrayed in this novel are either products of the author's imagination or are used fictitiously.

HIGH BLOODS

Copyright © 2009 by Penny Dreadful Ltd.

All rights reserved.

A Tor Book
Published by Tom Doherty Associates, LLC
175 Fifth Avenue
New York, NY 10010

www.tor-forge.com

Tor® is a registered trademark of Tom Doherty Associates, LLC.

Library of Congress Cataloging-in-Publication Data

Farris, John.
High bloods / John Farris.—1st ed.
p. cm.
"A Tom Doherty Associates book."
ISBN-13: 978-0-312-86696-9
ISBN-10: 0-312-86696-8
1. Werewolves—Fiction. 2. Hollywood (Los Angeles, Calif.)—Fiction. I. Title.
PS3556.A777H54 2009
813'.54—dc22

2009012921

First Edition: July 2009

Printed in the United States of America

0 9 8 7 6 5 4 3 2 1

High Bloods is fondly dedicated
to the many authors of the Good
Old Stuff who were published
by Gold Medal Books during the
fifties and early sixties, from
Edward S. Aarons to Harry Whittington.
I learned a lot from you guys.

And a special nod of thanks to
Steve Brackeen for putting me
through college.

THANKS TO:

Mr. Jimmy Webb of the clothing emporium Trash and Vaudeville in New York City for the line "I'm bewildered by life . . ." (quoted in *The New Yorker*, March 26, 2007), which I've given to Beatrice on page 97. And also for Mr. Webb's observation about rock 'n' roll, which is on page 95 (ibid).

The actress Kirsten Dunst for her comment on her strict requirements in matters romantic, which was quoted in *Us Weekly* magazine, I forgot which issue. I've given Miss Dunst's self-appraisal in slightly altered form to Chiclyn Hickey on p. 68.

Eric Hansen for information about Borneo that I found in his excellent memoir *Stranger in the Forest* (Houghton Mifflin, 1988).

And Peter John for tirelessly committing all of my manuscripts to hard disc for the convenience of everyone else in the book and magic-lantern business.

J. F.

In nature there are neither rewards nor punishments—there are only consequences.

—Robert G. Ingersoll

He who makes a beast of himself gets rid of the pain of being a man.

—Samuel Johnson

1

There were at least four upscale Lycan hangouts within a quarter mile of one another on Santa Monica Boulevard east of the Doheny gateway to Beverly Hills. We left the department Hummer on the center divider with the light bar winking and the no-touch repel charge on high. My partner Sunny Chagrin took the south side of Santa Monica. I took the other side, making my way around the usual debris, human and otherwise.

De Sade's always had a crowd waiting outside behind a velvet rope, advertising how popular and hard to get into the place was. Twin doorkeeps dressed in this year's big fashion statement, the Kansas farm-boy look, glanced at the gold shield on my belt and said nothing as I walked past them and opened the brass-bound leather door.

Inside the music came at me like turbocharged thunder. I winced and reached for my noise-canceling whisper tits. At one-fifteen on a Monday morning, Observance minus five, de Sade's was packed with their typical crowd: hot young media stars or the merely hopeful. Diamondbacker royalty and retro Hip-Hoppers in air-conditioned greatcoats, surrounded by street muscle and sweet sweet chocolate. Raptors of both sexes trying to act twenty years younger than they were. Yesteryear's big celebs who were back numbers now, all of them with the Malibu gloss that gave them an unreal digitally enhanced look. Maybe half the crowd were High Bloods, mingling with, hitting on Lycans, hoping for the sexual Nirvana such risky liasons promised. Or so the legends had it.

I was there looking for a postdeb named Mal Scarlett. The family was old rich, impeccable bloodlines except for Mal. She had been out of reach for nearly forty-eight hours, according to WEIR. Either Mal's Snitch had malfunctioned (a rare occurrence) and she didn't know it, or some illegal surgery had been performed. It was getting to be quite a thing with members of her set: rich kids with tenuous family ties, wanderlust, and no social consciences. If it was a fad it was a dangerous one.

Most people who go missing have patterns. Nine out of ten missing persons turn up within four miles of their homes, dead or alive. The tough cases involve those individuals who are instinctively distrustful, secretive loners—wanderers by habit or by nature. A good description of the rogue population of werewolves, which was already too big to manage effectively.

I was installing the second of my earbuds when a tall girl bumped into me, turned for a look. She gave me a bold, sparkly smile. She was blond, with a narrow, pretty face, an uppity nose. Her glam was Jazz Age: the beaded flapper dress, marcelled hair. She also was wearing one of the gold crosses combined with a wolf's head—an emblem of Lycan spirituality we were seeing a lot of lately.

She leaned on me, still smiling, and winked hello.

"I'm Chiclyn," she said in a broad Aussie accent. "Chickie Hickey."

"I'm Ducky Daddles," I said. "Is the sky falling?"

She brushed damp hair off her forehead and peered at me, an insolent glint of eyetooth in her crooked smile, mischief in her violet eyes. She'd been doing Frenzies or Black Dahls, but not for a while.

"I think I'm falling for *you*, Ducks."

I had to get a grip on Chickie, or she would've been at my feet. It was verging on heat wave in de Sade's and she was slippery as goldfish.

A couple of de Sade's scuffs may have decided I was cutting her out of the flock. They moved in on either side of us, smiling politely. That popular farm-boy look again: yellow coveralls, clodhoppers, neckerchiefs knotted at the side of the throat.

"She's maybe a tad young for you, Dads," one of the scuffs said.

I'd been silver-haired since my mid-thirties. He took a light grip on my upper-right bicep, and looked surprised. Power lifting is just one way I stay in shape.

None of them seemed to have noticed my ILC shield.

"Blow ahf!" Chickie sneered at them. She had locked both hands on my left forearm. Her fingers contained a Levantine's collection of baroque rings. "I choose my own company!"

"So do I," I said, with an inoffensive smile.

The scuff thought this over, then dropped his hand.

"Looking good for your age," he said. "Where do you train?"

"Home gym. Is Artie around tonight?"

"Who's asking?"

"Rawson. Lycan control."

With that Chickie was out of there, almost: I caught a wrist.

"We were having such a good time," I said.

"Piss in your face, Wolfer!" She tugged hard to free herself. I felt her terror as if I were holding a live wire.

I voiced "L-Scan" to my wristpac and her data came up. Legal name, full signal, full reservoir. I was surprised that she had one of the new, injectable LUMOs that WEIR had been testing.

Touching the girl's humid skin I felt a rush, the flash-contagion of her avid sexuality. And, deep in that part of the brain (the angular gyrus) where the ghosts of intuition live, I was receiving signals that prompted a different glandular reaction. A mystery took creaturely shape.

"I'd like to talk to you after I visit with Artie," I said.

"What for?" she said sullenly.

I stared at her. "I'll think of something, cutie."

She didn't try running again. She squared her shoulders and looked me defiantly in the eye.

"Meanwhile you can do me a favor by asking around for Mal Scarlett. Have you seen her tonight?"

"No. I don't even know her. Not personally." She squinted hostilely. "And I don't do fuck-all for Wolfers!"

"Maybe you'd enjoy a month in San Jack Town for some group therapy in positive attitudes."

She lowered her head, a corner of her mouth tweaking unhappily. I looked at the small ruby eye of the wolf's-head crucifix near the LUMO (for Lunar Module) site. I had a dull sense of foreboding. Religion, no matter how bizarre, meant organization and control.

Chickie looked at me again, more or less acquiescent.

"Good girl," I said. "Now go have your kicks."

She melted into the crowd of Ravers without a backward glance, pausing to adjust her earbud, which just about everybody nowadays called "whisper tit" because of the shape and size. Due to the noise level she manually accessed a number on her designer wristpac.

I was left with her spoor, the faint chemical traces of the girl's skin cells sloughed by the hand with which I'd been holding her. They had nearly the same effect on my nose as a gun fired off next to my ear would affect my hearing.

Someone who was having too much fun let out a series of wolf howls. He wasn't a good mimic. In some jurisdictions, like the Hills of Beverly, it's a misdemeanor, punishable by a few days' hard labor on the walls around the richest of all city-states.

In a place as liberal as de Sade's, it was just a forlorn way of denying a national malaise, the dark night of the popular soul.

There was some laughter, which got him going again. But enough was enough: one of the scuffs took off to find the yipper and put him on the street.

I looked at the other scuff. "Let's go see Artie."

Arthur Excalibur Enterprises occupied the third floor of the building he owned and which also housed de Sade's. The second floor, presumably, was packed solid with soundproofing. Except for occasional vibrations as if from weak earthquakes, nothing betrayed the presence of the club below.

I was announced; subsequently sixteen minutes went out of my life forever, with no music, laughter, good jokes, or the company of loved ones to ease their passing. I checked in with my partner Sunny, who had nothing useful to report about the social gadabout Mal Scarlett.

Then the door to Artie's inner sanctum was opened. One of his girls—tall, a glossy chestnut-brown color, and with a long elegant neck—beckoned to me. She was dressed like Peter Pan: couture tunic, unitard, half boots. Her name, I recalled, was Beatrice.

I followed her inside.

Artie was pacing around on a beautiful Savonnerie carpet, talking on his retro cell phone. He gestured to a lounge chair and winked at me. I hadn't thought he could manage that, considering the shape his eyes were in. Artie was an educated man with a jones for fine art. He collected paintings by Bosch, Bacon, Dali. He also had pursued a life in the ring long past the point where it would have been sensible not to answer the bell. Never going anywhere with it, except to various hospitals for stitches and X-rays. He fought a few names, but for most of his career he was just hamburger on some hack promoter's menu.

A poorly screened transfusion in a tank town infirmary gave Artie Lycanthropy, or LC disease. There are those, it seems, who like being werewolves in spite of the monthly wear and tear and limited life expectancy. Others just live with what, as time goes by and their numbers inexorably increase (one thing is certain: nature had never invented a more ghastly disease by which the majority of mankind paid for the fleeting ecstasy of sex), is less of a stigma, even a social distinction. Particularly among the young with their limited sense of mortality or lack of interest in the future of the human race.

Lycans contributed to the world's economies, or all semblance of civilization would have disappeared following World War II. For putting in a mandatory thirty-two-hour workweek, the Lycans known to ILC, or International Lycan Control, were wards of government everywhere, including the city-state republics that had replaced the centralized governments of North America.

Although lycanthropy is epidemic, for only a small segment of humanity is LC disease quickly fatal. Artie was in that subgroup. His choices, once infected, were to Off-Blood—which is an agonizing process—or go to an early grave. Artie had opted for living. Which meant a complete change of blood twice a year and the ambiguous status of the Off-Bloods.

Unlike those werewolves—about eighty percent of their estimated number—whose activities were monitored and controlled by ILC, Off-Bloods could do business with High Bloods, marry whom they pleased, easily obtain visas for travel outside their official places of residence. They enjoyed citizenship but couldn't hold public office.

And if they had a talent for making money, they could obtain licenses to do business on their own. But not in Beverly Hills, known as "the Privilege," the shining example of what regrouped civilization could aspire to and achieve. Neither Off-Blood nor Lycan was permitted to pass a night in Beverly Hills, unless they were being treated at a private clinic or the UCLA Medical Center. Those who lived in the Privilege and unluckily became infected, like Mal Scarlett, were expelled.

Expelled and frequently despised by High Blood families, lovers, former friends.

Those who had "the blood" made the rules.

Eventually (as my mother liked to say after about a half pint of Boodles, lemon twist) the fate of every culture seemed to come down to "damned if you do, double-damned if you don't." After a fourth martini Pym also was apt to conclude, "I like to think there's an afterlife. But we'll probably screw that one up also."

America had won a long and grueling war in the Pacific. What that war unearthed in a previously little-known, nearly inaccessible region of the Kalimantan then followed both victor and vanquished home—to Japan, Australia, the U.S. Another, even more terrible war began, and after more than eighty years no one could predict an end to it.

But, getting back to Artie, a victim who had made the best of things in a big way:

Arthur Excalibur Enterprises owned Mexican silver mines, real estate on three continents, vineyards in Sonoma, wind turbine farms in the deserts, small but rewarding pieces of casinos. With High Blood partners he was in the movie and music businesses, areas of popular culture dominated by Lycan talent. Because so many Lycans, off-Observance, were beautiful people, with that shadowy, ravishing mystique behind the eyes.

Perversely Artie was also in a business that could have brought heavy sanctions. He employed a stable of elite call girls, ten-thousand-a-night lovelies. Worth every penny to High Bloods who liked living dangerously. Girls guaranteed to be at their erotic best during the time just before an Observance known as the Aura.

It was a business he didn't need, but not within my area of enforcement. Artie claimed that he was in prostitution for the favors to be returned by grateful clients. Like all Lycans and most Off-Bloods, Artie despised High Bloods. Maybe with one exception. He couldn't afford the luxury of having me for an enemy.

In spite of expert makeup Artie wasn't looking well tonight. It was difficult for virologists to keep up with all the mutating viruses that thrived in human blood. Some were so new even advanced screening couldn't detect them.

"Sorry I kept you waiting," Artie said. "New girls from Budapest made the border an hour ago." Artie took a drag on his black cigarillo, exhaling with an expression that might have been bliss on a less-devastated face. "Romany bloods. I have a couple of media kings panting for those honeys already."

"All that time in quarantine must eat into profits," I said.

"Same for government regs and fees. So I use intermediaries in Mexico and skip the red tape. But you know me—all of my girls are Snitched before I expose them to Highs."

Or he wouldn't have been telling me about them. Artie had his back-channel contacts at WEIR. Off-Bloods were seldom bothered by werewolves, for whom they lack charisma or something. But the penalty for introducing an unregulated werewolf into the population was death. No appeal, no exceptions.

We were served refreshments by a Nordic beauty who shone like a polished silver loving cup. She wore de Sade's obligatory chains and leather, a coiled pink cat-o'-nine, boudoir-style, on her wide belt. She was new to me, trying not to react badly to my presence.

"Saw you when you came in," Artie said, glancing at a wall of surveillance screens monitored by two more of his girls. "Interested in somebody, or is this a social call?" He smiled cynically at the notion, then snapped his fingers and said to one of the girls who turned alertly to him, "Put Mr. Rawson up on number three."

So I was treated to a rerun of my encounter with Chickie Hickey after I had walked into de Sade's.

"Know her?" I asked Artie.

"Aussie. Minor roles in three movies. Her agent's Johnny Padre."

"Once she got on to me she was ginky. More than they usually are. I'll probably look her up again before I leave. How often do you see Mal Scarlett in the club?"

"Two, three times a week. Sometimes Mal and her entourage close up the place. They're good for business. You saw the paparazzi outside. Like flies on spoiled meat." He laughed softly, then went on about Mal. "Great body, birdshit for brains. Enough money to paper the Louvre. Guilt money. Mother Ida gave Mal the boot, of course, when she got infected. I don't have to tell you about Ida Grace." Artie sipped his tea, staring at me, a fat mauled lid nearly obscuring his left eye. "Mal's daddy died, didn't he?"

"A bug he picked up in the tropics conked both kidneys."

"The Rawsons live next to the Graces, so you must've known Mal when she was a kid. And her older sister. What was her name?"

"Elena Grace. Half sister."

"Disappeared too, didn't she? Ever learn what happened to her?"

As far as I knew I might have been the last one to see Elena alive. When she begged me to kill her. I was in love with her, so of course I hadn't. But sometimes, in the throes of the bad mean blues, with no clue to Elena's fate, I thought it might have been merciful to do what she'd asked of me.

"I don't think Mal has disappeared," I said. "Probably just holed up somewhere with the rock star du jour. WEIR reported that she went off-line at 0110 hours Friday."

"Off-line?" Artie mused. "Lose many that way?"

"More and more lately, it seems." My turn. "What do you know about the First Church of Lycanthropy?"

Artie cocked his head slightly, as if he might have detected a certain grimness in my question.

"How it got started? Don't know. One thing I can tell you, it's more entrepreneurial than religious."

"Or political?"

"All religion is politics. One way or another."

Beatrice looked up from her laptop and shook her shapely head, sprinkles of stardust in her close-cropped hair glinting at me.

"I've checked all the up-to-the-minute Bleat blogs," she said. "Mal Scarlett, she lay low."

"She'll turn up," Artie predicted. "No technology is perfect, I guess."

I had a hunch there was more Artie could have told me—about Mal, or the First Church of Lycanthropy. An oddball religion so astutely promoted had to be a cover for something else. But Artie always had been a miser with info that might eventually be worth a bundle to him. My resources as an ILC employee were limited.

I got up from the lounge chair to prowl around the office, a converted loft with fifteen-foot ceilings and two skylights. The she-Lycans didn't exactly bristle at my passing, but their tension was evident. Bea, on the other hand, was High Blood: she just grinned at me when I gave her a thank-you pat on one shoulder.

No visit to Artie's would have been complete without a look at the latest of his boojum trees that he couldn't manage to keep alive indoors in spite of compulsive pampering. But maybe that was his problem: too much love for something basically unlovable.

The boojum was a spindly, fuzzy-looking thing in the glow of full-spectrum lights trained on it. In the wild, and fully mature, they grew past fifty feet in height. This one was just getting a good start at ten feet; beneath one of the pyramidal skylights it still had room to grow.

Boojums are found only in Baja California and the Sonoran Desert of Mexico. Which meant that in the wild they survived the harshest imaginable conditions. Lack of water, intense heat, high winds, blistering sandstorms. They seemed to thrive only under the most terrible, destructive conditions nature could devise.

"Still trying, huh?" I said to Artie. I finished my bourbon.

"Yeah. But it's almost impossible to domesticate them. No matter how carefully you tend a boojum, they almost always go sour on you. What do you make of that?"

"They want to be wild," I said.

We looked at each other. Artie smiled sadly with his scar-intaglio'd lips.

"They're going to win, aren't they?" he said, keeping his voice even lower than its usual hoarse level. All those punches to the side of the neck.

He wasn't talking about boojums now.

"I don't have a head for technology," I said. "But where there's a problem there's always a fix."

I found myself looking for Beatrice, and discovered her looking back at me, with a small speculative smile that reminded me of how long it had been since I had wanted the company of any woman, pay-for-play or not.

"Sure," Artie said. "The answer to every desperate need in history has been human ingenuity. That's if time permits. Dysgenic research looks promising—but slow. I have inside information to that effect. While the inhuman race finds itself near a stage that you might call warp-speed Darwinism."

"That's the pessimistic view."

"You probably heard about that small pack of wilding Lycans that sacked a pueblo near Nogales during the last Observance. Now wasn't that interesting."

"What about them?"

"Crissake, you were raised by an anthropologist, Rawson! It's also rumored you have certain . . . preternatural skills that make you the top Wolfer in town. You know *Lupus canae* don't like being by themselves. They're highly sociable creatures. Very sensitive, family oriented. When they're removed from the wild, some of them just . . . pine away without the company of their own kind."

He looked at me, mildly exasperated. I have a graduate degree in wolf biology. But I didn't comment on Artie's little lecture. He'd taken some beatings in his ring days, now lived always on the brink. I would've thought there was no fear left in him.

"Werewolves, on the other hand—solitary. Loners. Hatred for anything warm-blooded. They're killing machines. They'll kill each other for shits and giggles."

"Yeah, I've seen it happen."

"What they don't do is hang out with their kind. Much less participate in pack activities. But it *happened.* Less than a month ago. Would you like another drink to settle your nerves?"

"My nerves are fine, Artie. Have to be going. Time to look up the Aussie and maybe get some religion."

Artie hunched his shoulders a little. He paused before walking away from his beloved boojum tree to snip with his fingernails a tiny bloom from one flowering branch. Whatever load was weighing on him he had shrugged off. He had that near-blissful look on his face again.

That's when the skylight above Artie and the tree exploded, showering glass everywhere. Something huge and smelling like a sack of shit came down feetfirst next to Artie. And with one bite through neckbones and muscle Artie's head wasn't on his shoulders anymore: it was bouncing like a football twenty feet away across the onyx top of his desk while the air around his still-standing body turned red from arterial spray.

2

My threat-reaction time, even to the totally unexpected, is about a third of a second. But, although the deluge of glass surrounding a tawny monster twice the size of a timberwolf was—to put it mildly—bizarre and shocking, some hint of danger in my reptilian brain such as a momentary shadow, a rooftop-prowling Lycan eclipsing the moon above Artie's skylight, had alerted the organism. Not in time to save Artie, because the monster had landed upright on huge paws between us. But I was able to keep from being seriously cut or blinded by flying shards.

I did what the old-time flyboys call a "Mongo Flip" and came down a little off balance, staggerng backward as I pulled my compact .45 from its quick-release holster. As Artie's head finished its trip down his desk and made a streak of red on the nearby wall beneath a horror show of a Francis Bacon painting, I shot three times through a jet of blood from Artie's toppling body, the shots counterpoint to the screams from Artie's girls.

If you're going to drop a werewolf stone-dead you shoot it through the heart or pineal gland. With silvertips. Otherwise you'll just annoy it. I missed the vital spots but the impact of high-velocity silvertips jolted her just long enough to allow me to scramble farther away—but only marginally beyond her leaping distance.

The she-wolf looked at me with rapt eyes that I found vaguely familiar. I hit her again dead center on the breastbone, which may have deflected most of the slug away from her heart. The she-wolf shuddered but didn't fall.

She howled then.

No matter how hardened you believe yourself to be by the terrors of combat or by the experienced hunter's realization that his dangerous prey might now be stalking him, when a werewolf howls, literally in your face, you pee like an infant in its diaper. No matter how many times you may have heard it, how many of them you've managed to kill, you can't help yourself.

Werewolves are half wolf, half human, with powerful jaws. And something a little extra to stupefy the senses: that nauseating fecal odor. But a ghostly imprint of humanness lurks in their hairy faces, particularly around the eyes. If you have to kill or be killed, that startle reaction to the imprint can be distracting for a fatal instant.

I wasn't likely to be distracted, or miss again.

But before I got off the killshot something winked in the air past my head. The blade of a silver throwing knife sliced into the monster a notch below her jaw, cutting off the howl she was raising.

The impact of the knife jolted the she-wolf. Pain flared in her yellow eyes. I sensed her losing interest in killing me, and eased the pressure of my finger on the trigger.

The she-wolf looked up, then leaped straight off the floor and caught the frame of the shattered skylight with one hand.

"Kill her!" Beatrice shouted at me.

But I didn't fire again. The she-wolf pulled herself up through the skylight space and swung out into the moonlight, already struggling and woozy. But she was able to bound away. A string of werewolf blood fell from some jagged glass into the corrupted air of the loft.

I hadn't finished her off for a couple of reasons. One, she had so much silver in her hide she wasn't going to last another hour anyway. And two: if she died before she skinnydipped then she couldn't tell me some things I needed to know, and fast.

"How do I get to the roof?" I yelled at Beatrice.

But she was already running past me, veering from the body of Artie Excalibur that was bleeding out and destroying the value of his rare carpet. Artie had always liked nice things. Probably there were worse places to die, although I would've preferred not to have *my* head thirty feet away, eyes still open and watching it happen.

"Follow me!" Beatrice yelled back.

"Where do you think *you're* going?"

I voiced Sunny Chagrin's ILC call sign on my wristpac.

"That knife cost me five thousand and I want it back!"

I couldn't blame her; the price of silver was now close to four thousand an ounce, in Beverly Hills Free Zone dollars, when you could find any for sale.

Beatrice had given me a little time. Somehow our she-wolf, an undiscriminating killer like all of them, had rationalized her situation and chosen to get the hell out of there. Showing any sort of reasoning ability or discretion was aberrant behavior for werewolves.

Besides silver there are other methods of defense against them, all problematical. Animal tranquilizers or anesthetics sometimes made werewolves a little giddy, but that was all. Wolfsbane temporarily befuddled the youngsters. Essence of wolfsbane in a spray bottle was a useful item, which we all carried in addition to our choice of firepower. But unlike junkyard dogs, werewolves seldom let you know they're around. There are those people who believe in spells, symbols, and incantations to keep werewolves away from the home place. It has been a thriving quack industry for decades.

Sunny answered. "What's up, R?"

"We've got a Hairball on the roof of Excalibur's. Artie has lost his head. The Hairball is toting silver and should be powering down."

"Wha—? A Hairball? Are you fuckin' *serious*?"

"We were nearly nose to nose for a few seconds. I want de Sade's and the immediate neighborhood iso'd. Roll the wagons, but no Zippos. We need remains, not ashes."

I sprinted after Beatrice, who was jumping nimbly up a spiral of iron stairs to the roof. Couldn't fault her for courage. But if the she-wolf still had any fight in her, Beatrice's head could roll too as soon as she set foot on the roof.

I caught up to her and grabbed her by her Peter Pan tunic before she could stick her head out into the night.

"What are you planning to do, take her on bare-handed?"

"Okay, *you* go first."

The building was oblong in shape, with a fire escape to the alley behind it. As soon as I reached the roof in the misty moonlight I heard the monster clattering down the fire escape. Mid-roof there was a trio of TRADs—for Taser Remote Area Denial—on their tripods, but for some reason none were operative. If they had been, the she-wolf would have been bouncing around the intersecting force fields like a shaggy tennis ball.

I pulled Beatrice up after me.

"Did Artie deactivate his TRADs?"

"Don't be ridiculous. Why would he do that?"

We ran to the fire escape just as the she-wolf made it to the alley between a couple of Dumpsters. She paused long enough to look up at us with eyes that shone like isotopes. I aimed my .45 to hobble her, but she was off like a streak. She jumped twelve feet from the alley to a barred window of the four-story apartment building next door, tore the bars out of the concrete, and disappeared headfirst inside, smashing through the window.

"This can't be happening," Beatrice said, licking her lips as if she were about to be sick. "Can it?"

We heard screams from inside the apartment the she-wolf had invaded.

"I guess it can," Beatrice said, still licking, her face momentarily blank from shock. Then she turned her head and threw up violently.

I raised Sunny again. She was breathing as if she were coming our way at a dead run.

"The Hairball's gone to ground," I said. "Montmorency apartments. How far away are you?"

"Block and a half."

"Get the PHASR out of the Humvee. As long as the bitch is alive I want to keep her that way. Sunny, you've got the atrium entrance to the building."

"You haven't explained how—"

"I don't have any answers. Maybe she's just one of Nature's little anomalies."

"We hope and pray. How do you know the Hairball is a she-wolf?"

"Because," I said, "she doesn't have a dick. Swell pair of boobs, though."

"Oh, ha-ha. R?"

"What?"

"Don't go in there after her. Wait for—"

"I'm closest, Sunny. And children may be sleeping in their beds. They don't need a nightmare like this one."

"So be a macho asshole. And good luck."

I went over the parapet to the fire escape and began climbing down. Beatrice finished retching and followed me.

"Go back," I told her.

"If I stop moving I'll shake myself to pieces. I'd rather be with you. Maybe I could help. And I still want my knife."

I wasn't going to get into the condominium the way the she-wolf had managed. The screams had stopped abruptly. But lights were coming on in the building. It was quiet now. Not a good quiet. My closest point of entry was the underground parking garage, locked down behind rolling gates. I headed for it. People were congregating at either end of the alley, attracted by the screams. I heard sirens; they were eight or ten blocks away.

I used my electronic jimmy to decode the key card access lock outside the gates. They parted slowly.

The building's basement garage was a single floor. Two slots per occupant was the norm in a condo like the Montmorency. I went down the ramp with my .45 in hand, Beatrice close behind me, our footfalls echoing. The lighting was barely adequate. The garage looked nearly full, chockablock with expensive sets of wheels, some of them wearing customized dust shrouds.

I took it slow getting to the stairs at the front of the building. Beatrice reached out to touch me a couple of times. Maybe to tell me she had my back, or just to reassure herself.

There was a small elevator next to the stairs. I started up to the lobby level, then heard the elevator's whine. My hair may have gotten a little whiter. I backed down to the basement floor, bumping into Beatrice.

"Stay put," I said. "And don't give me any sass."

In the alley outside, police vehicles screeched to a stop within a few seconds of each other. They would be SoCal Sheriff's deputies; the West Hollywood substation was nearby.

The elevator stopped. The door opened. I drew a bead with the .45.

There she was, overwhelming the small space inside, a foot planted on the crumpled remains of some unlucky soul. His gore dripped from her jaws.

We stared at each other.

Midway in the garage a deputy worked the slide on a shotgun while the other cast his light on our little tableau. The silver hilt of Beatrice's throwing knife gleamed at the base of the she-wolf's throat.

"Keep back!" I warned the uniforms. Not that they were eager or equipped to rush into the fray. To the she-wolf I said, "Be a good girl and don't give me any more trouble."

But her eyes were glazing from trauma as she came limping out of the cabinet-sized elevator toward me. She was bent over and making sounds of distress. Slowly she lifted her head again and tried to glare at me. I heard a ghostly, burbling voice.

"Piss . . . in your face, Wolf . . . er."

She choked then and coughed up a gout of blood. I heard the start-up roar of a powerful engine close by. Talk about ghosts. A gray-shrouded SUV with only a view slit at windshield level on the driver's side burned rubber leaving its space and barreled straight at me.

I had two blinks of an eye to throw myself from its path as Beatrice shouted a warning. I collided with a concrete pillar, left shoulder and the side of my head. I slumped to the floor with my field of vision full of sparklers as the SUV panic-stopped between the she-wolf and me.

The automatic in my hand felt as heavy as an anvil. I could barely lift it. What physical effort I was capable of went into crawling away from the path of the shrouded SUV. From the size of the tires, the shape of it, I figured Navigator or Escalade.

The driver gunned his engine as if he were thinking about making another run at me.

I crawled a little farther behind the pillar. The garage echoed voices. Flashlight beams overlapped on the walls of the garage. I rolled over onto my back like a whale rolling over on the ocean floor. My head throbbed and I tasted blood on my lower lip.

I raised my head but couldn't locate the she-wolf, and every passing second without knowing her whereabouts chilled my blood a degree lower.

There was a scuffle of feet on the side of the SUV away from me. A door slammed shut. Then the SUV burned rubber again. It was instantly pedal-to-the-metal and heading for the exit, taking hits from a couple of Remington police models, which slowed it not at all.

I made it to my knees in time to see the SUV scatter Socal-West sheriff's deps as it drove up the ramp, demolished the back end of a cruiser parked in the alley, and roared away.

Beatrice appeared cautiously from behind another pillar. I looked at the dead guy in the elevator. His head was where it belonged, meaning the she-wolf had only eviscerated him, a next-favorite target of the breed.

But the Hairball was nowhere to be seen.

How the hell?

Beatrice kneeled beside me. She gently wiped my bloody lip with the back of a wrist. Sheriff's deps were everywhere, some of them throwing down on me. The garage reeked of cordite and werewolf.

The confused deputies were yelling at me to put my gun down, as if I were a deranged felon.

"ILC!" I yelled back. "Anybody see where the Hairball went?"

"She's in the SUV," Beatrice said.

I didn't see how she could be. But I took Beatrice at her word and barked at the uniforms, "Get a stop on that SUV!"

All they wanted was for someone to act like he was in charge. I gave them a look at my shield and they backed off respectfully. I tried moving my shoulder. Sore, but the collarbone wasn't broken. Beatrice, grimacing, helped me to my feet.

"Take a look around upstairs," I said to the uniforms. "There could be other victims."

"Or other Hairballs?" one of them said.

"What you saw is not what you think you saw," I told them, the best Official Denial I could come up with on short notice.

"The hell it wasn't," another dep muttered, but none of them seemed too sure. I told them to get moving. They preferred action to uncertainty, and three of them went running up the stairs to the lobby. A fourth deputy looked into the elevator, then placed a coroner call.

"How did the Hairball get into an SUV that was wearing a dust shroud?" I asked Beatrice.

"Some sort of Velcro thing, you know, like a tent flap? On the left side over the rear door. Zip, they were out of the vehicle. They grabbed the—the Hairball and pulled her inside. She didn't resist. She looked half dead. Bloody all over. And she still has my—"

"They? How many?"

"Two big guys. Ninja dress. Black hoods. I couldn't tell you much about—"

"Hey, hero!" Sunny Chagrin called to me. Still sounding out of breath.

I looked around. She was toting the big-ass PHASR (Personnel Halting and Stimulation Response) rifle from our department Humvee. The rifle uses laser beams to cause temporary blindness, even in werewolves.

"Did you get a shot at that SUV?"

"Not a good one. Traveling too fast. I had to hit a foot-long slit in that dust cover that was maybe two inches wide. No time to steady this big bastard." She set it down carefully, muzzle up. "How many dead, R?"

"Other than Artie Excalibur? The vic in the elevator. Could be more bodies upstairs. The Montmorency gets a full thirty-day quarantine, although I don't think she was going to lair in this building." I paused to get my breath, thinking fast. Sunny opened a link with her wristpac to ILC Special Tactics. "All of Artie's building, including de Sade's, is now a crime scene. Detain everybody. But if we're lucky only half a dozen people outside this garage got a look at the Hairball. Chase Soc-w off this one and button it up tight. My authority. Total news blackout, of course."

"We wish," Sunny said, as she finished relaying my instructions to SPECTAC. "Know anything for sure, other than we have a Hairball out-of-phase?"

An out-of-phase Hairball in ILC jargon was an OOPs. Extremely rare but not unheard-of.

"This wasn't a random wilding," I said. "Artie was targeted."

Beatrice drew a sharp breath.

Sunny looked her over. Beatrice had the kind of looks that could give other women jealousy cramps. Or cause their short hairs to grizzle, depending on their sexual orientation. Sunny had been my partner and close friend for five years. She was half Filipino and half Hawaiian, and when it came to looks she didn't need points from any woman. Probably we would have got married long ago but for that matter of sexual orientation: Sunny was acey-deuce.

"This is Beatrice," I said. "Artie's executive assistant. An eyewitness to the killing. I'm taking her into protective custody."

Beatrice flashed me a look I chose to interpret as grateful; Sunny's reaction was a slight, knowing leer.

"You need to go home and change," Sunny said. "Put some ice on that bump."

"Plan to. West Hollywood should already have an APB out on our wanted vehicle. Of coure we don't know the make because of that shroud."

"Which they probably got rid of at the first opportunity."

"Sunny, check the ladies' lounge wastebaskets at de Sade's right away. We're looking for a robin's-egg flapper dress, jewelry, a Tiffany wristpac, a gold mesh swag bag, maybe a wolf's head crucifix."

"You've already ID'd this Lycan?"

"If it's who I'm thinking of we may be in luck. I'll meet you back at the office in a couple of hours."

Sunny looked at Beatrice again.

"Both of us," I said. "Oh, I'll need the Humvee."

"Jesus, R. You stink of werewolf. Among other things." But she tossed me the keys. She also handed Beatrice a half-ounce spray bottle of scent killer.

"I'll air the Humvee out after I clean myself up. Let's go, Beatrice."

There was a trace of envy simmering in Sunny's brown eyes. "Nice meeting you. Beatrice."

Beatrice nodded, expressionless. It wasn't out of rudeness. Her mind was far away.

In the Humvee, after we had cleared the Doheny gateway and entered the city-state of Beverly Hills, expanded years ago to incorporate all of Bel Air north to Mulholland Drive and L.A. west to the Santa Monica line, Beatrice said, "If you're dropping me at my place, I'm on Rexford south of Wilshire." Her tone said, *Please don't.*

"You don't really want to be alone right now."

She shook her head then looked away, at the bright corona of the Privilege: a blitz of casino lights, gold-leafed towers of the world's major financial institutions. The Privilege glittered 24/7 like perpetual Christmas beneath the powerful, sordid smog of the Los Angeles basin, surrounded by its Great Wall. The security the wall provided was enhanced by technology such as acoustic bouncers and heat rays: electromagnetic radiation that caused wall-scaling werewolves to suffer from intense burning sensations. If that didn't discourage them, there were plenty of Zippos at intervals atop the wall capable of throwing hundred-foot gushers of flame.

A few decades ago the sure method of dealing with the plague of werewolves—or almost anything else wearing fur during an Observance—was wholesale slaughter. Flamethrowers were popular. Spike guns, corrosive acids, chain saws. Then it became obvious that the world's population was declining drastically. Innocent people as well as Hairballs were being killed indiscriminately by the overanxious or trigger-happy. Neighbors were wiping out neighbors and, not infrequently, members of their own families.

But it occurred to those who had any common sense left after the initial years of hysteria that human beings afflicted with LC disease were indisposed or unproductive only for brief spells. Just a small percentage were hopelessly addicted to their monthly changes, which, as in the case of binge drinkers, amounted to a two- or three-day blackout.

So billions were poured into Lycanthropy research. Drugs that suppressed the triggering mechanism in the brain at the onset of the full moon were discovered and synthesized from rare specimens of jungle plants. My mom and her colleagues found some of those, and as a result Pym had a Nobel for her work. With the drugs cheaply available, International Lycan Control was established and financed by a consortium of the richest city-states around the world, including the one we were driving through.

ILC had roughly eighty percent of the Lycan population identified and Snitched. Snitches are surgically implanted, satellite-monitored transponders. Active life three years, then they must be replaced. They come with a microcomputer that controls a flow of drugs collectively known as TQs into the bloodstreams of Lycans for the forty-eight-hour period centered around the full moon each month. TQs put all Lycans into a state of twilight sleep after switching off the hairing-up impulse.

There was maintenance involved along with monitoring. The failure rate of Snitchers was less than two percent. The reservoirs had to be refilled six times a year at ILC clinics. Woe to the careless or forgetful Lycan, and the occasional smartass who deliberately ignores his responsibility. But there are always those people who just don't like being told what to do.

Harsher methods exist to deal with that triggering mechanism, but they leave the individual in a permanent vegetative state. Another expense the rest of us don't need. What we do need is the Lycans' cooperation. Because, for one instance, the North American population continues to shrink. It's illegal for Lycans to breed. High Blood women are continually encouraged, through financial incentives and massive doses of PR dupe, to have more children. Booty for High Blood babies. The various programs had all been failures. Women just didn't want to make babies anymore, and who could blame them?

"My mother is about your height," I said to Beatrice. "She's partial to old jeans and colorful native kit, but we'll find something for you to change into."

"Oh, I'm meeting your mother?"

"Not this visit. Last I heard from Pym, she was crossing the Plains of Bah in Sarawak, heading for her favorite rain forest."

"Ah." Beatrice exhaled softly. "Borneo. Where it began. As the legend has it."

"That's what Mom and her team would like to find out for sure."

"She's a biologist?"

"Anthropologist. I didn't catch your last name, Beatrice."

"Harp. Like I could be playing right now if you hadn't paid such a timely call on Artie."

"From where I saw it, you would've done a first-rate job of defending yourself."

Beatrice didn't say anything, only shuddered. She was still holding back a lot of fright and anguish. She began to lick her lips again. I put down the window on her side to let the night air stream in.

"I don't think there's much I'll be able to tell you," she said. "I mean—a motive. And since when do werewolves bear a grudge? Artie lived under the radar anyway. Always careful. Didn't make enemies."

"That you know of. I'm not so much interested at this point in the motive for his killing. What concerns me is that someone may have learned to control and direct the murderous impulse of a Hairball."

Beatrice looked at me. We were both thinking the same thing.

"Maybe that's the motive," she said.

At this time of night there was almost no traffic except for the near-silent glide of monorail trains and the automated Pacific Electric MagLev transit system. Few vehicles other than those used by tradesmen or others for official use were allowed on the streets of the Privilege. Requirements to own a private vehicle were strict.

Of the 28 million population of SoCal, about a third resided in the Privilege. Of that number nearly one hundred percent were High Bloods. I say "nearly" because we can never be completely sure. LC disease was always only a few careless moments of ecstasy away.

Private residences had become nearly nonexistent south of Sunset Boulevard. More than three hundred condominiums of thirty stories or better were jammed into the twelve square miles of the walled city, just enough room between them to allow for swaying in an R-8 earthquake. Anything stronger than that and much of the Privilege would, in less than sixty seconds, become a very large tribal burial mound for extraterrestrial archaeologists of the far future to puzzle over.

I turned right off Sunset at Benedict Canyon.

Breva Way was a serpentine road through a much smaller canyon like a barranca, with acacia-covered bluffs above it. The homes were tucked away from the road behind hibiscus hedges, pepper and eucalyptus trees, high brick and stone walls covered in roses or bougainvillea thick enough to conceal the coils of razor wire. The still air was redolent with the rich, dark, stinking fertilizer the gardeners spread over emerald lawns.

A private patrol pickup truck came slowly toward us. I blinked a code with my lights, because the Humvee had no ILC decal on it.

"You live around here?" Beatrice said. "I'm impressed."

"No, you're not," I said. "Anyway I'm just house-sitting."

I don't think she believed me. "What possessed you to become a Wolfer? It's less dangerous skydiving with an umbrella."

"*Faute de mieux*," I said.

"'For want of anything better,'" Beatrice translated. She didn't believe that either. When she looked at me this time she was able to smile. "Oh, yeah. Just a tough guy with the heart of an idealist."

"Maybe I think civilization is worth saving," I said. I stopped the Hummer to key in the code that opened the gates of 141 Breva Way. "What do you want from life, Beatrice?"

"To go on living it."

3

Those were the last words Beatrice said to me for quite a while, although she did favor me with a low, two-note whistle on her first look at the layout as we drove toward the house at the rear of a three-acre lot on a curving drive paved with brown river stones set in concrete.

My mother's house was Japanese, a three-thousand-square-foot *minka*, or farmhouse, with an entrance pavilion that enclosed a garden of raked gravel, more smooth round stones, and bonsai banyan trees.

My father had inherited tens of millions of oil money, which I suppose kept gushing in. He was the kind of luckless gambler who would have bet against the Trojan horse, so a lot of the wealth had gushed right out again. Maybe he'd have succeeded in getting us into receivership, but a faulty heart valve put an end to his high-rolling ways when he was one month shy of fifty.

I'd always liked him. We had fun together. He taught me, by example, never to draw to an inside straight.

It had never occurred to me to wonder what had attached my mother, whose name was Penelope but who liked to be called Pym, to my father. She was probably a genius, and he had coasted through an Ivy League school with a gentleman's C. They were both nearsighted, liked Boodles gin, and liked Sinatra. That was about it. Opposites do attract, of course. And once Pym had said to me, "He doesn't mean any harm and he never hurts my feelings," probably the only serious examination of their relationship she ever undertook.

I opened the front doors of the *minka*, which were never locked, for Beatrice. Clapped the recessed lighting on as she walked in, looked around, looked at me with a tense expression.

"Bathroom?" I gave directions.

She didn't forget to slip out of her boots before going briskly down a hallway floored in black slate. The hall separated a large minimally furnished living room from the tea room, each with twenty-five-foot bamboo ceilings. The post-and-beam construction mimicked that of Japanese farmhouses, but the posts were steel, better to handle seismic events. I went on to the kitchen, untypically modern: stainless steel appliances, a cooking island with a ceramic range top.

I pulled two bottles of Killian's Red from one of the side-by-side refrigerators, where I chilled the beer to a couple of degrees above freezing. Lord Killian probably would've had a fit, but that was how I liked my brew. I held the cold bottle against the bump over one ear, then drank the Killian's slowly, giving Bea the privacy she required.

The WC and separate spa were on two levels, walled in teak, skylighted, floored in big rectangles of rough-finished red quarry tile. The spa contained a sauna, a cold plunge, and an open-front shower I could lie down in should I be in no shape to stand.

Beatrice had turned on the water walls on two sides of the shower, along with the spectrachrome overhead lighting. I knocked on one of the *Shoji* doors.

"Cold beer here." I could see through a translucent door panel her ghostly shape in drifting warm mist.

I had expected her to reach out discreetly. Instead she slid one of the doors all the way open. She was neither bold nor shy about her nakedness. She drank most of the beer I handed her in three long swallows, her small breasts taut as she tilted her head back.

I stepped inside, closed the door behind me. When Beatrice had finished off the bottle she smothered a burp with one hand, shrugged in childlike embarassment, then turned and walked through the mist into the shower, a rainbow of lovely skin in the spectrachrome lights. While I was throwing off my clothes she played with jets spurting at all angles, luxuriating in the massaging sprays, dancing a little, coming fully alive. When I stepped in with her she was into my arms at a touch, holding me very tightly.

There wasn't much foreplay. Just high-burn sex, that urgent desire to banish, for a little while, dark and frightful images from our conscious minds.

Beatrice had had a few lovers before me, but she wasn't sexually experienced. In the shower her body had been telling her what she wanted, had to have, as quickly as possible.

But we made love again—in the best sense of those words—on the double futon in my bedroom, taking time for a leisurely appreciation of each other's bodies. The humanness of sexual need.

Once I thought, from the slow, deep rhythm of her breathing, that she had fallen asleep, I started to get up from the futon platform.

But Beatrice quaked in alarm and took a fierce grip on me.

"You're leaving?"

"Not going to work yet, but I need to report in. Find out how the investigation is going."

Premeditated murder by a werewolf—if that turned out to be the case—made hash of everything that ILC thought it knew about the species. Just the possibility was enough to give me a sick stomach.

Beatrice relaxed her grip. "Please don't be gone long." Her eyes were serious, meeting my gaze. "My body is yours now. Just don't ever fuck with my head."

"Not my style, Beatrice."

I touched one corner of her lips, then the other, then with a fingertip drew a smile on her relaxed face.

"No," she said. "I didn't think it would be."

Sunny and I conferred on the dedicated and encrypted ILC channel. I transferred her hologram to a breakfast-nook booth and sat opposite it.

"What have we got so far?"

"West Hollywood turned up that dust shroud in an alley off Melrose about a mile from de Sade's. It was custom, so—"

"Probably stolen from a similar SUV in storage. Trace the ownership anyway."

"Better news, we found the mesh purse you were talking about. Along with a dress, shoes, and the Lycan crucifix in the ladies' lounge stall where she haired-up. Other women using the facility had the good sense to stay locked in their own stalls while that was going on."

I nodded. The involuntary groans werewolves make during the hair-up is unmistakable, as terrifying as the act itself.

Sunny said, "The Lycan is, or was, Miss Chiclyn Hickey of Melbourne, Australia. But you knew that already, didn't you?"

"She came on to me in de Sade's like the Saturday Night Special, until I sort of let it slip that I was a Wolfer."

Sunny heard that with a wry smile.

"Not that you're a bad-looking guy, and the hair certainly works for you, but you know they're all just looking for someone who reminds them of daddy."

I ignored her; it was one of her favorite critiques, one I heard, along with not very subtle hints about a nose job, when she was feeling bitchy or miffed at me. After all, I'd left her with a crime scene to run.

"What about the designer wristpac?"

"We haven't come up with one yet."

"She may have passed it on to someone else. Which makes me think—"

"Chickie the Hairball might've had a little helper on the inside?"

"Someone who knew to disconnect the rooftop TRADs. Put Joel and Tink to work reviewing the discs from all the surveillance cams. And confiscate every cell phone or wristpac in de Sade's before you let the Ravers go home."

"We might need to strip-search."

"If it adds to your fun."

"Speaking of good times, R, how is your interrogation coming along?"

"Her full name is Beatrice Harp. I found out that much."

"How could she resist your, um, relentless probing?"

"Be nice."

"So tell me, did you take the local or the express with Beatrice? Were you up front with her, or did you go in the back way?"

"I'll see you at the office," I said. "Probably I'll be late. There's someone else I need to talk to."

After I finished talking to Sunny I made coffee, toasted a bagel, and turned on the five o'clock news.

The second-stringers who worked the A.M. beat were outside de Sade's, but the word there was mum and they had no one to interview who had a coherent story to tell. There had been screams, a shape in the night that could have been a large dog or someone wearing one of the popular Jazz Age chinchilla coats and a porkpie hat. Just as a formality ILC investigators were on the scene. There were rumors of bodies in the Montmorency. At this point nothing was confirmed.

Around the world the usual pointless but lethal squabbles were going on over this and that, as if the warring factions didn't have enough to do keeping Lycanthropy in check. A religious cult in Tierra del Fuego had played follow-the-leader in committing mass suicide; he had guaranteed them a better world somewhere else.

Cults always had been the first refuge for the emotionally immature, those who couldn't cope, even with the counsel of therapists and antidepressants, with the reality of the world they'd been born into.

Speaking of feel-good nostrums, Miles Brenta's pharma colossus near San Jack Town seemed to have come up with a hot new one as we cut to commercial. On-screen an ideal young couple, healthy and happy in a setting of green hills, blue skies, and fleecy clouds, exulted in their well-being, courtesy of a drug called SECÜR.

And back to the news as I poured a second cup of coffee: a rancher named Max Thursday had been found guilty in SoCal Superior Court of hosting a *mal de lune* hunt on his Seco Grande spread with Hairballs as prey. It had happened a few months ago. Because he had no priors, he received a fine and probation. A LALALY (Legal Assistance for Los Angeles Lycans) pro bono team had registered "strenuous objections" to the leniency of the sentence and were "filing motions of appeal"—as if their actions could hope to stop an increasingly popular sport on either side of the border.

A pair of young Lycans had been murdered in the backseat of a car parked in a trysting spot near Laguna Nigel. The boy's throat was cut. The girl, already conveniently naked and in heat, was gang-raped, then slaughtered. From tire tracks around the vehicle police estimated that at least a dozen bikers had been involved. They didn't go so far as to implicate Diamondbackers, who had much better lawyers than LALALY. And deeper pockets, going by the quality of the motorcycles they owned.

There was a public service spot featuring gang-pressed young Lycans whitewashing a handball wall on a playground, obliterating the spray-painted legend KILL ALL HI BLUDS. The voice-over narrator solemnly reminded us that promoting such violence only inspired more intolerance throughout the cultural in-group, namely High Bloods.

We all just had to try and get along, in the immortal words of someone whose name I had forgotten long ago.

The entertainment minute of the news was devoted to clips from the opening of another Miles Brenta resort in Paradiso Palms the previous Saturday night. I didn't pay attention. I was rinsing out my cup when I heard Miles say, ". . . seen a rough cut, and let me be the first to say Chickie is just fantastic in it; this girl is going to be a major star."

I turned from the sink in time to catch a few seconds of a radiant Chiclyn Hickey, wearing a stylish gown and a fall, snuggled next to Brenta, maybe bending her knees a little so as not to appear taller than the stocky billionaire. Brenta had a casual arm around her bare shoulders. They were onscreen long enough for me to tell that Chickie had left her wolf's-head crucifix at home: she had on a diamond choker with a small pendant instead.

Anyway Brenta would know that Chickie was Lycan; he wasn't careless about who he bedded.

Assuming Chickie had been his date for the evening, I wondered how that had gone over with Mrs. Brenta, who no longer made public appearances. She was one of the few survivors of a werewolf attack I knew of. All of whom were much the worse for the experience.

I went on the Internet and gave a couple of Lycan-oriented sites a fast look. Sometimes they were first to post stories the so-called legitimate media hadn't caught on to or were reluctant to report if they did know something. But this morning the pages were largely filled with gossip, wishful thinking, or just plain fantasy: UNBORN CHILD BECOMES WEREWOLF IN MOTHER'S WOMB and EVIDENCE THAT EARLY CHRISTIANS WERE LYCANS FOUND IN HIDDEN CAVE.

While I was choosing something to wear to a second breakfast from the *tansu* wardrobe in my bedroom, Beatrice rose up on one elbow, eyes still filled with sleep. I told her where I was going and how long I expected to be gone. She mumbled something and lay down again.

I kissed a bare shoulder, had a quick shave, inhaled enough upper vape to keep me awake and alert for the next twelve hours, dressed. I was on my way down to the Beverly Hills Hotel as the first rays of sun appeared on the high, dry hills and gently stirring acacia above the canyon.

Five mornings a week, as soon as the rising sun permitted his entrance into the Privilege, Johnny Padre took his place at a table for eight in the Polo Lounge for a power breakfast.

Johnny was a senior partner in the talent agency EiE (Excellence in Entertainment) located in Century City. The biggest of the Big Three. Always there were two or three Juniors in attendance, along with whatever talents and/or studio honchos EiE was wooing.

For all the Excellence in Entertainment execs, the Amish look was de rigueur: blue shirts with the collar buttoned, black trousers, suspenders, high-topped black shoes. Chin whiskers were optional. They all wore identical flat-crowned white straw hats with black bands, even at table. In sync sartorially as they were, aligned in dignity and humble power, they had the august presence that belied the truth of their profession, made up of numerous rival nests of frenzied, conniving, backbiting rats.

Johnny wasn't pleased to see me walk in. The client for whom they were negotiating a deal this morning was a longtime best-selling author, a tall, serious-looking octogenarian with a shaggy gray haircut and thick glasses. The A-list director also present already had turned several of the novelist's wildly popular Luke Bailiff western novels into cinema classics. Neither the author's fans nor moviegoers could get enough of Luke Bailiff or the western genre. The good old days of pioneer America. When there was still half of a country to be explored and settled, and most men—probably a few women too—felt energized by opportunity, fully in control of their destinies.

Almost no one felt that way anymore. The future was a black hole. Suicide rates all over the world were climbing in what statisticians called parabolic curves. The newest satellite maps no longer bore the ancient legend across empty quarters of ocean or trackless wasteland that read *Here there be monsters*. But they might as well have.

After introductions and a few pleasantries I asked the rest of the breakfast club to excuse Johnny Padre for a few minutes.

Because I had some power in my own line of work, Johnny, an Off-Blood, made the best of the interruption, cracking wise about being cited for sneaking too much Château Mouton-Rothschild '84 into his most recent blood-swap, and followed me to a banquette we both knew wasn't bugged.

Johnny had a pallid face and a chronically constipated expression. The little sideways lurch of his mouth when he attempted a heartless smile always reminded me of a math teacher I'd hated in high school because he never graded on the curve. Johnny sat hunched and watchful opposite me as if he were harboring a secret mean spirit.

"I'm loving this like a boil on my dick," he growled. "So give me the bad news first—as long as it's happening to somebody else."

"Chiclyn Hickey," I said.

"She's a client. Not what you'd call intellectual property, but the camera worships her. She's got the fucking star quality: young sin in her eyes and that sexy overbite. I've been bringing her along slowly, small but important roles with A-list directors. Now it's Chickie's time. Eight to five she breaks out in *Ghost Galleon.*"

"Is she fucking Miles Brenta?"

"How would I know? It's his money in the movie. He fucks who he wants. What's your interest in Chickie?"

"She's a Lycan."

"This is breaking news? In show business, who's not hairy these days?"

"When their time of the month comes around."

"Meaning?"

"Chickie's an OOPs."

Padre winced, looked down, dry-washed his thin pale hands worriedly.

"C'mon. Out-of-Phase Hairballs? That's just an urban legend."

"We do our best to promote it as such."

Artie fumbled in his shirt pocket for a blister pack of small white pills and swallowed one. He was beginning to look clammy.

"That's fucking swell. Potential five mil her next contract. What's she done that we can't plea-bargain or buy her out of?"

"She did a Hairball number on Artie Excalibur at de Sade's a few hours ago. Sorry, Johnny. But this you keep to yourself."

Johnny breathed through his mouth, a hand over his heart as if he were about to give sworn testimony.

"I love the kid like a daughter!" He looked up at me accusingly. "Is she dead? Did you kill her, Rawson?"

"I shot her. Not fatally. But she's missing. I doubt that there's much chance she's still alive. If my silver didn't do it, then whoever drove Chickie away from de Sade's has finished the job, maybe after she skinnydipped."

"Somebody had the stones to put a werewolf in his car? Reminds me of the old joke." Assuming I had heard it, he went straight to the punch line: "'*Thought it was the best pussy I'd ever had, until she told me she'd bikini-waxed her face.*'" Johnny squeezed his hands together so hard some color appeared in his cheeks, a mild pink flush.

"It was an SUV," I said. "Chickie was low sick by then, from the last look I had of her. Right now she's either in the upper Mojave under a pile of rocks or marinating in a dump. I hope we find her, although by the time we do there won't be a trace left of whatever they programmed her with."

"Program a werewolf? Last I heard, they don't take direction."

"Chickie did. I'm reasonably sure. Any idea of who might have found Artie expendable in their scheme of things?"

Johnny shrugged.

"He was in and out of some deals, always with a profit. Had a savvy eye for the next good thing, little start-ups that need cash bad. There's a lot of competish in those areas of investment. Artie couldn't crack an egg with his punches anymore, but his footwork was still fancy. Never stepped on any important High Blood toes that I know of."

"His word was his bond?"

"Good enough for me, yeah. He put me into a couple of real moneymakers. Wind turbine leases. That biodiesel utility company in Camarillo. Artie was big on saving the planet." Padre smiled cynically. "Maybe he thought there's gonna be somebody left to enjoy it."

"When did you see Artie last?"

"Our Thursday-night game. Upstairs at the Redondo casino he has a piece of. Two tables, regulars only, twelve or fifteen of us, depending. Kind of a who's who in SoCal, you know?"

He seemed pleased to be including himself.

"Miles Brenta one of them?"

"Doesn't gamble. Says he has no card sense. Poker would be the only thing he's not good at. I think he just prefers fast toys and hunting dangerous game for amusement."

Johnny glanced anxiously at the table where proposals were being floated without him.

"Listen. About Chickie. It's a tragedy. A great loss. Maybe what you find out, you could keep me in the loop? Like a daughter to me."

His look of compassion for the presumably departed Chickie was enough to bring tears to the glass eyes of a stuffed moose head.

"Aren't they all?" I said.

When I pulled up in front of the house on Breva Way I sat in the Humvee looking at a bed of red, white, and purple china asters, letting my mind slack off while my brain continued humming dependably along, putting out its steady twelve watts of electrical energy, impulses lighting up the glowworm cellular network that makes up the human—and animal—nervous system.

It took a little while before I consciously realized I was trying to connect with something. Like another energy field from another mind that lingered on the periphery of psychic recognition, a spirit not unknown but unnamable in the bright, suddenly creepy silence of early morning.

Human, animal, both? My internal séance, as they usually are, was unnerving. I broke it off and went into the house.

The washing machine was going in the laundry alcove off the kitchen. I found Beatrice in the courtyard wearing one of the dragon kimonos that were in most of the bedroom wardrobes, including mine. She was drinking coffee. The hand that held the cup still wasn't all that steady. Other than the pewter coffee service there was nothing on the table but a shiny steel cleaver from the kitchen's cutlery rack.

She looked around at me with a troubled face. But she relaxed her grip on the cleaver.

"Someone was here," she said. "She scared me so bad I nearly freaked. I guess you didn't have the time to tell me you had an ex-wife. Of course you didn't. We've barely talked at all. But you would've told me sooner or later, wouldn't you?"

4

It had been more than a year since I had seen or spoken to our closest neighbor, Ida Grace. She had lived alone in the next house up the canyon road since her daughter Mallory had gone Lycan at age seventeen and earned her banishment from hearth and home and the unforgiving wolfless society of the Privilege.

The loss of Mal and perhaps advancing age had turned Ida into a recluse whose household needs were met by a complement of service staff, particularly a houseman named Duke, who put on his chauffeur's cap whenever Ida ventured outside the walls of her brick colonial house, usually for medical reasons. She occasionally visited the gallery on Canon Drive that exhibited her paintings or the vet who looked after her dogs. She owned a white Maltese and two Neapolitan mastiffs, the only breed I knew capable of taking on a werewolf with some prospect of survival.

These days Ida's social life seemed to be limited to a weekly visit from a Buddhist priest. But I was convinced that during the earliest hours of his morning there had been another visitor.

Although it was still early, Ida had breakfasted and was at work on a painting in the orangerie/studio semidetached from the main house. I hadn't expected Duke to receive permission to bring me around, accompanied by the mastiffs, although I had stressed that it was important and not a social call.

Mal Scarlett had been the surprise offspring of Ida's second marriage, when Ida was fifty-one years of age. Mal was born two weeks after my father died. Now at seventy-four Ida was spare of motion, finely eroded, but still erect. She had put down her sable brush just as I walked into the glass-walled orangerie. She stared at the canvas on her studio easel, ignoring me.

I made myself at home on a two-piece wicker lounger and waited to be acknowledged. She was, as always, painting butterflies and hummingbirds and big splashy crimson flowers. The garden outside was filled with all three.

"I thought maybe by now you would've taken a whack at abstract expressionism—like Jackson Pollock's stuff," I said, just to get the conversational ball rolling.

"Those paintings are as ugly as bug guts on a windshield."

Ida turned then, slowly, with a certain arrogant tilt of her head, looking at me as if I were an afterthought. She had a butch haircut and a tough flat face, the ashen lack of expression that of a martyr who has long since squandered all of her passions but one. I thought she probably despised me, but that was nothing compared to how she felt about my mother.

She had a smudge of blue oil paint next to one flared nostril. I helpfully pointed that out to her. Ida sniffed contemptuously and glared at me.

"Well, then. Is she dead? Is that what you've come to tell me?"

"Pym? No. I don't think so. Although she's been out of touch for a while."

"Still searching for the magic cure, is she?"

"The secret of immunity she thinks is out there, just one more isolated, dawn-of-history tribe away."

"So if she *isn't* dead, this is going to be something likely to spoil my day," Ida said, with an understated smile of malice.

"Ida, why don't you let up on Pym? She didn't steal your husband. I don't think she slept with him either. They did go off together on an expedition. He admired—"

"*Admired?* Worshipped her, you mean. He was utterly spellbound by her fame. As for the sexual relationship you deny—my husband may have been a weak man, but he was damned attractive."

"I think he just wanted to accomplish something worthwhile in his life."

"Pitiful," she sneered. "Off on a jaunt, cavorting through jungles, hoping to discover—himself. I told him more than once. Only in relentless self-appraisal can one fashion character strong in purpose, touched by grace."

"On the other hand," I said, "you just may drive yourself to drink."

She studied me, something heavy in each of her dark eyes, like unshed tears lethal as mercury. I had been momentarily pissed at Ida, but I relented.

A fly buzzing near her unfinished painting distracted Ida. She swiped at it with her right hand, then began searching through a tall jar of brushes on her worktable.

"I suppose the real hell of life is that everyone has his reasons," she said. Quoting Jean Renoir.

Before she could decide I wasn't worth any more of her time I said to Ida, "Where's Elena?" My pulses were racing.

Her back was to me as she selected the brush she wanted. I couldn't tell by her reflection in one of the tall orangerie windows if there was a change of expression. But she might already have had a premonition of why I'd come calling, and had prepared herself for the question.

"How should I know? I suppose if she cared to see either of us she would have, years ago."

"Bullshit, Ida. Elena was here. Around sunrise. Maybe she called you first. You know I can find out. But she also came to see me. I wasn't home. She gave my houseguest a good scare. Elena's spoor was all over my bedroom, in the garden, right up to the wall between our properties."

Ida turned to glare at me.

"Sorry," I said. " 'Spoor' is Wolfer talk. I should've used a different terminology. Still, what Elena left behind was as obvious to me as my own face in the mirror. Her specific energy pattern. Vibes. You know."

"More of your vaunted 'Sixth Sense'?" she said, with an attempt at a sneer.

"It's nothing that all other human beings don't have. I'm just better able to tune in to the electrical fields connecting living minds. Or dead ones, in some cases. The newly dead."

Having selected the brush she wanted, Ida changed her mind about going back to work and put down her palette.

"There are seven gateways into Beverly Hills," I reminded her. "They're all monitored. Profilers, Snitch readers. Even though Lenie's not a registered Lycan, I won't have to go to any trouble to learn where she came in and what name she's using. So stop stalling me."

Ida crossed bare arms over her fin de siècle painter's smock, as if in response to an inner Arctic chill.

"I hadn't seen her for many months. She always—she shows up unannounced. Fugitive. A little frightened."

She *was* a fugitive. As are all rogue werewolves. But I didn't press the point with Ida, because I'd seen a moment of anguish spark in her desolate eyes, grief for a once-beloved child.

"Elena was alone?"

"No. She came with two—friends, I presume. On motorcycles. Bikers, is that what they're called? They wore identical jackets, a lot of silver around their necks, piled on their wrists."

"Were they Diamondbackers?"

"I wouldn't know. The dogs didn't like them. They kept their distance while Elena and I— Diamondbacker?"

"For the snakeskin tats they all have on their backs."

"Is that a club, or something more sinister?"

"They're the worst. Since all drugs were legalized they've made their livings by snatching celebrity Lycans for ransom. Or else they're werewolf killers, claiming the fat bounties some High Bloods are willing to post."

"I wouldn't know about that," she said unconvincingly. "I pay little attention anymore to what goes on out there." Ida nodded, agreeing with herself, with the propriety of her reclusive life, while she looked around at small beautiful objects on display in her orangerie, favorite paintings, the walled garden outside that protected her secular nunnery. "Does it really matter who she is with, what sort of life she leads now?"

Ida was giving me a headache. "Here's the reality. If Lenie's passing herself off as High Blood, she couldn't be in with a worse crowd." Although I couldn't figure that one out, what Elena's motive might be in running with Diamondbackers. "I'm not the only animal psychic around. If I can sniff out a rogue werewolf off-Observance, there are others who can do the same. Maybe in one of the Diamondbacker chapters. You don't want to know what they'll do to her if—"

That was nearly too much for Ida.

"No! I don't want to know! Because for seven years she has been as good as dead to me. Do you think I get any pleasure from her surreptitious little visits? Oh, she tries to put such a good face on her tragedy! Her efforts only serve to remind me of who she was and what I hoped she might become in spite of the iniquities of a maddened world. But there can be no hope, neither for Elena nor for Mallory—although Mal, if she possesses any self-awareness apart from vanity, must know she has gotten just what she deserved."

One of the mastiffs responded to her shrill tone with an anxious whine. Ida seemed momentarily as blind as the Sphinx, half buried in stifling drifts of old angers and recrimination.

"Speaking of Mal," I said, "she went off-line early Saturday morning."

Ida blinked a couple of times. She was lightly misted with perspiration around her eyes, at her temples.

"Oh?" she said vaguely.

Other than her eyeblinks she didn't move or betray any comprehension of what I was talking about. But the heavy beat of a pulse in her throat told me she already knew about Mal.

"Have you spoken to her lately?"

Ida roused herself from her sere purview and returned to form.

"She only calls when she needs more money."

"But she hasn't—"

"I do not encourage Mal to visit either. We have nothing to talk about. Except, perhaps, her father. Whom, I suppose, she misses. They were always—she adored—"

Ida seemed suddenly dazed. Too much vitriol was bad for aging hearts. There were a couple of crystal decanters on a low table in a part of the orangerie that contained a well-lighted reading corner and bookshelves of first-edition classics. I poured a snifter a quarter full of Armagnac and took it to Ida.

She found the fumes bracing; her eyes began to clear.

"Stop waving that under my nose," she snapped. She unclenched her hands, took the glass with a look of surcease and drank, her eyes closing as she did so. Then she breathed deeply and looked at me.

"Why don't you have one too?" she said grudgingly. "I feel shameful, drinking all by myself at this hour."

So I poured another shot. Seemed the right time for a strengthener. And some codeine to dodge the headache.

"I don't suppose you can find her," Ida said casually.

"Mal? We're looking, but—"

"Once that sensor is no longer embedded beneath her clavicle it can be difficult. I, ah, suppose."

Something in my glance disconcerted her.

"I learned about that watching a television program."

"Oh."

"I'm quite fond of the Discovery Channel."

"Sure." I wanted to talk about Elena. The fact that she was passing for High Blood off-Observance was neither the best nor the worst news I'd had since her disappearance. I was only glad that she was still alive.

"How did she look this morning?" I asked Ida.

"Elena?" Her expression softened almost impalpably. "As lovely as the day she had to leave me."

"Hard to believe." I was familiar with the ravages done to the human personas of werewolves who haired-up at each full moon.

"True." There was something malicious in the frankness of Ida's gaze. "How does that feel?"

"Like a kind of death."

"Good. You never deserved her, you know."

Not a topic for argument. Not now, anyway. "Why was she here? Something special about this day?"

"I've told you. Elena just turns up. I never know when that may be."

"But today was different from the other times. Because today she also paid a call on me. Except I wasn't there. What's going on? What did she have to say to you, Ida?"

"Nothing that would be of interest to you. Her visit was brief." Ida paused. "I asked her never to come again."

Like all poor liars—or those forced into a lie—Ida Grace spoke with an excess of conviction.

I didn't believe her. But there was no point in challenging her either. I finished my Armagnac. One of the mastiffs got up from the orangerie floor and went outside to pee in the garden. Two hummingbirds were visiting the feeder near the open door.

"Might I get back to work now?" Ida said with an edge of sarcasm. She was watching the tiny hummers, the speed of their wings like flashes of pale fire against the deep green backdrop of photinias.

"Thanks for your time, Ida."

I was giving up too easily; Ida knew it. That worried her. And if she was worried, it meant that next time I was going to see Elena and not just the vagueness of her doppelgänger haunting my house. I very likely would be seeing her soon.

Before I returned to Beatrice I ordered twenty-four-hour surveillance on Ida's house and on Ida herself.

On the short walk to my own doorstep I tried putting together some vague pieces of information I'd heard or intuited during my half hour with her.

There was what I considered to be the urgency of Elena's visit and her desire to see me—by climbing over the eight-foot wall in our secret place to my backyard. Which could have meant she didn't want her biker escorts to know where she was going. And she wasn't just taking a nostalgia trip. Elena had startled the half-awake Bea in my bedroom but said not a word to her. *Hey, sorry, kid; just wanted to say hello to R.* And she had left no message for me, either.

I now had good reason to believe that Mallory Scarlett was actually missing, in the bad sense of the word. It was a good bet that her Snitcher had been surgically removed. Elena knew that, and, I thought, she must also know why. Was Mal just another hostage for ransom, and had Elena been dispatched to pick up a gym bag full of money from their mother?

But I couldn't believe Elena would have any part in a kidnap plot involving her sister.

If it wasn't a kidnapping for profit, then it was something else that might have to do with a much larger sum than they could hope to wring out of an old lady. Even a Beverly Hills old lady.

Something much worse.

I took pity on Ida then, because it appeared both of her daughters were in some sort of jeopardy—estranged from their mother, of course, but still embedded deeply in her heart and soul where the good times and special moments remained, no matter how crushed she was by emotional hardship.

When I walked into the kitchen where good things had been prepared in the double ovens, Beatrice smiled shyly at me. She'd made huevos rancheros and guava popovers. I realized I was starved. We sat outside in the courtyard where the morning glories were just folding up for the day. I ate a lot and drank two cups of fresh coffee. My headache, or Ida-ache, had dulled down. Bea only nibbled while I finished telling her about Elena.

"You probably know from Artie that there is a major black market in the blood business." She nodded. "The big profits that used to come from the drug trade now attract the same racketeers to bootleg blood. Probably more than half of Off-Blooders can find themselves desperate to ensure a continuous supply. At any price. Particularly if they're a rare type like AB negative. A prosperous man such as Artie Excalibur must have had two or three blood cows for his exclusive use."

Beatrice nodded again.

"A woman in Thailand and a Danish avant-garde composer. I oversaw all of the purity evals for Artie. Each of his High Bloods receive a hundred thousand a year for their donations." She looked confused, frowning. "What does this have to do with Elena Grace?"

"Before I became a deputy director of ILC SoCal I worked undercover busting gangs who peddled tainted or artificial blood in bulk to Offs lacking Artie's bankroll. People who couldn't be all that choosy about the source of their refills, couldn't afford the rigorous screenings to detect a thousand and one viruses that could kill them in a few days. A risky way to live. So was the work I was doing. Especially when there was another Intel guy willing to break my identity to the wrong people to improve his career prospects."

Beatrice folded her lower lip between her teeth, afraid of what she imagined was coming next.

"Elena didn't know about my double life, of course. She trusted me in all things. I trusted myself to keep her safe. But I should have stayed away from her until I was rotated out of our bloodleggers unit."

"You were in love, so—" Beatrice shrugged. "You had to see her."

"Yeah. I had to see her. In little hideaways here and there. But after I was betrayed, four members of the gang caught up to us at a bed-and-breakfast near Ojai. I killed two of them. The other pair kicked my head in"—I tapped the slight indentation on my forehead beneath which lay a silver plate—"and were pouring gasoline on me when an off-duty CHP interrupted their play. They got away with Elena. She turned up three days later on a foggy stretch of Carillo beach, barefoot, half naked. They had raped her repeatedly. The one who spoiled her blood was a cousin of the gang leader, who hadn't showed up for my barbecue. I guess he planned to watch the DVD later. Anyway the rogue Lycan invited for the fun was named LouLou Morday."

"Oh God. So awful."

"I was in a coma for ten days, in the hospital three months. Spent more time recuperating at my mother's lodge up at Big Bear. Talking to the squirrels until I could recognize the sound of my own voice. I forced myself to walk until I could manage a mile without my right foot starting to drag. I had the kind of headaches steel-toed boots can give you. I still do. More months passed without a word from Elena. She never came to the hospital. Of course for a long while she was in miserable shape herself.

"Ida held me completely responsible for the attack on her daughter. She wouldn't tell me where Elena was. It was Mal who tipped me that she was in a psychiatric clinic in Canada, near Banff. With all of my resources at ILC I still couldn't get in to see her. So once I was ninety percent recovered and hoping for the best for Elena's sake, I turned to other matters."

It must have been the look on my face. Beatrice said, "You don't have to—"

"Why not? You want to know me, this is part of it. First I tracked down LouLou Morday and fed small chunks of him to a flock of wild geese. Until there wasn't much left that was essential to his continued existence."

Beatrice swallowed hard and got up quickly from the table, went to a far corner of the courtyard and made gagging sounds. Nothing came up. I guess it was for the best she hadn't eaten much breakfast.

"I was a little upset with him," I explained. "As for the guys who fled that night with Elena, a routine spike job was enough for them. By then I'd mellowed."

"What's a— No, don't tell me."

Bea got her composure back and came slowly to me. She stood behind me and put a hand lightly on the back of my bowed head. A blessing of sorts. My overheated blood drained slowly from my face.

"The gang leader, the one who planned to watch my immolation in the comfort of his Woodland Hills rec room with a bowl of popcorn and some cold brew, him I haven't been able to lay a hand on. His name is Raoul J. Ortega. He is, I've been told, important to ILC Intel. They want him alive and working at his game, whatever it is currently. But someday Raoul J. Ortega will be expendable to ILC. Raoul and I both know that. Knowing may give him some anxious moments. Because I can wait, and I'll never forget."

"And you never saw Elena again?" Beatrice said after a few moments.

"Only once," I said.

Because Artie Excalibur's office on Santa Monica was a crime scene, Beatrice said she could probably use her home computer to access Artie's business files and compile a list of associates.

Before I dropped her at the Radcliffe, a forty-story tower on Rexford where she had a one-bedroom apartment, I took from the safe in my home office a set of three throwing knives and showed them to her. The knives were Japanese-made, Damascus steel with laminated silver; each edge could cut through a railroad spike.

She studied the knives on dark blue velvet with her low, two-note whistle of appreciation.

"These are finer than anything I could hope to own," she said with a trace of wistfulness. "Priority hunk. The workmanship is *so* gorgeous."

"Want to try them?" I said.

Outside we crossed the arched red bridge over the koi pond to a sunlit expanse of lawn where there was room to throw at a scarred old piece of upright timber.

Beatrice was fast on the draw, her motion as deft as that of a conjuring magician. She whipped the knife from the quick-release scabbard that she wore midthigh and fired it underhand at the target. Like a fast-pitch softballer but with no windup. There was only a glint in the air, then that solid *thock* a second later as the blade bit deep into dry old wood.

She worked up some perspiration throwing each knife several times from a distance of eighteen feet. All of her throws were in a painted target area less than six inches in diameter.

I tried it Beatrice's way a few times to see how difficult it was. It was damned difficult. I was out of the money every time and a little embarrassed by my ineptitude.

"You're very good," I said.

"I know. If you're going to tote one, better know how to use it." Her eyes were alight with the pleasure of accomplishment. "My father taught me."

"What does he do for a living, travel with a circus?"

"No. MERC. Twenty years of it. All those places where egomaniacs were putting on wars that are largely forgotten. Now he aqua-farms salmon in Oregon. About half his moving parts are pross. I don't get up there often enough to visit him. But my stepmom spoils him rotten and I think he's a happy man." She whistled another low tune, sounding mournful. Then she looked up at me, possibly with a touch of nerves.

"How old are you, R?"

"Forty."

It may have been a happy surprise. "Oh—that's not so—I was thinking maybe—"

"Both my parents were white as doves when they were about my age. It's a family-gene thing."

"I'll be twenty-four in a couple of months," Bea said.

"Big for your age."

She laughed and gave me a shove. She might have been relieved that I wasn't a well-preserved fifty. She was going to use a handkerchief to blot her face when I stopped her.

"I like your sweat," I said, kissing her.

When we took a break from kissing she said regretfully, "I suppose we have to get going."

"There'll be tonight."

"Yes? That had better be a promise."

With a forefinger Beatrice sketched the letter *B* on my cheeks.

"There. You're branded. Glam rustlers beware. They'll have to get through me to get to you."

"Armed and dangerous. Which of these knives would you like to have?"

"You can't be serious! Each of them must be worth—"

"Right now they're only taking up space in a safe drawer."

"Well, then—" Bea looked them over again with an eye toward acquisition. "They're all choicely good." After a few moments she decided. "This one. The balance is exactly right for my grip, it might've been made for me."

Silver is too malleable to take a sharp edge. But the Japanese master craftsmen seamlessly melded carbon steel with razor edges and tips to the pure silver blades that meant sayonara for werewolves.

"Does this mean we're engaged?" she said, a hand on the hilt of the knife she slipped into its scabbard. Then, with a quick look at me, "Just kidding."

I felt a little better now that she had a weapon. I hadn't said anything and maybe Beatrice hadn't thought of it, but whoever had sent the out-of-phase Hairball Artie's way might have had two victims in mind. By sheer chance I'd been there, between the she-wolf and Bea. But if Bea as Artie's Girl Friday knew or could find out something about Artie's business dealings that represented a threat to the perpetrator—

I wished I could be with Beatrice constantly, but that wasn't possible. I had other investigations to run. I thought Bea would be secure locked in her apartment while accessing Artie's files. Either Sunny or I would be in touch with her at all times.

Even so, the night I had promised her and looked forward to with an unfamiliar but welcome ache around my heart seemed a very long way off.

5

Sunny Chagrin was looking flogged and sounding cranky when I made it to the office on Burton Way, a campus of white stone, five-story buildings devoted to the diverse activities of the ILC, and an acre of satellite dishes.

"Go home," I said to Sunny. "You look like a molting seagull."

"Fuck you. Something I need to show you first."

A couple of our technicians, Joel Picón and Tink Ladue, who were unrelated but looked like twins, had been at work for hours reviewing the surveillance discs from de Sade's. Sunny had directed them to clean up and enhance a promising segment recorded at three minutes and twenty seconds past midnight.

"Our gal in the flapper dress," Sunny said, when Chiclyn Hickey appeared in 3-D.

"That's our OOPs," I acknowledged. "Do we have her going into the ladies' lounge around one-thirty, twenty minutes to two?"

"Yes. But I wanted you to see this guy."

Chickie was talking to a couple of other girls, each of whom wore not much more than thongs and full-body appliqués, when the Guy showed up. There was what might be called an Awkward Moment, then the Guy and Chickie participated in what might be called a Heated Exchange. Enough heat involved to cause the

Laminates to promptly move away. Because of the camera angle there was no way to read their lips. But Chickie's body language revealed growing hostility.

When she tried to walk away from him the Guy put a hand on her arm. Not aggressively, as far as I could tell. He seemed to be pleading with her. He looked briefly toward the entrance to de Sade's. *Let's get out of here*. Chickie shook her head vehemently and pushed him away from her. For a couple of seconds her face was toward the camera, her lips moving. Eyes fierce and blazing.

Tink said, "Something about 'he wants me to—' All I can pick up."

Two seconds more and all that was visible of Chickie was the back of her blond head.

But the expression on the Guy's face was clear enough.

"Poor Bucky," Tink said. "She really gave him the axe."

"So you've got a name?" I said.

"That's Bucky Spartacus."

"Elucidate," I said.

Sunny yawned and was about to pop a tab of something unfamiliar to me when I blocked her.

"Uh-uh. Sleep first. You know how you get on that stuff."

She growled softly but put her pill container away. "It's just vitamins, R."

"Uh-huh. Anyway, about this Bucky—"

"Don't you know your rock stars?" Sunny said.

"Why would I? So he's a rock star."

"Not as big as he's going to get."

Tink said, "Bucky and Chickie have been all over the e-sites and fanzines. Should they or shouldn't they? Hottest couple in Hollywood. Just last week I was reading in *Teeze* magazine where she said, 'until Bucky I never met anyone who could deal with all the aspects of who I am.'"

"We know what Chickie's biological status is. Or was. So I'm guessing Bucky is High Blood."

"It's almost like *Romeo and Juliet,*" Tink said, sniffing a little.

"High Blood, or passing," Joel suggested, and looked at Sunny.

She smothered another yawn with the back of her hand. "Anyway, he's not in our system."

"So they were having a lover's quarrel," Tink said, still caught up in the romantic aspect of the scene we'd witnessed.

"I might buy that," I said, "if Chickie hadn't turned up a little while later to give Artie more than the sharp edge of her tongue." To Sunny I said, "Who reps the rocker?"

"Bucky? EiE, of course. What else?"

Lew Rolling, a recent hire I was beginning to think a lot of for his intuition as a detective and all-around smarts, looked in on us.

"Morning, R. The director says his office, ten sharp."

"Thanks." I looked at my watch. I had time for a couple of phone calls. Lew was walking away. I whistled him back.

"Yeah, R?"

"I've got a name buzzing around the back of my brain. It won't go away. Unrelated case already adjudicated. Sometimes I just have to humor myself. The name is Max Thursday. I want to know more about him and his case."

I told Joel and Tink I was pleased with their work. I told Sunny to go home and, privately, not to dip into her stash of feel-good pharma when she got there. Sunny was subject to sudden tailspins after back-to-back eighty-hour weeks. She'd had one lengthy stay in rehab. Another, and she couldn't be my chief investigator and trusted confidant anymore. That would have hurt both of us deeply.

In my office I told my wristpac what I wanted and eight seconds later was connected with a male assistant of Johnny Padre's.

"I'm sorry, but Mr. Padre is in a meeting."

"Get him out of the meeting," I said.

"I'm afraid that's not possible, sir, but he will return your call as soon as—"

"Now," I said. "My name is Rawson."

"And this would be in reference to—"

"Just tell him Rawson. And I hate to wait."

I didn't wait long.

"Chrissake, I'm loving this like a handjob from my ninety-three-year-old grandmother." He paused to claim some air, changed his tone, lowered his voice. "Is this about Chickie? She turn up? You know, alive?"

"No break there. You didn't mention that she was getting it on with somebody named Bucky Spartacus."

"So she's wailing on his meat flute. That's cold dish. Everybody fucks everybody in their set, it's a way of saying hello. Basically their big romance is a superhype number. Our promotions people put them together. With Miles Brenta's okay, of course."

"What does Brenta have to do with the kid?"

"Personal manager and father figure. Bucky was orphaned by Hairballs, some shitcan town in the Midwest."

"What's Bucky's rank in the Pantheon?"

"Ascending. He was front man for *Farewell Order*, now his solo album's looking triple-platinum. I just lined up a key supporting role for the Buckster in Disney's latest! It's the kind of movie that's landfill for the adolescent brain, but it'll gross a billion. Tomorrow night he's headlining with Chimera at that fund-raiser where the Rose Bowl used to be."

"Fund-raiser for what?"

"First Church of Lycanthropy."

"Whose bright idea—"

"Bucky's a very religious guy," Johnny said defensively. "And he's up-front about promoting harmony between the, you know, species." Johnny drew a deep breath. "I got people waiting, so give with the bad news."

"I don't have any right now."

"Chrissake, you get me out of a meeting—" He sounded almost disappointed.

"I know that Spartacus was with Chickie last night at de Sade's. They had a fight, she blew him off."

"So?"

"I didn't get the impression that it was a manufactured romance. Not on his part, anyway. Where would I find Spartacus?"

"At the beach, I suppose. Carbon Beach. He's renting until he hits the majors in take-home."

"I could use a phone number."

"You have to bother him?" Johnny said anxiously. "I mean, it's happening for him. But if he was into Chickie as deep as you seem to think, the news could bust him up pretty bad."

"I don't bother people, Johnny. Sometimes they get bothered all by themselves when I show up at the door. Anyway, I won't be saying anything about Chickie to the kid, so rest easy."

"A phone call from you is about as soothing as a double nitroglycerin on the rocks."

But Johnny had the assistant I'd talked to earlier provide me with Bucky's home phone number.

I called out there before going up to the director's office on the fifth floor. I watched an ILC helicopter lift off from one of the pads across Burton Way while I counted the rings. Eleven of them. Apparently the voice mail slot was full. Finally I got a sleepy voice, but no face on my wristpac.

" 'Lo?"

"Bucky Spartacus?"

"No. This is Cam. Who's this?"

"Someone who wants to chat with Bucky."

"Yeah?" He went from sleepy to surly. "How'd you get this number?"

"Johnny Padre gave it to me, Cam."

"Oh." I heard him yawn. "Okay. I'll get him for you. What time's it anyway?"

"Five minutes to ten."

"Jesus. Hang on."

He was gone from the phone a couple of minutes. I heard background voices. Other members of Bucky's entourage, I supposed. Then Cam returned.

"Doesn't seem like he's here, dude."

"Maybe he's jogging on the beach?"

"The Buckster? No way. Buck don't like exercise. Running, anyway. He's got that trick knee. So you try his girlfriend? She's down the beach about half a mile from here."

"Chickie Hickey?"

"Yeah, man." Cam paused to talk to someone else who had wandered into the room, then said to me, "Fitz is sayin' Buck didn't show last night. I'd try him at Chickie's. He was planning on hooking up with her. De Sade's or someplace. Didn't want any of us with him. Drove himself. I told him, man, you got to be careful now that you're happening. Thinks because he knows Tae Kwon Do he's invulnerable. I hope this ain't somethin' to worry about. Anyway, you need Chickie's cell?"

"Yes."

He scrolled through his own directory and gave me her number.

"When Bucky does show," I said, "have him call me." I spoke slowly and had him repeat my number back to me.

"You're with the agency, right?"

"One of them," I said.

After talking to Cam I called SoCal DMV and got the license number and make of Bucky Spartacus' wheels. He drove an old Cadillac Escalade. I found that interesting.

Then I called Chickie Hickey's number, and after two rings heard her voice again.

"Apologies, mate. Whoever you are, I love ya. Leave a goddamn number. Ciao."

I sighed, thinking of Chickie bright-eyed on whatever her favorite popsie was when first we'd bumped into each other. And then those reminiscent eyes in the gross figure of a mortally wounded werewolf, staring out at me from the bloodied cabinet elevator in the basement garage of the Montmorency.

Piss in your face, Wolfer.

Chickie had feared or hated me for what I was. I didn't hate her for what she was. Nor could I totally blame Chickie for Artie's fate. I was pretty sure that someone had done Chickie a terrible wrong.

It was one of those low moments when I hate my job.

Even more, I hated what the world had become.

Before going upstairs I stopped by Lew Rolling's desk and diverted him to finding Bucky Spartacus, by means of the GPS tracker in his Escalade.

Booth Havergal was a Brit who had put in time with the ILC in Paris and São Paulo before accepting the top job in SoCal. His background, like mine, was money. He dressed the part: three-piece pin-striped suits that were timeless in style, handmade shoes. When it came to clothes I made only a minimal attempt each day to clad my body in combinations that didn't provoke hysterical laughter from the fashion-conscious women in our offices. Booth was a little taller than I was and had a much better haircut. His nails were always buffed. He was smooth with the ladies and loved the charmed social circle of the Privilege. But beneath his polished surface and urbane nonchalance he was a tough guy who stayed on top of things.

Booth was researching OOPs when I walked into his penthouse office.

"Not much to go on, is there?" he grumbled. "The buggers just pop up now and then off-Observance. Scientific opinion amounts to conjecture, guesswork, and bullshit. What's your opinion?"

"We need a body," I said.

Booth nodded. "For genetic analysis. Do you think you'll come up with one, R?"

"No. The business at de Sade's was planned and carried out very efficiently."

"Leads?"

"Tenuous."

He stroked a cheek with his forefinger. "Just tell me what you're thinking, then."

"It's obvious someone went to a lot of trouble to kill Artie Excalibur when a long-range shot to the back of the head would've done the job just as well, without the theatrics. So if they wanted him to die gaudy it could've been payback for something unforgivable on Artie's part, or a warning to someone else we don't know about, or—"

"But in any case you're convinced it was premeditated murder."

"Yeah."

"Inasmuch as werewolves have no reasoning ability that we have been able to discover, they simply act out in the bloodiest ways imaginable, we seem to have a potentially catastrophic scenario on our hands."

"Programmable Hairballs. Artie knew something about this."

Booth nodded pensively. "He was a very intelligent man. I've never understood why he pursued a third-rate career in the ring."

"He liked the punishment. Needed it. As simple, or as complex, as that."

"So you had a chance to talk to Artie before the attack."

"For one thing, he was concerned about that little business in No Gal last Observance."

"Aren't we all?" Booth took a turn around his well-appointed office, stopping to watch the activity in a tropical aquarium.

" 'They're going to win, aren't they?' Those were his exact words," I said.

Booth grimaced. It was the one question never far from the thoughts of anyone who worked for ILC.

"He also said that dysgenic research had begun to look promising. Claimed to have inside information to that effect."

"For instance?"

"I don't know. Maybe something that he was funding quietly. I'm looking into it. I have his assistant, a bright girl named Beatrice Harp, more or less in protective custody. My personal custody. While she digs into Artie's business arrangements."

Booth took that in and smiled slightly. "All right. I won't begrudge you. You could use the right sort of distraction, but be discreet."

"Speaking of distractions—" I hesitated, not knowing just where to put this in the context of our immediate concerns.

Booth watched me patiently.

"Elena Grace dropped by the house this morning. Clandestinely. Very early."

"Oh. How long has it been?"

"More than six years."

"How is she?"

"I don't know. I wasn't there. Elena also visited her mother. This is a reach, but it may be that Elena showing up now has something to do with her kid sister going off-line. Although I couldn't get much out of Ida, she was clearly disturbed about Mal."

"Is that why you have a watch on the house? Do you think the expense is justified?"

"Just going with my gut," I admitted.

"No evidence yet that Mal is being held for ransom?"

"I have Lew checking phone logs. But I don't believe that's why Mal is missing. It's not another celebrity snatch. But if she's off-line—" I glanced at Booth's centuries-old Lunarium, which had been updated to also display the time, to the second, that remained before the next full moon. "About eighty-two hours from now Mal will hair-up. There are two reasons for that happening. One, Mal is just being a rebellious twenty-four-year-old brat. She's never been the cookie in the jar with the most raisins. Or else—and I'm still reaching—someone *wants* her to go Hairball, like Chickie Hickey."

"For a similar motive?"

I caught myself rubbing my stomach where it hurt, but deeper inside.

"Maybe. Or to be offered up as some kind of sacrifice."

"Sacrifice is another way of saying 'prey.'" Booth stroked his cheek, lost in thought. "There have been rumors, little wisps of speculation floating around the Privilege. A shoot is being set up. Very large money involved, perhaps even a loving cup. If one is going to chance hunting werewolves, even under controlled conditions, it's so much more prestigious as well as rewarding if the hunter bags a trophy werewolf: a celebrity. Dozens have been nabbed for ransoms, but how many are simply missing during the course of the last two years?"

I couldn't answer that one. Booth queried his computer and the tally blitzed back to us.

"Eleven in twenty-six months. Hadn't thought it was so many. Movie stars like Lance Rodd, Curt Cannon, and Shell Scott. That corporate swindler and deluxe party-giver Colorado Gaines. Jackie Kirk, a very funny bloke. Diane Richelieu, Paula von Hymen—top-tier, all of them, of whom no traces remain."

I said, "There's been one prosecution for staging a hunt. A rancher in Seco Grande named Max Thursday. Claimed he leased his property to a movie company for three days and went fishing. Much to his surprise there was a *mal de lune* shoot in his absence, and if any movies got made they were home movies. His story didn't quite sync up with reality, but all they nailed him with was a fine. What the hell, they were only Lycans. I was thinking of paying Max a call today, to see what I can jog loose from his memory. Like who approached him in the first place."

With Booth's approval I ordered a helicopter. While I waited for the chopper to be serviced, Lew Rolling got back to me about Bucky Spartacus' Escalade.

"The GPS aboard has either been disabled or yanked," Lew said. "Sorry, R."

"Let's find his ride anyway. I'm beginning to believe there's a possibility it was Bucky who spirited his girlfriend away from the Montmorency last night. With help from some members of his loyal entourage. One of them is Cam, the other is Fitz. They live in Carbon Beach."

"Chuck a werewolf, even a dying one, into your ride? That reminds me of the old joke—"

"Heard it," I said. "Just get on your way to Carbon and begin sweating Bucky's crew. I want that boy and I want him fast."

I called Beatrice. She answered on the second ring.

"How are you coming along?" I asked her.

"Wow. I had no *idea*. Artie was one secretive guy. Paranoid, even. His holdings are like mazes within labyrinths. There's a name I keep coming up with. Dr. Chant. As in Gregorian."

"Medical doctor?"

"Don't know."

"Local address?"

"Uh-uh. In the past couple of months he's e-mailed Artie from places like Rio and Darjeeling. Always on the move."

"What's in the e-mails? Wish you were here?"

"No, he keeps asking Artie, 'Does he have it yet?' Situation urgent, he says. Situation critical."

"Maybe he needed to close a deal. Keep digging, angel."

"I'm getting a headache," Bea complained.

I had an idea.

"I sent Sunny home to sleep, but I feel kind of one-armed without a partner. I'm about to hop over to Seco Grande, and I thought you might—"

"Where are you? Burton Way? I'll be there in five, make it five and a half minutes, the elevators in the Radcliffe are poky. So if I'm your partner, do I get sworn in or something? A badge like yours? Wow."

I had to laugh. "You get a free lunch. Now move your sweet—"

Beatrice had already hung up.

6

Anyone who wanted to get around the SoCal hinterland (an area almost three times the size of the state of Massachusetts) without spending hours on old, frequently dangerous roads in elderly vehicles and chancing bridges that could crumble into an arroyo without warning, traveled by air taxi. Or else they owned their choice of aircraft ranging from minijets to ultralight helicopters. The skies could be hazardous over thickly populated provinces.

Except for the rich enclaves like the Privilege or Paradiso Palms out in the desert or Laguna Nigel on the Pacific, the tax base of the rest of SoCal was inadequate to maintain infrastructure properly. There were brownouts and blackouts and bad water and worse sewage systems. Public schools were erratic. In some provinces police protection was subsidized and good. Fire protection throughout SoCal was excellent, a simple matter of self-preservation, financed by the wealthy with everything to lose and supported by celebrity fund-raisers. Otherwise vast areas of SoCal would have been nothing but charred stubble and we all would have choked to death on the dust raised by the Santa Anas.

The SoCal Lycan population, according to statistics kept by the ILC and never made public, was creeping up to sixty percent.

Out of 28 million souls. Rogue werewolves, a much smaller group, were a major headache for us and for large landowners with cattle and other livestock to protect. Low taxes and more subsidies kept the ranchers and growers flush and productive, even those whose cash crops were squantch and poppies, covering thousands of acres.

Max Thursday was a third-generation cattleman. His spread was twenty-five hundred acres of graze east of the Santa Ana Mountains and south of Corona. Good pasture cut through with arroyos and a couple of large barrancas that had water in them in August, probably from deep slow springs. There were maybe three hundred head of cattle on the hillsides. Closer to the home place on an additional, flatter thousand acres we saw wind turbines and a rectangular tank with a few dairy cows grazing in the shade of big cottonwoods.

Beatrice had been researching Max Thursday during our flight.

"One thing is for sure," she said. "Whatever he was paid for the use of his land, he didn't need the money. Majority stockholder in the Citizens' Bank of Riverside. Net worth eight million."

"Maybe he has ex-wives to support."

"One wife. Died four years ago. He lives with his granddaughter Francesca."

I put the ILC chopper down where I had been told to at the south end of an unpaved landing strip. There was a twin-engine Cessna parked beneath an aluminum sunshade and a couple of pumps for the underground tanks of aviation fuel. A golf cart was waiting there along with a teenaged Mexican boy wearing a tattered straw hat and an unbuttoned blue shirt. He smiled bashfully. We climbed aboard and were driven down a straight quarter-mile lane of California oak trees with their hard, sharply pointed little leaves that enabled the trees to thrive where daytime temperatures usually topped a hundred degrees this time of the year.

Irrigation equipment was idle in a flat green truck garden. It was already hot, and still. The house waiting for us at the end of the lane was one of those California old-timers completely alien to the landscape. Three stories high, not counting assorted chimneys bristling with lightning rods and peaked, jerkinhood eaves. The sort of thing that wealthy folk from Philadelphia, where my father was from, put up along the Jersey Shore as the twentieth century was getting off to a good start. This house rambled, with a deep covered porch on one corner and an enclosed solarium on the other side. It was shingle-sided with hand-adzed western cedar. Cross-mullioned windows were partly shielded against the Seco Grande winds and summer heat by the hooded eaves and dormers.

There were no fences except for stock pens and a corral. The usual sheds and equipment you find around ranches. The house was protected from werewolf incursions by the latest in electronic deterrence: a Humvee-mounted Zippo backed up by acoustic blasters (AUGIEs) on the roof of the house. Two TRADs stood at either end of the deep porch.

As if he had been watching us from the moment we landed from behind the screen door, Max Thursday came out of the house when we reached the top step of the porch. An old black-and-white dog limped at his heel. Max himself was eighty-four, standing about five-ten on bulldogger heels and lean to the bone in his Wranglers and pressed khaki work shirt. In the husk of his face old eyes seemed to yearn for greener years. He didn't offer to shake hands when I introduced us, but his good eye, the one without a sizable bloodknot, lingered in appreciation on Beatrice.

"Well, now. Said I would see you as a courtesy, but my lawyer has told me I don't need to say 'nother word about what went on here without my knowledge and consent. I was hoodwinked, as you must know."

"I'm aware of what you told the local law, Mr. Thursday."

"Much as I'm a cattleman, last thing I want is a bunch of werewolves turned loose. I told 'em, anybody who'd listen. It just ain't common sense. Not that I won't shoot a Hairball on sight, and I have kilt aplenty of them. But not for sport. There are laws, and I abide by them."

"Yes, sir."

"Pled nolo contendere as I was advised to do, and paid my fine. It's all behind me." To Beatrice he said with a one-sided smile, the other side of his face seeming to be without muscle tone, "You are a very pretty girl. Got that Creole coloring like some women I comed to know while I was serving in the U.S. Army at Camp Polk, Louisiana. That was in '64, before I was shipped off to that ruckus in Southeast Asia. Would you happen to hail from New Orleans?"

"My mom was from Baton Rouge."

He nodded. His gaze wandered, came to rest on the throwing knife Bea wore. It seemed to impress him.

"Mr. Thursday," I said, "what can you tell me about the movie company people who approached you?"

"There was two of them. Company they represented was called Luxor Pictures. Turned out to be a shell, but the bond they put up was good as gold. Made sure of that before I turned the keys over to them. Then I went fishing."

"By yourself?"

He looked at me with a weary contempt I had unknowingly earned.

"I can do anything now I could do when I was fifty years younger."

Way off in the bright blue distance there was a plume of dust from a motorcycle headed our way.

"In your deposition you said you didn't recall the names of the men from Luxor, and you misplaced their business cards."

He looked blankly at me, as if he'd momentarily misplaced himself. I repeated the question.

"Oh. That's how it was."

"Could you describe the men?"

"Messkins. One kind of stocky, with that long greaser hair tied in back. The other was tall, about your height. Had a couple of gold-lined teeth, and three scars under one eye, like some woman had got her nails into him. He called me *jefe*. Now, when some Messkins call you that, it's the same as calling you a pubic hair." Max Thursday's lip twitched sourly. "Not that I got anything again' the Messkin. Plenty a them's good people. Married myself to a woman from Hermosillo for forty-three years. She'd still turn heads in the street when she was sixty."

The motorcyclist must have been winding it up close to a hundred miles per hour on the straight farm road to the house. The old dog heard it coming although Max didn't seem to: the dog got creakily to his feet and huffed a couple of times, all the bark he had left in him.

"Where do you usually do your fishing, Mr. Thursday?"

"Got me a place in the San Gabes on the Hawknail River. Don't get up there often enough nowadays. Haven't been this year at all."

Beatrice and I looked at each other.

"Was there anything else?" Max asked me, and then to Beatrice, "You're a very pretty girl. You come again sometime. Always room in my house for a pretty girl."

"Thank you," Beatrice said, and with another, brief glance at me she turned to watch the approach of the biker.

"Ain't noontime yet," Max Thursday said, squinting at the sky. "Reckon why she's home early today."

"Is that Francesca?" I said.

It was Francesca. She sat idling twenty thousand worth of BMW road rocket near the steps to the porch and looked up at us from her bronze-tinted face shield before she killed the 1300 cc engine and swung a long leg out of the saddle. Halfway up the steps she took off her helmet and paused to shake out her thick mahogany-toned hair. She was smiling. Beatrice whistled softly, just for me to hear and interpret.

"Company, Max?" Francesca said, looking us over.

Introductions again. Francesca's last name was Obregon. She was in her mid-thirties, I guessed. But with many beautiful Hispanic women it could be hard to tell. She might have been as old as forty-five. Her cheekbones were so prominent they made the rest of her face look almost gaunt. She had bold dark slanting eyebrows and in the clear light of day her eyes looked as black as hot black coffee. She had a sharply notched upper lip and a full underlip; there was a certain proud as opposed to sullen stubbornness in the set of her mouth. She had the kinetic attitude of zest for risky things that went with the expensive hog she rode.

It was the cheekbones, the body language, the toss of her lovely head that prompted a sharp jab of recognition, the certainty that I knew her from somewhere.

"Call me Fran," she said, her free hand on her hip. Not quite a challenge-to-combat stance. "ILC, huh? What's it about this time?"

"Routine," I said, trying to look benign.

Fran shrugged slightly but with unmistakable disbelief and took Bea's measure, her eyes lingering on the throwing knife in Bea's scabbard.

"Hunky," she said. "For show?"

"No damn way," Bea said, as she looked at the silver handle of the knife Fran wore. She blinked a couple of times. "Yours looks kind of neat," she said slowly.

Almost in sync the two women drew their knives and offered them hilt-first to each other for inspection.

"They were just leaving," Max said, taking a couple of steps toward me with hands upraised as if to shoo me off his porch. Then he stumbled. I caught him. He felt as frail as a paper lantern in my grasp.

"Max, did Luz Marie check your blood sugar this morning?" He mumbled something unhelpful. To me Fran said, "Would you mind helping him inside?" And with swift concern she went into the house first, leaving Bea holding both of the throwing knives.

Max Thursday wanted to shake me off, protesting that he could walk five miles by himself anytime he wanted, but right now he wasn't able to keep his feet from crossing, so I kept a hand on his elbow and guided him across the threshold, then into a partly shuttered parlor with eighteen-foot ceilings and three paddle-bladed fans going overhead. He sank into an old rocker with a Navaho blanket thrown across the high back and looked vacantly at the floor while he breathed through his mouth. His spotted hands grappled weakly with each other.

Fran had disappeared momentarily, through an arched doorway where a beaded curtain was moving. Somewhere in the house parrots squawked, birds twittered; it sounded like a distant aviary. Bea stood by a stone fireplace studying pictures on the walls: horses, dogs, ancestors, portraits framed like museum pieces.

I watched the old man. After a little while he looked up at me.

"How do you do, sir."

"Doing okay. Can I get you anything?"

"A drink of water." He nodded his head toward a deal table where there was a pitcher and glasses. I poured some for him. He was looking around now, but seemed far from alert.

"Carlotta may have my room," he said. "She'll be more comfortable there."

"All right," I said. I helped him drink some water.

"Where did she go? She was just here, wasn't she?"

"Fran?" I said.

His brows knitted in feeble asperity. "No. Carlotta. I'm doing this for Carlotta."

"I see," I said.

Fran Obregon returned to the parlor followed by an anxious Mexican woman as plump as a bumblebee. Fran had a diabetics' kit with her. Luz Marie dithered.

"I check him at nine-thirty this morning. He okay then. *Dios mio.*"

"He asked for water," I said. "I gave him some. I hope that was okay."

Max Thursday had put his head against the back of the rocking chair. His eyes opened and closed, but he didn't appear to be in distress. Nonetheless Fran took a reading of his blood sugar. The level was within parameters and she seemed relieved. She pinched one of her grandfather's cheeks lightly.

"Max? You with us, darling?"

He focused on her with a dawning look of pleasure. "Is lunch ready?" he said.

"Almost." Fran glanced at Luz Marie, who ambled away. She looked at me.

"Obviously you put my grandfather under stress. I don't suppose you would mind leaving now."

"We just chatted," I said. I smiled at her but didn't move. "He thought you were someone else," I said, to see what that would get me.

"Did he?" There was something guarded in her eyes. Her lips parted, then closed on an unasked question. She looked at her grandfather again, with fondness and regret. "He gets this way. As we all will." Then she said, mostly to herself, "The years just vanish. Like flies in a sandstorm."

"Is it time for you to go back to work?" Max Thursday asked her in another moment of disconnect.

"Not yet, Max. We haven't had our lunch yet."

"Do you work near the ranch?" I said.

Francesca shrugged, maintaining patience. Just.

"I'm not far. San Jack Town."

Max looked at me. "I didn't ask them to stay for lunch," he said. His mind seemed to be clearing up.

"They won't be," Fran said, her hand on her hip again, fingers curling the way a jungle cat's tail twitches as she prepared to stare me down.

"What is it you do, Miss Obregon? Secretarial?"

That nettled her. "Hardly. I'm an executive of Brenta International. CEO of Nanomimetics, as a matter of fact."

"Oh, Miles Brenta. Do you see much of the big boss?"

"At board meetings."

"Not on social occasions?"

Her eyes narrowed.

"You've been asked to leave," Max Thursday said, energized by the hostility flowing my way. He tried to rise from the rocker. I lent a helping hand. Francesca moved to his other side.

"Who's Carlotta?" I said to her.

"Get out, Mr. Rawson. I mean business."

Beatrice came toward us and laid the silver knife on the deal table. She had sheathed her knife.

"Thanks for showing me this," she said to Francesca, and looked at me with a hint of pleading in her eyes. "We really *do* have to go."

I nodded amiably to Fran, who turned her back on me and guided the old man toward the doorway with the beaded curtain.

I heard Max say, "I'm not going to be in trouble, am I?"

The beaded curtain clacked softly behind them. Parrots squawked in the dimness beyond. Otherwise there was silence.

We walked outside. The Mexican kid looked up from a white wheelbarrow filled with geraniums he was watering and sprinted to the golf cart.

As we went down the steps Beatrice took a firm grip on my arm.

"Oh boy," she said, almost whispering. "Do I have something to tell you!"

"Okay."

"Not here. The farther we are from this place, the better."

I tried to find out why she was agitated, or what had spooked her. But on the trip back to the helicopter she shook her head resolutely and kept mum. She looked back twice at the house, as if checking to see if we were being watched.

I humored her. Once I had the helo airborne and we were headed west Bea let out her breath and opened up.

"There's no way I could actually prove this a hundred percent," she said. "And since my fingerprints are on it anyway . . . but I don't think I'm wrong. Francesca has my knife! The knife we last saw sticking out of the Hairball's throat in Artie's office!"

"It's a custom job?" She nodded. "Do you have your initials on it somewhere?"

"No, damn it. And I'm not saying there couldn't be a few thousand knives around that aerodynamically are virtually identical to mine."

"Then what makes you think—"

"I had the knife for five years almost! And I practiced with it a lot, at least three times a week at the Beverly Hills Knife and Gun Club. The handle is all silver. Nicks and scratches are unavoidable. But there's one particular deep nick where the ball of my thumb rested so that I knew each time my grip was right and my throw would be good. I made it myself with a nail file."

"It's not much to go on," I said. "We'll keep it in mind."

"I still want my knife back," Bea said, glowering. "And now I know where it is." She was quiet for a time. "What did you think of her?"

"*Mucha mujer*," I said, and pretended to dodge her look of displeasure.

"Is she High Blood?"

"She wasn't registering Lycan on my scanner."

"But that doesn't eliminate rogue."

"No, it doesn't. But almost always when I run into a wild one, I know. It's an instinct that has saved my life a couple of times."

I gained some altitude to put plenty of room between us and a trio of ultralights that were like migrating butterflies.

"There are lies in that house," I said. "But they aren't about family bloodlines."

Bea said, "You know that old man was lying, don't you? He's far too feeble to go fishing in the mountains by himself. He was there when they were shooting werewolves. And who do you suppose he had Francesca confused with?"

"Carlotta might be someone in Thursday's extended family who resembles Fran. If not her twin."

"There were at least a dozen beautiful women in those portraits hanging in the parlor," she said. "A lot of resemblances, now that I think about it." She watched me fly for a couple of minutes. "I don't see how you keep us in the air. Your hands barely move the controls."

"If I wagged the cyclic or collective enough for you to notice, we'd be all over the sky. It's a matter of feel, maintaining steady pressure. Want to try the controls yourself?"

"No, thanks. Flying makes me nervous as it is. It's like a circus up here; I keep looking for Dumbo." After a few moments she made another approach to what was on both our minds. "I know I'm not wrong about my knife. But that means Francesca had to be there last night."

"Or afterward, when Chickie's body was dumped."

"I guess so. If she *was* there at de Sade's, then she could've seen me. And she wouldn't have been so quick to hand over the knife." She shuddered slightly. "If she recognized both of us, she's really great at keeping her cool. Some psychopaths are adept at that, aren't they? This is getting complicated. I don't like complicated, and it scares me."

"Whether she was at de Sade's or not, Francesca is connected to both the *mal de lune* hunt and Artie's murder."

"Oh my God! I was hoping you were going to tell me not to worry!"

"When the name 'Carlotta' came up at Thursday's house, it helped me to tie some loose ends together."

"How?"

"Chickie Hickey and Bucky Spartacus are, or were, protégés of the same very wealthy man who likes to dabble in moviemaking. Miles Brenta is also, as you heard Francesca say, chairman of the company she works for. Brenta was, and I believe he still is, married to a woman who survived a werewolf attack. Which is rare enough to be called a miracle."

"And she's the Carlotta Max Thursday was talking about? What was it he said—'I'm doing this for Carlotta.' Doing what?"

"I don't know. What I would like to know meanwhile is how Carlotta Brenta and Fran Obregon are related."

"How hard can that be? I'll find out for you. So do you think Miles Brenta wanted Artie killed?"

"The idea isn't so far-fetched that I can dismiss it. But digging into Brenta's affairs—business or, especially, personal—is asking for trouble. The ILC isn't immune from political pressure."

My hand on the cyclic trembled involuntarily. I dumped the air cushion from beneath the disk like some novice just learning to fly and we sank swiftly enough to make Beatrice yelp in alarm.

Once I had control again and we were level in flight she said, "But you're going to do it anyway, aren't you?"

7

I treated Beatrice to lunch at my usual hangout, Doghouse Reilly's, which was on the ground floor of a thirty-story condo on Pico, one block west of the Wall. Reilly's was an old-fashioned saloon with deep cozy booths and dark oak paneling on two walls, mirrors elsewhere. There were the usual autographed celebrity photos. The beef brisket was good there, and Reilly's had the largest selection of microbrews in Beverly Hills.

A couple of the faces in the photos I recognized as being on the vanished list. But the stars remained in a glossy state of half-life on Reilly's walls, with the color in the photos and the stars' allure of yesteryear both fading slowly into showbiz twilight.

Beatrice said, staring into her glass of beer, "Did you bring Elena here?"

"She always wanted to come when the Dublin Pipers were in town. Reilly's has other good Irish bands on Thursday nights."

"You don't like talking about Elena. I understand. But that just makes me think about her all the more, and wonder—you know."

"You can ask me anything about Elena."

"She was always the Girl Next Door?"

"I remember when I was four or five rocking her in her pram. Later there were birthday parties, but little boys don't play that much with little girls. I think I first started paying attention to her when she was twelve or thirteen and I was getting my growth spurt and some fuzz on my cheeks."

Bea smiled at that. I'd been a little tense at first but as I opened up and found it easier to talk I began to relax, although not without a certain heaviness of heart.

"Her father died when Elena was fourteen. Both of them took Baird Grace's passing very very hard. Ida looks and sounds a lot tougher than she is. She had a breakdown, and Elena was obliged to finish her schooling in the east and in Europe. We wrote now and then but didn't see much of each other for a long time. While she was studying at the London School of Economics she got married—pretty much on impulse, she told me later. I tried and failed at a couple of things before I became an ILC investigator, which suited some talents I barely knew I had. Our two families had a falling-out over Ida's second husband. Ida was obsessed with the idea that my mom stole Ray Scarlett from her. I don't think that's how it was, but Scarlett did go off with Pym on a months-long expedition looking for the remnant of a lost tribe reputed to be immune to Lycan Disease."

"In Borneo?"

"Yeah. Unfortunately Ray got a fever and then his kidneys conked on him. Meanwhile Elena divorced her husband and headed home to Beverly Hills to see what she could do about keeping her kid sister on the rails. Didn't work out: Mal went Lycan at seventeen. The only good thing that came of it was Elena and I meeting again after more than a decade. And—it was—"

"What had been simmering for a lot of years came to a boil."

"Well, that. And by then we had the maturity to appreciate each other. We probably would have been married a month after she returned, if her family situation hadn't been such a mess. Ida claimed she would poison herself if Lenie didn't drop me. As you can probably figure, I was getting most of the fallout from my mom's adventuring with Ray Scarlett."

Beatrice nodded sympathetically. Our lunch came. Bea poked at a salad and I ate most of my corned beef on rye.

"Elena didn't say a word this morning when she found me in your bedroom. Just backed away and disappeared."

"You had every right to be in there. I don't know if I can say the same for Lenie. But it's not going to happen again."

"My being in your bedroom?"

I shook my head. "No, that's exactly where I want you. From now on."

"We haven't had a chance to simmer, much less—"

"Two things I never argue with. Natural selection and my *cojones*. When it's right it's right, Bea."

She whistled low, adding a happy, third note this time.

"I did want to hear that, although I was kind of roundabout getting there." She looked earnestly at me. "But if Elena comes again—"

"She's a woman in trouble, Beatrice. And we're old friends. Last time I saw Lenie she was half out of her mind from grief. Nothing left to offer me but the bad blood in her veins. She asked me to—finish the destruction. I think she must be well over that."

"Or she would've been dead long ago?"

"Yes."

We were having coffee when Joe Cronin stopped by our booth. Not just to say hello. When lawyers in Cronin's league pull up a chair to chat with me it's no coincidence that we happen to be in the same place at the same time.

"The last date I brought here," Cronin said, looking around, "thought 'cunnilingus' was an Irish troubadour."

He was a slight man with a type-A personality who spent most of his days in overdrive. He ran marathons on weekends to bleed off stress. His manner was usually chipper; but once he bore down on you his gaze could chip flint. He was tastefully dressed, as were all the fifty-odd male lawyers in his firm, like an Edwardian-era undertaker. Ah, fashion.

"Beatrice Harp, Joe Cronin," I said.

Cronin flashed a smile of pleasure, then didn't look at her again for five minutes. Because he was a notorious horndog, the fact that I was getting all of his attention meant that I'd probably rather be toasting my bare feet in hell.

"Understand you're looking for one of our clients," he said. His fists were knuckle to knuckle on the back of the chair he straddled.

"Prather Fitzhugh and Golightly has a hell of a client list," I said.

"Bucky Spartacus."

"Oh, Bucky. Yeah, I would like to talk to him. Know where I can find him?"

"Not offhand. He's a busy boy these days. What's it about?"

"I'm looking into a matter involving his girlfriend. Chickie Hickey."

"Another of our clients."

"Really?"

"So what is it all about, Rawson?"

"Ongoing investigation."

He stared at me; I stared back. Since he knew me well enough to know he wasn't going to get anything that way, he relaxed his fists and tempered his approach.

"Okay, so what has she done? Skipped her meds?"

"It may be a case of what's been done to her," I said.

"By Bucky?"

"I don't know yet. Haven't talked to him."

Cronin tried not to look exasperated. "What has Chickie had to say?"

"Can't find her either," I said. "Just not my day, I guess."

"So you have no evidence of a crime committed by either of our clients."

I let that one go, and permitted a meaningful silence to build.

"Anyway, Bucky's High Blood," Cronin said. "He doesn't come under your purview. He doesn't have to say dick to you if he doesn't want to."

"It would be a courtesy," I said.

Cronin thought about it.

"You know he's got this gig tomorrow night. A big boost to his career."

"I heard."

"Right now Bucky could be doing half a dozen things. Rehearsal. Picking out some new threads at Jerry Lee's." Cronin smiled slightly. "I asked him one time why he wore his jeans so tight. He said, 'Man, it ain't rock and roll if your jeans don't hurt.' "

"He's not back on Molochs, is he?" Molochs was another name for crystal meth.

Cronin looked amazed and indignant.

"Hey, that was just a kid thing! Lasted a couple of weeks, then his padrone caught on and had Bucky in rehab fast-fast." Cronin snapped his fingers twice to demonstrate just how on top of things Miles Brenta had been. "Nowadays Bucky's clean as angels. He has a serious nature. A student of TM. So like I'm saying, if he's temporarily out of touch it's because, hell, he's an artist. Needs some alone time to prepare for his gig. They're looking for upward of forty thousand over there in Pasadena."

"Doesn't solve my problem. I'll just keep on hoping I bump into Bucky before then."

Cronin looked over my bargaining chip and decided to call.

"Okay. Just lay off a little while and I'll introduce you to our boy tomorrow night at the fund-raiser. Once his gig is over, have a couple of beers with him. Ask him whatever's on your mind. But I sit in, Rawson."

"Looking forward to it," I said.

Then he took his time checking Beatrice out. Bea offered him a cool nod for his appreciation. The three of us left Doghouse Reilly's. After promising to be in touch about my "interview" with Bucky Spartacus, Cronin dodged a westbound Pacific Electric trolley and grabbed a pedicab for the short trip to his firm's offices on Wilshire.

Bea and I waited for the parking valet to bring my Land Rover. A street sweeper swished by. The Privilege was an immaculate place. No hoochers, curb roaches, bloodstains left by wingless angels. No dirt, bad air, birdcrap, butts, paper cups, gobs of coochputty, cracks in the sidewalks, weeds in the concrete planters. Pedicabs chirped like crickets so you wouldn't absentmindedly walk in front of one. MagLevs hummed along. A million solar-gain windows reflected clouds. A block from us a nearly forty-foot 3-D mural of Bogart, Bergman, and Paul Henreid in the penultimate parting scene from *Casablanca* dominated our shut-in view. Other murals of long-departed stars and their fabulous films were all over town, blown up to cloud-size, relieving the stark ugliness of miles of thick concrete wall. Tourists loved them; but then all of the Privilege must have seemed like heaven for the fantasy challenged of a traumatized society.

Bea said, "I started to get this odd feeling while the two of you were talking."

"What about?"

"Remember you told me how you bumped into Chickie at de Sade's before you came upstairs to see the boss?"

"Yes."

"And you scanned her."

"After she reacted badly to my being a Wolfer."

"So her Snitch was functioning okay?"

"She had one of the new models WEIR has just started using. A LUMO."

"What—"

"For Lunar Module. All updated microcircuitry. Chickie's LUMO was in perfect working order."

"Well—when her brain signaled a changeover in the ladies' lounge, shouldn't her supply of TQ have kicked in immediately and suppressed it? Put her to sleep right there on the pottie?"

"Unless at some point during the thirty-five or forty minutes between the time I saw her last and the Hairball appeared, Chickie's LUMO malfunctioned. No matter how rigorously they're tested, new gadgets sometimes get fritzy. There's another possibility. Someone, and I wouldn't rule out Spartacus, popped the Snitcher out of his gal-pal with the point of a knife, then triggered the mechanism that caused Chickie to go OOPs. Then by some means she was directed to climb to the roof, jump through the skylight, and chomp Artie's head off."

"If Chickie could be turned on like that, then she could also be turned off."

"Yeah. And transportation was waiting. Of course once she skinnydipped Chickie would have no recollection of what she'd been up to as a Hairball."

"Lord above," Bea said softly. She shuddered, although it was ninety-plus in the shade of the leaded-glass canopy above the entrance to Reilly's. I put an arm around her.

"By now," I said, "Joel and Tink ought to have a 3-D panel of mug shots for me to look at. The famous and the infamous who were hanging out at de Sade's last night."

"I should get back to work trying to make sense of Artie's business arrangements." Beatrice looked glumly down at the sidewalk. "Sometimes I'm bewildered by life," she said quietly. "But I try not to live in the bewilderment."

"About dinner," I said. "My house. I'll cook."

"Oh, you cook too?" Her mood improved quickly. She gave me a cheeky grin. "How lucky can I get?"

"We'll see," I said, feeling really full of myself.

At three-thirty Sunny Chagrin came into my office looking refreshed and upbeat. She'd had some sleep and gotten her nails done.

"Where were we?" she said, looking at the display that the virtual reality lab had put together from the surveillance discs ILC obtained from de Sade's. I'd been at it too long already, and my vision was blurring. "Oh, Bucky Spartacus. Talk to him yet?"

"Whereabouts currently unknown."

"Same for the Aussie actress who left her flapper dress behind. So what do we have?"

"Only a long list of things I wish we had. Like Chickie's wristpac. I'd like to know who she was calling in this sequence." I used my laser pointer. "But her body is blocking us from making out most of the number."

"Somebody had to turn off Artie's security."

"Could have been done from a mile away by someone with computer access. About a dozen people who worked at de Sade's were familiar with the system and knew the codes."

"Not necessarily an inside job."

"I doubt that it was."

Sunny slanted a look at me.

"That's disappointing. I thought there might be a chance your big tawny friend with the great ass knows more than she's telling."

"She doesn't," I said curtly. It was shaping up to be one of those days when Sunny was relentless about getting under my skin and on my nerves.

Joel Picón buzzed me from the computer lab.

"R? You wanted to know where Elena Grace entered the Privilege this A.M., and who she was with? We've got it."

Elena had come through the Wilshire gate at the Santa Monica city limits. By motorcycle, and possibly from the direction of the beach. Her ride was a Kawasaki. She wore leather and a biker's cap, but no helmet. The time was 6:17 A.M.

The quality of the Virtual Reality re-creation from surveillance digital wasn't great, but I would have known Elena immediately. Her ID was phony—she was using the name Lonnie Kruger, a variation of "Lenie," her childhood nickname.

Two bikers accompanied her. Joel had good detail of both.

"Sweet God of Mercy!" Sunny said, walking into the VR scene, peering closely at a biker. "I don't believe it!"

I sure as hell didn't want to believe it. My belly suddenly felt as if it were full of cold scrap iron. I turned away from the VR display. Joel looked at me, startled. Maybe it was the expression on my face.

"But what would she be doing with that son of a bitch?" Sunny said. "She has to *know*, doesn't she? Who he is and what he did to both of you?"

"Make use of your contacts in the Diamondbackers and fucking *find* her!" I said to Sunny. I started out of the lab.

"Where are you going, R?"

"Upstairs!"

I walked past Booth Havergal's secretaries and neither of them said a word in protest after a look at my face. When I barreled into his office Booth was vid-conferencing, speaking in French to someone overseas. I banged the door shut behind me. He dropped his feet to the floor and swung around in his palomino leather chair, ready to bark. But my expression must have startled him too. I stood by his boomerang-shaped desk while he told the other party that he'd have to get back to him.

"What the hell do you mean coming in here like that?"

"Raoul Jesus *Ortega*," I said, having trouble getting the name out because the muscles in my jaws were bunched like walnuts.

Booth mulled the name for a few seconds, then got up and crossed his office to his tropical fish tank, staring down at an arrowhead of tiny neon-blue fish hovering above an artificially sunny reef.

"Go on."

"It's been months since I've seen or heard anything about him. Now twice in the same day it comes to my attention that he's making personal appearances again."

"For instance?"

"I talked to Max Thursday at his ranch this morning. Before the old boy had a sinking spell he did a pretty good job of describing Ortega as one of the men who approached him about leasing out his spread for that *mal de lune* shoot. This morning Ortega is with Elena Grace coming into the Privilege via the west Wilshire gate to visit her dear old mother."

"Your Elena?"

"My Elena."

Booth mulled that one too, his face a little lopsided as if he were nursing a bad tooth.

"It doesn't make sense," he said. "What reason would she have for going anywhere near him?" He turned to look at me, fatalistically, I thought. "What do you want me to say?"

"For Christ's sake! Tell me what's going on. ILC Intel posted a *do not disturb* on Ortega. Why is he important to them? What is he up to and what do you know about it?"

Booth shook his head wearily. "Sorry, R."

My face was hot. "Seven years. Seven goddamn years!"

"I know."

"If you know where she is, at least tell me—"

"But I don't, R. This is a surprise to me as well."

I had worked for Booth for nearly four years. I was sure that although he could be evasive about certain political matters within ILC, he had never played me for a sap. If he were doing so now, it was a first. And if at some point I had proof of that, also it would be the last time.

"As for Ortega," he said. "He's still untouchable. That's all I can tell you for now."

There was a hint of sympathy in his hooded eyes, enough to take some of the edge off my temper and my anxiety. I realized I had pushed him as far as I could, or needed to.

I let out a slow breath and looked at the bubbling 250-gallon aquarium, the darting fish in a tranquil tropical setting, and felt fatigue dragging me down like an undertow.

I said nothing to Booth about already having ordered Sunny to track down Elena, working off what little might be learned from the gateway images: Elena on her Kawasaki, both coming and going from the Privilege. Sunny was a genius at getting the most from the smallest of clues.

8

After my last, unsatisfactory meeting with Booth Haver-gal, I called it a day and went home. I prepared a shopping list for the Korean housekeeper who kept nine-to-five hours and sent her in the Land Rover to a farmers' market that specialized in imported foods and condiments I would need to make dinner. It had been a while since I had wanted to cook anything; but I was in a mood to show off for Beatrice.

I worked up a sweat with the weights, bathed, and stretched out wearing only a small towel for a quick nap on my futon. But I was more flogged than I thought. The next thing I knew it was two hours later; Bea was bending over me and light was fading from the sky outside. She'd taken off her clothes. She plucked the towel away, then straddled me with the gleeful expectancy of a small child seating herself on a carousel horse.

After sex we put on short kimonos and went to the kitchen. I inventoried the grocery items Cho Lin had picked up for me. Bea and I had a couple of Killian's apiece, then I put on my chef's hat. She perched on a high stool at the breakfast bar and asked questions: how did I know how to prepare this and where did I find *those* as I made soup from the small nests of white swiftlets, a bird native to Borneo; red rice steamed inside cylinders of green bamboo; and tilapia fillets lightly sweetened with spiced brown cane sugar and baked in banana leaves.

"I learned to cook native while I was on a field trip with Pym," I told her.

"When was this?"

"I was fifteen and bored with school; 'educational dyslexic' is the unofficial term. So Mom figured it was time for my real education. I spent six months with her in the highlands where Sarawak and the Kalimantan come together. Nobody is sure where the border is up there. Nobody really cares, because that part of the world is almost totally uninhabited, thousands of square miles of it. Even the timber trade avoids the area."

"You were looking for the mysterious 'lost tribe?' "

"Rumored to exist, in spite of the werewolves that already had done a very good job of reducing the population of Borneo to a few fortified coastal cities. But we didn't see a soul deep in the jungle. Only scattered, tantalizing traces."

"She was taking quite a chance, though, I mean with her one and only son?"

"She said it was time to toughen me up. Mom left me in the highlands for another year, in the care of a tribe whose shaman she trusted."

"Shaman? Did you learn any, um, magic?"

"What I learned might seem magical to most people. It's not whisking doves out of silk handkerchiefs. I studied mind-body control. Learning to sense and visualize the extradimensional, the telemagical sympathies that connect all living things. My mother is great at it too."

"How tough is your mother?"

"She is six feet of pure, unalloyed mettle," I said, and spelled that for Bea. "So much scar tissue the leeches can't find a place to draw blood."

"You're exaggerating."

"Only a little," I said, and smiled at the thought of my being able to exaggerate anything where Pym was concerned. "There's a full-length portrait of her in her office. I'll show you around out there after we eat."

My mother's office, in a smaller but exact version of the *minka* and surrounded by formal Japanese gardens, was probably two-thirds museum, with all of the stuff she couldn't find room to display in the farmhouse: a large thirty-foot-square room filled with masks, weapons, fertility figures.

I opened a carved chest crammed with mementos and selected a rope of beads from perhaps a dozen native necklaces. I hung the chunky beads around Bea's neck.

"Present from Pym," I said. "I know she'd want you to have them."

"Thank you, Pym," Beatrice said, looking around the half-lit room. "If only I could thank you in person."

"You'll get the chance. Those beads, by the way, are helpful for interpreting dreams and foretelling the future."

"*Our* future?" Bea said, fingering the necklace and not looking at me. Until I put my thumb under her chin and lifted it and a smile suffused her solemn face with pleasure.

I lit an incense burner stocked with aloeswood to dispel the stuffy atmosphere of the room: Pym's office had been unvisited for months. Next I poured a little rice wine for us from a leather-clad decanter. A little is appropriate and advised because, other than suicide, there is only one known cure for a rice-wine hangover, if you happen to have a supply of a medicinal grass root called *gerangau mereh* handy. Rice-wine hangovers are legendary.

A camp lantern seemed to be what was required for ambience as I presented the unframed portrait of my mother to Bea. It was carelessly parked with her other paintings beside a wall-mounted display of *parangs,* which were two-foot-long knives suitable for hacking through jungle creeper and vines covered with barbs like fishhooks, swords for collecting heads, blowpipes for hunting small game, and a shotgun handmade by a clever Panan craftsman utilizing what happened to be available: some reinforced water pipe, an inner tube from an old bicycle, and umbrella springs. The stock and grip were hand-carved.

"I *know* her!" Bea exclaimed, two seconds after the camp lantern afforded her a good look at Pym's portrait.

"You probably saw her *Time* cover when she won the Nobel," I said. "Although that was a few—"

"No, R! I saw her *last week*!"

My grin felt a little funny on my face. "Come on."

"Honestly. It was her, and she was conferencing with Artie on just about the worst satellite feed I've ever seen." She continued to study Pym without a flicker of doubt.

There is no denying my mother is memorable: frizzy cloud of white hair, head of a lioness, incongruous little granny glasses. A passion for discoveries in her dark eyes.

"Artie knows my mother?" I said, completely bewildered.

"They seemed to be old friends. But old friends with a big problem."

"What were they talking about?"

"I was only there in Artie's inner office for a few seconds. But—" Beatrice took a few moments to think about it, still fascinated with the portrait in which my mom stood almost a foot taller than the nearly naked Panan nomads posed on either side of her. She was smiling, leaning nonchalantly on seven feet of staff. I smiled too, and realized that I missed her. I wondered if the first time the Panan glimpsed Pym striding in their direction way up there in the green cloud forest of Borneo they had thought she was a goddess.

Bea said, "Remember that name I came up with when I was researching Artie's holdings and participations? Dr. Chant?"

"Rings a small bell. His name was mentioned? By who?"

"Your mother."

"What else do you remember?"

"About their conversation? That's it. Didn't your mother ever say anything to you about being a business partner of Artie's?"

"I may have had three conversations with her in the past two years. And business has always been the last thing on Pym's mind. She has money; she trusts the bank officers who handle it for her. All of her accounts are POD in my name."

"Rich, huh?"

"Don't know, don't care. I'm well enough paid by ILC. As long as we're on the subject of businesses Artie may have had a piece of, can you give me some names?"

"XOTECH and MegaGenomics, so far. The areas of research are hush-hush. So are the rosters of scientists involved. I Googled their locations. XOTECH occupies most of a large box canyon near Antelope Valley; the road in has three separate checkpoints. MEGA-G is on a small island in a chain of islands in the Scottish Hebrides, accessible only by ferry or helicopter when the wind stops blowing, which is almost never."

My wristpac vibrated. "Rawson," I said.

I got nothing back for a while except for some gusts of stressful breathing.

"Are we going to have a meaningful dialogue," I said, "or can I finish cutting my toenails?"

Then a male voice, choked with grief, came through.

"She's dead, isn't she?"

I had a hunch who I was talking to. I tried raising his hologram, but he was calling me on a retro throwaway cell phone. They had become collectables.

"Is that you, Bucky?"

"Yes."

"Where are you, son?"

"Just . . . tell me. Is she dead?"

"Do you mean Chickie?"

"Yes."

"Bucky, I don't know for sure. I thought maybe you could help me with that."

He moaned softly. "I . . . I don't know either. I don't know . . . what they're trying to *do* to us! I begged Chickie . . ."

His voice broke completely. He sobbed incoherently in my ear.

"Listen, Bucky. I'm glad you called. I want to help you. But we don't need or want to have this conversation on wireless. Just tell me where I can find you. If you're in the area I'll be there in less than half an hour. It'll just be the two of us."

"That thing they gave me . . . something's wrong . . . I don't feel so good."

"Who are you talking about, Bucky?"

"I can't . . . but it doesn't matter. I'll live with it. Everybody does. I just want Chickie back! Please tell me . . . she's not dead!"

That chilled me. How much did he know? "I don't have conclusive proof that she is," I said. "Give me your locaton, Bucky."

A long pause. But he was listening. Hopefully, maybe. Breathing more quietly now.

"Valdemar," he said at last.

"The old Piers Andersson estate in the Palisades?"

"Yes. Shane L'Estrange owns it now. But . . . he's on tour. Lets me hang out at the house whenever."

"Stay put, Bucky. I'm coming."

"Thank you," he said, heartfelt, I thought. The connection was broken.

I looked at Beatrice and told her who I'd been talking to.

"I think he's alone, and certainly scared. I need to get moving."

"I'll be okay," she said.

"In exactly one hour," I said, checking the time, "I'll call you." It was ten-seventeen. "If I don't, notify ILC that my last location was Valdemar, and have them send a patrol."

"Oh Jesus," Bea said softly, snatching her hand away from the necklace she'd been toying with, as if the magical beads had given her a glimpse of the future, as I had suggested they could; and the future she saw was too hot to handle.

Valdemar was a huge Moorish-style house high in the Palisades at the head of a deep barranca with the Pacific Ocean below. The house had been built for a megalomaniacal film director (that's probably redundant) who for thirty years held the title of Meanest Bastard in Hollywood. He also owned a couple of Oscars for his work behind the camera. He never married, lived reclusively when he wasn't filming, and satisfied his erotic cravings with waifs of both sexes, for whom his longtime chauffeur trolled diligently on Hollywood Boulevard.

The twelve-foot-high iron gates at the end of a narrow and private road winding uphill from Sunset were standing open when I arrived. There was curling fog in the barranca that had risen almost to the level of the terrace on the side of the house that overlooked the ocean. I saw only a couple of lights inside.

If Bucky Spartacus had left the gates ajar for me, I hoped that he also had had the presence of mind to turn off the TRAD and the AUGIE brainblasters that a sign posted on the gate by Southland Security Systems warned about.

I looked for Bucky's vintage Cadillac Escalade SUV on the motor court where it most likely would have been, but the cobbled court was empty. The garage doors, all eight of them, were closed.

I drove through the gates and stopped in front of the house. But I didn't get out right away. Instead I was about to call Bucky's cell number when my own wristpac lit up.

An accented voice I didn't recognize said, "Have a look on the terrace, *jefe*."

"Why?"

"We drop off a little package for you."

"Who's this?" I tried to get a look at him, but that feature of his Pac was blocked. No image, no GPS fix. And no reply to my question. But he was still listening. He had a slight wheeze. Overweight, I guessed.

I ended the call, reached behind me and pulled my reliable old short-barrel Remington 12-gauge from its cradle. Six rounds, one already chambered. Guaranteed weight loss for a fat gut; the pounds just melt away.

If someone had wanted to kill me they'd already have shot the Land Rover to pieces and added flaming gasoline. I got out cautiously anyway, stayed low and still felt as exposed as a fly on a wedding cake. I listened but there wasn't much to hear. The scrape of my shoe on a cobble, the ticking of the Rover's engine. The rising fog acted as a blanket, smothering the noise of unseen traffic a mile or so distant on the Pacific Coast Highway.

I moved toward the barranca and the fog, looked down. The moon, rounding to full, was high above the fog bank, adding luster to the glass of terrace doors. I walked down a dogleg of stone steps to the terrace, all two hundred feet of it.

There was a central octagonal fountain populated by marble naiads almost luminously white by moonlight, all of them undraped and anatomically explicit, some erotically involved, others just lazing timelessly around. The package the Greaser had mentioned was there, near the dry fountain. They had dropped her off nude, barely conscious, and wrapped in razor wire. There was a lot of blood. It soaked into the knees of my khaki pants when I dropped beside her, said her name.

Her eyelids flickered.

"Hey. Rawson."

"Who did this, Sunny? Ortega?"

"Damn. I forgot . . . to ask."

"Did you find Elena? Did she have anything to do with it?"

I voice-accessed my wristpac, gave my call sign, and requested a medical team. The wristpac GPS signal would have an ILC chopper over us in less than twelve minutes.

"Limo," Sunny said. Then, "Mal."

"Mal? Mal Scarlett? What about her?"

Sunny was shivering. Each time she shuddered the barbs drew more blood. She licked her lips.

"Angel," she said. "Dead drop. Handicap."

She seemed to be talking in code. Or as if each breath she drew to speak might be her last.

"What do you mean, Sunny?"

"Angel Town."

"Say again."

She flinched like she was being sawn in half and cried out. I didn't want her to hear the fright in my voice. I bit down on my tongue.

"I have wire cutters in the Rover," I said. "I'll be right back."

I thought I saw her smile.

"Know you will," she said faintly.

I sprinted up to the motor court and located the cutters in my tool chest. But by the time I got back to Sunny, it wasn't any use.

9

Sunrise found me still sitting on the wall of the terrace at Valdemar, looking out on a slate-gray sea with a sheen on the horizon, where the moon had set. Nearer the shoreline a few early-rising surfers coasted on some moderate waves. Occasional vehicles southbound on PCH all had their headlights on. There was ground fog at the bottom of the barranca and the moon was down behind some trees like an eye about to close.

Evidence Response teams had finished their work in and around the house and on the terrace without turning up anything significant. If Bucky Spartacus had been there he hadn't left any trace behind. He had called me on a throwaway. So had the wheezing, taunting Latino it would someday be my pleasure to kill.

Raymond Chandler, poet laureate of a different L.A. in what we all nostalgically thought of as a better time, had written in one of his books that dead men are heavier then broken hearts. I looked at my bandaged hands that I had ripped on razor wire in my clumsy efforts to free Sunny and nursed my own broken heart. She had been family to me: smart, wry, a tough counterpuncher when my humor got a little too personal. Kid sister, partner, friend. I kept thinking how I'd sent her to someone or into something neither of us had been prepared for and how her blood was still drying on my clothes. They'd killed her brutally and indifferently and I didn't know why.

I heard my name twice before I looked up. Lew Rolling was standing a few feet away, tapping his wristpac.

"Huggins," he said. "Do you want to talk to him now?"

Ron Huggins and his partner Wade Miller had been the agents I had assigned to the graveyard shift to keep me informed of activity at Ida Grace's home. I nodded. Lew projected Ron's hologram toward me.

"R, we're so goddamned sorry about Sunny. Anything yet?"

"No." I glanced at the top of the steps to the terrace and saw Booth Havergal starting down with one of his bodyguards. "Did Ida have a peaceful night?" I asked Huggins.

"Uh-uh. She had her chauffeur drive her to Van Nuys airport at two this morning."

"Ida had travel plans?"

"The airport was as far as she got. Stayed in the limo when they arrived. At 0225 a helicopter showed up, one of those twelve-passenger jobs. As soon as the helo was on the ground Mrs. Grace left the limo and walked over to it. She was helped up the stairs and inside by a crew member. She stayed just shy of fifteen minutes, returned to the limousine, and was driven home. She arrived at 0300. The helicopter, by the way, is owned by Brenta Development."

"Thanks, Ron."

His hologram vanished. "Miles Brenta," I said to Lew. "Funny how his name keeps coming up. Or maybe it's not so funny."

"How do you mean?"

Booth Havergal came over to us, and dismissed Lew with a glance.

To me he said, "I was on a call with Joe Cronin. He has not heard from their rocker client."

"Or wouldn't admit it if he had."

Booth stroked his chin with a forefinger. He always looked freshly barbered no matter what hour of the day it was.

"I'm not easily lied to. I have to know that you're absolutely certain it was Bucky Spartacus you were talking to, inasmuch as you've never met the lad."

"He knew a couple of things about Chiclyn Hickey only the two of us should know. Bucky was convinced that she was dead. He said to me, direct quote, 'I don't know what they're trying to do to us.' Which to my way of thinking indicates complicity, however unwilling he might have been."

"Go easy, R."

I looked at the place by the fountain where each blood spot was being sampled while a couple of kneeling naiads looked on. In the mild light they seemed as if they might be mourning. I turned and leaned out over the wide flat-top railing and vomited stale coffee and what bile I had left into the barranca. I wiped my mouth on the back of a bandaged hand and stared at Booth, eyes running, trying to get my breath back.

"Easy's over with," I said. "I'll build a solid case if I can. But if I can't and it looks as if the ones responsible for Sunny might walk, then it'll be blood for blood."

"Take some medical days, R. Give the wounds a chance to heal."

"No."

"It's not a suggestion."

"I'm not out of control."

"Closer than you think, fella."

"I can deal with it. Anger doesn't make me blind and it doesn't make me stupid. You know that, Booth."

He was on the verge of suspending me. He studied my face as if looking for hex markings. I couldn't blame him. He had a shop to run and his reputation to think about. But once he made his decision reluctantly in my favor he set his jaw and nodded.

"Sunny was the best. I know what this case means to you. Get some sleep, get a tetanus booster, and I'll see you in my office at three this afternoon. We'll go over everything we have so far, and decide how to proceed. *I'll* decide."

Beatrice met me at the front door when I returned to the house on Breva Way. She took a startled step back when she saw me, as if she were witnessing an apparition at a séance. I'd called her hours earlier but I hadn't done much explaining; she only knew that Sunny was dead.

"Your hands—"

"Not as bad as it looks. Some gouges and scratches. I cut her out of the razor wire because I didn't want anyone else to see her like that."

"Oh God! Who could do such a vicious thing?"

"The world's full of them. I need a shower."

I started down the black slate hall, pulling off my shirt as I went.

Bea said, "Your neighbor's here."

"Who do you mean?"

"Ida Grace. I think. She wouldn't tell me her name, or much of anything else I could understand."

I went back to her. "Where is she?"

"I tried to make her comfortable in the tea room. I hope that's okay. It was a little past four, I think. I heard someone walking around outside, talking. Scared me. But when I looked out I saw it was only a small old woman in her dressing gown and slippers. She wasn't trying to get into the house. She sounded incoherent. I went out to the lanai and invited her in. She seemed in shock, but when I coaxed she followed me. She kept saying in this earnest, pleading tone, like she was answering a voice in her head, 'How could you? She's all I have left.'"

"Uh-huh," I said, neither making sense of that nor wanting to see Ida Grace myself right now.

"I looked in on her just a few minutes ago," Bea said. "She'd finally stopped talking to herself. Her eyes were closed. Maybe she fell asleep."

"Let her sleep," I said. "Give me twenty minutes. I could use something to eat. Toast, cereal. No coffee."

When I was out of the shower I put some adhesive bandage on my hands, enough to cover the worst of the gouges without impeding my fast draw. I dressed and took the bowl of oatmeal and sliced bananas Bea fixed for me into the tea room. Ida Grace's eyes were still closed, but the veined grayish lids twitched and a slippered foot jumped while I looked her over, noting smudges on her housecoat and pajamas, a tear at one elbow. I figured she had climbed over the eight-foot wall between our properties. No razor wire there, but a lot of climbing roses.

I wondered what had compelled her to try a stunt like that at her age, what she'd been escaping. I reached down and nudged Ida awake in the lyre-backed Chinese Chippendale chair.

"Uhh!" she exclaimed, knocked loose from the grip of an intolerable dream. She breathed harshly through her mouth for a few seconds as if she were still climbing the garden wall. She looked up at me, looked around the tea room.

"Just as I . . . remember it," she said.

I put my bowl of half-eaten oatmeal aside. My stomach felt better for having given it something to work on.

"Who did you meet at the Van Nuys airport?"

Ida licked dry lips. Beatrice gave me a barbed look and said, "You might at least offer her a cup of tea first."

Ida looked at her with a faint grateful smile.

"Yes. Tea. If it's no bother. I don't recall your name?"

"Beatrice. And it's no bother."

So we waited until Ida sucked up half a cup of green tea. Which did serve to steady her, and brought a trace of color to her cheekbones.

"Now then," I said. "You got some bad news a few hours ago, and you're here to see if I can do something about it."

"I thought . . . I could deal with the situation myself. After all . . . she did owe me. I could have betrayed her to her husband. I chose at the time not to . . . make a fuss, for all our sakes."

She looked at me as if all that were perfectly clear. I shook my head slightly.

"Of course you wouldn't know anything about it. Although I'm sure it isn't news that . . . my husband was a philanderer."

"Which husband?"

"Raymond. Scarlett." She looked around the tea room again, made a nervous gesture. "It must have been going on here too, under this roof."

"Alleged infidelity," I said. "My mother has better sense." I almost said, *And better taste*, but that would have amounted to piling on, and I didn't want to antagonize Ida unnecessarily. "It would help if you could tell me who you visited in the Brenta helicopter at Van Nuys airport."

She looked at me as if she were disappointed in my powers of perception.

"Carlotta, of course."

"Miles Brenta's wife." I saw Bea purse her lips, but she didn't whistle. I said, "How long ago did Ray and Carlotta have their affair?"

"Oh—quite a long time. I married Raymond twenty-five years ago. He'd had roundheels long before I married him. Don't know what made me think marriage would change him. But if there were others besides Carlotta—I cast a blind eye on that side of our relationship."

"So Ray Scarlett had Car Brenta as one of his lovers. This would have been well before she was chewed up by a werewolf, and that was—ten years ago?"

Ida quivered and slipped a little sideways in the chair.

"I never imagined that she would agree to see me. But Lenie had said that Carlotta was the one I must talk to. Only Carlotta could give Mal back to me. So I contacted her. To my surprise she—she seemed almost delighted to hear from me. At least that's how I interpreted her lengthy response to my e-mail message. I felt greatly relieved and encouraged. I had no way of knowing until I met with Carlotta in the—in person, that she is probably insane."

"As a result of the attack?"

"I believe so."

"Then why is Miles Brenta letting her run loose at two in the morning instead of keeping her under watch in a plush sanitarium like Lodge Pine or Quail Woods?"

Ida reached out and almost knocked the cup and saucer off the little table next to her. Bea rescued both and poured more tea.

"But she *was* watched. Discreetly, by young men I took to be male nurses. They must be a necessity. When I saw her, even in the low light of the helicopter's cabin—dear God, the damage! She had had her hair done. It wasn't much help. She was almost too talkative and animated, as if she were in the manic phase of bipolar disorder."

Ida blinked several times. After the last couple of blinks there were tears clinging to her eyelashes.

"Carlotta was wearing a black veil, much like a mantilla. And oh, she *smelled*. She smelled like a wretched excess of cheap perfume. But at the same time she also smelled of decay. An overpowering rottenness. She held out her hand to me, although she couldn't rise. I had to take her hand even though I was stifled by her lurid odor. The hand was dry and cold and had no strength in it.

"She said, 'So delighted to see you again, Ida. I sent flowers. Ray will always live in my memory.' She was talking about the service for Ray as if it had been only last week. Her voice was odd and slurred, she could barely pronounce some of her words. One of the attendants aboard the helicopter offered me brandy. I thought I had better have it to keep my gorge from rising. After it was brought to me I asked Car why she wasn't having one as well. That's when she pulled her veil aside and showed me her *face*. Obviously plastic surgeons had done their best. But severed nerves are beyond a surgeon's ability to repair. Car's lips are twisted and don't meet on the right side of her face. She drools constantly, into a towel that is wrapped around her throat. That was the smell all of her perfume couldn't mask. 'I drink through a straw,' she said. 'And I have trouble swallowing. Yet in spite of everything I have managed to keep up my appearance, don't you think?' "

Ida wiped at the tears on her cheeks.

"Once I thought I hated her," she said quietly.

"All right," I said. "What does Car Brenta have to do with Mallory?"

"I asked her if she'd seen my daughter. That didn't help, but when I described Mal she said yes, she thought she had seen her recently. 'Pretty young people come to our parties all the time,' she said. 'Miles invites them because he knows that I like to watch young people having a good time.' "

"Kind of a surreptitious social life," Bea observed. "But I guess one look at Carlotta would chill the party."

I said to Ida, "You told her Mal was missing and possibly has committed a class-three felony?"

"No! What do you mean, a felony?"

"Deliberately going off-line is just that. But if Mallory's Snitcher has been removed without her knowledge or consent, then someone else has committed a felony."

"Without her knowledge?" Ida said, surprised and alarmed. "But how could that be?"

"Maybe she's fallen in with a bad crowd. Like some of the people Elena is running around with. Kidnappers. Bloodleggers. Murderers for fun and profit." A grisly image of Sunny Chagrin hit my mind and I couldn't chase it away. I didn't as yet understand what the profit motive was in her death. But there would be one. Diamondbackers, like a lot of businessmen, were rigorous in their fidelity to greed.

Ida said, "It was Elena who told me—"

"Yeah, to try to get information from Car Brenta about Mallory. Implying two things: that Elena had reason to believe Carlotta might know something useful, and that Mal is in real jeopardy. But Lenie might not realize just how off in the head Carlotta is. I wonder—"

Beatrice had to give me a hard nudge; I had been staring holes in Ida while a far-fetched notion pinballed around my brain trying to find another, cockeyed notion it wanted to mate with.

"Wonder what?" Bea said.

"What other kinds of parties Miles Brenta likes to throw to keep his wife entertained."

That prompted a small gasp from Ida.

"When Carlotta spoke of pretty young people she also said, in a matter-of-fact tone of voice while she drooled into her towel and looked at me with such lifeless, haunted eyes, 'But as I said to Francesca, so many of them deserve to die, don't you think?' "

I couldn't sell it to Booth Havergal.

"*If* Mal Scarlett partied recently at Miles Brenta's house, there is no reason to assume it has anything to do with her disappearance. Hearsay and speculation by no means justifies trying to get through Miles's phalanx of lawyers to question him."

"There's a likely tie-in between the *mal de lune* shoot at Max Thursday's place a few months ago and Brenta himself," I argued.

"If you're talking about Francesca Obregon—" Booth shook his head.

"The Bleat blogs have linked them. And we know from a genealogy Website that Francesca and Carlotta are first cousins."

I composited the virutal reality images of Francesca and Car Brenta, before the werewolf attack on Car. Two beauties who easily could have been mistaken for each other. "And it wouldn't surprise me to know Francesca was quick to assume Carlotta's wifely duties in her husband's big brass bed."

"I wouldn't begrudge Miles whatever happiness he was able to find following such a tragedy," Booth said with a hint of cynicism. He iso'd Fran in the display. "She is a marvelous-looking woman. And very important to him in the business as well. WEIR just received a very large shipment of the LUMOs her firm designed and manufactures. Three million units initially."

Limo, Sunny had whispered to me as she was dying. Or was it more like *LUMO*? I hadn't thought about it again until now.

"As for Miles being involved in something like a *mal de lune*, however comfortably removed from liability he might be, well, he always has been a sharpshooter. Business or pleasure."

"You know him better than I do," I said. The Lunarium in Booth's office was reading fifty-seven hours and a couple of minutes to the next Observance. Mentally I felt hog-tied; physically I wanted to grab a couple of people and shake some truth out of them.

I had turned off my wristpac voicecom for the meeting with Booth, but I had a text message.

"Bucky Spartacus showed up for the sound check for tonight's big bash, and is currently sacked out in a borrowed starbus," I told Booth.

"So he's planning to go on tonight."

"Yeah. I'll be talking to him after his gig. Cleared it with Joe Cronin."

Booth was staring out a window, hands clasped behind his back. In the space between us, the VR heads of the women revolved slowly.

"Somewhere in all of this, werewolves amok, the murders, the disappearances, a motive must lie." When Booth was stressed he could sound like Hercule Poirot in an old Agatha Christie novel. "None of it is as random as it might seem. Let's crack on, then. Bring me evidence, R."

"Lew's trying to find out who Sunny was in touch with yesterday. But we don't know where her ride is and her wristpac's missing, so—Booth, about Sunny. The arrangements."

"I spoke to both of her parents this morning. Unfortunately they're too infirm to travel to SoCal for the departmental service; I've arranged for them to see it on a satellite feed. Then we'll send her body home."

Beatrice had spent a couple of afternoon hours shopping for an outfit to wear to the concert in Pasadena. When I picked her up at the Radcliffe she was wearing a cream-colored Capone with twenty-inch-wide cuffs and brown striping, a white shirt with a high collar that flattered her long neck, a plain black tie, and a high-crowned cream fedora with about four inches of black band. The brim of the fedora riding rakishly low, covering the tops of her ears.

She struck a pose, hands in her pants pockets, for me to admire.

"Priority hunk," I said. "But I thought we were going bowling."

"I really splurged," she said a bit ruefully. "Don't know what I'll do for a job now that Artie—" Her ebullient mood palled somewhat. "By the way, I made funeral arrangements. Cremation, once his body is released. His lawyer confirmed; it's in his will. He has no survivors that we know of."

"Where's his cash going?"

"Hospitals, orphanages, nursing homes. All of them listed as 'Pay on Death.' "

"You could run de Sade's," I said. "If and when it reopens."

She shrugged.

"Might as well. I was mostly running things anyway while Artie took his litle trips and holed up making mysterious phone calls."

"What kind of mood was he in after he talked to Pym last week?"

"Lous-y. He was, in fact, being a mean little prick. He'd get that way, out of frustration, I guess. More and more often during the last three months."

"Did he make any references you might not have paid attention to at the time?"

She was still thinking about that when we boarded the chopper at ILC along with Lew Rolling and two more agents, Ben Waxman and Harry Stiles. Lew had the controls. Bea and I sat together in the back.

"I did hear Artie mutter something like 'motherfuckers.' Then, a little later he looked at me, or through me is more accurate, and said, 'The only language greed knows is money. So okay, no eight-count. Go for the knockout.' "

"Knock out who? Or what?"

"How would I know? I sort of edged out of his line of sight and left him sitting behind his desk, staring at a blowup of himself in the ring, with a mouse eye but with his gloves above his head, doing a little victory prance. He couldn't have been more than twenty-five in that photo."

"Dreams of glory," I said. "Whatever he may have been planning this time, the opposition got wise and had him whiffed."

"Yes," Bea said with a stony expression. "I remember."

During our ten-minute flight I outfitted Bea with a pair of digicam glasses and an earbud the brim of her hat concealed. Then I handed her a backstage pass to wear. She was more impressed by the pass than by the junior-detective rigging.

"Where did you get *this*?"

"We're ILC," I said. "Ask, and if ye do not receive, counterfeit something. But that pass is the real deal."

"Why do we have so much company tonight?"

"To help me keep an eye on our boy. This gig was too important to his career for him to pass up, but afterward he might take a notion to dust. I don't feel like being stood up again."

"What do you want me to do, R?"

"Hang out with the rockers. Make friends, have a good time, and take a good look at anyone who comes within a few feet of our Bucky. Don't fiddle with the glasses; it's a giveaway. We'll be receiving everything you look at."

"How?"

"We have a tech van at the venue."

"Oh. You really want to talk to him bad."

"What I want is to nail Bucky's skinny ass and as many others as he'll cop to for conspiracy to commit murder."

Her lips pursed for a whistle, but because of the whine of the turbine overhead I didn't hear it. I did see a racing shadow of anxiety in her eyes.

"Where will you be, R?"

"Around," I said, and gave her hand a reassuring squeeze.

An earthquake snaking through Arroyo Seco a few years ago had heavily damaged the venerable Rose Bowl, particularly the stands on the Linda Vista Avenue side. That area was now a long grassy knoll. The part that had been salvageable was a thirty-five-thousand-seat arc preserving all of what had been the south end zone of the stadium. The stands had been refurbished as an amphitheater. The stage was an elaborate three-tier affair. Behind the stage there was parking for support groups, limousines, tour buses, satellite uplink trucks, and a warren of hospitality tents. There were also five helo pads, most of them for the use of law enforcement agencies.

We flew in with a sunset spilling into low clouds behind us like lava from a volcano.

The stands appeared to be filled already. The highly desirable infield was packed, probably another three thousand fans who wanted to mosh. More of them were spread across the grassy knoll in the last red glow of daylight, picnicking, getting high. They paid much less than those within the amphitheater and could watch the acts on a jumbotron screen mounted on massive steel scaffolding at the southwest corner of the stage.

The band opening for Bucky and the trash goddess Chimera was already into its set. As Lew descended to a helicopter pad marked ILC we had a look at a scale model of the church for which they were raising money that was displayed on one side of the stage. The church was architecturally impressive and—I remembered Artie's description of the fusion of Christianity with Lycanthropy—more entrepreneurial than religious.

There was a cable-suspended backdrop the width of the stage on which a tanned, athletic Jesus, wearing a white singlet with a gold cord at the waist and with His beard neatly trimmed, was surrounded by birds, both hawks and doves, and creatures of the wild—including, prominently, a wolf at His sandaled feet. Domestic variety. The right hand of Jesus was raised over the wolf's head in a gesture of peace and friendship.

"It's going to be a fun evening," Beatrice said. But not as if she were entirely sure of that, or herself.

10

I posted myself in the tech van where I could observe, on feeds from amphitheater security, everything that went on at the sprawling venue and keep in touch with Beatrice as she prowled backstage and tried not to trip over anything.

A line of stretch limos, each about half a city block long and escorted by motorcycle cops, arrived. High-level EiE talent agents and clients unloaded, mingled, drifted into the white vinyl hospitality hives. Johnny Padre, wearing casual chic tonight, dressed like a comedy sailor from the chorus of *Pirates of Penzance*, was there with his twenty-one-year-old actress-wife, who made the description "stunning" sound like faint praise. The Padres and a few others of similar rank or god-quality stardom formed ranks and trooped around to the starbuses to stick their heads inside for the obligatory good wishes.

Backstage Beatrice encountered the Reverend A. A. Kingworthy, pastor of the First Church of Lycanthropy, and his entourage. He was waiting to say a few words of welcome and offer the invocation before the evening's stellar attractions took stage. He smiled at Bea, liking what he saw, bowed slightly and called her "sister."

When she moved away Bea whispered in my ear, "Is the Rev a Lycan?"

"No. He's just a humble preacher with a love for all of God's creatures and what they can contribute to his personal well-being."

"You're such a cynic."

"Roger that. Over and out."

I had a look at another limo arriving. Three beefers got out, then the Man himself—Bucky Spartacus' mentor and, I presumed, confidant—Miles Brenta. Who turned to offer a helping hand to his female companion as she emerged.

I thought it was past time that I had a heart-to-heart with Brenta. And I didn't mind the prospect of seeing Francesca Obregon again.

Two of the beefers converged when I approached within twenty feet of Miles Brenta, who had his back to me and his head down as he said something to Francesca. She saw me over his shoulder and her eyes got bigger, her full mouth twisting a little in irritation. Which prompted Brenta to look around.

I had to stop in my tracks or start kicking beefer butt, but because they undoubtedly carried Tasers my choice was clear enough. So all I did was wave cheerily to Francesca.

"Hey there, Fran! We seem to be running into each other all over the place!"

Miles Brenta glanced curiously at Francesca, who shrugged. I included him in my greeting.

"Rawson," he acknowledged. He nodded to his beefers. "No problem. Let him come."

They stepped aside and I made it a threesome alongside their limousine. Fran was dressed Mexican-peasant style, the Zapata era: a blouse with full sleeves that was laced, not tightly, at her breasts; a clingy midcalf cotton skirt made for twirling and whirling; and rope sandals. Brenta, a man some distance into his fifties who obviously took great care of his body, wore a black T-shirt and black jeans and a Greek fisherman's cap. He was hard-boiled handsome with a somewhat liverish complexion and he didn't trim his graying eyebrows. He was one of those men who belong to money the way talons belong to a bird of prey.

Francesca was still annoyed. Brenta smiled thinly and said, "Where do you two know each other from?"

She drew a long breath but before she could speak I said, "I was visiting with her *abuelo* yesterday when she came cruising up to the home place on her Kraut Klipper."

"Max Thursday's house? More bother about that *mal de luner*? Old business, isn't it?"

"Not as long as we may be looking at the prospect of another one soon."

"Those things go on," Brenta said quietly. "But you've met Max. He couldn't have had anything to do with any of it."

"I've told him as much already," Fran said, a fist on her hip. One of these days she was going to take a swing at me. It was something to look forward to.

Although the windows of the stretch limo they'd stepped out of were tinted nearly full black, I noticed the flare of a cigarette lighter inside and had a glimpse of a long face, pale as a seed buried in a jar of jam. The window had been let down about an inch, as if someone were interested in hearing what we were talking about.

"Great turnout for Bucky's big night," I said, looking at the starry sky as I changed the subject. "For a while I was afraid he'd be a no-show."

Brenta looked at me with fading patience but not as if I had touched a nerve. Fran was a lot more uneasy. The woman just did not have a knack for keeping her thoughts, or worries, to herself.

"Just what do you mean by that?" Brenta asked.

"Oh—I thought he might have told you."

"No. I haven't spoken to Bucky for a couple of days. So many business matters taking up far too much of my time." He waited for me to explain. I wasn't in a hurry.

"Congratulations, by the way. On the success of your LUMO. WEIRs received about three million of them so far, I'm told."

Brenta nodded. "The honors belong to Francesca and her development team. I merely provide the financing. About Bucky—"

"He called me late last night. Sounded really broken up about his girlfriend. Another of your protégés, I believe."

"Do you mean Chiclyn? Yes, they've been keeping steady company, as all the world must know. What about Chickie?" He stared at me without blinking.

"Seems to be missing. When did you see her last?"

Brenta turned to Francesca. "Friday night, wasn't it? The party after we saw the rough cut of *Ghost Galleon*?"

"Umm," Fran murmured, looking at me as if I had brought up a family curse.

"Why do you believe she's missing?" Brenta said. "And what reason would Bucky have for contacting—"

"A Wolfer? I plan to ask him just that in a little while. I agreed to meet with him at Valdemar last night to find out what had him crying on the phone, who he was afraid of."

"Afraid?" Brenta said, looking more wary then puzzled. Francesca started a turn of her hand toward the limo, then checked herself.

"But he didn't show," I said. "There was no one at Valdemar but my partner Sunny Chagrin. She was wrapped naked in razor wire and bleeding out on the terrace. I'll be asking Bucky about that too."

"*Dios mio!*" Francesca said. I'd upset her; it was either Bucky or the razor wire. Or both.

"Take it easy, Cesca," Miles Brenta said, without sounding particularly annoyed. But the ice of his eyes seemed to have deepened as he studied me. "Are you alleging that Bucky had something to do with the murder of an ILC agent?"

"He asked me to meet him at the Valdemar estate. Then he

dusted, leaving a body behind. That's topic A for an intensive interrogation, wouldn't you think?"

"I assume that you recorded this conversation you say you had with Bucky."

"No, sir."

"Then I advise you, and Bucky's legal counsel also would advise, that you not pursue this."

"I wouldn't have grounds," I admitted, "if I couldn't prove that Bucky met Chickie at de Sade's early Monday morning. Surveillance cams showed them arguing heatedly. Shortly thereafter Chickie paid a visit to the ladies' lounge, haired-up in a bathroom stall, climbed to the roof of the building, jumped through a skylight, and beheaded Artie Excalibur with one good chomp of her girlish jaws."

I gave their reaction a three-count, then added: "I think Bucky knew it was going to happen, and why. Tonight he's going to tell me about it."

I made a fist below my belt buckle to indicate just where I had Bucky's nutmuffins, and how tight, and walked away.

"Meantime, enjoy the show."

Now and then I have this tendency to get a little cocky.

The opening band had finished its set. As I walked back to the ILC van the Reverend A. A. Kingworthy and his support group from local churches, including a gospel choir, were taking stage to a frenzied welcome from the crowd—most of whom, I supposed, were familiar with the Rev through his television ministry. Kingworthy was a veteran grifter who had learned his trade on the raise-'em-from-the-dead evangelical tent-show circuit, paying his dues in order to earn this exploitative shot at the Greater Glory.

I paused near the van to watch the multicamera action on the Jumbotron. My perspective was distorted; the crush of sound and flashing light show gave me the feeling that the trembling earth might open beneath my feet at any moment.

The man had style and presence, no denying that. He was nearly seven feet tall and probably more than three hundred pounds in a draped pearl-gray silk suit that glistened like sunlight on a waterfall. But he had the moves of a dancing pony and he didn't need amps to deliver his simple message. Each time he shouted "Brothers and sisters, Jesus loves you!" to a crowd that may have been ninety percent Lycan, their celebration reached a new height of ecstasy. Each time he wiped his streaming brow on a fresh white handkerchief and dropped the hanky into eager hands below the stage, more young and even middle-aged Lycans fell to the ground in paroxysms of religious fervor. In the stands tens of thousands of hands were thrust on high, shaking in spasms of emotional hunger, charging the air with an energy that ignited their tainted blood and empowered their nascent beasthood.

(So promise them, Brother Kingworthy, what no impalpable deity can hope to provide. Lead them all out of the wilderness, but to what? An even more violent and nightmarish wilderness.

Because if you disappoint them, and you will, see what happens to the civilization we're barely clinging to now.)

My chest was tightening. I felt angry. I hated the spectacle and was afraid of the ease with which the preacher inspired their frenzy, reminded each Lycan of his low earthly status and the fact of his captivity. I was hearing wolf-cries now. There was an underlying, malevolent potential in the Reverend Kingworthy's congregation, so close to becoming a mob. The moon was overhead at this hour, only a couple of days shy of peak power—the power in the blood of all Lycans that no wall could be built high enough or strong enough to resist.

Chimera had come out of her starbus with her band and her entourage and was on her way backstage. Bucky Spartacus appeared, likewise surrounded by his court, and the two luminaries paused to embrace. Chimera had a hit on the joint Bucky was smoking. There seemed to be a lot of in-group camaraderie.

Bucky was tall and splinter-thin. He wore an open leather vest that framed a full-torso tattoo elaborate as an epic poem. His low-slung leather jeans were ornamented in flashy silver. He had to have a high threshold for pain just to walk in those jeans, let alone strut a stage. Chimera's erotic laminates and usual see-through costuming made genital herpes seem almost wholesome. In the later years of a hard-boiled career she didn't just have a bad reputation; she had chronicles of infamy.

My wristpac vibrated. I had a text message.

I can't stop this or
I'll be exposed. It's
up to you. Bucky must
not get on that stage!!!

It was signed "E."

I looked up, then around the crew lot behind the big stage. There were only a couple of unpaved acres, surrounded by a chain-link fence. The lot was no better lighted than it had to be. A scrim of squantch-tainted smoke and pale dust further dimmed the lot's worklights. Faces less than thirty feet away were hard to make out. Most of the available space was devoted to limos, the starbuses, and at least ten large tractor-trailer rigs that belonged to the stage-lighting techs, the set construction gang, event staff, and the satellite network that was taping the concert.

I saw Miles Brenta and Francesca Obregon get back into their limo instead of heading for the show. Maybe they were bothered by all the dust. The star attractions were on their way up the wide ramp to the backstage area.

There was a shortcut down an alley between two eighteen-wheelers and I took it, wondering how the hell I was going to stop the show with no good reason for doing so, and on dubious authority. But Elena, no matter how elusive and mysterious she was acting now, whatever her state of mind might be, was someone I couldn't believe would, as Bea had put it, fuck with my head.

My mind and eyes were on Bucky Spartacus and I didn't pay as much attention as I should have to a couple of Latinos sitting high inside the cab of the big rig on my left. The one closest to the open door had a walkie-talkie to his ear. About sixty pounds of sagging gut spilled over his belt. I barely noticed the other one.

The next thing I was conscious of I was flat on my face in the dirt with Taser barbs in my neck, twitching out of control, the aftermath of a lightning bolt flickering through muscle, nerves, and brain.

El Gordo and his partner hauled me back into the shadowland between trailers and dumped me on my back. I was still powerless. They had quick hands, sorting through my pockets, yanking my earbud, gun, and wristpac and pitching them under a trailer.

"*Hola, jefe,*" El Gordo said, the ribbed sole of a boot on my neck. "You doan take a hint so good." He had a definitive wheeze, a voice that was familiar even in my befuddled state.

His partner smiled and walked away and waved a flashlight over his head, signaling somone.

I heard the whoosh of a truck's airbrakes being released. El Gordo's pocked swarthy face reddened from the tailights of a forty-foot trailer as the driver jockeyed his rig, warning beeper sounding, into the alley we occupied. Gordo's partner came back and I was hauled to my feet, strong-armed up against the ribbed side of a parked trailer. There we waited for the rig to come close enough to dump me under a set of wheels. I was an accident about to happen. I still had the Taser barbs in my neck and no fight in me. I could've used another thirty seconds. I wasn't going to get them.

A motorcycle headlight flashed at the other end of the trailer alley as the rider made a tight turn and came slowly toward us. The truck driver must have seen the bike in his rearview. He stopped his rig to assess the situation.

El Gordo and his partner stared at the oncoming biker, who was astride what looked like the 650 cc Kawasaki Ninja, maneuvering the sport bike with one hand and boots on the ground. The other gloved hand held a sawed-off shotgun. I didn't know whether to feel good or bad about that.

Gordo knew. His smile signaled a discreet retreat. His grip on me loosened. He shrugged and gave me a little push away from him.

"*Muy borracho,*" he explained to the unknown biker, and showed more of his teeth. I participated unwillingly in his charade by taking two wobbly steps and pitching to my knees. I squinted up into the headlight of the rice rocket, built for speed. So was the slender biker, anonymous in black from helmet and face shield to buckled boots.

The biker didn't say anything, to me or the Latinos. The double-barreled muzzle of the shotgun motioned me to my feet. I was happy to oblige. I looked back at El Gordo and partner. Each man was the soul of innocence. I knew that the fat man was at least partly responsible for the murder of Sunny Chagrin. I was breathing hard, feeling a flush climbing above my barbed neck to my temples. I would have trouble, given the condition I was in, taking him apart with my bare hands. But it was going to be done.

The biker may have sensed what was on my mind. The shotgun moved again, motioned me to follow as the Kawasaki was backed out of the trailer alley.

I backed up too, keeping my eyes on El Gordo, who took the walkie off his belt. He said a few words, then walked away, his belly fat bouncing. But he moved with deceptive speed; his partner scrambled to keep up.

The sky was rosy from fireworks. Concussions from FX mortars rolled around the amphitheater. All that noise and the screaming crowd deafened me. I glanced up at Bucky Spartacus and his band on the Jumbotron screen and almost fell over the Kawasaki. The biker shoved me away.

El Gordo and the other man climbed into the back of a limousine that could have been dark blue or purple—color values were distorted beneath the flush of sky and the dust-shrouded sodium vapor lights. The limo raised more dust in getaway mode.

I turned and grabbed the biker's shoulder.

"I'm ILC!" I yelled. "The fat bastard killed my partner! Give me the goddamn shotgun!"

Even though we were only a few feet apart, the biker probably didn't hear me. My intention was clear. I reached for the shotgun but had it yanked from my grip, which wasn't all that strong.

Then the biker wheeled about, the back tire spraying dirt in my face, and zoomed off in a direction opposite that which the limo had taken.

I was blinking and spitting mud when Lew Rolling showed up.

"Looking for you! Jesus, R! What the hell—"

"It's a dead-red," I told him. "Bucky Spartacus!"

"Jesus!"

I grabbed the handkerchief he handed me, wiped my eyes. Then I pulled Lew toward the tech trailer from which the lighting and stage effects were controlled. It was parked near the backstage ramp.

"Give me your piece!"

Lew was a little slow complying; I yanked the. 40 caliber auto from his belt holster and gave him a push. "Tell them to pull the plug! Stop the show! I'll get Bucky off the stage!"

"But are you—"

"Do it!" I yelled, still barely able to hear anything, including myself. I ran past Lew to the ramp. And a dozen feet up the ramp. And stalled there, as if the remainder of the ramp had become a vertical wall. I dropped to my hands and knees, trembling. Fucking Tasers!

This time the helping hand belonged to Beatrice Harp.

"What in the name of—"

"Bucky's about to be assassinated! Get me to the stage!"

Easier said than done. I had some trouble keeping my feet going in a straight line. Before we made it backstage we were attracting attention, including armed security personnel. Three of them, and I had a gun in my hand. Bea and I kept yelling "ILC!" but they weren't buying it. Taking into account how I must have looked, I couldn't blame them.

So I was disarmed, manhandled again in spite of Bea's screams of protest. While we fought not to have our wrists cuffed behind our backs the show went on, Chimera and Bucky Spartacus belting out a rocker.

I would've been on my way to the closest lockup, but Ben Waxman and Harry Stiles, alerted by Lew Rolling's signal, got there on the run and began trying to control the situation. I kept repeating "Dead-red!" and "Get Bucky off the stage!"

About then Bucky missed a riff on his Stratocaster and muffed a lyric out there. Chimera covered for him, but Bucky couldn't resume the beat. He looked glassy-eyed. Then he stopped trying to play altogether and took himself out of the show.

His head jerked back as Chimera put a hand on his shoulder. There was no spray of blood and brains from a sniper's shot. He began to convulse. Chimera backed off, looking our way for help. It was not just an impromptu sideshow and she knew it. I was still partially deaf but I could hear and feel the crowd reaction, a change in tone and mood. The boys in the band were looking at each other, but when Bucky dropped to his knees they finally stopped playing.

It wasn't the dead-red I had anticipated that soon had him

writhing and howling in torment while Chimera continued to back away, a hand pressed to her pouty mouth, eyes white from shock. If anything, considering the bloodlines of most of those watching, it was worse. Bucky Spartacus was hairing-up in front of a shitload of Lycans.

Bucky was a werewolf.

11

We all play a game with ourselves called "What If?" There has never been a winner.

Maybe *if* I had trusted my gut instead of accepting Joe Cronin's ground rules and had gone straight to Bucky when I arrived at the amphitheater, I would have sniffed the kid out before any harm came to him. There are two kinds of rogues, i.e., unregulated werewolves: those who know what they are and don't give a damn, and those so recently infected they have not yet felt the impact of their first full moon.

Of course the moon wasn't completely full when Bucky rose up howling onstage, tearing off what was left of his rocker duds. Which made him, like his girlfriend Chickie, an OOPs.

And there are two kinds of people who find themselves in the vicinity of a raging Hairball: the lucky and the seriously screwed.

The bass player was a few steps too close to his former front man, and a second too slow reacting.

When his mangled remains fell in the midst of the infield crowd, panic turned to havoc. Or maybe it was the other way around. Law-abiding Lycans and High Bloods alike were falling over one another to get out of range: an adult werewolf could leap nearly thirty feet from a standing start, and as much as twelve feet vertically. They had a lot of fast-twitch fiber in their bulked-up, zoomorphic thighs.

After killing the bass player the Hairball was having a look around. The other band members had climbed to a higher level on the stage, dragging Chimera along with them.

"Who's packing silver?" I yelled.

Nobody was. Wrong time of the month. I had silvertips as part of the load in my Glock, but it was still under a trailer in the lot.

The Hairball dropped to all fours, looking our way. Then it cast a yellow eye on a boom-mounted camera that was being remotely operated from the tech truck.

"There's a PHASR in our chopper!" Ben Waxman said, and added, "I think."

"Go!"

The Hairball howled again. Then in one leap it cut by half the distance to the fifty or so people still hanging around backstage. Now our area emptied out fast, led by the Reverend A. A. Kingworthy's gospel choir, all of them in good voice if you enjoy hysterical screaming, their robes billowing around us like a crimson tsunami.

The Rev, however, chose not to run. At his height and with his girth he was hard to miss, and the Hairball seemed to take an avid interest in him.

I backed up a couple of steps and bumped into Beatrice. I thought she'd fled along with the others. She grabbed my arm and I snarled at her.

"Would you get the hell out of here?"

Her mouth was ajar in a kind of cockeyed smile, or a poleaxed grimace. Hard to tell just how she was reacting, but I noticed that her eyes were focusing, clear of shock. Then she held up the throwing knife she'd concealed in the waistband of her loose-fitting trousers.

"Don't be stupid," she said. "I'm all we've got."

"Give me the blade. I'll do it."

"No you won't. Not to hurt your feelings, but you couldn't stick a pitchfork in an elephant's butt."

"I thought of that. I'll get in close enough to cut the Hairball's throat."

"*What*?"

"It can be done. You have to have the right moves."

"Bull*shit*," Bea said, holding me in a death grip. Then: "Wait a minute. Look! What does he think *he's* doing?"

Far from being intimidated by the imminent prospect of having his Mount Rushmore head chewed on by a werewolf, the Reverend A. A. Kingworthy was approaching, with firm step and squared shoulders and a hand raised in a gesture of beatification like the hand of Jesus on the painted backdrop, the Hairball alter ego of Bucky Spartacus.

And the werewolf, instead of attacking in a fit of maniacal bad humor, just crouched where it was and let him come.

Those in the crowd who were located far enough away so as not to have been panicked by the hairing-up of the pop idol greeted Kingworthy's bold appearance onstage with an outcry that was somewhere on a scale between dread and awe. And everything was being recorded, with at least three cameras active around the stage. ILC was going to have a tough time suppressing those images. In our official view, there was no such thing as an OOPs.

"Have you ever seen a werewolf lie low?" Beatrice said in my ear.

"Uh-uh." And I never had seen one retreat, which is just what the Bucky-Hairball was doing now.

"There are no alien creatures in *God's* universe!" Kingworthy proclaimed. He had a shapely and authoritative preacher's basso that could have been heard with perfect clarity for nearly a mile on a calm night. "There are only God's children! We are *all* the children of God! His way is the only Way! Let us give thanks and praise to the heavenly father, and *love* one another!"

God's child the werewolf raised its already blood-smeared chops a few inches higher. It stared at the Rev, who was less than ten feet away. I had thought I knew everything there was to know about werewolves. But this baby was writing a whole new chapter for my book.

Bea hadn't surrendered her knife to me.

"If I can get a little closer while it's not paying attention I can take my shot," she said. "Or else Kingworthy is dead meat."

My turn to lock her down.

"That's *his* problem."

"Welcome, child of Godddd!" Kingworthy said, holding out his arms to the werewolf.

And someone in the crowd screamed, "Lycan power!"

Uh-oh, I thought.

That's when the helicopter showed up.

Not one of ours. It belonged to Channel Two News. And suddenly a nasty situation had escalated into a crisis.

The chopper made a pass at the stage, coming in close, raising infield dust where the mostly youthful fans were still pushing and shoving to clear the area. There was a cameraman in an open doorway. The nearness of the helicopter and the rotor wash set the Reverend Kingworthy back on his heels, his shoulder-length Moses-style locks flowing back from his head like the tail of a comet.

The Hairball rose up with a snarl of fury, giving Channel Two News full frontal nudity. But that apparently wasn't enough for them. The pilot, just taking orders or momentarily forgetful of what they were dealing with, edged the helicopter closer to the stage.

Like a cat going after a bird the werewolf leaped to the helicopter, grabbed the cameraman, flung him and his digicam high into the dazzle of stage lights, then plunged into the cabin and killed the pilot.

The chopper autorotated out of control and smashed down hard on the infield. Busted rotor blades chopped lethally through the crowd.

From dust and smoke and flickers of flame the Hairball climbed slowly out of the broken chopper, showing signs of hard wear and brain fade. But it was able to stand erect on the fuselage and howl. I wasn't amazed to hear, from the crowd, ecstatic, hair-raising wolf calls.

The Reverend Kingworthy was stage front on his knees, praying.

"It's going to blow," I said. I didn't only mean the ruptured gas tank of the helicopter.

With the wolf calls there were isolated cries of "Lycan Power!" that became a chorus.

And then they started to applaud, and "Lycan Power" turned to shouts of "Bucky."

BUCKY. BUCKY! BUCKY!!!

"They've got their martyr," I said to Bea. "And for the rest of us the shit gets deeper."

Kingworthy stood and raised his hands to the sky and as if on cue the helicopter exploded thirty yards from him.

All he got was a face like rare prime rib and badly singed eyebrows.

By the time I reached the corpse of the ex-rocker and Out-of-Phase werewolf with a fire extinguisher, only blackened hide and briquettes of flesh and a toothy jawbone remained.

But a legend had been born from the ashes.

After a meticulous search of the area where the werewolf had fallen in flames, one of our Evidence Response techies came up with a tweezerload of twisted titanium, a bit of melted acrylic, and fused microwiring that might have been a Snitcher. The object went back to the lab for trace analysis.

If it was a Snitcher, WEIR didn't know anything about it. Bucky Spartacus was not on their roster as a Lycan. Miles Brenta's Nanomimetics Corporation held all the contracts to make Snitchers and the new LUMO upgrade exclusively for WEIR. So we knew that if the suspected implant hadn't served some legitimate medical purpose then Bucky, as he had seemed to fear when I talked to him, was or had been badly used. The purpose seemed clear to me.

"For the unification and further growth of the First Church of Lycanthropy," I explained to Booth Havergal. We were watching another forensics team comb the area where I had been ambushed by El Gordo. "A werewolf was born tonight. Out-of-Phase, so to the credulous it's a miracle birth. But not just another werewolf. An ordinary rock-and-roller becomes a mythic figure. I'm sure that's the kind of heavy dupe Kingworthy's PR will lay on it."

"The Elvis of Lycanthropy?" Booth said. "Do you think the Right-bloody-Reverend is behind this business?"

"I'm not sure. It's possible he was so cranked on Frenzies tonight he thought he was invulnerable. His press conference has been going on for forty-five minutes and he may keep it up till dawn." ILC had done its usual thorough job of sealing the crime scene, but we had no grounds for detaining Kingworthy, who after being patched up by the paramedics was now, along with his entourage, entertaining the media nearby but out of our jurisdiction. I gave the Rev some thought, then shook my head. "Religious grifters are different from the typical con men. They seldom have that deep hard core of cynicism and disdain for the human race. Kingworthy's a true believer of whatever part of his spiel he happens to tune into as it rolls off his tongue. I'll talk to him, but I have no leverage. I can't tie him into Miles Brenta."

"It's entirely coincidental, R."

"Sometimes I like coincidences. In the last forty-eight hours two of Brenta's celebrity pets have gone Hairball—but in freakish, atypical ways. Almost as if they were obeying commands. We don't have Chiclyn Hickey's body and we don't have much of Bucky left, but the fact that there was a microchip in that meltdown of a Snitch facsimile is one coincidence too many. If it can be traced to Nanomimetics—"

"Brenta's company is not the only one around capable of manufacturing one of those."

"But not legally. Brenta has the best technology, most of the patents, and the government contracts worldwide. He also has a nervous girlfriend I think I should see more of."

"What pretext?"

"I like making her nervous. Maybe it's sexual. On her part."

"Pay a call on Francesca if you think it may be useful. But walk the line, R. Don't make Miles Brenta nervous." He paused, not liking the prospect of a nervous and politically potent Miles Brenta. Then he said, "Control of Lycans is essential to human survival. But can you think of any reason why someone who might possess the necessary technology would want to control an actual werewolf?"

"They make ideal assassins. Artie never knew what hit him."

"If only we had a motive."

"Just before he was killed Artie was getting close to telling me something he'd learned that worried him. He'd been talking about those Hairballs in No Gal the last Observance." I had to take a look at the moon. It's a nearly irresistible twitch most people have around this time of the month. Look up. Look around. Be afraid. "I think Artie, who was heavily invested in research and technology companies, knew just how hairing-up can be triggered whenever it suits someone's purpose. And I have a strong hunch that Francesca Obregon also knows how it's done."

"You seem obsessed with her," Booth said disapprovingly.

It was an opportunity to tell him about Bea's conviction that Francesca had her knife.

"Enough for an arrest warrant?" I said.

"You know better. If there's anything to it, if your—if Miss Harp isn't mistaken, then undoubtedly Francesca has rid herself of the knife already."

But he had liked it. And he was frustrated. When the sun came up he had to face a largely hostile media throwing questions at him he couldn't answer.

"She's Brenta's mistress and both of them are in this up to their necks," I said.

He ignored me with an angry shake of his head.

"And aren't you overdoing protective custody? You involved a civilian in ILC business tonight."

"I needed a date for the prom."

"If she wants to be a detective let her take a course on the Internet."

We watched a tech guy making an impression of a portion of tire track left by the biker who had rescued me from El Gordo. Lifting the track was routine. It wasn't going to tell us anything useful. But I was pretty sure I knew the biker's identity. Booth listened pensively to my explanation.

"If it was Elena Grace, surely she'd have let you know."

"Couldn't risk it. Or so she implied in her text message a few minutes earlier. Christ, Booth! She's working undercover for ILC Intel. And you know it."

"What possible expertise or discipline would qualify her for that sort of work?"

"Qualify— Those Intel assholes use civilians all the time to make a case! *Mis*use them—they don't care whose blood gets spilled if they look good."

"Even if your hunch is correct," he said, "I can't afford a balls-out with Intel right now. I have too many problems as it is." He stared at me, rubbing his chin with the back of a hand. "Don't be another problem."

"One phone call," I said. "Whatever she's into, you can get her yanked. Do it for me, Booth."

He rocked slightly on his heels, looked around the back lot of the amphitheater. He was seething. But not at me.

"If you want Elena Grace back—"

"I just don't want her killed."

"—bring me someone else's head. Before the Observance."

I looked at the moon again. He was giving me forty-eight hours.

12

Where are we going?" Bea asked as, ninety minutes later, we left the gates of the house on Breva Way behind. "And *where* did you get that jazzbo ensemble? I don't know if I want to be seen with you."

"The suit was my father's. I think he bought it to wear to a costume party. If you're patient everything comes back into style."

"I wouldn't quote odds on that set of threads," Bea said skeptically.

I had added some gold chains to the sportin' life suit with its wide, wide lapels, a pleated black shirt open at the neck, and a pair of perforated black-and-white wingtip shoes that also had belonged to my father. I couldn't wear my Geekers—they were a dead giveaway that I was ILC. Instead I put on a pair of wrap-around shades that covered as much of my face as the Lone Ranger's mask. A pirate's black headwrap and a pale gray, snap-brim fedora concealed my white hair.

"I'm in disguise," I said. "Think you can impersonate a giddy newlywed?"

"I had the lead in my senior class play. Who are *you* supposed to be?"

"Just a rakehell gambler who got lucky at the Gold Spur

Casino tonight. Call me 'Reef,' doll. Because I'm feeling flush, we got ourselves married up in the casino's wedding chapel, and now we're—"

"I don't have a ring. I can't feel married without a ring."

I turned the Rover north onto Coldwater Canyon, then took a well-worn plush ring box from a pocket of the suit jacket and handed it to her.

Beatrice opened the box slowly, as women are apt to do.

"Omigod! That stone must be ten carats."

"About that. You're looking at my mother's wedding ring, angel."

"Omigod! And you want me to wear it? That'll make me giddy, all right."

"If you put Pym's ring on your own finger, it's Let's Pretend. If I put it on, that'll be for keeps."

Bea took a very long breath and wiped under one eye with a finger. She took another long breath.

"You haven't told me where we're going and why we're pretending."

"Forty-two thirteen West Burbank Boulevard. Angeltowne Livery and Exotic Car Rentals. Open twenty-four hours. Reef and Honeychile are looking for something stylish to drive up the coast on their honeymoon."

"Honeychile?" Her lip curled. "Okay, can we get serious? The real reason is—"

"I'm there to have a look around while you provide a diversion."

"You're on the job."

"Right."

"What is the job?"

"When Reef don't have much else to go on, Reef goes with his gut, doll."

"Would you *stop*? Why Angeltowne Livery? I know that Artie occasionally rented one of their limos."

"Yeah. They have white for weddings, black for funerals. And even a couple of purple ones as homage to Elvis. Old-time Lincoln Continentals sawed and stretched. I'm sure it was one of those Lincolns the greasers who tried to throw me under the truck scrammed in when their play didn't develop. Reef is still kind of chapped about that."

"There are a lot of limo places, and some of them may have purple ones."

"The last time I saw Sunny Chagrin she was able to say only a few words to me. She was dying and she knew it and she had to make the words count. Two of them were 'Angel Town.' Sunny could have meant Angeltowne Livery. And she may have found or seen something there that got her killed. Anyway, it's a place to start."

"I understand," Beatrice said in a subdued tone. "And we could be killed too."

"I'm not risking your life. Maybe it's just a blocked trail and I won't learn anything. But you're not going to be in there for more than five minutes."

"What about you?"

"I'll need more time to look around."

Bea crossed her arms and settled a little lower in her seat.

"I have a chill," she said faintly. "Would you turn down the air conditioner?"

Angeltowne Livery occupied a block with one diagonal side to it, a two-story stucco building. Their location was convenient to the movie studios where they probably did a sizable business renting out their antique cars to period productions awash in sentiment and nostalgia.

At 2 A.M. the showroom was brightly lighted; a crew was waxing and dusting an assortment of elegant automobiles: a 1956 Thunderbird, a pink tailfin Caddy, a Stutz Blackhawk. All of the window spaces on the second floor had been filled in and painted over.

I drove around the building before settling on a place to leave the Rover. They were busy in the back, where a courtyard surrounded by a chain-link fence topped with the obligatory razor wire protected a compound of limos. I saw a gleaming bale of the deadly wire sitting in the bed of a pickup truck outfitted with chromed pipes and handholds and a rack of off-roader lights. The truck had the bulky tires and shocks necessary for desert rambling.

A car carrier was being unloaded, half a dozen vehicles from the late 1940s—the beginning of an era on the drop-edge of an abyss of time, before anyone had fully realized what was in store for humanity. The big worry back then was the Bomb, which now seemed quaint. Man had made his peace with the atom. Any political redhot who wanted a big bang could have one, but so what? The true assassins were everywhere, as we drifted to extinction in the final season of our blood.

The returned cars were driven into the garage beneath the building. There was a guard on the gate, another patrolling the lot with a pair of Rottweilers and a burp gun slung across his chest. I counted four surveillance cameras.

While we were idling along a big Harley zoomed up from the hive of the garage and turned into the street behind us. The Harley headed west into North Hollywood. The biker looked like a Diamondbacker.

I found a parking spot on a lighted section of the diagonal side street half a block north of the livery. I opened the flask filled with Boodles that I had brought from the house and basted my whiskery chin, then added a few drops of gin to my shirt collar.

"Excuse me," I said to Beatrice. I gargled with the stuff, then spat it through an empty window.

Bea stared at me and pitched her voice higher, whining a little.

"Now, Reef! Baby, don't you think you've had about enough?"

"Hell, we just got married! Gettin' on my case already? I can drink more liquor than a freight train can haul! Now let's go grab ourselves a hunk set of wheels. I feel like flyin' tonighttt!"

With our act established I pocketed the flask. We strolled down to Burbank Boulevard hand in hand. Opposite Angeltowne Livery on the wide street there was a collection of low, drab-looking buildings housing businesses that were seedy, second-rate, or out-of-date. Chinese takeout. Dry cleaning. Porn books and collector DVDs. A gas station on the corner was closed. There was a yellow van partly visible behind it.

We went through a glass door marked RENTAL OFFICE and up a couple of steps. The agent stuck with the graveyard shift was, according to the plaque on his desk, T. Hollingsworth Sibley. He was watching TV. He had narrow shoulders, a hairpiece he might have borrowed from a poodle, and the disgruntled expression of a man who knows the joke is always on him.

His mood didn't improve when I leaned over his desk and breathed on him.

"Mr. Sibley, the little woman and me—she's been the 'litle woman' for, what is it now, a whole hour and a half, darlin'?" Bea simpered prettily. "Give Sib here a gander at your rock."

Bea flashed the diamond for him, posing this way and that with the toothy élan of a low-rent movie starlet. Then she turned and gawked at the cars on the showroom floor.

"The little woman and me are about to depart on our honeymoon, as you might have guessed," I said with a randy leer.

"Well, congrat—" Sibley murmured halfheartedly.

"Oh my gawdd, Reef! Have you ever seen more beautiful cars in your life? They are so *hot*. What's that red convertible there called? That's the one I want! Can you get it for us, baby?"

Sibley's thin eyebrows knitted in consternation. But before he could move from behind his desk to head us off I had Bea around the waist and was walking her into the showroom, managing to be a little unsteady on my feet.

"Uh, just a moment, please?"

Bea smiled at him over her shoulder. "Oh, he's okay. Reef's just celebrated a little too much. But I can drive just fine. I hardly ever touch a drop myself. Even though my first two husbands were slaves to the bottle."

"You never told me about two other husbands! Where the hell's this news coming from all of a sudden?"

"Oh, Reef. I was only a *kid* then. Tige and Randolph hardly count at all! They were just *practice* husbands. You're the only one I have ever really truly loved, and it'll be *forever,* baby. Now don't you sulk."

"I'll sulk if I want to!"

One of the Hispanic women in coveralls who were polishing the rolling stock looked up with a smirk. I dug out my flask and tippled.

Sibley said, "Oh, now, we can't have that! I must ask you—"

"Reef, you are going to give Mr. Sibley the impression we're not responsible people to rent to!"

Sibley undoubtedly had decided that already. I reinforced the bad impression I was making by gagging, then spraying gin on the windshield of a candy-apple-red Chevrolet Mako Shark II, such a beautiful machine that desecrating it was almost enough to give me guilt spasms.

Sibley sprang to the rescue with his own initialed handkerchief before either of the cleaning women could respond. He gave me a hateful look. I spat up a little more. Sibley pointed wildly down a hallway.

"Not here! First door on your right!"

"Oh, Reef!" Beatrice wailed. "Are you sick? Was it all that sushi?"

I nodded and stumbled away toward the bathrooms. LADIES and GENTS side by side. There were two other doors. The one at the end of the hall had a sign that read GARAGE—EMPLOYEES ONLY. The other one, next to the men's room, had no ID. Both doors required card key access.

I glanced back as Bea was carrying on, doing a good job of distracting or entertaining everyone. I ducked into the ladies'.

On the terrace at Valdemar as she lay dying Sunny had tried to guide me precisely to where she wanted me to go: *dead drop*, she had said, then: *handicap*.

The bathroom stall designed for wheelchairs. At least that's how I had it figured. Sunny had left something in there for future retrieval because someone might have made her and she knew her chances of walking out of Angeltowne Livery with whatever it was, borrowed or copied, were not all that good.

The ladies' was deserted. There were no cameras, although the showroom was lousy with them. It was a reputable business after all, at least on the surface. Employees could get used to being watched anywhere else but not on the john.

I closed the door of the big stall behind me. No need to look around. There was no tank for the toilet. I kneeled and felt around the bottom of the bowl. Something was stuck to the porcelain there. So I got down on my back and had a look.

Sunny had left me a card key, fastened to the porcelain with two corn plasters she probably found in her purse. I pulled it free, flushed the plasters, and got up, shrugging the kinks out of my neck and shoulders.

I heard Bea even before I cracked the door to the hall an inch. She was bawling, on Reef's case as Sibley tried to shush her. She felt so humiliated, sobbed Beatrice. Maybe she'd made a mistake after all. Men who drank might be fun for a while, but in the end they meant heartbreak. When would she ever learn?

Bea had maneuvered Sibley so that his back was to the hall. She had a hand on his arm in case he tried to look my way. She would keep it up for another minute or so, then her humiliation would get the best of her and she would leave in a final cloudburst of tears and wait for me in the Rover.

I slipped out of the ladies', tried the card key in the lock of the door next to the bathroom and got a green light. I went in fast and the door closed on Bea's squall of suffering. It was all I could do not to bust out laughing.

I went two at a time up a flight of stairs to a second-floor hall where a couple of fluorescent bulbs needed to be changed: they flickered and buzzed. There were offices or cubicles along the right side of the long hall. Most of the doors stood open. Nothing to hide. A big one-way window was set into the middle of the left-side wall. It overlooked the garage two floors below. Mechanics were at work. The zip-buzz of power wrenches. I saw choppers worth twenty thousand or better and several Diamondbackers working on them. Four more members of the Brotherhood were playing hold 'em and drinking beer from quart bottles in a brightly lit lounge area ringed with vending machines.

One of the players looked like El Gordo.

(So Angeltowne Livery was also a clubhouse for Diamondbackers. Was that what you wanted me to know, Sunny?)

I wasn't satisfied. I prowled the length of the hall and came to the last two doors. One was marked SECURITY. The other could have been an exit door with stairs beyond, but it also required a card key.

I put my ear to the first of the doors and listened. A faint hum of computers inside. I used my card key and the lock clicked open. So it was probably a master key that Sunny had left me, with access to any part of the building.

I peeked inside. One wall was all monitor screens for the surveillance cameras. A guy in a khaki uniform had his feet on a desk amid paper plates and cartons of Chinese. He was snoring softly.

I didn't go in, but I spent a little time looking at the monitors. I saw Bea leave the showroom downstairs and walk quickly along Burbank. I saw a basement area apart from the garage big enough to hold a couple of armored trucks. Nobody was there. And I saw a small, empty room with a narrow bed in it, nothing on the bed but a mattress. The walls appeared to be padded. There was a table, a molded plastic chair, a washbasin, and a lidless commode.

Furnished like a holding cell, but soundproofed. No clue as to where this room might be. But I wanted a closer look, if I could find it.

I left the surveillance room and the snoozing guard and opened the last door. Beyond it was a flight of stairs going down and another hallway along the east side of the building. More locked doors, which I opened one by one. Finding nothing of interest until I came to a chilly room in which there were six restaurant-sized stainless steel refrigerators. Each contained a hundred or so 500 cc bags filled with what appeared to be blood.

The door opposite the blood bank had a small window, about eight inches square, at eye level. I looked in at the cell-like soundproofed room I had seen on the surveillance monitor. What light there was came from the overhead fluorescent fixture in the hall.

I unlocked the door and went in. The window in the door was one-way from the hall. The air inside was stale but there was a faint linger of woman-odor, a mix of bodily effluvia: of skin and glands, of perfume and lotions, the merest trace one out of a few thousand noses might detect. I picked up the residue quickly. If a man had occupied this room for any length of time the air would've had a sharper, rye, rancid smell to me.

The room, or cell, was tonelessly dull visually, but clean. Not a hair to be found in the sink or a ring in the toilet. I kneeled and sniffed the mattress. She had spent a lot of time lying on the bed, asleep or drugged, and her odor was as definite as if she'd been there only moments ago.

I inhaled again, then stood and backed away to the center of the room, hoping that the guard on night security wouldn't wake himself with the velocity of his snoring, or his feet wouldn't fall off the desk. If I was going to raise her I needed another two or three minutes, and there was nothing I could do about the wide-angle security camera mounted in a corner of the room below the high ceiling.

I had been taught, in the long nights of the forest and the dark of the shaman's lodge where only a dim red glow from the ever-present fire provided necessary light for orientation purposes, what might have been called miraculous by the uninitiated, or black arts by the fearful. But there was nothing otherworldly or profane about it. With training almost anyone could do what I was about to do.

With a firm olfactory impression of her, what I needed now was to telepathically "see" as much of her as possible from the energy field she'd left behind.

I didn't look directly at the mattress, but at a place on the blank wall a few feet above the bed. Putting my mind at rest. She was there; I had only to let the energy field provide me with a glimpse of her spirit body.

"There have been rumors," Booth Havergal had said to me. *"Little wisps of speculation floating around the Privilege. A shoot is being set up. Very large money involved, perhaps even a loving cup. If one is going to chance hunting werewolves, even under controlled conditions, it's so much more prestigious as well as rewarding if the hunter bags a trophy werewolf: a celebrity."*

Mal Scarlett was an insolent little scatterbrain, but nobody deserved such a fate.

"Don't worry, sweetheart," I said softly as her image faded from my mind's eye. "Uncle R is coming to get you."

I had notice of an upcoming *mal de lune* shoot with Mal as the designated trophy, but I needed a line on where and when. To get that information I also needed to make good use of ten minutes, alone, with Raoul J. Ortega. President of the SoCal Diamondbackers, a criminal organization. Angeltowne Livery, judging by what I had already seen, was a favorite hangout of Diamondbackers. The refrigerators across the hall attested to the fact that they were still in the bloodlegging business. I didn't think I would have much difficulty finding out that Ortega was a silent partner in Angeltowne. Or a shell company called Luxor Films. And one of Ortega's least attractive ventures appeared to be setting up *mal de lune*s to amuse wealthy and morally deficient High Bloods.

I'd been hanging around Angeltowne a little too long. Bea would be safely back in the Rover and T. Hollingsworth Sibley might be wondering about me.

So I retraced my steps, not pausing to find out if the security guard was still asleep in front of his monitors, and went down the steps to the first floor. There didn't seem to be a reason for caution at this point, so I just barged out into the hallway where the bathrooms were.

And almost ran into El Gordo, smelling of beer and pomade and just maybe underarm flop-sweat from a bad couple of hours at the poker table.

I don't know how drunk he was. He sidestepped me, blinking, glanced off the opposite wall, mumbled something in Spanish, and went into the men's room, unzipping and hauling out his cock as the door closed behind him.

I took a couple of seconds to start breathing again, looking toward the showroom. I didn't see Sibley. The Hispanic women were running floor polishers.

My heart was pounding from rage, and there was nothing in my brain but an intense burning light.

I went into the men's room with no concern about stealth and went up behind El Gordo where he was blissfully relieving himself at a urinal and crooning a Mexican song under his breath. I drew my Glock and put a hand on his shoulder and when he turned his head to give me a blearily surprised look I lashed him backhanded across his fat face with the gun, opening a cheek to the bone. He staggered away from the urinal, pissing in spurts on the floor, and I hit him again with everything I had, coming across the other side of his face and smashing his nose.

He fell back into a stall and sprawled there, an arm across the toilet, his other hand going to his bleeding face. He stared up at me.

I pulled off my shades and leaned over him.

"It's Rawson, *cabrón*."

I pushed the muzzle of the .45 against his forehead and thought about Sunny in her cocoon of razor wire and thought about justifiable homicide. Drunk and hurt as he was, he saw it coming in my eyes and spasmed, swallowing blood.

But I didn't do it. I needed him alive, at least for another sixty seconds. I had two questions for El Gordo. And there was no alternative to pleasing me with his answers.

T. Hollingsworth Sibley looked up from the infomercial he was watching on the TV behind his desk when I approached him on my way out.

"You'll need a bucket and a mop in the men's room," I said.

Outside I walked back to the Rover, which was parked a block up the street. I didn't feel as good about my encounter with El Gordo as I wanted to feel. Because dead was dead and I wasn't going to get Sunny back no matter what I did now. As for Mal Scarlett—a sense of urgency was beginning to tick out of control next to my heart when I reached the Rover.

I opened the door. The light came on and it was obvious right away that Beatrice wasn't inside.

I turned around to call her name and someone who was both quick and confident put the muzzle of his gun into the notch of my throat.

"Rawson, you asshole," he said.

13

The tall man with the gun prodding my tonsils was strung together like a big wading bird, with an overhang of head and almost no shoulders. That made him a bad fit in off-the-rack suits. Instead of demonstrating the ease with which I could disarm anyone so clueless as to crowd me like that, I smiled forgivingly. And I let him take my piece from the shoulder rig.

"Well, well. It's Stork McClusky, right? Long time no see."

"You're going to be sorry you saw me tonight," he growled.

McClusky had backup, this one coming toward us from across the street, thumb of one hand hooked in his belt. The whites of his eyes gleamed in the available light. Him I didn't know, but it had been a while since I had worked ILC Intel.

McClusky took a step back but with his automatic, a big H and K two-tone, still close to my face.

"Get in the backseat, Rawson," he said. "I'll drive."

"Oh my," I said. "Two Intel boyos coming on hard to me. Just give me a few seconds while I finish peeing down my leg."

"I'm Maltese Greek," the other one said quietly, with a shrug and a smile to strum the heartstrings of the lovelorn. He had thick dark curly hair and thick glossy eyelashes. He wore a summer-weight blue mock-turtleneck with his faded jeans, a gold medallion on a chain centered on his breast, and a gold loop earring. Small loop. McClusky had a gun and a line of hard talk and he wasn't somebody I'd turn my back on. The kid was half McClusky's size, had a diffident way of speaking, a winsome smile, and a brand of deadliness he had no reason to advertise. It was just there, and anyone who'd had experience with his type would recognize it.

"Where's Beatrice?" I said.

"She went on ahead," McClusky said, giving me the bitch eye. "Now get in and be quick about it."

"If you shoved your gat in my girl's face," I said to McClusky, "we'll need to have a short discussion about your crummy manners before the night's over."

"She's all right," the Greek kid said reassuringly. "She handled herself fine."

I looked at him.

"It's just going to be conversation," he said. "About teamwork, or so I understand. We can't exactly chew you up and spit you out, now can we? My name's Paulo. By the way, I like your outfit."

"You seem to have a brain," I said. "That should have disqualified you right away for Intel."

He grinned, opened the door for me, and nodded politely. I climbed in without a fuss. McClusky put his gun away, put a finger on his earbud. He looked up and down the street, then said importantly to someone, "We got him. Leaving now. ETA about three minutes."

"If you make the lights," I said, and settled back to await developments.

McClusky drove us into North Hollywood, took some residential side streets in a cunningly evasive manner in case we were being followed, which we weren't. We came to a bungalow in the middle of a block of similar 1930s-sytle homes. There was a black wrought-iron gate across the drive and somone waiting near the gate in the dark front yard. He opened it when McClusky blinked the Rover's lights. At the end of the drive there was a small garage with the doors chained shut. A couple of sedans were parked haphazardly beneath jacaranda trees in the small backyard, which was surrounded by a seven-foot wooden privacy fence with bougainvillea spilling over from the yard behind it.

"Not much to show for your budget," I said idly. "And in this neighborhood all of you should be wearing T-shirts with SEXUAL PREDATOR logos."

"We know what we're doing," McClusky said.

"There's always a first time," I allowed. "But this probably ain't it."

McClusky left the Rover at the end of the driveway beside a large yellow van with JAKE'S JIFFY ELECTRIC in red script on the side. This van or a similar one, I remembered, had been parked at the gas station across from the Angeltowne Livery.

I followed Paulo the Greek onto a small back porch. A dog barked close by. McClusky hung back, ready and able to mow me down if I made a sudden break. The glass in the kitchen door had a blackout shade covering it. Nifty. Inside a couple of techie types, red-eyed in the wee hours, were hanging out waiting for a fresh pot of coffee to brew. We continued along a short hall. Bathroom, two bedrooms. McClusky rapped on a bedroom door as he went by. It didn't sound like a secret knock. But like I said I'd been away for a few years. Maybe they'd changed it.

There were two snug rooms at the front of the bungalow. A dining room with pocket doors half closed and a parlor. More blackout shades on windows that faced a roofed front porch and the street. The dining room contained utility shelves and a lot of audio and visual surveillance equipment. The latest and best available. Overhear a whispered conversation in a restaurant half a mile away. See through walls, clothing, locked safes. Peer into the hearts of desperate men. Or maybe they hadn't yet reached that level of snooper refinement.

In the dining room Paulo joined a tall, formidable-looking woman with his olive coloring. She wore all black: sweater, leather gloves, high-waisted slacks. She had been watching a TV monitor I couldn't see, but when Paulo spoke to her she turned and gave me a flat incurious stare. She said something to Paulo. He opened a pewter cigarette box on a table and lighted one, then took the cigarette from his lips and placed it between hers. Something wrong with her concealed hands; rheumatoid arthritis? The fitted gloves could only have worsened her pain. But maybe her vanity required them.

The woman had a severe, beautifully boned face, heavy eyebrows, and countersunk lightless black eyes like dark wells in a soothsayer's cave. I thought she might have passed through my life at some point like a messenger from the damned. But the hour was late, I was tired, and I couldn't place her.

I sat next to Bea on the sofa. Her eyes opened. She looked happy to see me, then worried.

"Did I screw up?"

"No," I said. "Did any of them lay a finger on you?"

"They've been nice enough. But they don't say much. Who are they? What's going on, R?"

"Remains to be seen."

In response to a summons on his wristpac Stork McClusky beat it back down the hall and briefly visited the bedroom behind the closed door. I squeezed Bea's hand.

"Whatever it is, we shouldn't be long."

"Good. Do you know any of them? Are they ILC?"

I nodded and looked at the Greek woman's profile. Still familiar, but elusive, just a shadow among shadows in memory. I shook my head, which needed clearing. McClusky returned and gave me a smug, hostile look. So I was about to get my nuts busted. But not by the likes of McClusky.

The bedroom had been turned into an office: standard rental stuff designed to take a beating. Gray steel, an eighth of an inch of padding on the chair seats. Nothing on the desk blotter but two landline scrambler phones and a micro recorder. Also a pair of hands under a fluorescent lamp, palms down. The nails were buffed. He'd always taken good care of them. He hadn't much liked the jobs that required him to get his hands dirty.

He motioned with his right hand. I sat down in one of the chairs that faced him squarely and we looked at each other. Nothing was said. After almost a minute of that he nodded slightly.

"How about taking off the shades, Rawson?"

I took them off and put them into an inside pocket of my coat. I had left the fedora in the Rover. I was still wearing my pirate's black do-rag. I kind of liked it.

"How long has it been?" he said in a disinterested, bored tone of voice.

"Not long enough."

When Cale DeMarco smiled, which was rare, it was a thin-lipped effort that always ended up with him sucking at a tooth somewhere in his mouth, making a noise like a minor expression of skepticism, or disgust. So he was seven years older, bearded now, a square salt-and-pepper job. Some men grew beards when their hair began thinning out. He wore glasses with a heavy-duty black frame. He'd been promoted twice while I was still in rehab after being nearly kicked to death by Raoul J. Ortega's Diamondbacker posse and now he ran it all: director of SoCal ILC Intelligence Division. The Head Spook. He had acquired the bookish, professional look that lent added distinction to his eminence. Just the right amount of high seriousness in his demeanor.

"How are the headaches these days, R?"

"How are your hemorrhoids?" I said.

His smile concluded with a sibilant *tsk*.

"I know you've never been convinced that I had nothing to do with—outing you."

"No, I still like you for it," I said.

"I'm sorry. There's nothing more I can say, is there?"

"No problem, Cale. Ortega's going to tell me all about it one of these days. Then I'll be back to see you. Speaking of headaches."

DeMarco sighed a little and spread his hands farther apart on the desktop. He looked down as if admiring the quality of his manicure.

"That attitude of yours is why you were always dangerous to work with," he said. "And one reason why you're about to be replaced at ILC SoCal."

I felt a pulse jump in my throat and my head was starting to throb under the tight do-rag. I don't think much of anything showed in my face. But whatever he saw there caused him to sit back warily in his ergonomic chair.

"Oh well," I said. "Down and out in Beverly Hills again. What do you have on me that you think will stick, or do I only get the particulars at Kangaroo Court?"

"I don't mind telling you." He had recovered his cool and gazed at me with a certain forbearance, as if he were counseling a backsliding drunk. His lips twitched a little and he made that sucking sound again. "Your clumsy, clownish actions at Angeltowne Livery tonight may have negated months of work on a vital investigation we've been conducting. I stress *vital*."

"An investigation that involves Raoul J. Ortega? If it's blood you're after, there are six big refrigerators of it in an upstairs storeroom. Assuming Ortega is connected to the limo place in some documented way, then you should have enough to put him in Rocky Peak for a few years."

"We're not interested in Ortega's bloodlegging activities. It isn't illegal for any citizen to stockpile blood."

"If he's selling it and the blood is tainted—"

"Try proving he knows it's tainted. We don't have any plans to put Ortega away. Let it go at that."

I stared at him. A few seconds' worth of astonishment and disbelief, then naked hate that choked me like something malignant growing in the throat.

"What about Mal Scarlett? And maybe a dozen other Lycan celebrities he's arranged to do their hairing-up at *mal de lune* shoots in the past?"

DeMarco raised a hand from the desk just enough to brush the suggestion of Mal away with two fingers, as if a fly had annoyed him.

"I don't know anything about that."

"The fuck. You know everything that's been going on at Angeltowne for weeks! You know Sunny Chagrin dropped by looking for Elena Grace, and now Sunny is dead. Mal Scarlett was a prisoner upstairs, probably not the first they've held there, until only a few hours ago. Where did they take her, DeMarco?"

"Wayward Lycans are your responsibility. *Were* your responsibility. I personally don't give a damn how many werewolves are slaughtered to raise the testosterone levels of Privilege bigshots with exaggerated notions of their prowess as hunters."

He pushed his chair back because he knew I was coming for him, right across the desk. I was out of my chair and he had his automatic half pulled from the shoulder rig he wore, looking at me expectantly, with the arrogant satisfaction his kind feel knowing they own somebody, dead or alive. He would have had a half second's advantage, and that half second might have been enough.

I exhaled, the blood in my head half blinding me. The door opened and the Greek kid named Paulo looked in and said casually, "Hey, easy, fellas. What's the ruckus about?"

We both glanced at him. He was smiling, but with a hard

light in his eyes that emphasized the winner of our kill-or-be-killed session wasn't going to have a chance to celebrate.

I wondered just who the hell he was, and who he worked for. It sure wasn't Cale DeMarco.

The gloves-wearing woman walked into the room behind him. Paulo fetched the other chair for her and she sat erect with her back to the wall, looking us over, her hidden hands lying twisted on one thigh. The ash of her cigarette was about an inch long. Paulo gently removed the half-smoked cigarette from her lips. She didn't look at him. Her eyes were on me. Paulo squashed the gasper on the wood floor and scuffed out the sparks remaining with the sole of a boot. Then he leaned against the wall a couple of feet from her with his arms folded. I was getting a crick in my neck looking around at them. I wondered if her hands were so useless she needed help getting dressed. Or undressed. And did Paulo in addition to bringing her a chair and fussing with her smokes do those chores as well? A very curious couple. I had the impression she found me interesting. But we all like to think we're interesting. They had DeMarco behaving like a kid suddenly called to the principal's office.

But he stopped fidgeting, joined his hands on the desktop, and took a firm tone with me.

"I want to know what you were doing at Angeltowne tonight. Why did you suddenly assault that Mexican in the men's room?"

"Let's get this straight," I said. "I don't have to answer questions about an ongoing murder investigation."

"Ah," he said, flicking his gaze at the impassive pair aligned along the bedroom wall. "So tonight was all about Sunny Chagrin?"

"The greaser in question," I said, "kindly phoned me up when I visited Valdemar a couple of nights ago and told me where I could find the package they'd dropped off for me. 'Dropped off' doesn't quite describe how Sunny came to be there on the terrace of the house. According to the forensic guys, she was dragged across a cobblestone-paved auto court and down a couple of flights of stone steps wearing nothing but razor wire. The greaser in question Tasered me a few hours ago, then attempted to dump me under the back wheels of a tractor-trailer rig. Elena Grace bailed me out of that one. You'll be happy to know she managed to do it without blowing her cover."

I waited for his reaction. He sucked at a tooth that might suddenly have pained him and said slowly, "Elena . . . Grace?"

"You have her working undercover," I said impatiently. Headache was causing my vision to blur. "Cozied up to Raoul Ortega for God knows what purpose."

DeMarco looked again at the Greeks auditing us like a couple of Furies from an obscure tragedy that had no name.

I said, "And with every breath she takes she's in danger of being killed herself."

DeMarco paid me full attention again, and shook his head.

"Elena Grace? What would she be doing with—"

"An evil murdering son of a bitch like Ortega? Good point. He knows exactly who she is, who she used to be, what we meant to each other, and what she became after she was raped. I can understand how it might all work for Ortega—a demented exercise in power, an ego thing—keeping his former victim and now a rogue werewolf dangerously close to him. A game he enjoys playing. For now. What I don't get is the leverage you must have used to persuade Elena to cooperate in *your* game. Because if there's hate in her bones, it's hatred of Ortega."

I was breathing too fast. It was injury on top of permanent pain to think of Elena with the man who had ordered me killed, who was laughing at me from behind the wall of immunity he enjoyed, a wall provided by Cale DeMarco.

"Leverage . . . ?" DeMarco said. He looked exasperated. "Elena Grace has nothing to do with us, Rawson. Jesus. I haven't spoken to her in years."

I heard the click of a cigarette lighter and turned for another look at the Greeks on my periphery. This time I thought there might be a family resemblance. The gloves-wearing woman puffed on the unfiltered cigarette that Paulo held for her. I made a grab from memory, retrieved and placed her. Yes. There she was, looking at me the length of a wide echoing hallway that was all marble, old gold, frescoes, thirty-foot ceilings hung with chandeliers. A former palace, now a palatial public building. Late sixteenth century, maybe. I had been there on business. ILC business. She was the only woman in a group of men, ministry level from the looks of them. She'd been smoking there too. I was crossing that hall with all the Renaissance statuary to a curved flight of stairs when our eyes met. We may have looked at each other for about three seconds while I hesitated a step. I hadn't learned then, or been curious enough to ask, who she was.

"You have a name?" I said rudely to her. I was fed up with the whole performance, for which she and the young Greek god-type seemed to have recruited me as an audience of one.

She stared at me unblinkingly through a blue cloud of expelled smoke. Paulo leaned on the wall again, agreeably holding her cigarette for her.

One of the sly phones on DeMarco's desk played part of the *Godfather* theme.

"Rome," I said to the gloves-wearing woman. "About four years ago, wasn't it? But you were only wearing a glove on one hand then."

This time she blinked.

Paulo smiled slightly and looked down at her and whispered something in Greek.

"*What?*" DeMarco yelled, or almost yelled, to whoever had called. He was exasperated again. I looked at him. He listened for a few more seconds, then slammed the phone receiver down.

"What the *fuck* did you do?" he demanded.

"The decent, humane thing," I said. "There was a badly injured man in the men's room at Angeltowne. I think he may have fractured his skull when he slipped and hit his head on the toilet. He also happens to be either a murderer or a material witness in a murder case. Which is why I notified ILC Medevac to transport him by helicopter to the prison hospital at San Jack Town for treatment. He'll be guarded twenty-four/seven in ICU where Ortega won't be able to get to him. Once El Gordo is on the mend and coherent there's a chance I'll get a statement from him implicating Ortega in Sunny's death. Sorry if that blows up some shit of yours, DeMarco."

"You have no damn idea of the trouble you've caused, how badly you've set us back! But that's it. You're gone, pal. You're history where ILC is concerned. I'll see to it personally."

"Mr. DeMarco?" Paulo said, before I could react. "I have a suggestion."

His words were polite, but his tone had an edge that denied politeness. It said, *Time for you to shut up and listen*.

14

Paulo took his leave from the wall he'd been holding up and seated himself on a corner of the gray steel desk, one foot on the floor. He formed a triangle with DeMarco and myself. His gold medallion glinted in the leak light from the gooseneck desk lamp. His face, turned to me, was sculptured shadow. DeMarco ran a hand over the top of his head where his hair was thinnest and looked about to say something to reestablish himself as the honcho of our little group.

The Greek gave an earlobe a tweak between thumb and forefinger and said, for DeMarco's benefit but without a glance at him, "I think Mr. Rawson might agree that it makes sense at this point to release a report that his material witness in hospital lapsed into a deep coma and is surviving on life support. Thus giving Raoul Ortega temporary peace of mind."

I grinned at him. "Did you say 'thus?' "

"Cambridge," he said. "I read medieval Middle European history."

"Run across any references to werewolves in the good old stuff?"

"Some. But I guess my interest in the species is the same as yours: finding a way to survive them."

"Okay. My material witness or whatever he is lingers near

death and there's no hope for him. Sound about right to you, Cale?"

"I—"

"Good," Paulo said. "Now, if you wouldn't mind leaving us alone for a few minutes, Mr. DeMarco?"

"What?"

"We'll get back to you shortly. By the way, you've been doing an outstanding job here in SoCal."

"But—"

"Thank you, Mr. DeMarco."

Cale's mouth was open. He breathed through it. Paulo didn't go to the trouble to look around at him. Cale coughed a few times, possibly reacting to the bile that had risen in his throat. When he had that under control he scraped his chair back. He stood and squared his shoulders and walked to the door where, his hand on the knob, he appealed with a glance to the gloves-wearing woman. She declined to save his manhood.

"I could use some coffee," I said, as he was opening the door.

He stiffened as if I'd touched a cattle prod to his tailbone.

"And I," Paulo said. "If you wouldn't be going to any trouble."

"Two coffees?" Cale said in a strangled voice, not looking around to confirm.

"Black," I said.

"Any old way," Paulo said indifferently.

The door closed. Paulo tweaked his earlobe thoughtfully, grinned to himself.

The ash on the woman's cigarette was growing too long again. Paulo got up and disposed of the ash and put the cigarette back between her lips. Probably from long practice he knew just where she liked it. He spoke to her again in Greek.

They were an interesting team. Interesting in a purely clinical sense. I had the kid figured for a killer fruit. And speaking of medieval, if souls wore clothing, hers would've been chain mail.

When Paulo finished talking the gloves-wearing woman nodded, looking straight at me.

I said to her, "How are we going to have a beautiful relationship if you won't tell me your name? Or am I just not your type?"

Lavishing the charm just as if I hadn't been through a world of crap tonight, with bowling balls knocking around inside my head. I needed codeine like a baby needs its pacifier, or I was going to start vomiting.

Charm got me nowhere either.

Paulo also ignored my overture to the woman as he took a slightly larger than letter-sized envelope from an inside jacket pocket. The envelope contained a few small lumps of something and a color photo, which he placed on the desk in front of me. Then he adjusted the lamp so I could see more clearly.

The photo was a head-and-shoulders portrait of a Middle Eastern or Indian-Asian male, late middle age as far as I could tell. You could see thousands just like him on streets from Damascus to Mumbai to Jakarta every day. A somewhat frowsy, dark mustache plastered to his upper lip, dull half-lidded eyes. Flat lighting. Maybe the fact that he'd been dead for hours or as much as a full day when the picture was taken in a morgue had everything to do with his lack of manly distinction.

"I know it's tough," Paulo said. "But—"

I shook my head. "Uh-uh. Any identifying scars I could look up? A unicorn-shaped birthmark on his tummy?"

"No."

"Murdered?"

"Yes. What is popularly known in SoCal as a spike job."

"Where?"

"Rome. We think he came to see us."

" 'Us' being the Home Office. Spook Central."

"Sure."

"Did the vic contact you?"

"Presuming the corpse in the photo and the one who left his name and a message are the same man. Matter of great urgency, he said. Before we could establish direct contact, apparently some owlhoots on his trail caught up to him."

"Owlhoots?"

"Bad guys. Dog heavies. I'm a Luke Bailiff junkie." Paulo grinned and swished his feathery dark eyelashes at me.

"Okay, so you don't have a positive ID?"

"They didn't leave him with his fingers when they dumped him in the Tiber, only the ice pick in the back of his neck. But the name we have checks out. There is only one Barsi Chanthar Vajracharya, alive or dead. Known to colleagues as 'Dr. Chant.' A renowned nanobiotechnologist. Until about six months ago Dr. Chant was director of R and D for the Nanomimetics Corporation in San Jack Town."

I nodded. "Was he fired?"

"As far as we've been able to learn, Dr. Chant took an abrupt and indefinite leave of absence and did his very best to disappear. Through airline sources we've placed him in recent weeks in five different cities around the world."

"Fiddle-footed," I suggested. "Or not very good at disappearing."

"We're just very good at tracking people who try. But so were the ones who wanted him dead. And they had a head start."

I looked again at the photo. "I have a bitch of a headache right now, but I hear a bell faintly ringing. What did the autopsy report have to say? High Blood? Lycan?"

"The man from the river was an Off-Blood. NANOMIM HR records confirm that Dr. Chant was Off-Blood. Best we can do without fingerprint confirmation, but it's a near-certainty they're the same man."

"Off-Bloods are a select group," I said. "Fewer than one thousand of them in SoCal. Most are men. It's almost a fraternity. No secret handshake, but they try to help one another. It's a difficult way to live. They share info on the availability of reliable blood cows. Off-Bloods like doing business with Off-Bloods. Nobody else seems to have much affection for them."

Cale DeMarco knocked, then backed into the room with two Styrofoam cups of black coffee. I felt in my pockets for my pill dispenser. A cody for my head, meth for stamina. I took both with the coffee, burning my tongue.

DeMarco looked curiously at the photo of the murdered man. And at me.

"Two murders that may tie in," I said. "I'm pretty good with murders. Would you mind asking Beatrice to come in? We need her."

Paulo didn't object. The gloves-wearing woman glanced at DeMarco when he was slow to react. He nodded tightly and left.

"Two murders?" Paulo said.

"Artie Excalibur's is the one I've been working on. He was done in by an OOPs named Chickie Hickey early Monday morning. In his office above de Sade's. Bea and I happened to be there. Chickie has yet to turn up. Probably dead herself. She was an actress and protégée, in the bird-in-nest sense, of Miles Brenta, who dabbles in movie production. Bucky Spartacus, the kid who went OOPs tonight at the concert, was more than a protégé of Brenta's; from what I've heard he was like a son to him. The two kids have been an item for publicity purposes, but I think it went deeper than that for Bucky: he was in love with Chickie, even though he might have known or guessed that Chickie was doing both him and Brenta, a double-dip career move. Chickie might have infected Bucky with LC disease, but that's guesswork. If Bucky, why not Brenta? It *is* plain fact that Bucky was toting an unregistered Snitcher, the remains of which we found in the little pile of burnt offering he turned into."

Paulo opened his envelope again and shook out three two-inch-square transparent evidence bags on the desk next to the photograph. I recognized the Snitcher recovered at the amphitheater.

"That's supposed to be in the ILC lab right now," I said.

"It will be," Paulo said. "But I doubt they'll learn anything from what's left."

"What are the other two for?"

"Number two is a standard-issue Snitch, the most recent upgrade, in use for nearly six years. There are tens of millions of them, reliable, maintaining what we hope is a balance of nature." He smiled a little sadly. "Number three, as you can probably tell without a magnifying glass, is smaller, injectable, state-of-the-art: a LUMO, probably a prototype."

"Where did you get it?"

"From the body of the late Dr. Chant. Slightly modified so that wolf-scanners like yours wouldn't detect it. But our chief pathologist in Rome is very thorough."

"Off-Bloods have no use for Snitchers. So he was on the run with a LUMO he helped design."

There was a polite tap at the door. Paulo got up from his perch on the desk and opened it.

Beatrice came in supressing a yawn, looked first at me, seemed relieved that I hadn't been given the third degree with a meat-axe. Although I could be sure it was part of their repertoire when needed. Then she looked at the gloves-wearing woman and smiled.

"We're keeping you up very late," the gloves-wearing woman observed with a hint of apology. She spoke out of the side of her mouth. The cigarette didn't move. Her voice had a lot of hard bark on it, probably due to a lifetime's affection for gaspers.

"Oh, that's okay, Arl. I know it's important."

"When did you two get chummy?" I said.

"Oh," Bea said, "we had a chance to chat before the Stork brought you."

Bea and the gloves-wearing woman seemed to find the allusion amusing, which made my mood and temper worse than they already were.

"Your name's Arles?" I said. "Like the French city?"

"For Arlequin," she croaked.

"I always thought 'Arlequin' was INTEL/INT code for something. But you spook types always play it so tight and cozy. Working with any of you is like bedding down with a python."

"Let's not be quarrelsome. Too much is at stake for discord. Why is Beatrice here?"

"Yes, why?" Beatrice said brightly.

"Have a look at the photo," I said to her.

Bea put a hand on my shoulder and leaned toward the desk.

"Ohh. Ugh. He's dead, isn't he?"

"Know him?"

Bea made herself take a longer look.

"I may have seen him. A few months ago, at Artie's digs. Late at night. Artie had asked me to bring him a spare computer from the safe at the office, the one he used at home had conked. Artie had me lock up all of his computers. I told you he was kind of paranoid about business matters."

Paulo said, "We think the man in the photo is Barsi Chanthar Vajracharya, a.k.a. Dr. Chant. Formerly employed by NANOMIM."

Bea's hand squeezed my shoulder. "Well—a lot of men look like this, dead or not. But remember I told you, R, about the e-mails Artie was getting from this Dr. Chant?"

"E-mails from where?" Paulo asked.

"South America. India. As if the two of them, Artie and Chant, had some big deal about to happen."

"It happened," I said. "They're both dead because of it."

"What sort of deal?" Bea said.

"Trafficking in stolen Snitchers. Maybe."

"Not Artie," Bea insisted. "He got a little shady sometimes, but he wasn't a criminal."

I looked at the gloves-wearing woman.

"Is that what you've had DeMarco working on? Yeah, it would be a step up for an old bloodlegger like Ortega. If there was enough money in it."

"There is not," she said hoarsely.

"I didn't think a deal like that would bring you here from Rome. Too much at stake, as you said." I gave it a few seconds, then shrugged and got up from my chair. "Okay, go on playing python, but I won't be your main squeeze. You've got DeMarco for that. I have two murders and a potential third to solve before the next full moon. That would be Mallory Scarlett, still missing and a potential trophy for werewolf hunters. Lycans are human too. In a manner of speaking. Besides, I sort of liked the little snot when she was living next door. Come on, Bea. Let's vamoose."

Paulo stood too, turning to me and smiling. I looked him in the eye.

"If you have no objections that I can't deal with," I said.

The gloves-wearing woman said in her half-ruined voice, "Perhaps we can help you with the Scarlett girl."

"Is that a fact?"

"Yes. She was taken from the Angeltowne Livery at 1230 hours yesterday in one of the armored trucks they keep over there."

"Taken where?"

Paulo said, "The helicopter DeMarco assigned for surveillance tracked the armored truck to the Crestline Highway a few miles north of San Bernadino. That's when the chopper had to turn back; apparently the EGT was running red-line."

"Swell," I groused. "Crestline? There's only about a hundred twenty square miles of forest and mountains we'll have to search in the next forty hours."

He shrugged. "The girl wasn't a priority with us. But if she's going to remain a prisoner until she hairs-up, probably there are only so many areas suitable to conduct a *mal de lune* up that way. One or two may be hunting lodges owned by prominent sportsmen. And all hunters like to brag, some of them in advance, about their prowess. You know. It's the Luke Bailiff, only-law-west-of-Dodge syndrome."

"Okay," I conceded. "You've given me a worthwhile lead. I apologize for being edgy with you. This OOPs business has me—"

It wasn't the tingle of a distant bell competing with the headache bongos that stopped me: it was a full-throated cannonade of Notre Dame–sized bells as the tumbrels rolled through Paris streets. I turned and stared down at the Snitchers neatly labeled in evidence bags—two that looked unused, one nearly destroyed.

"R?" Beatrice said tentatively. "What's wrong?"

An image of Chickie Hickey at de Sade's whipped through my mind like a ghost released from an attic.

"Jesus," I said. "Anything but that."

Paulo clicked his lighter to fire up another cigarette for the gloves-wearing woman. She was looking at me when I turned to them.

"Unfortunately, yes," she said with a nod.

Bea grabbed me pleadingly.

"Don't *look* like that," she said. "You're scaring me."

I picked up the evidence bag with the Snitcher leftovers from the amphitheater.

"Chickie had one of the new, injectable LUMOs," I said. "Different location in the body, no surgical scar to cover up. After she went OOPS I thought it was probably because her Snitcher had been cut out of her. Which couldn't have accounted for her actions after she haired-up. So it had to be the LUMO. And this one was Bucky's. Another LUMO? That leaves two possibilities." I went after those with the dedication of a soused rat in a maze. I'm always full of ideas. Sometimes they turn out to be good for something. I made my choice. "The LUMOs are defective. A design flaw. They can't stop a Lycan from hairing-up."

"Three years of testing," Paulo countered. "All the tests done to WEIR's specifications and under their supervision. A printout of all relevant data runs to about four thousand pages. Conclusion: no design flaws. All the prototypes, thousands of them, worked perfectly. And you're missing something."

"Of course I am. Because Out-of-Phase Hairballs are extremely rare. I know of six documented cases in twenty-five years. Now there have been two occurrences within four days. Two kids. Lovers. What are those odds?"

"Not worth calculating," the gloves-wearing woman said within her mystical haze of cigarette smoke. "And not at all necessary. At least three million LUMOs have already come off the line and most have been shipped to WEIR clinics in SoCal. If they should be recalled, what is there to look for? But that also is wasted effort. That the design is good is beyond question. A recall and lengthy reevaluation of the LUMO's integrity would accomplish but one thing. It is all a matter of critical timing for Miles Brenta and for Nanomimetics."

"No LUMOs, no big bucks for Brenta," I said. "And there's a domino effect. The patents his company holds on the old-model Snitchers expire in a few months. When that happens, anyone can tool up and manufacture Snitchers without paying licensing fees and royalties."

"Free-market economics will prevail," Paulo said dryly. "No monopoly, and no LUMOs. NANOMIM will be undersold everywhere."

"Bad luck and bad timing," I said. "Maybe. But if that's how it goes down, then we come to the Really Bad Thing."

Beatrice was still holding on to me. I felt her shudder.

"How bad?"

"A sizable percentage of the newly manufactured but old-style Snitchers likely would be counterfeit, knockoffs from sweatshops in twenty countries. Those Snitchers might work. Probably they would fail in wholesale lots and at unpredictable times."

"Oh my God," Bea said softly. "But—there's no need to recall the LUMOs. Maybe a couple of them failed, but the design is good. Isn't that what you both said, Paulo?"

She let go of me and reached for the little baggie on the desk containing the nodule that a pathologist in Rome had excised from the cold flesh of a corpse. She held it up.

"LUMOs are a major advance in technology and micro-whatever. So there wouldn't be a market for old-style anymore. Only WEIR buys Snitchers."

"There are thousands of WEIR clinics," I said, "but no central purchasing agency. The usual bureaucratic shuffle-and-deal. Clinic managers don't mind putting a few extra thousand into their own pockets. The yearly audits are a joke. Anyway, a flood of counterfeit Snitchers isn't the immediate worst-case."

Bea looked at all of us in turn. She was dead for sleep and we were making her miserable. She blinked her tearing eyes. The smoke in the room was getting to be oppressive.

"There's something worse than the Really Bad Thing?" Bea said finally.

"That item you're holding," I said, "is responsible for at least four deaths. So far. But I'd bet a pound of pure Mexican silver and a bottle of thirty-year-old Scotch that it isn't a LUMO. It's something else entirely."

15

After a further twenty-minute session with Paulo and the gloves-wearing woman I retrieved my gun, Range Rover, and Bea, and drove us to Beverly Hills, taking Laurel Canyon to Ventura, then Coldwater up into the hills where Coldwater merged with Mulholland for a mile or so before dropping south and into the Privilege through the Trousdale gate, which looked like a set left over from *The Ten Commandments*. With date palms.

Almost as soon as we had left the bungalow in North Hollywood Beatrice curled up as comfortably as she could manage with her long legs in the bucket seat next to me and went to sleep. She didn't want to talk and she didn't want to hear me talk. It had been a long rough night and she'd had her fill of shocks and forebodings; a few hours of oblivion were a necessity for her now.

For much of the way home I thought I was being followed. Motorcycle. Hanging back about a quarter of a mile behind us. Three-thirty in the morning and there was almost no other traffic. Because of the luminosity of the sky from the nearly full moon (Observance minus about forty-three hours), I could make out in my rearview the crouched shape of the biker low in the saddle.

At the Mulholland summit the biker turned west and became no more than a pencil of light amid the dark hills. I felt a little disappointed. Maybe I had wanted it to be Elena.

I left the Rover in front of the house on Breva Way. I had to shake the complaining Bea hard to get her out of the Rover. I walked her inside and down the black slate hall to my bedroom. Bea undressed to her bikini briefs with her eyes closed and a little help from me and collapsed on the futon with an unconscious sigh. I covered her with a satin throw and went to take a shower. There was a sour odor of old cigarette smoke clinging to my skin; I could taste it at the back of my throat.

The meth was keeping me awake and reasonably sharp. The hot shower and hotter sauna soothed my aches and scrapes. What was left of my headache vanished. I got dressed, made myself a cup of green tea with Kabuchka and ate a few rice crackers with almond butter. I reviewed the plan that I had more or less convinced the spooks from Rome would work. How well it would work depended on how far I was willing to stick my neck out. And it would still be necessary to convince Booth Havergal that I knew what the hell I was doing.

I left a DO NOT DISTURB sign on my bedroom door for the housekeeper, locked Bea inside the house, and drove to ILC on Burton Way for the six o'clock staff meeting I had called. I got there a little after five-thirty. There was a hint of daylight in the east and the birds in the greenspace eucalyptus were tuning up. The early PE trams were humming along the divider strip rails. I counted six satellite uplink trucks parked on the side street and there were lights in my eyes as I drove down to the basement parking levels beneath ILC headquarters. Bucky Spartacus' final performance had shocked the world; the media were swarming.

I had enough time to e-mail Booth Havergal a full account of my activities of a few hours ago, including my meeting with Cale DeMarco and the spooks of Rome. It was possible he didn't know they were in the neighborhood.

Then it was time for the meeting I'd called. My priority this morning was the armored truck last seen on the Crestline Highway, presumably with Mallory Scarlett inside. I sent two teams out to Crestline with instructions to enlist the local law and park rangers in our *mal de lune* investigation and come up with something. ILC business took precedence over all other law-enforcement activities. And the lunar clock was at Observance minus forty hours.

It was almost seven A.M. when I sat down with a mug of coffee in our Virtual Reality lab for a look at 3-D simulations made from the amphitheater digital surveillance files, concentrating on those from the crowded two-acre backstage lot. When you don't know what you're looking for, it's tedious and boring work.

But after only a few minutes' worth of compressed-time simulations I caught a glimpse of something I wanted to see again. The techie working with me provided an enhanced image that didn't leave much doubt in my mind. The figure was taller than the doorway he was framed in, so he had to stoop to look out. That characteristic and the starbus he was visiting had caught my eye: it was the bus Bucky Spartacus had borrowed for the concert.

On a monitor I saw Lew Rolling walking past the Virtual Reality lab and paged him. When he joined us he leaned on the back of my chair and looked at our Virtual of the man on the starbus: he had an ascetic, lugubrious face like you see in deathbed paintings by El Greco or Velásquez, a face made longer by the kind of beard they were wearing in those days.

"Could be Raoul Ortega," Lew said.

"It is."

"Where is he?"

"Visiting Bucky Spartacus before the show."

"So they knew each other?"

"Wouldn't surprise me. It's a tight little circle, getting tighter all the time. With Miles Brenta and probably NANOMIM at the nexus."

I had a text message from Booth Havergal, responding to my report.

Ys know spooks r here. Toss u a bone,
they want bigger bone back. Yr prop
one: squeeze the greaser, bring me poop.
prop two: no grnds warrant so no
fkg way unless u want to marry her.
prop three: legit approach within
bounds yr invest. B's lawyers
building walls already. Mat witness?
don't think so but keep digging. Hv
nice day.

"Been to the woodshed?" Lew said with a laugh.

"Like most days. Sometimes Booth leaves me a mousehole to crawl through. Can you get me a copy of Miles Brenta's schedule for today from his office?"

Lew got on it. I reread Booth's memo, looking for my mouse hole. Not this time. If he didn't want me leaning on Fran Obregon in my inimitable fashion, I could sort of agree on the need for caution. But with what I knew so far Fran was dirty and when I could corroborate that I would skin her alive. The thought made me temporarily happy.

I ordered a helicopter for ten o'clock, hoping I'd be finished reviewing VR surveillance by then.

The next sequence of interest that turned up almost had me jumping out of my seat.

"Again," I said to the techie beside me.

According to the time code what I was looking at had happened within moments of Bucky Spartacus' other, impromptu, hairy performance onstage.

I saw Miles Brenta exit the backseat of his limousine and take several running steps toward the backstage area. I saw Fran poke her head out as the beefer leaning against the trunk of the limo whirled and went after his boss. Fran followed.

They practically had to wrestle Miles Brenta to the ground. Even without a close look at his face it was obvious to me that he was screaming.

The techie repositioned the Virtual Reality figures to enhance Brenta's face. I could almost read the horror in his eyes.

"Son of a bitch," I said. "He didn't know. Give me Fran now."

The enhancement of Fran as she took a good grip on one of Brenta's arms revealed no such emotion, not even a hint of shock. She might have been thinking about what to make at her next pottery class.

"But *she* knew," I said.

I watched Fran Obregon and two beefers, because that's how many of them were needed to pull Brenta back into the limo, which raced away even before the door was shut. The last VR image was Obregon's hand reaching for the door handle.

"Freeze," I said, and sat back in the lab chair with my fingers locked behind my head. I was grinning as I stared at the VR detail of her outstretched hand: the chicly jeweled fingers, the expensive bracelets looped around her wrist.

"Shake hands with the devil, baby," I said. "It won't be long now."

I was halfway to San Jack Town at nine hundred feet over Seco Grande when Lew Rolling got back to me and said that Miles Brenta had canceled his schedule and was spending the day at home in Paradiso Palms, presumably in seclusion.

The prison hospital operated by WEIR was a collection of two-story adobe-style tan cubes with narrow tinted windows and solar panel roofs angled to acquire sunlight all day. Covered walkways connected the buildings. The complex was just north of San Jacinto; a quarter mile farther north the Colorado Aqueduct glittered like a silver vein in a thin concrete arm.

Two helo pads were located well away from the psychiatric unit, so the comings and goings of choppers wouldn't disturb the loony birds in residence. There was no shade but the facility provided hose connections to one-ton mobile APUs for cooling. Otherwise after only a few minutes on the ground the cabin temps could hit a hundred sixty degrees at noon on a hot day. And it was another hot day.

I rode the minibus to administration and checked in. El Gordo had been X-rayed and treated on arrival, then removed to an isolation unit where he was reported to be sedated but able to talk.

WEIR already had run his prints and I had his sheet. Four aliases, birth name Roberto Gallego, birthplace Guanajuato, Mexico. He had a trip to the main joint at Rocky Peak on his ledger, murder two bargained down to manslaughter, eight and out.

And at the moment he had a hairline fracture that would heal without intervention, a lump on the side of his head the size of a lemon. Twenty-two stitches had closed the trenchlike gash on his face opened up by the front sight of my Glock. His right eye was swollen shut. Probably he would have trouble breathing through his nose for the rest of his life, but what life expectancy he had came down to the toss of a coin, and I was doing the tossing.

There was a guard on his door. The charges were everything I could think of from suspicion of murder on down. When I mentioned the charges he showed me the underside of his lip like a nickering horse.

"*Abogado*," he said.

"Ortega knows you're here," I said. "By now he probably would've sent you a mouthpiece with a basketful of forget-me-nots. But the word is out you're in a coma and probably won't be needing anything but a priest and a cheap funeral. That's my favor to you, comprende, Roberto?"

"Fock tu madre."

"But any time I say, hombre, you'll have a rapid recovery. Before you know it you'll be out of your cozy room here and into the general population at the Peak. Where if you're not on the SN yard you might last, what, a day and a half? Before one of your fellow Diamondbackers gets the word and shanks you through the solar plexus."

He thought that one over; then his good eye moved in my direction, catching some of the filtered light through the single, six-inch-wide window opposite the hospital bed he occupied. He looked at me for two seconds, looked away. His fat mouth behaved this time. I took his lack of a sneer as a sign that he wanted to parlay. I made a bitter choice.

"You can do twenty-to-life for Sunny Chagrin," I said. "I'd like to see you do the time. I owe it to Sunny. But I don't think you can rat out Ortega on murder one and make it stick, even if you live long enough to go to trial. I'm willing to give it a shot, though. Unless you give me something else I want."

It was quiet for a while in the small hospital room, except for the tweeting of the vital-signs monitor. Then his good eye wandered back to me.

"Qué es?" he said.

"Where is Mal Scarlett?"

According to the monitor his pulse rate picked up. He breathed deeply through his mouth.

"No se, hombre."

"I can get you fixed up with a one-way back to Guanajuato," I said, hating myself for bargaining over Sunny's corpse. "Or I walk out the door and you're dead, amigo. Help your memory any?"

"I doan know about those bizness. *Cazando lobos. El jefe*, he arrange."

"You don't know where the next one is going to be, where they took Mal?"

He might have frowned, if his face could have handled the stress. His eyes closed briefly. He grimaced, showing off his gold bridgework.

"Yesterday they took her away from Angeltowne in an armored truck," I said. "I know that much."

"*Verdad.* But I no was there *el tarde*. I hear Pepito say—Pepito, he drive the trock, onnerstan? Always he drive. To take the lobos to the keeling place. Beeg stars, onnerstan? Mucho famoso."

"What did you hear Pepito say?"

"Pepito say, 'the beetch is go to catch her plane.' He laugh."

"The truck was headed up the Crestline Highway is the last information we have. There's no regional airport I know of up that way."

"I doan know," he moaned weakly, as if he were sinking under the weight of the painkillers they had him on. "Like a *chiste* he ees saying it. She catch her plane now. Ho-ho, beeg joke."

I didn't know of a regional airport north of San Berdoo, but if one existed there was little chance that Pepito and whoever else had been along for the ride would attempt to off-load a kidnapped ex-debutante with a face known all over the world and put her into a waiting plane. Day or night.

But if Mal was destined for a *mal de lune* site outside of SoCal where law enforcement was lax, corrupt, or nonexistent, there were numerous private fields with minimal services and not much supervision. Probably at least thirty of them, from the edge of the great Mojave west to Lancaster and Palmdale. In that sparsely populated corridor of SoCal, ultralights, small planes, or helicopters are essential if you wanted to make it down to the bright lights and sin spots of the L.A. basin without hard driving on bad roads.

I made the calls I had to make; but it was a lot of territory to cover in a short time with limited manpower.

While I was using my wristpac I heard a familiar, unforgettable voice and drifted to where it was coming from: a shaded rec area where a congregation of about thirty Lycan inmates—a few on crutches, a couple in wheelchairs—had gathered to enjoy some ice cream and hear the Word from the Rev. A. A. Kingworthy, pastor of the First Church of Lycanthropy.

His text dealt with lions, lambs, and Lycans. It didn't make a lot of sense to me, but his timing was great as always and he was rewarded with choruses of hallelujahs and amens. After his homily, which was the usual can of beans, he talked briefly to and blessed each inmate individually. The aftereffects of a helicopter blowing up in his face had left him looking like a great old dog with a bad case of mange. His hands and several fingers were bandaged. I had to admire his pluck.

Kingworthy blotted his perspiring brow with a succession of nacre handkerchiefs shaken out and delicately handed to him by an associate pastor, a man who was a third the size of the Reverend and twice as dark. The associate seemed in agony that not a drop of sweat fall on the Rev's immaculate white suit.

The inmates were herded back to the wards they had come from. Kingworthy helped himself to a quart bottle of root beer from a cooler.

I went over to him. His broad back was to me, his head tilted back as he took long swallows of his drink.

"Inspiring," I said. "I didn't know you also had a prison ministry."

He lowered the bottle and turned to me with a pleasant show of teeth.

"I take the Gospel wherever it is most needed."

He was still perspiring. They had run out of fresh handkerchiefs. The sting of salt must have been painful on his flash-burned skin. The associate was frantic; I assumed wringing out one of the used ones just wouldn't do. I handed Kingworthy my handkerchief.

"Thank you, and God bless you, sir." His eyes were blood-red today. He blinked a couple of times as if to bring me into sharper focus. I think he recognized me then. For a few seconds there was something guarded in his expression. Then the smile reappeared, with enough gleaming veneer to resurface a bowling alley. "Have we met?"

"Not formally. I was there last night, backstage."

"Ah," he said sorrowfully, his brow wrinkling. "Shocking and tragic. But perhaps it was a sign from the Lord. After long and prayerful contemplation, that is what I make of it."

Kingworthy bowed his head momentarily, his tongue nudging a blister on his lower lip.

"What exactly was the Almighty trying to impress upon us?" I said.

"I have no further interpretation to offer. The Lord's majestic inscrutability is often a great comfort to me. Are you a believing man?"

"I believe in truth, justice, and a square deal—when I can get one."

He nodded. He finished patting his tender face with my handkerchief, and stared at the initialed corner.

"Forgive me for not recalling your name."

"Rawson," I said. "I'm deputy director of ILC SOCAL, criminal investigations."

"Forgive me again—may I offer you something cold to drink, Mr. Rawson?"

"Sure. I'm partial to lemon-lime." I didn't add that I usually liked it with four ounces of freezer-chilled vodka on the side.

The associate pastor rolled up his starched shirt cuff, fished among the remaining chips of clear ice in the cooler, and came up with a can of soda for me. I pulled the tab and raised the can in a toast.

"Confusion to the enemy."

Kingworthy agreeably joined in with his quart bottle. His bandaged fingers could've gone around it twice. Damn, he was big.

"Whose name," Kingworthy added, "we all know to be Satan."

I watched a squadron of big-bellied flies around a wire trash basket half filled with ice-cream bar wrappers. The flies looked iridescent in streaks of sun. A hot wind blew dust and a couple of stray wrappers across the asphalt pavement of the rec yard. I thought I could hear the humming of the flies.

"I was thinking more of someone who could make a Lycan go werewolf any old time, even if he or she didn't want to."

Kingworthy eyed me in a troubled way and gently fingered a couple of the raw places on his broad face. I tried to remember all the plagues of biblical Egypt. Flies, of course, and [sored] flesh and a bloody tainted river. Like the bloodstreams of Lycans? Firstborns too. They had figured into it somehow. I was an only child. That probably should have made me nervous.

"Is such an abomination possible?" Kingworthy said.

Now it was an abomination, and not some inscrutable lesson from a deity.

"We both saw it happen last night. For me, it was the second such occurrence in little more than four days." The humming of flies seemed louder to me. I was besotted with symbolism. I needed more sleep or more meth or something to shut down the anger that was spilling too much adrenaline into my system. "So what was it, Reverend? An act of God or an act of Satan we witnessed last night at the amphitheater?"

As soon as I asked him that I realized I wasn't interested in whatever response he might give. It was a question for theologians. He was just a preacher. My true interest was earthly evil and those who had the capacity for it.

"Sorry," I said. "I didn't come over here to challenge your

faith. I hoped you might be able to help me with something else."

I took out a 3-D head shot of Raoul J. Ortega made from the VR surveillance discs.

"This man was at last night's concert. Do you know him or recall seeing him backstage with Bucky?"

He only needed a moment to look at the photo.

"Yes, I know him. That is our blessed brother Raoul. A great friend of the First Church of Lycanthropy, although like myself he is of the High Blood."

"Also he's president of the SoCal Diamondbackers, a known criminal organization. They all have a pathological hatred of Lycans."

That didn't faze Kingworthy.

"Brother Raoul has renounced his past sins. That was good enough for me, but most importantly he stands guiltless in the sight of Almighty God."

"God may not be the shrewd judge of character he's given credit for. I know how much Ortega enjoys organizing things. Was the fund-raiser his idea?"

"It was."

"He persuaded Bucky and Chimera to appear?"

"I left everything up to him. The choice of personalities. The venue."

"Chimera's style is kind of down and dirty for a church social."

He looked wearily at me. "Our church home will be costly to build. Everyone's contribution is welcome. I don't care for rock and roll myself. Our young parishioners like it. The greater good benefits from the lesser evil."

"Ortega's in the armored transport business. Was he also responsible for hauling the loot away?"

"Do you have a reason for doubting Brother Raoul's integrity and devotion to our church?"

"We could both keel over from heat prostration before I finish giving you all of my reasons."

I stepped a little closer to him. We were nearly toe to toe. If I had been five inches taller I could have unknotted his tie with my teeth. He looked down at me and didn't yield. I pitched my voice lower.

"Come on now, Reverend. Between you and me. You don't trust Ortega either, do you? How many of your associate pastors were riding shotgun with the strongbox last night? I mean just the ones licensed to carry bazookas with their go-to-meeting clothes."

I don't know what response I expected; something pious or indignant, maybe. What I got was a hearty laugh that nearly blew me back on my heels. The associate pastor with us smiled primly, hands folded at his beltline.

"But you probably had his split negotiated and packaged long before any of the money left the amphitheater," I said. "I don't know if you're a good bad man or a bad good man, Reverend Kingworthy. Maybe it's all malarkey; still I admire your dedication. It's hot out here and you probably haven't had any more sleep than I've had. But here's some advice: go play with real rattlesnakes and leave Diamondbackers alone. You'll live longer."

He nodded.

"Complications abound," he mused. "But worthwhile goals are never easily achieved." He paused, adding with a smile, "And things as they are are changed upon the blue guitar."

"The Gospel according to Wallace Stevens?"

"A favorite poet of mine. Deeply philosophical. Would you like to have your handkerchief back? Or may I have sent to you a dozen new ones with my compliments?"

"Thanks, but I'll just take the old one with me. After it dries I'll probably frame it and hang it over my mantel and spend long winter nights pondering your image when it appears."

He handed me the soggy handkerchief with just the faintest trace of amusement on his blistered lips.

"A pleasure speaking to you this morning, Mr. Rawson. Would there be anything else I can do for you? I'm afraid I have no idea where you might find Brother Raoul. He finds me, whenever he is in need of spiritual sustenance."

I let that notion blow by me like the grit picked up by the wind, nodded slightly, and walked away. I didn't get far. I turned to Kingworthy as he was opening a second quart of root beer.

"Raoul Ortega killed Bucky Spartacus," I said. "I don't know yet how he managed it, but I'll find out." The Rev was motionless, contemplating this charge. "One more question, Reverend."

"As you wish, sir."

"Did you know that Bucky's hair-up was coming?"

He looked gravely at me.

"How could I possibly anticipate such an ungodly thing?"

"But your reaction was—hell, call it suicidal. The Bucky-ball was like all the rest of them, an equal-opportunity killing machine."

"But I never gave dying a thought. I never felt in danger. Like all the rest of them? You will never convince me of that. What I saw was not just another werewolf. I saw the inner writhing of a tormented soul."

"Then you've got something I haven't got."

Kingworthy nodded. "Yes. Perhaps I do, Mr. Rawson."

16

Paradiso Palms was a designed community for the very well heeled and just plain heels, an immaculate watering hole where the worst problem any of the residents seemed to have was getting out of the sand traps at the golf club. The Palms, like the Prestige, was walled, but more handsomely, and very well policed. It was off-limits to Lycans at any time; even domestic help and staff at the two large resort hotels had to be High Bloods, who made twice the money Lycans could get in other, less choosy places.

Miles Brenta's real estate company had planned and built Paradiso Palms in the desert about five minutes by helicopter from WEIR's sprawling top-security complex at San Jack Town. Part of the Palms was nestled in the canyons on the southeast flank of San Jacinto Mountain. Brenta had reserved fully one-quarter of the entire community for his own estate, an enclave landscaped from scratch where before only the Joshua trees and ocotillo had stood much of a chance. Now, from the air, the terrain looked verdant and hilly, with date palm oases, streams stocked with rainbow trout, a couple of stair-step waterfalls, and another big-league golf course for the exclusive use of Brenta and his cronies. I didn't see anyone playing as I approached. A dozen groundskeepers were at work on the estate, scooting along trails in electric trucks. One of the largest wind farms and desalination plants in perpetually water-starved SoCal kept the hundred and sixty acres green as Ireland. A twenty-four-inch pipeline went directly to the Salton Sea. Lycan gangs had sabotaged it recently. There were probably two hundred thousand Lycans living out this way in human junkyards, or government-subsidized trailer parks, some who had a lot of free time to think up ways to vent their hatred of High Bloods.

Looking at the oncoming estate from eight hundred feet and the visible pleasures of being Brenta, I was reminded that in the old days the "sport of kings" consisted mainly of trying to stay alive.

As soon as I penetrated their airspace Brenta Security squawked me. I identified myself with the chopper's tail number and requested permission to land. They had three helipads near the main house, two occupied.

"Please give me your name and state the nature of your business, six-one-niner."

"Rawson. Here to see Miles Brenta."

"Circle at eight hundred feet and I'll get back to you."

"Roger that."

He needed a half minute to confirm what I'd already guessed the answer would be.

"Negative on your request to land, six-one-niner. Mr. Brenta is not seeing visitors today. Please return immediately to unrestricted airspace."

"This is not a social call," I said. "I'm ILC, here on official business."

"Continue circling."

I did, along with a couple of redtail hawks about half a mile away, who also probably didn't have permission to land. By and by I saw a lone rider pushing a black horse at what appeared to be full gallop along a hillside trail. I voiced "binocular" to my Geekers and the optics shifted to give me a close look at Miles Brenta, riding hell-for-leather as if he were outdistancing a fantasy posse. He wore chaps with his Wranglers, a red and white checkered shirt like John Wayne's in *The Searchers*, and a pale yellow, high-crowned Stetson.

I got back on the radio.

"Brenta Security, I'm getting excessive rotor vibe. It could be a laminate crack or a loose Jesus nut. My will's not up to date so I'm setting down until it's cool enough for me to have a look at the mast."

"Roger, six-one-niner. Stay with your helo on the ground and we'll send out a mechanic."

"Thanks for your hospitality," I said, and clicked off the radio.

Miles Brenta had eluded the posse and reined in his horse to a walk. The sleek Arabian appeared to be limping off the right foreleg. Brenta left the saddle to examine the horse's hoof and hock while the black stood patiently with the reins down.

As a courtesy to Brenta and because I didn't know how nervy the big black might be, I cut power, bottomed the pitch, turned into what was a pretty good breeze across rolling grassy hills that had been created by bulldozers from a few million cubic feet of nontoxic landfill, and drifted down to perch fifty feet from them like a bee on a buttercup.

Brenta looked up in annoyance. He was wearing a wild-west-style gun belt studded with cartridges. His hand moved toward the butt of a big holstered revolver like the Frontier-model .44 Colt as I stepped down from the helicopter. I took off my Geekers, wincing in the strong noon light, and let him have a look at me.

"It's Rawson, Mr. Brenta. I apologize for dropping in, but we need to talk."

He looked around, but there were no hired hands in sight. Getting up on his injured horse again wasn't an option. He didn't throw down on me but his hand stayed near his shootin' iron and his thumb twitched a couple of times. He hadn't shaved today. There were no clouds in the sky, but his eyes looked overcast, his face taut with trouble.

"You're close enough," he said. "I don't want to talk to you. No questions! There's nothing—" He took a deep breath, as if recovering from another in a series of body blows. "Serve me with a subpoena or leave me alone. And get your helicopter off my land."

I shook my head gently. The horse looked around at me.

"Emergency landing," I said. "Your security people told me they'd lend a mechanic to look for the problem. How is your horse?"

He seemed to have forgotten the black's lameness.

"Oh. I don't think it's—" Using the red bandana draped around his neck he dabbed sweat from his forehead. Then he called and notified someone at the stable to bring up a horse trailer for the Arabian and to send for the vet.

"I want to help you," I said, trying it a different way. "I may be the only one who knows enough to help you, Mr. Brenta."

Sometimes you get lucky—make a blind stab, say the right thing without knowing what it was. Miles Brenta was an operator, a tough guy, at the peak of his career the way cannibals are at the top of the food chain. He had money and power. But he was alone in his grief today, trying manfully to handle it, or so it seemed to me, acting out like a Bill Hickok throwback. Always the fastest gun in the deal or with the women who caught his eye. But the very wealthy seldom have close friends. They have enablers, competitors, supplicants, and enemies. Sometimes there's the love of a good woman. But Brenta's wife was a demented cripple and the closest thing he'd had for a son, Bucky Spartacus, had become a monster.

I thought that Bucky going Hairball had been a tipping point for Miles Brenta. The loss of Bucky was killing him and he simply had no one to talk to.

He didn't exactly come weeping into my arms. He scarcely changed expression. For an instant I saw confusion in his eyes. Then he turned away from me and lifted his head and squinted at the high sun, a hand going wearily to his forehead beneath the big brim of the old-fashioned cowboy hat.

"Looks close enough to noon," he said. "Offer you a drink? I sure as shit could use one."

Brenta didn't conduct a tour, but he pointed out to me that his house consisted of half a dozen interconnected villas: living space for Brenta, guests, and, I assumed, his wife. Although he didn't mention Carlotta. There were two villas for play and exercise and otherwise toning up the body and another for business when he was in residence. Pools, fountains, and green space were interspersed among the villas.

His duplex was whitewashed limestone with tall tinted lancet windows recessed in the thick walls. There was a moatlike pool on three sides of the villa: it looked big enough for kayaking. Brenta liked to do his thinking and drinking on a patio that he said was paved with blocks of fourteenth-century Jerusalem limestone, sheltered by feathery palms in square white planters and furnished with club chairs in nubby white fabric. The patio was two steps up from the surface of the pool, which was tiled with frescoes taken from an old Roman bath.

"I met your mother on a couple of occasions," he said, pouring the Scotch I had requested himself. He'd used a brass bootjack to remove his custom-made black cowboy boots. His own drink was chilled vodka with two drops of lemon peel oil. "She sent me a signed copy of one of her books. The one about how Lycans evolve as a social group in hostile cultures."

I nodded. "And how their restrictive social position evolves into a psychological imperative for revenge."

He dropped into one of his chairs and put his feet up on an

ottoman, ran a hand through thick, graying razor-cut hair. He looked at me the way men in his position and status group often looked at me, as if trying to decide how best I could serve some purpose beneficial to them. They can't help themselves. Just the old alpha-dog reflex.

Finally he lifted his glass in my direction in a halfhearted wordless toast and slugged some of the vodka down. I swallowed an ounce of the Glenlivet and maintained a benign expression.

"Okay," he said. "I think we can talk. I wasn't sure before. But anything I say, Rawson, is off the record. If I don't like the direction you're going—"

"Sure, I get it," I said. "Very informal. I'm not taping anything. This is man-to-man. There's a mystery to be fathomed. Could the key to our mystery be the late Bucky Spartacus?"

It sounded callous to me as soon as I spoke; he didn't like it either.

Brenta had begun his drinking with an eight-ounce tumbler nearly full of vodka; he took a second pull and the glass was almost empty when he set it down on the top edge of his big silver belt buckle. He licked his lower lip, then his mouth hardened savagely.

"I didn't *know* about Bucky!" he said. "God's truth. It had to have been recent. One of those curb roaches they all whore around with at the beach. Get a little careless, you're in hell for life."

"Or it could've been—"

He cut me off with a slash of the hand that wasn't holding the tumbler.

"No. Not Chickie. We both knew what she was. Knowing's one thing, resisting it is another, particularly during the Aura." He drained his glass, looked through it at me, as if he needed to put me at greater distance from his anger and grief. "Couldn't keep my hands off her, even though I knew what she was up to.

Bucky knew about us. He couldn't quit her either. I feel like—like I've taken a bad fall, but the falling isn't over yet. I just keep heading down. Once I'm all the way down, I won't be able to get back up. Not this time. Carlotta—I was years younger then. I could handle the shock, deal with her—her condition."

He looked at a corner of the patio where there was a fireplace framed in beautifully sculpted white marble. Above it, a full-length portrait of his wife, painted years before the werewolf attack.

"At least Bucky—he went fast," Brenta said. He turned his face back to me, licked his lower lip again. It appeared to be soring up in one corner, as if a fever blister were erupting there. "So we're talking. But all I hear is my own voice. I guess that's what you're good at. Waiting the other guy out. So I'll just be a clam until you tell me something I ought to know."

"I think someone came up with a way to make werewolves hair-up out-of-phase."

He moved in his club chair like a man winding himself tight to take a punch. He was still wearing that old single-action Colt.

I didn't elaborate on my suspicion. Brenta absorbed my silence until it made him hostile. He rose abruptly from the club chair, went to the granite-topped bar, took the vodka from the concealed refrigerator, and milked the bottle into his glass. This time he added a couple of ice cylinders, dropped in the curlicue of lemon peel. He sprawled in his chair again, not taking his eyes off me. He pressed the cold glass against his swelling underlip.

"The fuck," he said. "Where are you getting that from?"

"Here and there. Little pieces I've picked up. ILC INTEL/INT is one source, not the local clowns. Before I get into who and why, there's a couple of gaps I'd like to fill in, beginning with Artie Excalibur. The Chickie-ball killed him—"

"So you said," Brenta growled, with another slash of his free hand. "Allegation, or fact?"

"I was there when his head went flying. It was Chickie, all right."

He was trying to coil again, like a snake someone had a grip on just behind the head. His face suddenly looked old and bloodless. Even though an artery in his neck was working hard. For no good reason I wondered about the condition of his heart.

"You killed her?" he said coldly.

"No. But she's dead somewhere. They didn't have further use for Chickie, and she was carrying something in her body they didn't want found."

"They?"

"We'll come to it. So Artie was murdered. I don't know why. How well did you know him?"

Brenta shrugged dismissively. "An Off-Blood?"

"So you never did business with him."

"No." He drank more of his vodka. The artery in his neck stopped its violent pulsing. Something occurred to him. "There was this little deal. A year, maybe a year and a half ago. I wasn't directly involved in the negotiation. Francesca brought it to me. She felt it was a great opportunity. A good fit with NANOMIM. I trusted—I've always trusted her judgment. Without Francesca I—" He glanced again at the portrait of the youthful Carlotta, as if he'd felt the subtle impact of the eyes in the portrait on his soul. "Anyway, I said sure; go for it."

"Go for what?" I said patiently, and sipped my Scotch.

"Artie had this little company near Antelope Valley, a start-up he'd been pouring cash into. Enough cash so that he found himself strapped. Cesca negotiated a forty-nine percent interest. Five seats on the board."

"What was the name?"

Brenta looked momentarily unsure. "I'm into so much stuff—XOTECH. Yeah, that was it. Microtechnology R and D. There were some good brains involved. Good growth prospects.

Cesca will keep a close eye on XOTECH, but I probably won't see much of a return for two or three years."

"Fran's done a lot for you. Another good brain. CEO of a major corporation."

"Sound businesswoman," he agreed.

"And you take good care of her—financially, I mean."

"Francesca doesn't have any complaints. Where are you going with—"

"But I imagine it was hard on your long-term relationship, I'm talking about the personal arrangement, after you started fucking Chickie. That was kind of in the air when we all met last night, Fran trying to keep the deep sulks from showing when Chickie's name was mentioned. Or is it something more complex, because Francesca has always been in love with you?"

Brenta sat up straight and for a second I thought he was going to throw his glass at me. I could have dodged it, but I was aware of the six-gun again. I hoped he'd forgotten about it.

"That's it. Now get the hell out. We're through talking, Rawson!"

"And I've got a hell of a nerve, it's none of my business and so forth. I thought this was going to be man-to-man, Brenta." I showed him some locker-room lip, a knowing leer. "Do you think it's a secret that Francesca took over the wifely chores from her first cousin when Carlotta was mauled by that werewolf?" I gestured to the portrait. "Almost uncanny how they once resembled each other. Nothing ugly about what happened between you and Fran. It was human nature. A man's got to be a man. Then Chickie came along. That's when it got ugly. We both know what a woman with Francesca's pride and temperament can do when she feels betrayed. And brother, if she hasn't done it already she's getting close."

Brenta lunged from his chair but not as if he were coming for me. He wasn't even looking my way. His eyes were as blank as a blind man's. He walked slowly to the edge of the patio and stared into the turquoise water of the gently flowing pool, one hand flexing near the butt of the Colt on his thigh. I'd left my Glock in the helicopter because I hadn't thought his security people would let me keep it. I felt reasonably confident that it wasn't my day to get shot. I'd given Brenta something new to think about, which might already have been subconciously worrying him.

I finished my Scotch, watching him. After about a minute of staring into the pool he said in a low harsh voice, "She has a temper. And we've had our moments. But Francesca's a realist. She wouldn't hurt me."

"I didn't mean that Fran was working herself up to sticking a knife between your ribs. She carries one, but it's a cheap kind of revenge and then where is she? Like you say, Francesca's too smart to let her hot blood ruin her main chance. Revenge is a dish best eaten cold. I remember that's what my horoscope said yesterday." Now that I'd finished bullying him, at least temporarily, I adopted a more earnest tone. "Mr. Brenta, I'd like for you to look at something."

He touched a finger to the herpes sore on his lip.

"Always get these," he said. "Since I was a kid. Nerves." He turned and came back to me, on edge, newly belligerent. "What is it, Rawson? I'm getting tired of—"

I let dangle the LUMO-like object in a sealed bag, the one a scared little man had been hiding in his flesh while he ran for what was left of his life. Brenta glanced at it, and at me as if I were wasting his time.

"A hundred million worth of research and development. What about it?"

"Until this thing can be reconstructed by our lab techs I have no actual proof, but it's almost certainly not a LUMO. I don't know yet if it evolved accidentally in the course of development and was meant to be discarded after a few trials, or if it was purposely and privately tinkered together by Nanomimetics' resident genius Dr. Chant. If that was the case, he lived to regret it."

I explained where and how the object was recovered.

"He'd been missing about six months," I said. "But he was in touch with Artie Excalibur during his fugitive sabbatical. Artie sold you that interest in XOTECH. Something Artie also had cause to regret."

"What are you getting at?"

"I'll try to keep it simple. One way or another Dr. Chant came up with a device that can be used to control werewolves, most likely through low-frequency electrical impulses. But what if control isn't all that reliable? Let's say a nearby microwave oven could cause a hair-up out-of-phase. How about a hot-licks solo from a rock-and-roll bass player? There are a lot of possibilities when you think about it. Dr. Chant must have thought long and hard about what he had. Then, as head of NANOMIM R and D, he dutifully reported the existence of his little wolfmaker to his boss. Because of the chaos enough of the devices wrongly implanted in Lycans could cause, a responsible CEO would have ordered the wolfmaker's destruction and seen to it that all relevant research data was erased from files. It's a reasonable assumption that Francesca did order the deletions, because WEIR closely monitors everything that has to do with Snitchers at your firm. But the data first could have been transferred to XOTECH, away from WEIR's eagle eye."

"Because?" His dark stare was half-lidded. The thumb on his gun hand was twitching again.

"Francesca Obregon had a real need for the wolfmaker. It must have seemed ideal for implementing the revenge she wanted."

"I already told you—"

"The Hispanic temperament. Proud, strong, loving, lusty people. But the hate lies deep in many of them. The desire to destroy what they can no longer have. Tear down a life to bare bones, then crush those bones under dancing heels. Olé!"—I snapped my fingers—"Motherfucker."

Brenta smiled. Maybe because of the herpes sore it was painful for him.

"Miles Brenta doesn't tear down so easily," he said. "Your story is fantastic. And it's crap. Francesca and I aren't lovers anymore. But we still have something together and it's solid, Rawson."

"As solid as the relationship she has going with Raoul Ortega?"

He snorted in contempt.

"*Cabrón.* She uses him, that's all. To get back at me? So what? Like I care she's fucking a Diamondbacker? I get along with Diamondbackers. They come in handy sometimes."

"For staging *mal de lune*s to entertain your wife?"

"Car likes seeing werewolves killed. Do you blame her? What's another goddamn werewolf anyway?"

"Maybe nothing, until you find yourself up to your nutmuffins in H-balls with no place to hide. And werewolves have made you the fortune Francesca's about to take away from you."

"Are you dreaming this shit? You're wearing out your welcome."

"So call a couple of beefers to show me the door."

Instead he looked again at the probable wolfmaker I was holding. He touched his lip again.

"Need some ice for this," he said vaguely. "Get you another Scotch while I'm at it?"

"Okay. Thanks."

We were back to being more or less cordial. He busied himself at the patio bar, twisting cylinders of clear ice into a towel, getting a clean glass for me from a row on a glass shelf. He was laying off the vodka this round. My wristpac was vibrating. I looked at it. The calling number was my home phone. Probably Beatrice.

"I'll play along with this for a minute," Brenta said, bringing my second Scotch to me. "I could tell you how Francesca's twenty ways different from what you think she is, but okay: how do you figure she comes after me?"

He stayed close, on his feet, looking down. Because he hadn't shaved the little white scars from previous outbreaks of herpes showed more clearly on his underlip.

"Like I said, she's already begun. But let's clear up some murders, all of which involve her and, I think, Raoul Ortega."

"Partners in crime? She'd have to be the brains of *that* outfit."

He was trying to act as if he found the whole thing entertaining. But there was no laughter in the depthless obsidian of his eyes. He was tense, holding the towel-wrapped ice to his lip, and there was hazard in his tension.

I said, "I wouldn't underestimate Ortega. I did that once and nearly got killed. All right. First there was Dr. Chant, who dropped out of sight and was on the run until the Roman carabinieri fished him out of the Tiber a few days ago. That took care of the wolfmaker's inventor, who might not have been able to cope with a bad conscience. Then Artie got slabbed, because Dr. Chant had spilled to him everything about his little invention. Artie would've investigated, and I'm sure he found out that Fran was having wolfmakers secretly manufactured at XOTECH. That won't be hard to verify. Now Chickie: she and Fran were not pals, but Fran could have persuaded her to give up an old-style Snitcher for what Chickie was led to believe was a superior prototype. Money probably had something to do with it. Chickie was up-and-coming but not yet cashing any big paychecks. Expensive gifts from you wouldn't be enough for Chickie; she was just that kind of girl. As for Bucky—"

"That I don't get. Thirty days between Observances, give or take a day. Last month he was a High Blood. This month—"

"However he'd become infected, and having unprotected sex with Lycans isn't the only way, he'd have been frantic to keep it quiet, keep it from you."

"I suppose," Brenta said reluctantly, and looked away. "Anything wrong with your Scotch?"

"No," I said, and drank some of the Glenlivet.

"So in this fantasy epic of yours, Bucky shares the news with Chickie."

"Probably."

"Bucky is desperate to stay off WEIR's roster of Lycans. Chickie sends him to Francesca."

"Fran has access to both unregistered Snitchers and plenty of TQs."

There was a deep notch of pain between his eyebrows.

"She knew what Bucky meant to me. So she set the kid up to be slabbed?"

"And the other half of the partnership, Ortega, stands to profit in a big way from the increased awareness of the First Church of Lycanthropy. Which he chartered with the assistance of the Reverend Kingworthy. Ortega's rake-off last night was probably high six figures. Anything to do with Lycans is under our jurisdiction. We'll audit the shit out of them. We might be able to put both of them away for three or four years. But tax evasion's not how I want it to go down for Raoul Ortega."

Brenta went for another walk around his patio, came to a stop below the portrait of Carlotta with her reflective smile as she posed holding a vivid handful of amapola blooms. He stared up at her with that look of lingering pain and said in a voice almost too low for me to hear, "If it hadn't happened—"

I had another sip of Scotch. I empathized with his regrets. And I knew he had begun to accept that Francesca could have betrayed him.

Because of the way sunlight came through a bowl-shaped structure of redwood rafters overhead, his face when he turned to me was blurred like the face of an actor standing at the fringe of a high-intensity bolt of stage lighting.

"So Francesca threw Bucky to the wolves, so to speak, to get back at me. Is that where your revenge story ends?"

"Far from it," I said, blinking, trying to see him more clearly. I looked at the Scotch in my glass.

"No, it's over." Brenta said. "Because there's nothing else she can do. I've lost Bucky. But if she tries to rip me another way, she'll bleed just as bad."

"Think so? How many wolfmakers does Fran have left? We don't know. One OOPs, or two: no really big deal. But a couple of thousand Lycans hairing up at the movies or because of static electricity at a laundromat—very big deal." I sounded a little croaky; my throat was parched. I thought to ask for water, but instead I drank the rest of my Scotch. The rim of the tumbler clicked against my front teeth. My hand holding the glass felt oddly unrelated to the rest of me. "It would be an earthquake-magnitude blow to confidence in ILC, WEIR, and particularly NANOMIM. The foundation of Miles Brenta's financial empire.

I wondered vaguely why I was speaking of him in the third person—as if in a moment of confusion Miles Brenta had slipped away and a complete stranger stood in his place.

"A few thousand wolfmakers," I said, "included with millions of LUMOs will result in a recall of all LUMOs—the defective little bastards. Of course they aren't defective, but we'll be a long while making sure of that. Meanwhile billions in government contracts go into the shredder, and basic patents on old-style Snitchers expire."

"And Francesca stands to lose a couple hundred million in incentive bonuses and stock options. She wants revenge that bad? Bullshit."

"Bullship?" I said. My tongue felt like the backside of a gila monster. My heartbeat accelerated the way it used to when I was twelve years old and standing with my toes curled over the edge of a high-diving platform. While I looked down at the surface of the diving pool that was broken by sparkling jets of water. My face felt cold at that high altitude and I was teetering, trying to maintain my toe grip on the rough surface of the platform. I looked up because I couldn't focus well on the pool surface any longer. The blue of the sky hurt my eyes. But I didn't want to let them close. I'd lose my balance. My raspy tongue searched for the words I needed to say to Miles Brenta. He had come accommodatingly close and was staring gravely down at me. *Just give me a few seconds, Coach*, I thought. *Don't make me get off the platform. I'm not scared. I can do this dive.*

"No bullship," I said again. "She's too . . . fucking clever." I saw each word big as skywriting in my brain as I spoke. Then wisping away into the high blue. My eyelids were like sacks of lead shot. I was desperate to keep his attention. I wanted him to like me. Believe in me. Not cut me from the team.

"Listen," I said. "Fran . . . would give up money to make a lot more. Fran. Ore-tegga. What I think . . . they've been buying up little factories. South of the border. Bet on it. You listening? Turn out cut-rate . . . or counterfeit Snitch. Flood market once LUMOs recalled. You get me?"

Brenta nodded thoughtfully. Each movement of his head caused my own head to loll. I was doped, I thought craftily. Sure. That's how it was. He'd put one over on me. But I couldn't bring myself to dislike him for having done it. We were all friends here. Man-to-man.

"Maybe that makes sense," Brenta said. He wasn't loud but there was a lot of reverb inside my skull. Old bells tolling.

The tumbler slipped from my nerveless fingers. It was empty. Why struggle to hold on any longer? I'd expended too much energy already keeping my leaded eyelids off my cheeks.

Brenta reached down, a blurry motion at the edge of my shrinking field of vision, and caught the tumbler before it could shatter on the stone floor. I made an effort to sit up straight. He put his other hand flat against my chest and gently pushed me back against the seat cushion. I felt as light and airy as an oblivious gliding bird in the shadow of a hawk.

"Take it easy, Rawson," Brenta said. "Time for a little shut-eye."

"What . . . put in the Scosh?" I managed to hold my head still. I was able to squint with one eye. Sort of a wink. Just letting Brenta know that I was on to him.

He held up a small dark bottle. I stared at it for a few seconds but couldn't make out the printing on the label. No skull and crossbones, though. My eyelids sank again. So what? Anyway it was getting cloudy on the patio. I thought he was probably right. A little nap might be a good thing. If sleep was all he had in mind for me.

"It's just something we keep around in handy places in case Car throws one of her wingdings," Brenta said. "Calms her right down. The stuff won't hurt you. You might have a mild headache when you wake up."

"Should be going," I said thickly. Cautious is as cautious does. Very cloudy now. A purple twilight.

He kept his hand on my chest. His face receded in the velvety gloaming, along with his voice. Now he sounded as if he were talking to me from a villa next door.

"Francesca," he said. "So maybe you're able to get a warrant based on this LUMO lookalike you brought to me, and you go through your official routine the way you're supposed to. But what of it? She's a sidewinder in the sack, and she'll slither out of anything you try to get on her legally. No, my way's better and faster. Frontier justice, Luke Bailiff-style."

I felt a faint ticking of distress within my cocoon of blissful surcease.

"Damn fool. Don't try—"

He shook his head. His face was a blur that stayed blurry once his head was still. Nothing was clear except for the remote, cold light in his eyes.

"If Francesca was only trying to screw me financially—" Brenta shrugged. "It's only money. And I say the hell with money. I can always make more. But she crossed the line, and Bucky's dead."

I was going under and taking his voice with me, a voice thick with grief and murderous passion.

"She pays, and pays hard, for Bucky. Now. Today. I've known Cesca for a long time. So maybe I'm partly responsible for what she's done. It hasn't exactly been news to me, Rawson. But from here on it's my play. Thanks for stopping by and chinking up some gaps for me."

He did like me. I think I grinned at him. I felt a slight movement of the facial muscles responsible for grins and giggles. I tried, once more, to get my eyelids up for another peep at his face. But his hand wasn't on my chest anymore and all I saw was a flash of blue and light playing on the jets of water of the diving pool.

I wasn't afraid of it anymore, or the height of the platform. I was ready. *Watch this, Coach. Here goes Rawson. You old sonofabitch.*

17

I'm not sure what woke me up. It might have been the smell, like potatoes rotting in a musty old cellar, laced with a strong sting of perfume. Or it could simply have been the hindbrain (which never sleeps) warning of something morbid and dangerous creeping my way in semidarkness. Something or someone breathing asthmatically, a harsh snotty sibilance.

I had no idea where I was. My eyelids felt welded shut. I remembered fragments of my conversation with Miles Brenta. I had shown him the little wolfmaker I'd brought to his shining white villas in the desert. Mistake. My heartbeat on waking was too big, too rapid. I'd had a drink with him. Then another which he'd doped and which had plowed me under. Not six feet under, fortunately. He had said something about my having a headache when I woke up. I had the headache, which wasn't too bad. The idea that I'd been jobbed by Brenta was harder to bear.

I wondered fuzzily what Sunny would make of all this. Rawson's big screwup. Probably when I told her about it she'd—

But Sunny was dead. No more conversations with Sunny. A sense of loss side-slipped through me like an electric eel.

Come on, Rawson.

You're lying on your back, that much is obvious even to a dull boy like yourself. There's a mild tingling in your fingertips.

The air you're breathing is cool even though it's disgustingly tainted. That nearby sickening odor strong as a storm front. Get a grip, get up, find out what the smell is and where you are. Before—

The scream was feral, guttural, chilling. Not like anything I could recall hearing before. It got me going, all right.

I rolled hard to my left and fell off the low bed I'd been lying on. Plush carpet made the fall easy on my elbows. I kept rolling and bumped hard into the figure that had been creeping up on me, just as she was taking another step.

She sprawled across the bed I'd vacated with another scream and I saw the flash of a blade in low rainbow-tinted light like sundown through a church window.

She was mostly naked. Her long legs were badly scarred. She had on white bikini pants and a white T-shirt with SOCAL IRVINE and the school's mascot, an anteater, on the front of it. As she tried to get herself upright on the bed I made it to one knee, took a couple of deep breaths, and rose to my feet. I wasn't wearing my boots. Otherwise I was dressed as I had come: gray slacks, short-sleeved striped shirt unbuttoned at the throat. My throat was too dry for me to get a word out.

Carlotta Brenta put her feet on the floor and leaned toward me from the edge of the bed. In addition to the loose tee and nearly transparent panties, draped around her neck she wore a small soggy yellow-stained towel that seemed like a parody of the loosely knotted cowboy bandana that her husband had sported earlier.

Carlotta growled at me, making preliminary stabbing motions with the narrow blade.

Her face was the wreckage that had been described to me by Ida Grace. Plastic surgery had succeeded only in giving it a stiff, purplish-pink appearance. One eye was still misplaced, staring off in the general direction of hell on earth. Beneath the T-shirt she was missing a breast. That made me very angry. They could have done something about that. What was her husband thinking? Were there no mirrors where she spent most of her time now? But her shoulder-length hair was still dark, thick, and well brushed.

Obviously she'd eluded someone who was supposed to be watching her, had wandered and sniffed me out. A stranger. Also obvious that they should have gone to the trouble to keep sharp objects locked away from Carlotta. But once I took a closer look I saw that it wasn't a knife she was holding. More like a letter opener she'd snatched off a desk.

"Wolf," she said, getting up slowly and without physical awkwardness, her stench moving more forcefully in my direction. Her parted lips on one side formed a permanent savage-looking sneer.

"Mrs. Brenta?" I said. "Carlotta? I'm not a werewolf. I'm a friend of Miles. I think I—I had a little too much to drink for lunch, and Miles was letting me sleep it off in here."

With quick glances I was taking in a well-appointed bedroom suite. The bedchamber and a sitting room were separated by an archway. There were chrome-framed glass-front fireplaces in both rooms to take the chill off cold desert nights. In the dusky light I saw oblongs of furniture, sculpture, big folk-art paintings on every wall. In the trey ceiling over the bed were six small spotlights assuming a rosy glow in response to the lower light level outside the narrow windows. The overhead lights deepened the brute contours of her surgically recomposed face.

She tilted her head and the light above us was captured by the dark brown agate of her good eye. The light danced there. She gave her abundant hair a shake and some of it settled over the grosser part of her face, the baffled wayward eye. The half face that was turned to me retained hints of beauty lost, beauty defiled. The feeling in my constricted heart was a forsaken cold sorrow.

"I'm sorry," I said, "if I disturbed you. I need to be going now. But—if there's—is there anything I can do for you?"

The letter opener dipped slowly toward a scar-waxed thigh. She tilted her head a little more, inquiringly. Saliva gleamed on her lower lip and dripped into the towel.

"Who are you?"

"My name is Rawson."

"*Su nombre es Rawson*."

"Yes."

"Well . . . don't rush off. Meester Rawson."

Her tongue appeared and swiped along her lower lip. She made a noise in her throat like a sink unclogging.

"You want to do something . . . *por mi*." Her speech was badly slurred.

"If I can."

"*Conmigo?*" she said slyly.

When I didn't reply to the insinuation she said, "Do you have a big one, Rawson?"

I shook my head slightly.

"Miles does. *Muy largo*. But my husband won't do it to me no more."

She began to wag her head, dismally coquettish. The head wags became increasingly violent, waves of dark hair lashing across her face. Spit flew from the mouth she couldn't fully close.

"I am not too old! I could have a *nene* who would love me and not find me ugly. *Feo*. *Feo!* I say to my husband, I will wear my veil. I say to him, *mire*, *esposo:* you no have to look at me while we are doing it. But no. No, no, no! Never he is coming to my bed!"

I didn't say anything. She stopped the head-wagging before she succeeded in snapping her neck and looked away from me and began to make a low, sad sound: part whine, part tuneless humming.

"I really have to go now, Mrs. Brenta."

Without a flicker of warning she lunged at me, the letter opener flashing in her hand.

I caught her wrist without difficulty and squared away, thinking I was prepared for her strength. I wasn't. The wild demented ones, many smaller than Carlotta, require three trained psych techs to control them without causing serious injury. I remembered Miles saying something about Car and her "wingdings." Understatement. Carlotta Brenta would've been a handful even in a straitjacket. I didn't happen to have one with me.

"Carlotta!"

A woman's voice came from beyond the archway behind us as I fought to keep the letter opener out of my eye and Carlotta's knees away from my groin.

I felt as if I'd gone twelve rounds with a heavyweight contender before lamps brightened the suite. Suddenly Carlotta and I had a lot of company: two guys in male-nurse whites and white leather athletic shoes, a small plainly dressed nun in the gray and blue smock of her order, wearing a crucifix the size of a tuning fork.

They deftly took Carlotta off my hands and relieved her of the letter opener. Carlotta by then had wrung herself out emotionally; forgotten why she'd wanted to kill me, assuming she ever knew. Attacking me had been a release of something pent-up, orgiastic, incredibly violent. Now she was in the eye of that hurricane. She didn't look at me again as they led her away with soft soothing words.

I was breathing hard and felt as lathered as Miles Brenta's costly black Arabian after its long morning gallop. But at least I was wide awake when I turned to the fourth person who had come into the suite and who now watched me with a calm expression, a sense of inner detachment from the reality of who we were now, what we once had been to each other.

"Hello, R," Elena Grace said.

I tried to smile at her, but I didn't have the juice. I could only make a weak gesture of surprise, a perplexed hello.

For the past couple of days, since I'd caught that virtual reality glimpse of her in motorcycle leathers and as companion to a man I wanted to kill, I had been suppressing the anxiety that if I ever did come face-to-face with Elena I would be looking at a less drastic version of Carlotta. No obvious scars but a psychic difference, beauty marred by anger and shame, her mysterious, muted quality in repose gone forever.

The color of her eyes had changed but the capacity for contemplative silences had not left them. She had a confectionary swirl of white just off the right ear in her short dark brown hair, hair that always had had a stubborn quality no matter how many attempts she made to tame it. But the ruffled cat-fur look was her style, and suited her because she had no pretensions to glamour. Today instead of the unisex biker gear she was wearing a shantung navy pants suit with big white buttons on the short-sleeved jacket. A little eyeliner and pale pink lipstick on the long-bow arch of her perfect mouth: that was Elena as I remembered her. But the crucifix was something new. And it was not the Lycans' wolfshead symbol of ersatz Christianity.

"I don't know how much longer I can keep getting you out of pickles," she said, with a sidelong look at the rumpled bed. Then she canceled the verbal thrust with a puckish smile. "Just kidding," she said. But a pulse in her throat betrayed tension and uncertainty.

"Where did you leave your hog and that scattergun?" I said.

"The Kawasaki? It belongs to Miles. I borrowed the sawed-off from Ramon. He manages the stables for Miles."

"Miles, Miles, Miles," I said. "What else belongs to him?"

She gave me a deliberate look. "In a manner of speaking, I do," she said.

"I thought it was Raoul Ortega you were so damn chummy with."

Elena winced and shook her head.

"We're not getting anywhere like this."

"Okay. Where *are* we going and how do we get there?"

I glanced at my wristpac. It was four-twenty. I'd had a long nap. I also did an L-scan. It was active, but nothing showed on the black screen except the notation *O -31.10.* I looked up at Elena; she stared back at me. Her eyes were permanently wolf, that disturbing Saxony-green color. She must have worn brown contacts around Carlotta.

"I guess there are things about me you'd like to know."

"Well, no shit, Elena," I said, coming down hard on the sarcasm.

She was uncomfortable, and it made her hostile.

"Could we do this somewhere else?"

"How about your personalized Brenta villa? Or do you bunk in with the man himself?"

That caused her to flare, although she was making an effort to keep our unexpected reunion at least partly agreeable.

"We don't have that sort of relationship. And I don't live here."

"Where are you living?"

"At the mission," she said. "Would you like something to drink? To settle you down?"

"Love one. Where is Miles, by the way? He has something of mine and I want it back."

Elena reached into the pocket of her jacket and showed me the baggie with Dr. Chant's wolfmaker inside. At least I assumed it was the same one.

"Do you mean this? He left it with a note where I'd find it."

"He's gone?"

"Yes. I don't know where." She was visibly anxious about that. "If anyone else knows, they aren't telling me. I was supposed to meet Miles at four. Next thing I know Carlotta is screaming bloody hallelujah and we find you in here trying to teach her new dance steps."

"That's rich," I said. "Miles doped me and the next thing I knew loopy Carlotta was sneaking up on me in the dark with her letter opener. Can't top that for entertaining a houseguest. If it wasn't for the fact that she smells like buzzard puke with a Chanel chaser she might've—"

"Miles doped you?" Elena said sharply.

"To keep me on ice while he has a sit-down with Francesca Obregon before he kills her. Or hires it done."

Elena's eyes closed briefly. "*Dios mio!*" she said, prayerfully clutching the plain gold crucifix on her breast.

"About that drink," I said. "Make it a double."

She opened her eyes, turned, and with a follow-me wave of the hand Elena walked out of the bedroom suite. She walked with a limp.

"Make it yourself," she said.

On a patio not much different from the one outside Miles Brenta's villa but with more colorful bamboo-framed furniture (and without a portrait of Carlotta over the fireplace) I had my drink. Because I hadn't eaten much of anything since the meal I'd prepared for Bea almost forty-eight hours ago and my stomach was making noises, Elena asked the kitchen staff to bring over a buffet of fresh fruit and cold cuts. I made a prime rib sandwich. Elena nibbled some melon and sipped boysenberry lemonade because she didn't drink the hard stuff anymore. For a couple of minutes while I ate we didn't say anything, just listened to the sulfur-crested cockatoos in a gilded cage and the pleasant purling of clear water over big smooth stones in the pool below the patio.

I'd settled down and no longer was in the mood to flay her with hurtful recriminations, however justified I felt they might be. Elena's tense expression had softened. She was still shy about looking at me. There was a hell of a lot I wanted, needed to know, but it would just have to work its way to the surface gradually, with no hardcase interrogation on my part. And although I was nervous about and very angry with Miles Brenta for making me look and feel like a damn fool, dealing with Miles would have to wait a while longer.

I was halfway through my sandwich when my wristpac gave me some vibes. I looked at it.

"Is that your office?" Elena asked.

"No. It's Bea. I'll get back to her."

"Bea for Beatrice? I'm really glad you have someone now, R."

"I have yet to adopt celibacy as a way of life," I said, sounding like a jackass. Then I shrugged ruefully, man enough to let her know I knew it.

Elena smiled gently.

"I'd like to meet her sometime. When the, ah, lava crusts over and cools down and we can walk on it."

"Thought you'd already met."

Elena ignored me. She got up and helped herself to a slice of melon from the buffet cart.

"How long have you been a nun?" I said.

"I'm not. Yet. I may take my vows in a few months. There's no urgency. After all I've been through, God wants me to be certain about my vocation. I have time; He has patience. He's always been there, always will be."

"And it was Brenta who set you on the—what do you want to call it?—the straight and narrow? Because when I saw you last you were pitiful. All rogue and hungering for hell."

She looked up at me thoughtfully.

"I could've helped you," I said. "Put you in one of the programs."

"But I wasn't ready for redemption! I hadn't reached the depths I'd convinced myself I deserved. You had already suffered enough. Your hair had turned white. When you wouldn't put a bullet in my head I simply ran away. Ran and ran and ran."

"To Brenta. Strange choice, considering."

"But it was God who sent Miles to me."

"He's never struck me as being particularly religious."

Elena limped to the patio's edge with her plate. There were other things wrong with her physically. One shoulder lower than the other. An enlarged elbow joint. She had a little trouble picking up a piece of melon from her plate.

"What happened to your leg?" I asked.

"Surgery. Hip and knee."

"Fall off a cliff?"

"Too many Observances. I stayed wide awake and rogue. Punishing myself."

"Nothing that happened to you was your fault."

"I was angry. Deeply angry. I turned it against myself. A common psychological dilemma, I'm told. But during my—phases—I didn't want to hurt another human being, or animals. There's no way to control the impulse, so each month I found a lonely place and locked myself in chains that not even my werewolf's strength could break. Of course I damaged my joints and cracked some bones hairing-up in bondage like that."

"Where did Brenta come across you?"

"He was surveying property he owns in the high desert, where he wants to build another of his magical kingdoms for the very rich. There I was, dehydrated, sunburned, dragging bloody chains. One look at me and he knew the score. He sent his associates away and put the muzzle of a pistol against my head. *For Carlotta*, he said. I didn't know who she was then. I screamed at him. I was furious. 'For me!' I said. '*I* want it!' He could see that in my eyes, I'm sure. I was mad from the pain of being myself. But he lowered the gun. Or the hand of God pushed it away from my head."

"Killing anything that's looking at you in total surrender is only for hard-core psychopaths," I said.

Elena nodded.

"I know that you couldn't bring yourself to do it," she said.

My appetite was gone. I pushed half of my sandwich away. I didn't want the last couple ounces of Scotch either. I drank water instead.

"So Brenta couldn't shoot you either. What did he do?"

"He called his associates back. They were probably surprised to find me still breathing. I was loaded into the back of one of their off-roaders and driven ninety miles south to the mission."

"Which one?"

"Sisters of Saint Pius in Arroyo del Cobre, not far from—"

"I know where it is. It's been there for three hundred years. Why the mission and not a private hospital?"

"Because of Carlotta's condition, Miles already had an ongoing relationship with Mother Mary Aquinas, a certified psychiatrist. The Sisters is a medical order, tiny, but with longer than a thousand-year history. The Mission of Arroyo del Cobre deals primarily with Lycan females, some of them not yet teenagers but all of them alone in the world, psychologically disabled. A few are pregnant. And there are some terminally ill girls in hospice."

"So what is Brenta's connection?"

"That was Sister Lloyd you saw with Carlotta. She's a physician. Diseases of the blood. Sister Lloyd and I help Miles with Carlotta. Who some days needs a shitload of looking-after."

"I noticed. So your services are in exchange for a sizable donation from Brenta."

My wristpac vibrated again. I didn't even look this time. I didn't take my eyes off Elena, who had limped back to the buffet cart. She put her plate down. She wasn't forty yet, but moved like sixty-plus. Her eyes were clear, though, her face serene. She had the luxury of a confident heart.

"Without Miles's contributions, and the funds he's persuaded others to give, the order couldn't survive."

"And he allows a rogue werewolf in his home? Around his wife?"

"I'm Lycan now. I have been for almost four years."

"There's no record of you at WEIR. Believe me, I've checked often."

"Miles arranged for me to have a nonreg Snitcher. After all, his company makes them."

"Both of you are breaking the law."

"Did you like me better the way I was?" she said with a smile that had an edge to it.

I had no answer. I wasn't going to arrest her, so I changed the subject.

"I don't understand why Brenta didn't turn you over to Ida," I said.

"Because I told him nothing about myself except my nickname."

"Lenie."

"Yes."

"And he still doesn't know who you are?"

"He knows. I had to let him know eventually. I wanted to, in fact."

"You're the werewolf who came to dinner. And stayed. There has to be more to your relationship than you've been willing to tell me. First of all, the secrecy. Your e-mail message two nights ago. 'Get Bucky off the stage,' you said. 'I can't do it, I'll be exposed.' Exposed to what?"

"Not what, R. Who. Raoul Ortega. With whom I am also, how did you put it? Chummy."

There was a silver ice bucket on the buffet cart. It was big enough. I snatched it up, stuck my reeling head into the bucket, and held it there up to my ears in ice until my brain and my temper cooled down. Then I put the bucket back, brushed ice chips off my shoulders as I turned to stare at Elena. Ice water trickled down my face and neck.

"Poor old R," she said soothingly. "I'm confusing you."

"Just explain. Quickly. We're burning daylight and I've got trouble to deal with. I know you're a part of it, but I just hope like hell you're going to let me off easy."

"Okay. About Raoul. Three of us from the mission had been shopping at the supermarket in Del Lindo. We were loading a week's worth of groceries for the mission into the back of our Volvo wagon with two hundred thousand miles on it when Raoul and some of his fellow Diamondbackers came cruising through the lot. About six of them on their fabulous Harleys, right? Enough glitter to put your eyes out on a sunny day.

"They weren't all that interested in three nuns, or two nuns and one novitiate. I don't know how he happened to recognize me. Probably he wasn't all that sure at first, because they parked their bikes and went into the sporting goods store next to Ralph's. All but Raoul. He stayed in the saddle blipping his engine and staring at us. Then, when we were about ready to leave, he rode over slowly and stopped two feet from me. Sort of making it difficult for me to get into the wagon with the others."

"You knew who he was," I said.

"Some faces just get burned into your memory," Elena said. "Don't they."

"Raoul and I looked at each other and I didn't so much as blink and finally he said, 'I know you from somewhere.' "

"That was witty. And you said—"

" 'You should. I was engaged to a man named Rawson.' "

"Jesus, Elena!" But I felt a perverse pride in her.

"Ol' Raoul rubbed a hand across his beard and he was like, 'Oh yeah. Rawson. He doing okay?' I said, 'I haven't seen him for a long time.' He grinned and said, 'So you don't know if he still want to kill me?' I said, 'Oh no. I'm very sure he still wants to kill you.' Well. You can imagine how Sister Rosetta and Sister Thomasina reacted to *that*. It was hot in the Volvo, the air conditioner was broken again, and they just wanted to get away from there fast. But Raoul and I continued to stare at each other. Finally he said, 'And you into Jesus now?' I said I was into Jesus now. He said, 'How do you feel about me, Raoul? For what went down? You want to kill me, Sister?' I said no, I thank God for giving me this opportunity to forgive you."

"Forgive him? He must've eaten that up."

"Let's say it surprised him. Confused him, I think. And confusion quickly made him angry. He drove away without another word to me. But he didn't go far. I was still watching him when he turned around. Came roaring back and stopped with the front wheel of his Harley a foot away from me. I didn't flinch. He said, 'They teach you that, at the mission? *El perdón?*' 'No,' I said, 'I learned from Jesus how to forgive. My heart is cleansed and I have a new life now. What have you got?' "

"Taunting him wasn't a good idea."

"I don't taunt. It was an honest question. I think, despite what Ortega was and is, his godless ways, he recognized that I was sincerely interested in what he might have to say. His boys had come out of the sporting-goods store. And here *he* was, talking to a nun—as far as they knew. Ortega looked at them, then said to me, 'You got time to take a ride with me, Sister?' I said I hadn't, but I was willing to make time."

"So you went for a jaunt on his motorcycle along with a posse of Diamondbackers?"

"After I reassured the other sisters that I would be perfectly okay. I'd never been on a bike that size, with so much power. I really enjoyed it."

"Did you know what they could have done to you, on a whim?"

"Sure."

"You weren't afraid?"

"No. Because just a few miles down the road to Arroyo del Cobre something amazing happened. Let me call it what it was: a miracle straight from Heaven."

She smiled, thinking about it. I sneaked another glance at my wristpac. I wanted to be with her, to hear everything she had to say, but a foreknowledge of big trouble ahead had me jumpy.

"Elena?"

"Oh, I'm sorry—"

"About that miracle."

"Well, we must've been clipping along at close to a hundred miles an hour on a straight stretch of road with not much traffic. I know that we came up very fast on a truck hauling a double trailerload of scrap metal: old machinery, irrigation pipe, that sort of thing. Someone coming the other way must've had a blowout and veered into the path of the truck. The driver hit his brakes and then it was just a mess all over that two-lane highway, trailers flipping and the air filled with rusty flying stuff and nowhere to go."

"I get the picture," I said.

"There was no time to think about being killed. I was crouched down behind Ortega, wearing a helmet, of course, but if he had gone off the side of the road like the other bikers with us did, we probably wouldn't have survived. One of them didn't." Elena crossed herself. "Instead Ortega rode through the accident and tumbling chunks of metal and we came out on the other side without being struck. There wasn't a scratch on his bike. Do you understand? We were literally inside a hailstorm of flying metal for a few seconds and *nothing touched us*."

She looked at me triumphantly.

"God is my witness."

"As for Raoul Ortega," I said. "Is he a changed man?"

"I wish. But godless men—and women too—are often deeply superstitious. He does believe that he's alive today because I was with him on his motorcycle. It's no use trying to tell him otherwise. He doesn't want to hear it. Ortega calls me his '*amuleto*' "

"Lucky charm," I said. "Cute."

She made a wry face at me. "We go riding together three or four times a month now. That has its uses, R."

"I'm surprised Mother Mary Aquinas is letting you hang with a known scumbag."

"We aren't cloistered. And as I've said, I haven't taken my vows. Reverend Mother doesn't disapprove of the relationship because—well, I kind of brokered a deal between the Diamondbackers and the order."

"What was that about?"

"Before I joined the order, there had been a lot of incidents at the mission. Diamondbackers harassing the sisters and terrorizing the Lycan girls. They're notorious Lycan haters, as you well know."

"Yeah."

"Ortega makes the rules. They leave us alone now."

"He also knows you're a Lycan," I said.

"We've talked that out. He accepts me."

"Big of him. He was the one who—"

"Don't, R," she said, with a weary shake of her head. "It's behind me."

"But still front and center with me," I said. "Elena, how did you find out about Bucky Spartacus?"

"I overheard Raoul on his bike phone talking to someone."

"Do you recall his exact words?"

"I can come close. He was like, 'Bucky, don't anybody know yet, but he's a fuckin' werewolf.' I suppose he was asked how he knew this. He said, 'I can always tell. Be watching what happens at the fund-raiser, Bucky, he gonna have a million new fans when he hairs-up." She looked hopelessly at me. "I didn't understand how that could happen, out-of-phase. But I—I felt like I had to do something."

"Where's Mal, Elena? She's running out of time."

Elena stepped back awkwardly as if I had raised a fist to her face.

"But I don't know! I couldn't find out where she is. I thought if Mom saw Carlotta, maybe—it didn't do any good. Car's been in and out lately, you know the state she was in today."

"There's a way. Get Miles Brenta to call off the *mal de lune*."

"That's why I asked him to meet me this afternoon! What happened? What did you tell him about Francesca?"

"That she's dangerous. Just try to think of some way to get hold of Brenta. A cell number only a few others may have. Anything."

"But what if I don't speak to him in time?"

"Elena, what have you waited for?" I said, in a tone of voice that made her flinch.

"I thought that you—"

"I've got a couple of my top teams working on it. So far, nothing. Okay, Brenta's unavailable but there's another possibility. Your weird friendship with Ortega. Talk to him. He just might be willing to pull Mal out of the shoot."

Suddenly Elena was in tears, shaking her head.

"I don't know where Ortega is either! He comes around when he feels like it. But if I do say anything to him about a *mal de lune* and let him know about Mallory—you know how his mind works. He'll think if I know about the shoots he arranges, then maybe I know things about his other businesses I shouldn't know."

I hated the way that sounded. "Do you? Come on, Elena! Talk to me."

"There's something—I've been trying to find out for Miles," she said very quietly. She wiped her eyes with a paper napkin from the buffet cart. She was still breathing hard after her outburst. But she couldn't make herself look at me. "It was because of a remark Ortega made. 'If you have the gold, you make the rules,' he said. 'But if you control the werewolf, then you own the world.' I didn't know what he meant. But I told Miles. He was very upset."

"So Brenta has been using you to spy on Ortega? Is he out of his mind? Ortega and his kind feed like piranhas on suspicion. *Amuleto* or not, one little slip on your part and he'll have your throat cut, then shrink your pretty head and wear it on his key chain."

"*Don't.* I know I was wrong to—"

My wristpac was vibrating again. I'd been out of touch from everyone for more than five hours. Not a good day for that. I 3-D'd my e-mail for easier reading. It was from Bea, originating from her own wristpac.

PLEEZE!! NEED HELP!!

"Is it about Mal?" Elena said.

I glanced at her. "No. But I have thirty hours left and I *will* find her." I double-tapped the H box on the black screen of my pac and brought up Bea's hologram, showed it to Elena. "This is somebody else who I want to keep warm and breathing.

"Yes, I know," she said with a slight, sad inflection.

"Elena, I have to go. Stay here at Villa Brenta. If he comes back or calls, let me know immediately.

She nodded.

"Good seeing you. Let's do it again sometime."

"Go fuck yourself," Elena said spiritedly. Her eyes were dry and lively again. She was smiling.

I had given her reason to hope. I wished there was some left over for me.

18

One of Miles Brenta's security force, a middle-aged woman with wide shoulders and a personality like blunt trauma carted me up to my helicopter while I called Bea.

"R!" she answered. There was too much daylight and I couldn't receive her hologram. "Thank God! Where have you been all afternoon?"

I thought "unconscious" called for too much explanation. I heard music at her end, a Latin band with *mucho gusto*. If she was at a party, why the urgency? I didn't rumba.

"Doing my job," I said gruffly. "Mal Scarlett is still missing."

"That's why I have to talk to you! Ida is meeting someone here, I'm sure of that, and she's going to give him money, so I think it must have something to do with Mal. She won't tell me anything, but Ida has a big tote with her, and R, it is *bulging* with cash! I had a peek after she came out of the bank with Duke and got into the backseat of the car with me. The money is all in gold certs from the Bank of Beverly Hills. Large denominations. It just isn't safe for her to be carrying so much money around with her even though Duke is probably wearing a gun—" Duke Sanborn was Ida's longtime houseman and chauffeur.

"Bea, hold it right there!" I yelled.

I waited a few seconds until she caught her breath.

"Now back up. What are you doing with Ida Grace?"

"Oh. Well, after I woke up I was starving. So I fixed a huge lunch but had second thoughts about eating it all by myself. So then I thought, why not invite Ida to share it with me? That's what I did. I walked next door and—"

"Bea, get this jalopy into gear. Where—"

"No, wait, *wait*, this is important! She accepted my invitation but while we were eating—Ida seemed nervous and didn't have much of an appetite—she had two calls which she took where I wasn't supposed to hear her. But I have ears like a bat. I heard her say, 'That is all I can come up with on short notice.' She must have struck a deal, because then she said, 'No, not there. Do you think I'm a fool?' Pause. 'Not there either.' Long pause. Finally she said, 'That is agreeable. Five-thirty this afternoon at the Beverly Hills Hotel."

"That's where you are now?"

"Uh-huh. Poolside. There's a really groovy fashion show. Priority hunk. They have one every month. By invitation only. It's a big social thing in the Privilege."

"I know. Bea, where is Ida right now? Nowhere close, apparently."

"Ida had to go to the ladies' room. Again."

"She took the money with her?"

"No, I have it. Her tote, I mean. I'm not supposed to know what's inside. There's a little gold padlock, even if I *was* feeling snoopy. What I'm doing is sweating, with this tote between my feet. My pulses are going like those castanets. Could this be for real? Someone knows where Mal is and is trying to sell her back to Ida?"

"Ida would have to have good reasons for going along with it. Evidence that she's not being jobbed. A show-and-tell featuring Mal. Or a partial satellite map. The money buys the map coordinates." I checked the time as we came to a stop beside the helo. "It's twelve minutes to five. I can be there before five-thirty.

Whoever has approached Ida won't advertise himself in a crowd. But he's watching."

"You *had* to say that."

"If anybody comes too close to your table, throw a drink in his face. By the way, where's Duke?"

"He's at the bar. Probably fifty feet away. Just watching." She hesitated, lowering her voice. "Can we trust him?"

"I've known Duke all of my life. He's honest and loyal. He's also getting close to seventy." I was pouring sweat myself. As Johnny Padre might have put it, I was loving this like sex with a small amphibian.

"I have my knife with me," Bea said stoutheartedly.

Christ.

"You won't need it. It's strictly a cash transaction. There won't be any rough stuff. *Tranquila*, Bea," I pleaded.

The mechanic who had been keeping watch on the ILC helicopter got out of his van. He had been pumping the interior full of cool with a mobile auxilliary power unit, which he disconnected as I climbed aboard.

"Couldn't find a thing wrong up top, sir. You're preflighted and good to go."

The monthly high tea and fashion show at the sine qua non watering hole known as the Beverly Hills Hotel was, as Bea had reminded me, always a hot ticket. Booth Havergal made a point of attending with his wife Cerise. While I was flying back from the desert I received by e-mail a guest list from the hotel's social director. There were about two hundred names on it: High Bloods from the entertainment and fashion industries, a mélange of politicians, financiers, sportsmen, and a good many people who spent their lives doing nothing more strenuous than dressing for dinner.

Miles Brenta and Francesca Obregon were on today's list. I

knew that NANOMIM retained a very luxe bungalow at the hotel for certain business meetings and *intime* arrangements.

I was happy to see their names on the list. Maybe the day would turn out to be a winner after all.

Before I had reached cruising altitude I sent Lew Rolling and Ben Waxman to the hotel to clear a helo pad for me in air-taxi parking.

I touched down behind a windscreen of old cedars on the far side of the century-old hotel's gardens at five-eighteen. Lew and a security guard met me for the short trip by electric cart to the pool area.

I called Bea.

"I'm here," I said. "Do a good job of pretending you don't know me. Is Ida still at your table? Just say yes or no."

"Yes."

"Be cool," I said, and cut her off.

The theme of today's show was pre–World War II, with styles mimicking those of the period. The shake-and-bake Latin band was big and loud: when I walked through a gate at the northwest corner of the colonnaded cabana terrace the models were doing the boneyard shuffle on the runway to the tune of "She's a Latin from Manhattan." There was applause. The guests were basking in the first flush of a Southland sundown, the unclouded sky turning a deeper shade of blue. The fronds of tall palms around the pool area had begun to stir in a mild breeze. Everyone was keeping cool in drifting clouds of vapor from refrigeration units. The models wore pencil suits with very wide shoulders and skirts below the knee. They wore pill-box hats with peek-a-boo netting. Or they wore dresses with splashy flower prints and floppy hats, the brims as wide as beach umbrellas.

Everyone seemed to be having a good time pretending it was ninety years ago. When, except for a lingering economic malaise and a Teutonic paranoid-schiz with a bad haircut who was in

Middle European real estate the way Dillinger had been in banking, things looked pretty nifty to the hoi polloi.

In about fifteen hours (I didn't bother to touch the appropriate key on my wristpac that would give the exact time of peak full moon) the world these people actually lived in would begin fearfully to lock down. Some of the fashion-show guests might then be back here to drink their way through yet another Observance, in a werewolf-free zone, safety guaranteed by the wall around the Privilege and in-house protection on the order of TRADs and AUGIEs. If those babies ever did have to be put to use it would be hell on the guests as well. But then nothing compared to a werewolf attack, and more often than was commonly known they did show up, Privilege be damned. It was just a highly catchable disease, and social rank had nothing to do with it.

I made my way around the terrace perimeter behind pool lounge chairs and geraniums in massive pots. Waiters in mess jackets and hickory-striped pants hustled to and from the long bar with deftly balanced trays of drinks and mounds of minced-olive finger sandwiches. I checked the crowd for either Brenta or Obregon. Didn't see them. But the gloves-wearing woman and her associate or consort Paulo were at Booth Havergal's table. That was interesting.

Beatrice was throwing glances over her shoulder at me until I gave her the cut sign. Ida sat opposite her at their shaded table, her face turned toward the runway; I couldn't read her expression. The tote full of gold certificates wasn't visible either.

There were standees at the bar, most of them men, some in tennis whites. I edged in next to Duke Sanborn. He was wearing a medium gray suit with a black bow tie and a look of acute anxiety. He jumped when I touched the elbow that wasn't propped on the deeply lacquered, ebony surface of the bar.

"Mr. Rawson!"

"It's okay," I told him. "I'll take it from here."

There was a gleam of relief in his eyes before he said cautiously, "Well, I—I don't zackly know what you mean, sir."

"Yes you do. How long has it been since Ida attended one of these soirees? A year or two? She's here to pay off someone who could be conning her. Do you know what he looks like?"

Duke shook his head nervously.

"No, sir. Neither one of us knows. He never come to the house at all. Only sent video of Miss Mallory to prove she was alive."

"What else is he selling?"

"Well, he—he give to Miss Ida a location where she can find Mallory 'fore it's too late. But what he wrote was—"

"In code," I said. "Sure. Ida hands over the money, she gets the key to solving the code. Sounds jailhouse to me. How much does the perp want?"

"Fifty thousand," Duke said miserably. "At five-thirty, he said. Here at the hotel."

I checked the time. We had five and a half minutes. I looked at Ida again.

She was doing a lot of fidgeting in her chair. She glanced at the bar and was not happily surprised to see me next to Duke. She had the good sense to look away quickly. Bea leaned across the small table and spoke to her.

The girls of the runway, and a few well-bronzed guys, were showing off the latest in sportswear. The bandleader, a suave number with a hairline mustache and ravishing eyes he kept dancing toward the audience, kicked up the tempo a notch. A girl singer in a blouse with big ruffled sleeves and hips in overdrive launched into "Enjoy yourself—it's later than you theenk."

I wondered how the guy planned to collect his money.

Odds were he'd give Ida a call soon, have her walk into the hotel. The exchange, if there was going to be one, wouldn't happen in the lobby. Ida would never agree to meet him in a room upstairs. The way it would work best, he'd tell her to take an otherwise empty elevator, stop at the second or third floor, leave the tote and send the elevator to the service basement or VIP parking. Where he would be whistling and waiting near a convenient exit.

Once he was in the clear and if he was on the level, he would then call Ida and tell her where to pick up the code-break info, which he'd left for her in a will-call envelope at the front desk, probably hours ago when there was a different shift on.

But they were so seldom on the level.

I called Lew Rolling and told him what was going down.

"Grab yourself some hotel security and cover all sublevel entrances and exits. I'll take the lobby in case he's bold enough to stroll out through the front door."

"Who are we looking for, R?"

"No description. He'll probably have a gym bag with him, just large enough for stashing fifty G's worth of gold certs in a hurry."

Sure enough, half a minute later Ida had incoming.

I saw her stiffen. She cupped a hand around her whisper tit, nodded twice, then got up slowly from the table. She reached down for her tote, glanced at Bea with a weak smile and another excuse for taking a break. Then she looked up at us.

I put a hand on Duke's shoulder, also a signal to Ida.

"Stay put," I said to Duke. "It's routine now. I'll follow Ida and make sure she'll be okay."

"Yes, sir. Please don't let nothin' happen to her."

I had it figured beautifully, I thought.

But I was all wrong.

19

At just a few seconds past five-thirty either a computer malfunction (unlikely) or someone hacking into the hotel's deterrence system set off a couple of AUGIEs, which instantly spoiled what had been a good party.

An AUGIE, for Augmented Galvanomagnetic Intercept Effector, employs staggered electromagnetic fields with laterally vectored sonic pulses to mentally disorient and physically incapacitate anything in the vicinity that is warm-blooded and walks, flies, or crawls.

The overall effect was close to that of a Richter-10 earthquake. But only the air around us was moving, invisibly, with the staggering force of a tsunami; the aquamarine surface of the pool barely rippled and no roofs fell in. Everyone was holding their ears in pain. A dozen swans in their own pool, props for the fashion show, went squawking flapping nuts. Waiters reeled with their trays and crashed into tables. Anyone making it to his feet sprawled helplessly.

Most people have never been exposed to the devastating effects of an AUGIE—or TRADs or PHASRs. As part of my Wolfer training I had endured all three. But ILC also has countermeasures, unknown and unavailable to the public, that gives us the edge in dealing with temporarily brain-locked werewolves.

Duke Sanborn lurched against me. One hand clutched his chest in pain. I sat him down with his knees raised and his back to the bar. The tinted lenses in my Geekers already had darkened to full black and adjusted prismatically to neutralize the assault of the AUGIE pulses on my equilibrium. That left the skull-splitting low tones to deal with. I popped a spare whisper tit from a compartment on a sidebar of my Geekers and put it in my left ear, then manually activated the noise-cancel function on my wristpac.

Suddenly I had complete silence and the rest of my faculties. I was a secure island in a universe of pandemonium.

Booth Havergal and his guests from ILC Rome had eyewear similar to mine. Booth's wife didn't, unfortunately, and she was throwing up in her lap—that was a stage-two reaction to an AUGIE blast.

I looked at Duke, who was gasping. I wondered if he had a pacemaker. Not good. AUGIEs were hard on pacemakers.

Within my cone of silence I couldn't contact anyone; that feature of our wristpacs was blocked.

I got Duke on his feet again, intending to carry him to the lobby and call for help once I was out of AUGIE range. I glanced at Ida Grace's table. She had placed the tote on the table in front of her just before the AUGIEs went off. Now she was down on hands and knees along with Bea, torment in both their faces. I didn't think about the money in the tote; Duke was my priority here.

Then I saw the kid.

He was heading casually for Ida's table, sidestepping reeling or prostrate fashion show guests. He wore noise-canceling headphones and, unmistakably, a pair of Geekers. If he wasn't with ILC, it was a third-class felony for him to have them. He couldn't have been more than twenty years old. His glam was the tie-dye duds and love beads of an era decades in the past. He was tall, with shoulder-length, dirty blond hair and a pimply nose. He knew just where he was going and what he was there for.

I had Duke as deadweight in my arms and I couldn't react as the kid reached out while walking past Ida's table and snatched the moneybag. He headed for the hotel lobby with a broad smile on his face.

I followed, dragging Duke along with me.

Fortunately the kid was in no hurry. He was aces up and two more in the flop. His lips were pursed as if he were whistling a happy tune, although he couldn't have heard himself.

I reached the lobby with Duke as the kid was going out the front door. I put Duke down in a nearby lounge chair, kicked over another chair and lifted his feet up to the seat. He had both hands on his chest, fingers digging in, and was breathing with difficulty.

The AUGIEs were shut off. I could tell by the reaction of those hotel guests who were down on the carpet but no longer holding their ears in pain.

I popped out the spare whisper tit as my Geeker lenses lightened up. I signaled for a Catastrophe Med Team from Beverly Hills Providian Hospital and took off after the kid, pulling my Glock from the shoulder leather.

He had crossed the drive opposite the entrance and walked past a small crowd of pedicab operators untangling themselves on the greensward. Now he was loping down to Sunset, the tote slung over his shoulder, in more of a hurry because he'd seen a westbound Pacific Electric tandem streetcar that he apparently wanted to catch.

There was a bright red TRAD box mounted on one of the stucco columns supporting the canopy over the driveway. I busted the glass with the butt of my Glock and passed my other hand over the heat-sensitive arming eye. On the sunny open downslope of the lawn TRADs popped up like mechanical mushrooms, one of them about ten feet directly in front of the getaway kid. I keyed all six of the TRADs to active, folded my arms, leaned against the column and watched.

The kid was violently repulsed by the force field generated by the TRAD closest to him. It knocked him out of his Haight-Ashbury sandals and back a good fifteen feet. Where he encountered another field that bounced him into the air. He came down like someone being blanket-tossed, but he didn't touch the ground again. A third TRAD sent him windmilling toward the street and the three-foot-high chain-link fence isolating Pacific Electric's westbound track from those lanes on Sunset devoted to pedicabs, commercial, and emergency vehicle traffic.

He cleared that fence with room to spare and sprawled across the track. The juice was underground and he wasn't in danger of being electrocuted. But he'd come down hard, and the wind was knocked out of him. He staggered up and fled blindly into the path of the oncoming automated streetcar, which was slowing but still traveling about thirty miles an hour. He was knocked down and under the wheels as the sensors aboard applied the brakes.

I got there as fast as I could, feeling sick about the accident I'd caused. I heard sirens. I picked up Ida's tote that the kid had dropped on his way to a brutal end. I hopped the fence and had a look. Only about half of him was under the streetcar. The rest was lying faceup. He'd lost the Geekers in the impact with the front of the streetcar. I kneeled beside him.

"Sorry, kid." There wasn't much else to say.

His eyes were filming over. His arms shook. Blood bubbled from his mouth, and he died before I could ask him his name.

I didn't really need to know. He was just a delivery boy for whoever owned the Geekers.

They were lying a dozen feet away. Not in great shape. One of the complex and very expensive optical systems was shattered. Two Beverly Hills Police Department prowlies were speeding up Beverly from the Flats, followed by Fire and Rescue. I had the Geekers stowed away. Now this was just an accident scene within BHPD's jurisdiction.

By the time I had walked back uphill to the hotel the driveway was filling up with paramedic and EMT buses. I grabbed an EMT named Barbara as she stepped down from the back of her bus with her medical bag and marched her into the lobby where I'd left Duke Sanborn.

He was still conscious. "Chest pains?" the girl asked. Duke nodded. Barbara fed him baby aspirin, popped a nitro tablet under his tongue, put him on high-flow oxygen, and began attaching him to an EKG monitor. Efficiency was her game.

Duke was on a nonrebreather and couldn't talk to me. He rolled his eyes toward the tote I'd left on a chair.

"Ida's okay. So is her money." I interpreted the second question in his eyes. "Mal? That's what I'm going to find out next."

I left Duke in the hands of the EMT and caught up to Lew Rolling. He was wiping off his shirtfront with a handkerchief soaked in club soda.

"Bad day to leave your Geekers somewhere else," I admonished him as we went outside to the pool terrace. I handed over the pair the dead boy had been wearing and explained what had gone down. "Trace the serial number and find out who these were issued to."

"You think we have a bad apple?"

"Yeah."

There was a lot of milling around on the terrace, but only a few guests were trying to leave. Most were just catching their breath. There were a few cases of nerves, some loud and angry voices. The hotel manager was an old hand at dealing with the obscenely rich. He had the serving staff handing out brandies and ice wrapped in towels. Lawyers on the guest list probably were thinking about fat lawsuits and those doctors on hand were helping with the elderly who required more than a stiff shot to keep that other foot out of the grave. A few models were sitting on the edge of the runway, either looking sullen or nonchalantly touching up their makeup. The band was playing again. "Life Is Just a Bowl of Cherries." Catchy. Don't get serious. It's so mysterious.

Ida Grace looked up when I sat down opposite her. She eyed the tote gratefully.

"I wondered where that went."

"It's where it was supposed to go that interests me."

A waiter placed glasses of cognac on the table with a murmured apology. I swallowed mine in gulps, watching two swan wranglers climb precariously on the tiled roofs of cabanas trying to coax down a pair of the beady-eyed birds.

Beatrice and I looked at each other. She was holding hands with herself, probably because she still had the shakes. But she smiled.

"I wonder what's become of Duke?" Ida asked nervously, looking around.

I told them, and threw in a cheery prognosis. No harm in that.

"You didn't happen to see Francesca Obregon this afternoon?" I said to Bea.

"Yes! I mean, I only had a glimpse of her when she was dropped off at one of those big bungalows."

"Anyone with her?"

Bea shook her head.

"I didn't see anyone. Come to think about it, I don't believe she came to the show." She looked around at overturned tables and floating trash in the pool while the band played on. "Some people don't know how to have fun," Bea said. A different look came into her eyes. "Do you suppose she still has my knife?"

"Listen, Bea. I want you to take Ida home. I'll arrange transportation. Both of you stay at the *minka* tonight. I'll probably be delayed. Keep an eye on the loot until Ida can return it to the bank tomorrow. Meanwhile I'll have private security guards on the front gate all night."

Her eyes got a little bigger.

"What did you mean when you said where the money was *supposed to go*? There's still somebody who might come after it?"

"I don't think so. He'll probably be on the run, and in a different direction. Mexico is closest. I feel personally obligated to see that he doesn't make it."

Lew Rolling called.

"Got your boy. I wouldn't have believed it."

"Go."

"That pair of Geekers was issued to G. W. McClusky by ILC Scientific. Three years ago, when they first became field-approved."

"Stork McClusky."

"You know him?"

"Yeah. I need his exact location."

"Can't get it, R." He sounded exasperated. "He's Intel, and they're stonewalling. He's none of our business and besides they've never heard of him."

"The fuck," I said, and got up from the table. I looked at Bea, described her to Lew, and told him I had a job for him.

Then I headed straight for the table where Booth Havergal, his wife, and the Spooks from Rome were preparing to leave. Cerise Havergal looked ill, but she was able to smile. I knew Booth had been wondering what I was doing there.

"Sorry to be rude," I said to Booth, "but I have a lousy situation on my hands and the clock is ticking. I need some help from your guests."

Booth winced. Paulo was, as usual, lighting a cigarette for the gloves-wearing woman. She flicked her dark glance at me. Even by daylight her face seemed dense with secrets; the glowing tip of her cigarette failed to ignite a responsive spark in the deep stealth of her being. Apparently she had no identifiable emotions. Paulo smiled, as laid-back as ever.

"What is it, R?" Booth said, not too pleased with my usual lack of interest in the protocols of command. And whatever it was I'd brought to him, he didn't want Cerise listening.

"I'll wait in the lobby," she said. "Nice to see you again, R." She was one of those women endowed with a natural elegance but without artifice whom I wouldn't have minded being married to, if she hadn't been married to someone else.

I spoke to Booth as Cerise walked away.

"An Intel agent's gone sour," I said. "I need him and need him damn fast, because I think he knows where Mal Scarlett is. He tried to promote his knowledge into some ready cash from Ida Grace. It won't be too long before the Stork realizes the cash ain't coming and he's been burned." Now I included the Spooks from Rome. "Intel won't acknowledge McClusky or otherwise give me a thing I can use. But if you get hold of Cale DeMarco—"

The gloves-wearing woman exhaled a long streamer of smoke from her nose and looked at Booth, granting him permission to give me some inside dope.

"Cale DeMarco resigned as chief of ILC-Intel at ten this morning," Booth said.

"Oh," I said. But now I had a grasp of why McClusky was trying to get his hands on some fast money. The walls were caving in at Intel.

I looked at the gloves-wearing woman.

"So you're cleaning house. Just give me McClusky, that's all I ask."

The Latin band had finished with "Life Is Just a Bowl of Cherries" and were packing up their instruments. Paulo began whistling a cheerful tune, providing the next musical interlude. He eyed a model, who gave him the eye back. Male model.

"Paulo!" the gloves-wearing woman said a bit sharply. His

whistling stopped and his smile became a little sheepish. He looked at her.

She nodded in my direction.

"Find out whatever he needs to know, and go with him," she said.

As we were leaving the terrace I got in touch with Lew Rolling and told him to meet us out front in a department R-Two (Rapid Response Transport/Tactical Weapons Operations).

"All I need is McClusky's ILC call sign," I said to Paulo. "I think I know where he's going to be for the next fifteen minutes. After that he's long gone."

20

The largest transit station on the Sunset light rail line was UCLA North, where passengers transferred to the Westwood/Wilshire monorail loop. The tandem streetcar that the dead kid who had come for the money probably intended to catch was now held up indefinitely by the accident. It was scheduled to make three more stops before arriving at UCLA North, ETA 5:58 P.M.

That station was always busy: it served Bel Air as well as a campus of thirty-five thousand students. Most of the time even a Stork McClusky at six-six or so wouldn't attract a lot of attention as he waited for the arrival of his delivery boy.

"So what do you think?" Lew Rolling asked me. "If that's where McClusky is?"

"He could have planned it several ways. The simplest would be to get on the streetcar, locate the kid, sit or stand near him. Next stop the kid goes, leaves the bag, and Stork cuddles up to it. He rides to the Malibu terminus of the Sunset line, hires an air taxi there. Ten minutes later he's at LAX, and in Mexico City in time for a late dinner."

"No streetcar, no money," Paulo said. "Then what does he do?"

"What does INTEL/INT have on him?"

"Dipping too often into the black bag."

"Then he has money stashed somewhere else. Doesn't need the fifty grand that bad, so he dusts."

"Among his other bad habits," Paulo said, "was stiffing casinos."

"Okay. Then he might not be so well-off, and he's nervous. But the cash from Ida Grace would seem like such easy pickings. So he doesn't give up on it until he can't control his fidgety feet any longer."

We had passed the Beverly Glen light rail interchange. I told Lew to take a left at the top of the hill onto Hilgard, then approach the station by a circuitous route through the campus. McClusky, wherever he might be waiting, wouldn't miss an ILC heavy among the delivery trucks and an occasional restored old sport-ute on Sunset.

"Speaking of bad habits," I said to Paulo, "what about Cale DeMarco?"

"Racketeering. Charges to come later. He was advised to hire a good lawyer."

"I hope you can make that stick."

Paulo smiled confidently.

"My wife is very good at building airtight cases," he said.

"Arlequin? She's your— None of my business, of course, but I thought you—"

He nodded, still smiling.

"Sexual orientation is no matter to us. We are two old souls, and we've spent other lifetimes together. We have perfect accord spiritually."

"Oh, okay," I said. Old souls? I changed the subject. "The other night you told me that DeMarco had a helicopter tracking the armored truck from Angel Towne with Mal Scarlett in it. The pilot reported engine trouble and they had to break off surveillance. Do you think you can confirm that story? I have one I like better. McClusky was aboard; he faked the trouble call. The chopper continued to the next *mal de lune* site where Mallory was unloaded. Later Stork revisited the location, photographed Mal, who must have been hysterical from fear by then. But he didn't attempt to rescue her. Uh-uh, not McClusky. For which oversight I will take great pleasure in kneecapping him. He sent his proof of life to Ida Grace, with a polite request for a payoff. I don't think that he ever intended to give up the girl's whereabouts. For that I will be pleased to take out his other knee, which ought to be enough to get his tongue wagging."

Lew parked the R-Two on Circle Drive behind the Applied Math building and we got out. Lew unlocked the R-Two's arsenal. In addition to heavy stuff like the PHASR and compact zippos there was an array of small arms, each with silencer attachments and sonic stunners. I changed my shoulder holster to allow for the silencer I attached to my Glock.

From the roof of Applied Math Lew would have an unobstructed view of all levels of UCLA North station, which was about two hundred yards west. Paulo was to be his contact; they checked walkie reception on Paulo's whisper tit. Lew took binoculars and went upstairs. Paulo declined to choose a weapon.

"Guns make me uncomfortable," he said.

A monorail train passed overhead a few yards away, ghostly quiet but with that charge of momentum you felt in the gut; sunlight winked off its tinted windows. Summer session at the university was over and there were few students around as we walked toward the station.

"There really shouldn't be any need to shoot McClusky," Paulo said. "Rat that he is."

"Now don't go and spoil my day," I said.

Before we reached the southwest exit ramp of the station, Lew Rolling had positioned himself on the roof of UCLA's Applied Math building and had checked in on the walkie.

"I've got McClusky on the lower westbound platform," he said.

Paulo handed me the walkie.

"What's he doing?" I said to Lew.

"Moving around; checking the time; checking the arrivals board."

"Lew?"

"Yes?"

"Be careful where you aim those binoculars. The lenses aren't tinted. The sun is just at the right angle now to give you away if he looks in your direction."

"Roger that."

An eastbound triple-tandem streetcar was in the station; a crowd from the Malibu beaches was streaming toward us down the ramp. Most were college kids. Backpacks, beach blankets, folding chairs, a couple of surfboards.

"McClusky knows both of us on sight," Paulo said. "But he'll pick you out first. You're as obvious as an anthill on a putting green."

"Check," I said. I stepped in front of a gangly kid with zinc oxide on his prominent nose. He had his arm around a tink with a gamin haircut and merry close-set eyes. He was wearing one of those beach hats that are woven from palm fronds.

He looked startled, then anxious when I gave him a look at my ID folder.

"We're High Bloods."

I'd already scanned them. "I like your hat. Would you take a fifty for it?"

"Uh—what? You want to buy my hat?"

"Sure," the girl said, nudging him out of neutral with a sharp elbow. "Let's see the money."

I gave him the money and he gave me the hat.

"What's going down?" the girl said.

"Nothing to worry about," I said. "Just keep moving."

I put the hat on. It had a beachy tang and a faint beeriness. I was already wearing Reef's sunglasses. I looked at Paulo and said out of the side of my mouth, "Lothario in the sixth at Del Mar. Back up the truck on this one."

"You'll do," Paulo said. He checked the time. "Four minutes past the hour."

"We want ILC helo Interceptors and BHPD prowlies on the scene at ten after. Gives me time to have a chat with the Stork."

"If he takes off?"

"Then I've done a bad job of convincing him that he's wasting his time."

We split up. I stopped at a newsstand and bought a paper. Then I idled my way through a crowd descending from the monorail platform. I positioned myself next to the line at the pizza stand on the eastbound side and watched Stork McClusky grow more and more agitated on the platform across from me. Six minutes after the hour: he was scowling as he stared up Sunset for a glimpse of the late streetcar. He took out a blue handkerchief and blotted some sweat below the snap brim of his cocoa-colored Panama straw hat.

A groan ran through the crowd waiting with McClusky. More faces turned up to see what the arrivals board had to tell them. I couldn't see from where I stood but I had a good idea what the message was: ACCIDENT DELAY WESTBOUND.

Stork took in the bad news with his lips compressed. I saw indecision in his face. "Delay" could mean five minutes, or an hour.

Time to go for his balls, I thought.

I drew the Glock and concealed it with the folded newspaper. Then I transmitted McClusky's call sign on the ILC channel of my wristpac. A silent signal. He stared at his vibrating wristpac for a few moments, indecisive, then wary. But he responded wordlessly.

"Hi, Stork," I said. "Rawson. You were fucked as soon as you got the idea of extorting money from a woman who is just trying to salvage something of her family. But that's nothing compared to how fucked you're going to be if you don't tell me in the next couple of minutes where I can find Mallory Scarlett. Understand, asshole? You're not going anywhere. We're all over you like stink on a hand-me-down whore."

McClusky rubbed a hand angrily across his mouth. He glanced around. He looked up. Nine minutes past the hour. We both heard the helicopters. And sirens on Sunset.

I took off my palm-frond hat and waved it, so he could easily locate me.

He saw me. He hesitated for a couple of seconds, then smiled a savage smile.

"Fuck you, Rawson. Come and get me."

Then he headed for the escalator to the monorail platform. He shoved his way past a Little League team with parents and coaches, not in a panic, just in a hurry. As if he had an out prepared. He looked at me once as he ran up the escalator with a motion of his head as if he wanted me to follow.

I did, contacting Paulo on the run.

"McClusky wants to play. Westbound monorail. If he gets on the train, I'll take him off at Veteran or Sepulveda."

The five-car train that was operating on the west side of the loop was pulling in when I reached the platform above me. The ILC helicopters had arrived and were circling overhead. I crossed the bridge unhurriedly as passengers left the train. McClusky looked up at the helos, then boarded the middle car with that smile fixed on his face.

I strolled aboard along with the baseball kids, who were stuffing their faces with pretzels, pizza, and ice cream while chattering excitedly about the game they had won. I stood in the middle of the car as it filled up and looked at McClusky. He was facing me about ten feet away, one hand on an overhead grip rail, the other hand holding his panama hat against his chest, like in the good old days at the ballpark when they were playing the national anthem and Dimaggio was in his rookie year.

His whisper tit was in his ear. He hadn't disconnected us, as if he might be interested in talking while he stared fixedly at me over the heads of the small fry. He was perspiring. His eyes bothered me but not as much as his smile.

"This train ends up back where it started," I said, as patiently as if I were explaining to a child. "What's the point, Stork?"

"I know where I'm going," he said. "Where we'll all go if you don't leave me alone." He sounded petulant, aggrieved, and a little frightened. Falling out of touch with reality like someone falling from a high window.

The fully automated train started up smoothly. The next stop was about eight-tenths of a mile away, at Veteran and Gayley. Then it would continue on to the West Wilshire gateway to the Privilege at Sepulveda.

"You don't have anything to bargain with," I said. "Other than Mal Scarlett's life. Tell me where she is and I'll develop a bad memory about the extortion attempt. Let's get off at the next stop and we'll have ourselves some coffee and when it's confirmed that we've found Mallory—"

Below us were the playing fields and tennis courts of the university and the shadow of the passing train and another moving shadow, that of one of the helicopters keeping pace with us.

He stooped to look out at the black helicopter thirty yards away.

"SWAT, huh?" he said. He was breathing heavily and he had that smile again. Cunning and ruthless. "Get rid of them."

"I will. Just give me a reason for playing ball with you, Stork. Give me Mal Scarlett." I tried not to let emotion into my voice. "It's no beef against you. You didn't kidnap her."

But the look he flicked my way gave me reason to wonder. His eyes said, *Wouldn't you like to know?*

"You want to play ball?" he said. "Okay, let's play ball."

His smile, no longer senseless, was touched by a fleering evil.

He showed me what he had in his hat.

"How do you like your kids cooked, Rawson?" he said.

The tan grenade was an ILC Armory standard item. It was incendiary and the arming light was on, a pinhead red glow. Six seconds after it hit anything—the roof of the car, the floor, someone's body—the packed car would light up like an exploding star. At least twenty men, women, and children would die in one of the most frightful ways imaginable.

I had a clean shot at him with the silenced Glock. He knew I had a gun and didn't care. No point thinking about it. The grenade could not be allowed to explode.

"Okay," I said, trying without a lot of success to control my rage. "You walk, McClusky. There'll be another time."

I'd barely spoken when the girl standing close and belt-high to Stork said in a loud voice, "Mama, this man has a bomb in his hat!"

Screams.

And some damn fool hit the emergency stop button.

Half of those standing in the car lurched backward as braked tires smoked on the rail. Stork McClusky was piled into by bodies of assorted sizes. He had a tight grip on the overhead handrail and managed to keep one foot on the floor. But his upper body was wrenched violently to the right. His arm flew up past his shoulder and the thermite bomb, a little larger than a handball, popped up out of his hat like a lazy infield fly, grazed the ceiling, and began to arc down.

A chubby kid with a peeling nose who had kept his seat facing the aisle at the rear end of the car saw the grenade coming. I'd noticed him before, pounding a baseball into his catcher's mitt while he relived the game with a teammate seated beside him. Still into that game, he reached out instinctively to snag the falling grenade with his mitt.

He almost made the catch. But instead of nestling in the small pocket of the mitt, the grenade hit the front edge and teetered there. Distracted by the screaming and jostling, the kid made a determined effort to bring in the grenade, but his teammate gave him a shove off the seat and the grenade fell to the floor amid several pairs of feet in flip-flops, sneakers, and sandals.

Three seconds.

The grenade was going to explode, and there was nothing I could do about it.

But there are those moments—ask any athlete who makes his living in pro sports—when time on the field or court seems to slow down, allowing for an almost preternatural clarity of vision. Ted Williams had claimed he could see and sometimes count the seams on a fastball dished up to him at ninety-plus miles an hour in six-tenths of a second.

I had some of that, a clarity of vision prompted by extreme crisis, an acute appraisal of all options available to me. As the grenade rolled up the aisle and back to us while others scrambled frantically to get out of the way, I moved toward Stork McClusky, calmly aware of what I must do.

Two seconds.

His head was coming around as he shifted his feet to keep his balance and I hit him with a straight shot to the point of the chin. The punch traveled only about a foot but I had never thrown a better one. His eyes rolled up and out and he lost his grip on the handrail.

One second.

I caught McClusky by the lapels of his sports jacket as he began to sag, spun him around and threw him down between the scuffling feet of terrorized riders: threw him onto the incendiary grenade as it was detonated.

There was a muffled *whump* and McClusky's long body arced in a floppy sort of way like a broken jackknife, but rose only a few inches off the floor. At a temperature of around three thousand degrees Fahrenheit the magnesium accelerant produced enough thermal energy to burn instantly through most of his skinny torso and begin to melt the floor around and under him. Those closest to the flash also were burned: clothing, shoes, bare legs. But most of the force of the grenade had been directed downward by the dampening effect of McClusky. The burn would eat a hole in the floor of the car three feet in diameter before it slowed down. But the physical damage was contained. There was very little smoke; the stench was as ripe as a cannibals' cookout. There were maybe a dozen injuries, half of those serious.

I grabbed a large bottle of designer water from someone's backpack and used it to douse a screaming kid whose flips were melting. I grabbed her off the sizzling floor and shoved her into her mother's arms and yelled for more water, soda, aloe vera gel; anything to cool down other burn victims.

Paulo pushed his way inside from the car behind us, made a quick and accurate guess as to what had happened.

"SWAT wants to know our situation!"

"Help me empty this car and get the train moving again! We'll need medical at the next stop."

It may have been the same helpful idiot who had stopped the train in the first place who now thought it was a great idea to emergency-open the doors. Possibly forgetting that the train was between stations and about eighteen feet in the air. There was still a lot of panicky shoving going on as everyone tried to put distance between themselves and the steadily shrinking blackness of Stork McClusky. The smell; the horror. A bearded man with a guitar strapped across his back toppled backward into space, fell with a shriek. The guitar, I hoped, would absorb some of the shock from his fall.

When a kid was knocked off balance and almost rolled out through another door I'd had enough: I pulled the Glock, unclipped the silencer, and fired four quick shots into the ceiling of the car. It was a risky gamble. Either they all would continue to panic, or I would have a few moments to grab control of the situation.

Most of them froze, staring at me.

So I explained that the worst was over, I didn't want to hear any more goddamn screaming and yelling and anyone who chose not to cooperate could leave the car by the nearest exit.

Someone laughed nervously. But there was a noticeable easing of fear as they began to believe me.

"We have an emergency here! People are injured, but there are first-aid kits and fire extinguishers aboard. Use them. Get calm, get organized, and we'll soon be moving on.

"Any questions?"

I had a gun and the voice of authority. There were no questions.

A few minutes later the doors closed and the train was rolling again, slowly, to the next stop.

About half an hour after the train had been emptied, as twilight settled in and the sky had darkened to a tranquil shade of indigo and I could breathe again without smelling burned flesh, Paulo and I watched what little remained of Stork McClusky in a body bag being loaded into the back of the coroner's bus.

"Was there anyone at SoCal Intel who wasn't corrupt?" I said.

"We'll be sorting that out in the next few months. McClusky was just dirtier than most."

"While DeMarco looked the other way? I don't get why he's not in lockdown."

"No formal charges yet. He's cooperating with us."

I sighed and shook my head, looked at my wristpac. Cell call. It was Beatrice.

"Hiya."

"R?" She sounded tense.

"Who else?"

"W-where are you?"

She was tense, all right. Her voice low, tentative. As if she were afraid to talk, almost afraid to breathe. I tried to raise her hologram. The image was shaky tonight. My wristpac either needed a charge, or it had taken a beating when I clocked McClusky.

"Not far away," I said. "There was some trouble. It's sorted out. How's Ida?" Now I was tense, my teeth on edge, because Stork McClusky might have been my last hope for finding Mal Scarlett before the *mal de lune*.

"I—I'm not with her. I'm still at the hotel."

"Why?"

"You're going to be mad."

"No I'm not. What's going on?"

"It's about my knife—the silver one."

"Jesus, Bea. Not that again."

"Just listen! I found it."

"You—where?"

She took a long breath.

"It's, uh—oh, hell."

"Bea, are you where I think you are?"

Her blurry hologram trembled in the darkening air as a strong breeze flowed through the ficus trees behind me.

"Yes. F-Francesca Obregon's bungalow. She still has my knife, R. I mean—she's sort of wearing it?"

I let five seconds go by. Whistled three low notes.

"That mean what I think it means?"

"Uh-huh," Beatrice said tearfully.

"Are you alone?"

"Yes. Well—except f-for— R, it's getting dark and I'm kind of scared, can you—"

"Go to the door," I said. "Lock it. Wait. I'll be there in ten minutes."

21

Francesca Obregon was half reclining with a lot of colorful taffeta-covered pillows on a bed with a sateen pearl-gray spread and an ornate headboard of wrought iron painted white and accented with ormolu. The bedroom was half of the first-floor master suite of the bungalow leased by one of Miles Brenta's companies. The suite contained, among other luxuries and examples of Hollywood whimsy, two wood-burning fireplaces, a pink grand piano in a windowed alcove, and a standing harp with two stuffed lovebirds perched on it.

Francesca's beautiful nude lightly oiled body looked relaxed, as death first relaxes us all. Her long legs were crossed at the ankles and her thighs were primly together. Her large dark eyes were open and fixed on us behind the netlike brim of one of those summery hats two or three of the models at the fashion show had been wearing.

The silver hilt of Beatrice's throwing knife was canted at an upward angle and snug to the chest wall slightly below Francesca's breasts. I guessed that her eyes had been closed; postcoital nap, maybe. Then they had opened wide at the brute thrust of the blade, stayed that way as the blade ripped her heart nearly in half. A complete surprise to Francesca, obviously. Whoever had done it was both deft and strong. Filled with rage and poisoned passion or maybe just the sadness of saying goodbye in a lethal way.

My first thought was of Miles Brenta.

My second thought was, *Setup*.

"OhGodohGod," Beatrice said sofly behind me.

"Are you going to throw up?"

"I did already. In the toilet. I didn't make a mess. I've got such a headache. I didn't like her, but—how brutal. How awful."

I approached the bed. Bea said, "Do you have to touch her?"

"Yes."

"I'll wait in the front room for you."

Francesca's murder wasn't ILC business; she belonged now to BHPD's homicide division and the rest of the Privilege's efficient inquest process. I only wanted to get an estimate of how long she'd been dead.

There was congealed dark blood at one corner of her slightly parted lips. But no sign of rigor, which made TOD less than two hours.

I called homicide and asked for Burt Ferguson, whom I had known for years. Burt was in. Ten minutes, he said.

Then I joined Bea, who wanted to be held.

"My fingerprints—" she said.

"The cross-hatched hilt wouldn't take a print. The blade is clean from Fran's blood." Bea shuddered. "Forget about your knife. Here's your story. Short and simple. You ran into Obregon mid-afternoon in the hotel lobby. She invited you to stop in after the fashion show for a drink. You'd met her her at Max Thursday's hacienda and kind of hit it off, but you didn't know her very well. That's all you need to say. We'll be out of here in less than an hour."

"All right. Poor Max. He needed Francesca. I'm so sorry for him too."

She cried, and was getting over it when Burt Ferguson and a detective I didn't know walked in with a couple of uniforms.

They took a few minutes, then Evidence Response arrived, followed by the Beverly Hills ME. A lot of traffic, muted voices. Burt was a short guy with heavy brows and the introspective eyes of a priest bored with sinners. He spent less than ten minutes with Beatrice, two with me.

"You know the vic?"

"Not very well."

"No ideas, then?"

"Wish I could be of more help, Burt."

He shrugged. "I wonder how many Brenta execs besides her had the run of the bungalow? We could have a lot of DNA to process. Most of it might belong to Brenta himself."

"Wouldn't be surprised," I said.

"The help around here will be able to tell us if he was doing her on a regular schedule. So there she was, naked and waiting for him in her peekaboo hat. Why can't my wife think of something like that?" He looked back at the bedroom where the ER team was doing its meticulous work. "Ain't it just too good to be true?" he said, wistfully.

"I thought you'd never notice," I said. "Okay if I take Miss Harp home now?"

He'd already detected the nuances of a relationship. He grinned his feisty grin.

"You do all right for yourself. Have her come by the office tomorrow and we'll take a statement. What the hell is going down at ILC these days?"

My turn to shrug. "Nobody tells me anything."

"Yeah, I'll bet."

I walked outside with Bea. A couple of cops loitered near the door. It was full dark now. A stiff breeze earlier had become boisterous gusts of wind throwing the shaggy shadows of deodars across the flagged path that wandered among the bungalows. The path was lighted Hawaiian-style by torches. I thought we were probably in for a couple of days of Santa Anas. I looked up, saw clouds adrift around the moon like stuffing pulled from eviscerated dolls. I had a knot in my stomach as if something sharp were pointed at my navel.

I glimpsed someone standing behind trimmed shrubbery a few feet off the path. Too dark for me to make out a face.

He called to me, his voice just above a whisper.

"Rawson."

Bea loosened her grip on my right arm and stepped aside. I put my hand on the butt of my holstered Glock.

"Come out where I can see you."

He moved carefully in our direction. Bea sucked in a scared breath.

"Take it easy," he said. "It's Miles Brenta."

"The man we all want to see," I said, drawing the Glock but letting my gun hand fall slowly to the side away from him. "Go on in. The lights are on and the cops are waiting. The homicide dick in charge is Burt Ferguson."

"Is it Francesca?" he said. "Is she dead?" He might have been asking if she were putting on her makeup.

"Just the way you left her."

He looked slowly at the bungalow.

"I haven't seen her today."

"No?"

He looked back at me.

"I don't have anything to talk to cops about. But I need to talk to you."

"Do you want to get shot? Step over here where I can get a good look at you."

There were three types of murderers who lurked near the scene after they'd killed: a few who enjoyed the spectacle they had created, some who didn't care if they were caught, and those in an emotional blackout who couldn't remember having done it.

Brenta came a couple of steps closer to the lighted path, a flare of torches on the pupils of his dark eyes. I read what there was to read in his eyes. He wasn't enjoying himself and his mind was on other matters, not in a state of confusion. I didn't sense fear. But the herpes breakout on his lower lip still looked painful.

"I know what I told you this afternoon," he said. "But I got here just five minutes ago. I have witnesses to prove that."

"Then where have you been?"

"Taking care of business. I don't mean Francesca. How long has she been dead?"

"Long enough to keep you out of it if your story's good."

Brenta nodded, looked again at the bungalow. No regrets, just that long goodbye look. Either he was emotionally cold, or heartlessly pragmatic.

"Rawson, it had to be Raoul Ortega. I don't have time now to go into the whys and wherefores with the Beverly Hills police. But it was Ortega, all right."

"Why are you so sure?"

"This is the way the Diamondbackers dissolve partnerships they don't need anymore. Look, I can show you what I mean better than I can tell you. You'll just have to trust me."

"That's rich," I said. "Go ahead, hand me another laugh, Brenta."

He gestured; *follow me.*

"I have a helicopter waiting. We'll talk on the way."

"Prior engagement," I said.

He had turned away from us. He looked back with a frown of impatience, but he spoke calmly.

"There still may be time to stop Ortega from distributing those wolfmakers like the one you showed me."

Bea said softly, fear in her voice, "Is he talking about the Really Bad Thing?"

"Probably a lot more of them than I thought there would be," Brenta said. "Are you interested, Rawson?"

"Yeah," I said after a few seconds. "I'm interested."

We flew north over the San Gabriel Mountains to Antelope Valley in what I had heard described as the Ferrari of personal helicopters. There were only about a hundred of them in the world. This one was black and gold, needle nosed, and rocket fast. Very nearly soundproofed inside, loaded with communications gear. The cabin was outfitted clubroom-style in plush carpeting and pale leathers. There was ample space for eight passengers, a lavatory with gold fixtures, and a nicely stocked bar.

Besides Brenta and me there were two pilots and a flight attendant with hair the color of ginger ale and wide-set gray eyes that had the enchantment of the northern lights in them. I wasn't too tired to be enchanted.

I had arranged for Bea to be driven to the hospital where Ida Grace was waiting to see how Duke's tests came out. Afterward, because she didn't want to be alone at the *minka* even with guards at my gate, she would wait for me next door at Ida's.

I had e-mails from Booth Havergal chewing me out for not reporting back to ILC to be debriefed after the Stork McClusky fiasco. A lot of people were very angry with ILC and Booth Havergal in particular. The media was, as usual, recycling the limited amount of information they had. I was able to monitor three different channels as we flew. The flight attendant, whose name was Ulrike, opened a new bottle of Scotch and poured three fingers into a crystal tumbler. Where I could see and admire her, Miles Brenta drank black coffee. The single-malt whisky soothed my nerves somewhat; still we were edgy with each other. Brenta kept touching his sore underlip.

"The XOTECH facility was evacuated shortly before noon today," he told me. "Some bullshit about a security breach from an unnamed source. Everyone was dismissed for the day. There was no subsequent search of the premises, as there should have been. By four o'clock XOTECH was deserted except for a couple of security guards."

"I seem to recall there's only one road into the facility."

"That's right. A few minutes before five the Diamondbackers moved in. There were at least twenty of them, on Harleys or driving big rigs. They didn't meet with any resistance."

"What's the source of your information?"

"A ranger in a fire tower about three miles southwest of XOTECH."

"Where were you after you dumped me into a spare villa at your place?"

He had the integrity to look troubled by that action, although there was no apology. I didn't see the point of reminding him he'd committed a felony that could fetch him up to four years at Rocky Peak if I wanted to put him there. At some point in the future I might need a big favor from Miles Brenta; meanwhile I figured I had the bulge on him and I was content to hold his marker.

"Most of the afternoon I was at my office at NANOMIM initiating a review and search of outgoing shipments of LUMOs with supervisors."

His shrug indicated it hadn't gone too well.

"Did you speak to or make an attempt to contact Francesca?"

"Yes, I tried. You can have a look at my phone log if you'd like."

I shook my head and resumed soothing my nerves. I looked at Ulrike; she smiled and produced the bottle again.

Brenta said, "One of Cesca's assistants recalled hearing her say she needed to go up to XOTECH because of the security thing. And that's why I went there."

"And ran into Diamondbackers."

"Manner of speaking. They were all over the facility like ants on a sugar cube. I had Zeke—he's my pilot—circle near the fire tower I mentioned while I looked things over through binoculars. Dozens of cartons from Shipping were on the loading dock. They were being packed into the trailer of a semi. I think I forgot to say the Diamondbackers were armed to the teeth."

"Um-hmm. So you left the area."

"Yes."

"Why did you go to the hotel?"

He was beginning to look exasperated. Some red had seeped into his eyes.

"I hadn't slept since Bucky—I needed a hot shower, food, time to think. The hotel is much closer from here than Paradiso Palms."

"But you had no idea Francesca was in the bungalow."

"We've been through that. NO." He glared at me. "You're an obnoxious son of a bitch."

"I can get a lot worse, Brenta."

He didn't want to fight. He was still tired, still hungry, holding on to his poise and nerve like a hoocher clutching a threadbare coat around himself on a bone-chilling night.

"Mr. Brenta," Zeke the pilot said on the intercom, "we have XOTECH at three o'clock, range three-quarters of a mile."

The facility's perimeter floods made a yellow smudge on the underbellies of clouds above three one-story buildings. Wind-borne grit ticked against the helicopter's windows. The Santa Ana was bringing in a lot of dust off bare-bones desert east of Victorville, the lights of which were indistinctly visible as we crossed a forested ridgeline at about five hundred feet. From a left-side window I had a glimpse of two steadily glowing red lights atop the fire tower that Brenta earlier had referred to.

"Any sign of activity?" Brenta said. The copilot was glassing the floodlit surround.

"No, sir."

I couldn't tell if Brenta was disappointed or relieved.

"We should have a look inside. Take us down."

"Yes, sir," Zeke said, and lowered our airspeed to under a hundred knots.

The white adobe-style concrete buildings occupied a not very deep barranca that backed up to the northeast slope of the San Gabriel range. As we approached I saw a difficult fence, steel posts ten feet high, hedged in razor wire like a battlefield barricade. The fence continued on both sides of the paved road to a farm road about a mile east of XOTECH.

We pitched down toward a helipad in one corner of the parking lot a hundred yards from the loading dock. The Ferrari of the skies was buffeted by sudden explosive gusts of wind. Zeke had his hands full getting us down. Cartons and other trash skipped and danced across the asphalt below.

Ulrike came unsteadily out of the lavatory, dropped into a seat, and strapped herself in.

Three big tractor-trailer rigs were parked rear ends to the loading dock and about fifteen feet apart. They all looked road-weary, battered, dented, and scraped. None of the three had any sort of identification.

"Those trucks weren't here before," Brenta said. "There was only one new-looking semi that the Diamondbackers were loading the cartons into."

Zeke nosed the helicopter toward the pad, finding it difficult to read the wind, which sheared around the corners of the linked buildings. I thought he might be overcontrolling the tail rotor pedals, but what did I know? What I usually flew was temperamental junk compared to this aircraft.

He fine-tuned his landing a little too much and a hard gust lifted us back into the air. I didn't envy Zeke; set down too hard and bust something, try to be gentle and bounce around like a beach ball. Ulrike was making fists in her seat but she smiled gamely when I glanced at her.

"Those trucks all look like derelicts," Brenta said. "What are they parked here for?"

I don't know what it was about his observation that triggered the warning in my mind: *why indeed?* But it inspired a closer look at the parking lot as we descended again. Twelve feet from touchdown. *Eight*. Momentarily the winds were muted or absent. I recalled the small red arming eye of Stork McClusky's incendiary grenade and was puzzled, wondering why I should be seeing it again, a solemn red blinking behind the cab of the truck parked nearest the helipad.

"Zeke!" I yelled to the cockpit. "Get us off the deck *now*!"

There was probably a second's indecision on Zeke's part before his hand on the collective reacted and sent us soaring. But it was just enough time for the heel of the left skid to break the laser beam crossing the asphalt at a height of about four feet from the helipad to the big rig.

We rose straight up. Fast, but not fast enough. I had time to click on my safety harness. Then the fulminating black and orange, volcanolike cloud from the trailer truck exploding below caught up to us, engulfed the fuselage in a dazzling fury. There was a sensation of breathtaking compression and great violence. Shrapnel slammed through the metal skin around us. It fouled the steering and obliterated the electronics. My brain glowed with a fierce white light.

We all might have been screaming. I don't know. I know that we continued to fly, beyond the certain death of the subsequent fireballs from the other two rigs. The rotors had to have been damaged, but they didn't break apart.

Miles Brenta had been sitting opposite me; I didn't see him. There was a jagged hole toward the back of the helicopter where a window had been torn out. I saw the face of Ulrike, pale, young, uplifted, illuminated like a Madonna by churchlight. She coughed and blood ran from her mouth and she lowered her gaze apologetically to me, coughed up more blood and died. I felt a terrible wrenching sadness, aware that I probably wouldn't be far behind her.

The helicopter shook and flailed the air and I was very frightened. But, instead of breaking up, we autorotated. Hit something in the dark with a grinding crash, rebounded, fell again, tumbled down a hill or the side of an arroyo. The terrific jolting blacked me out.

When I was conscious again I smelled smoke and heard the crackling of fire. I wasn't strapped to the leather chair anymore. I didn't know where it was. I was lying faceup. I saw a few stars and heard the keening of the Santa Ana. I had dirt on my mouth. I heard voices. There were flashlights in the darkness.

One of the beams centered on my face. I raised a hand weakly in protest. The toe of a heavy boot nudged me in the ribs on my right side, which is how I learned that at least two of them were badly bruised or broken. My short scream attracted more attention.

Someone kneeled beside me. The light was still in my eyes. I turned my head, tasting blood along with the dirt. A white handkerchief appeared to float through my limited field of vision. Pure alcohol or 150-proof liquor stung my nose. Dirt was brushed from my face with the tequila-soaked handkerchief. It stung my dry lips. I licked a few drops. Tasted pretty good.

Breathing was an ordeal. I managed to speak to my samaritan.

"Is everybody dead?" I remembered Ulrike, who probably had taken some hot hard metal in vital places.

"*No todos uno.*" Not everybody. "But you lockier than most, hombre."

He laughed then. I was the joke and the punch line. I was the butt of his humor.

"Rawson. *Como el gato, no?*"

In the dark behind him another man snickered.

I knew then who I was talking to, he who had solicitously cleaned my face.

Raoul Jesus Ortega.

He placed the mouth of a bottle of tequila between my lips.

"Drink now," he said. "It relax you. Soon you feel no more pain."

22

Mr. RawSON," the girl's voice pleaded. "Mr. RAW-SON! Wake up! Get me out of here!"

Someone was always inviting me to have a friendly drink, I thought. Or two. Or in the most recent instance damn near a full fifth of tequila, whatever amount I hadn't been able to spit out. I was going to have to learn to choose my drinking companions more carefully.

I lay on my back, barely conscious, throbbing with pain and very goddamned drunk. *Why couldn't someone shut the brat up?* I thought. She was disturbing me. All I wanted was to catch a few winks and when I woke up again maybe the squirrels using the squeaky exercise wheel in my head would have stopped.

"Mr. Rawww-son!" she wailed again. "Please! It's almost time! Luvagod, help me!"

Time for what? I thought. *Don't be cryptic. Out with it, girl.*

"Where am I?" I muttered.

Wherever it was, there was a metallic resonance, a sort of hollow drainpipe effect when she screamed at me again.

"We're in an AIRplane!"

"Oh. Okay." But I missed the sensation of flight, the drone of engines.

"You sure?" I said witlessly.

"An *old* airplane! There's a lot of them parked here! Would you please *look* at me?"

So I rolled my head toward the sound of her voice. Which confirmed by the feel of rivets in steel plate that I actually was lying on a deck. Airplane. Submarine, maybe: because I had the sensation of being submerged, drowning in gloom. And we were moving, intermittently rocked by big gusts of wind. The Santa Ana. I had memories—of trucks blowing up in cataclysmic sequence and knocking a big helicopter around in a fiery sky until it crashed. The face of a lovely Nordic girl who never knew what hit her. There was sickness in my mouth, the back of my throat. Tequila had never been my drink of choice.

"I *hate* the wind! It's been blowing like this all day! It's driving me crazy!"

Complain, complain. My eyes felt as if they'd been spray-painted shut. I forced the lids to open, blinked away the sticky mucus until I was focusing. The light was very bad, just a brownish yellow stain from a single dim old lightbulb. Flying dust and bits of desert mica pecked at the skin of the fuselage. There was a steady low hum inside. The air was moving in drafts. At least it was breathable, piped in from a mobile APU.

I saw her crouched a dozen feet from me. Leaning forward in a hampered, crippled attitude like a street beggar. In the poor light I saw strain in her smudged, pretty, vapid face.

"Told you . . . I was coming, Mal," I said.

"What? You never told me *any*thing! And you're certainly no good to me the way you are! I WANT OUT OF HERE BEFORE THEY SHOOT ME!"

I tried to move my hands. They felt swollen and they tingled. They were fastened tightly together at my waist. I couldn't raise my head high enough to see what my hands were restrained with.

"How long have you been here?" I said to Mal. Just to keep the conversation going while I figured something out.

"I don't know! A couple of days! But it's almost time! I can feel it! The moon. It's about to *happen* to me! They're all here already! The hunters with their guns! They came in a couple at a time to stare at me. Like I'm a filthy animal! And I heard them laughing outside when they got into their trucks. Making bets with each other about who'll be the one to kill me!"

"It's not going to happen, Mal."

"What's going to stop them? I'll hair-up soon. I itch all over!" She sobbed. "They cut out my Snitcher! All they gave me was a local, and they didn't stitch the wound up. It hurts, I think it's infected."

This was a girl who needed a champion. Invulnerable in the flesh. But every move I made resulted in spasms, knife-edged pain. In movies the hard tough capable hero, ignoring contusions, a broken bone or two, and maybe some gunshot wounds in nonvital places, would cleverly free himself from his surly bonds and carry off the grateful damsel on his back while machine-gunning a dozen bad guys on his way out.

All in a day's work. All I could think about was how badly I needed to take a pee.

"Mal," I said, "is there some way you could—"

"I'm as close to you as I can get! I'm chained up. So are you! We're both chained to ringbolts in the floor and somebody will be coming back soon! Probably the tall greaser with the beard. He said when it got dark he'd come for the other guy!"

"What other guy?"

"He's all the way back there! Unconscious. Or maybe not—I did hear him groan a couple of times. But I know he must be in bad shape. He looked dead when they dragged the two of you inside. They gave him blood."

"Blood?"

"Do you have to repeat everything I say?"

"You mean like a transfusion?"

"I guess so. Now *please* think of something. Tell me what we're going to do!"

I made an effort to sit up, heard the rattle of a chain behind me on the deck. The pain in my left side was ferocious. I couldn't breathe very deeply. My hands were getting numb. I flexed my fingers, trying to restore feeling. I was secured at the wrists by one of the notched plastic temporary restraints cops used. Hands below my waist and back to back, putting strain on my arms; my shoulders ached.

"You can't move at all?" I said to Mal.

"J-just enough so I can use my b-bucket when I h-have to," she said, burbling with tears.

I saw the bucket referred to. I got slowly to my feet, rocked a little. The old fuselage of whatever aircraft it was resounded with a dull *boom* when struck by heavy gusts of the Santa Ana. My feet weren't shackled, which helped me keep my balance. I thought dimly that this oversight might turn out to be unlucky for someone.

I had about six feet of chain. It allowed me to move closer to Mal where she was kneeling, hunched on the floor with her hands together the way mine were tied. Her shirt was torn, her denim shorts filthy, and there was about her a faint odor of fleshly corruption. Her eyes were feverish. I felt sorry for her, but sorry didn't get it. What I wanted, had to be, was fired up, mad as hell. I wanted adrenaline. But my blood was sluggish; my brain was on a long slow-burning fuse.

I slid the slop bucket closer with one foot, fumbled my zipper down, and began relieving myself. Mal watched. The sting of urine in the stale air made her sneeze.

"Luvagod," she said after a minute or so had passed. "I didn't know anybody could hold that much."

I zipped up again. "Can you stand?" I said.

"Yes. Why?"

"Just do it," I said.

Mal was barefoot. She wore the same type of fancy tooled-leather biker's belt I had on, with snap-fastened pockets, a lot of studs and steel loops double-stitched to the leather.

"Let's see how close we can get to each other," I suggested.

I raised my bound palms-out hands toward her, shoulder joints popping audibly. She did the same and shuffled toward me, chain clinking behind her. I advanced another foot or so. We touched hands, kept straining toward each other. She had more slack than I did. When she was close enough I raised my arms higher and brought them down on either side of her head, resting them on her shoulders. Her hands were bent limply against my chest, elbows spread wide. Our foreheads came together. Mal felt feverish to me. We stayed like that a little while, saying nothing, just breathing, in a kind of helpless but loving communion. She breathed through her mouth, breath quickening gradually.

It's a bizarre biological imperative: the human species can be battered, dirty, terrified, trembling at the abyss, and still desire to mate. That was what was happening to us. There could be no consummation. But lust was useful; it caused the fuse in my brain to burn brighter and faster, gave me the first mild kick of adrenaline I needed to survive.

"How are your teeth?" I asked her.

"I have great teeth." Mal's eyes popped open; she studied me. "What the hell do you—oh. Like, chew through the plastic stuff?" She thought about it. "Yeah. Maybe I can. Then you'd have your hands free." Her eyes widened a little in anticipation of the hell to pay once that much of our freedom had been achieved.

I had to disappoint her.

"Won't do us much good. I'm still chained to the floor."

She grimaced.

"Fuck. *What*, then?"

"I need to get free of the damned chain. Nothing's going to budge that ringbolt in the floor. The weakest point is where the steel loop is sewn to the belt in back. Probably double-stitched, but if you can chew through enough of it I think I can yank myself free."

"Let's do it!"

We were face-to-face still, but our bodies were nearly two feet apart. I sensed for the first time a strangeness about Mal, a spoor of wolf. Her eyes looked different. Full-moon eyes shading from Delft blue to a yellow-gray. She licked her lips, smiled at me.

"What's wrong?" she said. "It's a great idea, R. It'll work."

"Yes," I said. "But we'd better get started."

The trick was to put my back to Mal and for her to have enough leverage to gnaw away at the tough saddle-stitching. She slid away from me and went down on one knee. I tried to twist myself all the way around but the chain pulled taut. I ended up standing a little better than sideways to her. Mal's long fingers and broken nails scrabbled against my slick khakis, groped higher. I twisted my head until the muscles of my neck burned to look down at her. Mal's teeth glinted and her jaw seemed to have a new, prognathic thrust; but the light was barely there and my perspective was distorted.

Confinement and hangover were giving me the jimmy-jams. I saw, before I had to change the angle of my head to relieve pressure, that sweat was beading on her swarthy brow and there were flickering disturbances beneath her skin as if nerves and muscles were firing out of control.

Part of the training to be an ILC Wolfer is, you have to watch a couple of them hair-up. The time it takes can vary considerably, depending on the power of the human organism to resist the profound physiological change.

I was able only to bring my hands up a few inches before the strain on my shoulders became excruciating. I still couldn't reach with my backward fingers the three small buckles that fastened the belt around my waist.

It was up to Mal, who had begun to slip away from me into a world where I had never been.

"You're not close enough!" Mal said, with a gnashing of her teeth. "Suck in your gut!"

I did. Mal then was able to hook her fingers onto the stout belt and pull hard, with more than girlish strength. She bent me back until there was a drastic curve to my spine. I was sweating too, and I barely could handle the pain of my injured ribs. Mal cried out in an agony of her own. Then she began to snuffle and chew, grinding her teeth into the tough stitching around the steel loop. I felt her hands on me, desperate, pawing.

When she needed to stop for breath she panted and whimpered.

"Rawson. It hurts—so bad."

"You are Mallory. Mallory Scarlett. Don't give in to the wolf! Say your name."

"Yes. I am—Mallory."

"Get me loose from this chain. Or we'll both be dead."

I heard a faint pleading voice from the dark rear section of the aircraft.

"Rawson?"

The voice sounded like Miles Brenta's.

"Hang on. I'm coming!"

Behind me Mal growled with renewed effort, tearing now at the heavy belt. The sounds she made chilled me. I couldn't afford the effort to look at her again. Nor did I want to see her eyes, the cold baleful beauty of wolf light.

Outside I heard the diesel engine of a truck or SUV approaching the plane that I thought might be an old Mitchell bomber from World War II. Most of them had been torched for scrap decades ago, but a few remained in the hands of collectors. The engine noise surged louder through the wind and hard sift of sand against the vinyl-sealed fuselage, then idled nearby.

And inside the odor of blood, birthing blood and a darker, saturating stain, absorbed my attention. I felt the sharp nudge of her teeth and distended physiognomy as she ravaged the biker belt with some remnant of purpose in her moon-drunk brain. But she was no longer satisfied to rip out stitching. She was devouring leather and still hungry for meat, muscle, bones; then the exposed sweets of liver and kidneys.

"Mal! Get me loose!"

The biker belt parted. I lurched away from her, tripped and fell heavily to the deck. I rolled onto my left side and made a grab for the slithering chain. I caught it with my right hand, pulled it out of the deck ring and rolled again farther away from Mal as she kneeled with her head thrown back, a howl beginning in her throat. Her teeth were bared in the snap, crackle, and pop agony of ongoing trauma and disfigurement.

A door opened in the left side of the plane. I saw a section of low canted wing forward of the door space. More sand than light filtered in. A man stepped off the ladder outside and climbed in with us. He wore gear that was useful in a blow like this: lace-up hunter's boots, a lightweight orange parka, a skier's darkly tinted face shield. The hood of the parka was pulled tight around his face. He carried a flashlight. As he ducked inside the wind caught the door and slammed it shut behind him.

The diffuse beam of his three-cell flashlight revealed Mal in the throes of hairing up.

"Jaysus Christ!" he said in shock. I thought I knew the voice.

The sight of the half-wolf girl bathed in his light transfixed him for eight or ten seconds. Mal was still restrained by the biker belt but her powerful shoulders and muscular forearms had easily allowed her to snap in two the plastic restraints.

I was out of range of the light, motionless, waiting. It occurred to the visitor that I wasn't sprawled unconscious and drunk where I ought to have been. He flashed the light on me then but I was already whirling to gain momentum. He may have heard the whip of the chain coming but couldn't move fast enough in those boots to skip completely out of the way. The chain lashed around his right ankle and I pulled hard. He flew up and back, losing his grip on the flashlight, and smacked the back of his head on the deck. The hood of his parka did little to cushion the jolt. He was knocked cold.

23

Mal Scarlett writhed on the floor of the barren old air-plane, another repetition of the devolutionary freak-show, the genomic calamity known as Lycanthropy. For her the changeover was excruciatingly slow. Her eyes, wild from the pain and the animal desire to be free of a trap, were fixed on me. The air inside the fuselage was thick, gamey, vile.

"Rawwwwsssson."

Her plea for help was the last intelligible thing she had to say to me. But there was nothing I could do now except try to protect her until her spell broke, which would be many hours, as much as a full day from now.

The unconscious man had a walkie on his belt that crackled with static and someone's faint inquiry. Others would be coming if he didn't respond.

I kneeled beside him. I needed a knife. He had one, in a woven leather belt scabbard. He also had a gun, a fourteen-shot Sig Sauer 9-millimeter automatic. Full magazine. Now I liked our chances better.

I was able to pull the knife without cutting myself. No way I could grip it usefully to slice through the tough plastic wrist restraint with the partly serrated, six-inch blade. I needed help.

"Brenta!" I called. "Can you hear me?"

He answered weakly. I got a grip on the flashlight with my other hand and hunched my way on the seat of my pants to the back of the plane.

Miles Brenta's eyes squinted shut when the light hit his face. He lay on his back on a slant ladder used for deplaning, an arm across his chest. The forearm was badly broken near the wrist, a compound fracture.

Into the AC vein at the elbow of his left arm a needle had been inserted and taped down. A small nearly noiseless transfusion unit had pumped about 250 cc from a bloodpack suspended from a ceiling hook overhead. The bloodpack was labeled with a big red O. Presumably Brenta's blood type; another type would have killed him quickly. Someone had taken care. I didn't think it was loving care, or that he'd been given blood to save his life, but to turn the life he had left into yet another revelation of hell on earth.

I let go of the flashlight and awkwardly peeled away the transparent tape, then pulled the needle from the antecubital vein. Blood welled from the small wound. He sucked in a breath.

"Oh Jesus. So much pain. I need a doctor."

"Brenta, can you use your left hand?"

"Use it . . . ?"

"Pay attention! My hands are still tied. The other guy is out but he may not be unconscious for long. I have his knife. I want you to cut my hands free."

"Try," he said. "Put the knife . . . in my hand."

I did the best I could. His fingers were slippery from blood, or nerveless. The blade rattled on the floor.

"Shit," he said dispiritedly.

Brenta breathed deeply then and there was a commotion in his chest that had him panting desperately. Blood came to his lips. He moved very slowly but closed his hand over the leather hilt of the knife.

"The blood. He did it."

"Who are you talking about?"

"Raoul Ortega. Gave me . . . bad blood, didn't he? Made me . . . one of them."

"I don't know," I said. I damn well did know.

Mal, her transformation nearly completed, howled and jerked at her chain. Maybe it would hold her. A full-grown male werewolf, forget it. I was a gusher of sweat, holding down the reasonable, primitive impulse to save myself and get out of there.

"The girl . . . my God. Not me! Not me." Brenta's eyes appeared delirious; his voice was breaking. The size and color of the swelling on his forehead looked dangerous. "Don't . . . let it happen to me, Rawson." His lips pursed in a childish way. He shook from terror. I was about to lose him to the terror.

"Cut me loose, damn it!"

Brenta moaned hopelessly but reacted with strength, hacking away with the blade, with enough accuracy to avoid slashing either of my wrists. Finally I could pull my hands apart. Brenta sank back on the ladder coughing, blood on his lower lip and chin. He moved the point of the hunting knife to the pulse of the carotid artery beneath his jaw.

"Help me. Do it. Spill it all out of me! I *will not*. Live like *them*."

Instead I took the knife away from him.

"It's not a given," I said. "If you know anything about Lycanthropy you know the virus is unstable in unrefrigerated blood. Maybe you'll get a break. But now I've got things to do if any of us are going to have a chance."

I went back to the man sprawled on the deck. He was snoring and wheezing through his parted lips. Mal the wolfgirl snapped and lunged at us.

"Calm down, sweetheart," I said. I undid the drawstrings of the man's parka, pulled off the protective face shield, revealing by flashlight the face of Cale DeMarco.

I felt as if my personal gods, whoever they might be, were nudging and winking at each other.

His walkie was staticky again. I sat DeMarco up, stripped him of his parka, and laid him back down. After I hogtied him with the chain I put the parka on, then the face shield. It was tinted to cut glare without reducing visual acuity. The Sig Sauer went inside my belt, his wristpac on my wrist. In a flap pocket of the orange parka I found a package of condoms and a container of a popular vasodilator for men. That gave me another reason to dislike Cale DeMarco. He'd come back to the old warplane just before the kickoff of tonight's *mal de lune* for a grungy hack at a helpless girl, no doubt inspired by the tales of just how eager and passionate young female Lycans could be during their Auras and just before the hairing-up cycle began.

I checked the Lunarium stored in DeMarco's wristpac. We were less than an hour from peak moon.

Mallory was momentarily quiet, watching me, back on her haunches.

Something of Mal remained, vaguely, in the long stare, the dark muzzle of the distorted face. But the impression was weak now, apparitional, overwhelmed by cold diabolism. I wondered if in her new shape she might suddenly twist and squirm free of the encompassing biker's belt and be all over me in an instant. She made a low sound in her throat and stared. Stared heartlessly. The knife I had was not silver. Nor were the bullets in the Sig auto. But DeMarco would have had full silvertip loads in the rifle he'd probably left in his vehicle.

I flashed the light on Brenta. He was motionless, suffering. His eyes were open, looking straight up. There was more blood on his lower lip.

"Get me out . . . of here. I'm dying, Rawson."

I used up half a minute finding out if the wristpac I had taken from DeMarco was going to work here. But the steel fuselage of the airplane and the strong winds outside blocked access to a satellite.

I slapped DeMarco a couple of times. He groaned but didn't open his eyes. A hard man to wake up. So I picked up the slop bucket, which was about half full, and let him have all of it in the face.

He sputtered and choked himself awake, gagged.

"Where's Raoul Ortega?" I said.

"Rawson?" His eyes must have been stung by the urine. He was having trouble making out my face behind the amber shield. He looked anxious. "Why did you tie me up like this?"

"Did you hear the question, DeMarco?"

He struggled with the chains. "You son of a bitch!"

Behind him Mal Wolfgirl growled.

DeMarco twisted his head painfully to get a look at her.

"Oh—*shit*."

"One more time before you two get cozy. Where's Ortega?"

"The hangar. With the others. Most of the others."

"Having themselves a swell party? Yeah, I'll bet. Just where are we?"

"Old airfield. Ten miles from Barstow. Flight line of old World War Two junk. They get rented out to movie companies."

"How long have you and Ortega been buddied up?"

"Awhile. I had an opportunity. I took it. Let me out of this, Rawson. Ortega is the one you want anyway."

"Where are the wolfmakers that were trucked away from XOTECH yesterday?"

DeMarco acquired a stubborn look.

I put the flashlight down, grabbed him off the floor, and dumped him a couple of feet closer to Mal Wolfgirl.

"You two have a good time."

"You're not going to leave me with *that*?"

"Why, yes I am, numbnuts. Thanks for asking."

"Rawson. Rawson! *Please*. We can deal."

"Who's outside waiting for you? Diamondbackers?"

"Just Vollmer and McQuarrie."

Vollmer, I knew, was governor of the Privilege. McQuarrie was in the casino business. They would be seasoned *mal de luners*. I wondered how they were going to like hunting werewolves with sticks and stones.

"How many Lycans are in the hunt tonight? Besides Mal."

"Three more; one female. They're just rogue trash. Nobody who'll ever be missed. That's how we always do it."

"Where are they?"

"Stashed along the flight line. One to a plane, of course. They're tied, but the rope can't stand up to a werewolf's strength when its time comes."

"What kind of planes? Like this one?"

"No. One is a Liberator. There's a Fock-Wulf Kondor sitting next to it, and a B-17 with a chin turret opposite them on the runway. Rawson? I know where the wolfmakers went. But that's my get-out-of-jail card. Ortega has to be out of the picture, savvy? You've been wanting your shot at him. This is it."

"Jail? Hell, you must be feeling lucky. What do you think is going to get you out of the garbage when Mal is finished with you?"

He started screaming at me, which set Mal off. I had DeMarco's wallet and I silenced him by cramming it into his mouth. Then I returned to Miles Brenta.

"Do you think you can walk?" I asked him.

He licked his swollen lips. Blood had dried and looked hard as nail polish in the cracks.

"Try."

"Your broken arm is a big problem. I can loop my belt around your neck to serve as a makeshift sling. But if you pass out on me I'll have to leave you until I can get a MedEvac chopper in here."

". . . Be okay. Let's just do it."

I half carried Brenta to the middle of the plane and forced the door open against the wind. I sat him in the doorway, jumped past him to the ground. It hurt. When I had my breath back I went looking for help.

The crew cab diesel pickup that had delivered DeMarco to his anticipated tryst was idling twenty yards off the left-side wing of the Mitchell bomber. Multiple high beams sizzled through the gritty tempest battering the flight line. I saw more than a dozen antique aircraft in long-term storage, sealed against scouring winds and blistering daytime temperatures with thick coats of sprayed-on vinyl. All the engines were missing propellers. Sand had formed small dunes around the landing gear.

I thought of a couple of once-powerful eagles I had seen in a taxidermist's dusty window.

Halfway to the heavily shocked-up truck I heard a werewolf's howl. The sound stopped me in my tracks. But it wasn't Mallory. The howling came from the dark beyond the flight line, out of the reach of the truck's high-beamers. For four or five seconds I peered through the sandblast for something bounding my way. I didn't see any immediate threat and moved on.

I wrenched open a door of the crew cab. Vollmer sat high in the front seat with McQuarrie behind him. He was loading a banana box for an Uzi semiauto with silvertips. I lit up their faces with the flashlight. Because I was wearing DeMarco's orange parka they were appropriately jolly and foulmouthed about DeMarco's supposed conquest until I raised the 9-mil.

"Rawson, ILC. Get out of the truck. McQuarrie, lay that chatter gun on the seat beside you."

"R-Rawson?" Vollmer sputtered. "Now listen, Rawson, we—"

I put a bullet past his nose through the window of the door on the driver's side.

Vollmer had short legs and a barrel chest. He fell getting down from the high cab, looked up at me on all fours, face reddening in anger and humiliation.

"Where's Cale?" he demanded.

"Miami Beach."

"Do you know who I am?"

That bullshit. I sneered tiredly at him.

We all heard the werewolf this time. *Same one*, I thought. If I hadn't felt so bad I might have laughed at the expression on Vollmer's face. His eyes were hectic from fear behind his shooter's glasses.

McQuarrie was a different breed, with an acquired urbanity that hid his alley-rat origins.

"So one of them has haired-up already. Sounds close by. I think given the circumstances I should have my gun back."

From the belly of the Mitchell bomber Mal Wolfgirl answered the other werewolf's cry. The only difference in werewolf howls was the degree of murderous rage expressed.

"Two," I said.

"Help me up!" Vollmer pleaded. His voice a high squeal.

I wasn't about to lend a hand I couldn't spare. McQuarrie assisted.

"You two get over there to the Mitchell and help Miles Brenta," I said.

"Miles? What happened to him?" Vollmer said.

"Helicopter crash. He has a broken arm, concussion, probably internal injuries."

Vollmer looked at the mothballed bomber. Miles Brenta was still sitting in the doorway, legs dangling, face turned away from the stinging wind, and I was afraid he would be blown to the ground.

"Are you crazy?" Vollmer said. He was out of breath already

just from falling out of the truck. "There's a werewolf in that plane. *She's* the fucking trophy!"

"I used to change her diapers. Nothing's going to happen to Mal tonight or my wrath and my vengeance will be without equal. How many of you intrepid sons of bitches are in the competition?"

"There are six of us," McQuarrie said calmly. "Miles was to have been the seventh." He looked steadily at me through his face shield, ignoring the Sig that was pointed at his navel. He wasn't out of breath, and appeared to be health-club fit in spite of his sixty-odd years. "Now, I would like to have my rifle back, Rawson." He had the cool nerve to smile. "Be a sport. I have a very large bet tonight, and I don't like to lose. Tonight Mal Scarlett has the opportunity to settle up for all the markers she's left at my casinos. Besides—what's another werewolf to a Wolfer?"

I almost slugged him with the steel barrel of the flashlight. But I needed the strength my outrage would give me for someone more deserving.

"Get over to the plane now, both of you, before I start shootng off toes."

I put a round into the earthquake-crumbled runway for emphasis. It missed the sole of one of Vollmer's boots by a hair. They got going. I climbed into the truck to back it up.

In the distance I saw lights coming our way, half a dozen bouncing beams of motorcycles speeding over rough terrain. Above the low whistle of hot wind blowing through the bullet hole in the window next to me I heard the roar of engines.

I had a few moments of apprehension; then I felt a strange surge of satisfaction.

Maybe I wouldn't have to go looking for Raoul Ortega after all. It appeared that he was coming to me.

24

Vollmer and McQuarrie handed Miles Brenta down to me in the bed of the pickup. I laid him on his back and turned his head to one side so that whatever came into his mouth—blood, vomit—he wouldn't aspirate. The hot and nerve-racking wind had everybody else perspiring, but Brenta was cold to the touch and his eyes were back in his head.

McQuarrie jumped down beside me, looked at Brenta.

"He won't make it," McQuarrie said dispassionately.

"Brenta's a tough guy. Let me have your safari jacket."

He didn't argue with me. I covered Brenta as well as I could with the jacket.

"Six hunters? How are you dispersed?"

"Pickup trucks like this one. Two to a truck. DeMarco's just a driver, not a hunter."

Inside the Mitchell bomber Mal Wolfgirl was putting on a show. She wasn't just being territorial. It took a lot of energy to hair-up, she was hungry and she knew other werewolves were around, with their own claims to the food supply. Which was us.

Vollmer was standing weak-kneed in the doorway, glancing over his shoulder. Probably as close to a live one as he'd ever been.

"What about DeMarco?" he yelled.

Diamondbackers were getting closer on their big Harleys, accompanied by more lights mounted at the rooflines of the pickups. There was some hoorahing going on, a real wild-west roundup.

"What about him?" McQuarrie said to me.

I shrugged. "Go get DeMarco if you want him."

McQuarrie smiled edgily and shook his head.

"I don't think anyone wants him that badly. If I can't have my chatter gun, then I'd just as soon head for home."

"Let's roll!" I called to Vollmer. "Get in the goddamned truck!"

He was still quaking, unable to bring himself to jump the short distance into the pickup's bed. Maybe with all of the weight he was carrying above the beltline he had bad feet.

Hesitation cost him. He screamed suddenly, almost lost his footing, teetered in the doorway, arms windmilling. But he had to take that last look back.

I jumped from the bed of the pickup to the running board and squeezed into the cab behind the steering wheel, cracked ribs like knives in my side. I'd left the engine running, of course. I shifted to low and the oversized tires spun through the sand that covered the old runway.

McQuarrie grabbed a chrome handhold as the back end of the truck slewed away from the plane. I glanced at Vollmer.

He was still in the doorway, his mouth open in a scream. He looked rigid from fear.

Then I saw Mal Wolfgirl as she loomed behind Vollmer, put a hand on his shoulder, gripped his neck with jaws that had so much more power than the bite of any other canine. She leaped from the plane with him. Vollmer hit the ground with his head half severed. The she-wolf let go of him and looked in our direction.

McQuarrie made it into the front seat the same way I had.

"Suppose we get the hell out of here," he said.

The CB radio in the cab squawked as I accelerated.

"DeMarco? You have finish with the girl, hombre? Cut her loose. We are coming. Already there are Hairballs. DeMarco? Come back."

I grabbed the mike and answered him.

"DeMarco's run into a little tough luck, Ortega. You're next."

"Rawson? That you, amigo?"

"*Mal de lune*'s over, Ortega. No more 'amuleto.' It's you and me tonight, asshole. Come back."

"You and me." He laughed. "Interesting. I accept."

"What's going on here?" McQuarrie said nervously. "Is this some kind of personal vendetta?"

"You bet it's personal."

"Listen, I don't want any part of this."

The headlights of half a dozen Harleys and the racks of pickup roof and side lights were in full flood inside the cab. Dazzling. They were all about a hundred yards away and, in spite of the blow, they lit up the flightline like an ancient arena. I saw a rogue Hairball scramble over the top gun turret of a Flying Fortress. One of the trucks swerved toward it and tracer rounds were fired from the bed. The Hairball wasn't damaged but the old bomber took a beating. The Hairball drew everyone's attention except for one biker. While bikes and trucks circled the plane with the werewolf on it, Raoul Ortega—I could be sure it was him—came straight toward us.

I looked back for Mal Wolfgirl, who was clearly visible in the throw of the headlight on Ortega's motorcycle. She was crouched near the leftovers of the late governor of the Privilege, her eyes like liquid fire in the light. McQuarrie turned in his seat and reached behind him for the tricked-up, bright blue steel assault weapon with its night optics and thirty-round box loaded with silvertips. I suppose a gambler like McQuarrie would have called his high-powered rifle the "House vig."

Some fucking sportsman.

As he turned around again cocking the rifle, I hit the truck brakes. He sprawled forward into the dash. The rifle's front sight hit him in the mouth and removed the veneers from his front teeth. I took the Uzi away from him. He sat back, dripping blood from a split lip, looking dazed.

I threw the pickup into reverse.

"What the hell are you *doing*, Rawson?"

He spat out blood as I headed backward toward Mal Wolfgirl. Raoul Ortega, tall in the saddle, was only about fifty yards distant and closing. One of the lookalike pickup trucks had peeled away from the action around the Flying Fortress and was joining Ortega's chase.

He was back on the radio.

"Rawson? That is someone especial to you, no? I keel her first, then you, *cabrón*."

"What does it look like I'm doing?" I said to McQuarrie. "I'm going back for Mal. I promised her mother."

And still Mal Wolfgirl didn't seem to understand the danger she was in. Or else she was paralyzed by the light show and shooting carnival careening helter-skelter her way.

In spite of the pain from his bloody lip McQuarrie managed an ironic chuckle.

"You're going to put a werewolf in this truck? That's an old joke."

"Heard it. Mal may be a werewolf, but she's *my* werewolf."

McQuarrie had recovered from getting his teeth chipped. Or at least thought he was clearheaded.

"I'd like to find out how you're going to pull this off," he said. "But I think I should get off here."

Without haste he opened the door and put a foot out on the running board and jumped.

But he had misjudged the speed at which we were traveling. Also he jumped straight out instead of in the direction we were going. Momentum whirled him around twice in a running, stumbling attempt to maintain balance. The wind against him, with its velocity, might have kept him from nosing down in a flat sprawl. Instead he was sideswiped by Raoul Ortega's big flashy machine.

McQuarrie sat down hard and was getting up slowly when the oncoming pickup truck drove straight over him. Those massive chrome radiator guards can be lethal. Either the driver wasn't able to see McQuarrie through the swirling dust and with my six-pack of halogen lights full in his face, or his reflexes were a little slow after the happy hour preceding the *mal de lune*.

Ortega's motorcycle wobbled but stayed upright; he poured on the speed and shot up to the left side of my truck. I saw the shotgun in his right hand. I thought it was more to scare me than anything else but I tromped the brakes again and ducked. Half of the windshield turned into a blizzard above my head.

Cautious is as cautious does, Pym always liked to say.

The pickup trailing Ortega's Harley loomed when I glanced up. If the driver hadn't seen McQuarrie in time, there was no way he was going to miss a mirror image of his own vehicle squarely in his path. He veered hard left and straight into the wingtip of the Mitchell bomber, which took out the windshield, sheared through the cab, and demolished the smaller rear window, splattering the driver like a blueberry pie flung against a white tile wall and probably killing both of the shooters who had been standing and braced in the bed of the pickup.

Tonight's *mal de lune*, I thought in a giddy, near-hallucinatory moment, was officially FUBAR. For another instant I had a sense of World War II flyboys in their leather jackets and cocky flight caps lined up along the spine of their bomber and laughing indulgently, but that image disappeared when I was distracted by a bloom of light like a desert rose beneath the impaled pickup.

Fucked Up Beyond All Recognition, wasn't that what they used to say? I'd never been in a war, but this night's confrontation would do.

Raoul Ortega had accelerated past me following the buckshot-blowout of my windshield and was bearing down on Mal Wolfgirl. His left arm was raised and away from his body, shotgun extended.

Buckshot. Another sportsman.

The miserable bastard shot Mal Wolfgirl. In the back, from less than thirty feet away.

Mal went down in a cowering hairy bloody heap, but her head came up and her eyes blazed as she watched Ortega make a cautious wide sweep around her. Then he turned his sexy chromed superbike in her direction, a single bright eye lighting up Mal as she jerked her head toward him and red froth sprayed in the wind.

For a few seconds he sat on the Harley with one foot down, gunning the engine as if he dared her to come bounding after him. I don't think he was paying attention to me. He might have thought I was busy picking glass out of my eyeballs. Or bleeding to death.

When he lifted his foot and raised the shotgun again I screamed something no one could hear, yanked the big pickup around in a 180, and drove straight at him.

That kind of challenge Ortega didn't care for. He didn't like it that I had a gun too. When he saw the muzzle-wink and his headlight blew up, leaving him with only a few small running lights, he forgot about finishing off the wolfgirl and drove his bike between a torpedo bomber and a C-47 transport parked close to each other on the line, ducking low in the saddle to clear the right wing of the bomber.

I had no room to maneuver and took the same wing half off as I followed him, losing my rooflights. The flight line was quickly behind us; we were in terrain laced with arroyos hidden by manzanita and sagebrush, all of it so dry a spark from the exhaust pipe of either machine could ignite it. I glanced back once but didn't see Mal Wolfgirl. Maybe, as hurt as she had to be, instinct had made her seek shelter in the dark.

Both Ortega and I had power to spare. The pickup I drove was equipped for desert running. His Harley couldn't cope with the loose desert drybed for long. He was already enjoying a clumsy ride. He had to change his tactics or take a breakneck spill. And he had the shotgun.

We had traveled no more than half a mile into the full force of the harsh wind when he steered his bike down into a narrow arroyo. I couldn't follow. All I could do was block the arroyo at my end and hope that there was no way out for Ortega except on foot.

I killed the pickup's engine but kept the lights on. The wind slackened long enough for me to hear Miles Brenta coughing and moaning in the bed of the truck. I had been too busy for a while to give him any thought. It was a small miracle that bouncing around back there hadn't finished killing him.

I also heard werewolves, some distance behind me. A howl was answered by another even farther away. No surprise if the Hairballs on the loose already had attracted desert-dwelling rogues. I heard shouts, saw gunflashes along the flightline. The pickup that had driven into the Mitchell was a pyre, smoke rolling sky-high with the wind.

What I didn't hear was Ortega's Harley. With no way to drive out of the arroyo he'd shut the engine off. All I saw of the bike was a red speck of taillight some three hundred feet away and deep in the brush-thick arroyo.

The wind picked up again with its moaning sweep and dust devils like small tornadoes, but where I was crouched beside the truck the mesquite around me barely trembled. There was no movement in that part of the arroyo illuminated by the truck's headlights. From where I was with the blue-steel Uzi I could still make out the Harley's taillight.

Miles Brenta thumped in the bed of the truck and made a pathetic low noise that was almost like the yowl of a run-over animal.

"Well, *jefe*," Raoul Ortega said chummily on the CB radio, startling me with the nearness and clarity of his voice, "what we do now?"

I wondered if McQuarrie had loaded tracer rounds as the first feeds in the Uzi magazine: helpful for homing in on a loping Hairball in the darkness. Maybe I could have burned Ortega out of his end of the arroyo.

But I did nothing, only waited.

"But maybe you don't want to kill me," Ortega speculated. "Because, you know, I have the *amuleto* like you say. I don't mean she is with me now. But arrangements have been made. I go down, she goes down. And all the rest of them. The seesters. The Mission of Arroyo del Cobre. Soch a shame if that old place is destroyed one night. It have historical value, no?"

We both listened to the wind a little while longer.

"What am I worth to you dead, amigo? Nothing. The cost is too great. So why don't you back that truck up out of there and we go our separate way."

This time he didn't give me the chance to respond, if I had wanted to. The speculation was back in his voice.

"Or maybe you no in condition to drive. What a shame."

More than my physical self had taken a pounding during the last forty-eight hours. The sixth sense that had almost always looked after me was AWOL. I was crouched there like a dummy, eyes fixed on the taillight and picturing Ortega also sensibly crouched away from his machine with the cord of the CB mike stretched to its limit, shotgun in his other hand, waiting for his own instincts to plan his next move for him.

But handheld CBs were commonplace, particularly in areas where wristpacs lacked range, and it was more than likely Ortega had been chatting me up while circling slowly toward me with the wind in his face, shotgun ready.

I brought up the muzzle of the Uzi, turning at the same time. He spoke to me again, but not in his radio voice.

"*Buenas noches*. Put down the chatter gun."

I set the Uzi on the running board, otherwise not moving. I assumed he wanted to talk some more, enjoy his moment. Or I would have been dead before I knew he was there.

"*Mira me*," he said.

I let out a breath and looked up and around. He was standing in the aura of a sidelight on the truck, above me and about eight feet away. Both hands on his shotgun.

"Just leave Elena alone," I said, and added with a bitter taste in my mouth, "please."

I could see nothing of his face inside the protective hive of his headgear. What I saw reflected on the face shield was something he wouldn't have noticed with his head tilted down, his eyes fixed on me.

"*Por supuesto*," Ortega said graciously. "But your other one—*mucha mujer*. I will look her up. Take good care of her for you, *jefe*. So—now you can die."

He should have punctuated his last statement by blowing off my own helmeted head, but maybe he was enjoying himself too much. Or he wanted to hear me scream for mercy, the way some of the condemned will do. That would've been worth waiting a few extra moments for. The death scream.

Which turned out to be Ortega's.

The werewolf that was still partially Miles Brenta leaped from the bed of the truck and dragged Ortega to the ground. A load of buckshot put a hole in the door but above my head as I grabbed the Uzi. Ortega was getting to his feet, hurling the crippled wolf-thing away from him, when I trained the Uzi on his midsection and emptied the box. He never got off another shot.

The virus in the blood that Ortega had pumped into Miles

Brenta had only half done its work. There was hair and there was beast and there were the human eyes of a dying man as he got to his feet, a human broken arm dangling, fingers useless.

"My turn," he said. His voice calm, not pleading.

The Uzi was empty. I dropped it. And slowly reached for the 9-mil Sig on my belt.

I don't know how long I drove around the desert looking for Mal. But the sky was lightening in the east when I had a glimpse of a naked female body half hidden in sagebrush.

The wind had died down. I got out of the pickup and walked slowly toward her, saying her name. But she didn't respond until I put a hand on the back of her neck.

I took off the parka and dressed her in it. Then I sat on the ground holding her for a few minutes. ILC helicopters came and went in the distance. I watched them with sore eyes and thought about being alive. Dawn thoughts.

"It was so stupid!" Mal sobbed, clinging to me for what warmth I had to give her. "I thought it would be, you know, *fun* to be that big and powerful and scary. Most of my friends were already Lycans. But I don't want to be a werewolf anymore! Luvagod, isn't there something that somebody can *do*?"

I kissed a salty cold cheek, smoothed her hair back from her forehead. She shuddered in my arms, fetched a hopeless sigh, and closed her dreary blue eyes.

"I'm not giving up," I said.

I got to my feet with her; somebody else could have built a house in the time it took to pull that off. Mallory cried in pain and I was mindful of the double-aught silver pellets embedded more than skin-deep in her back.

Last of the Beverly Hills werewolves. I carried Mal to the battle-worn truck and laid her on her tummy on the backseat and drove slowly toward the pall of smoke above the old warplanes on the flight line. They were just a hazy vision now of what had been indomitable in an old war, in another time. But all wars ended, faded from memory. The latest war, against a tiny virus casting its malevolent spell from an unknown fortress deep in the brain, also would end. Because it had to.

I just didn't know how, or when.

25

At eight o'clock in the morning I dropped Mal Scarlett off at her mother's house in Beverly Hills. She was wearing church barrel–casual and old running shoes and was wobbly on her feet. But halfway up the walk, as the front door opened, Mal put a hand on my arm and looked up at me with a wan smile.

"I'll be okay the rest of the way."

She continued to the front steps. Ida Grace had come outside. I saw Duke in the foyer of the house, not looking too bad off.

All's well that ends well—until the next time, when it probably won't. So went my thoughts, but then it had been a long twenty-four hours and my mood demanded hot black coffee.

Mother and daughter looked at each other for a few moments. If either of them said anything I didn't hear. Then Ida put an arm around Mal to guide her into the house.

On the threshold Ida paused and looked back at me. There wasn't enough expression on her face for me to tell what was going through her mind.

Then she nodded.

Probably all the thanks I would ever get from Ida. It was enough.

Beatrice had dozed off in the front seat of the ILC Humvee

I had requisitioned at the *mal de lune* site. When I got in gingerly, feeling the ache of effort in most of my body parts, she opened her eyes.

"Nobody can say we don't have fun together," I said.

It didn't earn me a smile.

"I was thinking about those missing wolfmakers," she said. "There must be a way of tracking them. Give me a few hours on my computer and I'll locate them for you."

"I know you will," I said. "Meantime, how about coffee? A roll in the hay is optional, if I don't have to do the rolling."

Bea studied me critically. "How about a week in the hospital?"

"I hate hospitals. Okay, maybe a couple of stitches. I'll be good as—"

Bea looked incredulous. I saw a shine of tears before she turned her face away.

"Are you nuts? That is *not* brave. It's not being tough, either. It's just, it's dumb. You survived a helicopter crash and werewolves. You're bloody and you're hurt and being smartass about being hurt doesn't make you half the man you think you are!"

"Hey!" I said, surprised and maybe a little pleased by her outburst.

She looked at me again, wiping away tears.

"And I, I don't know what I'm going to do with you except—just—just keep on doing it!"

We looked at each other. Bea sniffed a couple of times.

"Does that make sense?" she said finally.

"Does to me," I said.

I leaned awkwardly toward her and kissed her. Except for the fact that I was, as she'd correctly pointed out, pretty well flogged and needing a bath and redolent of werewolf, Bea didn't seem to mind.

"I hope your mother will like me," she said.

"Which reminds me," I said.

Bea glanced at me.

"I'm entitled to a few weeks off. I'd better use most of them trying to locate Pym. If she could have come to me, by now she would have. Instead she was having conversations with Artie X. I need to know what that was all about."

"Unless Artie erased those e-mails, shouldn't be hard for me to—R?"

I put the Humvee in reverse and backed out of Ida Grace's driveway.

"What?"

"You look worried."

"I am. Because Pym may have made a discovery."

"Discovery? Do you mean—?

"Yeah. The Holy Grail. The cure for Lycan disease she's spent most of her adult life looking for."

"But why—"

"Go to Artie with it? Don't know. What I do know is that Pym has had failed trials and errors in the past. The bad news is, she was always too willing to use herself as a subject of preliminary trials."

We waited for the gates of the *minka* to open.

"Oh, no," Bea said softly.

I nodded.

"You can't cure what you don't have," I said.

I drove up to the house. Parked, took my hands off the wheel, and watched them tremble.

"So your mother can't come home again."

"Two ways. As ashes in a vase, or after she's finally found the means to change the fate of the rest of us poor benighted bastards."

I got down out of the Humvee and that was it, I couldn't take a step. So I just leaned against the side breathing like a foundered horse until Bea came up beside me, turned my head gently, and kissed me.

"When do we leave?" she said.

GLOSSARY

Acey-Deuce
Bisexual.

AUGIE (Augmented Galvanomagnetic Intercept Effector)
Used for werewolf deterrence.

Beefer
Bodyguard; any man vain about his physique.

Bitch Eye
Hostile look.

Black Dahls
Stimulants; uppers.

Bleat Blog
Internet gossip sites devoted to celebrities.

Bloodleggers
Dealers in black-market, frequently tainted blood.

Boneyard Shuffle
High-fashion show with ultrathin models.

Capone'd
Women wearing the male clothing of Prohibition-era gangsters.

Cold Dish
Stale gossip.

Coochputty
Birth-control chewing gum for Lycans.

Curb Roach
Teenage Lycan hooker.

Dead-Red
Assassination target.

Flogged
Tired to the point of exhaustion.

Frenzies
Stimulants; uppers.

Gas Attack
Any speech by a politician running for office.

Geekers
Very high-tech, as opposed to stylish, sunglasses. Used by ILC agents only.

Gold Certs
Bank-issued certificates redeemable 100 percent in gold.

Hairball
Slang term for werewolf.

Hairing-up
The process of becoming a werewolf.

Heavy Dupe
Excessive public relations drumbeating, usually with spin.

ILC
International Lycan Control.

Jesus Nut
Indispensable item that holds the rotors onto a helicopter's mast.

LUMO
For ***Lu***nar ***Mo***dule, referring to an injectable type of Snitcher.

Lycan
Any human being infected with the werewolf virus.

Mal de lune
Literally "moon sickness." In popular usage, a staged werewolf hunt.

Molochs
Crystal meth.

Mongo Flip
Aerobatic or gymnastic maneuver.

No Gal
For Nogales, capital of the ARIMEX border territory.

Observance, the
Full-moon period of about twenty-four hours during which the world locks down and rogue werewolves roam at will.

Off-Bloods
Persons who must change their blood at least twice a year to remain completely free of LC disease.

OOPs
Out-of-phase werewolf.

PHASR (Personnel Halting and Stimulation Response)
Pulse rifle used for werewolf deterrence.

Priority Hunk
Fabulous example of just about everything.

Privilege, the
Smart term for the rich city-state of Beverly Hills.

Scuff
Tough guy with an affinity for high fashion; also bouncer.

SECÜR
Proprietary name for popular antipsychotic found in everything from toothpaste to breakfast food. Just to get the day off to a good start.

Silvertip
Any bullet intended for defense against werewolves.

Skinnydip
Changing from a werewolf back to human form.

Slabbed
Killed; most often used in murder cases.

Snitcher or Snitch
ID and tranquilizer implant mandatory for Lycans.

Squantch
Marijuana.

Tink
Small-breasted woman.

TRAD (Taser Remote Area Denial)
Force field effective for repelling werewolves.

TQs
(From the Spanish, *tranquilo.*) The most effective drug for suppressing the hairing-up impulse in Lycans.

WEIR (Werewolf Identification and Records)
A division of ILC.

Whisper Tit
Popular name for the earpiece companion to the wristpac, so-called because of its shape.

Wingless Angel
Someone who commits suicide by jumping from a high place; an almost weekly occurrence in the Privilege.

Zippo
Any type of flamethrower used as defense against werewolves.

S0-AHR-930

Canadian Securities Course Volume 2

Prepared and published by

CSI

200 Wellington Street West, 15th Floor
Toronto, Ontario M5V 3C7

Telephone: 416.364.9130
Toll-free: 1.866.866.2601

Fax: 416.359.0486
Toll-free fax: 1.866.866.2660

www.csi.ca

Where leaders learn financial services.

Copies of this publication are for the personal use of properly registered students whose names are entered on the course records of CSI Global Education Inc. (CSI)®. This publication may not be lent, borrowed or resold. Names of individual securities mentioned in this publication are for the purposes of comparison and illustration only and prices for those securities were approximate figures for the period when this publication was being prepared.

Every attempt has been made to update securities industry practices and regulations to reflect conditions at the time of publication. While information in this publication has been obtained from sources we believe to be reliable, such information cannot be guaranteed nor does it purport to treat each subject exhaustively and should not be interpreted as a recommendation for any specific product, service, use or course of action. CSI assumes no obligation to update the content in this publication.

A Note About References to Third Party Materials:

There may be references in this publication to third party materials. Those third party materials are not under the control of CSI and CSI is not responsible for the contents of any third party materials or for any changes or updates to such third party materials. CSI is providing these references to you only as a convenience and the inclusion of any reference does not imply endorsement of the third party materials.

Notices Regarding This Publication:

This publication is strictly intended for information and educational use. Although this publication is designed to provide accurate and authoritative information, it is to be used with the understanding that CSI is not engaged in the rendering of financial, accounting or other professional advice. If financial advice or other expert assistance is required, the services of a competent professional should be sought.

In no event shall CSI and/or its respective suppliers be liable for any special, indirect, or consequential damages or any damages whatsoever resulting from the loss of use, data or profits, whether in an action of contract negligence, or other tortious action, arising out of or in connection with information available in this publication.

© 2008 CSI Global Education Inc.

All rights reserved. No part of this publication may be reproduced, stored in a retrieval system, or transmitted in any form by any means, electronic, mechanical, photocopying, recording, or otherwise, without the prior written permission of CSI Global Education Inc.

ISBN: 1-894289-65-x

First printing: 1997
Revised and reprinted: 2000, 2001, 2002, 2003, 2004, 2005, 2006, 2007, 2008

Copyright © 2008 by CSI Global Education Inc.

INTRODUCTORY COURSES

- Canadian Funds Course
- Canadian Insurance Course
- Canadian Securities Course™
- Conduct and Practices Handbook™
- CSI Prep Series™
- Investment Advisor Training Program
- Investment Representative Training
- New Entrants Course

COMPLIANCE AND TRADING

- Branch Managers Course
- Canadian Commodity Supervisors Exam
- Chief Compliance Officers Qualifying Examination
- Chief Financial Officers Qualifying Examination
- Options Supervisors Course 
- Partners, Directors and Senior Officers Course
- Trader Training Course

FINANCIAL PLANNING AND WEALTH MANAGEMENT

- Canadian Securities Course™
- Professional Financial Planning Course™
- Wealth Management Techniques™
- Wealth Management Essentials

CHARTERED PROFESSIONAL *STRATEGIC WEALTH*

- Building High Net Worth - Advanced Strategies for Accumulating and Preserving Wealth
- Managing High Net Worth - Advanced Strategies for Optimizing Retirement Income and Transferring Wealth
- The Strategic Wealth 360

RISK MANAGEMENT AND DERIVATIVES

- Derivatives Fundamentals Course™
- Energy Markets Risk Management Course
- Financial Markets Risk Management Course
- Futures Licensing Course
- Options Licensing Course
- Options Strategies Course
- Technical Analysis Course

PORTFOLIO MANAGEMENT

- Canadian Securities Course™
- Investment Management Techniques™ 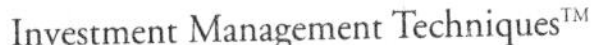
- Portfolio Management Techniques™

INSURANCE

- Canadian Insurance Course

CONTINUING EDUCATION

- Anti-Money Laundering
- Broker Liability
- Compliance Program
- Charts and Formations
- CPH for Industry Professionals
- Corporate Governance
- Covered Call Writing
- Estate Planning
- Ethics Module and Case Study Retail Version 
- Ethics Module and Case Study Institutional Version
- Exchange Traded Funds
- Fixed Income Investing
- Hedge Funds Essentials for Today's Financial Professional
- How Mutual Funds and Hedge Funds Use Derivatives
- Income Trusts
- Industry Trends
- Investor Confidence
- Portfolio Theory, Asset Allocation and Performance Measurement
- Principal-Protected Notes
- Quantitative Analysis
- Pre-Retirement Planning
- Retirement Planning
- Segregated Funds
- Single Stock Futures
- Socially Responsible Investing
- Trust Structures
- Understanding Margin: Benefits and Risks

DESIGNATIONS

Chartered Professional (Ch.P.) *Strategic Wealth*

Fellow of CSI (FCSI)™

Derivatives Market Specialist (DMS)

Canadian Investment Manager (CIM)™

Financial Management Advisor (FMA)

VOLUME 2

Contents

SECTION FIVE
INVESTMENT ANALYSIS

© CSI GLOBAL EDUCATION INC. (2008)

© CSI GLOBAL EDUCATION INC. (2008)

SECTION SIX
PORTFOLIO ANALYSIS

© CSI GLOBAL EDUCATION INC. (2008)

© CSI GLOBAL EDUCATION INC. (2008)

© CSI GLOBAL EDUCATION INC. (2008)

© CSI GLOBAL EDUCATION INC. (2008)

© CSI GLOBAL EDUCATION INC. (2008)

SECTION EIGHT

WORKING WITH THE CLIENT

© CSI GLOBAL EDUCATION INC. (2008)

© CSI GLOBAL EDUCATION INC. (2008)

© CSI GLOBAL EDUCATION INC. (2008)

SECTION FIVE

Investment Analysis

© CSI GLOBAL EDUCATION INC. (2008)

Chapter 13

Fundamental and Technical Analysis

© CSI GLOBAL EDUCATION INC. (2008)

13

Fundamental and Technical Analysis

CHAPTER OUTLINE

© CSI GLOBAL EDUCATION INC. (2008)

LEARNING OBJECTIVES

By the end of this chapter, you should be able to:

1. Compare and contrast fundamental, quantitative and technical analysis, and evaluate the three market theories explaining stock market behaviour.
2. Describe how the four macroeconomic factors affect investor expectations and the price of securities.
3. Analyze how industries are classified and explain how industry classifications impact a company's stock valuation.
4. Calculate and interpret the intrinsic value and the price-earnings ratio (P/E) of a stock using the dividend discount model (DDM).
5. Define technical analysis and describe the tools used in technical analysis.

THE ROLE OF INVESTMENT ANALYSIS

A great deal of information is available when making an investment decision. There is market and economic data, stock charts, industry and company characteristics, and a wealth of financial statistical data. The amount of this information can be overwhelming and, at the same time, can add clarity and perspective to the investment-making process.

Fortunately for investors and advisors, there are different branches of analysis which helps to organize the information. Some analysis focuses relatively narrowly on companies themselves, while some looks more broadly, using an international and market perspective. Our focus here is to gain a better understanding of how analysts use the information available to value a security and make a recommendation on its purchase or sale.

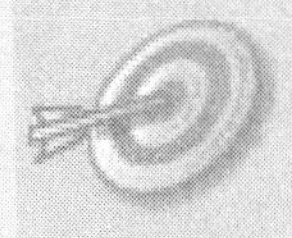

In the on-line Learning Guide for this module, complete the Getting Started activity.

Although these fundamental and technical analysis techniques are widely used and reported in the financial press, their use and interpretation is often misunderstood. An advisor or investor considering an investment based on an analyst's interpretation of these techniques, or on their own analysis, must have a clear understanding of what the techniques measure, how they are determined, and how they are interpreted.

For example, suppose you are considering an investment in the stock of a cyclical company and there are reports that an economic slowdown is imminent. What does that mean for the industry, the economy and your investment? This chapter will give you the necessary tools to answer those questions and others.

© CSI GLOBAL EDUCATION INC. (2008)

KEY TERMS

Advance-decline line
Blue chip
Continuation pattern
Contrarian investor
Cycle analysis
Cyclical industry
Cyclical stock
Defensive industry
Dividend Discount Model (DDM)
Economies of scale
Efficient Market Hypothesis
Elliott Wave Theory
Emerging growth industry
Fundamental analysis
Growth industry
Head-and-shoulders-formation
Industry rotation
Mature industry
Moving average
Moving Average Convergence-Divergence (MACD)
Neckline
Oscillator
Price-earnings ratio
Quantitative analysis
Random Walk Theory
Rational Expectations Hypothesis
Resistance level
Return on equity (ROE)
Reversal pattern
Sentiment indicator
Speculative industry
Support level

© CSI GLOBAL EDUCATION INC. (2008)

OVERVIEW OF ANALYSIS METHODS

Fundamental Analysis

Fundamental analysis involves assessing the short-, medium- and long-range prospects of different industries and companies. It involves studying capital market conditions and the outlook for the national economy and for the economies of countries with which Canada trades to shed light on securities' prices. In fact, fundamental analysis means studying everything, other than the trading on the securities markets, which can have an affect on a security's value: macroeconomic factors, industry conditions, individual company financial conditions, and qualitative factors such as management performance.

By far the most important single factor affecting the price of a corporate security is *the actual or expected profitability of the issuer.* Are its profits sufficient to service its debt, to pay current dividends, or to pay larger dividends? Fundamental analysis pays attention to a company's debt-equity ratio, profit margins, dividend payout, earnings per share, sales penetration, market share, interest, asset and dividend coverages, product or marketing innovation, and the quality of its management.

Quantitative Analysis

Quantitative analysis involves studying interest rates, economic variables, and industry or stock valuation using computers, databases, statistics and an objective, mathematical approach to valuation. In quantitative analysis, the analyst is looking for patterns and the reasons behind those patterns in order to identify and profit from anomalies in valuation. Quantitative methods can be applied in economics, fundamental analysis and technical analysis to measure factors that influence investment decisions.

The science of valuation requires an extensive use of computers and mathematical concepts, both of which have become increasingly common in economics and finance. Considerable time has been spent quantifying virtually everything in finance theory, including market psychology. Quantitative techniques often use statistics to determine the likelihood of a particular investment outcome.

One of the great advantages of using computers in quantitative analysis is their ability to store decades of information and to perform repetitive calculations on this information quickly. Quantitative research provides another way to produce better investment decisions by scientifically studying the factors that influence valuation.

Technical Analysis

Technical analysis is the study of historical stock prices and stock market behaviour to identify recurring patterns in the data. Because the process requires large amounts of information, it is often ignored by fundamental analysts, who find the process too cumbersome and time-consuming, or believe that "history does not repeat itself."

Technical analysts study price movements, trading volumes, and data on the number of rising and falling stock issues over time looking for recurring patterns that will allow them to predict

© CSI GLOBAL EDUCATION INC. (2008)

future stock price movements. Technical analysts believe that by studying the "price action" of the market, they will have better insights into the emotions and psychology of investors. They contend that because most investors fail to learn from their mistakes, identifiable patterns exist.

Investors who favour technical analysis find that this approach makes better sense of market gyrations than fundamental analysis alone. They point to the market crash of 1987, when stock markets around the world fell by 20% to 40% as proof that there is no true value for a stock, and that investors do not always act rationally.

In times of uncertainty, other factors such as mass investor psychology and the influence of program trading also affect market prices. This can make the technical analyst's job much more difficult. Mass investor psychology may cause investors to act irrationally. Greed can force prices to rise to a level far higher than warranted by anticipated earnings. Many feel greed was the underlying motivation for the phenomenal rise in prices of Internet or "dot-com" stocks. Conversely, investor uncertainty can cause investors to overreact to news and sell quickly, causing prices to drop suddenly. Program trading can trigger mass selling of stocks, in a way that is unrelated to the expected earnings of the stocks.

Market Theories

Three theories have been developed to explain the behaviour of stock markets.

The **efficient market hypothesis** assumes that profit-seeking investors in the marketplace react quickly to the release of new information. As new information about a stock appears, investors reassess the intrinsic value of the stock and adjust their estimation of its price accordingly. Therefore, at any given time, a stock's price fully reflects all available information and represents the best estimate of the stock's true value.

The **random walk theory** postulates that new information concerning a stock is disseminated randomly over time. Therefore, price changes are random and bear no relation to previous price changes. If this is true, past price changes contain no useful information about future price changes because any developments affecting the company have already been reflected in the current price of the stock.

The **rational expectations hypothesis** assumes that people are rational and make intelligent economic decisions after weighing all available information. It also assumes people have access to necessary information and will use it intelligently in their own self-interest. Past mistakes can be avoided by using the information to anticipate change.

The efficient market hypothesis, the random walk theory and the rational expectations hypothesis all suggest that stock markets are efficient. This means that at any time, a stock's price is the best available estimate of its true value.

Many studies have been conducted to test these theories. Some evidence supports the theories, while other theories support market inefficiencies. For example, it seems unlikely that:

- New information is available to everyone at the same time;
- All investors react immediately to all information in the same way; and
- All investors make accurate forecasts and correct decisions.

© CSI GLOBAL EDUCATION INC. (2008)

If all investors reacted to new information in the same way and at the same time, no investor should be able to outperform others. However, there have been times when investors have been able to consistently outperform index averages like the S&P/TSX Composite Index. This evidence suggests that capital markets are not entirely efficiently priced.

For example, investors do not react in the same way to the same information. One investor may buy a security at a certain price hoping to receive income or make a capital gain. Another investor may sell the same security at the same price because that investor simply needs the cash at that moment. Also, not everyone can make accurate forecasts and correct valuation decisions. Finally, mass investor psychology and greed may also cause investors to act irrationally. Even when investors do act rationally, thorough stock valuation can be a complex task.

Since stock markets are often inefficient, a better understanding of how industry factors, company factors, and macroeconomic factors influence stock valuation should lead to better investment results. These three factors all help to determine changes in interest rates and in the actual or expected profitability of companies. In the following section we examine some pricing models based on these factors.

FUNDAMENTAL MACROECONOMIC ANALYSIS

Many factors affect investor expectations and therefore play a part in determining the price of securities. These factors can be grouped under the following categories: fiscal policy, monetary policy, international factors and business cycles.

Sudden unpredictable events can affect – favourably or unfavourably – the Canadian economy and the prices of securities. Such events include international crises such as war, unexpected election results, regulatory changes, technological innovation, debt defaults, and dramatic changes in the prices of important agricultural, metal and energy commodities. Many commodity price swings can be predicted by examining supply/demand conditions. Other price changes may not be easy to predict because they depend on price-setting agreements or on the action of cartels such as the Organization of Petroleum Exporting Countries (OPEC), which sets oil prices.

The Fiscal Policy Impact

The two most important tools of fiscal policy are levels of government expenditures and taxation. They are important to market participants because they affect overall economic performance and influence the profitability of individual industries. They are usually disclosed in federal and provincial budgets.

TAX CHANGES

By changing tax levels, governments can alter the spending power of individuals and businesses. An increase in sales or personal income tax leaves individuals with less disposable income, which curtails their spending; a reduction in tax levels increases net personal income and allows them to spend more.

© CSI GLOBAL EDUCATION INC. (2008)

Corporations are similarly affected by tax changes. Higher taxes on profits, generally speaking, reduce the amount businesses can pay out in dividends or spend on expansion. Increases in corporate taxes also limit companies' incentive to expand by lowering after-tax profit levels. On the other hand, a reduction in corporate taxes gives companies an incentive to expand.

Several factors limit the effectiveness of fiscal policy. One is the lengthy time lag required to get parliamentary approval for tax legislation. There is also a lag between the time fiscal action is taken and the time the action affects the economy. Also, politicians are not always able to change tax levels when conditions warrant. Although easing fiscal policy through reducing taxes is a highly popular move with voters, the introduction of restraint through increased taxation is very unpopular.

GOVERNMENT SPENDING

Governments can affect aggregate spending in the economy by increasing or decreasing their own spending on goods, services and capital programs. However, public spending seldom starts or stops on short notice. Planning periods are long, budget procedures are slow, and there are many delays before any capital construction begins.

Some fiscal policy measures are intended to help certain sectors of the economy. For example, tax incentives have been used to stimulate the housing and film production industries. Import quotas and tariffs have been used to shield domestic shoe, clothing and automobile producers from foreign competition. Sales taxes have been temporarily reduced to spur the sales of domestic manufacturers of cars and consumer durable goods.

Fiscal policies can also be designed to achieve government policy goals. For example, the dividend tax credit and the exemption from tax of a portion of capital gains were designed to encourage greater share ownership of Canadian companies by Canadians.

Savings by individuals can be encouraged by measures such as Registered Retirement Savings Plans. Such policies increase the availability of cash for investments, thereby increasing the demand for securities.

On the simplest level, an increase in government spending stimulates the economy in the short run, while a cutback in spending has the opposite effect. Conversely, tax increases lower consumer spending and business profitability, while tax cuts boost profits and common share prices and thereby spur the economy.

GOVERNMENT DEBT

Up until the later part of the 1990s, most Western governments accumulated massive debts and continued to add to these annually with deficit budgets. In Canada, this trend has reversed in recent years. After peaking in 1996-97, net Canadian federal debt is actually declining – both in absolute terms and, more importantly, as a percentage of Gross Domestic Product.

Today, consumer debt is at record-high levels as consumers have been spending more and saving less. This could have the long-term effect of increasing interest rates and dampening future economic growth.

The main problem with a large government debt is that it restricts both fiscal and monetary policy options. Fiscal and monetary policy choices affect the general level of interest rates, the rate of economic growth and the rate of corporate profit growth, and all of them affect the valuation of stocks. With high levels of government and consumer indebtedness, the government's ability to reduce taxes or increase government spending is impaired.

© CSI GLOBAL EDUCATION INC. (2008)

The Monetary Policy Impact

It is the responsibility of the Bank of Canada to maintain the external value of the Canadian dollar and encourage real, sustainable economic growth by keeping inflation low, stable and predictable. The Bank will take corrective action if these goals are threatened, that is, it will change the rate of monetary growth and encourage interest rates to reflect the change. If, during a period of economic expansion, demand for credit grows and prices move upwards too quickly, the Bank of Canada will try to lessen the pressure by restraining the rate of growth of money and credit. This usually leads to higher short-term interest rates. On the other hand, if the economy appears to be slowing down, the Bank of Canada may pursue an easier monetary policy that increases the money supply and the availability of credit, leading to lower short-term interest rates.

Changes in monetary policy affect interest rates and corporate profits, the two most important factors affecting the prices of securities. Therefore, it is important to understand Bank of Canada policy and how successful it is in achieving its aims. At times, perhaps more often in the United States than in Canada, market participants try to gauge the impact of each piece of economic news on future Federal Reserve Board policy. Rumours about likely Federal Reserve action also influence expectations and therefore the prices of securities.

MONETARY POLICY AND ACCUMULATED DEBT LEVELS

Monetary policy has always played a crucial role in economic growth. The significance of monetary policy has also increased as government indebtedness has restricted fiscal policy. Although some observers have argued that changes in monetary policy are less visible in terms of their effect on interest rates, this is probably not true. In fact, the growth in accumulated government debt has made it even more important to understand the interaction between short-term interest rates (such as bank rates) and long-term interest rates (represented by long-term bond yields). The interaction between short-term interest rates set by the central bank and long-term rates in the bond market is an explicit indication of changing monetary policy.

Since monetary policy tends to influence short-term interest rates and interest rates tend to influence the Canadian dollar, these issues are treated as monetary policy factors. It is crucial therefore, to understand how both the currency market and the bond market influence monetary policy.

When Canada offers foreign investors higher real interest rates than other countries, it is because Canada is trying to stabilize or improve the value of the Canadian dollar. Higher real rates to attract capital and increased currency volatility are two effects of relying on foreigners to finance a substantial portion of a country's increasing government debt.

MONETARY POLICY AND THE BOND MARKET

Throughout the 1970s and 1980s, the growth in accumulated debt created a massive U.S. and Canadian bond market. When economic growth begins to accelerate, bond yields rise rapidly, thereby tempering higher inflation. If the U.S. Federal Reserve does nothing to calm the bond market's fear of inflation, then bond yields may soar, possibly leading to a crisis in debt markets affecting trillions of dollars of debt.

As a result, the Federal Reserve must raise short-term interest rates to slow economic growth and contain inflationary pressures. This may lead to a more moderate economic growth rate or even a growth recession (a temporary slowdown in economic growth that does not lead to

© CSI GLOBAL EDUCATION INC. (2008)

a full recession). If U.S. long-term rates fall while short-term rates rise, then the bond market temporarily signals its approval of the degree of economic slowing.

For example, if the Federal Reserve raises short-term interest rates to slow economic growth and bond yields fall simultaneously, reflecting the perceived success of this policy, then the Federal Reserve has maintained the balance between economic growth and the needs of the bond market.

During the next twenty years, debtor nations will be trying to expand their economies so that their levels of accumulated debts become smaller by comparison. Therefore, central bank monetary policy walks a fine line and investor confidence is crucial. Because equities compete directly with the level of bond yields, stocks will be affected by the bond market for at least the next ten to twenty years.

MONETARY POLICY AND THE YIELD CURVE

When long-term bond yields fall while short-term rates rise, this is called an inverting or a tilting of the yield curve. It suggests a temporary reprieve from short-term interest rate pressure and less competition for equities from the level of bond yields. The process is as follows:

- Rapidly rising bond yields cause a collapse in bond prices.
- As short-term interest rates rise, the rate at which bond yields increase slows down.
- As this rise in short-term rates continues, the economy usually slows, bonds begin to stabilize and briefly fall less than equities. This is due to the fact that a slowing of economic growth benefits bonds at the expense of stocks.
- Suddenly, with each short-term interest rate increase, the long-term rate begins to fall. This is crucial evidence that the bond market is satisfied with the slowing of economic growth.

Strong evidence exists to show that the S&P/TSX Composite Index and S&P 500 are sensitive to yield curve tilting. A decline in long-term rates not only reduces competition between equities and bonds, it may also result in lower short-term rates. Less upward short-term rate pressure relative to the prevailing market return on equity (ROE) growth is, on the whole, good for stocks. On the other hand, higher real bond yields over time increase the degree of competition between bonds and equities and slowly undermine equity markets. A tilting yield curve is, however, very different from periods in which the whole yield curve is falling, as it does in the late stages of a recession.

The Flow of Funds Impact

The flow of funds is important to stock valuation. When the relative valuation of stocks and bonds or stocks and T-bills changes, capital flows from one asset class to the other. These flows are determined largely by shifts in the demand for stocks and bonds on the part of Canadian retail and institutional investors and of foreign investors. These shifts are caused largely by changes in interest rate levels. However, understanding why these shifts occur can be important to determining if a rise or fall in stock market levels is sustainable.

NET PURCHASES OF CANADIAN EQUITY MUTUAL FUNDS

Net purchases of Canadian equity mutual funds influence the TSX. Since falling interest rates tend to improve the value of stocks relative to bonds, equity mutual fund purchases should rise as interest rates fall. Figure 13.1 illustrates that, for the most part, this has generally proven to be true. However, the figure also shows that between 2000 and 2002, both T-bill yields and net purchases of mutual funds fell. This irregularity is attributed to the uncertainty caused by the

© CSI GLOBAL EDUCATION INC. (2008)

prolonged bear market beginning in 2000 that drove retail investors out of the market, causing net purchases of Canadian equity mutual funds to fall despite the fall in T-bill yields. The net purchase of equity funds recovered in 2003 and have recorded strong increase from 2004 onwards.

FIGURE 13.1 91-DAY T-BILL YIELD VS. NET PURCHASES OF CANADIAN EQUITY MUTUAL FUNDS – 1990 TO 2007

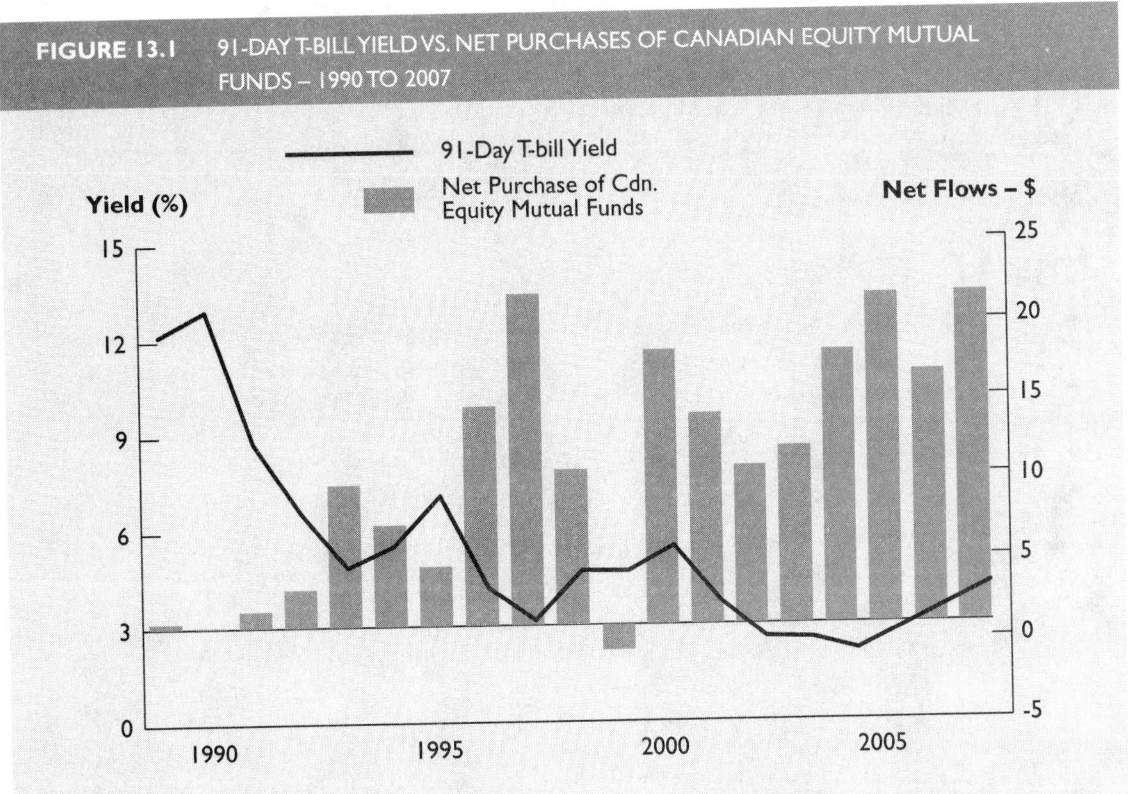

Sources: Bank of Canada website, Banking and Financial Statistics, February 2008; Investment Funds Institute of Canada website.

NON-RESIDENT NET PURCHASES

Another factor that influences the direction of markets is new demand by foreign investors for Canada's stocks and bonds. Although this demand can help sustain a stock market rise or decline, it lags behind other changes. Non-resident net purchases tend to increase after a rise in the market and tend to persist even after it starts to fall.

Non-resident net purchases of stocks are largely determined by the currency trend and the market trend, which are, in turn, affected strongly by changes in interest rates and, therefore, by changes in monetary policy. However, foreign investors still tend to view an appreciating market and a strengthening currency as good reasons to buy that country's stocks.

The Inflation Impact

In North America, from 1950 to 1970, the annual increase in the inflation rate, as measured by changes in the Consumer Price Index (CPI), was seldom regarded as a problem. The average annual increase in the two decades before the mid-1960s was less than 2.5%, with periodic fluctuations coinciding with variations in the business cycle. Figure 13.2 shows that between 1978 and 1982, inflation was higher than in any other period in history, averaging 10.3% a year.

© CSI GLOBAL EDUCATION INC. (2008)

Inflation fell dramatically after 1982 and then again after 1992, both instances largely the result of monetary policy actions of the Bank of Canada. Over the last several years, inflation in Canada has remained within historically low levels.

FIGURE 13.2 CANADIAN CONSUMER PRICE INDEX (CPI) ANNUAL PERCENTAGE CHANGE 1965 TO 2007

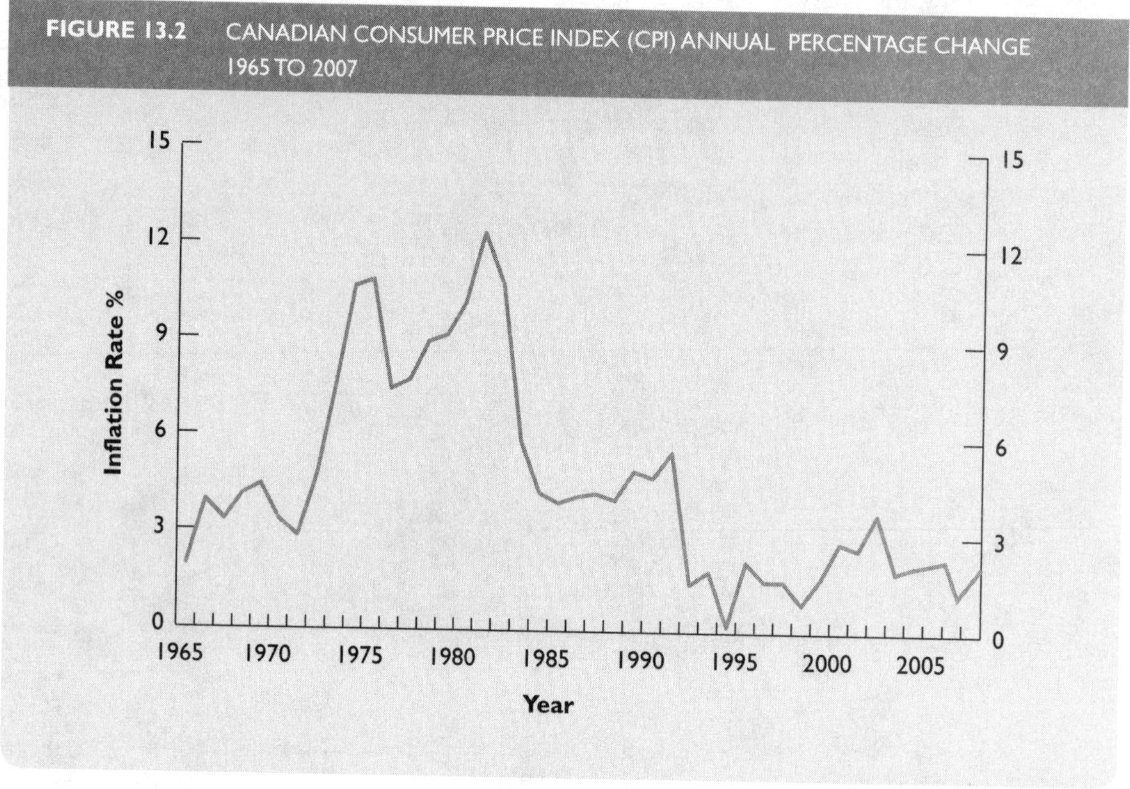

Inflation creates widespread uncertainty and lack of confidence in the future. These factors tend to result in higher interest rates, lower corporate profits, and lower price-earnings multiples. There is an inverse relationship between the rate of inflation and price-earnings multiples.

Inflation also means higher inventory and labour costs for manufacturers. These increases must be passed on to consumers in higher prices if manufacturers are to maintain their profitability. But higher costs cannot be passed on indefinitely; buyer resistance eventually develops. The resulting squeeze on corporate profits is reflected in lower common share prices.

FUNDAMENTAL INDUSTRY ANALYSIS

It has often been suggested that industry and company profitability has more to do with industry structure than with the product that an industry sells. Industry structure results from the strategies that companies pursue relative to their competition. Companies pursue strategies that they feel will give them a sustainable competitive advantage and lead to long-term growth. Pricing strategies and company cost structures affect not just long-term growth, but the volatility of sales and earnings. Therefore, industry structure affects a company's stock valuation. It is a framework that can easily be applied to virtually every industry. Many investors and IAs rely on research departments and other sources of information on industry structure.

© CSI GLOBAL EDUCATION INC. (2008)

Classifying Industries by Product or Service

Most industries are identified by the product or service they provide. For example, the S&P/TSX Composite Index classifies stocks into 10 major sectors based on the Global Industry Classification Standard (GICS). The U.S. market has about 90 different industry groups. However, an astute investor can understand the competitive forces within an industry by classifying industries based on their prospects for growth and their degree of risk. These two factors help determine stock values.

ESTIMATING GROWTH

The initial approach is to study an industry's reported revenues and unit volume sales over the last several years, preferably over more than one business cycle. Three basic questions must be asked:

1. How does the growth in sales compare with the rate of growth in nominal Gross Domestic Product (GDP)?
2. How does the rate of change in *real* GDP compare with the industry's rate of change in unit volumes?
3. How does the industry's price index compare with the overall rate of inflation?

By extending this approach to all companies in the same industry, it is possible to assess how effectively any one company is competing. For example, is the company acquiring a growing share of a growing industry, a growing share of a stable industry, a growing share of a declining industry or a declining share of a declining industry?

Furthermore, a company's revenues result from a combination of the prices they charge and the volume of unit sales. Revenue growth may result from higher prices or increased sales volume. Is recent revenue growth improving? How stable are prices or volume? The degree of stability is important in understanding the degree of investment risk and the possible timing of the investment during a business cycle.

LAWS OF SURVIVORSHIP

In theory, all industries exhibit a life cycle characterized by initial or emerging growth, rapid growth, maturity and decline. However, the length of each stage varies from industry to industry and from company to company. For example, the entire railway industry life cycle from its beginnings to its present maturity or decline is more than 150 years. Some high-technology industries have gone through a complete life cycle in a few years or even a few months.

Each stage in the industry life cycle affects the relationship between a firm's pricing strategies and its unit cost structure, as sales volume grows or declines. For example, the biotechnology industry is still relatively new. Recent technological breakthroughs have created opportunities for high profits and high profit margins. On the other hand, the steel industry has been in operation for many years and is in the mature to declining stage of its life cycle. Growth has slowed and competition has forced prices down, to the point at which some competing steel companies have been forced out of business.

Often, as the size of a market increases, a decline in unit costs occurs due to **economies of scale**. These may result from experience gained in production or volume price discounts for raw materials used in production. A change in unit costs may affect pricing strategies aimed at gaining market share, which in turn determines profit margins, earnings and long-term growth. The lowest cost

© CSI GLOBAL EDUCATION INC. (2008)

producer in an industry is best able to withstand intense price competition, either by pricing its product to maximize profits or setting prices at low levels to keep potential competitors from entering the business.

Since companies constantly strive to establish a sustainable competitive advantage, a firm usually becomes either:

- A low-cost producer capable of withstanding price competition and otherwise generating the highest possible profit margins; or
- A producer of a product that has real or perceived differences from existing products. These differences may make it possible to achieve higher profit margins while avoiding intense price competition.

Often some smaller market segments or niches are left unserviced by firms focusing on either of these strategies. These niches may be filled by smaller, specialized companies, known as niche players.

The competitive landscape is constantly changing because new investment capital always tends to flow to industries that have above-average returns. New sources of competition tend to lower profit margins. Furthermore, capital usually moves away from industries where returns are low, particularly if rates of return are expected to stay below the level of relatively risk-free returns such as T-bill rates. These competitive forces are the basic laws of survivorship and assure that rates of return move toward average levels over time.

Classifying Industries by Stage of Growth

EMERGING GROWTH INDUSTRIES

New products or services are being developed at all times to meet society's needs and demands. The transportation industry is an example of companies and industries moving from a stage of growth to maturity and then being faced with new competition from emerging businesses. For example, railways had to face competition, first from cars, trucks and buses, and then from the growth of airlines. Today, rapid innovation is particularly evident in software and hardware development in the computer industry.

Emerging growth industries may not always be directly accessible to equity investors if privately owned companies dominate the industry, or if the new product or service is only one activity of a diversified corporation.

Emerging industries usually demonstrate certain financial characteristics. For example, a new company or industry may be unprofitable at first, although future prospects may appear promising. Large start-up investments may even lead to negative cash flows. It may not be possible to predict which companies will ultimately survive in the new industry.

GROWTH INDUSTRIES

A **growth industry** is one in which sales and earnings are consistently expanding at a faster rate than most other industries. Companies in these industries are referred to as growth companies and their common shares as growth stocks. A growth company should have an above-average rate of earnings on invested capital over a period of several years. It should also be possible for the company to continue to achieve similar or better earnings on additional invested capital. The

© CSI GLOBAL EDUCATION INC. (2008)

company should show increasing sales in terms of both dollars and units, coupled with a firm control of costs.

Growth companies often have able and aggressive managements that are willing to take risks in their use of capital. Many growth companies, especially those in the United States, tend to spend heavily on research to develop new products. During the rapid growth period, the companies that survive lower their prices as their cost of production declines and competition intensifies. This leads to growth in profits. Cash flow may or may not remain negative. Growth stocks typically maintain above-average growth over several years and growth is expected to continue.

Growth companies often finance much of their expansion using retained earnings. This means that they do not pay out large amounts in dividends. However, investors are willing to pay more for securities that promise growth of capital. In other words, growth securities are characterized by relatively high price-earning ratios and low dividend yields. Growth companies also have an aboveaverage risk of a sharp price decline if the marketplace comes to believe that future growth will not meet expectations.

MATURE INDUSTRIES

Industry maturity is characterized by a dramatic slowing of growth to a rate that more closely matches the overall rate of economic growth. Both earnings and cash flow tend to be positive, but within the same industry, it is more difficult to identify differences in products between companies. Therefore, price competition increases, profit margins usually fall, and companies may expand into new businesses with better prospects for growth. Where consumer goods are concerned, product brand names, patents and copyrights become more important in reducing price competition.

Mature industries usually experience slower, more stable growth rates in sales and earnings. The reference to more stable growth does not suggest that they are immune from the effects of a recession. However, during recessions, stable growth companies usually demonstrate a decline in earnings that is less than that of the average company. Companies in the mature stage usually have sufficient financial resources to weather difficult economic conditions.

In general, during recessions, the share prices of mature industries fall less than an index like the S&P/TSX Composite Index. However, their share prices are not immune from declining. For example, over the last 30 years, there were six prolonged declines in stock market prices. The average length of these declines was about 11 months. During these prolonged declines, the S&P/TSX Composite Index recorded an average price decline of 15.1%. By comparison, a broadly defined basket of mature industries fell about 11.9%, while more economically sensitive stocks fell about 17.9%.

DECLINING INDUSTRIES

As industries move from the stable to the declining stage, they tend to grow at rates comparable to overall economic growth rate, or they stop growing and begin to decline. **Declining industries** produce products for which demand has declined because of changes in technology, an inability to compete on price, or changes in consumer tastes. Cash flow may be large, because there is no need to invest in new plant and equipment. At the same time, profits may be low.

© CSI GLOBAL EDUCATION INC. (2008)

Classifying Industries by Competitive Forces

Michael Porter, in his book *Competitive Advantage: Creating and Sustaining Superior Performance*, described five basic competitive forces that determine the attractiveness of an industry and the changes that can drastically alter the future growth and valuation of companies within the industry.

1. The ease of entry for new competitors to that industry: Companies choose to enter an industry depending on the amount of capital required, opportunities to achieve economies of scale, the existence of established distribution channels, regulatory factors and product differences.
2. The degree of competition between existing firms: This depends on the number of competitors, their relative strength, the rate of industry growth, and the extent to which products are unique (rather than simply ordinary commodities).
3. The potential for pressure from substitute products: Other industries may produce similar products that compete with the industry's products.
4. The extent to which buyers of the product or service can put pressure on the company to lower prices: This depends largely on buyers' sensitivity to price.
5. The extent to which suppliers of raw materials or inputs can put pressure on the company to pay more for these resources; these costs affect profit margins or product quality.

In the final analysis, companies can thrive only if they meet customers' needs. Therefore, profit margins can be large only if customers receive enough perceived value.

Classifying Industries by Stock Characteristics

Industries can be broadly classified as either **cyclical** or **defensive**. Few, if any, industries are immune from the adverse effects of an overall downturn in the business cycle, but the term *cyclical* applies to industries in which the effect on earnings is most pronounced.

CYCLICAL INDUSTRIES

Most cyclical S&P/TSX Composite Index companies are large international exporters of commodities such as lumber, nickel, copper or oil. These industries are sensitive to global economic conditions, swings in the prices of international commodities markets, and changes in the level of the Canadian dollar. When business conditions are improving, earnings tend to rise dramatically. Interest expenses on the debt of cyclical industries can accentuate these swings in earnings. In general, cyclical industries fall into three main groups:

- *commodity basic cyclical*, such as forest products, mining, and chemicals
- *industrial cyclical*, such as transportation, capital goods, and basic industries (steel, building materials)
- *consumer cyclical*, such as merchandising companies and automobiles

The energy and gold industries are also cyclical, but tend to demonstrate slightly different cyclical patterns.

Most cyclical industries benefit from a declining Canadian dollar, since this makes their exportable products cheaper for international buyers. However, the rate of expansion or contraction in the U.S. business cycle is still the single greatest influence in determining the profitability of cyclical Canadian companies. The currency is an important secondary factor.

© CSI GLOBAL EDUCATION INC. (2008)

DEFENSIVE INDUSTRIES

These industries have relatively stable ROE. Since defensive industries tend to do relatively well during recessions, this category includes blue-chip and income stocks. These are actually overlapping categories. For example, the term **blue-chip** denotes shares of top investment quality companies, which maintain earnings and dividends through good times and bad. This record usually reflects a dominant market position, strong internal financing and effective management.

In both the United States and Canada, some consumer stocks have generated such stable long-term growth that they are considered defensive. However, a blue-chip stock offers no guarantee of continued performance; company fortunes can and do change. For example, the U.S. publishing industry was once considered blue-chip until industry maturity led to a decline in stock prices. The utility industry, however, would be considered a defensive blue-chip industry.

Many investors consider shares of the major Canadian banks to be blue-chip industries. However, banks are also typically high-yielding stocks (that is, income stocks) and are sensitive to interest rates. As interest rates rise, banks must raise the rate they pay on deposits to attract funds. At the same time, a large part of their revenue is derived from mortgages with fixed interest rates. The result is a profit squeeze when interest rates rise. Bank stock prices are therefore sensitive to changes in the level of interest rates and particularly the level of long bond yields. Utility industry stocks also tend to be sensitive to interest rates, because they tend to carry large amounts of debt.

SPECULATIVE INDUSTRIES

Although all investment in common shares involves some degree of risk because of ever-changing stock market values, the word *speculative* is usually applied to industries (or shares) in which the risk and uncertainty are unusually high due to a lack of definitive information.

Emerging industries are often considered speculative. The profit potential of a new product or service attracts many new companies and initial growth may be rapid. Inevitably, however, a shakeout occurs and many of the original participants are forced out of business as the industry consolidates and a few companies emerge as the leaders. The success of these leaders in weathering the developmental period may result from better management, financial planning, products or services, or marketing. Only an experienced analyst should try to select the companies that will emerge as dominant forces in a fledgling industry.

The term speculative can also be used to describe any company, even a large one, if its shares are treated as speculative. For example, shares of growth companies can be bid up to high multiples of estimated earnings per share as investors anticipate continuing exceptional growth. If, for any reason, investors begin to doubt these expectations, the price of the stock will fall. In this case, investors are "speculating" on the likelihood of continued future growth which may, in fact, not materialize. The current interest in wireless technology stocks is a good example. Companies like Research in Motion have seen their shares grow exponentially – by more than 1000% during 1999, only to see them plummet by 44% in one day in April 2000.

RETURN ON EQUITY (ROE)

To compare cyclical and defensive industries, it is important to understand the concept of **return on equity (ROE)**. This ratio is important to shareholders because it reflects the profitability of their capital in the business. Return on total equity is calculated using the following formula:

$$\frac{\text{Net earnings (before extraordinary items)}}{\text{Total equity}} \times 100$$

© CSI GLOBAL EDUCATION INC. (2008)

To calculate return on common equity only, subtract preferred dividends from net earnings and divide by common equity.

Analysts often track the ROE of an industry in which they are interested, as well as the ROE of the S&P/TSX Composite Index, in order to establish benchmarks for the companies within the industry. As a rule, the ROE of a defensive industry typically varies by about a third during a single business cycle. For cyclical industries, if the ROE of the S&P/TSX Composite Index varies by about 55%, the ROE of a cyclical industry will vary by at least 100%.

The variability in S&P/TSX Composite Index ROE generally reflects the cyclical industries within the S&P/TSX Composite Index. During economic downturns, defensive industries also demonstrate falling ROE, but their ROE falls less dramatically than those of cyclical industries. During economic upturns and periods of prolonged economic growth, the ROE of defensive industries tends not to rise as much as that of cyclical industries.

Complete the on-line activity associated with this section.

Defensive industries tend to outperform cyclical industries during recessions. Because the ROE of a cyclical industry falls faster than the ROE of a defensive industry during recessions, cyclical stock prices also fall faster. Therefore, stocks with a stable ROE demonstrate defensive price characteristics. However, during periods of sustained economic growth, the superior growth in the ROE of cyclical industries tends to produce superior price performance in those industries. This is one of the basic factors influencing a pattern of alternating industry leadership during a business cycle. This pattern is referred to as industry rotation and the pattern is used by portfolio managers.

FUNDAMENTAL VALUATION MODELS

Dividend Discount Model

The widely used **dividend discount model** (**DDM**) illustrates, in a simple way, how companies with stable growth are priced, at least in theory. The model relates a stock's current price to the present value of all expected future dividends into the indefinite future.

In Chapter 7, we showed you how to calculate the value of a bond – the present value of the coupon payments plus the present value of the principal payment at maturity. The dividend discount model assumes that there will be an indefinite stream of dividend payments, whose present values can be calculated. It also assumes that these dividends will grow at a constant rate (g – the growth rate in the formula).

The discount rate used is the market's required or expected rate of return for that type of investment. We can think of the required rate of return as the return that compensates investors for investing in that stock, given its perceived riskiness. The mathematical formula that represents this model is:

$$\text{Price} = \frac{\text{Div}_1}{r - g}$$

© CSI GLOBAL EDUCATION INC. (2008)

Where:

Price is calculated as the current intrinsic value of the stock in question

Div_1 is the expected dividend paid out by the company in one year

r is the required rate of return on the stock

g is the assumed constant growth rate for dividends

It is technically incorrect to assume that r in the denominator is equal to the general level of interest rates or that g is simply equal to growth in corporate profits. However, these simplifying assumptions make it possible to illustrate how changes in interest rates and corporate profits affect stock price valuation during a business cycle. There are other, more complex formulas that accommodate changing dividends and changing growth rates.

Although the dividend discount model has many practical limitations, it is a useful way to think of stock valuation.

EXAMPLE: ABC Company is expected to pay a $1 dividend next year. It has a constant long-term growth rate (g) of 6% and a required return (r) of 9%. Based on these inputs, the DDM will price ABC at a value of:

$$\text{Price} = \frac{Div_1}{r-g} = \frac{\$1}{0.09-0.06} = \$33.33$$

The DDM tells us that, based on the expected dividend, the required return and the growth rate of dividends, the stock has an intrinsic value of $33.33. We can interpret the DDM in the following way: If ABC is selling for $25 in the market, the stock is considered undervalued because it is selling below its intrinsic value. Alternatively, if ABC is selling for $40, the stock is considered overvalued because it is selling above its intrinsic value.

The true value of an investment should be equal to the present value of all future cash flows that accrue to the investor. If the only cash flows are dividends, then:

$$\text{Price} = \frac{Div_1}{(1+r)^1} + \frac{Div_2}{(1+r)^2} + \ldots + \frac{Div_\infty}{(1+r)^\infty}$$

Where:

r = discount rate

However, this is an oversimplification, since future stock dividends are not predictable. Furthermore, a stock does not have a defined maturity, like a bond.

Using the Price-Earnings Ratio

The dividend discount model also allows an investor to estimate the basic price-earnings (P/E) ratio, based on certain assumptions. For example, assume that earnings growth is constant and that the rate at which dividends are paid out is constant (the percentage of earnings paid out as dividends is known as the *dividend payout ratio*). Then the price of the stock, divided by next year's earnings, will be equal to the payout ratio divided by $r-g$.

$$\frac{P}{E} = \frac{\text{Payout Ratio}}{r-g}$$

© CSI GLOBAL EDUCATION INC. (2008)

For example, if a company is earning \$5.00 a share and pays \$2.75 in dividends, it would have a payout ratio of 0.55 (2.75 ÷ \$5.00). If the market capitalization rate (*r*) was assumed to be 9% while the growth rate (*g*) was assumed to be a constant 6%, the P/E ratio for a company could be calculated as:

$$\frac{P}{E} = \frac{0.55}{0.09 - 0.06} = 18.3 \text{ times}$$

Given two similar companies that pay out a large proportion of earnings, the company that can maintain these payout levels has a more dependable earnings stream. Therefore, all things being equal, a company with more stable earnings should have a higher P/E ratio than a similar type of company with less stable earnings.

Furthermore, a growth company will have a higher P/E only if the long-run growth rate (*g*) is expected to accelerate. Of course, a decline in long-run growth is likely to produce a decline in a stock's P/E ratio. In practice, companies that investors expect will produce a tremendous growth rate in earnings (*g*) typically have a higher P/E ratio than companies that have a lower growth rate in earnings.

The P/E can be used to forecast a future price of a stock. For example, an equity analyst has found that over time, software stocks trade at a P/E ratio of about 20 during a period of economic growth. If the analyst feels that it is currently a time of economic growth and the company should earn \$3.00 per share over the next year, the stock should be priced at \$60 (\$3 × 20 = \$60).

Figure 13.3 shows that the P/E levels of the S&P/TSX Composite Index and S&P 500 are inversely related to the prevailing level of inflation. For example, when inflation was 2–3% in the early 1960s, the S&P/TSX Composite Index P/E traded between 15 and 20 times, averaging about 18 times. As inflation rose during the mid- to late 1960s, the average P/E fell to 16 times. During the inflation of the 1970s, the S&P/TSX Composite Index and S&P 500 P/E averaged about 8 times and 10 times respectively. From 1982 to the late 1990s, P/E averages rose as inflation fell. However, during the bear market that took hold in 2001, the S&P/TSX Composite Index fell into negative territory. With lower inflation over the last few years, both the S&P/TSX Composite and S&P 500 have increased.

© CSI GLOBAL EDUCATION INC. (2008)

FIGURE 13.3 S&P/TSX COMPOSITE P/E, S&P 500 P/E, CANADIAN INFLATION RATE (RIGHT AXIS) ANNUAL PERCENTAGE - 1980 TO 2007

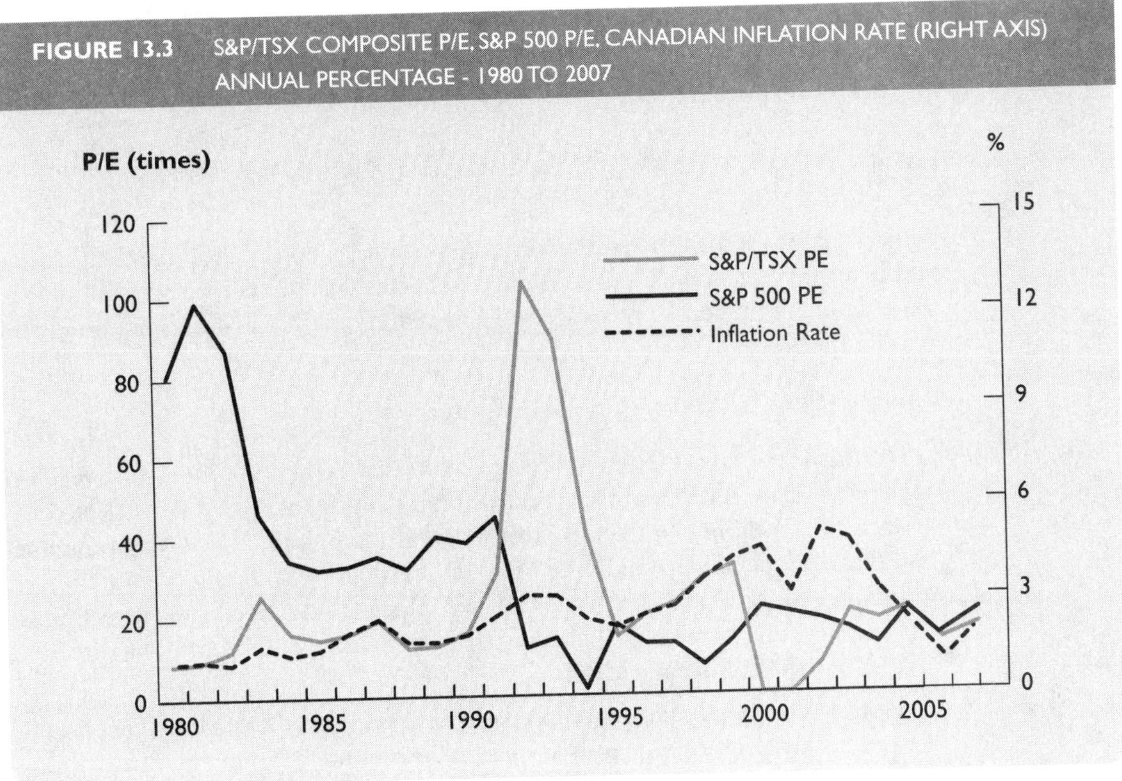

Generally it is assumed that when confidence is high, P/E ratios are also high, and when confidence is low, P/E ratios are low. However, P/E levels are strongly inversely related to the prevailing level of inflation and, therefore, to the prevailing level of interest rates.

The P/Es of individual stocks are even more variable and are affected by many factors specific to individual companies, such as comparative growth rates, earnings quality, and risk due to leverage or stock liquidity. Analysts consider individual company P/Es in relation to the relevant market index or average and compare that number with an average relative P/E over some prior time period, such as three years or five years.

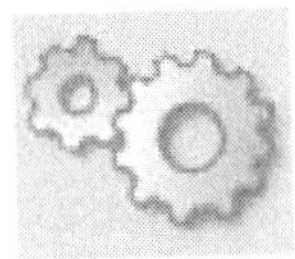

P/Es are volatile, because earnings vary. In some cases, highly cyclical or economically sensitive companies may have losses or low levels of earnings that produce unrealistic or unusable P/Es. To the extent the market is efficient, a low P/E may result from the market's ability to correctly anticipate an imminent decline in earnings. Therefore, the P/E may actually decline before the decline in earnings, and normal P/E levels may appear after the anticipated decline in earnings occurs.

TECHNICAL ANALYSIS

Technical analysts view the range of data studied by fundamental analysts as too massive and unmanageable to pinpoint price movements with any real precision. Instead, they focus on the market itself, whether it be the commodity, equity, interest rate or foreign exchange market. They study, and plot on charts, the past and present movements of prices, the volume of trading,

© CSI GLOBAL EDUCATION INC. (2008)

statistical indicators and, for example in the case of equity markets, the number of stocks advancing and declining. They try to identify recurrent and predictable patterns that can be used to predict future price moves.

In the course of their studies, technicians attempt to probe the psychology of investors collectively or, in other words, the "mood" of the market.

Technical analysis is the process of analyzing historical market action in an effort to determine probable future price trends. As mentioned, technical analysis can be applied to just about any market, although the focus of this section is on equity markets. Market action includes three primary sources of information – price, volume and time.

Technical analysis is based on three assumptions:

- All influences on market action are automatically accounted for or *discounted* in price activity. Technical analysts believe that all known market influences are fully reflected in market prices. They believe that there is little advantage to be gained by doing fundamental analysis. All that is required is to study the price action itself. By studying price action, the technician attempts to measure market sentiment and expectations. In effect, the technical analyst lets the market "do the talking," believing that the market will indicate the direction and the extent of its next price move.
- Prices move in trends and those trends tend to persist for relatively long periods of time. Given this assumption, the primary task of a technical analyst is to identify a trend in its early stages and carry positions in that direction until the trend reverses itself. This is not as easy as it may sound.
- The future repeats the past. Technical analysis is the process of analyzing an asset's historical prices in an effort to determine probable future prices. Technicians believe that markets essentially reflect investor psychology and that the behaviour of investors tends to repeat itself. Investors tend to fluctuate between pessimism, fear and panic on the one side, and optimism, greed and euphoria on the other side. By comparing current investor behaviour as reflected through market action with comparable historical market behaviour, the technical analyst attempts to make predictions. Even if history does not repeat itself exactly, technical analysts believe that they can learn a lot from the past.

Comparing Technical Analysis to Fundamental Analysis

In comparing technical analysis with fundamental analysis, remember that the demand and supply factors that technicians are trying to spot are the result of fundamental developments in company earnings. The main difference between technical and fundamental analysis is that the technician studies the effects of supply and demand (price and volume), while the fundamental analyst studies the causes of price movements. Where a fundamental analyst might suggest a bull market in equities will likely come to an end due to rising interest rates, a technical analyst would say that the appearance of a head-and-shoulder top formation indicates a major market top.

Studying fundamentals can give an investor a sense of the long-term price prospects for an asset. This might be the first step in investment decision-making. However, at the point of deciding when and at what level to enter or leave a market, technical analysis can serve a vital role, particularly when investing or trading leveraged investment products such as futures or options.

© CSI GLOBAL EDUCATION INC. (2008)

Commonly Used Tools in Technical Analysis

Mastering technical analysis takes years of study. It takes skill and experience to read price action and know which indicators work best in which markets. Even then, the success of most technical systems relies on expert money management rules and execution skills.

The four main methods used by a technical analyst to identify trends and possible trend turning points are chart analysis, quantitative analysis, analysis of sentiment indicators and cycle analysis. They are often used in conjunction with one another.

CHART ANALYSIS

Chart analysis is the use of graphic representations of relevant data. Charts offer a visual sense of where the market has been, which helps analysts project where it might be going. The most common type of chart is one that graphs either the hourly, daily, weekly, monthly, or even yearly high, low and close (or last trade) of a particular asset (stock, market average, commodity, etc.). This type of chart is referred to as a bar chart, and often shows the volume of trading at the bottom. Figure 13.4 is an example of a bar chart. Other price charts, not discussed here, include candlestick charts, line charts, and point and figure charts.

FIGURE 13.4 SAMPLE BAR CHART

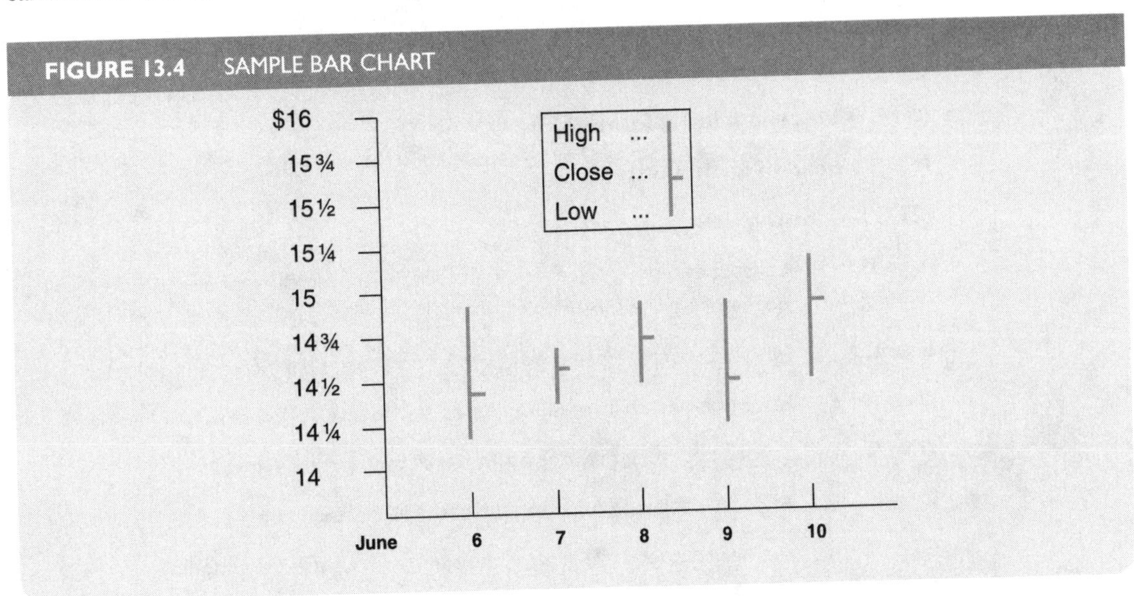

Technical analysts use price charts to identify support and resistance levels and regular price patterns. Support and resistance levels are probably the most noticeable and recurring patterns on a price chart. The most common types are those that are the highs and lows of trading ranges.

- A **support level** is the price at which the majority of investors start sensing value, and therefore are willing to buy (demand is strong), and the majority of existing holders (or potential short sellers) are not willing to sell (supply is low). As demand begins to exceed supply, prices tend to rise above support levels.
- **Resistance levels** are the opposite. At this point, supply exceeds demand and prices tend to fall.

Chart formations reflect market participant behavioral patterns that tend to repeat themselves. They can indicate either a trend reversal (reversal pattern), or a pause in an existing trend (continuation pattern).

© CSI GLOBAL EDUCATION INC. (2008)

Reversal patterns are formations on charts that usually precede a sizeable advance or decline in stock prices. Although there are many types of reversal patterns, probably the most frequently observed pattern is the **head-and-shoulders formation**.

This formation can occur at either a market top, where it is referred to as a head-and-shoulders top formation, or at a bottom, where it is called either an inverse head-and-shoulders or a head-andshoulders bottom formation.

Figure 13.5 demonstrates a head-and-shoulders bottom formation.

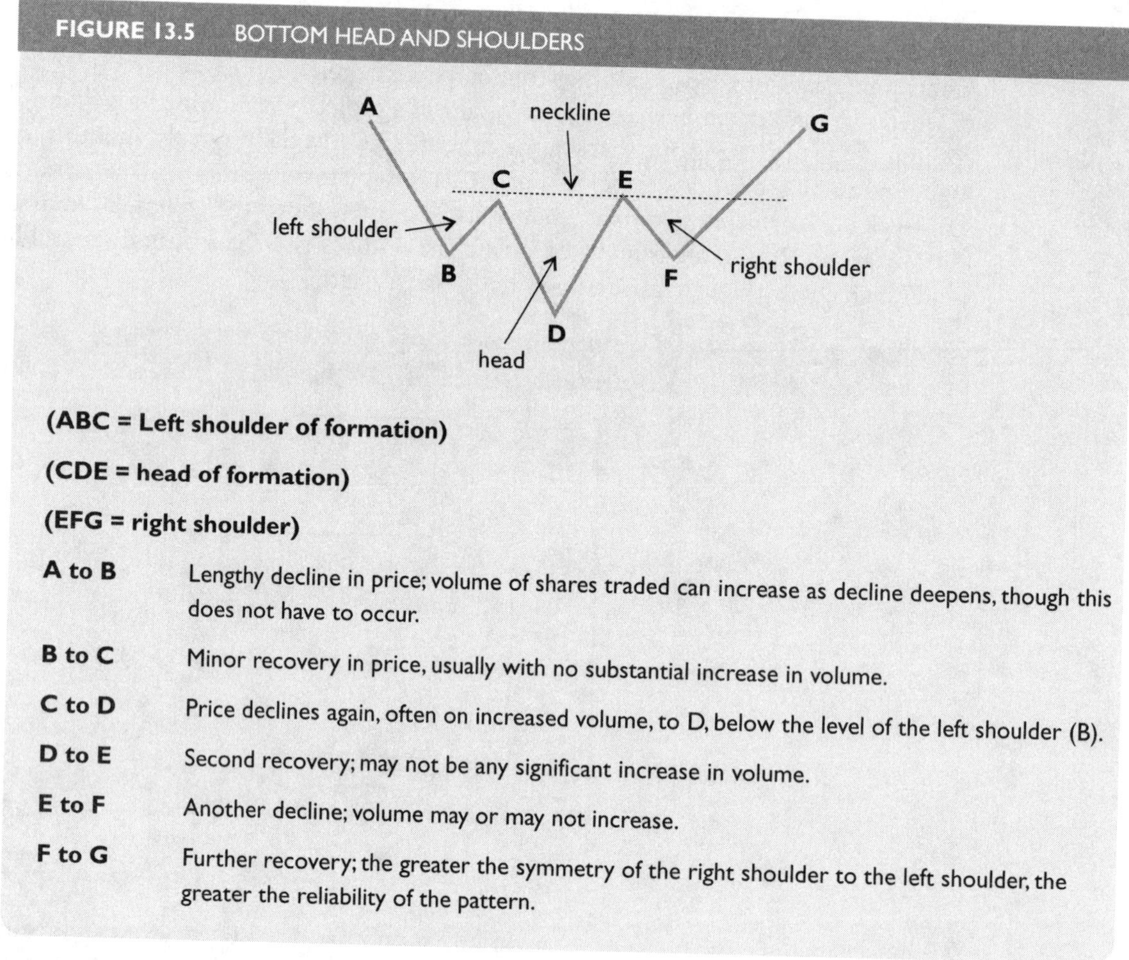

FIGURE 13.5 BOTTOM HEAD AND SHOULDERS

(ABC = Left shoulder of formation)

(CDE = head of formation)

(EFG = right shoulder)

A to B	Lengthy decline in price; volume of shares traded can increase as decline deepens, though this does not have to occur.
B to C	Minor recovery in price, usually with no substantial increase in volume.
C to D	Price declines again, often on increased volume, to D, below the level of the left shoulder (B).
D to E	Second recovery; may not be any significant increase in volume.
E to F	Another decline; volume may or may not increase.
F to G	Further recovery; the greater the symmetry of the right shoulder to the left shoulder, the greater the reliability of the pattern.

Joining the two recovery points C to E (indicated by the broken line) produces the **neckline**, which can be extended out to the right of the chart pattern. The final step that confirms the reversal pattern is an advance that carries the stock above the neckline on increased volume. Then, an *upside break-out* has taken place. Although some analysts are skeptical about the validity of this chart pattern, experience has confirmed its reliability, probably three times out of four.

Continuation patterns are pauses on price charts, typically in the form of sideways price movements, before the prevailing trend continues. These patterns are referred to as a consolidation of an existing trend. They are quite normal and healthy in a trending market.

One such pattern is called a symmetrical triangle, and is shown in Figure 13.6.

© CSI GLOBAL EDUCATION INC. (2008)

FIGURE 13.6 TRIANGLE

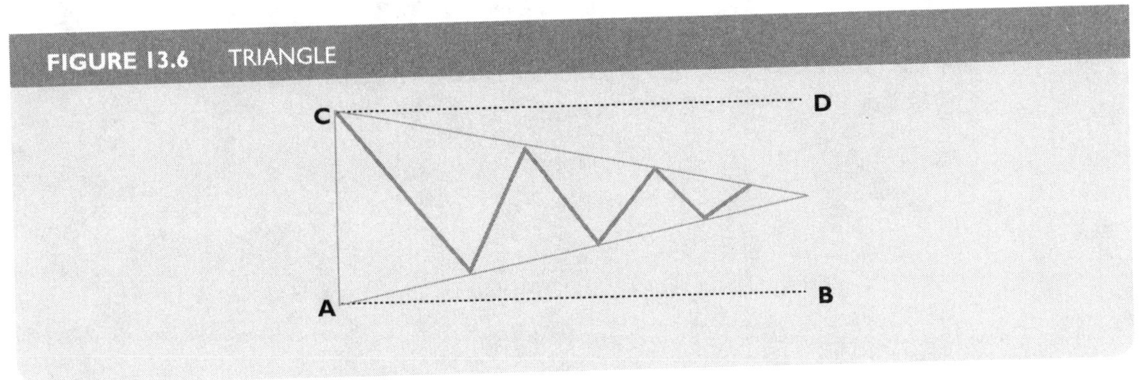

In this formation, the stock trades in a clearly defined area (CD – AB), during a period ranging from three weeks to six months or more. The rectangle represents a fairly even struggle between buyers and sellers. The buyers move in at the bottom line (AB) and the sellers move out at the top line (CD). This activity repeats itself back and forth until one side proves stronger.

In most cases, a symmetrical triangle is just a pause in a bull or bear market (continuation pattern). At times, however, it can indicate a reversal formation. There is no clear method of distinguishing whether a triangle will be a continuation or a reversal, so close attention must be paid to the direction of the break-out.

QUANTITATIVE ANALYSIS

Quantitative analysis is a relatively new form of technical analysis that has been greatly enhanced by the growing sophistication of computers. There are two general categories of statistical tools: moving averages and oscillators. They are used to supplement chart analysis, either by identifying (or confirming) trends, or by giving an early warning signal that a particular trend is starting to lose momentum.

A **moving average** is simply a device for smoothing out fluctuating values (week-to-week or dayto- day) in an individual stock or in the aggregate market as a whole. It shows long-term trends. By comparing current prices with the moving average line, the technician can see whether a change is signalled.

A moving average is calculated by adding the closing prices for a stock (or market index) over a predetermined period of time and dividing the total by the time period selected (see Table 13.1).

© CSI GLOBAL EDUCATION INC. (2008)

TABLE 13.1 CALCULATION OF FIVE-WEEK MOVING AVERAGE FOR A PARTICULAR STOCK CLOSING PRICE

Week One	$17.50
Week Two	18.00
Week Three	18.75
Week Four	18.35
Week Five	19.25
Total	91.85
Average (divided by 5)	$18.37

An amount of $18.37 would be plotted on a chart at the end of Week Five. At the end of Week Six, a new five-week total would be calculated for Weeks Two to Six, dropping Week One. If Week Six's closing price was $19.50, the total would be $93.85 and the average would be $18.77, which would be plotted on the chart next to the previous week's $18.37.

Although we have shown a five-week average in the example for simplicity, a 40-week (or 200-day) moving average is most common, because it is more closely aligned with the primary trend of the market and with Dow's basic assumption that the market moves in broad trends.

If the overall trend has been down, the moving average line will generally be above the current individual prices, as shown in Figure 13.7.

FIGURE 13.7 BUY SIGNAL

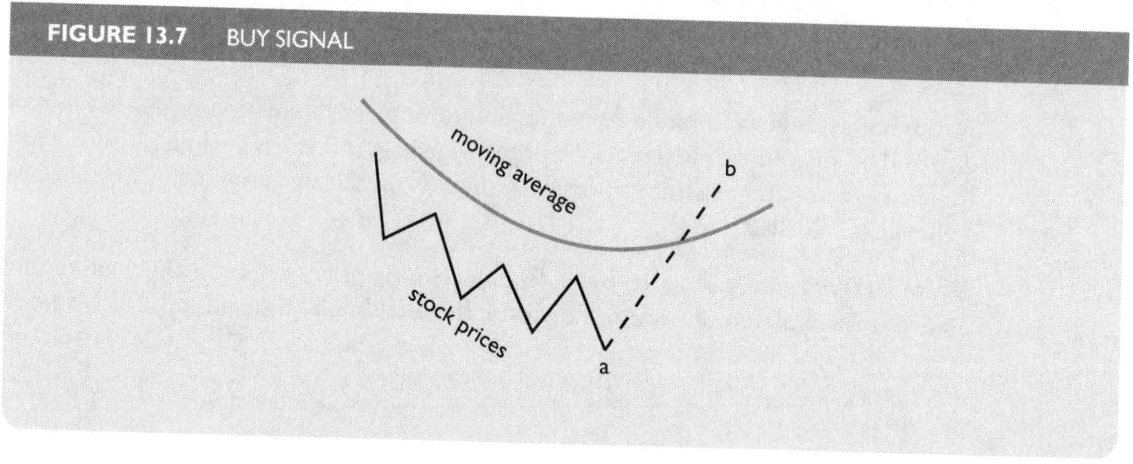

If the price breaks through the moving average line from below on heavy volume (line a–b) and the moving average line itself starts to move higher, a technician might speculate the declining trend has been reversed. In other words, it is a *buy signal.*

If the overall trend has been up, the moving average line will generally be below the current individual prices, as shown in Figure 13.8.

© CSI GLOBAL EDUCATION INC. (2008)

FIGURE 13.8 SELL SIGNAL

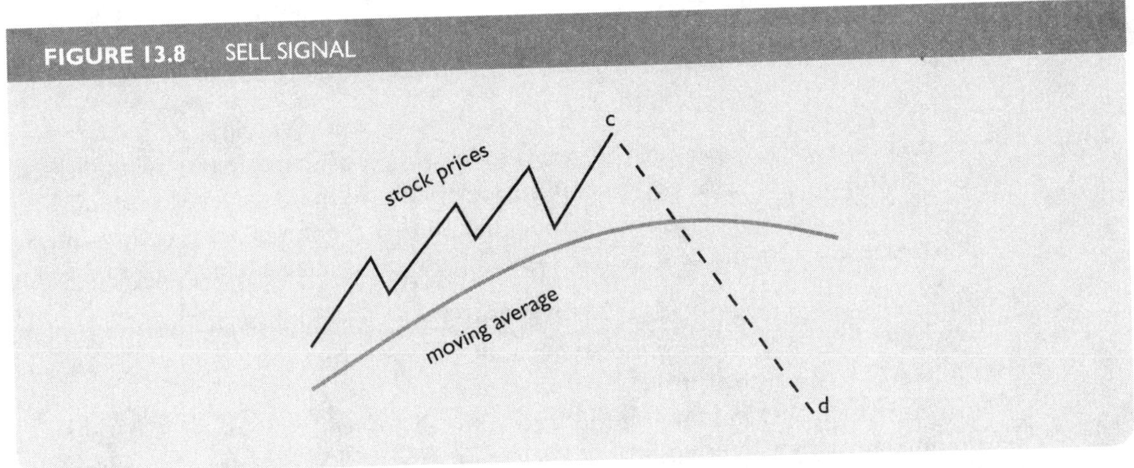

If the price breaks through the moving average line from above on heavy volume (line c–d) and the moving average line itself starts to fall, the upward trend is reversed. This is a *sell signal.*

Oscillators are indicators that are used when a stock's chart is not showing a definite trend in either direction. Oscillators are most beneficial when a stock is moving in either a horizontal or sideways trading pattern, or has not been able to establish a definite trend.

There are several different types of oscillator indicators. The readings from an oscillator will fluctuate either from 0 to 100 or -1 to +1. This indicator can be used in one of three ways:

- When the oscillator reading reaches an extreme value in either the upper or lower end of the band, this suggests that the current price move has gone too far. The market is said to be overbought when prices are near the upper extreme and oversold when near the lower extreme. This warns that the price move is overextended and vulnerable.
- A divergence between the oscillator and prices when the oscillator is in an extreme position is usually an important warning that a trend may be weakening.
- The crossing of the zero line can give important trading signals.

The **moving average convergence-divergence** (**MACD**) is probably the most popular indicator for tracking momentum and conducting divergence analysis. The MACD oscillator takes the difference between two moving averages so that you can measure any shift in trend over a period of time (i.e., momentum). The standard periods used are a 12-day and 26-day moving average of a specific stock. The MACD is calculated by subtracting the 26-day moving average from the 12-day moving average.

That difference is then smoothed by a 9-day moving average and this is called the signal line. Signals are generated when the MACD crosses the signal line.

The MACD indicator is also used to identify divergences. If a stock is moving higher but the MACD is trending lower, this could be interpreted as a warning signal that the market is losing its upward momentum. Likewise, a series of higher MACD highs when the market for that stock is moving down may indicate a market bottom may be near.

SENTIMENT INDICATORS

Sentiment indicators focus on investor expectations. **Contrarian investors** use these indicators to determine what the majority of investors expect prices to do in the future, because contrarians move in the opposite direction from the majority. For example, the contrarian believes that if the

© CSI GLOBAL EDUCATION INC. (2008)

vast majority of investors expect prices to rise, then there probably is not enough buying power left to push prices much higher. The concept is well proven, and can be used as evidence to support other technical indicators.

A number of services measure the extent to which market participants are bullish or bearish. If, for example, one of these services indicates that 80% of those surveyed are bullish, this would indicate that the market may be overbought and that caution is warranted. As mentioned above, however, contrarian indicators should only be used as evidence to support other indicators.

One tool used to measure overall market sentiment is the bullish and bearish consensus. A number of American organizations, such as Consensus Inc. and the American Association of Individual Investors, construct consensus indicators based on the bullish or bearish leanings of market participants and publish the results, usually to paid subscribers. Consensus Inc. compiles sentiment data on all futures markets, including the S&P 500 Index. According to its Consensus Index of Bullish Market Opinion, when 75% or more of those surveyed are bullish, the market is considered to be overbought and may be ripe for at least a temporary decline. When only 25% are bullish, the market is oversold and may be near a point from where it will rebound.

CYCLE ANALYSIS

The tools described above help technical analysts forecast the market's most probable direction and the extent of the movement in that direction. **Cycle analysis** helps the analyst forecast when the market will start moving in a particular direction and when the ultimate peak or trough will be achieved.

Cycles can last for short periods of time, such as a few days, to decades. What makes cycle analysis complicated is that at any given point, a number of cycles may be operating.

Cycle analysis is used to accurately predict events in nature: bird migrations, the tides, planetary movements and seasons. The prices of many commodities, particularly in the agricultural complex, reflect seasonal cycles as well. Although the task of applying cycles to financial assets is more complex, there are at least four general categories of cycle lengths:

- Long-term (greater than two years)
- Seasonal (one year)
- Primary/intermediate (nine to 26 weeks)
- Trading (four weeks)

One of the better-known cycle theories is the Elliott Wave Theory.

The **Elliott Wave Theory** is a complicated theory based on rhythms found in nature. Elliott argued that there are repetitive, predictable sequences of numbers and cycles found in nature and similar predictable patterns in the movement of stock prices.

According to this theory, the stock market moves in huge waves and cycles. Superimposed on these waves are smaller waves, and superimposed on the smaller waves, even smaller waves, and so on. Elliott found that the market moves up in a series of five waves and down in a series of three waves. These larger waves may have smaller waves superimposed on them. In addition, there are various refinements. For example, the third wave should be longer than waves one and five.

© CSI GLOBAL EDUCATION INC. (2008)

Unfortunately, because of so-called extensions of waves, whereby odd waves are sometimes broken down into five smaller waves, it is often difficult to determine which part of the cycle we are in at any given time. However, at times, this theory has given experienced interpreters a clear indication of the direction in which markets are heading.

OTHER INDICATORS IN EQUITY MARKET ANALYSIS

In addition to the tools mentioned above, technical analysts look at other indicators to gauge the overall health of equity markets.

Volume changes: Although volume plays an important role in technical analysis, it is used mostly to confirm other indicators. In a bull market, volume should increase when prices rise. This tells investors that the weight of money is on the buying side of the market. When prices rise and volume does not increase, the market may be in the beginning stages of a potential bearish reversal. A bear market should see the opposite, namely, heavier volume on price declines and reduced volume on the subsequent corrective rallies.

Breadth of market: Breadth monitors the extent or broadness of a market trend. If, in an uptrend, breadth measurements are persistently weak, the trend has a higher probability of failing. If, in a downtrend, breadth reverses before the major averages, it could be a significant indicator that the market is close to bottoming. There are several ways to measure breadth.

The cumulative **advance-decline line** is the most popular way of measuring breadth. It is a nonprice measure of the trend of the market. Starting with an arbitrary number such as 1,000, the analyst takes the difference between the issues advancing and the issues declining. If more issues advanced than declined, add this difference to the starting line. If more issues declined than advanced, subtract the difference. Continue this procedure daily until an advancing or declining line has been plotted. Technical analysts compare advance-decline lines to the Dow Jones Industrial Average, to see if both are telling the same story.

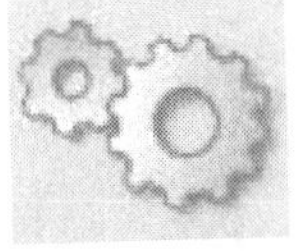

Review the on-line summary or checklist associated with this section.

Like the advance-decline line, the new highs and new lows indexes take into account the market as a whole and therefore measure its breadth. Daily or weekly, the number of stocks making new highs is divided by the number of issues traded to give the new highs index, and a similar calculation is done for new lows. Each index is then plotted separately.

The market is considered strong when new highs are increasing and weak when new lows are increasing. Technical analysts who use this index believe:

- The number of new lows reaches unprecedented peaks at the end of a bear market;
- The number of new highs begins to increase very early in a bull market; and
- The number of new highs begins to decline long before the advance-decline line or the Dow Jones Industrial Average tops out.

© CSI GLOBAL EDUCATION INC. (2008)

SUMMARY

By the end of this chapter, you should be able to:

1. Compare and contrast fundamental, quantitative and technical analysis, and evaluate the three market theories explaining stock market behaviour.
   - Fundamental analysis focuses on assessing the short-, medium- and long-range prospects of different industries and companies to determine how the prices of securities will change.
   - Quantitative analysis involves studying interest rates, economic variables, and industry or stock valuation using computers, databases, statistics and an objective, mathematical approach to valuing a company.
   - Technical analysis looks at historical stock prices and stock market behaviour to identify recurring and predictable price patterns that can be used to predict future price movements.
   - The main difference between technical and fundamental analysis is that technicians study the effects of supply and demand (price and volume), while fundamental analysts study the causes of price movements.
   - The Efficient Market Hypothesis states that at any given time a stock's price will fully reflect all available information and thus represents the best estimate of a stock's true value.
   - The Random Walk Theory assumes that new information concerning a stock is disseminated randomly over time. Therefore, price changes are random and bear no relation to previous price changes.
   - The Rational Expectations Hypothesis assumes that people are rational and make intelligent economic decisions after weighing all available information.
2. Describe how the four macroeconomic factors affect investor expectations and the price of securities.
   - There are four categories of macroeconomic factors: fiscal policy, monetary policy, the flow of funds and inflation. A change in any one of these factors requires a re-thinking of current investment strategies.
3. Analyze how industries are classified and explain how industry classifications impact a company's stock valuation.
   - Most industries are identified by the product or service they provide.
   - Investors and advisors who understand the competitive forces in an industry can consider the prospects for growth and degree of risk, which are two factors that help determine stock values.

© CSI GLOBAL EDUCATION INC. (2008)

4. Calculate and interpret the intrinsic value and the price-earnings ratio (P/E) of a stock using the dividend discount model (DDM).
   - The Dividend Discount Model is used to value a company so that a decision can be made on whether the company's stock is under- or overvalued relative to its current price.
   - The price-earnings ratio can also be used to forecast a future price of a stock. In practice, companies that are expected to produce strong growth in earnings typically have a higher P/E ratio than companies that have a lower growth rate in earnings.

5. Define technical analysis and describe the tools used in technical analysis.
   - Technical analysts plot on charts and study the past and present movements of security prices, the volume of trading and other statistical indicators.
   - The analysis focuses on trying to identify recurrent and predictable patterns that can be used to predict future price movements.
   - Three key assumptions underlie technical analysis: all market influences are automatically accounted for in price activity, prices move in trends and those trends tend to persist for relatively long periods of time, and the future repeats the past.

Now that you've completed this chapter and the on-line activities, complete this post-test.

© CSI GLOBAL EDUCATION INC. (2008)

Chapter 14

Company Analysis

© CSI GLOBAL EDUCATION INC. (2008)

14

Company Analysis

CHAPTER OUTLINE

© CSI GLOBAL EDUCATION INC. (2008)

LEARNING OBJECTIVES

By the end of this chapter, you should be able to:

1. Identify the factors involved in performing company analysis to determine whether a company represents a good investment.
2. Explain how to analyze a company's financial statements using trend analysis and external comparisons.
3. Describe the different types of liquidity ratios, risk analysis ratios, operating performance ratios and value ratios, and evaluate company performance using these ratios.
4. Evaluate the investment quality of preferred shares and summarize preferred share ratings.

THE COMPONENTS OF COMPANY ANALYSIS

The decision to invest, or not invest, in the securities of a company is a conscious choice. In making that choice, an advisor or investor exercises independent judgment. As we learned in the previous chapter, advisors and investors generally perform some form of fundamental analysis of relevant factors in an effort to make successful, rather than unsuccessful, investment choices.

The reality of investing is that there are no guarantees; all investment has risk of one type or another. One of the goals of performing company analysis before investing in a company's securities is to help identify risks and opportunities, which can help reduce, although never eliminate, potential surprises regarding the investment decision.

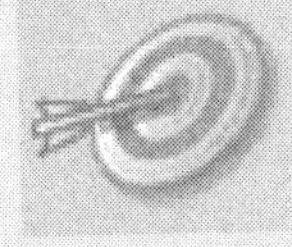

In the on-line Learning Guide for this module, complete the Getting Started activity.

Company analysis is used to look at company-specific factors that can affect investment decisions. The approach involves looking at a company and deciding: Is it a good investment? Does it fit into an investment strategy? How will changes in specific or general economic or market factors affect the company? Are there risk factors or strengths hidden in the financial statements not readily apparent after a quick review of the company? Is there more to the company than is reported in company press releases or news stories? In short, what do the financial numbers tell us about the company?

Being able to rigorously analyze the financial statements of a company is key to an advisor's or investor's ability to answer the above questions.

© CSI GLOBAL EDUCATION INC. (2008)

KEY TERMS

Apparent tax rate
Asset coverage ratio
Capital structure
Cash flow
Cash flow/total debt ratio
Current ratio
Debt/equity ratio
Dividend payout ratio
Dividend yield
Earnings per common share (EPS)
Enterprise Multiple
Enterprise value
Financial Ratio
Gross profit margin ratio
Interest coverage ratio
Inventory turnover ratio
Liquidity ratio
Net profit margin
Net tangible assets (NTA)
Operating cash flow ratio
Operating performance ratio
Operating profit margin ratio
Percentage of capital ratios
Preferred dividend coverage ratio
Pre-tax profit margin
Price-earnings ratio (P/E ratio)
Quick ratio
Return on common equity (ROE)
Risk analysis ratio
Trend ratio
Value ratio
Working capital

© CSI GLOBAL EDUCATION INC. (2008)

OVERVIEW OF COMPANY ANALYSIS

Fundamental industry analysis was the main subject of Chapter 13. The subject of this chapter is fundamental company analysis, which means looking at a company to determine whether it is a good investment. Company analysis uses the financial statements to determine the financial health and potential profitability of the company. You may want to review the accounting principles learned in Chapter 12 before proceeding through this chapter.

Earnings Statement Analysis

The analysis of a company's earnings tells the investor how well management is making use of the company's resources.

SALES

A company's ability to increase sales (or total revenues) is an important indicator of its investment quality. Clearly, sales growth is desirable while flat or declining sales trends are less favourable; high rates of growth are usually preferable to low or moderate rates of increase. The analyst will look for the reason for an increase, such as:

- An increase in product prices
- An increase in product volumes
- The introduction of new products
- Expansion into a new geographic market (such as the United States)
- The consolidation of a company acquired in a takeover
- The initial contribution from a new plant or diversification program
- A gain in market share at the expense of competitors
- A temporary increase in sales due to a strike at a major competitor
- Aggressive advertising and promotion
- The favourable impact of government legislation on the industry
- An upswing in the business cycle

With this knowledge, the analyst can isolate the main factors affecting sales and evaluate developments for their positive or negative impact on future performance.

OPERATING COSTS

The next step is to look at operating costs to assess the overall efficiency of operations. Operating costs include the cost of goods sold, selling and administrative costs, and other expenses considered direct costs necessary to generate sales. Operating costs do not include interest charges, amortization charges, or income taxes. Although amortization is often considered an operating cost, it is excluded in this discussion because it does not represent an actual outlay of funds.

By calculating operating costs as a percentage of sales (operating profit margin), it is possible to determine whether these costs are rising, stable, or falling in relation to sales. A rising trend over several years may indicate that a company is having difficulty keeping overall costs under control and is therefore losing potential profits. A falling trend suggests that a company is operating cost effectively and is likely to be more profitable.

© CSI GLOBAL EDUCATION INC. (2008)

The analyst should determine the main reasons for any changes in the operating margin. Although it may be difficult to identify the causes, they are important in understanding what affects the company's cost structure. For example:

- Cost of goods sold is a major component of operating costs. Therefore, the cost at which a company obtains its raw materials has a major impact on its operating margin. Companies that rely on commodities such as copper or nickel, for example, have to cope with wide swings in raw material costs from one year to another.
- Capacity utilization can be a factor. As a general rule, the closer a company operates to its total production capability, the more efficient its operations. Certain fixed costs that must be met whether output is high or low can be spread over a greater number of units.
- Expenditures to modernize equipment or to bring a new and efficient plant into production increase operating costs.
- The introduction of new products or services with wider profit margins can improve profitability.
- Employee costs are particularly important for companies that are labour-intensive.
- Costs and problems related to the start-up of a new plant can adversely affect profit margins.

DIVIDEND RECORD

The analyst will also want to look at a company's historical dividend record; for example, how much does the company generally pay out in the form of dividends to shareholders. An unusually high dividend payout rate (more than 65%, for example) may be the result of:

- Stable earnings that allow a high payout;
- Declining earnings, which may indicate a future cut in the dividend;
- Earnings based on resources that are being depleted, as in the case of some mining companies; or
- Earnings paid to controlling shareholders to finance other ventures.

Similarly, a low payout may reflect such factors as:

- Earnings ploughed back into a growth company's operations;
- Growing earnings, which may indicate a future increase in the dividend;
- Cyclical earnings at their peak and a company policy to maintain the same dividend in good and bad times;
- A company policy of buying back shares rather than distributing earnings through higher dividend payout; or
- A company policy of periodically paying stock dividends in lieu of cash.

Balance Sheet Analysis

Fundamental analysts also pay attention to a company's overall financial position. A thorough analysis of the balance sheet helps them understand other important aspects of a company's operations and can reveal factors that may affect earnings. For example, a company with low interest coverage will be limited in its dividend policy and financing options.

© CSI GLOBAL EDUCATION INC. (2008)

THE CAPITAL STRUCTURE

The analysis of a company's capital structure provides an overall picture of a company's financial soundness (that is, the amount of debt used in its operations). It may indicate the need for future financing and the type of security that might be used (such as preferred or common shares for a company with a heavy debt load). Analysts also look for:

- A large debt issue approaching maturity, which may have to be refinanced by a new securities issue or by other means;
- Retractable securities, which may also have to be refinanced if investors choose to retract (a similar possibility exists for extendible bonds);
- Convertible securities, which represent a potential decrease in earnings per common share through dilution; and
- The presence of outstanding warrants and stock options, which represents a potential increase in common shares outstanding.

THE EFFECT OF LEVERAGE

The earnings of a company are said to be *leveraged* if the capital structure contains debt and/or preferred shares. The presence of senior securities accelerates any cyclical rise or fall in earnings. The earnings of leveraged companies increase faster during an upswing in the business cycle than the earnings of companies without leverage. Conversely, the earnings of a leveraged company collapse more quickly in response to deteriorating economic conditions.

Table 14.1 illustrates the leverage effect of preferred shares on common share earnings. However, a similar effect will occur in a company that uses debt to finance its operations. In either case, a relatively small increase in sales or total revenues can produce a magnified increase in earnings per share; the reverse is true when sales decline. The market action of shares in leveraged companies shows considerable volatility.

TABLE 14.1 THE EFFECT OF LEVERAGE ON PER SHARE EARNINGS

Assume that two companies, A and B, each have a total capitalization of $1 million and each earned (after taxes and amortization):

Year One – $ 50,000
Year Two – $100,000
Year Three – $ 25,000

Company A's capitalization consists of 100,000 common shares, no par value.

Company B's capitalization consists of 50,000 5% preferred shares of $10 par value and 50,000 common shares of no par value. Note the effect of this variation in earnings on the earnings per common share for the two companies.

© CSI GLOBAL EDUCATION INC. (2008)

TABLE 14.1 THE EFFECT OF LEVERAGE ON PER SHARE EARNINGS (*Cont'd*)

	Year One	Year Two	Year Three
Company A (No Leverage)			
Earnings available for dividends	$ 50,000	$100,000	$25,000
Preferred dividends	Nil	Nil	Nil
Available for common	$ 50,000	$100,000	$25,000
Per share	$ 0.50	$ 1.00	$ 0.25
% Return earned on common shares	5%	10%	2 1/2%
Company B (50% Leverage)			
Earnings available for dividends	$ 50,000	$100,000	$25,000
Preferred dividends	$25,000	$25,000	$25,000
Available for common	$25,000	$ 75,000	Nil
Per share	$ 0.50	$ 1.50	Nil
% Return earned on common shares	5%	15%	0%

The stock of Company A is less risky than the stock of Company B, which must pay out interest on senior preferred capital before it can pay dividends to common shareholders. Stock A has more stable earnings, because it is less vulnerable to shrinkage in earnings, though it is also less sensitive to any increase in earnings.

Other Features of Company Analysis

Qualitative analysis: Qualitative analysis is used to assess management effectiveness and other intangibles that cannot be measured with concrete data. The quality of a company's management is unquestionably a key factor in its success. The ability to evaluate the quality of management comes from years of contact with industry and company executives, experience, judgment, and even intuition. It is not a topic that we can cover in this course.

Liquidity of common shares: Liquidity is a measure of how easy it is to sell or buy a security on a stock exchange without causing significant movement in its price. Trading should be sufficient to absorb transactions without undue distortion in the market price. Institutional investors dealing in large blocks of shares require a high degree of liquidity.

A common stock listed on an exchange must meet a certain standard of liquidity as a requirement for listing; however, even listed shares may be thinly traded. Information on trading volume is readily available from most financial newspapers and stock exchange publications.

Timing of purchases and sales: The timing of share transactions is a critical factor in determining an investor's ultimate return. Share prices in general tend to follow the prevailing trend of the stock market through bull and bear market cycles. Changing investor psychology, either optimistic or pessimistic, produces a broad ebb and flow in equity prices. Many books have been written and many theories devised to help investors time their buy and sell transactions. However, it is difficult to be consistently successful using market timing as a money management style.

© CSI GLOBAL EDUCATION INC. (2008)

Nevertheless, investor expectations about future economic conditions and corporate earnings are a major factor in determining investor behaviour. Investors should understand the business cycle and know which phase it is in at any point.

Continuous monitoring: When an investor decides to buy shares in a company, he or she should monitor the operations of the company for changes that might affect the price of the shares and the dividends that the company pays. Quarterly financial reports to shareholders are an especially important source of information and analysts scrutinize them in detail. They also glean useful material from prospectuses, trade journals, and financial publications.

INTERPRETING FINANCIAL STATEMENTS

Caution must be used when analyzing and interpreting financial statements. While there are a number of disclosure requirements and accounting rules that a company must adhere to, GAAP conventions provide flexibility. For example, inventory valuation methods, amortization periods, and revenue recognition procedures (i.e., when does the company record revenue) all have a substantial impact on the net profit of a company. The management of the company may select accounting practices that make the company look as healthy and prosperous and in as good a financial shape as possible, in order to attract investors or make management look successful.

Before delving into ratio analysis, it is also important to look over the statements in general first, and read the notes to the financial statements. There are often clues that the financial health of the company may be deteriorating, before financial ratios relay the same information.

An analyst reads the notes to the financial statements very carefully. A few of the most common warning signs are listed in Table 14.2 for informational purposes only.

TABLE 14.2 SOME WARNING SIGNS FOUND IN THE NOTES TO THE FINANCIAL STATEMENTS

Changes in accounting practices or auditors

- Look for changes in accounting practices which increase revenue, or decrease expenses, when the actual operation of the company did not change. The company may be trying to appear more prosperous than it really is.
- Look for changes in accounting practices that decrease revenue, or increase expenses, when the actual operation of the company did not change. The company may be trying to deflate profit now, so that it appears to be growing in profitability in the next few years.
- A change in the auditors of a company may signal a fundamental disagreement between the auditors and company management concerning how certain transactions should be treated.

Long-term commitments

- Look for long-term commitments, such as long-term commodity purchase agreements, which may be detrimental to the company in the future if the market for that product changes.

A series of mergers and takeovers

- Companies have been known to acquire a series of smaller companies, often unprofitable, in order to manipulate the consolidated balance sheet in their favour, or to hide the unprofitability of the original company.

© CSI GLOBAL EDUCATION INC. (2008)

Does this mean that if any of the above notes are present, the company is a bad investment? Not necessarily; the point is to be aware of these issues and dig further for explanations. Companies often change accounting practices in response to new situations, changes in industry practice or directives from the accounting boards such as the Canadian Institute of Chartered Accountants.

Trend Analysis

Ratios calculated from a company's financial statements for only one year have limited value. They become meaningful, however, when compared with other ratios either *internally*, that is, with a series of similar ratios of the same company over a period, or *externally*, that is, with comparable ratios of similar companies or with industry averages.

Analysts identify trends by selecting a base date or period, treating the figure or ratio for that period as 100, and then dividing it into the comparable ratios for subsequent periods. Table 14.3 shows this calculation for a typical pulp and paper company:

TABLE 14.3 PULP AND PAPER COMPANY A – EARNINGS PER SHARE

Year	Year 1	Year 2	Year 3	Year 4	Year 5
EPS	$1.18	$1.32	$1.73	$1.76	$1.99
	1.18	1.32	1.73	1.76	1.99
	1.18	1.18	1.18	1.1	1.18
Trend	100	112	147	149	169

The above example uses Year 1 as the base year. The earnings per share for that year, $1.18, is treated as equivalent to 100. The **trend ratios** for subsequent years are easily calculated by dividing 1.18 into the earnings per share ratio for each subsequent year.

A similar trend line over the same period for Pulp and Paper Company B is shown in Table 14.4.

TABLE 14.4 PULP AND PAPER COMPANY B – EARNINGS PER SHARE

Year	Year 1	Year 2	Year 3	Year 4	Year 5
EPS	$0.71	$0.80	$0.90	$0.84	$0.78
	.71	.80	.90	.84	.78
	.71	.71	.71	.71	.71
Trend	100	113	127	118	110

The trend line of each of these two companies shows the characteristic fluctuations of pulp and paper company earnings. For example, adding new machinery often causes temporary over-capacity and reduces earnings until demand catches up with supply. The trend line for Company B suggests some over-capacity in recent years, as earnings show a decline.

© CSI GLOBAL EDUCATION INC. (2008)

Trend ratio calculations are useful because they clearly show changes. They are also simple to do and easier to interpret than the alternative, which is the two-step method of calculating percentage changes from year to year.

A trend line will be misleading if the base period is not truly representative. It is also impossible to apply the method if the base period figure is negative, that is, if a loss was sustained in the base year.

External Comparisons

Ratios are most useful when comparing financial results of companies in the same or similar industries (such as comparing a distiller with a brewer). Differences shown by the trend lines not only help to put the earnings per share of each company in historical perspective, but also show how each company has fared in relation to others. Different industries may have different industry standards for the same ratio. In fact, a range is often employed rather than a specific target number.

In external comparisons, not only should the companies be similar in operation, but also the basis used to calculate each ratio compared should be the same. For example, there is no point comparing the inventory turnover ratios (discussed later) of two companies if one calculation uses "cost of goods sold" and the other uses "net sales." This comparison would be inaccurate since the basis of calculation is different.

Determining which items on a financial statement should be included in a ratio can be difficult. An investor may not be able to make a valid comparison between companies ABC Ltd. and DEF Ltd. if the research on each came from two different analysts. Different assumptions can result in one analyst including an item while an equally competent analyst may choose not to include it. For example, one analyst may include a bond maturing in five years as short-term debt while another analyst may consider that same security to be a long-term debt.

In addition to comparisons between companies in the same industry, industry ratios can be used to compare the performance of individual companies. Industry ratios represent the average for that particular ratio of all the companies analyzed in that specific industry.

Industry standards are different from industry ratios in that the industry ratio, the average of the industry, will change each year depending on performance of the industry as a whole. Industry standards are relatively static, that is, they remain the same regardless of the performance of the industry or the economy. Standards provide a longer-term view of the industry. For example, a company being analyzed may have a ratio that is above all the others in the industry, but due to a recession, all companies within the industry may be below the industry standard. The company may be seen as a top performer; however, the industry itself is not performing. To be thorough, an analyst must compare the company to both the current average of the industry, as well as the historical industry standard.

At this point, you should be able to interpret the ratios that follow and apply them in assessing the merits of securities.

To make it easier to follow and understand the method of calculating ratios, we have numbered the items used in the following examples to correspond to the relative items in the sample financial statements of Trans-Canada Retail Stores Ltd. These statements can be found in Appendix A. Appendix B provides a sample ratio analysis, comparing two companies.

© CSI GLOBAL EDUCATION INC. (2008)

FINANCIAL RATIO ANALYSIS

Having learned what the financial statements reveal about the financial condition of a company, the next step is to put that knowledge to work by testing the investment merits of the company's bonds and stocks. The tool most commonly used to analyze financial statements is called a ratio, which shows the relationship between two numbers.

Four types of ratios are commonly used to analyze a company's financial statements:

1. **Liquidity ratios** are used to judge the company's ability to meet its short-term commitments. An example is the working capital ratio, which shows the relationship between current assets and current liabilities.
2. **Risk analysis ratios** show how well the company can deal with its debt obligations. For example, the debt/equity ratio shows the relationship between the company's borrowing and the capital invested in it by shareholders.
3. **Operating performance ratios** illustrate how well management is making use of the company's resources. The net return on invested capital, for example, correlates the company's income with the capital invested to produce it. These ratios include profitability and efficiency measures.
4. **Value ratios** show the investor what the company's shares are worth, or the return on owning them. An example is the price-earnings ratio, which links the market price of a common share to earnings per common share, and thus allows investors to rate the shares of companies within the same industry.

Ratios must be used in context. One ratio alone does not tell an investor very much. Ratios are not proof of present or future profitability, only clues. An analyst who spots an unsatisfactory ratio may suspect unfavourable conditions. Conversely, analysts may conclude that a company is financially strong after compiling a series of ratios.

The significance of any ratio is not the same for all companies. In analyzing a manufacturing company, for example, analysts pay particular attention to the working capital ratio, which is a measure of the use of current assets. In an electric utility company, however, the working capital ratio is not as important, because electric power is not stored in inventory, but produced at the same time that it is used.

Liquidity Ratios

Liquidity ratios help investors evaluate the ability of a company to turn assets into cash to meet its short-term obligations. If a company is to remain solvent, it must be able to meet its current liabilities, and therefore it must have an adequate amount of working capital.

By subtracting total current liabilities from total current assets, we obtain the company's **working capital**, also referred to as *net current assets*.

© CSI GLOBAL EDUCATION INC. (2008)

WORKING CAPITAL RATIO OR CURRENT RATIO

The ability of a company to meet its obligations, expand its volume of business, and take advantage of financial opportunities as they arise is, to a large extent, determined by its working capital or **current ratio** position. Frequent causes of business failure are the lack of sufficient working capital and the inability to liquidate current assets readily.

The working capital for Trans-Canada Retail would be calculated as follows:

Current Assets (item 6)	$12,238,000
Less: Current Liabilities (item 17)	$4,410,000
Equals: Working Capital	$7,828,000

This relationship is often expressed in terms of a ratio. In this example, the working capital ratio would be expressed as:

$$\frac{\text{Current assets}}{\text{Current liabilities}} \text{ or } \frac{\text{Item 6}}{\text{Item 17}} = \frac{\$12,238,000}{\$4,410,000} = 2.78:1$$

Current assets are cash and other company possessions that can be readily turned into cash (and normally would be) within one year. Current liabilities are liabilities of the company that must be paid within the year. Trans-Canada Retail Stores Ltd. has $2.78 of cash and equivalents to pay for every $1 of its current liabilities.

The interpretation of the ratio depends on the type of business, the composition of current assets, inventory turnover rate, and credit terms. A current ratio of 2:1 is good but not exceptional, because it means the company has $2 cash and equivalents to pay for each $1 of its debt. However, if 50% of Company A's current assets were cash, whereas 90% of Company B's current assets were in inventory, but each had a current ratio of 2:1, Company A would be more liquid than B because it could pay its current debts more easily and quickly.

Also, if a current ratio of 2:1 is good, is 20:1 ten times as good? No. If a company's current ratio exceeds 5:1 and it consistently maintains such a high level, the company may have an unnecessary accumulation of funds which could indicate sales problems (too much inventory) or financial mismanagement.

Different businesses have different working capital requirements. In some businesses (such as distilleries), several years may elapse before the raw materials are processed and sold as finished products. Consequently, these businesses require a large amount of working capital to finance operations until they receive cash from the sale of finished products. In others (such as meat packers), the manufacturing process is much shorter. Cash from sales is received more quickly and is available to pay current debts. Such businesses can safely operate with less working capital.

QUICK RATIO (THE ACID TEST)

The second of the two most common corporate liquidity ratios, the **quick ratio**, is a more stringent test than the current ratio. In this calculation, inventories, which are generally not considered liquid assets, are subtracted from current assets. The quick ratio shows how well current liabilities are covered by cash and by items with a ready cash value.

© CSI GLOBAL EDUCATION INC. (2008)

$$\frac{\text{Current assets} - \text{Inventories}}{\text{Current liabilities}}$$

$$\frac{\text{Item 6} - \text{Item 4}}{\text{Item 17}} \text{ or } \frac{\$12{,}238{,}000 - \$9{,}035{,}000}{\$4{,}410{,}000} \text{ or } \frac{\$3{,}203{,}000}{\$4{,}410{,}000} = 0.73:1$$

Current assets include inventories that, at times, may be difficult to convert into cash. As well, because of changing market conditions, inventories may be carried on the balance sheet at inflated values. Therefore, the quick ratio offers a more conservative test of a company's ability to meet its current obligations. Quick assets are current assets less inventories. In this example, the ratio is 0.73 to 1, which means there are 73 cents of current assets, exclusive of inventories, to meet each $1 of current liabilities.

There is no absolute standard for this ratio, but if it is 1:1 or better, it suggests a good liquid position. However, companies with a quick ratio of less than 1 to 1 may be equally good if they have a high rate of inventory turnover, because inventory that is turned over quickly is the equivalent of cash. In our example, however, a quick ratio of 0.73:1 is probably satisfactory, since the company we are looking at is a retail store chain, an industry characterized by large inventories and a high turnover rate.

OPERATING CASH FLOW RATIO

Cash flow from operations is an important measure as it indicates the company's ability to generate cash from its day-to-day operations. A company needs cash inflows on a continual basis to pay its bills, finance growth and pay dividends. A positive cash flow from operating activities shows that the company was able to generate cash from its current business activities. Companies with negative cash flow from operating activities for periods of time will need to find other sources of funds such as borrowing, share issuance, or the sale of assets.

The **operating cash flow ratio** shows how well liabilities to be paid within one year are covered by the cash flow generated by the company's operating activities:

$$\frac{\text{Current flow from operations}}{\text{Current liabilities}}$$

$$\frac{(\text{Item } 43 + 32 + 49 + 41 - 42 - 50)}{\text{Item 17}} \text{ or } \frac{\$1{,}298{,}000}{\$4{,}410{,}000} = 0.29:1$$

This ratio is used to assess whether or not a company generates enough cash from operations to cover its current obligations. An absolute standard does not exist for this ratio. However, if the ratio falls below 1.00, the company is not generating enough cash to meet its short-term requirements. When this occurs, the company may be forced to find other sources to fund its day-to-day operations or it may need to find ways to reduce the amount of cash being spent. For Trans-Canada Retail, an operating cash flow ratio of 0.29 means there are 29 cents of operational cash flow available for every $1 of liabilities. Such a low ratio may highlight a potential liquidity problem for the company. It may also emphasize other problems. Trans-Canada Retail carries a fairly high level of inventory on its balance sheet. The longer it takes for the company to turn inventory into sales, the longer the time lag in receiving the cash needed to finance its operations.

© CSI GLOBAL EDUCATION INC. (2008)

Risk Analysis Ratios

The analysis of a company's capital structure enables investors to judge how well the company can meet its financial obligations. Excessive borrowing increases the company's costs, because it must service its debt by paying interest on outstanding bank loans, notes payable, bonds or debentures.

If a company cannot generate enough cash to pay the interest on its outstanding debt, then its creditors could force it into bankruptcy. If the company must sell off its assets to meet its obligations, then investors who have purchased bonds, debentures, or stock in the company could lose some or all of their investment.

ASSET COVERAGE

This ratio shows a company's ability to cover its debt obligations with its assets after all liabilities have been satisfied. The ratio shows the **net tangible assets** of the company for each $1,000 of total debt outstanding. It enables the debtholder to measure the protection provided by the company's tangible assets (that is, assets other than goodwill, intellectual property, or similar intangibles) after all liabilities have been met.

Assets with a value that is much higher than a company's total debt are normally required to generate the earnings necessary to meet interest requirements and repay indebtedness. At the same time, asset coverage shows the amount of assets (at their book value) backing the debt securities. However, at best, asset values should be treated with extreme caution, as the realizable value of assets in liquidation could be substantially less than their book value when the company is a going concern.

Asset values are usually calculated over a number of years to identify a trend.

$$\frac{\text{Total assets} - \text{Deferred charges} - \text{Intangible assets} - [\text{Current liabilities less short-term debt such as bank advances and the current portion of long-term debt}]}{\text{Total debt outstanding (i.e., short-term debt + long-term debt)} \div \$1{,}000}$$

$$\frac{\text{Item 11} - \text{Item 9} - \text{Item 10} - [\text{Item 17} - (\text{Item 12} + \text{Item 16})]}{(\text{Item 12} + \text{Item 16} + \text{Item 20}) \div \$1{,}000}$$

$$\text{or } \frac{\$19{,}761{,}000 - \$136{,}000 - \$150{,}000 - [\$4{,}410{,}000 - (\$1{,}630{,}000 + \$120{,}000)]}{(\$1{,}630{,}000 + \$120{,}000 + \$1{,}350{,}000) \div \$1{,}000}$$

$$= \frac{\$16{,}815{,}000}{3{,}100} = \$5{,}424 \text{ per } \$1{,}000 \text{ total debt outstanding}$$

Note: The debtholder's claim on assets ranks before future income taxes and non-controlling interest in subsidiaries.

Debtholders need to know the asset value behind each $1,000 of total debt outstanding. Normally, debtholders have a claim against all the company's assets after providing for liability items, which rank ahead of their claims. To be conservative, deferred charges and intangible assets such as goodwill and patents are first deducted from the total asset figure.

In our example, there is $5,424 of assets backing each $1,000 of total debt outstanding after providing for current liabilities, other than bank advances and the current portion of long-term debt, both of which are included in total debt outstanding. For example, if the industry standard

© CSI GLOBAL EDUCATION INC. (2008)

for this ratio is that retail companies should have at least $2,000 of net tangible assets for each $1,000 of total debt outstanding, Trans-Canada Retail Stores Ltd. meets, and in fact, exceeds this standard.

Industry standards for this ratio vary due, in part, to the stability of income provided by the company. Utilities, for example, have a fairly stable source of income. They are characterized by heavy investment in permanent property, which accounts for a large part of their total assets. They are also subject to regulation, which ensures the utility a fair return on its investment. Consequently, there is a greater degree of earnings' stability and continuity than for retail stores.

This calculation uses book values, which usually have no relationship to current market values, especially for fixed assets. Fixed assets, except for land, may have no value except to a continuing business, so it would be pointless to sell them to satisfy debtholders.

Trans-Canada Retail Stores Ltd. has only one issue of long-term debt outstanding (item 20). The calculation of net tangible assets (NTA) for each $1,000 of total debt outstanding is, accordingly, relatively straightforward. If more than one issue were outstanding, the NTA coverage calculation would include that debt figure as well, but of course the senior issue would be better covered than a junior issue, because of the senior issue's higher priority in interest and liquidation proceeds.

PERCENTAGE OF TOTAL CAPITAL RATIOS

These ratios simply show what percentage of total invested capital each type of contributor provided or is entitled to. (A percentage is a ratio in which a number is related to 100 instead of 1. Thus, 46% is the same as the ratio 46:100 or 0.46:1.) Common shareholders are usually entitled to more than they contributed, because retained earnings have accumulated to their credit over the years. Long-term debtholders and preferred shareholders are either entitled to par value or par plus a small premium.

Short-term debt	Item 12	$ 1,630,000
	+Item 16	120,000
+ Long-term debt	+Item 20	1,350,000
+ Par value of preferred shares	+Item 21	750,000
Common equity		
+ Stated value of common shares	+Item 22	1,564,000
+ Contributed surplus	+Item 23	150,000
+ Retained earnings	+Item 24	10,835,000
+ Foreign exchange adjustment	+Item 25	60,000
= Invested capital		$ 16,459,000

Percentage of **capital structure** attributable to debtholders (short- and long-term):

$$\frac{\text{Item 12} + \text{Item 16} + \text{Item 20}}{\text{Invested capital}} \times 100$$

$$\text{or} \quad \frac{\$1,630,000 + \$120,000 + \$135,000}{\$16,459,000} \times 100$$

$$= \frac{\$3,100,000}{\$16,459,000} \times 100 = 18.83\% \text{ (Debtholders – short and long-term)}$$

© CSI GLOBAL EDUCATION INC. (2008)

Percentage of capital structure attributable to preferred shareholders:

$$\frac{\text{Item 21}}{\$16{,}459{,}000} \times 100$$

$$\text{or } \frac{\$750{,}000}{\$16{,}459{,}000} \times 100 = 4.56\% \text{ (Preferred shareholders)}$$

These balance sheet relationships are helpful in determining the soundness of a company's capitalization. In our example, 18.83% of the capital structure is in short- and long-term debt, 4.56% is in preferred stock, and the balance of 76.61% is in common equity.

A high proportion of debt in the capitalization may mean that the company will have difficulty in meeting heavy interest and sinking fund charges in periods of low earnings. On the other hand, if a company can earn a higher rate of return on its invested capital than the cost of borrowed funds, it is good financial management to have a debt component in the capital structure. Debt can be used to expand the size of the company, with resulting benefits.

FUTURE INCOME TAXES AND INVESTED CAPITAL

Future income taxes and non-controlling interest in subsidiaries may also be validly regarded as sources of invested capital. Some analysts regard future income taxes as, in effect, an interest-free loan from the government and therefore part of debt. Others regard it as part of common equity since, in effect, it represents earnings that have not been allowed to flow through to retained earnings.

If the invested capital of Trans-Canada Retail Ltd. included future income taxes (item 18 on the balance sheet), then invested capital would total $16,944,000. However, in this text, invested capital does not include future taxes.

There is no general rule to determine what constitutes acceptable capitalization. The relationship of debt to total capitalization varies widely for companies in different industries. It is normal for public utility, pipeline, and real estate companies, for example, to have a fairly substantial proportion of their capital structure made up of debt. But if a company engaged in manufacturing products, subject to wide fluctuation in demand, showed a debt ratio as high as that normal in public utilities, the soundness of its capital structure would be questioned.

Analysts develop a sense of what is acceptable capitalization based on their experience. Utilities, for example, are expected to have total debt outstanding less than 60% of total capital, taking the equity component at book value.

DEBT/EQUITY RATIO

The **debt/equity ratio** shows the proportion of borrowed funds used relative to the investments made by shareholders in the company. If the ratio is too high, it may indicate that a company has borrowed excessively, and this increases the financial risk of the company. If the debt burden is too large, it reduces the margin of safety protecting the debtholder's capital, increases the company's fixed charges, reduces earnings available for dividends, and in times of recession or high interest rates, could cause a financial crisis.

$$\frac{\text{Total debt outstanding (i.e., short-* and long-term)}}{\text{Book value of shareholders' equity}}$$

* In this example, bank advances and first mortgage bonds due within one year.

© CSI GLOBAL EDUCATION INC. (2008)

$$\frac{\text{Item 12} + \text{Item 16} + \text{Item 20}}{\text{Item 21} + \text{Item 22} + \text{Item 23} + \text{Item 4} + \text{Item 25}}$$

$$\text{or } \frac{\$1,630,000 + \$120,000 + \$135,000}{\$750,000 + \$1,564,000 + \$150,000 + \$10,835,000 + \$60,000}$$

$$= \frac{\$3,100,000}{\$13,359,000} \times 100 = 23.21\% \ (0.23{:}1)$$

Thus, the debt/equity ratio for Trans-Canada Retail Stores Ltd. is 23.21% or 0.23:1, which is acceptable if it does not exceed the industry standard for retail stores.

Sometimes, analysts will make adjustments to this ratio by including total liabilities to the calculation. We have excluded other liabilities from the calculation to focus the ratio on a company's financial risk or leverage through the use of debt.

CASH FLOW/TOTAL DEBT OUTSTANDING

Cash flow from operations is a measure of a company's ability to generate funds internally. Other things being equal, a company with a large and increasing cash flow is better able to finance expansion using its own funds, without the need to issue new securities. The increased interest or dividend costs of new securities issues may reduce cash flow and earnings, while issuing convertibles and warrants may dilute the value of common stock.

The **cash flow/total debt ratio** gauges a company's ability to repay the funds it has borrowed. Bank advances are short-term and must normally be repaid or rolled over within a year. Corporate debt issues commonly have sinking funds requiring annual cash outlays. A company's annual cash flow should therefore be adequate to meet these commitments.

Before calculating this ratio, it is important to define cash flow from operations and consider its significance.

Cash flow is:

- A company's net earnings;
- *Plus* all deductions not requiring a cash outlay, such as amortization, non-controlling interest in subsidiaries and future income taxes;
- *Minus* all additions not received in cash, such as equity income.

Because of the substantial size of non-cash deductions on earnings statements (operating charges, which do not involve an actual outlay of funds), cash flow from operations frequently provides a broader picture of a company's earning power than net earnings alone. Consequently, cash flow from operations is considered by some analysts a better indicator of the ability to pay dividends and finance expansion. It is particularly useful in comparing companies within the same industry. It can reveal whether a company, even one that shows little or no net earnings after amortization and write-offs, can meet its debts.

Proper use of cash flow means considering it in relation to a company's total financial requirements. In financial statements, the cash flow statement puts cash flow from operations into perspective as a source of funds available to meet financial requirements.

© CSI GLOBAL EDUCATION INC. (2008)

A relatively high ratio of cash flow to debt is considered positive. Conversely, a low ratio is negative. Analysts use minimum standards to assess debt repayment capacity and provide another perspective on debt evaluation. For example, the industry standard for cash flow/total debt outstanding for retail stores might be that annual cash flow in each of the last fiscal five years should be at least 20% (0.20:1) of total debt outstanding.

$$\frac{\text{Current flow from operations}}{\text{Total debt outstanding (i.e., short- and long-term)}} \times 100$$

$$\frac{\text{Item 43} - \text{Item 42} + \text{Item 41} + \text{Item 49 (future portion only)} + \text{Item 32 +/- Item 50}}{\text{Item 12} + \text{Item 16} + \text{Item 20}} \times 100$$

$$\text{or } \frac{\$1{,}298{,}000}{\$1{,}630{,}000 + \$120{,}000 + \$1{,}350{,}000}$$

$$= \frac{\$1{,}298{,}000}{\$3{,}100{,}000} \times 100 = 41.87\% \ (0.42:1)$$

The preceding calculation shows that the cash flow/debt ratio for Trans-Canada Retail Stores Ltd. is 0.42:1, which is acceptable, since it exceeds the 0.20:1 industry standard.

Analysts usually calculate the cash flow to total debt outstanding ratio for each of the last five fiscal years. An improving trend is desirable. A declining trend may indicate weakening financial strength, unless the individual ratios for each year are well above the minimum standards. For example, if the latest year's ratio was 0.61 (Year 5) and preceding years' ratios were 0.60 (Year 4), 0.63 (Year 3), 0.65 (Year 2), and 0.70 (Year 1), there would seem to be no cause for concern, because each year's ratio is so strong.

INTEREST COVERAGE

The **interest coverage ratio** reveals the ability of a company to pay the interest charges on its debt and indicates how well these charges are covered, based upon earnings available to pay them. Interest coverage indicates a margin of safety, since a company's inability to meet its interest charges could result in bankruptcy.

It is essential to take into account *all* interest charges, including bank loans, short-term debt, senior debt, and junior debt. Default on any one debt may impair the issuer's ability to meet its obligations to the others, and lead to default on other debts.

Interest coverage is generally considered to be the most important quantitative test of risk when considering a debt security. A level of earnings well in excess of interest requirements is deemed necessary as a form of protection for possible adverse conditions in future years. Overall, the greater the coverage, the greater the margin of safety.

To assess the adequacy of the coverage, it is common to set criteria. For example, an analyst may decide that an industrial company's annual interest requirements in each of the last five years should be covered at least three times by earnings available for interest payment in each year. At this level, the analyst would consider its debt securities to be of acceptable investment quality.

© CSI GLOBAL EDUCATION INC. (2008)

A company may fail to meet these coverage standards without ever experiencing difficulties in fulfilling its debt obligations. However, the securities of such a company are considered a much higher risk, because they lack an acceptable margin of safety. Thus, the interest coverage standards are only an indication of the *likelihood* that a company will be able to meet its interest obligations.

It is also important to study the year-to-year trend in the interest coverage calculation. Ideally, a company should not only meet the industry standards for coverage in each of the last five or more years but increase its coverage. A stable trend, which means that the company is meeting the minimum standards but not improving the ratio over the period, is also considered acceptable. However, a deteriorating trend suggests that further analysis is required to determine whether the company's financial position has seriously weakened.

Aberrations in the trend may occur, for example, as the result of a prolonged strike, which may cause earnings to drop within a single year, but which will probably not impair the company's basic financial soundness in succeeding years.

However, a steep decline in earnings, particularly if it is prolonged or caused by a fundamental deterioration in the company's financial position, should prompt a revaluation of the investment quality of a debt issue. A sudden reversal from a profit to a loss also merits close scrutiny. Other changes, such as a rapid build-up in short-term bank loans, could also reduce the investment calibre of a company's debt securities. Thus, analysts must monitor companies to ensure that developments do not adversely affect its ability to fulfill its debt obligations.

$$\frac{\text{Earnings before interest and taxes (EBIT)}}{\text{Total interest charges}}$$

$$\frac{\begin{array}{c}\text{Net earnings (before extraordinary items)}\\ -\text{ equity income} + \text{non-controlling interest earnings of subsidiary companies}\\ +\text{ all income taxes} + \text{total interest charges}\end{array}}{\text{Total interest charges}}$$

$$\frac{\text{Item 43} - \text{Item 42} + \text{Item 41} + \text{Item 40} + \text{Item 38} + \text{Item 37}}{\text{Item 37} + \text{Item 38}}$$

$$\text{or } \frac{\$1,086,000 - \$5,000 + \$12,000 + \$880,000 + \$168,300 + \$120,700}{\$120,700 + \$168,300}$$

$$= \frac{\$2,262,000}{\$289,000} = 7.83 \text{ times}$$

The calculation shows that Trans-Canada Retail Stores Ltd.'s interest charges for the year were covered 7.83 times by net earnings available to pay them. Stated in another way, it had $7.83 of net earnings out of which to pay every $1.00 of interest.

Again, industry standards will vary from industry to industry. Standards vary, not only for companies in different industries, but also for companies in the same industry, depending upon their past earnings records and future prospects. The record of a company's interest coverage is particularly important, because a company must meet its fixed charges both in good times and bad. Unless it has already demonstrated its ability to do so, it cannot be said to have met the test.

© CSI GLOBAL EDUCATION INC. (2008)

In general, the lower the ratio the more a company is burdened by interest expense to cover its debt. For example, a ratio below one indicates a company's inability to generate enough revenue to cover its interest expense.

A high interest coverage ratio is not required for utility companies. They have a licence to operate in specific areas with little or no competition, and rate boards establish rates that enable them to earn a fair return on their capital investment. By contrast, the earnings of retail companies are likely to be more volatile, so a higher coverage ratio is necessary to provide a greater margin of safety. In addition to meeting the minimum standards for each of the last five fiscal years, companies should show a steady or rising trend in their year-to-year earnings available for interest charges and in their year-to-year interest coverage figures over the same period. A weakening or declining pattern is usually a danger signal.

PREFERRED DIVIDEND COVERAGE RATIO

Like interest coverage, the **preferred dividend coverage** ratio indicates the margin of safety for preferred dividends. It measures the amount of money a firm has to pay dividends to preferred shareholders. It is essentially an extension of the interest coverage calculation to include preferred dividends. The higher the ratio the better, as it indicates the company has little difficulty in paying its preferred dividend requirements.

The formula is as follows:

$$\frac{\begin{array}{c}\text{Net earnings (before extraordinary items)}\\ -\text{ equity income} + \text{non-controlling interests in earnings of subsidiaries}\\ +\text{ all income taxes} + \text{total interest charges}\end{array}}{\text{Total interest charges + preferred dividend payments before tax}}$$

$$\frac{\text{Item 43} - \text{Item 42} + \text{Item 41} + \text{Item 40} + \text{Item 38} + \text{Item 37}}{\text{Item 37} + \text{Item 38} + \text{Item 47 (before tax)}}$$

$$\text{or} \quad \frac{\$1{,}086{,}000 - \$5{,}000 + \$12{,}000 + \$880{,}000 + \$168{,}300 + \$120{,}700}{\$120{,}700 + \$168{,}300 + \dfrac{(\$37{,}500 \times 100)}{(100 - 44.60)}}$$

$$= \frac{\$2{,}262{,}000}{\$289{,}000 + \$67{,}690} = \frac{\$2{,}262{,}000}{\$356{,}690} = 6.34 \text{ times}$$

Since dividends are paid to shareholders from net income (after tax has been paid) and interest is paid before tax, it is necessary to *gross-up* the amount of the preferred dividend to its pre-tax equivalent as shown. This is because in order to have enough funds available to adequately cover the preferred dividend requirement, a company must have even higher pre-tax profits, as some of these profits will be paid in taxes and are therefore not available to distribute as dividends.

Trans-Canada Retail Stores Ltd.'s preferred coverage is 6.34 times interest, more than adequate coverage. Industry standards for a retail company are that the combined debt and preferred charges in each of the last five fiscal years should be covered at least three times by earnings available in each respective year.

While dividend coverage for the most recent fiscal year is important, it should not be looked at in isolation. As with interest coverage, the year-to-year trend, as well as the results in each of the last five fiscal years, should be examined to see if the situation is weakening or improving.

© CSI GLOBAL EDUCATION INC. (2008)

Trans-Canada Retail Stores Ltd., has only one preferred share issue outstanding (Item 21). If more than one issue were outstanding, the calculation would be similar, but preferred dividends of all preferred issues would be used, even if the intention was to assess one particular issue.

Typically, preferred dividend coverage is calculated for the last five years, and a trend is plotted. Ideally a rising or stable trend is revealed. However, even large, well-established companies will record a declining trend after one or two isolated bad years. Strikes, unusually heavy capital requirements, a cyclical industry or economic downturns are examples of events that could cause a declining trend. Analysts allow for temporary distortions and look at the overall five-year trend. They check that year-to-year coverage figures are above required minimums. If so, preferred dividend payments are likely to be continued without undue financial strain.

A clear deterioration in a company's dividend coverage trend over three or more years would be serious. Such a company would be subjected to re-appraisal to re-assess financial strength and ability to meet fixed income requirements. Generally speaking, the closer the preferred is to industry standards, the more closely the security is watched for signs of improvement or deterioration. Preferreds in cyclical industries, such as heavy industry and textiles, should be chosen with great care if coverage is near the minimum.

Operating Performance Ratios

The analysis of a company's profitability and efficiency tells the investor how well management is making use of the company's resources.

GROSS PROFIT MARGIN

The **gross profit margin ratio** is useful both for calculating internal trend lines and for making comparisons with other companies, especially in industries such as food products and cosmetics, where turnover is high and competition is stiff. The gross margin is an indication of the efficiency of management in turning over the company's goods at a profit. It shows the company's rate of profit after allowing for the cost of goods sold.

$$\frac{\text{Net sales} - \text{Cost of goods sold}}{\text{Net sales}} \times 100$$

$$\frac{\text{Item 28} - \text{Item 29}}{\text{Item 28}} \times 100$$

$$\text{or} \quad \frac{\$43,800,000 - \$28,250,000}{\$43,800,000} \times 100$$

$$= \frac{\$15,550,000}{\$43,800,000} \times 100 = 35.50\%$$

OPERATING PROFIT MARGIN

The **operating profit margin ratio** is a more stringent measure of the company's ability to manage its resources, as it takes into account the sales, general, and administrative expenses incurred in producing earnings. One advantage is that it makes it possible to compare profit margins between companies that do not show "cost of goods sold" as a separate figure and for

© CSI GLOBAL EDUCATION INC. (2008)

which, consequently, gross profit margin cannot be calculated. In computing the operating profit margin ratio for companies subject to excise taxes, such as tobacco companies, it is important to use "net sales *after* excise taxes" as the net sales figure in the calculation.

$$\frac{\text{Net sales} - (\text{Cost of goods sold} + \text{selling, administrative and general expenses})}{\text{Net sales}} \times 100$$

$$\frac{\text{Item 28} - (\text{Item 29} + \text{Item 31})}{\text{Item 28}} \times 100$$

$$\text{or} \quad \frac{\$43,800,000 - (\$28,250,000 + \$12,752,000)}{\$43,800,000} \times 100$$

$$= \frac{\$43,800,000 - \$41,002,000}{\$43,800,000} \times 100$$

$$= \frac{\$2,798,000}{\$43,800,000} \times 100 = 6.39\%$$

PRE-TAX PROFIT MARGIN

The figure for net earnings before income taxes represents the level of sales after all costs, except taxes, have been deducted. By calculating this amount as a percentage of sales over several years, it is possible to identify trends in the pre-tax profit margin. A rising trend may indicate improving cost control and efficiency; a declining trend may indicate the reverse.

Comparing the pre-tax profit margin ratio with the operating margin ratio is useful. For example, a rising operating margin but a falling pre-tax profit margin indicate proportionately large increases in interest and/or amortization charges.

Analyzing these ratios may uncover the cause of a change in the trend. Higher interest charges may result from the initial payment of interest on a new debt security issue, a build-up in short-term bank loans, the higher interest payments required for floating rate securities, and so forth. Similarly, any extraordinary changes in amortization charges should be analyzed. A company's amortization policy is usually explained in the notes to the financial statements; any changes in policy are noted.

$$\frac{\text{Net income before income taxes}}{\text{Net sales}} \times 100$$

$$\frac{\text{Item 39}}{\text{Item 28}} \times 100$$

$$\text{or} \quad \frac{\$1,973,000}{\$43,800,000} \times 100$$

$$= 4.5\%$$

© CSI GLOBAL EDUCATION INC. (2008)

NET PROFIT MARGIN

Net profit margin is an important indicator of how efficiently the company is managed after taking both expenses and taxes into account. Because this ratio is the result of the company's operations for the period, it effectively sums up management's ability to run the business in a single figure.

$$\frac{\text{Net earnings (before extraordinary items)} - \text{Equity income} + \text{non-controlling interest in the earnings of subsidiaries}}{\text{Net sales}} \times 100$$

$$\frac{\text{Item 39} - \text{Item 42} + \text{Item 41}}{\text{Item 28}} \times 100$$

$$\text{or } \frac{\$1{,}086{,}000 - \$5{,}000 + \$12{,}000}{\$43{,}800{,}000} \times 100$$

$$= \frac{\$1{,}093{,}000}{\$43{,}800{,}000} \times 100 = 2.50\%$$

To make comparisons between companies or from one year to another, the net profit must be shown before non-controlling interest has been deducted and equity income added in, since not all companies have these items. The sales figure used in this calculation should be net of excise taxes.

PRE-TAX RETURN ON INVESTED CAPITAL

Pre-tax return correlates income with the invested capital responsible for producing it, without reference to the source of that capital. In other words, this ratio shows how well management has employed the assets at its disposal.

$$\frac{\text{Net earnings (before extraordinary items)} + \text{income taxes} + \text{total interest charges}}{\text{Invested capital*}} \times 100$$

*The components of this item were discussed earlier.

$$\frac{\text{Item 43} + \text{Item 40} + \text{Item 37} + \text{Item 38}}{\text{Item 12} + \text{Item 16} + \text{Item 20} + \text{Item 21} + \text{Item 22} + \text{Item 23} + \text{Item 24} + \text{Item 25}} \times 100$$

$$\text{or } \frac{\$1{,}086{,}000 + \$880{,}000 + \$120{,}700 + \$168{,}300}{\$16{,}459{,}000} \times 100$$

$$= \frac{\$2{,}255{,}000}{\$16{,}459{,}000} \times 100 = 13.70\%$$

NET (OR AFTER-TAX) RETURN ON INVESTED CAPITAL

The differences between **net return** and the pre-tax return are that income tax is not included in the numerator in this case, and total interest charges after tax instead of total interest charges are added to net earnings (before extraordinary items).

© CSI GLOBAL EDUCATION INC. (2008)

$$\frac{\text{Net earnings (before extraordinary items)} + \text{total interest charges (after tax)}}{\text{Invested capital}} \times 100$$

$$\frac{\text{Item 43} + (\text{Item 37} + \text{Item 38} - \text{both after tax})}{\text{Item 12} + \text{Item 16} + \text{Item 20} + \text{Item 21} + \text{Item 22} + \text{Item 23} + \text{Item 24} + \text{Item 25}} \times 100$$

or $$\frac{\$1,086,000 + [\$120,700 + \$168,300) \times .554^*]}{\$16,459,000} \times 100$$

$$= \frac{\$1,246,106}{\$16,459,000} \times 100 = 7.57\%$$

* Calculated as 1 minus apparent rate.

NET (OR AFTER-TAX) RETURN ON COMMON EQUITY

The **return on common equity (ROE)** ratio shows the dollar amount of earnings that were produced for each dollar invested by the company's common shareholders. The trend in the ROE indicates management's effectiveness in maintaining or increasing profitability in relation to the common equity capital of the company. A declining trend suggests that operating efficiency is waning, although further quantitative analysis is needed to pinpoint the causes. For shareholders, a declining ratio shows that their investment is being employed less productively. This ratio is very important for common shareholders, since it reflects the profitability of their capital in the business.

$$\frac{\text{Net earnings (before extraordinary items)} - \text{preferred dividends}}{\text{Common equity}} \times 100$$

$$\frac{\text{Item 43} - \text{Item 47}}{\text{Item 22} + \text{Item 23} + \text{Item 24} + \text{Item 25}} \times 100$$

or $$\frac{\$1,086,000 - \$37,500}{\$1,564,000 + \$150,000 + \$10,835,000 + \$60,000} \times 100$$

$$= \frac{\$1,048,500}{\$12,609,000} \times 100 = 8.32\%$$

INVENTORY TURNOVER RATIO

The **inventory turnover ratio** measures the number of times a company's inventory is turned over in a year. It may also be expressed as a number of days required to achieve turnover, as shown in the example below. A high turnover ratio is considered good. A company with a high turnover requires a smaller investment in inventory than one producing the same sales with a low turnover.

$$\frac{\text{Cost of goods sold}}{\text{Inventory}}$$

$$\frac{\text{Item 29}}{\text{Item 4}}$$

or $$\frac{\$28,250,000}{\$9,035,000} = 3.13 \text{ times}$$

© CSI GLOBAL EDUCATION INC. (2008)

To calculate inventory turnover in days, divide 365 (days) by the inventory turnover ratio:

$$\frac{365}{3.13} = 116.61 \text{ days}$$

To be meaningful, the inventory turnover ratio should be calculated using the cost of goods sold. If this information is not shown separately, the net sales figure may have to be used.

$$\frac{\text{Net sales}}{\text{Inventory}}$$

$$\frac{\text{Item 28}}{\text{Item 4}}$$

$$\text{or } \frac{\$43,800,000}{\$9,035,000} = 4.85 \text{ times}$$

This ratio may also be expressed in terms of the number of days required to sell current inventory by dividing 365 days by the ratio.

$$\frac{365}{4.85} = 75.26 \text{ days}$$

This ratio indicates the management's efficiency in turning over the company's inventory and can be used to compare one company with others in the same field. It also provides an indication of the adequacy of a company's inventory for the volume of business being handled.

Inventory turnover rates vary from industry to industry. For example, companies in the food industry turn over their inventory more rapidly than companies engaged in heavy manufacturing, because a longer period of time is required to process, manufacture, and sell finished products.

Examples of high-turnover industries: baking, cosmetics, dairy products, food chains, meat packing, industries dealing in perishable goods, quick-consumption low-cost item industries.

Examples of low-turnover industries: aircraft manufacturers, distillers, fur goods, heavy machinery manufacturers, steel, and wineries.

If a company has an inventory turnover rate that is above average for its industry, it generally indicates a better balance between inventory and sales volume. The company is unlikely to be caught with too much inventory if the price of raw materials drops or the market demand for its products falls. There should also be less wastage, because materials and products are not standing unused for long periods and deteriorating in quality and/or marketability. On the other hand, if inventory turnover is too high in relation to industry norms, the company may have problems with shortages of inventory, resulting in lost sales.

If a company has a low rate of inventory turnover, it may be because:

- The inventory contains an unusually large portion of unsaleable goods;
- The company has over-bought inventory; or
- The value of the inventory has been overstated.

Since a large part of a company's working capital is usually tied up in inventory, the way in which the inventory position is managed directly affects earnings and the rate of return earned from the employment of the company's equity capital in the business.

© CSI GLOBAL EDUCATION INC. (2008)

Value Ratios

Ratios in this group – sometimes called market ratios – measure the way the stock market rates a company by comparing the market price of its shares to information in its financial statements. Price alone does not tell analysts much about a company unless there is a common way to relate the price to dividends and earnings. Value ratios do this.

PERCENTAGE DIVIDEND PAYOUT RATIOS

Dividend payout ratios indicate the amount or percentage of the company's net earnings that are paid out to shareholders in the form of dividends. There are two kinds of payout ratios:

- On combined preferred and common dividends
- On common dividends only

Note the different divisor in each case.

$$\frac{\text{Total dividends (preferred + common)}}{\text{Net earnings (before extraordinary items)}} \times 100$$

$$\frac{\text{Item 47 + Item 48 in Retained earnings statement}}{\text{Item 43 in Statement of earnings}} \times 100$$

$$\text{or } \frac{\$37,500 + \$350,000}{\$1,086,000} \times 100$$

$$= \frac{\$387,000}{\$1,086,000} \times 100 = 35.68\%$$

$$\frac{\text{Dividend on common}}{\text{Net earnings (before extraordinary items)} - \text{preferred dividend}} \times 100$$

$$\frac{\text{Item 48}}{\text{Item 43} - \text{Item 47}} \times 100$$

$$\text{or } \frac{\$350,000}{\$1,086,000 - \$37,500} \times 100$$

$$= \frac{\$387,000}{\$1,048,500} \times 100 = 33.38\%$$

Deducting the percentage of earnings being paid out as dividends from 100 gives the percentage of earnings remaining in the business to finance future operations. In our first example, 35.68% of available earnings were paid out as dividends in the year, therefore 64.32% was reinvested in the business.

Dividend payout ratios are generally unstable since they are tied directly to the earnings of the company, which change from year to year. The directors of some companies try to maintain a steady dividend rate through good and poor times to preserve the credit rating and investment standing of the company's securities. If dividends are greater than earnings for the year, the payout ratio will exceed 100%. Dividends will then be taken out of retained earnings, a situation that erodes the value of shareholders' equity.

© CSI GLOBAL EDUCATION INC. (2008)

EARNINGS PER COMMON SHARE

The **earnings per common share (EPS)** ratio shows the earnings available to each common share and is an important element in judging an appropriate market price for buying or selling common stock. A rising trend in EPS has favourable implications for the price of a stock.

In practice, a common stock's market price reflects the anticipated trend in EPS for the next 12 to 24 months, rather than the current EPS. Thus, it is common practice to estimate EPS for the next year or two. Accurate estimates for longer periods are difficult because of the many variables involved.

Along with dividend per share, this is one of the most widely used and well understood of all ratios. It is easy to calculate and is commonly reported in the financial press.

$$\frac{\text{Net earnings (before extraordinary items)} - \text{preferred dividends}}{\text{Number of common shares outstanding}} \times 100$$

$$\frac{\text{Item 43} - \text{Item 47}}{\text{Number of outstanding common shares per Item 22}} \times 100$$

$$\text{or } \frac{\$1,086,000 - \$37,500}{350,000} \times 100$$

$$= \frac{\$1,048,500}{350,000} = \$3.00 \text{ per share}$$

Because of the importance of EPS, analysts pay close attention to possible dilution of the stock's value caused by the conversion of outstanding convertible securities, the exercise of warrants, shares issued under employee stock options, and other changes.

Fully diluted earnings per share can be calculated on common stock outstanding plus common stock equivalents such as convertible preferred stock, convertible debentures, stock options (under employee stock-option plans), and warrants. This figure shows the dilution in earnings per share that would occur if all equivalent securities were converted into common shares. Since Trans-Canada Retail Stores Ltd. has no convertible securities, let us consider Company ABC, which had the following:

- 1,000,000 shares of $2.50 Cumulative Convertible Preferred Shares, $25 par, that are convertible into common on a 1-for-1 basis;
- 2,800,000 common shares, no par value; and
- Net earnings (before extraordinary items) of $10,455,000.

Earnings per common share using the formula above would be calculated thus:

$$\frac{\$10,455,000 - \$2,500,000}{2,800,000} \times 100$$

$$= \frac{\$7,955,000}{2,800,000} = \$2.84 \text{ per share}$$

© CSI GLOBAL EDUCATION INC. (2008)

Fully diluted earnings per common share would require the following adjustments:

- Since the preferred dividends would not have to be paid if the preferred shares were converted into common shares, the earnings available for the common shares would increase by the amount of the preferred dividends deducted in formula; the total would be $10,455,000.
- The number of common shares would increase by one million, since a million preferred shares would be converted on a 1-for-1 basis.

The formula is then:

$$\frac{\text{Adjusted net earnings (before extraordinary items)}}{\text{Adjusted common shares outstanding}} \times 100$$

$$= \frac{\$10,455,000}{2,800,000 + 1,000,000} \times 100$$

$$= \frac{\$10,455,000}{3,800,000} = \$2.75 \text{ fully diluted earnings per share}$$

Earnings from operations after all prior claims have been met belong to the common shareholders. The shareholders therefore will want to know how much has been earned on their shares. If net earnings are high, directors may declare and pay out a good portion as dividends. Even in growth companies, directors may decide to make at least a token payment because they realize that most shareholders like to feel some of the profits are flowing into their pockets. On the other hand, if net earnings are low or the company has suffered a loss, they may not pay dividends on the common shares.

Describing net earnings in terms of common shares shows shareholders the profitability of their ownership interest in the company and whether dividends are likely to be paid. In the Trans-Canada Retail Stores example, net earnings are $3.00 for each common share. Since regular dividends of $1.00 per share per year are being paid on common shares, the calculation also indicates that the dividend is well protected by earnings. In other words, earnings per common share are $2.00 more than regular dividend payments.

Since common share dividends are declared and paid at the discretion of a company's board of directors, no rules can be laid down to judge the amount likely to be paid out at a given level of earnings. Dividend policy varies from industry to industry and from company to company.

Estimating the dividend possibilities of a stock may take into account:

- The amount of net earnings for the current fiscal year
- The stability of earnings over a period of years
- The amount of retained earnings and the rate of return on those earnings
- The company's working capital
- The policy of the board of directors
- Plans for expanding (or contracting) operations
- Government dividend restraints (if any)

Before a company can pay a dividend, it must have sufficient earnings and working capital. It is up to the directors to consider the other factors and reach a decision on whether to pay a dividend and how large the payment should be.

© CSI GLOBAL EDUCATION INC. (2008)

DIVIDEND YIELD

The **yield** on common and preferred stock is the annual dividend rate expressed as a percentage of the current market price of the stock. It represents the investor's return on the investment.

$$= \frac{\text{Indicated annual dividend per share}}{\text{Current market price}} \times 100$$

Assuming current market prices of $49 for the preferred and $26.25 for the common shares of Trans-Canada Retail Stores, the yields are:

Preffered: $\frac{\$2.50}{\$49} \times 100 = 5.10\%$

Common: $\frac{\$1.00}{\$26.25} \times 100 = 3.81\%$

Dividend yields allow analysts to make a quick comparison between the shares of different companies. However, to make a thorough comparison, the following factors must also be considered:

- The differences in the quality and record of each company's management
- The proportion of earnings re-invested in each company
- The proportion of preferred and common shares in each company's capitalization
- The equity behind each share
- In the case of preferred shares, the difference in preferred dividend coverage

All these factors should be taken into account in addition to yield – preferably over several years. Only then can an analyst make an informed evaluation.

PRICE-EARNINGS RATIO OR P/E MULTIPLE

The **price-earnings ratio** or **P/E ratio** is probably the most widely used of all financial ratios because it combines all the other ratios into one figure. It represents the ultimate evaluation of a company and its shares by the investing public.

Formula: $\frac{\text{Current market price of common}}{\text{Earnings per share (in latest 12-month period)}}$

Assuming that the current market price of Trans-Canada Retail Stores' common stock is $26.25 and that its earnings per common share is $3.00, the P/E ratio is:

$\frac{\$26.25}{\$3.00} = 8.75{:}1$ or 8.75 times

P/E ratios are calculated only for common stocks, not for preferreds. The only relevance of earnings to most preferred shareholders is how well (or by what margin of safety) they cover preferred dividends. The "preferred dividend coverage ratio" measures this best.

The main reason for calculating earnings per common share – apart from indicating dividend protection – is to make a comparison with the share's market price. The P/E ratio expresses this comparison in one convenient figure, showing that a share is selling at so many times its actual

© CSI GLOBAL EDUCATION INC. (2008)

or anticipated annual earnings. P/E ratios enable the shares of one company to be compared with those of another.

EXAMPLE: Company A – Earnings per share: $2; price: $20
Company B – Earnings per share: $1; price: $10

P/E ratio for Company A: $\frac{\$20}{\$2} = 10:1$

P/E ratio for Company B: $\frac{\$10}{\$1} = 10:1$

Though earnings per share of Company A ($2) are twice those of Company B ($1), the shares of each company represent equivalent *value* because A's shares, at $20 each, cost twice as much as B's. In other words, both companies are selling at 10 times earnings.

The elements that determine the quality of an issue – and therefore are represented in the P/E ratio – include:

- Tangible factors contained in financial data, which can be expressed in ratios relating to liquidity, earnings trends, profitability, dividend payout, and financial strength (balance sheet ratios)
- Intangible factors, such as quality of management, nature and prospects for the industry in which the issuing company operates, its competitive position, and its individual prospects.

All these factors are taken into account when investors and speculators collectively decide what price a share is worth.

To compare the P/E ratio for one company's common shares with that of other companies, the companies should usually be in the same industry. Table 14.5 shows P/E ratios for various sub industry indexes of the S&P/TSX Composite Index.

TABLE 14.5 P/E RATIOS FOR SELECTED INDUSTRY SUB-GROUPS OF S&P/TSX COMPOSITE INDEX MAY 2008

Industry Sub-Groups	P/E Ratio	Industry Sub-Groups	P/E Ratio
Consumer Discretionary	13.8	Software/Services	15.6
Financials	14.1	Food Retail	14.3
Utilities	13.8	Consumer Staples	19.8
Transportation	11.2	S&P/TSX Composite	17.7

Source: TSX Review, May 2008.

In the Trans-Canada Retail Stores example, we calculated the price-earnings ratio on the earnings of the company's latest fiscal year. In practice, however, most investment analysts and firms make their own projections of a company's earnings for the next twelve-month period and calculate P/E ratios on these projected figures in relation to the stock's current market price. Because of the many variables involved in forecasting earnings, the use of estimates in calculations should be approached with great caution. The P/E ratio helps analysts determine a reasonable value for a common stock at any time in a market cycle. By calculating a company's P/E ratio over a number of years, the analyst will find considerable fluctuation, with high and low points. If the highs and lows of a particular stock's P/E ratio remain constant over several stock market cycles,

© CSI GLOBAL EDUCATION INC. (2008)

they indicate selling and buying points for the stock. A study of the P/E ratios of competitor companies and that of the relevant market subgroup index also helps to provide a perspective.

The P/E ratio comparison assists in the selection process. For example, if two companies of equal stature in the same industry both have similar prospects, but different P/E ratios, the company with the lower P/E ratio is usually the better buy.

As a rule, P/E ratios increase in a rising stock market or with rising earnings. The reverse is true in a declining market or when earnings decline.

Since the P/E ratio is an indicator of investor confidence, its highs and lows may vary from market cycle to market cycle. Much depends on changes in investor enthusiasm for a company or an industry over several years.

THE ENTERPRISE MULTIPLE (ENTERPRISE VALUE TO EBITDA)

The Enterprise Multiple (EM) is a commonly used measure of a company's overall value, and is frequently used in capital-intensive industries such as the biotechnology, telecommunications, industrial and steel industries. It looks at a company's enterprise value to its earnings before interest, taxes, depreciation and amortization, or EBITDA. Enterprise value (EV) is a measure of total company value at any given time and is calculated as the market value of the company's common equity, preferred equity, and debt less the value of cash and cash equivalents recorded on its balance sheet. In this way, enterprise value reflects the actual cost to purchase the company as a whole.

Since the Enterprise Multiple takes into account the market value of company debt, it may be a more appropriate measure of value when comparing companies, particularly when analyzing companies with different debt levels. For example, because EBITDA uses pre-interest earnings whereas EPS uses post-interest earnings, the EM may provide a better measure of comparison compared to the P/E multiple.

Assume that the current market price of Trans-Canada Retail Stores' common stock is $26.25, the market price of its preferred shares is $55.00, and that the value of the company's debt is the value recorded on the balance sheet. For simplicity of this illustration, assume that the market value of the company's debt is par. Enterprise value is calculated as:

Market value of common equity	350,000 × $26.25	$9,187,500
+ Market value of preferred shares	15,000 × $55	$825,000
+ Market value of debt	Item 12 + Item 16 + Item 20	$3,100,000
– (Cash and cash equivalents)	Item 1 + Item 2	($2,169,000)
= Enterprise Value		$10,943,500

EBITDA is calculated as:

Earnings before extraordinary items	Item 43	$1,086,000
+ Income taxes	Item 40	$880,000
+ Interest	Item 37 + Item 38	$289,000
+ Amortization	Item 32	$556,000
= EBITDA		$2,811,000

© CSI GLOBAL EDUCATION INC. (2008)

The Enterprise Multiple for Trans-Canada Retail is:

$$\frac{\text{Entreprise value}}{\text{EBITDA}}$$

$$= \frac{\$10,943,500}{2,811,000}$$

$$= 3.89$$

Enterprise multiples can vary depending on the industry and, similar to the P/E ratio, there is no standard. Trans-Canada Retail's measure of 3.89 says nothing on its own. However, when compared with another company within its industry and with the industry standard itself, we can determine whether Trans-Canada is over- or undervalued relative to its peers. Higher enterprise multiples generally exist in high-growth industries, while lower multiples are found in slower-growth or mature industries.

EQUITY VALUE (OR BOOK VALUE) PER SHARE

Preferred shares rank before common shares in any liquidation, winding up, or distribution of assets. When their prior claims have been met, the holders of common shares are entitled to what is left.

The two **equity value ratios** measure the asset coverage for each preferred and each common share.

$$\frac{\text{Preferred and common share capital} + \text{contributed surplus} + \text{retained earnings} + \text{foreign exchange adjustement}}{\text{Number of preferred shares outstanding}}$$

$$\frac{\text{Item 21} + \text{Item 22} + \text{Item 23} + \text{Item 25}}{\text{Number of preferred shares as per Item 21}}$$

$$\text{or } \frac{\$750,000 + \$1,564,000 + \$150,000 + \$10,835,000 + \$60,000}{15,000 \text{ shares}}$$

$$= \frac{\$13,359,000}{15,000 \text{ shares}} = \$890.60 \text{ per preferred share}$$

As the foregoing example shows, each preferred share is backed by $890.60 of equity in the company. Since the par value of the preferred is $50 (as stated in the balance sheet), the equity backing is $890.60 ÷ $50, or 17.81 times. Analysts like to see that the minimum equity value per preferred share in each of the last five fiscal years is at least two times the dollar value of assets that each preferred share would be entitled to receive in the event of liquidation. Trans-Canada's equity backing of 17.81 times far exceeds the minimum requirement.

If the preferred shares were redeemable at a premium on liquidation, the premium would be added to the par value in this calculation, slightly reducing the coverage. For example, a premium of $2.50 on liquidation would result in equity backing of $890.60 ÷ $52.50, or 16.96 times.

As well as meeting the minimum standard for the industry, equity value per preferred share should also show a stable or, preferably, a rising trend over the same period.

© CSI GLOBAL EDUCATION INC. (2008)

$$\frac{\text{Common share capital} + \text{contributed surplus} + \text{retained earnings} + \text{foreign exchange adjustment (less preferred dividend arrears, if any)}}{\text{Number of common shares outstanding}}$$

$$\frac{\text{Item 22} + \text{Item 23} + \text{Item 24} + \text{Item 25}}{\text{Number of common shares as per Item 22}}$$

$$\text{or } \frac{\$1{,}564{,}000 + \$150{,}000 + \$10{,}835{,}000 + \$60{,}000}{350{,}000 \text{ shares}}$$

$$= \frac{\$12{,}609{,}000}{350{,}000 \text{ shares}} = \$36.03 \text{ per common share}$$

Complete the on-line activity associated with this section.

There is no simple answer as to what constitutes an adequate level of equity value per common share. Although a per-share equity (or book) value figure is sometimes used in appraising common shares, in actual practice the equity value per common share may be very different from the market value per common share. Equity per share is only one of many factors to be considered in appraising a given stock. Many shares sell for considerably less than their equity value, while others sell for far in excess of their equity value.

Review the on-line summary or checklist associated with this section.

This disparity between equity and market values is usually accounted for by the actual or potential earning power of the company. The shares of a company with a high earning power will command a better price in the market than the shares of a company with little or no earning power, even though the shares of both companies may have the same equity value. Thus, we cannot quote a meaningful standard for an adequate book value per common share.

ASSESSING PREFERRED SHARE INVESTMENT QUALITY

The investment quality assessment of preferred shares hinges on three critical questions:

- Do the company's earnings provide ample coverage for preferred dividends?
- For how many years has the company paid dividends without interruption?
- Is there an adequate cushion of equity behind each preferred share?

In addition to the equity value per preferred share ratio already covered, analysts study a number of factors to answer these questions. The four key tests employed to finalize an assessment are:

- Preferred Dividend Coverage (covered previously in the Risk Analysis Ratios section)
- Equity (or Book Value) per Preferred Share (covered previously in the Value Ratios section)
- Record of Continuous Dividend Payments
- An Independent Credit Assessment

© CSI GLOBAL EDUCATION INC. (2008)

Dividend Payments

Has the company established a record of continuous dividend payments to its preferred shareholders? This information is obtained from individual company Historical Reports and *The Dividend Record* published by The Financial Post Datagroup in Toronto. Other sources of information regarding dividend payments include company annual reports and company studies by investment dealers.

Credit Assessment

Just as with bonds, a company's preferred shares may be rated by one of the recognized bond rating services. If it is, what is the rating and is it high enough to merit investment?

In Canada, the two independent bond rating services – Dominion Bond Rating Service (DBRS) and Standard & Poor's Rating Service – assign ratings to a number of Canadian preferred shares.

Dominion Bond Rating Service assigns rating classifications to preferred shares ranging from Pfd-l (Superior Credit Quality) (preferreds of the highest quality) to "D" (in arrears) (the lowest rating provided). DBRS ranks preferred shares as follows in Table 14.6.

TABLE 14.6 DOMINION BOND RATING SERVICE PREFERRED SHARE RATINGS

Rating	Description
Pfd-1	Preferred shares rated "Pfd-1" are of **superior credit quality**, and are supported by entities with strong earnings and balance sheet characteristics. "Pfd-1" generally corresponds with companies whose senior bonds are rated in the "AAA" or "AA" categories.
Pfd-2	Preferred shares rated "Pfd-2" are of **satisfactory credit quality**. Protection of dividends and principal is still substantial, but earnings, the balance sheet, and coverage ratios are not as strong as "Pfd-1" rated companies. Generally, "Pfd-2" ratings correspond with companies whose senior bonds are rated in the "A" category.
Pfd-3	Preferred shares rated "Pfd-3" are of **adequate credit quality**. While protection of dividends and principal is still considered acceptable, the issuing entity is more susceptible to adverse changes in financial and economic conditions, and there may be other adversities present which detract from debt protection. "Pfd-3" ratings generally correspond with companies whose senior bonds are rated in the higher end of the "BBB" category.
Pfd-4	Preferred shares rated "Pfd-4" are **speculative**, where the degree of protection afforded to dividends and principal is uncertain, particularly during periods of economic adversity. Companies with preferred shares rated "Pfd-4" generally coincide with entities that have senior bond ratings ranging from the lower end of the "BBB" category through the "BB" category.
Pfd-5	Preferred shares rated "Pfd-5" are **highly speculative** and the ability of the entity to maintain timely dividend and principal payments in the future is highly uncertain. The "Pfd-5" rating generally coincides with companies with senior bond ratings of "B" or lower. Preferred shares rated "Pfd-5" often have characteristics which, if not remedied, may lead to default.
D	This category indicates preferred shares that are **in arrears** of paying either dividends or principal.

Source: DBRS website

© CSI GLOBAL EDUCATION INC. (2008)

To arrive at a preferred share rating, the rating services subject company reports to a rigorous evaluation. An acceptable rating for a preferred helps to confirm the conclusions of tests such as those done on Trans-Canada Retail.

An unexpected change in the rating of a preferred share issue will usually affect the shares' market price. An unexpected downgrading to a lower rating has negative implications. An upgrading to a higher rating is a favourable development.

The question of whether or not an investment in a preferred share is warranted on the basis of a specific rating is difficult to answer in general terms. Both the issue and its rating must be compatible with a client's investment objectives before a purchase is made.

Selecting Preferreds

In addition to the four key tests just covered, other factors should be investigated before a purchase decision is reached. When choosing any equity security, marketability, volume of trading and research coverage by investment firms should be investigated. Find out on which exchanges the security is listed on, or why it isn't listed. Questions specific to preferreds include:

- What features (e.g., cumulative dividends, sinking funds) and protective provisions have been built into the issue?
- What is the relation of the preferred's call price to the market price? If the market price is above the call price, what is the likelihood of the preferred being redeemed?
- Is the yield from the preferred acceptable compared to yields from other, similar investments?

In addition to the checkpoints cited for selecting straight preferred shares, the following should be considered for convertible preferreds:

- Is the outlook for the common stock positive? A conversion privilege is valuable only if the market price of the common rises above the exercise price during the life of the conversion privilege.
- Is the life of the conversion privilege long enough? The longer the life of the conversion privilege, the greater the opportunity for the market price of the common and preferred to respond to favourable developments. Preferably, there should be at least three years before the conversion privilege expires.
- If there is a premium of conversion cost present, is it reasonable?
- How does the premium compare with premiums on other comparable convertible preferreds?
- Is the convertible preferred selling above its call price? If so, is it a candidate for a forced conversion?

Unfortunately there are no easy answers to the above questions. Successful selection entails a combination of common sense, experience, and familiarity with applicable investment principles.

How Preferreds Fit into Individual Portfolios

With characteristics of both debt and equity, preferred shares provide a link between the bond and debenture section of a portfolio and the common equity section.

Few investors are unsuited to owning some type of preferred shares because of the wide variety available. However, because of the differences in investment goals and needs, it is impractical to devise a guideline to determine the percentage of assets that should be invested in preferred shares that could be applied generally.

© CSI GLOBAL EDUCATION INC. (2008)

Table 14.7 attempts to match types of preferred to types of investor.

TABLE 14.7 HOW PREFERREDS FIT INTO INDIVIDUAL PORTFOLIOS

Type of Preferred	Type of Investor
Fixed-Rate Preferreds	
Top quality	Conservative
Medium to high quality	Moderately aggressive
Low quality to speculative	Aggressive, experienced investors and speculators
Special Types of Preferreds	
(High quality assumed)	
Convertible	Aggressive and moderately aggressive
Retractable	Conservative
Variable dividend	Aggressive and sophisticated
Preferreds with warrants	Aggressive and moderately aggressive
Participating	Conservative and moderately aggressive
Foreign-pay	Aggressive and sophisticated

SUMMARY

After reading this chapter, you should be able to:

1. Identify the factors involved in performing company analysis to determine whether a company represents a good investment.
   - Analysis of company earnings indicates how well management is making use of company resources (e.g., the trend in the operating profit margin).
   - Analysis of the balance sheet helps to better understand important aspects of company operations and can reveal factors that may affect earnings (e.g., the amount of debt currently reported).
2. Explain how to analyze a company's financial statements using trend analysis and external comparisons.
   - Financial ratios become meaningful when compared with other ratios over a period. A series of similar ratios for the same company can be compared; or the company's ratios can be compared to those of similar companies or industry averages.
   - Ratios are most useful when comparing financial results of companies in the same or similar industries. Trend lines help to put the ratios of each company in historical perspective and identify how each company has fared in relation to others.

© CSI GLOBAL EDUCATION INC. (2008)

3. Describe the different types of liquidity ratios, risk analysis ratios, operating performance ratios, and value ratios, and evaluate company performance using these ratios.

   - Liquidity ratios are used to evaluate a company's ability to turn assets into cash to meet its short-term commitments. Ratios in this category look at the relationship between assets and liabilities, specifically, how well current liabilities are covered by the cash flow generated by the company's operating activities.
   - Risk analysis ratios show how well a company can meet its debt obligations. Because financial risk can increase with higher levels of debt, these ratios help to show whether a company has sufficient earnings to repay the funds it has borrowed and its ability to make regular interest payments on its outstanding debt.
   - Operating performance ratios illustrate how well management is making use of company resources. These ratios focus on measuring the profitability and efficiency of operations. They look specifically at the company's ability to manage its resources by taking into account sales and the costs and expenses incurred in producing earnings.
   - Value ratios show the investor what the company's shares are worth, or the return on owning them, by comparing the market price of the shares to information in the company's financial statements. For example, these ratios look at the earnings available to common shareholders, the dividend yield or return on company shares, and the ultimate valuation of a company through the price-earnings ratio.

4. Evaluate the investment quality of preferred shares and summarize preferred share ratings.

   - The investment quality assessment of preferred shares hinges on three critical questions: Does the company generate enough earnings to cover its preferred dividend obligations? How consistently has the company paid dividends without interruption? What is the equity cushion behind each preferred share?
   - The preferred dividend coverage ratio, the equity (or book value) per preferred share, the record of continuous dividend payments, and independent credit assessments can be used to analyze the quality of a company's preferred shares.
   - The Dominion Bond Rating Service (DBRS) and Standard and Poor's Rating Service assign ratings to a number of Canadian preferred shares.

Now that you've completed this chapter and the on-line activities, complete this post-test.

© CSI GLOBAL EDUCATION INC. (2008)

APPENDIX A – COMPANY FINANCIAL STATEMENTS

The financial statements on the following pages should be referred to when reviewing this chapter. To make them easier to understand, these financial statements differ from real financial statements in the following ways:

1. Comparative (previous year's) figures are not shown.
2. No *Notes to Financial Statements* are included.
3. The consecutive numbers on the left hand side of the statements which are used in explaining ratio calculations do not appear in real reports.

Note: It is assumed that Trans-Canada Retail Stores Ltd. is a non-food retail chain.

© CSI GLOBAL EDUCATION INC. (2008)

Trans-Canada Retail Stores Ltd.

CONSOLIDATED BALANCE SHEET

as at December 31, 20XX

ASSETS		
CURRENT ASSETS		
1. Cash and bank balances		$ 129,000
2. Temporary investments – at cost, which approximates market value		2,040,000
3. Accounts receivable (less allowances for doubtful accounts – $9,000)		975,000
4. Inventories of merchandise – valued at the lower cost or net realizable value		9,035,000
5. Prepaid expenses		59,000
6. Total Current Assets		12,238,000
7. Investment in affiliated company		917,000
8. CAPITAL ASSETS, at cost		
Land	$ 1,370,000	
Buildings	2,460,000	
Equipment	6,750,000	
	10,580,000	
Accumulated amortization	(4,260,000)	6,320, 000
9. DEFERRED CHARGES (unamortized expenses and discount on bond issue) INTANGIBLE ASSET		136,000
10. Goodwill		150,000
11. TOTAL ASSETS		$ 19,761,000
LIABILITIES		
CURRENT LIABILITIES		
12. Bank advances		$ 1,630,000
13. Accounts payable		2,165,000
14. Dividends payable		97,000
15. Income taxes payable		398,000
16. First mortgage bonds due within one year		120,000
17. Total Current Liabilities		$ 4,410,000
18. FUTURE INCOME TAXES		485,000
19. NON-CONTROLLING INTEREST IN SUBSIDIARY COMPANIES FUNDED DEBT (due after one year)		157,000
20. 11% First Mortgage Sinking Fund Bonds due Dec. 30, 2027		1,350,000
		6,402,000
SHAREHOLDERS' EQUITY		
CAPITAL STOCK		
21. $2.50 Cumulative Redeemable Preferred – Authorized 20,000 shares, $50 par value – issued and outstanding 15,000 shares		750,000
22. Common – Authorized 500,000 shares of no par value – issued and outstanding 350,000 shares		1,564,000
23. CONTRIBUTED SURPLUS		150,000
24. RETAINED EARNINGS		10,835,000
25. FOREIGN EXCHANGE ADJUSTMENT		60,000
26. Total Shareholders' Equity		13,359,000
27. Total Liabilities & Shareholders' Equity		$ 19,761,000

Approved on behalf of the Board:

[Signature], Director

[Signature], Director

© CSI GLOBAL EDUCATION INC. (2008)

Trans-Canada Retail Stores Ltd.

CONSOLIDATED EARNINGS STATEMENT

as at December 31, 20XX

OPERATING SECTION		
28. Net Sales		$ 43,800,000
29. Less: Cost of goods sold		28,250,000
30. Gross Operating Profit		15,550,000
31. Less: Selling, administrative and general expenses	$ 12,752,000	
32. Less: Amortization	556,000	
33. Less: Directors' remuneration	110,000	13,418,000
34. Net Operating Profit		2,132,000
NON-OPERATING SECTION		
35. Income from investments		130,000
36. TOTAL OPERATING AND NON-OPERATING SECTION		2,262,000
CREDITORS' SECTION		
37. Less: Bank interest	$ 120,700	
38. Less: Bond interest	168,300	289,000
OWNERS' SECTION		
39. Earnings before income taxes		1,973,000
40. Less: Income Taxes:		
Current	$ 830,000	
Future	50,000	880,000
41. Less: Non-controlling Interest in earnings of subsidiary companies		12,000
42. Equity Income – affiliated company		5,000
43. Earnings before extraordinary item		$ 1,086,000
44. Extraordinary gain on sale of capital assets (net of taxes)		200,000
45. Net earnings		$ 1,286,000

Trans-Canada Retail Stores Ltd.

CONSOLIDATED RETAINED EARNINGS STATEMENT

as at December 31, 20XX

46. Balance at beginning of year		$ 9,936,500
45. Net earnings for the year		1,286,000
		11,222,500
Deduct Dividends -		
47. on preferred sahres ($2.50 per share)	$ 37,500	
48. on preferred sahres ($1.00 per share)	350,000	387,500
24. Balance at end of year		$ 10,835,000

© CSI GLOBAL EDUCATION INC. (2008)

Trans-Canada Retail Stores Ltd.

CONSOLIDATED CASH FLOW STATEMENT

as at December 31, 20XX

OPERATING ACTIVITIES	
43. Earnings before extraordinary items	$ 1,086,000
32. Add items not involving cash – Amortization	556,000
49. Future income taxes	50,000
41. Non-controlling interest in income of subsidiary companie	12,000
42. Equity income – affiliated company	*(5,000)
50. Net change in operating working capital items	(401,000)
CASH FLOWS FROM OPERATING ACTIVITIES	1,298,000
FINANCING ACTIVITIES	
51. Proceeds from share issue	750,000
52. Repayment of long-term debt	(400,000)
53. Borrowing of long-term debt	50,000
54. Dividends paid	(387,500)
CASH FLOWS FROM FINANCING ACTIVITIES	12,500
INVESTING ACTIVITIES	
55. Acquisitions of capital assets	(900,000)
56. Proceeds from disposal of capital assets	75,000
57. Dividends received from affiliated company	2,000
CASH FLOWS FROM INVESTING ACTIVITIES	(823,000)
58. INCREASE IN CASH AND TEMPORARY INVESTMENTS	487,500
59. CASH AND TEMPORARY INVESTMENTS – BEGINNING OF YEAR	1,681,500
60. CASH AND TEMPORARY INVESTMENTS – END OF YEAR	2,169,000
SUPPLEMENTAL INFORMATION	
61. INTEREST PAID	289,000
62. INCOME TAXES PAID	$ 432,000

* ( ) = deduction

AUDITORS' REPORT

To the Shareholders of Trans-Canada Retail Stores Ltd.

We have audited the balance sheet of Trans-Canada Retail Stores Ltd. as at December 31, 20XX and the statements of earnings, retained earnings and cash flows for the year then ended. These financial statements are the responsibility of the company's management. Our responsibility is to express an opinion on these financial statements based on our audit.

We conducted our audit in accordance with Canadian generally accepted auditing standards. Those standards require that we plan and perform an audit to obtain reasonable assurance whether the financial statements are free of material misstatement. An audit includes examining, on a test basis, evidence supporting the amounts and disclosures in the financial statements. An audit also includes assessing the accounting principles used and significant estimates made by management, as well as evaluating the overall financial statement presentation.

In our opinion, these financial statements present fairly, in all material respects, the financial position of the company as at December 31, 20XX and the results of its operations and the cash flows for the year then ended in accordance with Canadian generally accepted accounting principles.

Toronto, Ontario

February 8, 20XX Signature of Auditors

© CSI GLOBAL EDUCATION INC. (2008)

APPENDIX B – SAMPLE COMPANY ANALYSIS

This appendix demonstrates how to analyze and compare two companies in order to evaluate their investment quality. Remember that ratios must be used in context. One ratio alone does not tell an investor very much. Ratios are not proof of present or future profitability, only clues. An analyst who spots an unsatisfactory ratio may suspect unfavourable conditions and wish to investigate further. Conversely, analysts may conclude that a company is financially strong after compiling a series of ratios. The significance of any ratio is not the same for all companies.

Description of the Companies under Evaluation

An analyst needs to understand what the company does, how large it is and how it operates. The two companies being analyzed are the fictitious *Westcoast Communications Inc.* and *Provincial Teleprises Inc.* Both companies operate in the telecommunications industry.

	Westcoast Communications Inc.	**Provincial Teleprises Inc.**
Business Description	The company owns and operates the principal telephone system in Western Canada, providing telecommunication services to residential and business customers. Westcoast Communications Inc. is the third-largest publicly owned telephone company in Canada. Through 52%-owned The Peninsula Telephone Company Limited, the company provides telecommunications services to islands off the coast of British Columbia. Customer services include residential services, business services including private branch exchanges (PBXs) and business telephone systems, data and facsimile transmission, and network services which provide cellular and interconnect services to other areas.	The company is the principal supplier of basic telecommunication services in Newfoundland and Labrador. It also manufactures and distributes specialized marine instrumentation, electronic subassemblies, and computer hardware software products, and provides cellular telephone services.
Major Segments	• business services • residence services • network services	**Telecommunications** including Voice Information Services, Message Management Services 800 Plus service, and Advantage Vnet as well as data services and wireless communication services. **Non-regulated businesses** including office automation, electronic engineering and manufacturing, and financial services.

Most profitable business segment	**Long distance service**	**Local service**
Total Assets	$ 1,477,136,000	$ 732,683,000
Operating Revenues	$ 594,956,000	$ 324,229,000
Net Income	$ 47,659,000	$ 30,550,000

© CSI GLOBAL EDUCATION INC. (2008)

Ratio Analysis of Westcoast Communications Inc. and Provincial Teleprises Ltd.

When analyzing a company or comparing two companies, you need to look at several financial ratios. In isolation, these ratios do not mean much. Observe the trend of the ratio over the last five years and compare the ratios to other companies and to the industry averages. Many ratios have accepted industry standards that should be met. The following questions should be answered with respect to each ratio.

(i) What does each ratio measure and does it have an accepted industry standard (IS)? If there is an industry standard, how does each company measure when compared to this standard? In this example, we provide the industry standard.

(ii) How has the industry as a whole performed over the same five-year period? Has it met the IS?

(iii) How has *Westcoast Communications Inc.* performed through the five-year period when compared to the industry as a whole?

(iv) How has *Provincial Teleprises Ltd.* performed through the five-year period when compared to the industry as a whole?

(v) How have *Westcoast Communications Inc.* and *Provincial Teleprises Ltd.* performed compared to each other? Has one company outperformed the other?

This sample analysis will illustrate how this analysis is performed for a few of these ratios. Ultimately you should come to a decision as to whether the companies are good investments.

WESTCOAST COMMUNICATIONS INC. LIQUIDITY & DEBT RATIOS

	Sales ($)	Quick Ratio (x:1)	Asset Coverage ($)	Debt/ Equity (%)	Cash Flow	Cash Flow/ Total Debt (%)
Year 1	543,349.00	.71	2,339.22	97.73	186,679.00	34.13
Year 2	545,045.00	.70	2,238.04	106.37	200,672.00	33.40
Year 3	546,617.00	.72	2,072.45	129.14	205,097.00	29.85
Year 4	568,442.00	.72	2,035.09	130.95	192,785.00	27.70
Year 5	594,956.00	.56	2,190.96	111.37	195,362.00	31.82
Average	559,681.80	.68	2,175.15	115.11	196,119.00	31.38
% growth	9.50%	-21.13%	-6.34%	13.96%	4.65%	-6.77%

© CSI GLOBAL EDUCATION INC. (2008)

PROVINCIAL TELEPRISES LTD. LIQUIDITY & DEBT RATIOS

	Sales ($)	Quick Ratio (x:1)	Asset Coverage ($)	Debt/ Equity (%)	Cash Flow	Cash Flow/ Total Debt (%)
Year 1	285,058.00	.64	2320.85	90.96	102,511.00	36.00
Year 2	295,338.00	.25	2071.82	111.01	104,715.00	32.96
Year 3	295,371.00	.52	2308.11	91.91	101,766.00	35.62
Year 4	313,275.00	.70	2210.52	96.58	98,869.00	31.79
Year 5	324,229.00	.81	2418.03	83.71	112,222.00	40.86
Average	302,654.20	.58	2265.87	94.83	104,016.60	35.45
% growth	13.74%	26.56%	4.19%	-7.97%	9.47%	13.50%

WESTCOAST COMMUNICATIONS INC. VALUE & PROFITABILITY RATIOS

	EPS ($)	Operating Profit Margin	Price-Earnings (times)	Book Value per Common Share ($)	Net Profit Margin (%)	Return on Equity (%)
Year 1	2.00	52.48	10.25	16.54	12.47	12.11
Year 2	1.89	53.81	11.80	17.24	11.64	10.97
Year 3	1.58	53.01	15.19	17.49	9.48	9.06
Year 4	1.01	49.21	20.18	17.25	6.30	5.83
Year 5	1.52	52.17	14.64	17.63	8.72	8.64
Average	1.60	52.14	14.41	17.23	9.72	9.32
% growth	-24.00%	-0.59%	42.83%	6.59%	-30.07%	-28.65%

PROVINCIAL TELEPRISES LTD. VALUE & PROFITABILITY RATIOS

	EPS ($)	Operating Profit Margin	Price-Earnings (times)	Book Value per Common Share ($)	Net Profit Margin (%)	Return on Equity (%)
Year 1	1.69	52.97	11.39	16.56	11.25	10.23
Year 2	1.68	53.05	12.68	17.04	10.72	9.85
Year 3	1.88	12.68	11.57	17.76	11.07	10.56
Year 4	1.41	52.05	14.23	17.88	8.20	7.91
Year 5	1.70	48.27	13.16	18.22	9.55	9.31
Average	1.67	49.87	12.61	17.49	10.16	9.57
% growth	0.595%	51.24%	15.54%	10.02%	-15.11%	-8.99%

© CSI GLOBAL EDUCATION INC. (2008)

SELECTED INDUSTRY RATIOS

	Net Profit Margin (%)	Return on Equity (%)	Quick Ratio (x:1)	Operating Profit Margin	Debt/ Equity (%)	Price-Earnings (times)	Cash Flow/ Total Debt (%)
Year 1	9.21	2.04	0.82	34.37	154.00	15.4	17.46
Year 2	5.30	8.67	0.82	35.41	9.00	11.3	20.29
Year 3	6.95	7.30	2.05	28.94	2.00	12.5	26.27
Year 4	(1.08)	6.03	0.93	30.97	44.00	12.7	20.53
Year 5	0.04	8.36	0.92	29.24	46.00	12.6	24.16
Average	4.08	6.48	1.11	31.79	51.00	12.9	21.74
% growth	-99.57%	309.80%	12.20%	-14.93%	-70.12%	-18.18%	38.37%

CASH FLOW/DEBT

	Year 1	Year 2	Year 3	Year 4	Year 5	5-Year Average
Industry	17.46	20.29	26.27	20.53	24.16	21.74
Westcoast Communications Inc.	34.13	33.40	29.85	27.70	31.82	31.38
Provincial Teleprises Ltd.	36.00	32.96	35.62	31.79	40.86	35.45

i) This ratio gauges a company's ability to repay funds it has borrowed. A company's cash flow must be adequate to meet its commitments. Industry Standard (IS): at least 30% in each of the last five fiscal years. *Provincial Teleprises Ltd.* has consistently met the IS but *Westcoast Communications Inc.* slipped below it in Year 3 and Year 4.

ii) The industry results are very different, being consistently less than the IS in each year. (If these results are acceptable as standards for the industry, *Westcoast Communications Inc.* and *Provincial Teleprises Ltd.* may be under-utilizing their cash resources.) Industry results have been volatile, with cash flow/debt rising in Year 2 and Year 3 but dipping back down in Year 4 before rising again in Year 5.

iii) *Westcoast Communications Inc.* has outperformed the industry consistently, despite its dip in Year 2 and Year 3.

iv) *Provincial Teleprises Ltd.* has also outperformed the industry consistently. While less consistent than *Westcoast Communications Inc.*, it has never fallen below the IS.

v) *Provincial Teleprises Ltd.* has outperformed Westcoast in every year, except in Year 2. This shows superior performance for the company and indicates that it is in a better position for growth and as a potential investment.

© CSI GLOBAL EDUCATION INC. (2008)

DEBT/EQUITY

	Year 1	Year 2	Year 3	Year 4	Year 5	5-Year Average
Industry	1.54	0.09	0.02	0.44	0.46	0.51
Westcoast Communications Inc.	0.98	1.06	1.29	1.31	1.11	1.15
Provincial Teleprises Ltd.	0.91	1.11	0.92	0.97	0.84	0.95

i) This ratio pinpoints the relationship of debt to equity and can be a warning that a company's borrowing is excessive. The higher the debt/equity, the higher the financial risk. IS: no greater than 0.5:1. Both *Westcoast Communications Inc.* and *Provincial Teleprises Ltd.* exceed the IS guidelines consistently.

ii) The industry meets the IS guidelines, with the exception of Year 1. Results have been very volatile with debt/equity falling dramatically in Year 2 and Year 3 before beginning a recovery in Year 4, as companies took on more debt.

iii) *Westcoast Communications Inc.* has had a more stable performance over the past five years than that of the industry as a whole. However, levels have consistently fallen above acceptable limits. In fact, its five-year average is more than double that of the industry. There was a steadily rising trend until Year 5.

iv) *Provincial Teleprises Ltd.* has also had a stable performance compared to both the industry and *Westcoast Communications Inc.* However, levels remain above acceptable standards. Debt/equity has been falling since Year 2, a positive indication that the situation may be improving. Note also that Year 5 levels are currently below Year 1 levels.

v) *Provincial Teleprises* outperformed Westcoast over the five-year period. However, levels remain above acceptable standards. Debt/equity has been falling since Year 2, a positive indication that the situation may be improving. Note also that Year 5 levels are currently below Year 1 levels.

RETURN ON EQUITY

	Year 1	Year 2	Year 3	Year 4	Year 5	5-Year Average
Industry	2.04	8.67	7.30	6.03	8.36	6.48
Westcoast Communications Inc.	12.11	10.97	9.06	5.83	8.64	9.32
Provincial Teleprises Ltd.	10.23	9.85	10.56	7.91	9.31	9.57

i) This ratio correlates income, on an after-tax basis, with the invested capital (provided by common shareholders) responsible for producing it. It reflects the profitability of their capital in the business. There is no IS for this ratio. Investors would prefer to see their IS increasing. *Westcoast Communications Inc.* has been declining steadily since Year 1. By Year 4 it was less than half what it was in Year 1. It rebounded in Year 5 but is still substantially less than Year 1 levels. *Provincial Teleprises Ltd.* has shown a similar downward trend, but not as dramatic. It, too, rebounded in Year 5.

ii) Industry performance was very poor in Year 1. In Year 2 performance improved to more acceptable limits but trended back down over Year 3 to Year 4.

© CSI GLOBAL EDUCATION INC. (2008)

iii) *Westcoast Communications Inc.* outperformed the industry in all years except Year 4. Overall performance trended downward until Year 5, when, similar to the industry, it rebounded.

iv) *Provincial Teleprises Ltd.* has consistently outperformed the industry despite dips in Year 2 and Year 4. Overall performance has deteriorated somewhat over the period. Like Westcoast Communications Inc. and the industry, the ROE improved in Year 4.

v) *Westcoast Communications Inc.* had a higher ROE than *Provincial Teleprises Ltd.* in Year 1 and Year 2, but the positions reversed in Year 3, and Provincial Teleprises Ltd continues to outperform *Westcoast Communications Inc.* through to Year 5.

PRICE-EARNINGS RATIO

	Year 1	Year 2	Year 3	Year 4	Year 5	5-Year Average
Industry	15.40	11.30	12.50	12.70	12.60	12.90
Westcoast Communications Inc.	10.25	11.80	15.19	20.18	14.64	14.41
Provincial Teleprises Ltd.	11.39	12.68	11.57	14.23	13.16	12.61

i) This ratio allows a comparison to be made between a stock's earnings per share (EPS) and its market price. Price-earnings (P/E) ratios reflect the views of thousands of investors on the quality of an issue. There is no IS for this ratio. The P/E ratio of *Westcoast Communications Inc.* has increased steadily until Year 5, when it declined. *Provincial Teleprises Ltd.* has had a more erratic trend. Since Year 3, *Westcoast Communications Inc.* has had a higher P/E ratio than *Provincial Teleprises Ltd.*

ii) After dipping in Year 1, industry levels rebounded slightly and remained stable.

iii) At *Westcoast Communications Inc.*, the trend has been less stable than the industry. However, since Year 2, the P/E ratio has consistently been higher than the industry.

iv) The P/E ratio of *Provincial Teleprises Ltd.* has been stable, and closer in line to that of the industry. It has exceeded the industry P/E ratio in three of the last five years.

v) *Westcoast Communications Inc.* has consistently shown higher P/E levels than *Provincial Teleprises Ltd.* since Year 3. This may reflect greater investor confidence in the company in terms of future growth potential.

NET PROFIT MARGIN

	Year 1	Year 2	Year 3	Year 4	Year 5	5-Year Average
Industry	9.21	5.30	6.95	(1.08)	0.04	4.08
Westcoast Communications Inc.	12.47	11.64	9.48	6.30	8.72	9.72
Provincial Teleprises Ltd.	11.25	10.72	11.07	8.20	9.55	10.16

i) Net profit margin is an important indicator of how efficiently the company is managed after taking into account both expenses and taxes. Because this ratio is the end result of the company's operations for the period, it effectively sums up in a single figure management's ability to run the business. There is no IS for this ratio, although an increasing trend is favourable. The net profit margin of *Westcoast Communications Inc.* has shown a seriously declining trend until Year 4, when it was almost half what it was in Year 1. It rebounded

© CSI GLOBAL EDUCATION INC. (2008)

in Year 5 but is still well below Year 1 levels. The net profit margin of *Provincial Teleprises Ltd.* has shown a downward trend as well, although not as dramatic as that of *Westcoast Communications Inc.* Similarly, it rebounded in Year 5.

ii) Industry performance has trended downward over the period, with a huge drop in Year 4 (showing a negative net profit margin for the year) followed by only a marginal improvement in Year 5.

iii) *Westcoast Communications Inc.* has consistently outperformed the industry but performance has deteriorated over the period with only a slight rebound in Year 5.

iv) *Provincial Teleprises Ltd.* has also outperformed the industry with more consistent overall results over the period.

v) *Provincial Teleprises Ltd.* has consistently outperformed *Westcoast Communications Inc.* in terms of net profit margin for the last three years.

OPERATING MARGIN

	Year 1	Year 2	Year 3	Year 4	Year 5	5-Year Average
Industry	34.37	35.41	28.94	30.97	29.24	31.79
Westcoast Communications Inc.	52.48	53.81	53.01	49.21	52.17	52.14
Provincial Teleprises Ltd.	52.97	53.05	52.05	48.27	49.87	51.24

i) This ratio measures the company's ability to manage its resources. It is a more stringent measure than gross profit margin since it also takes into account the selling, general, and administrative expenses incurred in producing earnings. It allows profit margin comparisons between companies that do not show "cost of goods sold," and those that do. There is no industry standard against which to compare the company's performance. The higher the operating profit margin, the more likely it is that the company will be profitable. *Westcoast Communications Inc.* has shown a relatively stable operating profit margin. *Provincial Teleprises Ltd.* has experienced a similar operating profit margin. For the last three years, it has been slightly lower than the operating profit margin of *Westcoast Communications Inc.*

ii) The industry operating profit margin has been substantially lower than the operating margin of either of the two companies. Performance improved marginally in Year 2 (up 3.0%) only to deteriorate markedly in Year 3 (down 18.27%). Profit margins have improved since then but have not regained Year 1 levels. Overall performance has fallen 14.93% over the five-year period.

iii) *Westcoast Communications Inc.* has consistently outperformed the industry by at least 50%. Performance has not mirrored that of the industry, with levels staying relatively stable other than in Year 4 when the profit margin fell 7.17% from the previous year.

iv) *Provincial Teleprises Ltd.* has also outperformed the industry. Performance has mirrored *Westcoast Communications Inc.*'s rather than that of the industry. In Year 4 the profit margin fell 7.26% from the previous year. It has not yet regained Year 1 levels.

v) Despite starting with a slightly better operating profit margin than that of *Westcoast Communications Inc.* in Year 1, Provincial Teleprises Ltd. has not been able to maintain its performance levels. *Provincial Teleprises Ltd.*'s profit margins were lower than *Westcoast Communications Inc.*'s in Year 1 and Year 2, the dip was greater in Year 4, and recovery was slower in Year 5 (3.31% vs. 6.02%).

© CSI GLOBAL EDUCATION INC. (2008)

Which Is the Better Investment?

Provincial Teleprises Ltd. is currently the better investment choice for the following reasons:

Westcoast Communications Inc. has:	Provincial Teleprises Ltd. has:
Declining cash flow/debt, generally meets IS for this ratio.	Higher cash flow/debt, exceeds IS.
Generally rising debt/equity ratio. Meets IS in each year.	Lower debt/equity, meets IS.
Declining return on equity, outperforming industry results.	Return on equity surpassing *Westcoast Communications Inc.* and industry.
Price-earnings surpasses industry. Rising except for Year 5.	P/E more stable than *Westcoast Communications Inc.*
Declining net profit margin but better than industry.	Declining net profit margin but overtaking *Westcoast Communications Inc.* and industry.
Operating profit margin generally stable, substantially higher than the industry, slightly higher than *Provincial Teleprises Ltd.*	Operating profit margin generally stable, substantially higher than the industry, slightly lower than *Westcoast Communications Inc.*

© CSI GLOBAL EDUCATION INC. (2008)

SECTION SIX

Portfolio Analysis

© CSI GLOBAL EDUCATION INC. (2008)

Chapter 15

Introduction to the Portfolio Approach

© CSI GLOBAL EDUCATION INC. (2008)

15

Introduction to the Portfolio Approach

CHAPTER OUTLINE

© CSI GLOBAL EDUCATION INC. (2008)

LEARNING OBJECTIVES

By the end of this chapter, you should be able to:

1. Describe the relationship between risk and return, calculate rates of return of a single security, identify the different types and measures of risk, and evaluate the role of risk in asset selection.
2. Explain the relationship between risk and return of a portfolio of securities, calculate and interpret the expected return of a portfolio, and identify strategies for maximizing return while reducing risk.
3. Discuss the steps in the portfolio management process.
4. Evaluate investment objectives and constraints and explain how to use them in creating an investment policy for a client.
5. Describe the content of an investment policy statement and explain the purpose of an IPS.

PORTFOLIO ANALYSIS

No perfect security exists that meets all the needs of all investors. If such a security existed, there would be no need for investment and portfolio management, and no need to measure the return and risk of an investment. Advisors and portfolio managers spend a great deal of time selecting individual securities, allocating investment funds among security classes, and managing risks and returns.

In the on-line Learning Guide for this module, complete the Getting Started activity.

Recognizing that there are no perfect securities, investors and advisors use measures and methods to estimate risk and predict return. Based on these results, they construct portfolios designed to fit the particular needs and circumstances of individual investors. Building portfolios that correlate to specific investor needs is key to being successful in the investment industry. Generating the highest returns is not enough; higher returns that require exposure to risky investments may not be appropriate for a particular investor.

In this chapter, we integrate information about individual securities, the markets, and the different analysis techniques to focus on developing securities portfolios designed to meet the specific needs of investors. There are many factors to consider, including developing a portfolio based on specific circumstances, justifying portfolio selections and estimating the risk and return for a portfolio. Effective portfolio management requires attention to varied information..

© CSI GLOBAL EDUCATION INC. (2008)

KEY TERMS

- Alpha
- Beta
- Business risk
- Capital asset pricing model (CAPM)
- Correlation
- Default risk
- Diversification
- Ex-ante return
- Ex-post return
- Foreign exchange rate risk
- Holding period return
- Inflation rate risk
- Interest rate risk
- Investment policy statement
- Liquidity risk
- Market timing
- Non-systematic risk
- Political risk
- Rate of return
- Real rate of return
- Risk premium
- Risk/return trade-off
- Risk-free rate
- Security market line
- Systematic risk
- Time horizon
- Variance
- Volatility

© CSI GLOBAL EDUCATION INC. (2008)

RISK AND RETURN

It is every investor's dream to be able to get a very high return without any risk. The reality, however, is that risk and return are interrelated. To earn higher returns investors must usually choose investments with higher risk. The "Holy Grail" of investing is to choose investments that maximize returns while minimizing risk.

Given a choice between two investments with the same amount of risk, a rational investor would always take the security with the higher return. Given two investments with the same expected return, the investor would always choose the security with the lower risk.

Investors are risk averse, but not all to the same degree. Each investor has a different risk profile. This means that not all investors choose the same low-risk security. Some investors are willing to take on more risk than others are, if they believe there is a higher potential for returns.

In general, risk can have several different meanings. To some, risk is losing money on an investment. To others, it may be the prospect of losing purchasing power, if the return on the investments does not keep up with inflation. Risk could also refer to not meeting return objectives. For example, a retail investor may need to earn a 10% return in order to maintain a certain lifestyle. Institutional investors may have a target rate of return that they must meet each year. They may be investing to meet anticipated future cash flows. Thus, risk to an institutional investor may result from investing inappropriately, so that these cash flows do not materialize at the appropriate time.

Most retail investors feel that the prospect of losing money is an unacceptable risk. Institutional investors, on the other hand, are more concerned with the long-term rate of return on the portfolio, and less concerned about the prospect of losing money on one security.

Given that all investors do not have the same degree of risk tolerance, different securities and different funds have evolved to service each market niche. Guaranteed investment certificates (GICs) and fixed-income funds were developed for those seeking safety, while equities and equity funds were developed for those seeking growth or capital appreciation.

Few individuals would invest all of their funds in a single security. This being the case, a portfolio is designed around an asset allocation based upon the client's propensity for risk. The creation of a portfolio, or an asset allocation approach, allows the investor to diversify and reduce risk to a suitable level. The advisor, in turn, needs to understand how risk and return are related so that the client's questions can be answered intelligently.

To maintain and increase their purchasing power, investors "rent out" their money. In other words, they expect some sort of compensation for the use of their money. If investors did not expect some kind of return, it would not be classified as an investment – it would be a "donation" without a tax receipt!

Consider the following possible investments and the types of return generated:

Investment		Return
Canada Savings Bonds	–	interest income
Common shares	–	dividend income, capital gain
Gold bars	–	capital gain
Rental property	–	rental income, capital gain

© CSI GLOBAL EDUCATION INC. (2008)

An investor who buys Canada Savings Bonds expects to earn interest income (cash flow). An investor in common shares expects to see the stock grow in value (capital growth) and may also be rewarded by dividends (cash flow). An investor in a gold bar hopes the price of gold will rise (capital growth), and an investor who purchases a rental property expects to receive rental income (cash flow) and an increase in the value of the rental property (capital growth). The caveat on all this is that returns are rarely guaranteed, and that is why returns are often called "expected returns."

While an investment may be purchased in anticipation of a rise in value, the reality is that values can decline. A decline in the value of a security is often referred to as a capital loss. Therefore, returns can be reduced to some sort of combination of: cash flows and capital gains or losses. The following formula defines the expected return of a single security:

EXPECTED RETURN

Expected Return	=	Cash Flow + Capital Gain (or – Capital Loss)
Where:		
Cash Flow	=	Dividends, interest, or any other type of income
Capital Gain/Loss	=	Ending Value – Beginning Value
Beginning Value	=	The initial dollar amount invested by the investor
Ending Value	=	The dollar amount the investment is sold for

Rate of Return

Returns from an investment can be measured in absolute dollars. An investor may state that she made $100 or lost $20. Unfortunately, using absolute numbers obscures their significance. Was the $100 gain made on an investment of $1,000 or an investment of $100,000? In the first example the gain may be significant, while in the latter it could signal a dismal investment.

The more common practice is to express returns as a percentage or as a rate of return or yield. Within the investment community it is more common to hear that "a fund earned 8%" or "a stock fell 2%." To convert a dollar amount to a percentage, the usual practice is to divide the total dollar returns by the amount invested.

$$\text{Return } \% = \frac{\text{Cash Flow} + (\text{Ending Value} - \text{Beginning Value})}{\text{Beginning Value}} \times 100$$

The following example illustrates:

© CSI GLOBAL EDUCATION INC. (2008)

RATE OF RETURN ON AN INDIVIDUAL STOCK

1. If you purchased a stock for $10 and sold it one year later for $12, what would be your rate of return?

$$\text{Rate of Return} = \frac{\text{Zero Cash Flow} + (\$12 - \$10)}{\$10} \times 100 = 20\%$$

2. If you purchased a stock for $20 and sold it one year later for $22, and during this period you received $1 in dividends, what would be your rate of return?

$$\text{Rate of Return} = \frac{\$1 + (\$22 - \$20)}{\$20} \times 100 = 15\%$$

3. If you purchased a stock for $10, received $2 in dividends, but sold it one year later for only $9, what would be your rate of return?

$$\text{Rate of Return} = \frac{\$2 + (\$9 - \$10)}{\$10} \times 100 = 10\%$$

The above examples illustrate that cash flow and capital gains or losses are used in calculating a rate of return. It should also be noted that all of the above trading periods were set for one year, and hence the percent return can also be called the annual rate of return. If the transaction period were for longer or shorter than a year, the return would be called the **holding period return.** Adjustments would have to be made to the formula to convert it to an annual rate of return. The above generic formula will form the basis of yield calculations described later in this chapter.

Rates of return can be **ex-ante**, a projection of expected returns, or **ex-post**, meaning looking back at the actual returns previously earned (historical returns). Investors estimate future returns, i.e., ex-ante returns, to determine where funds should be invested. Ex-post returns are calculated in order to compare actual results against both anticipated results and market benchmarks.

The biggest problem with the rate of return measurement is that it does not take risk into account.

EX-ANTE AND EX-POST RATES OF RETURN

An investor purchases an equity fund in the expectation that the unit value will rise from $10 per unit to $12 per unit by the end of the year. The investor's expected rate of return would be:

$$\text{Rate of Return}_{\text{ex-ante}} = \frac{\text{Zero Cash Flow} + \$2 \text{ Capital Gain}}{\$10} \times 100 = 20\%$$

At the end of the year the unit's value was actually $10.50. The investor's actual rate of return was:

$$\text{Rate of Return}_{\text{ex-post}} = \frac{\text{Zero Cash Flow} + \$0.50 \text{ Capital Gain}}{\$10} \times 100 = 5\%$$

Choosing a realistic expected rate of return can be a very difficult task. One common method is to expect the T-bill rate plus a certain performance percentage related to the risk assumed in the investment. Corporate issues with a higher risk profile would be expected to earn a higher rate of return than the more secure federal government issues.

© CSI GLOBAL EDUCATION INC. (2008)

HISTORICAL RETURNS

An understanding of historical returns is important to the investor. Insights into the market can be gained by studying historical data. These insights are used to determine appropriate investments and investment strategies.

Consider the following rates of return in Table 15.1:

TABLE 15.1 COMPARATIVE TOTAL RATES OF RETURN ON SPECIFIC SECURITY CLASSES

Annual Total Return (% Change in Value Indices, December to December)

Annual Returns	T-Bills 90-Day (%)	Long-Term Bonds* (%)	S&P/TSX Composite Stocks (%)
1990	13.48	4.32	-14.80
1995	7.57	26.34	14.53
2000	5.49	12.97	7.41
2001	4.72	6.06	-12.57
2002	2.52	11.05	-12.44
2003	2.91	9.07	26.72
2004	2.30	10.26	14.48
2005	2.58	13.84	24.13
2006	3.93	6.47	15.63
2007	4.13	5.12	7.16

*Average term to maturity of long bonds is 16.47 years.

Source: Scotia Capital Fixed Income Research – Investment Returns, 2007.

A study of Table 15.1 reveals that the highest rates of return were achieved by securities that had the greatest *variability* or risk as measured by **standard deviation**, a measure of risk that will be explained later. The above historical information serves to illustrate that risk and return are related. Figure 15.1 demonstrates this relationship graphically.

© CSI GLOBAL EDUCATION INC. (2008)

FIGURE 15.1 RISK AND RETURN RELATIONSHIP

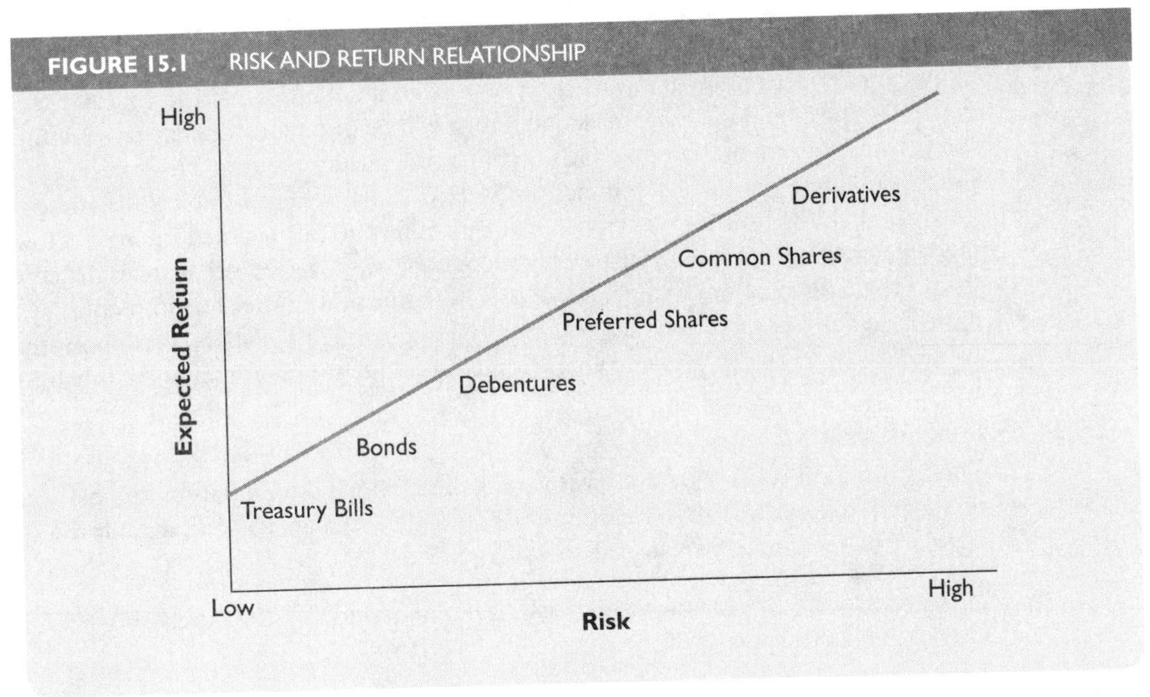

NOMINAL AND REAL RATES OF RETURN

So far we have looked only at a simple rate of return (i.e., the nominal rate of return). For example, if a one-year GIC reports a 6% return, this 6% represents the nominal return on the investment. However, investors are more concerned with the real rate of return – the return adjusted for the effects of inflation.

EXAMPLE: A client earned a 10% nominal return on an investment last year. Over the same period, inflation was measured at 2%. What was the client's approximate real rate of return on this investment?

The approximate real rate of return is calculated as:

Real Return = Nominal Rate – Annual Rate of Inflation

The client in the above example earned a real rate of return of 8% on the investment, calculated as:

Real Return = 10% – 2% = 8%

This calculation, however, does not take tax into account. If you assume that the return is 100% taxable, an investor with a return of 10%, having a tax rate of 30%, would have an after-tax return of 7%, calculated as 10% x (100% – 30%). Taking inflation into account (at 2%), the investor's approximate real return would be 5% (7% – 2%).

THE RISK-FREE RATE OF RETURN

A study of historical returns reveals that treasury bills usually keep pace with inflation and therefore provide a positive return. Since T-bills are considered essentially risk-free, all other securities must at least pay the T-bill rate plus a risk premium in order to entice clients into investing.

T-bills often represent the **risk-free** rate of return as there is essentially zero risk associated with this type of investment. The yield paid on a T-bill is roughly determined by estimating the short-term inflation and adding a real return.

© CSI GLOBAL EDUCATION INC. (2008)

Risk

As has already been pointed out, there is no universal definition of risk. In a statistical sense, it is defined as the likelihood that the actual return will be different from expected return. The greater the variability or number of possible outcomes, the greater the risk. This can be illustrated in a simple fashion. If an investor purchases a $500 Canada Savings Bond (CSB) and cashes the bond one year later, the investor will receive exactly $500 (plus any accrued interest). However, suppose the same investor purchased $500 worth of common stock at $25 per share in the expectation that the price would rise from $25 per share to $40 in one year's time. The investor may receive much more than $40 per share or much less than the original $25 per share. Common stocks would be defined as riskier than Canada Savings Bonds since the future outcomes are much less certain.

TYPES OF RISKS

The financial press talks about a great variety of risks including inflation rate risk, business risk, political risk, liquidity risk, interest rate risk, foreign exchange risk and default risk. These types of risks (the list is not all-inclusive) are defined below.

Inflation rate risk: As explained previously, inflation reduces future purchasing power and the return on investments.

Business risk: This risk is associated with the variability of a company's earnings due to such things as the possibility of a labour strike, introduction of new products, the state of the economy, and the performance of competing firms, among others. The uncertainty regarding a company's future performance is its basic business risk.

Political risk: This is the risk associated with unfavourable changes in government policies. For example, a government may decide to raise taxes on foreign investing, making it less attractive to invest in the country. Political risk also refers to the general instability associated with investing in a particular country. Investing in a war-torn country, for example, brings with it the added risk of losing one's investment.

Liquidity risk: A liquid asset is one that can be bought or sold at a fair price and converted to cash on short notice. A security that is difficult to sell suffers from liquidity risk, which is the risk that an investor will not be able to buy or sell a security at a fair price quickly enough due to limited buying or selling opportunities.

Interest rate risk: When an investor purchases a fixed-income security, for example, he or she expects to earn a certain return or yield on the investment. As we learned in the chapter on fixed-income securities, there is an inverse relationship between interest rates and bond prices. If interest rates rise, the investment will fall in value; on the other hand, it will rise in value if rates fall. Interest rate risk is the risk that investors are exposed to because of changing interest rates.

Foreign exchange risk: Foreign exchange risk is the risk of incurring losses resulting from an unfavourable change in exchange rates. Investors who invest abroad or businesses that buy and sell products in foreign markets run the risk of a loss whenever the exchange rate changes against foreign currencies.

Default risk: When a company issues more debt to finance its operations, servicing the debt through interest payments creates a further burden on the company. The more debt the company acquires, the greater the risk that it may have difficulty servicing its debt load through its current operations. Default risk is the risk associated with a company being unable to make timely interest payments or repay the principal amount of a loan when due.

© CSI GLOBAL EDUCATION INC. (2008)

SYSTEMATIC AND NON-SYSTEMATIC RISK

Certain risks can be reduced by **diversification**. The risks known as **systematic risks** cannot be eliminated, as these risks affect all assets within certain classes. Systematic risk is always present and cannot be eliminated through diversification. This type of risk stems from such things as inflation, the business cycle and high interest rates.

Systematic (or market risk) is the risk associated with investing in each capital market: When stock market averages fall, most individual stocks in the market fall. When interest rates rise, nearly all individual bonds and preferred shares fall in value. Systematic risk cannot be diversified away; in fact, the more a portfolio becomes diversified within a certain asset class, the more it ends up mirroring that market.

Non-systematic risk, or **specific risk**, is the risk that the price of a specific security or a specific group of securities will change in price to a different degree or in a different direction from the market as a whole. Stelco may rise in price, for example, when the S&P/TSX Composite Index falls, or Stelco, Dofasco and Co-Steel (all steel companies) as a group may fall more than the Index.

Specific risk can be reduced by diversifying among a number of securities. This type of risk theoretically could be eliminated completely by buying a portfolio of shares that consisted of all S&P/TSX Composite Index stocks, using index funds or buying ETFs based on the Index. The fund manager could also be asked to create a fund that mirrors an index.

MEASURING RISK

Investors may expect a given return on an investment, but the actual results may be higher or lower. To get a better feel for the possible outcomes and their probability of occurrence, several measures of risk have been developed. The three common measures of risk are variance, standard deviation and beta.

Variance measures the extent to which the possible realized returns differ from the expected return or the mean. The more likely it is that the return will not be the same as the expected return, the more risky the security. When an investor purchases a T-bill, the return is predictable. The return cannot change as long as the investor holds the T-bill until maturity. With other securities (e.g., equities), the outcomes are more varied. The price could increase, stay the same or decrease. The greater the number of possible outcomes, the greater the risk that the outcome will not be favourable. The greater the distance estimated between the expected return and the possible returns, the greater the variance. The risk of a portfolio is determined by the risk of the various securities within that portfolio.

Standard deviation is the measure of risk commonly applied to portfolios and to individual securities within that portfolio. Standard deviation is the square root of the variance. The past performance or historical returns of securities is used to determine a range of possible future outcomes. The more volatile the price of a security has been in the past, the larger the range of possible future outcomes. The standard deviation, expressed as a percentage, gives the investor an indication of the risk associated with an individual security or a portfolio. The greater the standard deviation, the greater the risk.

Complete the on-line activity associated with this section.

Beta is another statistical measure that links the risk of individual equity securities to the market as a whole. As we saw earlier, the risk that remains after diversifying is market risk. Beta is important because it measures the degree to which individual stocks tend to move up and down with the market. Once again, the higher the beta, the greater the risk.

© CSI GLOBAL EDUCATION INC. (2008)

PORTFOLIO RISK AND RETURN

Once you have a better understanding of the client's financial objectives and tolerance for risk, you will need to determine the broad categories from which investments will be selected. Investment assets can be grouped into three main asset classes: cash or near-cash equivalents; fixed-income securities; and equity securities. Near-cash items ensure some liquidity and include money market instruments and money market funds. Fixed-income securities offer safety and income and include bonds, preferred shares and fixed-income funds. Preferred shares, although technically a type of equity security, are generally considered to be fixed-income securities from a portfolio management standpoint. Growth securities usually include common shares and various types of equity funds. As their name implies, growth securities provide potential for growth or capital gain.

Asset allocation involves determining the optimal division of an investor's portfolio among the different asset classes. For example, depending on the client's tolerance for risk and the investment objectives, the portfolio may be divided as follows: 10% in cash, 30% in fixed-income securities, and 60% in equities.

Consider the following examples:

Jenny is a young, healthy, single professional with good investment knowledge and a high risk tolerance, a moderate tax rate and a long investment time horizon. She might benefit from the following asset mix:

Cash	5%
Fixed-income	25%
Equities	70%

Ahmed is a retired individual in a low tax bracket with no income other than government pensions, a medium time horizon and a low risk tolerance. He requires income from his portfolio. He might benefit from the following asset mix:

Cash	10%
Fixed-income	60%
Equities	30%

It should be noted that clients' needs and objectives will change over their lifetimes. Asset allocation will have to be adjusted to take into account these shifting needs.

Portfolio managers and investors will also alter asset allocation to take advantage of changes in the economic environment. For example, when the economy enters a period of rapid growth, the portfolio manager must decide how best to take advantage of the market. He or she will likely decide that a heavier "weighting" in equities would generate better returns than holding more of the portfolio in fixed-income securities or cash. Alternatively, if the portfolio manager believes the market is entering a recession, a heavier weighting in cash or fixed-income securities may be pursued to generate higher returns. This process of altering a portfolio's asset allocation to take advantage of changes in the economy is one meaning of the term market timing.

© CSI GLOBAL EDUCATION INC. (2008)

THE IMPORTANCE OF ASSET ALLOCATION

Investment returns are derived from:

1. The choice of an asset mix
2. Market timing decisions
3. Securities selection
4. Chance

Asset allocation is the single most important step in structuring a portfolio. It is estimated that it accounts for approximately 90% of the variation in returns on an investment portfolio.

Table 15.2 lists the top-performing securities between the years 1990 and 2007:

TABLE 15.2 TOP PERFORMING SECURITY CLASSES IN CANADA 1990 – 2007

Year	Security Class	Total Return (%)
1990	Corporate Paper	13.94
1995	Long Bonds	26.34
2000	Long Bonds	12.97
2001	Short Bonds	9.37
2002	Long Bonds	11.05
2003	Equities	26.72
2004	Equities	14.48
2005	Equities	24.13
2006	Equities	15.63
2007	Equities	7.16

Source: Scotia Capital Fixed Income Research – Investment Returns, 2007, TSX Group FactBook 2007.

While historical returns provide insight into the long-term performance of the market, it is obvious from the above that past performance is not necessarily indicative of future performance. Since it is extremely difficult to predict the future, an investor should employ the concept of diversification – diversification among asset classes – to reduce risk.

Calculating the Rate of Return on a Portfolio

The expected return on a portfolio is calculated in a slightly different manner from the rate of return of a single security. Since the portfolio contains a number of securities, the return generated by each security has to be calculated.

© CSI GLOBAL EDUCATION INC. (2008)

PORTFOLIO RETURNS

The return on a portfolio is calculated as the weighted average return on the securities held in the portfolio. The formula is as follows:

Expected Return: $R_1(W_1) + R_2(W_2) + \ldots + R_n(W_n)$

Where:

R = The return on a particular security

W = The proportion (weight or %) of the security held in the portfolio based on the dollar investment

The following example illustrates:

RATE OF A RETURN ON A PORTFOLIO

A client invests $100 in two securities – $60 in ABC Co. and $40 in DEF Co. The expected return from ABC Co. is 15% and the expected return from DEF Co. is 12%. To calculate the expected return of the portfolio, an advisor or investor would look at the rate expected to be generated by each proportional investment.

Since the total amount invested was $100, ABC Co. represents 60% ($60 ÷ $100) of the portfolio and DEF Co. represents 40% ($40 ÷ $100) of the portfolio. If ABC Co. earns a return of 15% and DEF Co. earns 12%, the expected return on the portfolio is:

Expected return = (0.15 × 0.60) + (0.12 × 0.40)

= 0.09 + 0.048

= 0.138 (or 13.8%)

Measuring Risk in a Portfolio

While diversification is important, investment managers must also guard against too much diversification. When a portfolio contains too many securities, superior performance may be difficult to achieve and the accounting, research and valuation functions may be needlessly complex. It is estimated that virtually all non-systematic risk in an equity portfolio is eliminated by the time 32 securities are included in the portfolio.

Investment managers have developed a number of strategies for limiting losses on individual securities or on a portfolio. Most of these strategies involve the use of derivatives. For example, they may use put options on individual equities or on investments such as gold, silver, currencies, and so on. Additionally, the portfolio manager can hedge an entire portfolio by using futures and options on stock index or long-term bond options.

© CSI GLOBAL EDUCATION INC. (2008)

Combining Securities in a Portfolio

This section addresses portfolio construction for the purpose of maximizing return and reducing risk. In doing so, it brings together the concepts of risk and return. Portfolio management recognizes the fact that while future returns are usually beyond the control of an individual or fund manager, risk to a certain extent can be managed.

Portfolio management stresses the selection of securities for inclusion in the portfolio based on the securities' contribution to the portfolio as a whole. This suggests some synergy or some interaction among the securities that results in the total portfolio being somewhat more than the sum of the parts.

As has been explained previously, if investors place all of their savings in a single security, their entire portfolio is at risk. If the investment consists of a single equity security, the investment is subject to business risk and market risk. Alternatively, if all of the investor's funds are invested in a single debt security, the investment is subject to default risk and interest rate risk.

Some of these risks can be eliminated or reduced through diversification. However, diversification must be done carefully and the methodology for combining securities must be understood. Combining any two securities may not diversify the portfolio if the risk characteristics of the two securities are extremely similar.

CORRELATION

Correlation looks at how securities relate to each other when they are added to a portfolio and how the resulting combination affects the portfolio's total risk and return. To illustrate the concept, consider the following:

An investor takes all of his or her savings and invests 100% of those savings in a gold mining stock. Obviously, if the price of gold rises, the company does well and the client makes money. If the price of gold declines, the gold mining company does not do well and the investor loses money. In order to reduce this risk, the investor diversifies into another stock, which happens to be another gold mining company. Has the investor's portfolio been diversified?

The investor's advisor points out that the portfolio has not been adequately diversified. Not understanding, the investor breaks up the portfolio and invests in five different companies chosen at random; unfortunately, they all turn out to be gold mining companies.

It is clear that the securities in the portfolio are linked – their value is tied to the fortunes of gold. The portfolio thus has a high correlation with the fortunes of gold. In fact, if the security price movements mirrored each other exactly, they would have a perfect positive correlation, which is denoted as a correlation of +1 (see Figure 15.2). The investor does not reduce his or her risk by adding securities that are perfectly correlated with each other.

© CSI GLOBAL EDUCATION INC. (2008)

FIGURE 15.2 COMBINING TWO PERFECTLY POSITIVELY CORRELATED SECURITIES

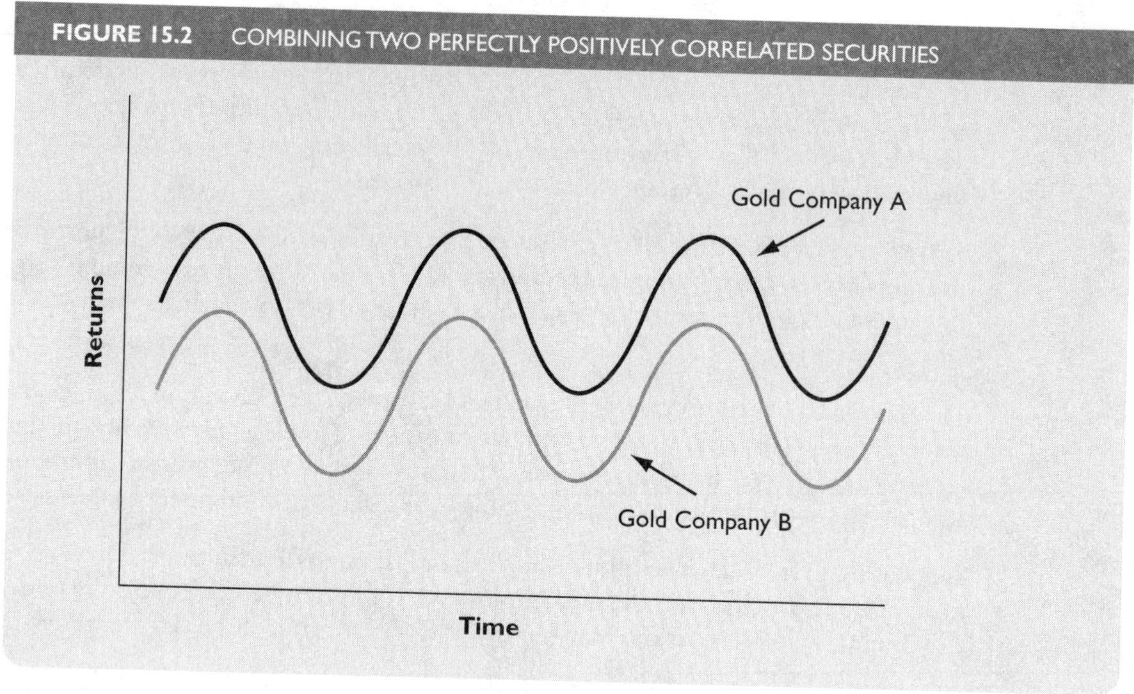

Figure 15.2 shows that the returns on both Gold Company A and Gold Company B have a tendency to move together in tandem – they rise and fall at the same time. These two stocks are said to exhibit perfect positive correlation. If an investor held only these two stocks, the portfolio would not be diversified against any market downturns. Therefore, holding securities with perfect positive correlation does not reduce the overall risk of the portfolio.

What if the stocks moved in opposite directions? Consider the following example:

An investor creates a portfolio of two securities – an airline company stock and a bus company stock. In good economic times people fly, but in bad economic times they save money by taking the bus. In good times, the investor's airline company shares increase in value. In bad times, the airline stock declines but the loss is offset by an increase in the price of bus company shares. Since the stock prices move exactly in the opposite direction, the investor earns a positive return with little risk (there is always the possibility of market risk). These securities have a perfect negative correlation, denoted as -1 (see Figure 15.3).

© CSI GLOBAL EDUCATION INC. (2008)

FIGURE 15.3 COMBINING TWO PERFECTLY NEGATIVELY CORRELATED SECURITIES

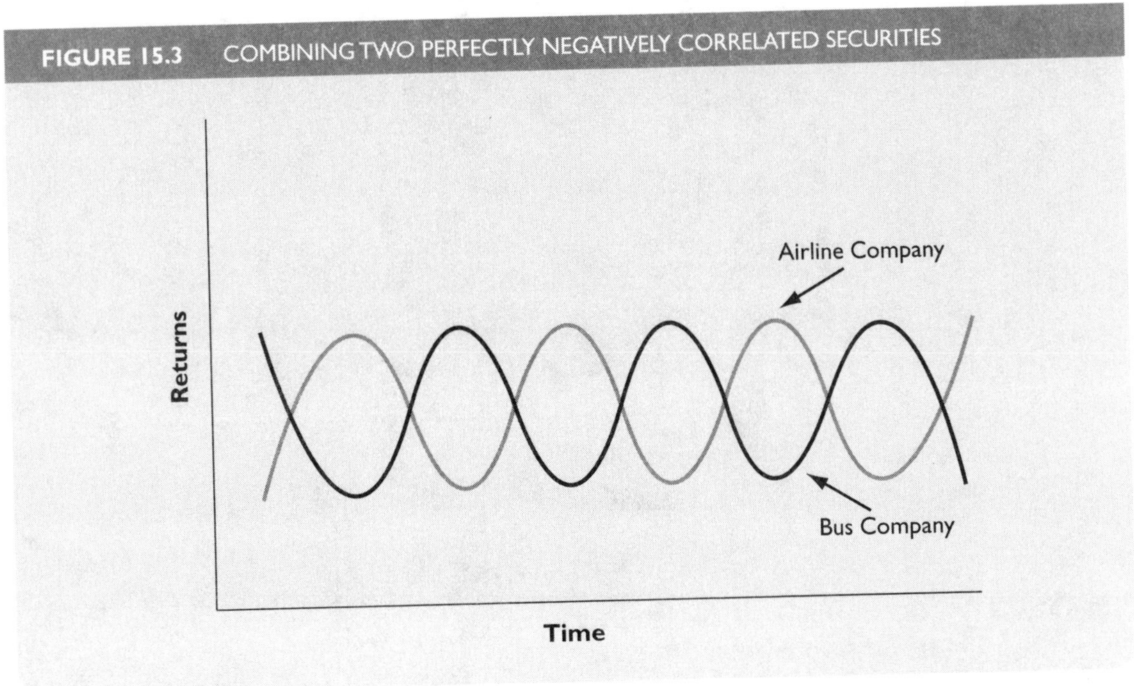

Figure 15.3 shows that the returns on the two companies move in completely opposite directions. When one rises, the other falls. With perfect negative correlation, there is no variability in the total returns for the two assets – thus, no risk for the portfolio. Therefore, the maximum gain from diversification is achieved when securities held within the portfolio exhibit perfect negative correlation. In reality, however, it is very difficult to find securities with such a high level of negative correlation.

Unfortunately, the above airline/bus example is not entirely correct. In bad times people tend to stay at home and travel less. So the stocks are not completely negatively correlated. In fact, research has found that most equities are correlated to some degree with the Canadian economy. When the economy does well, most stocks also do well – but not to the same degree.

Further research has revealed that adding poorly correlated securities to a portfolio does in fact reduce risk. However, each additional security reduces risk at a lower rate. In fact, once there are 32 securities in the portfolio, additional risk reduction is minimal. Since the securities in the portfolio are still positively correlated to some degree, the portfolio is left with one risk that cannot be eliminated – systematic or market risk. This concept holds true whether you are dealing with equity securities or debt securities.

Figure 15.4 shows reduction of risk by adding securities to a portfolio.

© CSI GLOBAL EDUCATION INC. (2008)

FIGURE 15.4 RISK IN A PORTFOLIO

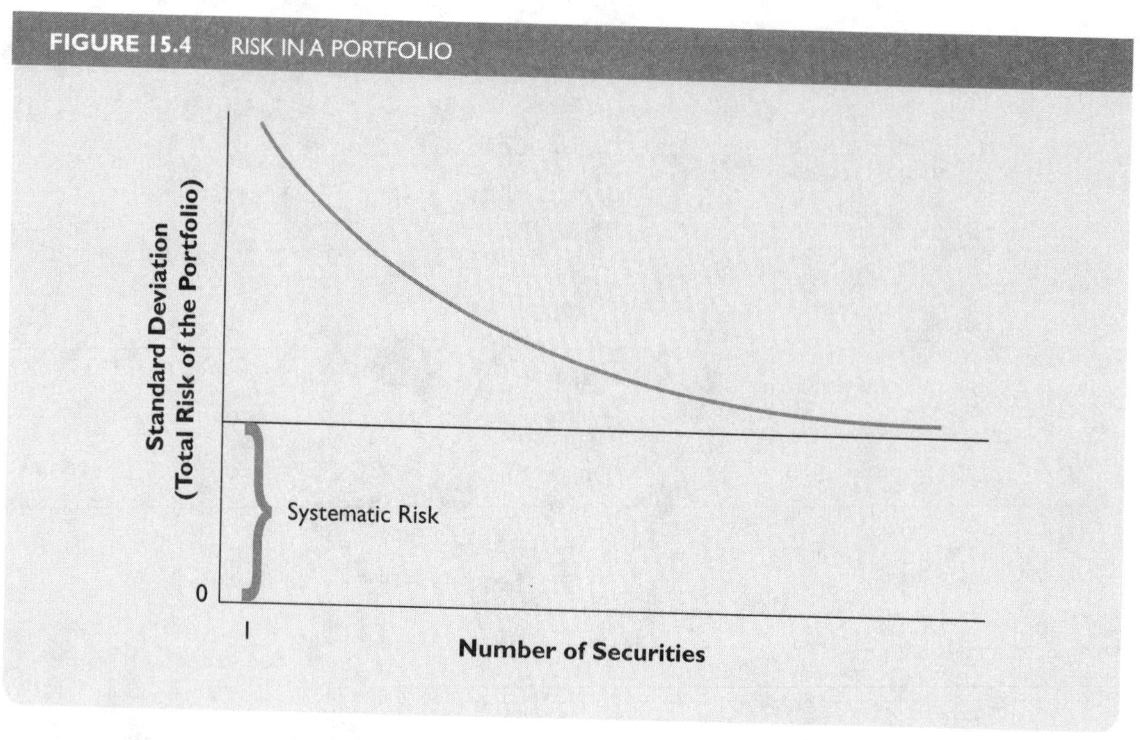

The total risk of the portfolio falls quite significantly as the first few stocks are added. As the number of stocks increases, however, the additional reduction in risk declines. Finally, a point is reached where a further reduction in risk through diversification cannot be achieved. Therefore, the main source of uncertainty for an investor with a diversified portfolio is the impact of systematic risk on portfolio return.

PORTFOLIO BETA

As was previously explained, the beta or *beta coefficient* relates the volatility of a single security to the volatility of the stock market as a whole. Specifically, beta measures that part of the fluctuation in a stock price that is driven by changes in the market. **Volatility** in this context is a way of describing the changes in a stock's price over a long time frame. The wider the range in market prices, the more volatile the stock and the greater the risk. The same concept can be applied to equity portfolios.

Any security, or portfolio of stocks, that moves up or down to the same degree as the stock market has a beta of 1.0. Any security or portfolio that moves up or down more than the market has a beta greater than 1.0, and a security that moves less than the market has a beta of less than 1.0.

If the Toronto Stock Exchange, as measured by the S&P/TSX Composite Index, rose 10%, a stock or equity fund with a beta of 1.0 could be expected to advance by 10%. If the Index fell by 5%, the stock or fund would fall by 5%. If a stock had a beta of 1.30, it would rise 13% (1.3 × 10%) when the Index rose 10%. A stock with a beta of 0.80 would only rise 8% when the Index rose 10%.

In real life, most portfolios have a beta between 0.75 and 1.40, indicating a positive correlation between equities and the stock market. Industries with volatile earnings, typically cyclical industries, tend to have higher betas than the market. Defensive industries tend to have betas that are less than the market, that is, less than 1. This implies that when the market is falling in price, a defensive stock would normally fall relatively less and a cyclical stock relatively more.

© CSI GLOBAL EDUCATION INC. (2008)

Simplistically, it could be stated that in a rising market it is better to have high beta stocks and in a falling market it is better to have defensive, low beta stocks. However, this is an over-generalization and presumes that history repeats itself.

Table 15.3 shows examples of betas for selected companies. Note not only how they differ from each other, but also how the beta changes over time.

TABLE 15.3 BETAS FOR SELECTED COMPANIES AS OF DECEMBER 2007

Company	52-Week Beta	3-Year Beta	5-Year Beta
Nortel	1.02	3.14	2.25
BCE	0.23	0.21	0.78
TD Bank	0.37	0.64	1.03
Royal Bank	0.47	0.36	0.56
Rogers Communications	0.48	1.17	1.22
Sears Canada	0.56	0.99	1.10
Ballard Power Systems	1.44	2.32	2.48
S&P/TSX Index Fund	1.00	1.00	1.00

Source: Bloomberg online, www.bloomberg.com.

PORTFOLIO ALPHA

Quite often, individual stocks outperform the market and move more than would be expected from their beta. The additional movement is due to the fundamental strength or weakness of the company. This strength, or weakness, could be due to the company's expertise, or lack of expertise, in marketing, production or management. An advisor's or fund manager's skill lies in picking those securities that will outperform others. This is known as the stock's **alpha**. Mathematically, it measures the portion of an investment's return coming from specific risk.

Those portfolio managers and individuals who can choose the "best" investments, and create a portfolio with a positive alpha, will earn higher returns than those who do not. In other words, their portfolios will dominate other weaker portfolios. To be able to create portfolios that dominate others, the individual investor, or portfolio manager, must be capable of analyzing both the company and the market. This is not an easy task. Given that most individual investors have neither the skills nor the time, professional managers usually represent a better choice. Professional management is considered one of the main advantages of investing in mutual funds.

Capital Asset Pricing Model (CAPM)

As we have seen, beta represents the best measure of a stock's risk compared with that of the overall market. Since investors generally hold a portfolio of securities, rather than just one security in isolation, we can now look at the riskiness of a security in terms of its contribution to the riskiness of the portfolio.

The **capital asset pricing model** (CAPM) was developed in the 1960s to recognize the trade-off between risk and return. The underlying assumption of this model is that investors who take on more risk expect higher returns.

© CSI GLOBAL EDUCATION INC. (2008)

The CAPM demonstrates graphically how investors are rewarded for assuming this risk. The difference between the risk-free return on Treasury bills and the return on the market is called the **risk premium**. This risk premium compensates investors for taking on additional risk. As we have seen already, the risk premium reflects market or systematic risk and is measured by beta.

Figure 15.5 illustrates the CAPM and the **risk/return trade-off**.

FIGURE 15.5 CAPITAL ASSET PRICING MODEL

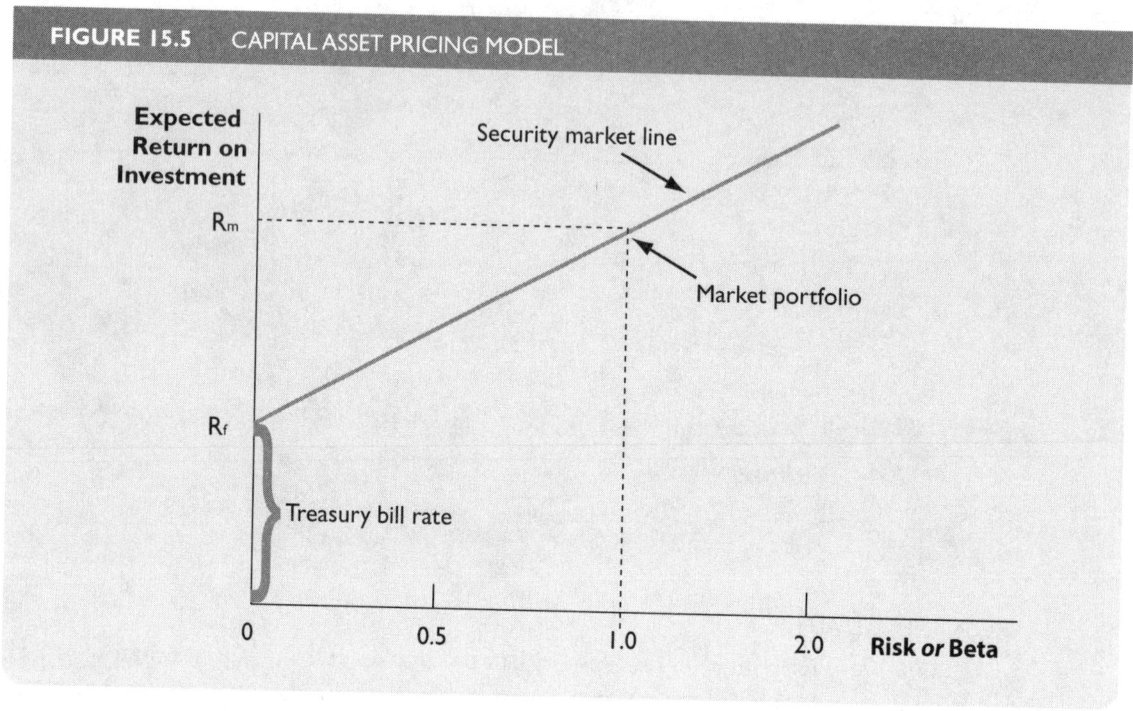

The CAPM produces a formula that can be used to calculate the expected return on a stock or portfolio. The **security market line** shows the relationship between risk and return.

We can write the security market line relationship as:

Expected Return = Return on T-bills + Risk Premium

Mathematically, this is written as

$$R_p = R_f + \beta(R_m - R_f)$$

Where:

R_p	=	the expected return on a security or a portfolio of securities
R_f	=	the risk-free rate of return
R_m	=	return on the market portfolio
β	=	beta
$(R_m - R_f)$	=	the market risk premium

To put this relationship in words, the security market line says that the expected return on a security or portfolio, R_p, is equal to the return on a security that has no risk, R_f, plus a risk premium, $(R_m - R_f)$, multiplied by beta, β, the relative riskiness of the stock or security in question.

© CSI GLOBAL EDUCATION INC. (2008)

For example, a client asks an advisor what the expected return is on a particular fund. The fund has a beta of 1.1, and the advisor knows that the return on the S&P/TSX Composite Index has historically been 10% (representing the return on the market) and that the T-bill rate (the risk-free rate) is currently 4%. Employing the formula:

$$R_p = R_f + \beta (R_m - R_f)$$

$$= 0.04 + 1.1(0.10 - 0.04) = 10.6\%$$

In other words, the expected return on this fund is 10.6%.

Note that the above return is only an estimate of the expected return – actual results may differ. The formula does, however, address the client's question as to what could be expected for a specific portfolio or individual equity security.

OVERVIEW OF THE PORTFOLIO MANAGEMENT PROCESS

While securities are sometimes selected on their own merits, portfolio management stresses the selection of securities for inclusion in the portfolio based on that security's contribution to the portfolio as a whole. As the previous section on risk and return has shown, there is some synergy, or some interaction, among the securities, which results in the total portfolio effect being something more than the sum of its parts. While the return of the portfolio will be the weighted average of the returns of each security, the risk of a portfolio is almost always less than the risks of the individual securities that make up the portfolio. This results in an improved risk-reward tradeoff from using the portfolio approach.

Security selection decisions, then, are made in a context of the effect on the overall portfolio, rather than as discrete decisions that ignore the effect of one security on another in the portfolio.

For this reason, a portfolio approach is much more desirable than a series of unco-ordinated decisions. The portfolio management process is a continuous set of six basic steps, with the word process indicating that when the sixth step is completed, work begins anew on the first step. The six parts to the portfolio management process are:

1. Determine investment objectives and constraints
2. Formulate an asset allocation strategy and select investment styles
3. Design an investment policy statement
4. Implement the Asset Allocation
5. Monitor the economy, the markets, the portfolio and the client
6. Evaluate portfolio performance

In this chapter, we focus on investment objectives and constraints and the investment policy statement. The remaining steps are described in Chapter 16.

© CSI GLOBAL EDUCATION INC. (2008)

OBJECTIVES AND CONSTRAINTS

Having discovered the client's objectives and constraints, the next step in designing an investment policy is to summarize this information in terms of the investment objectives. It is these objectives that will help determine the appropriate asset allocation for that client.

All the information learned from the client through interviews, questionnaires and follow-up discussions should be distilled into a return objective and a risk objective. These objectives must address the following questions:

- What rate of return does the client need to attain his or her goals?
- What risk is he or she willing and able to take to achieve them?

Return and Risk Objectives

The return objective is a measure of how much the client's portfolio is expected to earn each year on average. The return objective depends primarily on the return required to meet the client's goals, but it must also be consistent with the client's risk tolerance. An investor must determine whether a strategy of return maximization, in which assets are invested to make the greatest return possible while staying within the risk tolerance level, is preferable to a strategy in which a required minimum return is generated with certainty. The emphasis in the latter strategy is on risk reduction. In addition, the policy should be designed to take into account the client's tax position and needs with respect to the proportion of interest income, capital gains and dividend income to be generated.

The risk objective is a specific statement of how much risk the client is willing to sustain to meet the return objective. The risk objective is based on the client's risk tolerance, which in turn is dependent upon the client's willingness and ability to bear risk.

There are many ways to assess the risk tolerance of a particular investor, from the very rudimentary to the very sophisticated. Each has its value in measuring what degree of risk the client is prepared to take. Assessment of risk tolerance is a vital element in the ultimate design of the portfolio, as it will govern the selection of securities to be included.

Besides the risk the client is willing to assume, there must be a measure of the risk of each security to be considered for inclusion in the portfolio. As mentioned in Chapter 7, term to maturity and duration are two measures of a bond's risk. Such statistics as beta and standard deviation are used to measure the risk of equities. Other measures, too, exist, such as independent rating agency assessments and member firm research reports.

It is important to recognize the difference between the risk of an individual security and the risk of the portfolio as a whole. Because the risk of a portfolio is less than the average risk of its holdings, the client's risk tolerance should be matched to the risk of the overall portfolio, and not to the risk of each security.

Although most retail clients will need some degree of inflation protection, the extent will vary. A retired person with a long time horizon and the goal of using the portfolio to generate income will be very concerned about what the purchasing power of the cash flow from the portfolio will be. Another person using short-term trading strategies and interested in maximization of capital gains may concentrate less on this particular factor. It is important to remember that there are no

© CSI GLOBAL EDUCATION INC. (2008)

certainties with any client; just because a client is a "trader" and is young does not automatically mean he or she is not concerned about inflation. Careful listening to and discussion with the client should always replace assumptions and generalities based on such things as age and wealth.

The role of the investment manager in constructing a portfolio is to ensure that it will generate returns while taking into account the investor's own particular level of risk tolerance. Therefore, managing risk is a major focus of portfolio management. While an increase in returns should result from an increase in risk, high-risk portfolios do not always turn out to be high-return portfolios.

While grouping equities by level of risk is more subjective, the four definitions in Table 15.4 provide a basis for risk differentiation. The differences between the four equity risk categories are largely a function of differences in capitalization, earnings performance, predictability of earnings, liquidity and potential price volatility. Since these variables apply to all common shares in all industry groups, each industry may have companies whose securities could be ranked in any of the four groups. Also, because companies are not static, the risk in an individual security can change over time and may warrant a higher or lower ranking. Table 15.4 shows some of the alternatives available in constructing a portfolio.

TABLE 15.4 SAMPLE RISK CATEGORIES WITHIN EACH ASSET CLASS

Cash or Cash Equivalents:	
1. Government issues (less than a year)	Lowest risk, highest quality
2. Corporate issues (less than a year)	Highest risk, lowest quality
Fixed-Income Securities:	
1. Short term (from one to five years)	Low risk, low price volatility
2. Medium term (from five to ten years)	Medium risk, medium price volatility
3. Long term (over ten years)	High risk, maximum price volatility
Equities	
1. Conservative	Low risk; high capitalization; predictable earnings; high yield; high dividend payouts; lower P-E ratios; low price volatility.
2. Growth	Medium risk; average capitalization; potential for above average growth in earnings; aggressive management; lower dividend payout; higher P-E ratios; potentially higher price volatility.
3. Venture	High risk; low capitalization; limited earnings record; no dividends; P-E of little significance; short operating history; highly volatile.
4. Speculative	Maximum risk; shorter term; maximum price volatility; no earnings; no dividends; P-E ratio not significant.

© CSI GLOBAL EDUCATION INC. (2008)

Investment Objectives

In general, investors have three primary investment objectives – (1) *Safety of Principal*, (2) *Income* and (3) *Growth of Capital* and two secondary objectives – (4) *Liquidity* and (5) *Tax Minimization*. These investment objectives are described below in the context of choosing among different securities.

Consultation should continue with the client right through this stage in the portfolio process. When necessary, the advisor can explain each objective to the client, and together, they can come to a joint conclusion as to the appropriate balance among the objectives. It may be difficult for clients to communicate their wishes in non-tangible ways, but allocation to each major objective, on a percentage basis, is recommended. It adds clarity to both parties and will translate well into the **New Account Application Form** (**NAAF**) categories (refer to the copy of the NAAF shown in Chapter 23). Some firms have sub-categories to the major ones on the NAAF, which add exactness to the overall objectives, and for which the percentages will also be useful.

SAFETY OF PRINCIPAL OR PRESERVATION OF CAPITAL

One major objective is to have some assurance that the initial capital invested will largely remain intact. If this is the main concern among the three major objectives, the client is effectively saying that, regardless of whether a small, large or nil return is generated on the capital, the advisor should try to avoid erosion of the amount initially invested. This objective is expressed in constant dollars (i.e., not counting inflation).

If the highest degree of safety is required, it may be obtained by accepting a lower rate of income return and giving up much of the opportunity for capital growth. In Canada, a high degree of safety of principal and of certainty of income is offered by most federal, provincial and municipal bonds, if held to maturity. Selected high-grade corporate bonds also fall in this category. Shorterterm bonds also offer a high degree of safety because they are close to their maturity dates. Government of Canada treasury bills offer the highest degree of safety – they are virtually risk-free.

There is one simple strategy to make the preservation of an investor's principal fairly certain. Assume an account size of $100,000, and a T-bill rate of approximately 3%. Roughly $97,000 can be invested in T-bills, which are considered risk free, and which will mature in one year's time at $100,000, restoring the principal amount. The other $3,000 can be invested in some other venture, even a speculative one, and even if the full $3,000 is lost completely, the investor will receive the principal back (pre-tax).

Examples of individual investors who might be seeking safety as a principal investment objective include:

- A widow whose primary source of income is her securities portfolio.
- A young couple who are investing their savings for the eventual purchase of a house.
- A businessman who is temporarily investing the funds he will be using to buy out his partner in six months' time.

The choice of preservation of capital as the major investment objective is a result of the interaction of several objectives and constraints, including risk, market timing, inflation, return and emotion.

© CSI GLOBAL EDUCATION INC. (2008)

INCOME OBJECTIVE

This major objective refers to the generation of a regular series of cash flows from a portfolio, whether in the form of dividends, interest or some other form, and is a broader definition than the basic minimum income referred to as a constraint. The taxation of dividends and interest income will be a major determinant of the split between income received from debt or equity securities. This split is decided at the time the asset mix is set.

An investor seeking to maximize the rate of income return usually gives up some safety if he or she purchases corporate bonds or preferred shares with lower investment ratings. The term "usually" is used because there are times when the informed investor with access to accurate and current information may be able to obtain bargains. In general, however, safety goes down as yield goes up. But it should not be assumed that as the yield goes down the safety of the bond or preferred share improves, because other factors may affect price and yield.

Careful selection and periodic review of securities owned are necessary to obtain maximum income consistent with safety.

Examples of investors who might emphasize income as a primary investment objective include:

- A salaried individual who relies on the additional income from investments to meet the cost of raising and educating a family.
- A retired couple whose pension income is insufficient to provide for all living expenses.
- A very conservative investor who, temperamentally, is not comfortable with common share investments and fluctuating market values.
- A conservative person who, in a self-directed Registered Retirement Savings Plan (RRSP), is seeking the benefits of long-term, tax-deferred compounding of reinvested income.

The choice of income as a major investment objective is influenced by return, risk, inflation and basic minimum income, among others.

GROWTH OBJECTIVE

Growth of capital, or capital gains, refers to the profit generated when securities are sold for more than they cost to buy. When capital gains are the primary investment objective, the emphasis is on security selection and market timing, and generally a trade-off against preservation of capital is required. In recent years, capital gains have been taxed more favourably than interest income, which provides some incentive for choosing this objective over income generation.

The choice of capital gains as a major investment objective involves considering many factors, including risk, return, market timing and emotions, as well as others.

Examples of investors primarily seeking growth include:

- A well-paid young executive with excess income who wishes to build his or her own pool of capital for early retirement.
- A vice-president of a corporation who is seeking above average returns through common share investments.
- Well-to-do members of an investment club who seek capital gains but who can also sustain potential losses.
- A couple who, as a result of a substantial inheritance, are in a position to invest more aggressively and who are temperamentally prepared to accept a higher degree of investment risk.

Table 15.5, in very broad terms and disregarding inflation and its effects, shows the four major kinds of securities and evaluates them in terms of the three basic investment objectives.

© CSI GLOBAL EDUCATION INC. (2008)

TABLE 15.5 SECURITIES AND THEIR INVESTMENT OBJECTIVES

Type of Security	Safety	Income	Growth
1. Short-Term Bonds	Best	Very steady	Very limited
2. Long-Term Bonds	Next best	Very steady	Variable
3. Preferred Stocks	Good	Steady	Variable
4. Common Stocks	Often the least	Variable	Often the most

MARKETABILITY OBJECTIVE

A fourth goal sought by many investors is marketability, which is not necessarily related to safety, income return or capital gain. It simply means that at nearly all times there are buyers at some price level for the securities (usually at a small discount from fair value). For some investors who may need money on short notice (i.e., liquidity), this feature is very important. For others, it may not be vital. Most Canadian securities (excluding some real estate–related securities) can be sold in reasonable quantities at some price, usually within a day or so.

TAX OBJECTIVE

When assessing the returns from any investment, the investor must consider the effect of taxation. The tax treatment of any investment varies depending on whether the returns are categorized as interest, dividends or capital gains. Thus, tax treatment of the returns influences the choice among investments.

Investment Constraints

Constraints provide some discipline in the fulfilment of a client's objectives. Constraints, which may loosely be defined as those items that may hinder or prevent the investment manager from satisfying the client's objectives, are often not given the importance they deserve in the policy formation process. Perhaps this is because objectives are a more comforting concept to dwell on than the discipline of constraints.

TIME HORIZON

A major factor in the design of a good portfolio is how well it reflects the **time horizon** of its goals. Fundamentally, the time horizon is the period of time from the present until the next major change in the client's circumstances. In other words, just because a client is 25 years of age and normal retirement is at age 60, this does not necessarily mean the time horizon is 35 years. Clients go through various events in their life, each of which can represent a time horizon and a need for a complete rebalancing of their portfolio. For example, finishing university, planning for a career change, the birth of a child, the purchase of a home, and many other events besides retirement represent the end of one time horizon and the beginning of a new one.

While some major events in a client's life cannot be predicted, such as a serious health problem or loss of employment, a client's time horizon should still be the period of time from the present to the next major *expected* change in circumstances.

© CSI GLOBAL EDUCATION INC. (2008)

LIQUIDITY REQUIREMENTS

In portfolio management, liquidity means the amount of cash and near-cash in the portfolio. While there are no set rules in portfolio management, a rough guide is that wealthy, risk-tolerant clients should have about 5% of their portfolio in cash and very risk-averse clients with more modest accounts should hold approximately 10% in cash.

This is not to say that the cash component in a portfolio never rises above 10%. Typically, 10% may be held for liquidity purposes (payment of fees and unexpected expenses). The cash component could be higher during certain parts of the market cycle, such as when securities are judged to be overpriced or too risky for that client, or when the yield curve is inverted and the returns on cash are high.

TAX REQUIREMENTS

An investor's marginal tax rate will dictate, in part, the proportion of income that should be received as dividends, which are eligible for a tax credit, versus other types of income. Different marginal tax rates will help to dictate the proportion invested in preferred shares versus other fixedincome securities such as bonds. Taxation levels and rates will also guide the choice of tax-advantaged securities such as some limited partnerships, as well as the choice of tax deferral plans such as RRSPs and others. High tax rates, which significantly erode the final return on more traditional investments like GICs, are often a reason for a client to seek out the higher returns available from securities.

LEGAL AND REGULATORY REQUIREMENTS

Certainly any investment activity that contravenes an act, by-law, regulation, rule or the *Criminal Code* must be considered a constraint. For example, a client must be married (or living commonlaw) in order to participate in a spousal RRSP, and therefore from its benefits of income splitting. Also, a client may be an insider or own a control position. These types of clients must comply with all applicable regulatory guidelines. RRSP rules preclude certain transactions, and institutions and corporate charters may pose additional limits. Persons under the age of majority also pose important potential problems. Possible legal constraints are numerous, and would include proper use of margin accounts, good delivery, settlement, and many other matters covered in CSI's *Conduct and Practices Handbook Course.*

All firms have compliance personnel and many have legal counsel on staff. It is recommended that the investment advisor consult these resources when there is any question about legal issues.

UNIQUE CIRCUMSTANCES

Unique circumstances are specific to each client and must be considered in the creation of an effective investment policy. Examples of unique circumstances include the desire for ethically and socially responsible investing, among others discussed below. It is clear that client preferences are a legitimate concern and must be taken into account.

Moral and ethical considerations: Some transactions and investment activities may not be against the law, but should invariably be treated by the portfolio manager as if they are. While clients may have preferences for certain types of securities, they may also have strong aversions to certain others. For example, perhaps because of personal convictions, a client may instruct that no alcohol or tobacco stocks be purchased. Although it is not normally against the law to purchase these types of securities, and although these securities may fit the client's other objectives perfectly, if the client has instructed the manager not to purchase them, then that order must be respected.

© CSI GLOBAL EDUCATION INC. (2008)

Emotional factors: As full an assessment as possible should be made of the client's temperament. Through discussion and active listening, the manager can fulfil much more of the Know Your Client requirements than if this area is given only cursory treatment. One consideration is investment knowledge. Should a certain strategy be followed if the client clearly does not understand it? For example, writing covered options or using protective puts and other positions may be warranted by the client's circumstances, but the client may not understand them, and particularly will not if they end up losing money! However, serious discussion with the client, coupled with active listening, can result in a clearer definition of what may be bought and what must be excluded.

It is the responsibility of the investment manager to explain the investment process to the client, especially when the client is not sophisticated but is interested. Over time, even a novice client can become quite knowledgeable and more inclined to accept advanced strategies such as hedges.

Another aspect of the client's personality is risk tolerance. Although risk was mentioned above in the context of market volatility, here it relates to the client's level of comfort with volatility in income and volatility in principal. If a client is invested only in Government bonds and makes worried calls several times a day for a quote, chances are that this product is not appropriate for this client. An extra 1% return annually is not worth it if the client cannot sleep in the meantime because of the extra risk involved. On the other hand, a client may be quite comfortable with complicated options strategies and speculative positions, because of much higher risk tolerance.

Market timing: Two approaches to investing include the buy-and-hold approach and the market timing approach. As the name indicates, buy-and-hold means long holding periods through various market cycles for long-term growth and income. Market timing involves timing the short-term entry and exit points in the market in pursuit of quick trading gains over and above the commissions incurred. Clients generally have a preference for one of these approaches over the other. Some clients enjoy the excitement of trading for gains very much, and will increase their risk tolerance to accommodate this desire.

Income requirements: A key constraint is the basic minimum level of current income required or expected from the portfolio. Suppose a client has living expenses that are not covered by salary, pension and other income. The client requires $10,000 per year in cash flow from the portfolio to meet these expenses. The portfolio should be structured to generate a good total return, but it must also be designed to ensure that there is $10,000 in current income available from the portfolio or the client will not be able to live on the income.

There are two caveats to this point. The first is that the hypothetical $10,000 is current income generated by the portfolio. The required $10,000 is not expected to be met by liquidating securities and thereby eroding the portfolio value. The second caveat is that the current income should be spaced so that it matches as closely as possible the client's needs for spending throughout the year, rather than have cash flowing in at only one or two points in the year. Both the fixed-income and equity components of a portfolio can usually be structured to provide a fairly even monthly income if this is desirable.

Realism: An investment advisor will attempt to provide as realistic an approach to investing as possible. When the desires of a client are unrealistic, it is incumbent on the IA to point this out to the client. For example, in the discussion on basic minimum income outlined above, a hypothetical $10,000 in current income was used as an example of what the client desired to support the basic cost of living. If the client's total portfolio was valued at only $50,000, it would be very unlikely that current income of $10,000 could realistically be generated from the

© CSI GLOBAL EDUCATION INC. (2008)

portfolio. The client should be advised to reconsider objectives and perhaps spending patterns. Unfortunately, part of good communication sometimes involves saying "no" to a client.

In addition to having unrealistic expectations about the amount of current income that could be generated from a portfolio, a client could have expectations of extraordinary returns from the portfolio. In addition, a client could reveal a lack of investment knowledge by professing too low a level of risk tolerance.

Other objectives and constraints: Questions related to each of the points above can reveal a great deal about the client's attitudes and constraints. However, there is also a place for a final overall question, such as, "Is there anything else that we haven't yet talked about, which might be important?" It is surprising what can come from such a question. The client might reveal pertinent facts such as a family member who is an insider (legal constraint), the presence of a serious illness (income and time horizon implications), the size of the account (very small or a huge lottery winning) or a pending marital breakup, which somehow did not get uncovered in previous conversation.

Clients usually do not communicate their goals to their advisors in terms of return, risk, etc. Instead, primary investment goals might be stated as a desire to retire at a certain age, the acquisition of a business, vacation property or sailboat, or the pursuit of some other tangible goal. With care and explanation to the client, the IA can translate such events into the objectives above with the client's full agreement and understanding.

However, some objectives will not fall easily into the above categories. These are most properly spelled out in the investment policy statement under this category of "Other". It should be made clear that the objectives above do not often occur in isolation from other objectives. While return maximization, or risk reduction, may be an objective for some clients, usually more than one objective is chosen. In particular, liquidity and taxation are not objectives in and of themselves. No person invests in liquid securities simply to experience the enjoyment of selling them; rather they invest in them because they have appropriate investment merits and are also liquid. Similarly, no person should invest in a security simply for tax relief. The landscape is littered with miserably failed investments with great tax advantages. Instead, the investment merits of the security should be considered first, and then the tax relief aspects.

Managing Investment Objectives

The ultimate in safety of principal, income, capital gain and marketability is never found in one security. Some compromise is always necessary. If safety and income are high, yield tends to be comparatively low, because those who seek safety and regular income bid the price up and the yield falls. Similarly, if the growth prospects of an investment security are high, eager buyers create a demand, which pushes up the price and pushes down the yield.

Investment considerations are determined from a thorough discussion with and knowledge of the client's needs, preferences and resources. Major considerations are:

THE BALANCED PORTFOLIO

Reconciling the divergent factors of safety, income, growth and marketability may best be accomplished by diversification. It is usual to limit the investment in any one security to no more than 10% of the value of the portfolio. As the portfolio grows, the maximum figure may be reduced towards 5% or below.

© CSI GLOBAL EDUCATION INC. (2008)

A balanced portfolio includes securities from the three major asset classes: cash equivalents, fixedincome securities (bonds and preferred shares), and common shares. The actual weighting of each asset class in a portfolio (the asset allocation) is determined by the investment objectives of its owner.

As well as diversification by asset class, a portfolio can also be diversified by type of security, industry, geographical location and, in the case of bonds, by maturity.

A portfolio may have a defensive side emphasizing safety and a steady income return (usually via bonds and some high-quality preferred and common stocks) and an aggressive side that emphasizes capital gains (some growth common shares).

An individual's portfolio should be reviewed at least once a year to see if changes in investment objectives, risk tolerance, economic conditions or individual securities in the portfolio dictate a readjustment of the composition of the portfolio. Institutional investors review portfolio balance much more frequently, often daily.

RISK PREFERENCE: INVESTMENT VERSUS SPECULATION

Conservative investors normally seek investment-quality securities to form the main portion of their largely defensive portfolios. Many middle-aged to elderly individual investors and most institutional investors fall into this category. In contrast, younger and moderately wealthy individuals may be prepared to accept greater degrees of risk in selecting securities for their more aggressive portfolios. In so doing, they buy securities that others may consider speculative or even hazardous.

Unfortunately, no clear dividing line exists between investment-grade and speculative securities. It is better to look at the range of securities available as a broad spectrum ranging from top-quality, high-grade investments, through securities offering greater and greater degrees of risk, to those that are outright gambles.

The distinction is one of quality rather than form, because both bonds and stocks may be suitable either as investments or as speculations. And quality is never permanent; some degree of risk is always present. Changing circumstances of the securities issuer can turn an investment into a speculation and vice versa.

The problem for all investors is to determine the degree of safety or risk that best suits their investment program. Investors should determine the quality of each security as it is added to their portfolio and they should review both their objectives and their risk tolerance against the holdings in the portfolio on an ongoing basis to see if they continue to match.

THE INVESTMENT POLICY STATEMENT

The **investment policy** contains the operating rules, guidelines, investment objectives and asset mix agreed to by the manager and the client. It can be a lengthy, written and signed document that acts as a job description for the manager, or it can be derived from the New Account Application Form in accordance with the Know Your Client rule. Regardless of its formality, the investment policy is the result of many complex inputs. These inputs can usefully be classified into four areas: investment considerations of the client, constraints, major investment objectives, and manager style.

© CSI GLOBAL EDUCATION INC. (2008)

The investment policy statement forms the basis for the agreement between the manager and the client and is, in effect, the manager's job description. Policy statements can be either elaborate or quite simple, but most cover the objectives and constraints of a portfolio, a list of acceptable securities and a list of prohibited securities, as well as the method to be used for performance appraisal.

A copy of a sample policy statement for a retail client follows in Exhibit 15.1.

EXHIBIT 15.1 DETAILED INVESTMENT POLICY STATEMENT

The purpose of this statement of objectives is to provide a framework within which the assets of this account will be managed.

1. The Account belongs to John Smith, a Canadian (B.C.-based) citizen.

2. Revenues from the account will be taxed at the minimum [current] rates:

Interest Income	43.7%
Dividend Income	31.6%
Capital Gains	21.8%

3. Cash Flow Characteristics

   - For the next two years Smith should generate sufficient cash flow to satisfy taxes generated by the portfolio and pay the operating costs (i.e., P.M.L. Management and Custodial Fees). After the initial two years, the total portfolio must provide for $80,000 in annual income after tax.
   - A monthly withdrawal of $2,400 will be made from the account.

4. Investment Objectives

   - The primary objective of the portfolio is to provide a modest level of current income with a significant commitment to long-term growth.

5. Qualitative and Quantitative Constraints

   a. Asset Classes Eligible for Investment From time to time, and subject to this Policy Statement, the Fund may invest in any or all of the following asset categories. These assets may be obligations or securities of Canadian or non- Canadian entities.
      i. Publicly traded Canadian and non-Canadian common stocks, convertible debentures or preferred securities;
      ii. Bonds, debentures, notes or other debt instruments of Canadian and non-Canadian governments, government agencies, or corporations;
      iii. Mortgages;
      iv. Private placements, whether debt or equity, of Canadian agencies or corporations;
      v. Cash, or money market securities issued by governments or corporations.

   b. Constraints by Asset Class

Canadian Equities

- Maximum in single industry group: TSX weight plus 10%.
- Maximum in single company: greater of 10% or twice TSX weight.
- Maximum of 15% in companies with capitalization of less than $100 million.
- Restricted securities: ABC Canada, DEF Ltd., GHI, JKL, MNO Technology.

© CSI GLOBAL EDUCATION INC. (2008)

EXHIBIT 15.1 DETAILED INVESTMENT POLICY STATEMENT *(Cont'd)*

U.S. Equities

- Maximum of 15% in a single company.
- Maximum of 15% in companies with capitalization of less than $500 million.
- Specified restrictions: None.

International Equities

- As per Investment Policy Statement and Guidelines for the P.M.L. Private Management Ltd. International Equity Fund.

Fixed-income

- Bond Quality
  - Minimum BBB rating as defined by a recognized bond rating service.
  - 20% Maximum in BBB.
  - 10% Maximum in single issuer, except government guaranteed.
  - 30% Maximum in single industry.
- Private Placements
  - Minimum BBB rating as defined by a recognized bond rating service.
  - 20% Maximum.
  - 4% Maximum in a single issuer.
- Preferred Shares
  - Minimum P3 rating as defined by a recognized rating service.
  - 20% Maximum in P3s.
  - 10% Maximum in a single issuer.
- Mortgages
  - 20% Maximum.
  - NHA First Mortgage, or conventional loans with a maximum 75% Loan-to-Value ratio.
- Duration
  - +/– 1 yr of the duration of the ScotiaMcLeod Universe Index.
- Foreign Currency Bonds
  - 50% Maximum in foreign currency bonds and debentures.
  - Specified restrictions are as per the Investment Policy Statement and Guidelines for the
  - P.M.L. Private Management Ltd. Foreign Currency Bond Fund.

Cash and Equivalent

- Money Market securities must be rated R-1 or equivalent.
- Maximum term of any single investment not to exceed one year.

Use of Derivative Products

- Risk management forwards, futures, swaps, options and similar products may be used at all times or as circumstances warrant to hedge against interest and exchange rate risks. To the extent possible, use will be made of hedging products that are traded on recognized exchanges. Where this is impracticable, transactions will be entered into only with brokers or financial institutions of sound financial standing.
- Cost Effectiveness Equity derivative products involving futures, swaps or similar techniques may be used to reduce transaction costs and to facilitate the management process. To the extent possible, use will be made of products that are traded on recognized exchanges. Where this is impracticable, transactions will be entered into only with brokers or financial institutions of sound financial standing.

© CSI GLOBAL EDUCATION INC. (2008)

EXHIBIT 15.1 DETAILED INVESTMENT POLICY STATEMENT *(Cont'd)*

6. Performance Objectives

The primary objective by which P.M.L.'s performance will be measured is to achieve a rate of return that will exceed the return achieved by the Long-Term Investment Policy benchmark, as stated below, by 1.15% over the majority of market cycles as determined by performance over four to six years.

The following table illustrates the performance objectives of the IPS.

Asset Class	Policy Measurement	Minimum	Benchmark	Maximum
Cash and Equivalent	91-Day Cda T-bills	2%	10.0%	100%
Bonds, Mortgages and Preferreds	DEX Universe	0%	35.0%	98%
Preferreds		0%	–	50%
Foreign Currency Bonds	JP Morgan Govt. Bond	0%	5.0%	30%
Total Fixed-Income		25%	50.0%	100%
Canadian Equities	S&P/TSX Composite Index	0%	15.0%	75%
U.S. Equities	S&P 500	0%	25.0%	75%
International Equities	EAFE	0%	10.0%	15%
Total Equities		0%	50.0%	75%
Total Foreign Currency Bond and International Equity exposure		0%		40%

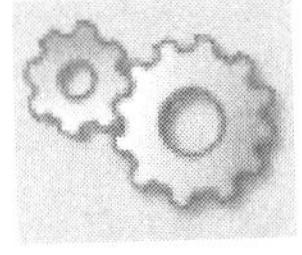

Review the on-line summary or checklist associated with this section.

7. Conflicts of Interest

All investment activities must be conducted in accordance with the CFA Institute code of ethics.

© CSI GLOBAL EDUCATION INC. (2008)

SUMMARY

After reading this chapter, you should be able to:

1. Describe the relationship between risk and return, calculate rates of return of a single security, identify the different types and measures of risk, and evaluate the role of risk in asset selection.
   - Generally, to achieve higher returns, investors must be willing to accept a higher degree of risk.
   - Returns from an investment can be measured in absolute dollars but are usually expressed as a percentage, or as a rate of return or yield. Historically, the highest rates of return have been achieved by securities that had the greatest variability or risk as measured by standard deviation.
   - There is no universal definition of risk. In statistics, it is defined as the likelihood that the actual return will be different from the expected return. A variety of risks are present when investing. Systematic risk represents non-diversifiable risk, as it is always present and affects all assets within a certain class. Non-systematic risk is the risk that the price of a specific security or group of securities will change to a different degree or in a different direction from the market as a whole. Non-systematic risk can be reduced through diversification. Three common measures of risk are variance, standard deviation and beta:
     - Variance measures the extent to which the possible realized returns differ from the expected return or the mean. The greater the variance, the greater the risk.
     - Standard deviation is the square root of the variance. Expressed as a percentage, it gives an indication of the risk associated with an individual security or a portfolio. The greater the standard deviation, the greater the risk.
     - Beta measures the degree to which individual stocks tend to move up and down with the market. The higher the beta, the greater the risk.
2. Explain the relationship between risk and return of a portfolio of securities, calculate and interpret the expected return of a portfolio, and identify strategies for maximizing return while reducing risk.
   - Asset allocation involves determining the optimal division of an investor's portfolio among the different asset classes of cash, fixed income and equities to maximize portfolio return and reduce overall risk.
   - There is a variety of measures available to assess the risk and return of a portfolio:
     - The return on a portfolio is calculated as the weighted average return on the securities held in the portfolio. While future returns are not controllable, risk can be managed to a certain extent by effective portfolio management.
     - Correlation looks at how securities relate to each other when they are added to a portfolio and how the resulting combination affects the portfolio's total risk and return.

  - A portfolio with a beta of 1.0 is considered as risky as the market; a beta less than 1.0 is less risky than the market; and a beta greater than 1.0 is more risky than the market.
  - Alpha measures the degree to which an individual security outperforms the market more than would be expected from beta.
  - The capital asset pricing model (CAPM) graphically shows the trade-off between risk and return. The underlying assumption of this model is that investors who take on more risk expect higher returns.

3. Discuss the steps in the portfolio management process.
   - The six parts to the portfolio management process are: determining investment objectives and constraints; formulating an asset allocation strategy and selecting investment styles; designing an investment policy statement; implementing the asset allocation; monitoring the economy, the markets, the portfolio and the client; and evaluating portfolio performance.

4. Evaluate investment objectives and constraints and explain how to use them in creating an investment policy for a client.
   - An advisor must determine what rate of return a client needs to attain his or her goals, and what risk he or she is willing and able to take to achieve them.
   - In general, investors have three primary investment objectives: safety of principal, income and growth of capital. Two secondary objectives are liquidity and tax minimization.
   - The balance between these objectives will determine constraints on investments and drive the final investment policy.
   - Constraints are essentially considerations that may hinder or prevent the investment manager from satisfying the client's objectives, including time horizon, liquidity requirements, tax requirements, and legal considerations.

Now that you've completed this chapter and the on-line activities, complete this post-test.

5. Describe the content of an investment policy statement and explain the purpose of an IPS.
   - The investment policy statement contains the operating rules, guidelines, investment objectives and asset mix agreed on by the manager and the client. The policy statement forms the basis for the agreement between the manager and the client and is, in effect, the manager's job description.
   - Most investment policy statements cover the objectives and constraints of a portfolio, provide a list of acceptable securities and a list of prohibited securities, and outline the method to be used for performance appraisal.

© CSI GLOBAL EDUCATION INC. (2008)

Chapter 16

The Portfolio Management Process

© CSI GLOBAL EDUCATION INC. (2008)

16

The Portfolio Management Process

CHAPTER OUTLINE

© CSI GLOBAL EDUCATION INC. (2008)

LEARNING OBJECTIVES

By the end of this chapter, you should be able to:

1. Describe the asset mix categories and evaluate strategies for setting the asset mix.
2. Compare and contrast the portfolio management styles of equity and fixed-income managers.
3. Discuss the benefits of asset allocation, distinguish strategic asset allocation from the types of ongoing asset allocation techniques, and differentiate active and passive management.
4. Describe the steps in monitoring and evaluating portfolio performance in relation to the market, the economy and the client.
5. Describe how portfolio performance is evaluated, calculate and interpret the total return and risk-adjusted rate of return of a portfolio, and evaluate an equity and fixed-income return expectation analysis.

PORTFOLIO ANALYSIS

Portfolio management is a process because financial markets and individual circumstances are ever changing, thus portfolio managers must be flexible to adapt to change. As we have seen before, there is no "one size fits all" solution to investing, and finding the right fit is critical to achieving financial objectives.

For an advisor, portfolio management involves analyzing a great deal of personal and financial information about a client to determine an asset mix that will best suit their unique circumstances. The asset mix can be allocated between cash, fixed-income securities and equities in any number of ways. A portfolio is never made up of one security; rather, it is a mix of a variety of securities that add up to something that is, or should be, more than the sum of its individual parts.

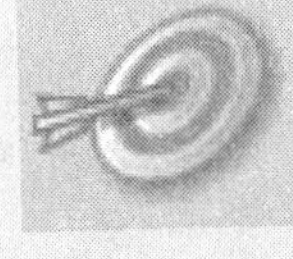

In the on-line Learning Guide for this module, complete the Getting Started activity.

It is often quoted that the asset allocation decision has a significant impact on the overall return of a portfolio. Consequently, understanding what is involved with arriving at the asset mix decision is crucial for portfolio performance. When working with a client, an advisor must be able to explain the decisions and asset choices they made. Also, advisors must be prepared to react to changing markets, investor objectives and economic factors.

This chapter discusses some of the key theories, practices and measurement standards employed by the investment industry in the process of managing investment portfolios. Understanding this information is important because it can significantly contribute to how well an investor or advisor is able to comprehend and apply the language and skills of portfolio management.

© CSI GLOBAL EDUCATION INC. (2008)

KEY TERMS

- Bear market
- Benchmark
- Bottom-up investment approach
- Bull market
- Dynamic asset allocation
- Indexing
- Integrated asset allocation
- Passive management
- Return forecasting
- Sector rotation
- Sharpe ratio
- Strategic asset allocation
- Tactical asset allocation
- Top-down investment approach

© CSI GLOBAL EDUCATION INC. (2008)

DEVELOPING AN ASSET MIX

After designing the investment policy (which you read about in Chapter 15), it is necessary to determine the broad categories from which investments will be selected.

To decide the exact make-up of the portfolio, i.e., to put together the appropriate asset mix, it is critical to understand the relationship between the equity cycle and the economic cycle and to use this understanding to plan the weighting to give to each asset class. In addition, it is essential to consider the individual characteristics and risk tolerance of the client.

The Asset Mix

The main asset classes are cash, fixed-income securities and equity securities. More sophisticated portfolios may also include an international asset class, a derivatives asset class, and alternative investments such as private equity capital funds, currency funds or hedge funds.

CASH

Cash includes currency, money market securities, Canada Savings Bonds, GICs, bonds with a maturity of one year or less, swaps and all other cash equivalents. Cash is required to pay for expenses and to capitalize on opportunities, but is primarily used for liquidity purposes in case of emergencies.

In general terms, cash usually makes up at least 5% of a diversified portfolio's asset mix. Investors who are very risk averse may hold as much as 10% in cash. While cash levels may temporarily rise greatly above these amounts during certain market periods or portfolio rebalancings, normal longterm strategic asset allocations for cash are often within the 5%–10% range.

FIXED-INCOME

Fixed-income products consist of bonds due in more than one year, strips, mortgages, fixed-income private placements and other debt instruments, as well as preferred shares. Convertible securities are not considered to be fixed-income products in the asset allocation process. The purpose of including fixed-income products is primarily to produce income as well as provide some safety of principal, although they are also sometimes purchased to generate capital gains.

From a portfolio management standpoint, preferred shares are simply another type of fixed-income security. They have a stated level of income, trade on a yield basis, offer many of the same sweeteners, are subject to the same protective provisions, and have a reasonably definable term. The only difference is that they pay dividends rather than interest, and dividends are taxed more favourably than interest income. For this reason, preferred shares can often be substituted for bonds to provide a tax benefit for the investor – of course, within the bounds of intelligent diversification. Although legally preferreds are an equity security, they are listed in portfolios as part of the fixedincome component because of the price action and cash flow characteristics listed above.

Diversification can be achieved in this part of the asset mix in several ways. Both government and corporate bonds can be used, a range of credit qualities from AAA to lower grades can be chosen, and foreign bonds may be added to domestic holdings. A variety of terms to maturity,

© CSI GLOBAL EDUCATION INC. (2008)

or *durations*, are often used (this is called *laddering*, with the various consecutive maturities mimicking rungs on a ladder), and deep discount or stripped bonds can be chosen alongside high-coupon bonds.

The amount of a portfolio allocated to fixed-income securities is governed by several factors:

- the need for income over capital gains
- the basic minimum income required
- the desire for preservation of capital
- other factors such as tax and time horizon

In very rough terms, fixed-income products generally account for at least 15% of a diversified portfolio, and under special circumstances up to 95% of a portfolio.

EQUITIES

Equities include not only common shares but also derivatives such as rights, warrants, options, iShares, LEAPS, instalment receipts, etc., and both convertible bonds and convertible preferreds. Although a dividend stream may flow from the equity section of a portfolio, its main purpose is to generate capital gains either through judicious trading or long-term growth in value. Objectives and constraints that influence the allocation to equities include risk, return, time horizon, inflation and emotion. Equities make up from 15% to 95% of a diversified portfolio.

OTHER ASSET CLASSES

While portfolios of most retail clients consist of cash, fixed-income and equities, it is possible to diversify even further by adding other investments that do not lend themselves to being included in one of the major asset classes. Many portfolio managers believe that **income trusts** and **hedge funds** should be considered separate asset classes.

It is also possible to invest directly in real estate, precious metals and collectibles, such as art or coins. Many of these investments, such as gold, are considered to be a good hedge against inflation.

Setting the Asset Mix

The four phases of the equity cycle (which traces movements in the stock market) are expansion, peak, contraction and trough. Understanding the equity cycle provides a useful approach for a general understanding of stock market movements. Figure 16.1 shows the S&P/TSX Composite Index over the last two decades and illustrates (with shading) the different phases. It is important to note that within a stock market expansion phase, which may last several years, there are also serious setbacks or corrections to stock prices which may last as long as a year.

© CSI GLOBAL EDUCATION INC. (2008)

FIGURE 16.1 BROADLY DEFINED EQUITY CYCLES: S&P/TSX COMPOSITE INDEX PRICE 1982 – 2007

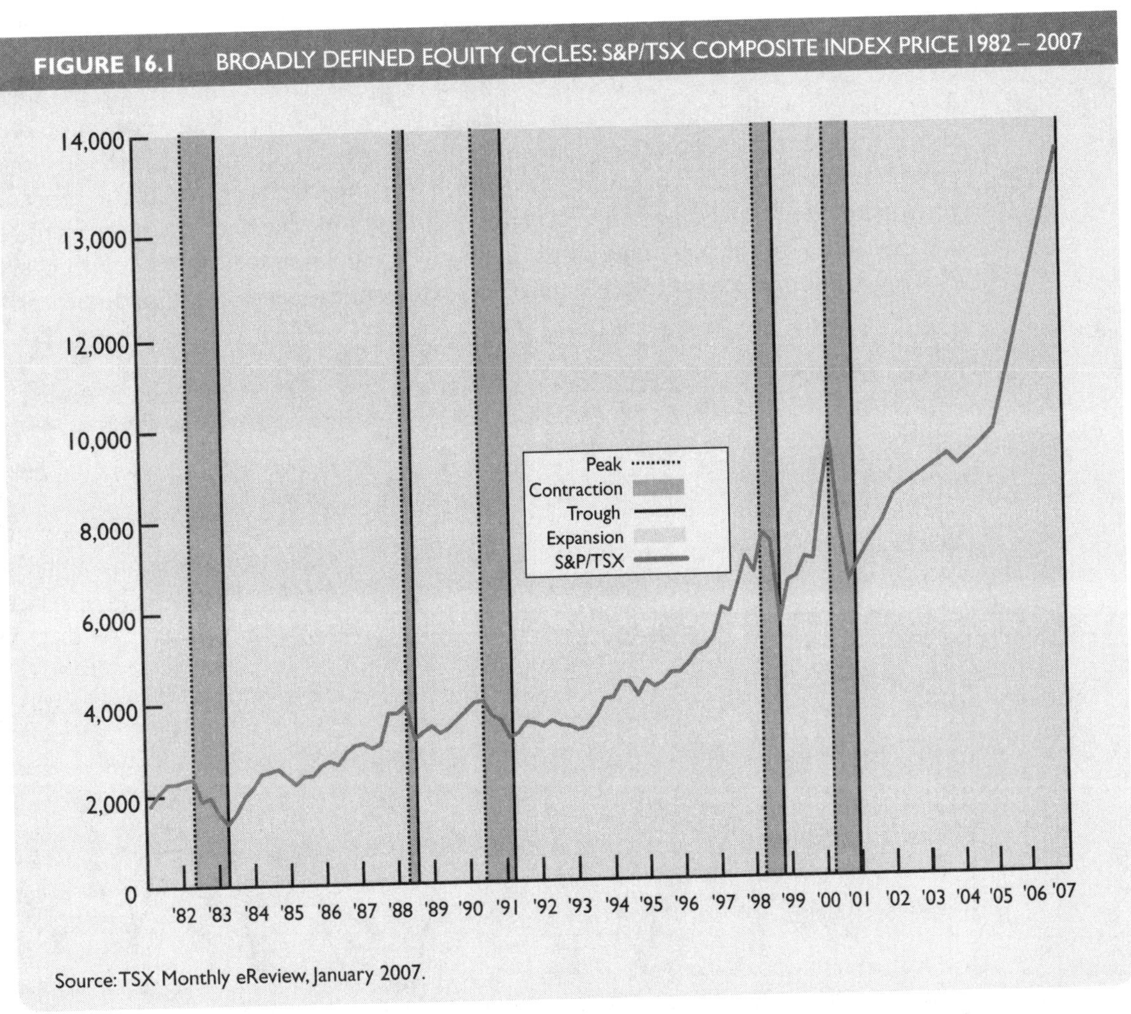

Source: TSX Monthly eReview, January 2007.

Over the last twenty-five years, T-bills have provided positive steady returns. Stock total returns have been the most volatile, but over this period they have outperformed bonds and T-bills. Bond total returns have tended to begin to rise before stock total returns.

ASSET CLASS TIMING

The general framework that follows outlines the most basic strategies for investors who choose to time stock, bond and T-bill investments. The benefits from successfully timing asset class selections are impressive. However, this presupposes that the investor has successful asset mix analytic tools available that indicate when to make shifts between stocks, bonds and T-bills. In reality, most investors would have trouble determining whether a rise in interest rates is designed to slow economic growth or will actually lead to a recession and, therefore, a contraction phase in stock prices.

The rationale behind asset class timing is that investors who recognize when to switch from stocks to T-bills, to bonds and back to stocks can improve returns. In addition, if at the time in question bonds are the best asset class, then it should make sense to lengthen the term of bond holdings to maximize returns. Similarly, if stocks are the best asset class, then certain strategies can be implemented to maximize stock market gains. Asset mix decisions affect both industry and stock selection. Generally, asset mix factors appear to account for 90% or more of the variation in the total returns of investment portfolios. Investment analysts have developed sophisticated computer models that assist in the timing of asset class shifts.

© CSI GLOBAL EDUCATION INC. (2008)

THE LINK BETWEEN EQUITY AND ECONOMIC CYCLES

In order to understand stock market strategies, it is essential to understand that there is a link between equity cycles and economic cycles. In general, the equity and economic cycles are very similar except that the equity cycle tends to lead. Figure 16.2 shows that the sustained economic growth in nominal GDP beginning in 1983, 1995 and 2002 fits closely the generally sustained rise in stock prices over that time. It is important to note that the beginning of the equity cycle actually preceded the beginning of the economic cycle by several months during 1982–1983 and 1995–1996, underscoring the Toronto Stock Exchange's role as a leading indicator.

FIGURE 16.2 S&P/TSX COMPOSITE, CANADIAN GDP (AVERAGE ANNUAL % CHANGE) 1974 – 2007

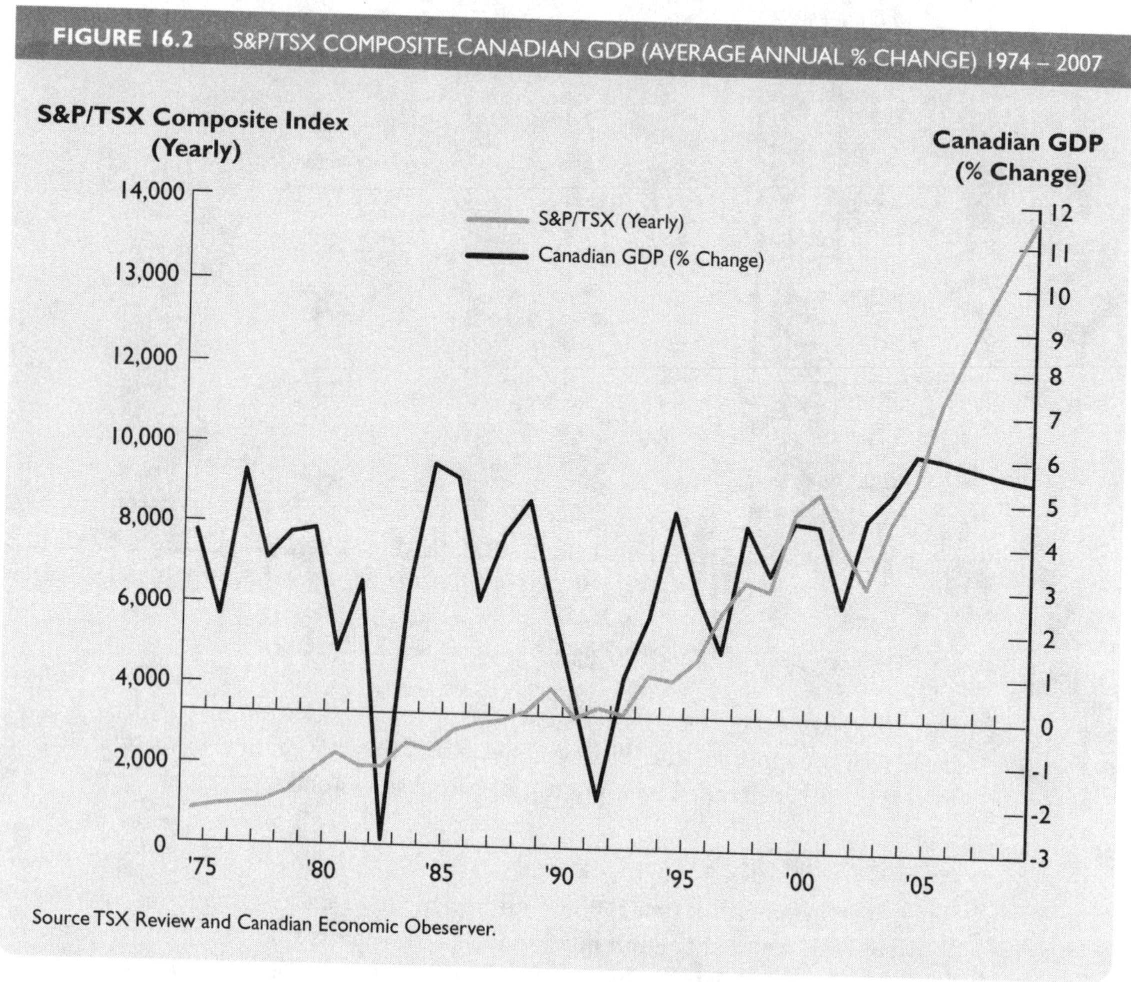

Source TSX Review and Canadian Economic Obeserver.

For investors who understand the relationship between economic and equity cycles, it is possible to follow the general investment strategies outlined in Table 16.1.

© CSI GLOBAL EDUCATION INC. (2008)

TABLE 16.1 GENERAL INVESTMENT STRATEGIES

Equity Cycle	Business Cycle	Strategy
1. Contraction Phase	End of expansion through peak, into the contraction phase	• Recession conditions are apparent. • *Recommendation:* Lengthen term of bond holdings, e.g., sell short-term bonds and buy mid- to long-term. Try to maintain same yield (income). Avoid or reduce stock exposure
2. Stock Market Trough	End of contraction phase, into the expansion phase	• The bottom of the business cycle has not been reached but has begun to advance because of falling interest rates and the expectations of an economic recovery. • *Recommendation:* Sell long-term bonds since they rallied ahead of stocks in response to falling interest rates. Common stocks usually rally dramatically; often the largest gains occur in the higher-risk cyclical industries.
3. Expansion Phase	Expansion phase	• *Recommendation:* Increase common stock exposure as sustained economic growth generally allows stocks to do well.
4. Equity Cycle Peak	Late expansion nto peak phase	• Economic growth has been sustained; however, this has also led to higher interest rates and the Bank of Canada may be tightening its monetary policy. Short-term interest rates tend to be higher than long-term rates, i.e., the yield curve is inverted. • *Recommendation:* Reduce common stocks exposure and invest in short-term interest-bearing paper. The equity cycle peak is generally followed by the contraction phase.

The problem with these general strategies is that they do not account for the many important variations that occur during an equity cycle. These variations may dramatically affect stock and bond market performance for 12 months or longer. For example, during the expansion phase of 1982 to 1989, the stock market experienced sharp declines due to high interest rates for six months in 1984 and during the stock market crash of 1987. Finally, the 1994 collapse in bond prices was unprecedented in magnitude when compared with the prior 50 years. While the general strategies appear attractive, variations within a cycle can affect asset class performance. The following section describes an equity cycle much more precisely by explaining the underlying causal factors.

Changes in the S&P/TSX Composite price level result, generally, from changes in interest rates or economic growth. The relationships between interest rate trends and economic trends (and therefore corporate profit trends) are of the greatest significance to equity price levels. These two factors, in combination, generally account for 80%–90% of the change in stock market prices.

© CSI GLOBAL EDUCATION INC. (2008)

As a result, these factors are often used together in asset mix models. As interest rates are used by central banks as a policy tool for managing economic growth, changes in rates tend to lead changes in economic growth.

THE DIVIDEND DISCOUNT MODEL (DDM) AND THE EQUITY CYCLE

The *Dividend Discount Model* (DDM), explained in Chapter 13, serves as a guide to understanding the way an economic cycle influences an equity cycle. It is useful to remember that when the economy is expanding (contracting), corporate profitability is usually growing (falling) as well.

Table 16.2 illustrates how interest rate changes and corporate profit changes are related and how changes in each component of the DDM affect equity prices at different stages of the equity cycle. We will assume that most of the short-term change in the discount rate (*r*) results from changes to the general level of interest rates. Changes in expected long-term growth (*g*) are influenced by recent changes in corporate profits.

The DDM can be used to illustrate four different periods of an equity cycle. The model in Table 16.2 assumes a constant dividend.

TABLE 16.2 THE DIVIDEND DISCOUNT MODEL AND THE EQUITY CYCLE

Point in Equity Cycle	Changes in Denominator	Cause of Changes in Denominator
A. Contraction Phase • End of equity cycle. • Examples: 1981, 1990. • Recession related decline in stock prices.	• r is still rising, and g is beginning to fall. Therefore, prices are expected to fall. • This period often lasts one to two years. $\downarrow P = \frac{Div_1}{\uparrow r - g \downarrow}$	• Interest rates are rising because of central bank policy aimed at causing a slowdown and because of currently robust economic growth. • Higher interest rates are designed to reverse the recently higher inflationary trend. The higher interest rate policy is beginning to take its toll. The economy is beginning to slow and corporate profits are beginning to fall.

© CSI GLOBAL EDUCATION INC. (2008)

TABLE 16.2 THE DIVIDEND DISCOUNT MODEL AND THE EQUITY CYCLE *(Cont'd)*

Point in Equity Cycle	Changes in Denominator	Cause of Changes in Denominator
B. Stock Market Trough • Interest rate–driven rally in stock prices. • Examples: August 1982 – July 1983 and October 1990 – April 1991. • The beginning of a new equity cycle. Short-term rally in stock prices.	• *g* is still falling; however, *r* is falling at a faster rate. Therefore, prices are temporarily assumed to be bid up. • This period has often lasted five to thirteen months. $\uparrow P = \frac{Div_1}{\Downarrow r - g \downarrow}$	• The rapid decline in *r* reflects the recent decline in interest rates owing to the recession and an attempt by the central bank to direct a new economic expansion, in part, by using lower interest rates. • Stock prices tend to rally rapidly owning to the more rapid fall in r and g. Investors also anticipate a recovery in corporate profit growth that should result from an economic recovery. • As T-bill rates fall, the implied return in stocks begins to look relatively more attractive and a sudden flow of hot capital from T-bills to equities tends to produce a rapid but unsustainable rise in stock prices.
C. Expansion Phase of the Equity Cycle • Early cycle interest rate shock and brief decline in stock prices. • Examples: 1976, 1983–1984.	• g is beginning to rise with a new economic recovery; however, *r* briefly rises more rapidly. Therefore, prices are expected to fall during a sudden adjustment to higher interest rates. • This period often lasts six to nine months. $\downarrow P = \frac{Div_1}{\Uparrow r - g \uparrow}$	• Interest rate policy tends to serve as a tool for directing economic expansions and contractions. Because interest rates tend to overshoot on the downside (as well as on the upside), there is a period at the beginning of a new economic cycle where rates are temporarily too low and must be raised or "normalized" in order to moderate the rate of new economic growth. This causes a rate shock.

© CSI GLOBAL EDUCATION INC. (2008)

TABLE 16.2 THE DIVIDEND DISCOUNT MODEL AND THE EQUITY CYCLE *(Cont'd)*

Point in Equity Cycle	Changes in Denominator	Cause of Changes in Denominator
D. Expansion Phase to Peak • The profit driven cycle in stock prices. • Examples: 1978–1980, 1988–1989.	• *r* is stable or rising, but rising less quickly than g. *g* is expected to continue growing with the sustained and later cycle economic recovery. Therefore, prices are expected to rise. This period of the equity cycle often lasts one to three years. $\uparrow P = \frac{Div_1}{\uparrow r - g \Uparrow}$	• Generally stock prices appreciate *steadily*, though less rapidly than in period B. As long as the economic expansion leads to a rise in *g*, which exceeds the rate of rise in *r*, prices should rise. However, the economic cycle is getting older and any unexpected upward inflation pressure can lead to sudden increases in *r*, possibly resulting in an interest rate shock as in C or leading to the end of that equity cycle as in A.

INDUSTRY ROTATION

When the equity cycle is defined in terms of changes in interest rates and changes in economic growth, it is possible to implement industry strategies based on turning points in the economic cycle.

To avoid confusion, the following description of industry rotation looks at how various industries might be expected to perform relative to the equity cycle (e.g., relative to the S&P/TSX Composite Index). Since all stock prices tend to move together, industry rotation can only be illustrated by comparing relative performance. One investment objective for an investor with an appropriate risk tolerance should be to outperform the stock market average. The distinctive industry price patterns that emerge within the Index often result from investors trying to identify which groups will benefit first from an economic recovery.

Industry rotation is concerned with trying to outperform the market averages such as the S&P/TSX Composite Index. For example, during the last stages of recession, bank stocks may rally first, to be followed by consumer growth stocks, consumer cyclical stocks, and thereafter those stocks that tend to benefit even later in an economic cycle, such as those for capital goods and commodity-based industries. Successfully shifting between these groups can produce greater returns than just buying and holding a diversified portfolio of stocks. However, industry rotation can be very complicated.

The most basic industry rotation strategy involves shifting back and forth between *cyclical* and *defensive* industries. During periods in which stock prices are falling, cyclical stocks tend to fall relatively faster. Defensive stocks, such as banks or utilities, tend to preserve capital by falling relatively more slowly. However, during periods in which stock prices are rising, cyclical industries, such as paper and forestry or integrated mines, tend to rise relatively faster because their profit growth is more robust during an economic expansion.

© CSI GLOBAL EDUCATION INC. (2008)

Industry rotation strategies become more complex once additional industry types are considered and variations in economic cycles are taken into account. For example, some industry groups are *interest rate sensitive* and follow a pattern that conforms almost entirely to the interest rate cycle. However, growth industries may do consistently well in most economic environments because of sustained growth in corporate profits. A minority of industries are counter-cyclical or lag the market averages. For example, gold stocks are occasionally inversely related to the S&P/TSX Composite Index. Specifically, gold stock prices occasionally rise during recessions while stock market average price levels are falling.

Variations in the economic cycle can also have a dramatic bearing on the timing of industry selection. Generally, two-thirds of a new economic recovery is being driven by an increase in consumer spending. This tends to lead to the need for businesses to add to plant and capacity, which results in an increased demand for capital goods and provides a boost for the stocks of capital goods makers.

In a normal cycle, U.S. investors, who have a broader, better diversified, less cyclical selection of industries to choose from, may follow a pattern of industry rotation that focuses on the consumer growth, transportation, consumer cyclical, energy and capital goods industries in that order.

PORTFOLIO MANAGER STYLES

A final requirement when designing an investment policy for the portfolio is disclosure by the investment manager of any particular style he or she follows. Sometimes a core manager is used for the overall portfolio, with sub-managers contributing their individual style and expertise for a particular asset class. A good fit between the client's objectives and the manager's method of achieving them is highly desirable. For example, if the client likes to trade and the manager prefers to pursue long-term growth through a buy-and-hold process, both the client and the investment manager may be happier not doing business together.

Sometimes a core manager is used for the overall portfolio, with sub-managers contributing their individual style and expertise for a particular asset class.

Equity Manager Styles

GROWTH MANAGERS

In the **bottom-up investment approach**, growth managers will focus on current and future earnings of individual companies, specifically earnings per share (EPS). Growth managers are looking for "earnings momentum" and they will pay more for companies if they feel the company's growth potential warrants the higher price. Stocks in this type of portfolio usually have a lower dividend yield, or provide no dividend at all, and managers may turn over the securities in the portfolio more often.

Risk Features

- If EPS falters, it can cause large percentage price declines.
- Reported EPS, above or below analysts' expectations, produces high portfolio volatility.
- These types of securities are highly vulnerable to market cycles.

© CSI GLOBAL EDUCATION INC. (2008)

Valuation

- High Price-Earnings Ratios
- High Price/Book Value
- High Price/Cash Flow

Long-term total return is gathered mostly through capital appreciation. Growth managers are usually not concerned with quarterly portfolio fluctuations. They can outperform in up markets and hope to survive down markets. Clients must be more risk tolerant (i.e., they do not panic in down markets) and have long-term investment horizons.

The growth manager's challenge is to avoid paying too much. Often managers try to buy stocks at P-E ratios that are less than the stock's expected earnings growth rate. Growth investing is a matter of expectations and growth stocks seldom seem cheap today. But, if the company continues to grow as expected, then today's stock price will represent a good investment a year or two from now.

Some managers who use the growth style are able to outperform the market in the short term. They identify companies with competitive advantages, such as new technology or original ideas, and that hold greater promise for market appreciation than established or less innovative companies.

The growth style works best in rising markets, however, as stocks with above-average prices are more vulnerable in bear markets. The style is appropriate for investors who are aggressive or who favour momentum investing, and who enjoy making spectacular gains in rising markets.

The growth style holds greater potential for capital appreciation because of faster earnings growth. Growth stocks tend to reinvest more of their earnings. However, this style has greater volatility, hence risk, since more of the total return of the portfolio is derived from capital appreciation, rather than dividend income, which tends to be more stable. Also, growth stocks may fall more rapidly than other stocks in a declining market.

Since portfolio turnover tends to be higher, investors in taxable accounts may be liable for increased amounts of capital gains tax every year.

VALUE MANAGERS

For value investing managers, the focus is on specific stock selection. They are bottom-up stock pickers as well, with a research-intensive approach. Security turnover is typically low, as the manager will wait for a stock's intrinsic value to be realized. Since a stock is often cheap for a reason (it is out of favour), realizing its intrinsic value can take some time. Out-of-vogue, overlooked, disliked, cheap stocks that investors, institutions and analysts alike have given up on, have quit following and probably don't own are what the value manager seeks.

Risk Features

- Lower annualized standard deviation
- Lower historical beta
- Stock price is already low, so the downside is low

Valuation

- Low Price-Earnings ratios
- Low Price/Book Value
- Low Price/Cash Flow
- High dividend yield

© CSI GLOBAL EDUCATION INC. (2008)

Over the long term, value investing has produced total returns virtually identical to those of growth investing but with higher current dividend yield and less portfolio volatility. This style tends to perform best in down markets with some participation in up markets.

Because of the lower volatility associated with this style of management, value managers can be used as core managers for low-to-medium market risk tolerant clients with long-term investment horizons. This style of investing requires patience. The patience comes from waiting for the value of the underpriced bargains to be realized by the market.

By screening stocks for cheap fundamentals, and investigating a company's management, products or services, and competitive position, managers can buy stocks at discounts that should eventually rise in price. Because turnover in portfolios with a value bias tends to be low, investors incur fewer capital gains. This allows more of the capital to grow inside the fund. Value investing largely ignores short-term market fluctuations.

A value manager's picks may not be immediately recognized as undervalued by the market. Value investing is more successful in inefficient markets, when stock prices may be out of line with corporate fundamentals, or in a stagnant or declining market, when there is greater emphasis on preserving capital or minimizing short-term losses.

One drawback to the value style of investing is that in efficient stock markets, the price of individual securities tends to reflect all that is known about them. Thus, an individual stock may be trading at a low price for a good reason that does not show up in its financial statements.

Because of the focus on "good value," value managers may also overlook or fail to purchase shares in excellent companies with above-average prospects for earnings growth and share-price appreciation. They may be drawn to companies that are in need of a turnaround to overcome financial or competitive difficulties.

Some value managers avoid some industries, such as high technology and health care, that tend to have high market values. These exclusions steer the value manager's portfolio away from highgrowth sectors with a strong potential for capital appreciation. Since value managers have no particular bias in their portfolio with respect to industry sectors, they will not benefit from strong gains in any particular sector.

SECTOR ROTATOR

Sector rotation applies a **top-down investing approach**, focusing on analyzing the prospects for the overall economy. Based on that assessment, the managers invest in the industry sectors expected to outperform. These managers typically buy large-cap stocks to maximize their liquidity. They are not as concerned with individual stock characteristics. Their primary focus is to identify the current phase of the economic cycle, the direction the economy is headed in, and the various sectors affected. In other words, industry selection is more important than stock selection, and the manager often tries to identify emerging trends.

Risk features include high volatility caused by industry concentration and rotation between industries and greater risk if the manager's economic scenario is wrong and the favoured industries do not perform as expected.

Over short periods, managers and investors who use sector rotation may significantly underperform the market benchmark. The turnover for a sector rotation–style portfolio also tends to be high. This pushes up trading costs and the expenses charged to the fund. The higher turnover may create problems for taxable accounts, since capital gains are paid on the fund's

© CSI GLOBAL EDUCATION INC. (2008)

frequent trades. Also, the style's emphasis on industry sectors means that the merits of individual companies get less scrutiny and good individual stocks may be overlooked.

The emphasis on large, liquid companies that lead their particular sector also means that the actual stocks picked may not necessarily represent the performance of the entire sector. Stock-specific circumstances may cause an individual holding to behave very differently from its industry peers.

Fixed-Income Manager Styles

Fixed-income managers invest in fixed-income products. Their choices may vary, depending on the term to maturity, credit quality, or their expectations of what will happen with interest rates and how this will affect the prices of the fixed-income products.

TERM TO MATURITY

Short-term managers will hold T-bills and short-term bonds with maturities less than five years. There is less volatility when interest rates rise since the portfolio has investments maturing that can be reinvested at the higher rates.

Mid-term managers' term to maturity will range from five to ten years. Mortgage funds are a good example. These funds generally invest in high-quality residential mortgages (usually NHA insured) with terms of five years.

Long-term managers will hold bonds maturing in ten years or longer.

CREDIT QUALITY

Bond quality of investment-grade bonds ranges from high (AAA) to low (BBB). High-quality issuers are typically federal and provincial governments and some very well-capitalized corporations. Generally, the lower the quality of the bond, the higher the coupon rate it must have, so managers must balance the return potential with the risk of default. Many bond portfolios have predetermined credit quality limits under which they will not go.

High-yield bonds are bonds that are not investment grade. They are often called junk bonds. Bonds in this category should pay higher interest, but they face greater credit risk. To mitigate this risk, managers often invest in high-yield bonds maturing in less than three years.

Because of the higher credit risk, corporate issues have higher yields than comparable Government of Canada issues. Thus, by selecting higher-quality corporate issues, a manager can improve a portfolio's yield without taking on much additional risk. This strategy also involves taking advantage of pricing anomalies in the market. For example, the gaps between yields on government bonds and those on corporate issues could be wider because of special situations.

Another factor to consider with corporate issuers is liquidity. Lower-rated bonds have less liquidity than government issues. In a declining market, trading spreads may widen or it may be difficult to find a buyer for this kind of debt. Some very low-quality securities (junk bonds) can be highly speculative. Credit default could lead to a total loss on one of these securities.

These bond funds are suited to somewhat aggressive investors who want higher yields and are willing to trade off a higher yield for higher default risk.

© CSI GLOBAL EDUCATION INC. (2008)

INTEREST RATE ANTICIPATORS

Some managers feel they can add value by anticipating the direction of interest rates and structuring their portfolios accordingly. They will extend the average term on their bond investments when they anticipate a decrease in the general level of interest rates. If they anticipate an increase in interest rates, they will shorten the term. The amount of trading done in this type of portfolio is relatively low, but the risks can be greater given the importance of correctly predicting the direction of interest rates.

Interest rate anticipation, sometimes also referred to as a form of duration switching, works best when the yield curve is normal – that is, there is a wide gap between short-term and long-term rates. If the yield curve is flat, it is not advantageous to extend the term to maturity of the portfolio. As explained in Chapter 7, the higher the duration of the portfolio, the greater the gain from falling interest rates and the greater the potential for capital gains.

SPREAD TRADERS

Spread traders look for opportunities to profit from the differences in rates between federal, provincial and corporate bonds. Trading in this type of portfolio is relatively high, but the risks tend to be lower since the manager is dealing with "what is" and not with "what will be."

ASSET ALLOCATION

All of the above steps do nothing to benefit the client unless the portfolio is actually created by purchasing suitable securities. This selection stems from the equity and fixed-income analysis discussed in earlier chapters. Because the portfolio approach is being emphasized, an important consideration is how the securities interact with each other. Even more important is how the asset classes perform against each other, with each generating returns while offsetting some of the others' risks.

Table 16.3 demonstrates the importance of the asset mix in determining overall portfolio return. In Part A, Annual Return by Asset Class, Portfolio Manager X outperforms Portfolio Manager Y by 22% in cash, 100% in fixed-income securities and 50% in equities. However, Part B highlights the actual allocation of assets in each portfolio. Clearly, Portfolio Manager X invested more heavily in fixed-income securities whereas Portfolio Manager Y emphasized equities in his portfolio. Part C shows the total return realized by each portfolio manager in a $1,000 portfolio. (Total return is calculated by multiplying the amount invested in each asset group by the rate of return for that group and adding the results.) Even though Portfolio Manager X significantly outperformed Manager Y in each asset class, the asset mix decision enabled Manager Y to achieve a higher total return in the portfolio.

© CSI GLOBAL EDUCATION INC. (2008)

TABLE 16.3 ASSET MIX & TOTAL RETURN

Asset Group	Index or Average	Portfolio Manager X	Portfolio Manager Y
A. Annual Return by Asset Class			
Cash	10%	11%	9%
Fixed-Income Securities	6%	8%	4%
Equities	25%	30%	20%
B. Actual Asset Mix			
Cash		5%	5%
Fixed-Income Securities		70%	25%
Equities		25%	70%
C. Total Return on a $1,000 Portfolio			
Cash		$5.50	$4.50
Fixed-Income Securities		56.00	10.00
Equities		75.00	140.00
Total Return		**$136.50**	**$154.50**
Total % Return		**13.65%**	**15.45%**

The conclusion is clear. When seeking to maximize the total return of a balanced portfolio, it is more important to emphasize the correct asset group than to outperform an index or market average within an asset group. This is particularly true when capital markets are volatile.

To document performance differences, Table 16.4 compares annual and compound total rates of return on certain asset classes over the period from 1970 to 2007. And as summarized in the table, the astute portfolio manager who emphasized the correct asset group in each year would have realized a total return that was significantly above average.

© CSI GLOBAL EDUCATION INC. (2008)

TABLE 16.4 COMPARATIVE TOTAL RATES OF RETURN ON SPECIFIC SECURITY CLASSES

Nominal Annual Total Return

(% Change in Value Indices, December to December)

	T-Bills 91-Day (%)	Mid-Term Bonds (%)	Long-Term Bonds (%)	S&P/TSX Composite Stocks (%)	S&P 500 Stocks US$ (%)
Annual Returns					
1970	6.70	N/A	16.39	-3.57	3.93
1975	7.41	N/A	8.02	18.48	37.30
1980	14.97	6.26	2.18	30.13	32.40
1985	9.88	21.92	26.68	25.07	31.95
1990	13.48	7.63	4.32	-14.80	-2.91
1995	7.75	21.80	26.34	14.53	37.53
2000	5.49	10.91	12.97	7.41	-9.15
2001	4.72	7.90	6.06	-12.57	-11.91
2002	2.52	10.46	11.05	-12.44	-22.15
2003	2.91	6.83	9.07	26.72	28.68
2004	2.30	7.77	10.26	14.48	10.88
2005	2.58	5.68	13.84	24.13	4.91
2006	3.97	4.08	4.08	17.26	15.79
2007	4.43	3.33	3.44	9.83	5.49
Compound Rates of Return					
(Ending 12/31/2007)					
20 years	5.80	9.03	10.37	10.23	12.75
15 years	4.31	7.94	9.46	12.07	10.49
10 years	3.83	6.36	7.50	9.47	5.91
5 years	3.24	5.53	7.92	18.32	12.83

Source: Scotia CapitalTM Inc.,Annual Investment Returns, January 2007 and Fixed Income Research, 2007 in Review.

Balancing the Asset Classes

The next step in the asset allocation process is to determine the appropriate balance among the selected asset classes. Using only cash, fixed-income and equity asset classes to make up a suitable portfolio, the following are examples of some approximate asset mixes. Note that they are provided for illustration only. The full set of client circumstances must be known to set an asset mix rather than simply choosing the closest example below.

© CSI GLOBAL EDUCATION INC. (2008)

- A young, healthy, single individual professional with medium investment knowledge, high risk tolerance, moderate tax rate and long time horizon:

Cash	5%
Fixed-Income	25%
Equities	70%
Allocation	100%

- A senior citizen in a low tax bracket with no income other than government pensions, a medium time horizon and low risk tolerance:

Cash	8%
Fixed-Income	62%
Equities	30%
Allocation	100%

- A middle-aged line factory worker, married with three teenaged children, who is a homeowner with great concerns about future employment and funding college education, and with low investment knowledge:

Cash	10%
Fixed-Income	40%
Equities	50%
Allocation	100%

Strategic Asset Allocation

Investment management firms, both large and small, often have proprietary, highly sophisticated models to forecast security prices. Here we show how asset allocation is determined through historical results, as shown in Table 16.5. Considering only stocks and bonds, and with 10% increments in the asset mix, the following are the expected returns for the various asset mixes.

© CSI GLOBAL EDUCATION INC. (2008)

TABLE 16.5 EXPECTED RETURNS FOR THE VARIOUS ASSET MIXES

Asset Mix		Historical Returns		Expected Return on Portfolio (%)
Stocks (%)	**Bonds (%)**	**Stocks (%)**	**Bonds (%)**	
0	100	10.0	4.4	4.40
10	90	10.0	4.4	4.96
20	80	10.0	4.4	5.52
30	70	10.0	4.4	6.08
40	60	10.0	4.4	6.64
50	50	10.0	4.4	7.20
60	40	10.0	4.4	7.76
70	30	10.0	4.4	8.32
80	20	10.0	4.4	8.88
90	10	10.0	4.4	9.44
100	0	10.0	4.4	10.00

The table illustrates an analysis which considers stock/bond combinations of 0% stocks/100% bonds, 10%/90%, 20%/80%, and so on to 100% stocks/0% bonds. The expected return of each asset mix combination is calculated by the manager. After viewing the possibilities outlined above, and considering the relative riskiness of stocks versus bonds, the manager will choose the optimal combination in consultation with the client. This asset mix is usually expressed in terms of percentage holdings, such as a 60/40 stock/bond mix. If the manager chooses a 60/40 stock/bond mix, the portfolio will have an expected return of 7.76%.

This base policy mix is called the **strategic asset allocation**. This is the long-term mix that will be adhered to by monitoring and, when necessary, rebalancing. As was just shown, to determine the strategic allocation, a limited number of asset mixes is analyzed to determine the expected return of each combination. In close consultation with the client, the manager then reviews the range of outcomes and chooses one, to determine the long-term policy, or strategic, asset mix.

This base policy mix does not necessarily imply a buy-and-hold strategy, because shifting values of the asset classes will cause the allocation to "drift" from the strategic mix. For example, suppose a $100,000 portfolio is invested $60,000 in equities and $40,000 in fixed-income, for a 60/40 asset mix. If the stock market rose 10% while the bond market sagged 10%, the investor's portfolio mix would be higher than 60% stocks, and lower than 40% bonds, after the change in market values. This is shown in Table 16.6 below.

© CSI GLOBAL EDUCATION INC. (2008)

TABLE 16.6 SECURITIES PRICE CHANGES AND ASSET MIX

Type of Security	Before Change	Change	After Change
Stocks	$60,000	+$6,000	$66,000
Bonds	$40,000	-$4,000	$36,000
Asset Mix	60 / 40		64.7 / 35.3

Ongoing Asset Allocation

Once the asset mix is implemented, the asset classes will begin to change in value with fluctuations in the market. Dividends and interest income will flow into the cash component. As a result, the asset mix will begin to change. For example, a portfolio starting out with an asset mix of 10% cash, 40% fixed-income and 50% equities could see its cash increase to 15% through cash flows from interest, dividends and maturing bonds, and the equity component could rise to 55% through capital gains. Although the fixed-income class might be higher in value than before, proportionately it would now be underweighted, at only 30% of the total portfolio value versus the original 40%. This calls for a rebalancing back to the original policy mix of 10%/40%/50%. Investment managers rebalance in a disciplined manner, acting before the mix gets too out of balance, while remaining conscious of transaction costs. The manager will typically specify that an asset class must move by a certain percentage (i.e., 3% to 4%) before it will be rebalanced.

DYNAMIC ASSET ALLOCATION

Dynamic asset allocation is a portfolio management technique that involves adjusting the asset mix to systematically re-balance the portfolio back to its long-term target or strategic asset mix. Re-balancing may be necessary for a variety of reasons:

- There is a build-up of idle cash reserves, possibly from dividends or interest income cash flows, that have not been re-invested.
- There are movements in the capital markets. These movements can cause abnormal returns, such as the 1987 market crash or the 1998 Asian flu crisis.

The portfolio manager follows a policy that places a limit on the degree to which each asset category can drift above or below the long-term target mix. Re-balancing becomes necessary once an asset category moves above or below this range. For example, the policy may call for a re-balancing if equities rise by more than 5% above their target weighting.

A dynamic re-balancing approach can be demonstrated using the example in Table 16.7. The strong performance in the stock market has altered the target asset mix to 64.7% equities and 35.3% bonds. One method of re-balancing the portfolio back to its target mix involves the direct buying and selling of the securities in the portfolio. The table demonstrates that to restore the target mix, a dynamic approach would involve:

- Selling $4,800 worth of equities
- Buying $4,800 worth of bonds

© CSI GLOBAL EDUCATION INC. (2008)

TABLE 16.7 DYNAMIC REBALANCING

Asset Class	Asset Mix After Rise in Stock Market	New Asset Mix	Dynamic Re-balancing	Re-balanced Portfolio	New Asset Mix
Equities	$66,000	64.7%	-$4,800	$61,200	60%
Bonds	$36,000	35.3%	+$4,800	$40,800	40%
Asset Mix	$102,000	100.0%		$102,000	100%

Under the dynamic approach, re-balancing dampens returns in a strong market period since the portfolio manager is reducing the strongest-performing component. It enhances returns in a weak market period through the purchase of under-performing asset classes at reduced price levels.

The dynamic strategy is suitable for the risk-averse investor, such as a defined benefit pension plan or a retired individual with low risk tolerance. The tax situation of the investor should be reviewed carefully, as such active management will result in more capital gains and losses.

TACTICAL ASSET ALLOCATION

Strategic asset allocation need not be an absolutely rigid approach. While the investment policy statement may indicate a long-run mix of 60% stocks and 40% bonds, the statement may also allow for some short-term, tactical, deviations from the strategic mix to capitalize on investment opportunities in one asset class before reverting back to the long-term strategic allocation mix. This is known as **tactical asset allocation**. For example, if the bond market is depressed and poised for an upswing, the manager may overweight the portfolio in fixed-income products well over the strategic allocation mix for as long as a few months and then, having profited from this move, move back to the long-term strategic asset allocation. This enables the manager to exercise any market timing skills he or she may have, while investing for the expected return indicated by the strategic mix. In such a case, a strategic allocation could be considered a mid- to long-term strategy, with tactical deviations a short-term strategy.

Though not a passive strategy, this approach is only moderately active, and is appropriate for the long-term investor who is interested in market timing. Such investors might include defined contribution pension funds, growth mutual funds and high-income individuals.

INTEGRATED ASSET ALLOCATION

All of the above types include consideration of capital market expectations, but only some take into account changes in capital markets or client risk tolerance. **Integrated asset allocation** refers to an all-encompassing strategy that includes all of these factors. The other asset allocation techniques are partial versions of the integrated approach.

Passive Management

The preceding asset allocation techniques are all active techniques. **Passive management** is consistent with the view that securities markets are efficient – that is, securities prices at all times reflect all relevant information on expected return and risk. The passive portfolio manager does

© CSI GLOBAL EDUCATION INC. (2008)

not believe that it is possible to identify stocks as underpriced or overpriced, at least to an extent that would achieve enough extra return to cover the added transactions costs. These managers use a buy-and-hold system.

Complete the on-line activity associated with this section.

Index funds are a type of passive management. Indexing is a portfolio management style that involves buying and holding a portfolio of securities that matches the composition of a benchmark index. This method does not require much trading or managerial expertise, since most of the work can be done on a computer (i.e., program trading). The exception to this would be when the underlying stocks in the index change. Then the manager must trade, in order to keep the index fund matching the index. The use of indexing with index funds such as iShares and SPDRs is common.

PORTFOLIO MONITORING

Having set the investment policy and designed and implemented an asset mix, the next step in the portfolio process is to monitor all fronts. The three key areas of focus are the market, the client and the economy.

Constructing a portfolio is only a beginning. Managing one is an ongoing process. It is, therefore, essential to develop a system to monitor the appropriateness of the securities that comprise the portfolio and the strategies that govern it. The process is twofold as it involves monitoring:

- The changes in the investor's goals, financial position and preferences; and
- Expectations for capital markets and individual companies.

Monitoring the Markets and the Client

Keeping informed of client objectives is critical. Investors may change their tolerance for risk, their need for liquidity, their need for savings, and their tax brackets. Therefore, client profiles must be updated on a regular basis. The New Account Application Form sets out the original profile of a client's income and asset levels, investment knowledge and goals. These basic facts should be reviewed and kept current. If any significant change occurs, an amended New Account Application Form should be completed.

Capital markets are also constantly changing to reflect changes in government and central bank policies, economic growth or recession, and sectoral shifts in prosperity within the economy. The portfolio manager must be constantly alert to the direction of monetary policy, forecasts for GDP and the inflation rate, shifts in consumer demand and capital spending, and the potential impact of all these factors on the strategic asset mix or on individual holdings. The challenge for the portfolio manager is to anticipate change and systematically adjust the portfolio to reflect both current return expectations and the objectives of the client. The process of adjusting a portfolio follows the same methodology that is used when constructing it.

Monitoring the Economy

The asset mix decision involves an analysis of all capital markets and is complex. Virtually all information that may affect each asset class has to be incorporated into the decision-making process. The scope of this material includes expected activities in the private and public sectors,

© CSI GLOBAL EDUCATION INC. (2008)

both nationally and internationally. It includes government policies, corporate earnings, economic analysis, existing market conditions and the forecaster's interpretation of the data.

Because of the complexity of the data and the subjectivity in interpretation, it is very difficult to make an accurate prediction about the magnitude of change in a particular asset class. For this reason, forecasts are sometimes expressed in ranges, with a minimum and maximum level. The use of a range not only reflects the unpredictability of capital markets, but it can also indicate the degree of risk anticipated.

The width of the ranges used in an asset mix return forecast will vary with the level of confidence the portfolio manager has in the forecast. When capital markets are volatile, market risk increases. The forecasting process is more difficult and so the ranges will tend to widen.

The expected total returns for each asset group are calculated by adding the expected annual income to the expected capital gain or loss for each group. For example, if stock prices are expected to increase 10% and dividend yields are forecast to be 4%, then the expected total pre-tax return for equities would be 14%.

RETURN FORECASTING

Rates of return are forecasted after analyzing the outlook for those factors that may affect them. While there are many factors to include in the analysis, not all will be of equal importance at all times. Frequently one or two factors, such as inflation or interest rates, will dominate the direction of capital markets. When this occurs, it is necessary to give greater weight to these factors in the analysis.

Quantifying the factors in each group is complex. For this reason, the words "positive," "neutral," or "negative" are frequently used to measure the impact of each factor in subjective terms. Qualifiers, such as "moderately," "very" or "extremely" can be added to positive and negative to give added emphasis to a particular factor. Once each individual factor has been rated, a consensus is taken and the outlook for the group is formed. The outlook is expressed as a minimum and maximum expected total return (capital gain or loss plus expected income) for the group. The following examples (Tables 16.8 to 16.12) are provided to demonstrate the process of return forecasting. The numbers and range of expectations will change depending on the economic situation at the time the result is being forecast.

EQUITY GROUP ANALYSIS

Since asset mix decisions are based on the comparison of entire asset classes, the direction and magnitude of change in a stock market index must be forecast when assessing the outlook for equities. On this basis, an analysis of Canadian markets would conclude by forecasting a future level for the S&P/TSX Composite Index and in the United States by forecasting future levels for the Dow Jones Industrial Average (DJIA) or the Standard & Poor's 500 Stock Index.

The indicators that help assess future stock prices fall into four general categories: fundamental, technical, economic and value indicators. While the factors under each heading can vary according to the preferences of the analyst, the factors shown in Table 16.8 provide a basic model upon which to analyze and forecast equity prices.

© CSI GLOBAL EDUCATION INC. (2008)

TABLE 16.8 SAMPLE EQUITY GROUP ANALYSIS

Factors	Rating
Fundamental Indicators:	
• Corporate Earnings	Positive
Technical Indicators:	
• S&P/TSX Composite Index Chart	Neutral
• DJIA Chart	Negative
Economic Indicators:	
• Leading Indicators	Positive
• Coincident Indicators	Neutral
• Lagging Indicators	Neutral
Value Indicators:	
• Composite P-E Ratios	Negative
• Composite Dividend Yields	Neutral
Consensus or Outlook	Neutral

When the analysis is complete, each factor shown in the table would be rated positive, neutral or negative, reflecting expectations that levels will rise, fall or remain constant. Then, using the same terminology, a consensus for the group would be formed.

For example, suppose the S&P/TSX Composite Index was expected to fall significantly. This would be reflected in a negative rating under technical indicators. There would be a flow-through effect in the value indicators. The rating for price-earnings ratios would be negative if prices were expected to fall more than expected earnings. Dividend yields would be rated positively if dividend payouts stayed constant despite falling prices.

The next step is to express the word(s) used in the consensus as a percentage to reflect the expected gain or loss for the group. As explained earlier, a range is used because the predictability of capital markets is limited. For example, if the consensus for equities was neutral, then the expected change in the S&P/TSX Composite Index would be plus or minus an equal percentage. If, on the other hand, the consensus was positive, the expected change in the S&P/TSX Composite Index might reflect only a small percentage decline and a greater percentage rise. Finally, as shown in Table 16.9, the expected income or dividend yield is added to the expected capital gain (or loss) to determine the expected total return for equities. Note that the dividend yield on the S&P/TSX Composite Index is often used as an approximation for the Expected Income Yield.

© CSI GLOBAL EDUCATION INC. (2008)

TABLE 16.9 SAMPLE TOTAL RETURN FORECAST – EQUITIES

	Minimum	Maximum
Expected Gain/Loss of Capital	-5%	5%
Expected Income Yield	3%	3%
Expected Total Return	-2%	8%

Note: The values given in this table are only examples. A neutral consensus in a different economic environment might result in a return forecast for equities greater or less than that outlined above.

FIXED-INCOME GROUP ANALYSIS

The method used to determine the expected total return for fixed-income securities is similar to that used for equities. However, the focus of the analysis is more specific. Here, in order to calculate an expected total return, an investment manager must forecast future levels for interest rates.

Unlike equity prices, interest rates are influenced by governments to achieve specific economic goals. Therefore, when forecasting interest rates, an investment manager assesses the potential effect of certain factors on the supply/demand equilibrium for money and how changes in that relationship may affect government policy. Factors assessed include monetary policy, fiscal policy, economic indicators, inflation and the value of the Canadian dollar. Since interest rates are international, these factors should be examined from both the Canadian and foreign perspective when feasible.

Table 16.10 provides a model with which to analyze and forecast interest rates. Since declining interest rates increase bond and preferred share prices, those factors that may currently cause rates to drop are said to be bullish, those having no effect, neutral, and those that may contribute to higher interest rates, bearish. As in the equity market analysis, the qualifiers "moderately," "very" or "extremely" may be used to modify a manager's feelings about a particular factor.

At different points in the economic cycle, ratings might lead to different conclusions in terms of anticipated interest rate changes as the market makes valuations on central bank policies.

TABLE 16.10 SAMPLE INTEREST RATE ANALYSIS

Factors	Status/Trend	Anticipated Impact on Interest Rates
Monetary Policy:		
• Canada	Neutral	Neutral
• United States	Neutral	Neutral
Fiscal Policy:		
• Canada	Neutral	Neutral
• United States	Neutral	Neutral

© CSI GLOBAL EDUCATION INC. (2008)

TABLE 16.10 SAMPLE INTEREST RATE ANALYSIS *(Cont'd)*

Factors	Status/Trend	Anticipated Impact on Interest Rates
Economic Indicators:*		
• Employment	Rising	Bearish
• Producer Price Index (PPI)	Rising	Bearish
• Money Supply (M1)	Rising	Bearish
• U.S. Composite Leading Index	Rising	Bearish
Canadian Dollar:	Falling	Bearish
Consensus or Outlook:		**Bearish**

*These are a sample of the economic indicators analysts will incorporate into thier analysis.

When the analysis of the factors is complete, a consensus is taken and the outlook for interest rates is formed. The portfolio manager needs to relate the interest rate analysis to the terms to maturity relevant for the securities being considered for the portfolio. For example, when considering midterm bonds, the portfolio manager needs to make decisions about expectations for mid-term interest rates.

The consensus from the analysis is expressed as an expected increase or decrease in absolute interest rates. To reflect the reality that interest rates are also difficult to predict, a range of rates is sometimes used to describe the potential change. For example, if the consensus for interest rates is neutral, then they may be expected to increase or decrease by an equal amount and remain within this range for the period being forecast. Should the consensus forecast for interest rates be bearish, the percentage decline expected will be less than the percentage rise expected.

The expected gain or loss of capital is calculated by determining the present value of a representative bond, in the example in Table 16.11, an 8%, semi-annual bond that matures in five years with a yield to maturity of 5.2%. The present value of this bond is then recalculated taking into account the expected rise or decline in interest rates consistent with the consensus outlook forecast earlier. The percentage change in present value from that derived in the original interest rate scenario equals the capital gain or loss to be expected under the forecast interest rate change.

To calculate the expected total return for the fixed-income group, it is necessary to add in the income component of the return. Thus, the coupon or interest rate is added to the expected gain or loss that would result from the projected interest rate change.

TABLE 16.11 FIXED-INCOME SECURITIES RETURN FORECAST USING 8% BOND, 5 5-YEAR MATURITY, WITH A 5.2% YIELD TO MATURITY

	Interest Rate Change	
	+1%	**-0.5%**
Expected Gain/Loss of Capital*	-4.06	2.11
Coupon (Interest Rate)	8.00	8.00
Expected Total Return	3.94%	10.11%

* Calculated using present-value method described in Chapter 7.
Note: Interest rate forecasts vary under different economic scenarios.

© CSI GLOBAL EDUCATION INC. (2008)

CASH OR CASH EQUIVALENTS GROUP ANALYSIS

This asset group is generally viewed as one through which managers can obtain a guaranteed rate of return with little risk to capital. Because cash investments are short term, the returns on cash and cash equivalents are the easiest to forecast.

The basis for estimating cash returns is a short-term interest rate (i.e., one year or less) forecast. For example, if interest rates are expected to increase, the portfolio manager takes current cash rates, adjusts them upwards to reflect the forecasted increase, and averages the returns over a 12-month period. The resulting figures are the expected rates of return for cash for the year (see Table 16.12). This return, since it is considered risk free, provides a standard upon which to measure the relative attractiveness of the riskier groups: fixed-income securities and equities. To shift capital from cash to other asset groups, the portfolio manager must feel that the added return potential offsets the added risk.

Continuing from the analysis above, the portfolio manager applies the interest rate changes of 1% and -0.5% to the current yield on cash. It is quite possible for short-term interest forecasts to range between a positive and negative value.

TABLE 16.12 EXPECTED RATES OF RETURN – CASH

	Percentage Return	
	Minimum	**Maximum**
A. Current Yield on Cash (i.e., 91-day Treasury Bills)	2.75%	2.75%
B. Expected Interest Rate Change	–0.50%	1.00%
C. Adjusted Yield on Cash	2.25%	3.75%
D. Expected Rate of Return (A + C) ÷ 2	2.50%	3.25%

Note: Interest rate forecasts vary with different economic scenarios.

The expected minimum and maximum returns for the three asset classes based on the above analysis are summarized in Table 16.13.

TABLE 16.13 RETURN EXPECTATION SUMMARY

	Minimum	**Maximum**
Cash and Equivalents	2.50%	3.25%
Fixed-Income Securities	3.94%	10.11%
Equities	-2.00%	8.00%

© CSI GLOBAL EDUCATION INC. (2008)

A Portfolio Manager's Checklist

Because of the complexity of the capital markets, the portfolio manager must remain abreast of many factors to be effective. The following list highlights some of these factors.

General Points

- Is the portfolio constructed in accordance with the individual's needs, objectives and ability to tolerate risk?
- Is the asset mix appropriate for the client and the outlook for the market?
- Is the portfolio over-diversified and complicated to manage?
- Are there likely to be cash withdrawals from the portfolio? If so, how often and how much?
- Is the portfolio concentrated in a few issues, creating an unnecessary risk?
- Are there sufficient liquid reserves to provide for emergency cash needs and for future buying opportunities?
- If the portfolio is subject to current taxes, is the maximum advantage being taken of the dividend tax credit? If the portfolio's income is not currently taxable, is the maximum advantage being taken of compounding high current income?
- What other assets are held that do not appear in the portfolio, e.g., mortgages, promissory notes or shares in a private company?
- Are there likely to be further funds available for investment from time to time? If so, how often and how much?
- Are there any weak securities that should be sold?
- Is the degree of leverage appropriate to the investor and the state of the market?
- Does the portfolio generate sufficient income?
- What are the current opinions of research analysts?
- Has the client been adequately informed of the current market outlook?

Cash and Cash Equivalents

- Should the terms of deposits be lengthened or shortened?
- Should the quality of the deposits be increased or reduced?
- Should some Canada Savings Bonds be cashed to obtain a better return?

Fixed-Income Securities

- Has the credit rating of any of the issuers changed?
- Is the average term to maturity of the bond portfolio appropriate?
- Does the yield spread between high-quality and low-quality bonds provide a switch opportunity without incurring inappropriate risk?
- Should the portfolio have high-coupon or low-coupon bonds?
- Do purchases of bonds by purchase funds provide a selling opportunity?
- Are there deadlines approaching for exercising conversion privileges?
- Are any securities selling well above their redemption prices?
- Are election periods for retractable or extendable securities approaching?
- Does the weighting between interest-bearing securities and dividend-paying securities maximize the after-tax income?
- Are the interest and dividend payments of individual holdings adequately covered by earnings?

© CSI GLOBAL EDUCATION INC. (2008)

Equities

- Is the risk level in the equity component appropriate?
- Is the portfolio diversified across industry sectors?
- Are the industry weightings appropriate for this stage of the economy?
- Are there sound reasons for important industries or economic sectors not to be represented in the portfolio?
- Are there sound reasons for duplications or overlapping investments (e.g., two bank stocks)?
- Are there any odd lots? If so, should they be sold or increased to board lots?
- Have any rights been declared on any of the issues? If so, should they be sold or exercised?
- Have the portfolio manager's and the client's records been updated?
- Are there shares which have better prospects for capital appreciation than the ones presently held?
- Are there foreign securities in the portfolio which might cause estate tax problems in the event of death?
- Are dividends secure?
- Are any warrants or options about to expire?
- Can the equity component be more easily diversified by using options?
- Can the current holdings be hedged by writing call options or buying puts?
- Should the outlook for any individual company be reviewed in depth?
- Are there any issues regarding taxes that should be reviewed?

EVALUATING PORTFOLIO PERFORMANCE

The success of a portfolio manager is determined by comparing the total rate of return of the portfolio being evaluated with the average total return of comparable portfolios. In this way, the portfolio manager and the client can compare their returns to industry norms and estimate their approximate ranking in relation to other portfolio managers.

For most individual investors, the ranking can be estimated most easily by comparing their performance with the averages shown in one of the Surveys of Funds appearing regularly in financial publications. Not only is it convenient, but many different funds are measured in the surveys and the portfolio manager can compare both the total return and the component returns of the portfolio. For example, the equity component of a diversified portfolio can be compared with the equity funds shown.

Managers are often measured against a predetermined **benchmark** that was specified in the investment policy statement. One common benchmark is the T-bill rate plus some sort of performance benchmark, perhaps the T-bill rate plus 4%. On portfolios that have low turnover to avoid capital gains taxes, performance against the market benchmark may not be appropriate. What investors are interested in is the protection and growth of their purchasing power.

Measuring Portfolio Returns

One very simple method of computing total return is to divide the portfolio's total earnings (income plus capital gains or losses), or the increase in the market value of the portfolio, by the average amount invested in the portfolio. The average amount invested is equal to the opening market value of the portfolio plus one-half of the net contributions made during the measurement period. Net contributions are calculated by subtracting funds withdrawn from the portfolio from funds deposited.

© CSI GLOBAL EDUCATION INC. (2008)

For example, assume that in the course of a particular year a portfolio had a market value of \$106,000 on January 1, and that the investor deposited \$3,000 on March 5 and withdrew \$5,000 on July 10. Assume also that the market value of the portfolio on December 31 was \$110,000. On this basis, the return for the portfolio for the year would be 5.71%, as calculated using the total return formula (pre-tax).

$$\text{Total Return} = \frac{\text{Increase in Market Value}}{\text{Average Amount Invested}}$$

$$= \frac{\text{Closing Value} - [\text{Opening Value} + \text{Net Contributions (or} - \text{Net Deductions)}]}{\text{Opening Value} + \dfrac{\text{Net Contributions (or} - \text{Net Deductions)}}{2}}$$

$$= \frac{\$110,000 - (\$106,000 - \$2,000)}{\$106,000 + \dfrac{(-\$2,000)}{2}}$$

$$= \frac{\$110,000 - \$104,000}{\$106,000 - \$1,000}$$

$$= \frac{\$6,000}{\$105,000}$$

$$= 5.71\%$$

If the total return of a portfolio is required for a shorter period, or if a return for only a component of the portfolio is needed, the same method can be used with the appropriate modification (i.e., as to time frame or relevant components).

Although this formula provides a total return percentage, it is subject to certain distortions. For example, if large withdrawals of funds occur towards the end of the measurement period, the average amount invested will be understated and the total return overstated. Conversely, if large contributions are made late in the period, the average amount invested will be overstated and the total return understated. When deposits or withdrawals distort the total return percentages, performance comparisons are inappropriate and should not be used.

Calculating the Risk-Adjusted Rate of Return

It is not enough merely to compare the returns of two portfolios to measure performance, without factoring in the risk assumed to earn those returns. The **Sharpe Ratio**, used by mutual fund companies and portfolio managers, compares the return of the portfolio to the riskless rate of return, taking the portfolio's risk into account. It measures the portfolio's risk-adjusted rate of return using standard deviation as the measure of risk.

$$S_p = \frac{R_p - R_f}{\sigma_p}$$

© CSI GLOBAL EDUCATION INC. (2008)

Where:

S_p = Sharpe Ratio

R_p = Return of the portfolio

R_f = Risk-free rate (typically the average of the three-month Treasury bill rate over the period being measured)

σ_p = Standard deviation of the portfolio

A good manager should be able to earn a risk-adjusted rate of return that is greater than the riskfree rate. If the risk-adjusted rate of return is lower than the risk-free rate, the portfolio is assuming more risk than is necessary.

If a manager is being measured against a benchmark, the portfolio's Sharpe ratio can be compared to the Sharpe ratio of the applicable benchmark. The larger the Sharpe ratio, the better the portfolio performed. A group of portfolios can therefore be ranked by their risk-adjusted performance. A money manager with a Sharpe ratio greater than the Sharpe ratio of the benchmark outperformed the benchmark. A portfolio's Sharpe ratio that is smaller than the benchmark's signals underperformance. A negative Sharpe ratio means the portfolio had a return less than the risk-free return.

Other Factors in Performance Measurement

In addition to return distortions, dissimilarities in portfolios also make accurate performance comparisons difficult. For example, portfolios may have different risk characteristics and/or special investor constraints or objectives, and the method used to calculate the returns may differ. When such factors affect returns, the conclusions drawn from the performance comparisons should be adjusted to reflect the impact of the variables.

Review the on-line summary or checklist associated with this section.

Because of the large number of variables in the management and measurement of portfolios, assessing investment performance is difficult. Regardless, when performance comparisons are made, investors should be concerned primarily with longer-term results since they best measure a manager's ability in all phases of the business cycle. Also of importance are consistency of results and the trend of performance as indicated by the results over the last few measurement periods.

SUMMARY

After reading this chapter, you should be able to:

1. Describe the asset mix categories and evaluate strategies for setting the asset mix.
   - The basic asset classes are cash, fixed-income securities, and equities:
     - *Cash* includes currency, money market securities, Canada Savings Bonds, GICs, and bonds with a maturity of one year or less.
     - *Fixed-income securities* include bonds due in more than one year, GICs, mortgage-backed securities, fixed-income mutual funds and other debt instruments, as well as preferred shares.
     - *Equities* include common shares, derivatives, exchange-traded funds, equity mutual funds, and convertible bonds and preferreds.

© CSI GLOBAL EDUCATION INC. (2008)

- Asset class timing is the practice of switching among industries and asset classes with a goal of maximizing returns and minimizing losses.
- The link between equity and economic cycles allows investors to attempt to maximize returns on equity investments by acquiring or divesting holdings based on the stage of the equity and/or economic cycle.
- The dividend discount model (DDM) can be used to identify four different periods of an equity cycle, thus allowing for implementation of relevant strategies to time switching between asset classes.

2. Compare and contrast the portfolio management styles of equity and fixed-income managers.
   - Equity growth managers use the bottom-up style of growth investing by focusing on current and future earnings of individual companies, with a key consideration being earnings per share (EPS).
   - Equity value managers focus on specific stock selection, buying stocks that research indicates are undervalued.
   - Equity sector rotators apply a top-down investing approach, focusing on analyzing the prospects for the overall economy. Based on that assessment, managers invest in the industry sectors expected to outperform.
   - Fixed-income managers make choices based on the term to maturity, credit quality, and their expectations of changes in interest rates and how this will affect the prices of fixed-income products.
3. Discuss the benefits of asset allocation, distinguish strategic asset allocation from the types of ongoing asset allocation techniques, and differentiate active and passive management.
   - *Strategic* asset allocation is the long-term asset mix that will be adhered to by monitoring and, when necessary, rebalancing a portfolio. It is the initial mix developed and is based on an evaluation of a client's personal and financial circumstances.
   - *Dynamic* asset allocation involves adjusting the asset mix to systematically rebalance the portfolio back to its long-term strategic asset mix.
   - *Tactical* asset allocation involves short-term, tactical deviations from the strategic mix to capitalize on investment opportunities in one asset class before reverting back to the longterm strategic allocation.
   - *Integrated* asset allocation is an all-encompassing strategy that takes into account changes in capital markets and client risk tolerance.
   - *Passive* management is the philosophy that securities markets are efficient and securities prices at all times reflect all relevant information about expected return and risk. Index funds are a type of passive investment strategy.
4. Describe the steps in monitoring and evaluating portfolio performance in relation to the market, the economy and the client.
   - Monitoring a portfolio refers to evaluating portfolio decisions in light of changes in the investor's goals, financial position and preferences, relative to changing expectations for capital markets and individual securities.

© CSI GLOBAL EDUCATION INC. (2008)

- Monitoring the economy refers to evaluating the changes in the economy as a whole and revisiting portfolio decisions based on changes in the economy and in light of changing personal or financial circumstances.

5. Describe how portfolio performance is evaluated, calculate and interpret the total return and risk-adjusted rate of return of a portfolio, and evaluate an equity and fixed-income return expectation analysis.

   - The success of a portfolio manager is determined by comparing the total rate of return of the portfolio being evaluated with the average total return of comparable portfolios.
   - Managers are often measured against a predetermined benchmark specified in the investment policy statement.
   - One very simple method of computing total return is to divide the portfolio's total earnings (income plus capital gains or losses), or the increase in the market value of the portfolio, by the average amount invested in the portfolio.
   - The Sharpe Ratio measures the portfolio's risk-adjusted rate of return using standard deviation as the measure of risk. Higher Sharpe Ratios are preferred.

Now that you've completed this chapter and the on-line activities, complete this post-test.

© CSI GLOBAL EDUCATION INC. (2008)

SECTION SEVEN

Analysis of Managed Products

© CSI GLOBAL EDUCATION INC. (2008)

Chapter 17

Mutual Funds: Structure and Regulation

© CSI GLOBAL EDUCATION INC. (2008)

17

Mutual Funds: Structure and Regulation

CHAPTER OUTLINE

© CSI GLOBAL EDUCATION INC. (2008)

LEARNING OBJECTIVES

By the end of this chapter, you should be able to:

1. Define a mutual fund and describe the advantages and disadvantages of investing in mutual funds.
2. Compare and contrast mutual fund trusts and mutual fund corporations, explain and calculate how mutual fund units or shares are priced, calculate a fund's net asset value per share (NAVPS), and analyze the impacts of charges associated with mutual funds.
3. Describe the mutual fund regulatory environment and the disclosure documents necessary to satisfy provincial requirements, identify mutual fund registration requirements, and discuss restrictions that sellers of mutual funds must observe..

INVESTING IN MUTUAL FUNDS

The Canadian mutual fund industry has experienced tremendous growth over the past decade, both in choice of products available to investors and in the dollar value of assets under management. Accordingly, the industry offers advisors and investors numerous opportunities and challenges. Are mutual funds ideal for all investors? As we have discussed previously in this course, there is no one perfect security that suits all investors; however, mutual funds have become important investment products for many investors.

In the on-line Learning Guide for this module, complete the Getting Started activity.

Although they may seem simple and nearly universally available, mutual funds are in fact a complex investment vehicle. Available in a variety of different forms and through a variety of different distribution channels, they may be one of the most visible vehicles for many investors, from the smallest retail client to the largest institutional investor. The funds themselves are subject to a range of unique provisions and regulations; thus, it is important to ensure a full understanding of this particular investment vehicle.

Do you fully understand what funds can, and cannot, do for a portfolio? Can you provide an educated explanation about the different charges and fees that apply and what the implications are? Can you identify what needs to be done to stay within the regulations? In this first chapter on mutual funds, we explore the structure and regulation of the mutual fund industry.

© CSI GLOBAL EDUCATION INC. (2008)

KEY TERMS

Back-end load
Clone fund
Early redemption fee
F-class fund
Front-end load
Management expense ratio (MER)
Money market
Mutual fund
National Instrument 81-101
National Instrument 81-102
Net asset value per share (NAVPS)
No-load fund
Offering price
Open-end trust
Pre-authorized contribution plan (PAC)
Redemption price
Simplified prospectus
Switching fee
System for Electronic Document Analysis and Retrieval (SEDAR)
Trailer fee

© CSI GLOBAL EDUCATION INC. (2008)

WHAT IS A MUTUAL FUND?

A **mutual fund** is an investment vehicle operated by an investment company that pools contributions from investors and invests these proceeds into a variety of securities, including stocks, bonds and money market instruments. Individuals who contribute money become share or unitholders in the fund and share in the income, gains, losses and expenses the fund incurs in proportion to the number of units or shares that they own. Professional money managers manage the assets of the fund by investing the proceeds according to the fund's policies and objectives and based on a particular investing style.

Mutual fund shares/units are redeemable on demand at the fund's current price or **net asset value per share (NAVPS)**, which depends on the market value of the fund's portfolio of securities at that time. The mutual funds industry in Canada has experienced tremendous growth since 1980. Figure 17.1 illustrates this growth.

FIGURE 17.1 MUTUAL FUND NET ASSETS 1980 TO 2007

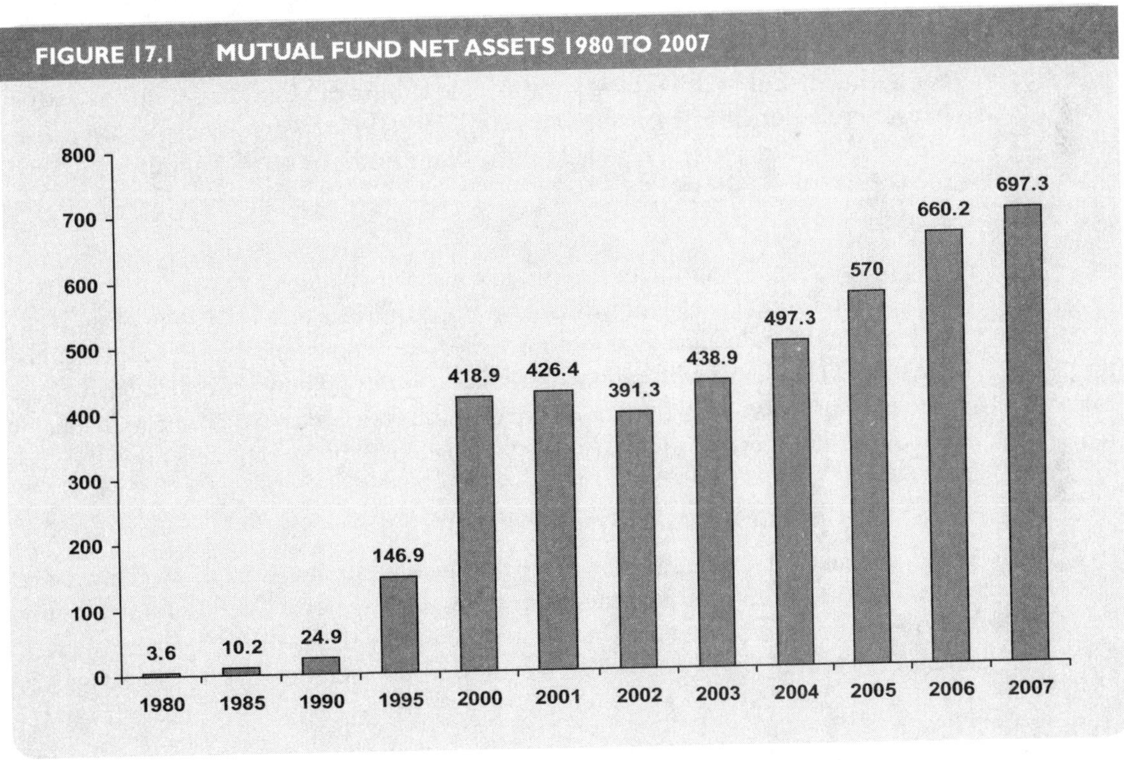

A fund's prime investment goals are stated in the fund's prospectus and generally cover the degree of safety or risk that is acceptable, whether income or capital gain is the prime objective, and the main types of securities in the fund's investment portfolio.

Individuals who sell mutual funds, whether they be investment advisors or mutual fund sales representatives, must have a good understanding of the type and amount of risk associated with each type of fund. As is true with other financial services, the salesperson must carefully assess each client profile to ensure that the type of mutual fund that is recommended properly reflects the client's risk tolerance and investment goals. The mutual fund salesperson also recognizes that a client's goals and objectives are never static and that the review process is ongoing, not

© CSI GLOBAL EDUCATION INC. (2008)

transactional. Finally, he or she recognizes that proper diversification means that a client's portfolio will contain an asset mix allocated among: cash or near-cash investments, equity investments and fixed-income investments.

Advantages of Mutual Funds

Mutual funds offer many advantages for those who buy them. Besides offering varying degrees of safety, income and growth, their chief advantages are:

LOW-COST PROFESSIONAL MANAGEMENT

The fund manager, an investment specialist, manages the fund's investment portfolio on a continuing basis. Both small and wealthy investors purchase mutual funds because they do not have the time, knowledge or expertise to monitor their portfolio of securities. This is an inexpensive way for the small investor to access professional management of their investments.

This is perhaps one of the main advantages that mutual funds offer. The fund manager's job is to analyze the financial markets for the purpose of selecting those securities that best match a fund's investment objectives. The fund manager also plays the important role of continuously monitoring fund performance as a way of fine-tuning the fund's asset mix as market conditions change. Professional management is especially important when it comes to specialized asset categories, such as overseas regional funds, sector funds or small-cap funds.

DIVERSIFICATION

A typical large fund might have a portfolio consisting of 60 to 100 or more different securities in 15 to 20 industries. For the individual investor, acquiring such a portfolio of stocks is likely not feasible. Because individual accounts are pooled, sponsors of managed products enjoy economies of scale that can be shared with mutual fund share or unit holders. As well as having access to a wider range of securities, managed funds can trade more economically than the individual investor. Thus, fund ownership provides a low-cost way for small investors to acquire a diversified portfolio.

VARIETY OF TYPES OF FUNDS AND TRANSFERABILITY

The availability of a wide range of mutual funds enables investors to meet a wide range of objectives (i.e., from fixed-income funds through to aggressive equity funds). Many fund families also permit investors to transfer between two or more different funds being managed by the same sponsor, usually at little or no added fee. Transfers are also usually permitted between different purchase plans under the same fund.

VARIETY OF PURCHASE AND REDEMPTION PLANS

There are many purchase plans, ranging from one-time, lump-sum purchases to regular purchases in small amounts under periodic accumulation plans (called **pre-authorized contribution plans** or **PACs**). One of the main advantages of mutual funds is the low cost to invest. With as little as $100, an investor can begin to purchase units in a fund through a PAC. Again, with as little as $100 a month, they can continue to contribute. At redemption, there are also several plans from which to choose.

© CSI GLOBAL EDUCATION INC. (2008)

LIQUIDITY

Mutual fund shareholders have a continuing right to redeem shares for cash at net asset value. National Instrument 81-102 requires that payments be made within three business days in keeping with the securities industry settlement requirements.

EASE OF ESTATE PLANNING

Shares or units in a mutual fund continue to be professionally managed during the probate period until estate assets are distributed. In contrast, other types of securities may not be readily traded during the probate period even though market conditions may be changing drastically.

LOAN COLLATERAL AND MARGIN ELIGIBILITY

Fund shares or units are usually accepted as security for a bank loan. Fund shares or units are acceptable for margin purposes, thus giving aggressive fund buyers both the benefits and risks of leverage in their financial planning.

VARIOUS SPECIAL OPTIONS

Mutual funds consist of not only an underlying portfolio of securities, but also a package of customer services. Most mutual funds offer the opportunity to compound an investment through the reinvestment of dividends.

Sponsors of mutual funds file a variety of reports annually to meet their regulatory disclosure requirements. These reports include the annual information form (AIF), audited annual and interim financial statements and an annual report, among others. The reports must be provided to unitholders or any person on request. They are easily retrieved through **SEDAR** (the **System for Electronic Document Analysis and Retrieval**) at www.sedar.com. Increasingly, these reports contain useful educational features such as manager commentaries.

Other benefits associated with managed products include record-keeping features that save clients and their advisors time in complying with income tax reporting and other accounting requirements.

Disadvantages of Mutual Funds

COSTS

For most people, a weakness in investing in a mutual fund is the perceived steepness of their sales and management costs. Historically, most mutual funds charged a front-end load or sales commission and a management fee that was typically higher than the cost to purchase individual stocks or bonds from a broker. Competition in the market has subsequently reduced both load and management fees, and investors are now offered a wider choice of investment options.

UNSUITABLE AS A SHORT-TERM INVESTMENT OR EMERGENCY RESERVE

Most funds emphasize long-term investment and thus are unsuitable for investors seeking short-term performance. Since sales charges are often deducted from a plan holder's contributions, purchasing funds on a short-term basis is unattractive. The investor would have to recoup at least the sales charges on each trading transaction. This disadvantage does not apply to money market funds, which are designed with liquidity in mind.

© CSI GLOBAL EDUCATION INC. (2008)

With the exception of money market funds, fund holdings are generally not recommended as an emergency cash reserve, particularly during declining or cyclically low markets when a loss of capital could result from emergency redemption or sale.

PROFESSIONAL INVESTMENT MANAGEMENT IS NOT INFALLIBLE

Like equities, mutual fund shares or units can suffer in falling markets where unit values are subject to market swings (systematic risk). Volatility in the market is extremely difficult to predict or time, and is not controllable by the fund manager.

Complete the on-line activity associated with this section.

TAX COMPLICATIONS

Buying and selling by the fund manager creates a series of taxable events that may not suit an individual unitholder's time horizon. For example, although the manager might consider it in the best interests of the fund to take a profit on a security holding, an individual unit holder might have been better off if the manager had held on to the position and deferred the capital gains liability.

THE STRUCTURE OF MUTUAL FUNDS

An investment fund is a company or trust engaged in managing investments for other people. By selling shares or units to many investors, the fund raises capital and the money raised is then invested according to the fund's investment policies and objectives. The fund makes money from the dividends and interest it receives on the securities it holds and from the capital gains it may make in trading its investment portfolio.

A mutual fund may be structured as either a trust or a corporation.

The most common structure for mutual funds is the **open-end trust**. The trust structure enables the fund itself to avoid taxation. Any interest, dividends or capital gains income, net of fees and expenses, is passed on directly to the unitholders. The fund itself does not incur any tax liability. Any income that has flowed through to the unitholder is taxed in the hands of the unitholder and the tax is based on the type of income that the fund generated.

The **trust deed** establishing the unincorporated mutual fund sets out:

- The fund's principal investment objectives;
- Its investment policy;
- Any restrictions on the fund's investments;
- Who the fund's manager, distributor and custodian will be, or any trustee power given to others to enter into contracts to provide their services; and
- Which of the fund's units are to be sold to the public. Normally, only one class of units is issued by mutual fund trusts.

Privileges attached to these mutual fund units are specified in the trust instrument. One that is always included is the holder's right to redeem the units at a price that is the same as, or close to, the fund's current net asset value per unit. However, unitholders of a trust may or may not be given voting rights under the terms of the trust agreement. Voting rights, if any, should be clearly understood before purchase, by consulting the prospectus.

Regardless of the voting rights specified in the trust agreement, the governing policy for mutual funds requires that, in most cases, funds must convene a meeting of security holders to

© CSI GLOBAL EDUCATION INC. (2008)

consider and approve specific issues. These issues include such matters as a change in the fund's fundamental investment objectives, a change in auditor or fund manager, or a decrease in the frequency of calculating net asset value.

Mutual funds may also be set up as federal or provincial corporations. Provided they meet certain conditions set out in the *Income Tax Act*, investment fund corporations are eligible for a special rate of taxation. Under the Act, the corporation's holdings must consist mainly of a diversified portfolio of securities. The income that it earns must be derived primarily from the interest and dividends paid out by these securities and any capital gains realized from the sale of these securities for a profit. Investors in mutual fund corporations receive shares in the fund instead of the units that are sold to investors in mutual fund trusts.

Investment funds established as corporations lack the flow-through status of investment fund trusts. However, the corporation can achieve a virtually tax-free status by declaring dividends during the course of the year that are equivalent to the corporation's net income after fees and expenses. These dividends are then taxed in the hands of the shareholder.

Organization of a Mutual Fund

Directors and trustees: The directors of a mutual fund corporation, or the trustees of a mutual fund trust, hold the ultimate responsibility for the activities of the fund, ensuring that the investments are in keeping with the fund's investment objectives. To assist in this task, the directors or trustees of the fund may contract out the business of running the fund to an independent fund manager, a distributor and a custodial organization. While the fund itself issues and redeems its own securities, it may enter into detailed contracts (with independent managers, distributors and custodians) which spell out the services each will provide and the fees and other charges to which each is entitled.

Fund manager: The fund manager provides day-to-day supervision of the fund's investment portfolio. In trading the fund's securities, the manager must observe a number of guidelines specified in the fund's own charter and prospectus, as well as constraints imposed by provincial securities commissions.

The manager must also maintain a portion of fund assets in cash and short-term highly liquid investments so as to be able to redeem fund shares on demand, pay dividends, and make new portfolio purchases as opportunities arise. A manager's ability to judge the amount of cash needed, and still have fund assets as fully and productively invested as possible, has a direct bearing on the success of the fund.

Other responsibilities of a fund's manager include calculation of the fund's net asset value, preparation of the fund's prospectus and reports, supervision of shareholder or unitholder recordkeeping, and providing the custodian with documentation for the release of cash or securities. The fund manager receives a management fee for these services. This fee is accrued daily and paid monthly. It is calculated as a percentage of the net asset value of the fund being managed.

Distributors: Mutual funds are sold in many ways: by investment advisors employed by securities firms, by a sales force employed by some organizations that control both management and distribution groups (e.g., Investors Group), by independent direct sales organizations and by "inhouse" distributors. The latter includes employees of trust companies, banks or credit unions who have duties other than selling.

In selling mutual funds, the distributor's representatives must explain the objectives and terms of various funds in language that is understandable to new, often unsophisticated investors.

© CSI GLOBAL EDUCATION INC. (2008)

They also mail out confirmations of sales, handle client inquiries about features of the fund, and accept and transmit orders for fund share redemptions. In the process, they offer clients financial planning assistance that involves "know your client" and suitability standards that are as important in mutual fund sales as they are in the general securities business. As compensation for these services, the distributor usually receives a sales fee.

Custodian: When a mutual fund is organized, an independent financial organization, usually a trust company, is appointed as the fund's **custodian**. The custodian collects money received from the fund's buyers and from portfolio income and arranges for cash distributions through dividend payments, portfolio purchases and share redemptions.

Sometimes the custodian also serves as the fund's **registrar** and **transfer agent**, maintaining records of who owns the fund's shares. This duty is complicated by the fact that the number of outstanding shares is continually changing through sales and redemptions. Fractional share purchases and dividend reinvestment plans further complicate this task.

To better keep track of account activity, the mutual fund industry increasingly makes use of a book-based system for settling account transactions. In this system, purchases and sales of fund units are recorded in a client's account so that no actual share or paper certificates change hands. Instead of issuing certificates, the custodians periodically issue statements showing each owner's current holdings.

Pricing Mutual Fund Units or Shares

Mutual fund shares or units are purchased directly from the fund (often through a distributor) and are sold back to the fund when the investor redeems his or her units. Given that they cannot be purchased from or sold to anyone other than the fund, mutual funds are said to be in a continuous state of primary distribution. Similar to other new issues, a purchaser must be sent a prospectus.

The price an investor pays for a share or unit is known as its **offering price**. In the financial press the offering price is expressed as the **net asset value per share** or **NAVPS**. This price will be based on the NAVPS at the close of business the day the order was placed. The NAVPS is the theoretical amount a fund's shareholders would receive for each share if the fund were to sell all its portfolio of investments at market value, collect all receivables, pay all liabilities, and distribute what is left to its shareholders. It is also used to calculate the **redemption price**, which is the amount (subject to redemption fees, if any) a shareholder receives when he or she redeems the shares.

If a mutual fund does not charge a sales commission to purchase a share or unit, an investor would pay the fund's current NAVPS. NAVPS is calculated as:

$$\text{NAVPS} = \frac{\text{Total Assets} - \text{Total Liabilities}}{\text{Total Number of Shares or Units Outstanding}}$$

For example, ABC fund has $13,000,000 in assets, $1,000,000 in liabilities and 1 million units outstanding. The offering price (the price paid by an investor for 1 unit) is calculated as:

$$\text{NAVPS} = \frac{\$13{,}000{,}000 - \$1{,}000{,}000}{1{,}000{,}000} = \$12 \text{ per unit}$$

This is also the redemption price if the fund does not levy any sales charges or fees.

© CSI GLOBAL EDUCATION INC. (2008)

Since most funds calculate an offering or redemption price at the close of the market each day, a specified deadline during the day is set. Orders received after that deadline are processed on the following business day. Mutual fund salespersons are expected to transmit any order for purchase or redemption to the principal office of the mutual fund on the same day that the order is received. While payment for purchases is usually made in advance, payment for redeemed securities must be made within three business days, according to National Instrument 81-102, from the determination of the NAVPS which for most, but not all, funds is done on a daily basis.

The frequency with which mutual funds calculate NAVPS varies. Rules outlined in **National Instrument 81-102** state that *new* funds must calculate NAVPS at least once a week. At the same time, funds that computed NAVPS on a monthly basis when the Instrument came into effect continue to have the option to do so. In reality, most large funds calculate NAVPS each business day after the markets have closed. If a fund computes its NAVPS less frequently than daily, sales and redemptions will be made at the next valuation date. If computed monthly, a fund may require that requests for redemption be submitted up to ten days before the date of the NAVPS computation. One exception to these rules is real estate funds. They must compute the NAVPS at least once a year, although most funds make the calculation on a quarterly basis.

Charges Associated with Mutual Funds

Mutual funds can be categorized on the basis of the type of sales commission, or load, that is levied. If loads are charged when the investor initially makes the purchase, they are called **front-end loads**; if they are charged at redemption, they are called **back-end loads**. Most load funds have optional sales charges that let the investor choose between front-end or back-end charges. The actual level of the sales charge levied by load funds depends on the type of fund, its sponsor and method of distribution, the amount of money being invested, and the method of purchase (i.e., lump sum purchases versus contractual purchases spread out over a period of time). A client may be able to negotiate with the salesperson over the front-end load, especially if a large amount of money is involved, as it is set by the distributor. The back-end load is set by the dealer and not negotiable.

Trying to calculate the impact of the various types of fees on mutual funds can be very complicated. The Ontario Securities Commission and Industry Canada's Office of Consumer Affairs have developed a new online calculator that allows investors to determine the impact mutual fund fees have on investment returns over time. The Mutual Fund Fee Impact Calculator is located at www.investored.ca.

NO-LOAD FUNDS

Many mutual funds, primarily those offered by direct distribution companies, banks and trust companies, are sold to the public on a no-load basis, with little or no direct selling charges. However, some discount brokers may levy modest "administration fees" to process the purchase and/or redemption of no-load funds. These funds, like other funds, do charge management or other administrative fees.

There was a great deal of controversy when no-load funds were first introduced. Many felt that the fund had to make the money somewhere. The no-load funds were said to have higher management fees. Prospective purchasers of no-load mutual funds should read the prospectus carefully, as this may or may not be true. Higher management fees may allow some no-load funds to compensate the salespeople through ongoing trailer or service fees, which are described in more detail below.

© CSI GLOBAL EDUCATION INC. (2008)

FRONT-END LOADS

A front-end load is payable to the distributor at the time of purchase. It is usually expressed as a percentage of the purchase price or NAVPS. The percentage typically decreases as the amount of the purchase increases.

Investors should be aware that the front-end load effectively increases the purchase price of the units, thereby reducing the actual amount invested. For example, a $1,000 investment in a mutual fund with a 4% front-end load means that $40 (4% × $1,000) goes to the distributor by way of compensation while the remaining $960 is actually invested.

Regulations require that front-end loads must be disclosed in the prospectus both as a percentage of the purchase amount and as a percentage of the net amount invested. In the example above, the prospectus would state that the front-end load charge would be 4% of the amount purchased ([$40 ÷ $1,000] ×100) and 4.17% ([$40 ÷ $960] × 100) of the amount invested.

To determine a fund's offering or purchase price when it has a front-end load charge, you must first determine the NAVPS and then make an adjustment for the load charge. Using a NAVPS of $12 and a front-end load of 4%, the offering or purchase price is calculated as:

$$\text{Offering or Purchase Price} = \frac{\text{NAVPS}}{100\% - \text{Sales Charge}}$$

So:

$$\text{Offering or Purchase Price} = \frac{\$12}{100\% - 4\%} = \frac{\$12}{1.00 - 0.04} = \frac{\$12}{0.96} = \$12.50$$

Note that the sales charge of 4% of the offering price is the equivalent of 4.17% of the net asset value (or net amount invested):

$$4\% \text{ of } \$12.50 = \$0.50$$

$$\frac{\$0.50}{\$12} = 4.17\%$$

BACK-END LOADS OR DEFERRED SALES CHARGES

A growing number of funds apply no sales charges on the original purchase, except for perhaps a nominal initial administrative fee, but instead levy a fee at redemption. This type of fee is known as a back-end load, redemption charge, declining sales or **deferred sales charge**. The fee may be based on the original contribution to the fund or on the net asset value at the time of redemption.

In most cases, deferred sales charges on a back-end load fund decrease the longer the investor holds the fund. For example, an investor might incur the following schedule of deferred sales charges with this type of fund:

© CSI GLOBAL EDUCATION INC. (2008)

TABLE 17.1 BACK-END LOAD SCHEDULE

Year Funds Are Redeemed	Deferred Sales Charge
Within the first year	6%
In the second year	5%
In the third year	4%
In the fourth year	3%
In the fifth year	2%
In the sixth year	1%
After the sixth year	0%

For example, an investor purchases units in a mutual fund at a NAVPS of $10. If the investor decides to sell the units in the fourth year when the NAVPS is $15, the fund will charge a 3% back-end load or commission.

If the back-end load is based on the *original purchase amount*, the investor would receive $14.70 a unit, calculated as follows:

Selling/Redemption Price	=	NAVPS – Sales commission
	=	NAVPS – (NAVPS • sales percentage)
	=	$15 – ($10 × 3%)
	=	$15 – $0.30
	=	$14.70

If the back-end load is instead based on the *NAVPS at the time of redemption*, the investor would receive $14.55, calculated as follows:

Selling/Redemption Price	=	$15 – ($15 × 3%)
	=	$15 – $0.45
	=	$14.55

TRAILER FEES

Another kind of fee is the **trailer fee**, sometimes called a service fee. This is a fee that a mutual fund manager may pay to the distributor that sold the fund. This fee is paid to the salesperson annually as long as the client holds the funds. Service fees are usually paid out of the fund manager's management fee.

The justification for paying this fee is that the salesperson provides ongoing services to investors such as investment advice, tax guidance and financial statements. Proponents of trailer fees argue that the ongoing services are a valuable benefit to investors and that salespeople must be compensated for their work. Critics believe that such charges have the potential to produce a conflict of interest for the salespeople who could encourage investors to stay in the fund even when market conditions might indicate that they should redeem their shares. Critics of trailer fees also argue that investors who hold funds for the long term end up paying higher overall fees than they would if they had paid a one-time front- or back-end load.

© CSI GLOBAL EDUCATION INC. (2008)

OTHER FEES

A small number of funds charge a set-up fee, on top of a front-end load or back-end load.

A variation of the redemption fee is the early redemption fee. Some funds, even no-load funds, note in the prospectus that funds redeemed within 90 days of the initial purchase may be subject to an early redemption fee, such as a flat fee of $100 or 2% of the original purchase cost. These fees are charged to discourage short-term trading and to recover administrative and transaction costs.

For example, $5,000 is invested in a fund that charges a 2% early redemption fee. If the investor redeems the units 45 days later, the early redemption fee is $100 ($5,000 × 2%).

SWITCHING FEES

Switching fees may apply when an investor exchanges units of one fund for another in the same family or fund company. Some mutual fund companies allow unlimited free switches between funds, while others permit a certain number of free switches in a calendar year before fees are applied. In many cases, the financial advisor may charge a negotiable fee to a maximum of 2% of the amount being transferred, but an advisor may choose to waive this fee altogether. A common requirement for switching is that the funds involved are purchased under the same sales fee options.

In other words, clients generally aren't allowed to switch between a front-end fund and a back-end fund, or vice versa.

As well, switching fees generally do not apply if a fund merges with another or is being terminated for any other reason. In such cases, the investor would be allowed to transfer to the existing fund or withdraw the cash value of the contract without incurring withdrawal fees.

MANAGEMENT FEES

The level of management fees varies widely depending on the type of fund, with fees ranging from less than 1% on money market and index funds to as much as 3% on equity funds. In general, fees will vary depending on the level of service required to manage the fund. For example, the management fees associated with money market funds are low, in the range of 0.50% to 1%. The management of equity funds (with the exception of index funds) requires ongoing research and therefore the management fees are higher, ranging from 2% to 3%. Index funds try to mirror the market with occasional rebalancing. Since this strategy is largely a passive buy-and-hold strategy, management fees are usually lower. In all cases, the management fees charged would be outlined in the prospectus.

Management fees are generally expressed as a straight percentage of the net assets under management. For example, "an annual fee of not more than 2% of the average daily net asset value computed and payable monthly on the last day of each month." This method of compensation has been criticized because it rewards fund managers not on the performance of the fund, but on the level of assets managed. Of course, a fund that consistently underperforms will find that its assets will fall as investors redeem their holdings.

The management fee compensates the fund manager, but it does not cover all the expenses of a fund. For instance, other operating expenses like interest charges, all taxes, audit and legal fees, safekeeping and custodial fees, and provision of information to share or unit holders are charged directly to the fund. The **management expense ratio (MER)** represents the total of all management fees and other expenses charged to a fund, expressed as a percentage of the fund's average net asset value for the year. Trading or brokerage costs are excluded from the MER calculation because they are included in the cost of purchasing or selling portfolio assets.

© CSI GLOBAL EDUCATION INC. (2008)

MER is calculated as follows:

$$\text{MER} = \frac{\text{Aggregate Fees and Expenses Payable During the Year}}{\text{Average Net Asset Value for the Year}} \times 100$$

For example, if a fund with $500 million in assets has total annual expenses of $10 million, its MER for the year is 2% ($10 ÷ $500).

All expenses are deducted directly from the fund, not charged to the investor. As such, these fund expenses decrease the ultimate returns to the investors. For example, if a fund reports a compound annual return of 8% and an MER of 2%, it has a gross return of roughly 10%. This means that the MER, expressed as a percentage of returns, is 20% of the return ([2% ÷ 10%] × 100).

Published rates of return are calculated after deducting the management expense ratio, while the NAVPS of investment funds are calculated after the management fee has been deducted. Funds are required by law to disclose in the fund prospectus both the management fee and the management expense ratio for the last five fiscal years.

F-CLASS FUNDS

Many financial advisors are moving to providing fee-based, rather than commission-based, accounts. The client is charged a percentage of the assets under management, rather than a commission or fee for each transaction. Buying mutual funds within these programs was expensive, as the client was charged an MER that included compensation to the IA, as well as being charged the asset-based fee. To accommodate fee-based financial advisors, a number of mutual fund companies, such as AGF, Mackenzie and Royal Bank, now offer F-class mutual funds. An F-class fund is identical to the regular fund, but charges a lower MER, thus reducing or eliminating the double charge.

REGULATING MUTUAL FUNDS

The Canadian securities industry is a regulated industry (see Chapter 3). Each province has its own securities act regulating the underwriting and distribution of securities in order to protect buyers and sellers of securities. Securities regulations related to mutual funds are based upon three broad principles: personal trust, disclosure and regulation.

The success of these principles in promoting positive market activities relies largely on ethical conduct by industry registrants. The following outlines a code of ethics also presented in the Canadian Securities Institute's *Conduct and Practices Handbook Course (CPH)* and the *Branch Managers Course (BMC)*.

This code of ethics establishes norms for duty and care that incorporate not only compliance with the "letter of the law," but also respect for the "spirit of the law." These norms are based upon ethical principles of trust, integrity, justice, fairness and honesty. The code distills industry rules and regulations into five primary values:

- Mutual fund salespeople must use proper care and exercise professional judgement.
- Mutual fund salespeople should conduct themselves with trustworthiness and integrity, and act in an honest and fair manner in all dealings with the public, clients, employers and employees.

© CSI GLOBAL EDUCATION INC. (2008)

- Mutual fund salespeople should conduct, and should encourage others to conduct, business in a professional manner that will reflect positively on the individual registrant, the firm and the profession, and should strive to maintain and improve their professional knowledge and that of others in the profession.
- Mutual fund salespeople must act in accordance with the securities act of the province or provinces in which registration is held, and must observe the requirements of all Self-Regulatory Organizations (SROs) of which the firm is a member.
- Mutual fund salespeople must hold client information in the strictest confidence.

Mutual Fund Regulatory Organizations

Investment firms that are members of one or more of the Canadian self-regulatory organizations (SROs), and the registered employees of such member firms, are subject to the rules and regulation of these SROs (see Chapter 3). Furthermore, all securities industry participants are subject to provincial securities law in their particular provinces and in any other province where the relevant securities administrators may claim jurisdiction.

The Mutual Fund Dealers Association (MFDA) is the mutual fund industry's SRO for the distribution side of the mutual fund industry. It does not regulate the funds themselves. That responsibility remains with the provincial securities commissions, but the MFDA does regulate how the funds are sold. The MFDA is not responsible for regulating the activities of mutual fund dealers who are already members of another SRO. For example, IIROC members selling mutual fund products will continue to be regulated by IIROC.

In Québec, the mutual fund industry is under the responsibility of the Autorité des marchés financiers and the Chambre de la sécurité financière. The Autorité is responsible for overseeing the operation of fund companies within the province, while the Chambre is responsible for setting and monitoring continuing education requirements and for enforcing a code of ethics. A co-operative agreement currently in place between the MFDA and the Québec regulatory organizations will help to avoid regulatory duplication and to ensure that investor protection is maintained.

National Instruments 81-101 and 81-102

Canadian funds fall under the jurisdiction of the securities act of each province. Securities administrators control the activities of these funds, and their managers and distributors, by means of a number of National and Provincial Policy Statements dealing specifically with mutual funds, and by provincial securities legislation applicable to all issuers and participants in securities markets. **National Instrument 81-101 (NI 81-101)** deals with mutual fund prospectus disclosure. **National Instrument 81-102 (NI 81-102)** and a companion policy contain requirements and guidelines for the distribution and advertising of mutual funds.

General Mutual Fund Requirements

Since investors in a mutual fund buy the fund's treasury shares rather than previously issued and outstanding stock, the fund must be registered for sale in each jurisdiction. With certain exceptions, the fund must annually file a prospectus or simplified prospectus (described below) which must be acceptable to the provincial securities administrator.

© CSI GLOBAL EDUCATION INC. (2008)

Many Canadian mutual fund securities are qualified for sale in all provinces. Most funds, particularly the smaller ones, file a prospectus or a simplified prospectus only in provinces where sales prospects appear favourable. Selling a fund's securities to residents of provinces in which the fund has not been qualified is prohibited. It is important, therefore, that mutual fund salespeople deal only in those funds registered in their own jurisdiction.

Since mutual funds are considered to be in a continuous state of primary distribution, investors must receive a prospectus upon purchase. Due to the nature of the industry, the completion of a full prospectus is considered cumbersome. To adhere to the disclosure requirements of a prospectus and yet allow the industry to function smoothly, a simplified prospectus system was introduced.

Mutual funds predominantly use the simplified prospectus system to qualify the distribution of mutual fund securities to the public. The actual requirements of this system are set out in NI 81-101, but the system differs from the long or full prospectus system for other securities in that the information is divided into parts.

The disclosure documents included as part of the simplified prospectus system consist of:

- A simplified prospectus;
- The annual information form;
- The annual audited statements or interim unaudited financial statements; and
- Other information required by the province or territory where the fund is distributed, such as material change reports and information circulars.

The Instrument requires only the delivery of the simplified prospectus to an investor in connection with the purchase of a mutual fund, unless the investor also requests delivery of the annual information form and/or the financial statements.

The Simplified Prospectus

A mutual fund prospectus is normally shorter and simpler than a typical prospectus for a new issue of common shares. Under the simplified prospectus system, the issuer must abide by the same laws and deadlines that apply under the full prospectus system. As well, the buyer is entitled to the same rights and privileges.

The **simplified prospectus** must be filed with the securities commission annually, but need not be updated annually unless there is a change in the affairs of the mutual fund.

Investors purchasing a mutual fund for the first time must be provided with the simplified prospectus and any other information required by the province. The mailing or delivery of the prospectus must be made to the purchaser not later than midnight on the second business day after the purchase. For further purchases of the same fund, it is not necessary to provide the simplified prospectus again unless it has been amended or renewed. If it has been amended or renewed, the investor has the right to withdraw from the investment within two business days after the document has been provided.

National Instrument 81-101 has ensured that investors will receive a shorter, more user-friendly type of fund summary. The information must be in plain language and set up in a specific format so that it is easier for the investor to find the information.

© CSI GLOBAL EDUCATION INC. (2008)

The simplified prospectus consists of two sections:

- *Part A* provides introductory information about the mutual fund, general information about mutual funds and information applicable to the mutual funds managed by the mutual fund organization.
- *Part B* contains specific information about the mutual fund.

The simplified prospectus may be used to qualify more than one mutual fund, as long as Part A of each prospectus is substantially similar and the funds belong to the same mutual fund family, administered by the same entities and operated in the same manner.

The simplified prospectus must contain the following information:

- Introductory statement describing the purpose of the prospectus and identifying the other information documents which the fund must make available to investors
- Name and formation of the issuer, including a description of the issuer's business
- Risk factors
- Description of the securities being offered
- Method used to set the price of the securities being sold or redeemed, and disclosure of any sales charges
- Method of distribution
- Statement of who has the responsibility for management, distribution and portfolio management
- Fees paid to dealers
- Statement of management fees and other expenses, including the annual management expense ratio for the past five years
- The fund's investment objectives and practices
- Information on the amount of dividends or other distributions paid by the issuer
- In general terms, the income tax consequences to individuals holding an investment in the fund
- Notice of any legal proceedings material to the issuer
- Identity of the auditors, transfer agent and registrar
- Statement of the purchaser's statutory rights
- Summary of the fees, charges and expenses payable by the security holder

The prospectus must be amended when material changes occur, and investors must receive a copy of the amendment.

As stated earlier, issuers using this simplified system must send or hand-deliver the prospectus to the buyer, no later than the second business day after an agreement of purchase has been made. This practice is followed because of the purchaser's rights of withdrawal and rescission and because the prospectus itself is an excellent sales tool, informing the buyer of the nature of the fund and its securities.

Certain types of mutual funds may not use the simplified prospectus system under National Instrument 81-101. These are mutual funds that invest in real property and those that constitute a commodity pool program.

© CSI GLOBAL EDUCATION INC. (2008)

OTHER FORMS AND REQUIREMENTS

Delivery of the **annual information form** (**AIF**) is available to investors on request. Much of the disclosure required in the AIF is similar to that provided in the simplified prospectus. The AIF contains, in addition to the above, information concerning:

- Significant holdings in other issuers
- The tax status of the issuer
- Directors, officers and trustees of the fund and their indebtedness and remuneration
- Associated persons, the principal holders of securities, the interest of management and others in material transactions
- The particulars of any material contracts entered into by the issuer

As part of the simplified prospectus system, a fund must provide its investors with financial statements on request. Annual audited financial statements must be made available to the securities commission(s) where the fund is registered on or before the deadline set by the commission(s). These statements must be made available to new investors and are described below.

Unaudited financial statements as at the end of six months after the fund year-end must also be submitted to the securities commissions, usually within sixty days after the reporting date. These statements must also be given to new investors.

The *balance sheet* (or statement of financial position/statement of net assets) shows the fund's assets, liabilities and equity. Mutual fund balance sheets are usually much simpler than those of other companies. The statement is dominated by a single asset category, the fund's investments at market value, and there are few liabilities to report. The equity, when divided by the number of outstanding shares or units, gives the NAVPS. This calculation of assets, liabilities and equity must be done each time the fund calculates its NAVPS.

The *income statement* shows all revenues earned and expenses incurred by the fund. The source of the revenues is most often interest or dividends from the securities in which the fund invests. The source of revenue ultimately depends on the nature of the fund, so for example, a real estate fund may report revenues as "Rent from Income Properties," while a bond fund will report interest income.

The management fee payable to the fund manager usually dominates the expenses. Other expenses include items like auditor's fees, administrative charges not covered by the management fee, etc.

The total expenses of the fund are deducted from the revenues to arrive at its net income. The net income is distributed to the fund's share or unit holders. The vast majority of funds qualify as mutual fund trusts for income tax purposes and the funds distribute their net income to investors, so the funds themselves are not subject to income tax.

The *statement of investment portfolio* (or statement of investments and other net assets) provides details on the securities (or other assets) that the fund is holding. For example, the statement lists any equities held by the fund, showing both the cost price and current market value. Bonds held by the fund are listed at cost and market value, and the coupon rate and maturity date may also be shown.

© CSI GLOBAL EDUCATION INC. (2008)

The *statement of changes in net assets* is the mutual fund equivalent of a company's statement of changes in financial position. The statement begins with the net assets in the fund at the beginning of the year and then shows all the factors that increased and decreased net assets and resulted in the net assets at the end of the year.

The *statement of portfolio transactions* provides disclosure details on a number of matters, such as:

- The name of each issuer of every security purchased or sold
- The total cost of purchasing securities
- An itemized list of debt securities and other securities held in the fund
- Other required disclosure statement

This statement is not usually included in the financial statements, but the notes to the financial statements inform investors that the statement may be requested without charge from the fund manager.

Registration Requirements for the Mutual Fund Industry

Mutual fund managers, distributors and sales personnel must all be registered with the securities commissions in all provinces in which they operate (and with the Autorité des services financiers if they operate in Québec) and must regularly renew their registrations. The commissions also insist that they be informed within five business days of any important change in personal circumstances, such as a change of address or bankruptcy.

Education qualifications: Salespeople must have passed a mutual funds course such as the *Canadian Securities Course* (CSC), the *Investment Funds in Canada (IFC)* course, or another qualified education program.

Registration requirements: An application for registration is filed electronically with the **National Registration Database** (Form NRD 33-109F4), with the appropriate fee. Provincial securities acts set the requirements for initial and continuing registration. In Québec, the salesperson must register with the Autorité des services financiers. These requirements include, but are not limited to, the following:

- Generally, mutual fund salespersons must be employed by the distribution company.
- Mutual fund salespersons are not permitted to carry on other forms of employment without the prior approval of the appropriate Administrator(s) and the industry association(s) of which their firms are members. Many provinces have issued policy statements permitting persons to be dually registered as mutual fund salespersons and life agents.
- Applicants must complete a detailed application about their past businesses, employment and conduct and submit to a police review.

The application asks questions about the salesperson and any companies with which the salesperson has been associated in certain capacities, such as:

- Any action against the salesperson regarding any government licence to deal in securities or with the public in any other capacity requiring registration
- Any disciplinary action regarding an approval by any securities commission or other similar professional body
- Any past criminal convictions or current charges or indictments
- Any bankruptcies or proposals to creditors
- Any civil judgment or garnishment

© CSI GLOBAL EDUCATION INC. (2008)

Notices of changes: The mutual fund salesperson has the obligation to notify the provincial administrator within five business days (ten days in Québec) of any changes in the information required in their provincial application. These include:

- A change in address
- Disciplinary action of a professional body
- Personal bankruptcy (Ontario and Québec)
- Criminal charges
- Civil judgements

Renewal of registration: A mutual fund salesperson must renew his or her registration on a regular basis. In most provinces, this must be done annually. If not renewed, it expires. The renewal application must set out any changes in the applicant's circumstances that have occurred since the applicant last made an application for registration. In every province, a registration fee is payable when submitting an application for registration as a salesperson. In Québec, an annual fee is payable.

Transfer of registration: As soon as a salesperson ceases to work for a registered dealer, registration is automatically suspended. The employer must notify the provincial Administrator of the termination of the employment and, in most provinces, the reason why. Before a salesperson's registration can be reinstated, notice in writing must be received by the Administrator from another registered dealer of the employment of the salesperson by that other dealer. The reinstatement of the registration must be approved by the Administrator.

If the Administrator does not receive a request for reinstatement and transfer to a new company within the permitted period of time, the registration lapses. The salesperson will have to apply again for registration. This period could be as short as 30 days or as long as 6 months (in Québec).

Mutual Fund Restrictions

The fund manager provides day-to-day supervision of the fund's investment portfolio. In trading the fund's securities, the manager must observe a number of guidelines specified in the fund's own charter and prospectus, as well as constraints imposed by provincial securities commissions.

PROHIBITED MUTUAL FUND MANAGEMENT PRACTICES

Some funds may have all the restrictions listed below, some may not. Restrictions that might be specified include:

- Purchases of no more than 10% of the total securities of a single issuer or more than 10% of a company's voting stock
- Funds cannot buy shares in their own company (for example, a fund owned by a bank cannot buy shares in that bank)
- Purchases of no more than 10% of the net assets in the securities of a single issuer or 20% of net assets in companies engaged in the same industry (specialty funds excepted)
- No purchases of the shares of other mutual funds, except in certain cases where no duplication of management fees occurs
- No borrowing for leverage purposes
- No margin buying or short selling
- Normally a prohibition on commodity or commodity futures purchases
- Limitations on the percentage holdings of illiquid securities such as those sold through private placement and unlisted stocks

© CSI GLOBAL EDUCATION INC. (2008)

USE OF DERIVATIVES BY MUTUAL FUNDS

Subject to strict regulatory controls, mutual fund managers are allowed to incorporate specific "permitted" derivatives as part of their portfolios. Recall that derivatives are contracts whose value is based on the performance of an underlying asset such as a commodity, a stock, a bond, foreign currency or an index. Options (puts or calls), futures, forwards, rights, warrants and combination products are among the permitted derivatives used by mutual fund managers.

The three most prominent applications of derivatives among mutual fund managers are to hedge against risk, to facilitate market entry and exit and the creation of clone funds. A **clone fund** tries to mimic the performance of a successful fund within a family of funds. It is often cheaper and quicker to enter the market using derivatives rather than purchasing the underlying securities directly.

For example, a fund manager may have experienced a rapid growth in the value of her portfolio, but is concerned that the market may fall. To protect herself against a fall in value, she purchases put options on the iUnits S&P/TSX 60 Index Fund (i60s). If the market declines, the fall in value of the portfolio is offset by an increase in the value of the put options. Other managers may sell call options on shares they already own in order to enhance the fund's income. When fund managers deal internationally, they may use futures contracts as protection against changes in currency values.

One focus of National Instrument 81-102 is to allow the use of derivatives to benefit investors by minimizing overall portfolio risk while, at the same time, ensuring that portfolio managers do not use derivatives to speculate with investors' money. This regulation covers such topics as:

- The total amount (10% maximum as a percentage of the net assets of a fund) that can be invested in derivatives
- How derivative positions must be hedged by the assets of the fund (based on daily portfolio valuations)
- Expiry dates on different option products
- Permitted terms
- The qualifications required by portfolio advisors to trade these instruments

There are exceptions to these rules. Clone funds, for example, make extensive use of derivatives in their strategies. Substantially more than 10% of their assets would be in derivatives. Hedge funds are exempted from these rules. As well, commodity pools are permitted to use derivatives in a leveraged manner for speculation.

The use of permitted derivatives must be described in a mutual fund's simplified prospectus. Briefly, the discussion must explain how the derivative(s) will be used to achieve the mutual fund's investment and risk objectives, and the limits of and risks involved with their planned use.

PROHIBITED SELLING PRACTICES

There are a number of sales practices that are clearly unacceptable to regulators. Engaging in these and other types of overselling and unethical behaviour could lead to a loss of registration.

Quoting a future price: When an investor places an order to buy or sell a mutual fund, the price per unit or share that he or she will be paying or receiving is not known. This is because the purchase or sale price is based on the net asset value on the next regular valuation date. Depending on the time of day in which the order is entered, the NAVPS may be priced at the end of the current business day or at the close of business on the next business day. Mutual fund companies specify the time by which a trade must be entered to receive the closing price for the

© CSI GLOBAL EDUCATION INC. (2008)

current business day. Consequently, it is unlawful for a salesperson to backdate an order in an attempt to buy shares or units at a previous day's price.

Offer to repurchase: Salespeople may not make offers to repurchase securities in an attempt to insulate investors from downturns in price. Of course, investors have the normal right of redemption should they wish to sell their mutual fund investments.

Selling without a licence: As mentioned, mutual fund salespeople must be licenced in each province where they intend to sell mutual funds, and this requires registration with each provincial regulatory authority under which they intend to work. They must renew their registration as required by the provincial authorities and keep authorities informed of material changes in their personal circumstances that could affect their registration status.

Furthermore, it is illegal for a mutual fund salesperson to sell products for which the salesperson is not registered. For example, a mutual fund salesperson cannot sell stocks, bonds or insurance unless licensed to do so in that province.

Advertising the registration: Salespeople may not advertise or promote the fact that they are registered with a securities authority, as this may imply that regulatory authorities sanction the salespersons' conduct or the quality of the funds.

Promising a future price: Salespeople may not make promises that a fund will achieve a set price in the future.

Sales made from one province into another province or country: While telecommunications have given access to the entire country, the filling of orders from non-provincial residents, even unsolicited, is not permitted unless the mutual fund salesperson is registered in the client's province. Selling mutual funds to clients in another province or to non-Canadian residents may result in the cancellation of the mutual fund salesperson's registration.

Sale of unqualified securities: Mutual funds must also be approved in the province in which mutual fund salespersons are registered. It is forbidden to sell mutual funds that have not been approved by the provincial regulator. Fortunately, most mutual funds available on the market are approved in every Canadian jurisdiction.

GUIDELINES AND RESTRICTIONS

There are also guidelines and restrictions with respect to what distributor firms and fund managers are permitted to do. These guidelines obviously have an impact on the salesperson.

Prohibited sales practices include:

- The provision by fund managers of money or goods to a distributor firm or its salesperson in support of client appreciation.
- While the rate of commission set for a new fund may differ from rates of commission set for already established funds, the rate of commission on a fund cannot be changed unless the prospectus for that fund is renewed.
- A fund manager may not provide co-operative funds for practices which are considered general marketing expenses, such as general client mailings.
- Fund managers may not financially subsidize skill enhancement courses such as effective communications, improving presentation skills, etc.
- There are strict guidelines with respect to the provision of non-monetary benefits. They are forbidden unless they are of such minimal value or frequency that the behaviour of a salesperson would be influenced (such as pens, T-shirts, hats and golf balls).

© CSI GLOBAL EDUCATION INC. (2008)

This is not an all-inclusive list. It is the responsibility of the salespersons to be aware of what is, and is not, allowed. The Investment Funds Institute of Canada (IFIC) puts out Sales Practices Bulletins, which interpret and give examples of acceptable and unacceptable sales practices.

SALES COMMUNICATIONS

NI 81-102 and NI 81-105 outline specific guidelines with respect to sales communications. The following is a brief summary of these policies, but a mutual fund salesperson should be familiar with both these instruments. These rules are common whether the communication comes from the salesperson, the salesperson's firm, the fund's promoter, manager or distributor, or anyone who provides a service to the client with respect to the mutual fund. When in doubt, the salesperson should always consult with their branch manager or compliance officer. Their approval is needed before any sales communications is sent out.

These guidelines apply to any type of sales communication, including advertising or any oral or written statements that the salesperson makes to a client.

Sales communications can include:

- A description of the fund's characteristics
- Comparisons between funds under common management, funds with similar investment objectives or a comparison of the fund to an index
- Performance information – there are very specific rules with respect to how this information must be calculated and presented (see Comparing Mutual Fund Performance)
- Advertising that the fund is a no-load fund

Any information or comparisons must include all facts, that if disclosed, would likely impact on the decision made or conclusions drawn by the client.

Of paramount importance is that the communication cannot be misleading. The communication cannot make an untrue statement, omit any information that if omitted would make the communication misleading, nor present information in a way that distorts the information. All information must agree with the information found in the prospectus.

Distribution of Mutual Funds by Financial Institutions

There are some rules that apply specifically to the distribution of mutual funds by financial institutions (such as banks, trust companies, insurance companies and loan companies).

The rules dealing with financial institutions' (FI) distribution of mutual funds require the following:

1. *Control of Registrant:* An FI can sell mutual fund securities in its branches only through a corporation ("dealer") which it controls directly or indirectly, or with which it is affiliated. The dealer must be registered in each province or territory where the mutual fund securities are sold.
2. *Registration of Employees:* Only registered salespersons can sell mutual funds.
3. *Dual Employment:* Employees of an FI who engage in financial services activities can also become registered as salespersons of the dealer and therefore sell mutual fund securities, provided that dual employment is permitted by the legislation to which the FI is subject.
4. *Conflicts of Interest:* Conflicts of interest can arise as a result of dual employment. For example, FI employees who are compensated on the basis of their sales of mutual fund securities but not other products are motivated to sell mutual funds to a client, even if other products would be more suitable for the client. A conflict can arise even when dually

© CSI GLOBAL EDUCATION INC. (2008)

employed salespersons are paid on a salary-only basis where the salespersons also have the ability to approve client loans (e.g., to fund mutual fund purchases).

To address these concerns, dealers must have in place supervisory rules to prevent conflicts of interest arising as a result of dual employment of salespersons. These supervisory rules must address potential conflicts and must be approved by the relevant provincial securities administrator unless such rules provide that:

- Dually employed salespersons are paid salary only; and either
- A dually employed salesperson cannot make loans to finance purchases of mutual fund securities sold by that salesperson, or
- Any loan made by a dually employed salesperson in order to finance the purchase of mutual fund securities sold by that salesperson must be approved by a senior lending officer of the FI.

5. *In-House Funds:* The requirements in these principles are based on the assumption that the only mutual fund securities traded by the dealer through branches of the FI will be those issued by a mutual fund sponsored by the FI (or a company controlled by or affiliated with the FI). If an FI wanted to sell mutual fund securities sponsored by a third party, this should be discussed with the relevant securities regulator to determine what amendments, if any, are needed to the rules regulating the sale of such securities.
6. *Proficiency:* Officers, directors and salespersons of the dealer must satisfy normal proficiency requirements, which will be set out by the applicable securities commission.
7. *Premises and Disclosure:* The dealer must carry on its business in such a way that it is made clear to clients that the business of the dealer and the FI are separate and distinct. Separate premises within a branch are not required, although adequate disclosure of the distinction must be made to customers of the FI.

   The disclosure must advise clients that the dealer is a separate corporate entity from the FI and that the investment is not insured by the CDIC or any other government deposit insurer, is not guaranteed in whole or part by the FI, and is subject to fluctuations in market value. This disclosure must be printed in bold face type and must appear on the following documents:

   - *Fund prospectuses:* The disclosure must be contained in the body of prospectuses; on renewals, the disclosure must appear on the face page;
   - *Subscription or order forms:* If these forms are used (e.g., order forms may not be required for processing telephone transactions) then disclosure must appear on them;
   - *Confirmation slips*;
   - *Promotional material:* The disclosure must appear on all promotional material appearing or handed out in any branch of the FI.

Review the on-line summary or checklist associated with this section.

The FI may lend money to a client in order to facilitate the purchase of mutual fund securities sold by the dealer. The dealer must disclose to the client that the full amount of the loan must be repaid even if the value of the mutual fund securities (purchased with the loan) decline in value. Note: The Nova Scotia provincial securities administrator may require further details of such a loan.

© CSI GLOBAL EDUCATION INC. (2008)

SUMMARY

After reading this chapter, you should be able to:

1. Define a mutual fund and describe the advantages and disadvantages of investing in mutual funds.
   - A mutual fund is an investment vehicle operated by an investment company that pools contributions from investors and invests these proceeds in a variety of securities, including stocks, bonds and money market instruments. A professional money manager manages the fund and follows a particular investing style.
   - Contributions from investors are pooled and invested in various asset classes according to the fund's policies and objectives.
   - Individuals that contribute money become unitholders in the fund and share in the income, gains, losses and expenses the fund incurs in proportion to the number of units that they own.
   - Mutual fund units are redeemable on demand at the fund's current net asset value per share (NAVPS), which depends on the market value of the fund's portfolio of securities at that time.
   - Advantages of mutual funds include low-cost professional management, diversification, transferability, variety of purchase and redemption plans, liquidity, ease of estate planning, and eligibility for margin and as loan collateral.
   - Disadvantages of mutual funds include costs, unsuitability as a short-term investment and/or emergency cash reserve, fallibility of professional management and tax complications.
2. Compare and contrast mutual fund trusts and mutual fund corporations, explain and calculate how mutual fund units are priced, calculate a fund's NAVPS, and analyze the impacts of charges associated with mutual funds.
   - An open-end trust does not incur tax liability. Any income flows through to the unitholder to be taxed in the hands of the holder based on the type of income the fund generates.
   - Mutual funds may also be set up as federal or provincial corporations and can be eligible for a special tax rate. This structure requires the holdings to be mainly a diversified portfolio of securities, and income must be derived primarily from capital gains, interest, and dividends generated by those securities.
   - The corporation distributes income through dividends that are taxed in the hands of the unitholder, which allows the corporation to avoid paying taxes on income.
   - Mutual fund units are purchased directly from the fund company, usually through a distributor, and are sold back to the fund when redeemed.
   - The offering price is the net asset value per share and is the price an investor pays for a unit. This price is based on the NAVPS at the close of business on the day an order is placed.
   - The NAVPS is calculated as:

$$\frac{\text{Total Assets} - \text{Total Liabilities}}{\text{Total Number of Units}}$$

© CSI GLOBAL EDUCATION INC. (2008)

- NAVPS is the amount a fund's unitholders would receive for each share if the fund were to sell its entire portfolio of investments at market value, collect all receivables, pay all liabilities, and distribute what is left to its unitholders.
- The redemption price is the price a shareholder receives when he or she redeems units, and is also based on the NAVPS.
- Purchases and redemptions can be subject to a range of fees that differ from fund to fund.
  - A front-end load is a percentage of the purchase price paid to a distributor or fund company at the time of purchase.
  - No-load funds are sold with low to no direct percentage selling charges; however, an administration fee may be charged for purchase and/or redemption.
  - Back-end load funds levy a fee at redemption, also referred to as a redemption charge or deferred sales charge. The fee may be based on the original contribution to the fund or on the net asset value at the time of redemption, and it may decline the longer an investor holds a fund.

3. Describe the mutual fund regulatory environment and the disclosure documents necessary to satisfy provincial requirements, identify mutual fund registration requirements, and discuss restrictions that sellers of mutual funds must observe.

   - The Mutual Fund Dealers Association (MFDA) is the industry's self-regulatory organization (SRO) for the distribution of mutual funds. In Québec, the mutual fund industry is the responsibility of the Autorité des marchés financiers and the Chambre de la sécurité financière.
   - The regulation of Canadian mutual funds falls under the jurisdiction of the securities act of each province.
   - National Instrument 81-101 regulates mutual fund prospectus disclosure. NI 81-102 and a companion policy contain requirements and guidelines for the distribution and advertising of mutual funds.
   - Because mutual funds are in a continuous state of primary distribution, investors purchasing a mutual fund for the first time must be provided with the simplified prospectus, which is a shortened form of a full prospectus that contains certain specific components. Investors also need to receive any other information required by the province.
   - Mutual fund managers, distributors and sales personnel must be registered with the securities commissions in all provinces in which they operate (and with the Autorité des marchés financiers if they operate in Québec).
   - Mutual fund sales registration must be renewed annually. Registration is subject to employment status with a registered dealer and has the requirement of notification to the relevant administrator, within time limits, of any changes in specific information.
   - The fund manager provides day-to-day supervision of the fund's investment portfolio and must observe a number of guidelines for securities trading as specified in the fund's charter and prospectus, and the constraints imposed by the securities commissions.
   - Prohibited sales practices include, among others, quoting a future price, making an offer to repurchase, selling without a licence, advertising registration, promising a future price, selling from one province into another, and selling unqualified securities.
   - There are specific rules that apply to the distribution of mutual funds by financial institutions (such as banks, trust companies, insurance companies, and loan companies).

Now that you've completed this chapter and the on-line activities, complete this post-test.

© CSI GLOBAL EDUCATION INC. (2008)

Chapter 18

Mutual Funds: Types and Features

© CSI GLOBAL EDUCATION INC. (2008)

18

Mutual Funds: Types and Features

CHAPTER OUTLINE

© CSI GLOBAL EDUCATION INC. (2008)

LEARNING OBJECTIVES

By the end of this chapter, you should be able to:

1. Describe the types of mutual funds and discuss the risk-return trade-off of investing in each type.
2. Evaluate mutual fund management styles.
3. Calculate the redemption/selling price of a mutual fund, explain the tax consequences of redemptions, and describe the four types of withdrawal plans and the appropriate use of each plan for an investor.
4. Describe how mutual fund performance is measured and how the comparative performance of mutual funds is determined.

CHOOSING MUTUAL FUNDS

There are myriad choices for mutual fund investors and many factors to consider when selecting one or more funds for investment. Mutual funds can be categorized based on the types of investments held in the portfolio, the level of risk and reward, and how the fund is managed. It is important to understand the various categories and the implications of choosing a particular mutual fund, including the available methods of withdrawal and the tax implications.

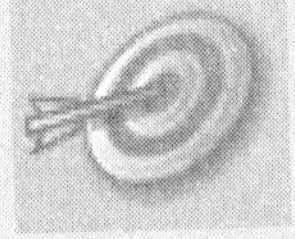

In the on-line Learning Guide for this module, complete the Getting Started activity.

Of course, both before and after an investor chooses a mutual fund, assessing that fund's performance is important. There a number of ways to measure fund performance and a number of different benchmarks. In Canada there are regulations about performance measures to help investors make comparisons between similar mutual fund investments.

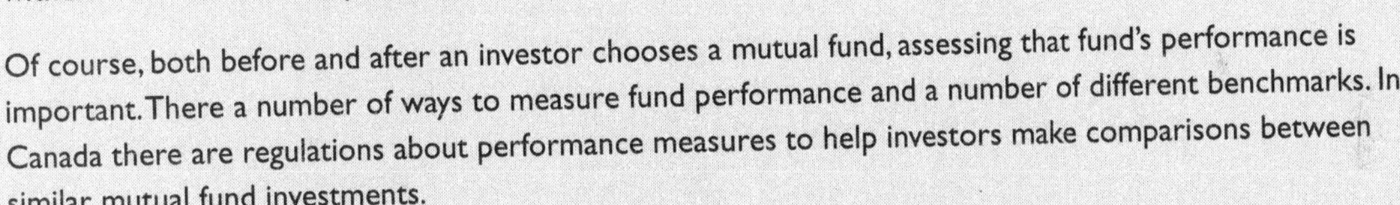

There are literally thousands of funds to choose from. Understanding the risk and return characteristics of the different types of funds is important and necessary to make an intelligent, well-informed and effective decision on the type of mutual fund to invest in.

© CSI GLOBAL EDUCATION INC. (2008)

KEY TERMS

Adjusted cost base
Asset allocation fund
Balanced fund
Bond fund
Closet indexing
Daily valuation method
Dividend fund
Equity fund
Fixed-dollar withdrawal plan
Fixed-period withdrawal plan
Index fund
Indexing
Modified Dietz method
Mortgage fund
Peer group
Ratio withdrawal plan
Real estate fund
Socially responsible fund
Systematic withdrawal plan
T3 Form
T5 Form
Time-weighted rate of return (TWRR)

© CSI GLOBAL EDUCATION INC. (2008)

TYPES OF MUTUAL FUNDS

Mutual funds offer different risks and rewards to investors and, as explained earlier, mutual fund salespersons have a fiduciary obligation to match the appropriate fund with the needs of their clients.

Mutual funds are distinguished by their basic investment policy or by the kind of assets they hold. The Investment Funds Standards Committee (IFSC) classifies Canadian domiciled mutual funds into 34 categories within four broad groups:

- Cash and equivalent funds
- Fixed-income funds
- Balanced funds
- Equity funds

To highlight the diversity of funds available in the marketplace, Table 18.1 shows the net assets invested in the different mutual funds and compares the years 2006 and 2007.

TABLE 18.1 NET ASSETS BY FUND TYPE

(all amounts in billions of dollars)

Fund Type	2007	2006	Year-to-Year Change (%)
Canadian Balanced	154.8	161.1	–3.9
Canadian Equity	145.3	120.2	20.9
Global and International Equity	98.0	98.6	–0.6
Canadian Bond & Income	48.8	65.7	–25.7
Foreign Bond & Income	7.3	5.4	35.2
Canadian Dividend & Income	37.2	29.4	26.5
U.S. Equity	22.8	25.8	–11.6
Canadian Money Market	51.2	41.9	22.2
U.S. Money Market	3.6	2.1	71.4

Source: Investment Funds Institute of Canada website.

Cash and Equivalent Funds

As their name implies, these funds invest in near-cash securities or money market instruments, such as Treasury bills, bankers' acceptances, high-quality corporate paper and short-term bonds. Government obligations may have a maximum maturity of 25 months, otherwise the maximum is 13 months for corporate debt securities. Funds in this category include:

- Canadian money market
- U.S. money market

© CSI GLOBAL EDUCATION INC. (2008)

Money market funds add liquidity to a portfolio and provide a moderate level of income and safety of principal. They are considered the least risky type of mutual fund.

A feature of these funds is a constant share or unit value, often $10. To keep NAVPS constant, the net income of the fund is calculated daily and credited to unitholders. The earned interest is paid out as cash or reinvested in additional shares on a monthly (or sometimes a quarterly) basis.

While risk is low, money market funds, as is true of all mutual funds, are not guaranteed. While fund managers try to maintain a stable NAVPS, rapid increases in interest rates could reduce the value of the shares or units. Money market funds are therefore subject to interest rate risk.

Distributions received from a money market fund are taxable as interest income when held outside of a registered plan. Investors would add the interest to their income and pay taxes at their marginal rate.

Fixed-Income Funds

Fixed-income funds are designed to provide a steady stream of income rather than capital appreciation. The main funds in this category are mortgage and bond funds and include:

- Canadian bond
- Canadian income trust
- High-yield bond
- Canadian short-term bond and mortgage
- Foreign bond

BOND FUNDS

Bond funds are designed to generate a steady stream of income in combination with the safety of principal. Bond funds invest primarily in good-quality, high-yielding government and corporate debt securities. Their degree of volatility is related to the degree of interest rate fluctuation, but fund managers will attempt to change the term to maturity, or duration, of the portfolio and the mix of low- and high-coupon bonds to compensate for changes in interest rates.

Interest rate volatility is the main risk associated with this type of fund. If the fund also invests in corporate bonds, the fund would also be exposed to default risk.

The primary source of returns from non-registered bond funds is in the form of interest income. The mutual fund investor may also receive a capital gain if the fund sells some of its bonds at a profit.

Balanced Funds

Balanced funds invest in both stocks and bonds to provide a mix of income and capital growth. These funds offer diversification, but unless the manager adds value by shifting investment proportions in anticipation of market conditions, investors might as well develop their own balanced portfolio by putting their money into more than one fund. Funds covered in this category include:

- Canadian balanced
- Canadian income balanced
- Global balanced and asset allocation
- Canadian tactical asset allocation

© CSI GLOBAL EDUCATION INC. (2008)

The main investment objective of balanced funds is to provide a "balanced" mixture of safety, income and capital appreciation. These objectives are sought through a portfolio of fixed-income securities for stability and income, plus a broadly diversified group of common stock holdings for diversification, dividend income and growth potential. The balance between defensive and aggressive security holdings is rarely 50-50. Rather, managers of balanced funds adjust the percentage of each part of the total portfolio in accordance with current market conditions and future expectations. In most cases, the prospectus specifies the fund's minimum and maximum weighting for each asset class. For example, a balanced fund may specify a weighting of 60% equity and 40% fixed income.

Asset allocation funds have objectives similar to balanced funds, but they differ from balanced funds in that they typically do not have to hold a specified minimum percentage of the fund in any class of investment. The portfolio manager has great freedom to shift the portfolio weighting among equity, money market and fixed-income securities as the economy moves through the different stages of the business cycle.

In addition to asset allocation funds, some firms offer asset allocation services. These services shift an investor's funds among a family of funds (Canadian equity, U.S. equity, bond, dividend, etc.). In some cases, the allocation service is personalized in the sense that the allocation is based on the personal circumstances and investment objectives of each investor.

An investor in balanced and asset allocation funds would be subject to market and interest rate risk, depending on the split between fixed-income and equity securities. Likewise, the tax implications are the same. The investor may receive a combination of interest, dividends and capital gains.

Equity Funds

Equity funds are the most popular type of fund and therefore have the most classifications:

- Canadian and U.S. equity
- Canadian dividend
- Canadian and U.S. small- and mid-cap equity
- International equity
- European equity
- Emerging markets equity
- Asia/Pacific rim equity
- Japanese equity

The main investment objective of equity funds is long-term capital growth. The fund manager invests primarily in the common shares of publicly traded companies. Short-term notes or other fixed-income securities may be purchased from time to time in limited amounts for liquidity and, occasionally, income. The bulk of assets, however, are in common shares in the pursuit of capital gains. Because common share prices are typically more volatile than other types of securities, prices of equity funds tend to fluctuate more widely than those funds previously mentioned, and are therefore considered riskier.

There are equity funds that invest entirely in the Canadian market and more specialized funds that invest in a variety of markets outside of Canada, including the United States, Europe, Asia, and other emerging countries. These funds are designed to benefit from the perceived advantage of diversifying into markets that offer the greatest opportunity for growth on a global basis.

© CSI GLOBAL EDUCATION INC. (2008)

Accordingly, investments in markets outside of Canada are subject to foreign exchange rate risk. As with common stocks, equity funds range greatly in degree of risk and growth potential. These funds are all subject to market risk. Some equity funds are broadly diversified holdings of blue chip income-yielding common shares and may, therefore, be classified at the conservative end of the equity fund scale. Other equity funds adopt a slightly more aggressive investment stance, for example, investing in young growing companies with an objective of above-average growth of capital. Other equity funds are of a more speculative nature – aggressively seeking capital gains at the sacrifice of safety and income by investing in certain sectors of the market (precious metals, health care, biotechnology) or certain geographical locations (China, Latin America, Japan).

The tax implications are the same as for any fund that holds equity securities. The distributions will be in the form of capital gains and dividends and are taxed accordingly.

SMALL-CAP AND MID-CAP EQUITY FUNDS

Canadian equity funds that limit investments to companies with capitalization below those of the hundred largest Canadian companies are considered to be small- to mid-cap Canadian equity funds. Because smaller companies are considered to have higher potential for growth than large, well-established ones, these funds offer opportunities that theoretically differ from general Canadian equity funds. Small-cap companies generally have a market capitalization of $250 million to $1 billion and mid-caps are in the range of $1 billion to $9 billion. These companies do not usually pay dividends, as they are young and reinvest profits into expansion.

Along with the potential for greater gains, there is more volatility than is typically experienced with an equity fund that invests in mature blue chip equities. Distributions in this type of fund will be primarily in the form of capital gains.

DIVIDEND FUNDS

Canadian dividend funds provide tax-advantaged income with some possibility of capital appreciation. Dividend funds invest in preferred shares as well as high-quality common shares that have a history of consistently paying dividends. The income from these funds is in the form of dividends, which have the tax advantage of receiving the dividend tax credit. There may be capital gains as well.

The price changes that lead to capital gains or losses on dividend funds are driven by both changes in interest rates (interest rate risk) and general market trends (market risk). Price changes in the preferred share component of the fund are driven by interest rate changes, while general upward or downward movements in the stock market most heavily affect the common share component. Recall that preferred shares rank ahead of the common shares but below bondholders, in the event of bankruptcy or insolvency. Consequently, dividend funds are considered riskier than bond funds, but less risky than equity funds.

Specialty and Sector Funds

Not all funds fit easily into one of the above categories. Some funds are more narrowly focused and concentrate their assets into one main area – a specific industry or region, for example. Funds in this category may include:

- Science and technology
- Natural resources
- Precious metals

© CSI GLOBAL EDUCATION INC. (2008)

- Real estate
- Financial services
- Health care
- Socially responsible (or ethical)

This type of equity fund seeks capital gains and is willing to forgo broad market diversification in the hope of achieving above-average returns. Because of their narrower investment focus, these funds often carry substantial risk due to the concentration of their assets in just one area.

While still offering some diversification, these funds are more vulnerable to swings in the industry in which they are specializing or, if they have a portfolio of foreign securities, in currency values. Many, but not all, tend to be more speculative than most types of equity funds.

REAL ESTATE FUNDS

Real estate funds invest in income-producing real property in order to achieve long-term growth through capital appreciation and the reinvestment of income. The valuation of real estate funds is done infrequently (monthly or quarterly) and is based on appraisals of the properties in the portfolio. Real estate funds are less liquid than other types of funds and may require investors to give advance notice of redemption. During periods of weak real estate markets, several of these funds have been forced to suspend redemptions and others have converted from open-end to closed-end funds in an attempt to deal with the problem of redemptions.

SOCIALLY RESPONSIBLE OR ETHICAL FUNDS

Socially responsible funds (or ethical funds) invest only in companies that meet the criteria of certain moral guidelines or beliefs. These criteria vary from fund to fund. One ethical fund may avoid investing in companies that profit from tobacco, alcohol or armaments, while another fund may invest according to certain religious beliefs.

Index Funds

An index fund sets out to match the performance of a broad market index, such as the S&P/TSX Composite Index for an equity index fund or the DEX Universe Bond Index for a bond index fund. The fund manager invests in the securities that make up the index they imitate, in the same proportion that these securities are weighted in the index. For example, if the chosen index is the S&P/TSX Composite Index and the Bank of Montreal represents 0.75% of the Index, the index fund must include 0.75% of Bank of Montreal stock.

Overall, the management fees associated with index funds are usually lower than those of other equity or bond funds. As a result, investing in an index fund represents a low-cost way for an investor to pursue a passive investment strategy.

The investment objective of an equity index fund is to provide long-term growth of capital. Equity index funds are subject to market risk because the portfolio is tied to the performance of the market. With a bond index fund, the main risk is interest rate risk.

The distributions will depend on the type of index being matched. A fund matching a bond index will obviously have primarily interest income, with some capital gains. An index fund matching an equity index may have dividend and capital gains distributions.

© CSI GLOBAL EDUCATION INC. (2008)

Comparing Fund Types

As the discussion above highlights, the mutual fund industry has created a variety of funds designed to meet the diverse needs of the Canadian investing public. Because each fund type or group will hold different types of securities and will pursue different investment objectives, the risk and return between the various funds will also differ.

Figure 18.1 illustrates the risk-return trade-off between the different types of mutual funds.

FIGURE 18.1 RISK AND RETURN BETWEEN DIFFERENT TYPES FO MUTUAL FUNDS

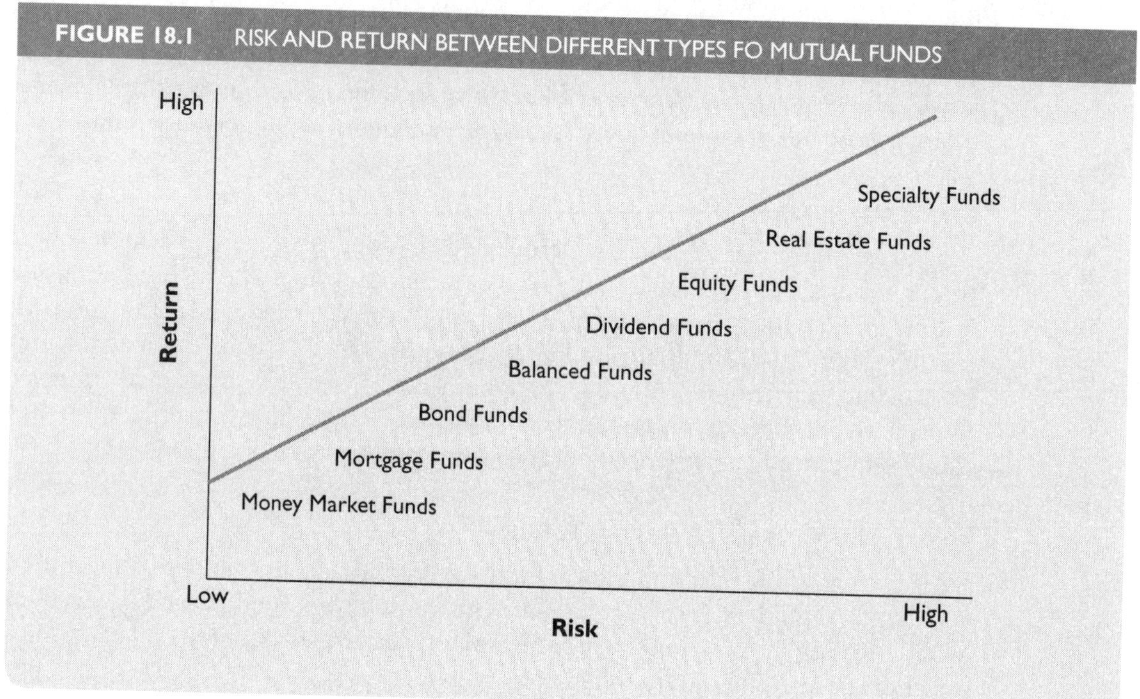

Complete the on-line activity associated with this section.

FUND MANAGEMENT STYLES

The absolute and relative return of a portfolio can be attributed first to the choice of asset class, and second to the style in which it is managed. Understanding investment styles is important in measuring fund performance. Managers employing a particular strategy may outperform or underperform others using a different strategy over the same periods.

Management style can be divided into two broad categories: passive and active. A **passive investment strategy** involves some form of indexing to a market or customized benchmark. In contrast, most equity styles are active. Active managers try to outperform the market benchmarks. There are many different **active investment** styles. At any one time, several of these styles may be in favour and others may be out of favour. Overall, funds that follow a passive strategy generally report lower management expense ratios (MERs) while funds that pursue an active strategy typically report higher MERs.

Active management may involve individual company selection, or over-weighting in favoured segments of industry sectors, or country selection for regional funds. In choosing to take an active approach, advisors may diversify their clients' portfolios by growth, value or other management style. This same strategy holds true with mutual funds. To diversify a client's portfolio, an advisor

© CSI GLOBAL EDUCATION INC. (2008)

may recommend both a value mutual fund and a growth mutual fund. In this way, volatility is reduced, and there continues to be an opportunity for higher returns than those made by the market as a whole.

The various equity and fixed-income manager styles were described in Chapter 16, and these styles also apply to mutual funds. We discuss two other mutual fund manager styles below.

Indexing and Closet Indexing

Indexing represents a passive style of investing that attempts to buy securities that constitute or closely replicate the performance of a market benchmark such as the S&P/TSX Composite Index or the S&P 500 Composite Index. The indexing style is a low-cost, long-term, buy-and-hold strategy. There is no need to conduct individual securities analysis. Many index funds, particularly those that provide foreign exposure, rely on a combination of stock index futures and Canadian treasury bills.

Closet indexing does not replicate the market exactly, but sticks fairly closely to the market weightings by industry sector, by country or region, or by average market capitalization. Some active managers are closet indexers. This can be determined by how closely their returns, their volatility and their average market capitalization correspond to the index as a whole.

The concept of index funds is generally simpler for investors to understand than other management styles. These funds simply buy the same stocks as the index. Because they do not need analysts for stock selection, management fees are lower than for actively managed funds. A final advantage is that indexing makes for low portfolio turnover, which is an advantage for taxable accounts.

The indexing style, being essentially a strategy to mirror the market, represents a loss of opportunity to outperform it. Also, after the payment of fees and expenses, index mutual funds or indexed segregated funds return somewhat less than the market benchmark in the long term. Another disadvantage of this style is that distributions in the form of derivative-based income are taxable as income, rather than as capital gains.

Multi-Manager

In multi-manager funds, the portfolio is divided into two or more portions that are managed separately, using different investment styles. For example, the fund may be split between a bottomup value manager, a bottom-up growth manager, and a top-down manager who uses a blend of styles to manage part of the portfolio. The rationale for this approach is that it is difficult or impossible to predict which style will outperform the others, so it is preferable to take a long-term strategic approach. At the same time, since all the portfolios are actively managed, the fund has the potential to outperform the broader market.

The multi-manager style features lower volatility than funds with single styles. It is less risky than funds managed in one single style because it avoids making a "bet" on any particular strategy. It should work well at most stages of the economic or stock market cycle and is unlikely to be one of the biggest losers in its category in a market slump.

A potential drawback is that weak performance by one manager may offset strong performance by another, and it is often difficult to analyze the performance of individual managers or manager firms within the fund. Also, the higher costs associated with multiple managers may be reflected in larger management fees and expenses.

© CSI GLOBAL EDUCATION INC. (2008)

REDEEMING MUTUAL FUND UNITS OR SHARES

After acquiring shares in a mutual fund, the investor may wish to dispose of his or her shares or units and use the proceeds. The mechanics of disposing of fund units are fairly straightforward. The client contacts his/her advisor (or discount brokerage) and makes a request to sell or redeem fund units. The broker then places the trade request with the fund, or the fund's distributor. At the end of the valuation day, the fund calculates the net asset value and the proceeds are sent to the investor.

Most funds also offer the investor a variety of methods of receiving funds if the investor does not want to redeem a specific number of shares or units.

Recall that most funds do not issue physical share or unit certificates. They operate a book-based system where the fund's transfer agent or custodian keeps track of the number of shares owned. When an investor wishes to sell the shares or units, the transfer agent knows the exact extent of the investor's holdings. Where an investor has taken delivery of the certificates, most mutual funds require that the certificates be delivered prior to their liquidation.

Tax Consequences

Mutual funds redeem their shares on request at a price that is equal to the fund's NAVPS. If there are no back-end load charges, the investor would receive the NAVPS. If there were back-end load charges or deferred sales charges, the investor would receive NAVPS less the sales commission. Mutual funds can generate taxable income in a couple of ways:

Through the distribution of interest income, dividends and capital gains realized by the fund
Through any capital gains realized when the fund is eventually sold

ANNUAL DISTRIBUTIONS

When mutual funds are held outside a registered plan (such as an RRSP or RRIF), the unitholder of an unincorporated fund is sent a **T3 form** and a shareholder is sent a **T5 form** by the respective funds. This form reports the types of income distributed that year – foreign income and Canadian interest, dividends and capital gains, including dividends that have been reinvested. Each is taxed at the fund holder's personal rate in the year received.

For example, an investor purchases an equity mutual fund for $11 per share and in each of the next five years receives $1 in annual distributions, composed of $0.50 in dividends and $0.50 in distributed capital gains. Each year the investor would receive a T5 from the fund indicating that the investor would have to report to the Canada Revenue Agency an additional $1 in income. The T5 may indicate offsetting dividend tax credits (from dividends earned from taxable Canadian corporations).

It is sometimes difficult for mutual fund clients to understand why they have to declare capital gains, when they have not sold any of their funds. There is, however, a simple explanation. The fund manager buys and sells stocks throughout the year for the mutual fund. If the fund manager sells a stock for more than it was bought, a capital gain results. It is this capital gain that is passed on to the mutual fund holder. Unfortunately, capital losses that arise when selling a stock for less than it was bought cannot be passed on to the mutual fund holder. The losses are held in the fund and may, however, be used to offset capital gains in subsequent years.

© CSI GLOBAL EDUCATION INC. (2008)

DISTRIBUTIONS TRIGGERING UNEXPECTED TAXES

During the year a mutual fund will generate capital gains and losses when it sells securities held in the fund. Capital gains are distributed to the fund investors just as interest and dividends are distributed. If the distribution of capital gains is carried out only at year end, it can pose a problem for investors who purchase a fund close to the year end.

Consider an investor who purchased an equity mutual fund through a non-registered account on December 1 at a NAVPS of $30. This fund had a very good year and earned capital gains of $6 per share. These capital gains are distributed to the investors at the end of December either as reinvested shares or as cash. As is the case with all distributions, this caused the NAVPS to fall by the amount of the distribution, to $24. At first glance, one might think that the investor is just as well off, as the new NAVPS plus the $6 distribution equals the original NAVPS of $30. Unfortunately, the $6 distribution is taxable in the hands of the new investor, even though the $6 was earned over the course of the full year. For this reason, some financial advisors caution investors against buying a mutual fund just prior to the year end without first checking with the fund sponsor to determine if a capital gains distribution is pending. Exhibit 18.1 provides an example.

EXHIBIT 18.1 DISTRIBUTIONS AND TAXES

An investor with a marginal tax rate of 40% purchases a mutual fund with a NAVPS of $30.The portfolio is valued at $30.The fund distributes $6 as a capital gains dividend or distribution.The value of the investor's portfolio after the distribution and the tax consequences would be:

Value of portfolio before distribution:	$30.00
Value of portfolio after distribution:	
NAVPS	$24.00
Cash or Reinvested Dividends	$ 6.00
	$30.00

Tax Consequences:

Assuming that the $6 was a net capital gain: 50% × $6.00 × 40%
= $1.20 Taxes Payable

Note: Even though the fund may call this distribution a "dividend" it is simply a distribution of capital gains. No dividend tax credit would apply.

CAPITAL GAINS

When a fund holder redeems the shares or units of the fund itself, the transaction is considered a disposition for tax purposes, possibly giving rise to either a capital gain or a capital loss. Only 50% of net capital gains (total capital gains less total capital losses) is added to the investor's income and taxed at their marginal rate.

Suppose a mutual fund shareholder bought shares in a fund at a NAVPS of $11 and later sells the fund shares at a NAVPS of $16, generating a capital gain of $5 on the sale. The investor would have to report an additional $2.50 in income for the year (50% × $5 capital gain). This capital gain is not shown on the fund's T5, as this was not a fund transaction.

© CSI GLOBAL EDUCATION INC. (2008)

ADJUSTING THE COST BASE

A potential problem may arise when an investor chooses to reinvest fund income automatically in additional non-registered fund units. The complication arises when the fund is sold and capital gains must be calculated on the difference between the original purchase price and the sale price. The total sale price of the fund will include the original units purchased plus those units purchased over time through periodic reinvestment of fund income. This mix of original and subsequent units can make it difficult to calculate the **adjusted cost base** of the investment in the fund. If careful records have not been kept, the investor could be taxed twice on the same income. Many investment funds provide this information on quarterly or annual statements. If these statements are not kept, it may be very time consuming to attempt to reconstruct the adjusted cost base of the investment.

For example, consider the case where an investor buys $10,000 of fund units. Over time, annual income is distributed and tax is paid on it, but the investor chooses to reinvest the income in additional fund units. After a number of years, the total value of the portfolio rises to $18,000 and the investor decides to sell the fund. A careless investor might assume that a capital gain of $8,000 has been incurred. This would be incorrect, as the $8,000 increase is actually made up of two factors: the reinvestment of income (upon which the investor has already paid taxes) and a capital gain. The portion of the increase due to reinvestment must be added to the original investment of $10,000 to come up with the correct adjusted cost base for calculating the capital gain. If, for example, the investor had received a total of $3,500 in reinvested dividends over the course of the holding period, the adjusted cost base would be $13,500 (the original $10,000 plus the $3,500 in dividends that have already been taxed). The capital gain is then $4,500, not $8,000.

Reinvesting Distributions

Many funds will, unless otherwise advised, automatically reinvest distributions into new shares of the fund at the prevailing net asset value without a sales charge on the shares purchased. Most funds also have provisions for shareholders to switch from cash dividends to dividend reinvestment, and vice versa.

The reaction of the NAVPS to a distribution of funds is similar to that of a stock the day it begins to trade ex-dividend. The NAVPS will fall by an amount proportionate to the dividend. Since most investors receive their dividends in the form of more units rather than cash, the net result of the distribution is that the investor owns more units, but the units are each worth less.

For example, the NAVPS of a fund is $9.00 the day before a dividend distribution. The fund decides to pay a dividend of $0.90 per unit. After the distribution is made, the NAVPS of the fund will fall by $0.90 to $8.10. As Table 18.2 shows, if this fund had 1,000,000 units outstanding, the NAVPS before the distribution would be $9,000,000 ÷ 1,000,000 = $9.00. The NAVPS after the distribution would be $8,100,000 ÷ 1,000,000 = $8.10.

© CSI GLOBAL EDUCATION INC. (2008)

TABLE 18.2 IMPACT OF A DISTRIBUTION ON TOTAL NET ASSETS

	Before Distribution	After Distribution	When Distributions Are Reinvested
Assets			
Portfolio	$8,075,000	$8,075,000	$8,075,000
Cash	950,000	50,000*	950,000
Liabilities			
Expenses	(25,000)	(25,000)	(25,000)
Total Net Assets	**$9,000,000**	**$8,100,000**	**$9,000,000**

* Distributions payable: $950,000 cash – ($0.90 dividend × 1,000,000 units outstanding).

Because the investors receive their distribution in new units, the fund now has 1,111,111.11 units worth $8.10 each ($900,000 ÷ $8.10 = 111,111.11 plus the original 1,000,000 units). Total fund assets are still $9,000,000. The $900,000 never actually leaves the company, but is reinvested in the fund.

What impact does this have on the individual investor? As stated above, the investor ends up with more units worth less each. The net effect is that the investor's portfolio is worth the same amount. Table 18.3 illustrates this. Assume that the investor owned 1,000 units of the fund. The investor would receive a distribution worth $900.00 (1,000 units × $0.90). The distribution is invested into new units. These new units now have a NAVPS of $8.10. The investor would receive $900 ÷ $8.10 = 111.11 units. The investor now has a total of 1,111.11 units (1,000 + 111.11).

TABLE 18.3 IMPACT OF DISTRIBUTION ON VALUE OF INVESTMENT

	Before Distribution	After Distribution
1,000 units × $9.00	$9,000	
1,111.11 × $8.10		$9,000

Types of Withdrawal Plans

A mutual fund's shareholders have a continual right to withdraw their investment in the fund simply by making the request to the fund itself and receiving in return the dollar amount of their net asset value. This characteristic is known as the **right of redemption** and it is the hallmark of mutual funds.

To help investors who need periodic income, and who wish to stay invested within the fund, many funds offer one or more systematic withdrawal plans. In simple terms, instead of withdrawing all the money in a mutual fund, the investor instructs the fund to pay out part of the capital invested plus distributions over a period of time. Withdrawals may be arranged monthly, quarterly or at other predetermined intervals.

© CSI GLOBAL EDUCATION INC. (2008)

If the fund invests its assets successfully and its portfolio increases in value, the increased worth of the fund's shares helps offset the reduction of principal resulting from the planned withdrawal over the specified period. However, the investor's capital will shrink if the net asset value of the fund does not increase more than the take-out. The possibility that the investor's entire investment will be extinguished by payouts is a real one and must be emphasized to investors contemplating withdrawal plans.

RATIO WITHDRAWAL PLAN

Here the investor receives an annual income from the fund by redeeming a specified percentage of fund holdings each year. The percentage chosen for redemption usually falls between 4% and 10% a year depending on the amount of income the investor requires. Obviously, the higher the percentage, the more rapid the rate of depletion of the investor's original investment. And, since the payout is a set percentage of the value of the fund, the amounts will vary each time.

Table 18.4 shows an example of a ratio withdrawal plan. We have assumed in this example, and each of the examples that follow, that the portfolio will grow by a steady 8% per year. In this example, we have also assumed that the investor wishes to withdraw 10% at the beginning of each year.

TABLE 18.4 RATIO WITHDRAWAL PLAN

The value of each withdrawal will vary from year to year.

	Value at Beginning of Year				Value of Withdrawal					Value at End of Year
Year 1	$100,000	×	10%	=	$10,000	($90,000	×	1.08	=	97,200)
Year 2	$97,200	×	10%	=	$9,720	($87,480	×	1.08	=	94,478)
Year 3	$94,478	×	10%	=	$9,448	($85,030	×	1.08	=	91,833)
Year 4	$91,833	×	10%	=	$9,183	($82,650	×	1.08	=	89,262)
Year 5	$89,262	×	10%	=	$8,926	($80,336	×	1.08	=	86,763)

FIXED-DOLLAR WITHDRAWAL PLAN

This plan is similar to a ratio withdrawal plan except that the fund holder chooses a specified dollar amount to be withdrawn on a monthly or quarterly basis. Funds offering this type of plan often require that withdrawals be in "round amounts" (e.g., $50 or $100, etc.). If the investor's fixed withdrawals are greater than the growth of the fund, the investor will encroach upon the principal.

Table 18.5 shows an example of a fixed-dollar withdrawal plan.

© CSI GLOBAL EDUCATION INC. (2008)

TABLE 18.5 FIXED-DOLLAR WITHDRAWAL PLAN

In this case, a constant or fixed amount of $10,000 is withdrawn at the beginning of each year.

	Value at Beginning of Year		Value of Withdrawal					Value at End of Year
Year 1	$100,000	–	$10,000	($90,000	×	1.08	=	$97,200)
Year 2	$97,200	–	$10,000	($87,200	×	1.08	=	$94,176)
Year 3	$94,176	–	$10,000	($84,176	×	1.08	=	$90,910)
Year 4	$90,910	–	$10,000	($80,910	×	1.08	=	$87,383)
Year 5	$87,383	–	$10,000	($77,383	×	1.08	=	$83,574)

When amounts withdrawn are greater than the increases in the portfolio, the principal can be encroached upon and eventually may reach zero.

FIXED-PERIOD WITHDRAWAL PLAN

Here a specified amount is withdrawn over a pre-determined period of time with the intent that all capital will be exhausted when the plan ends. For example, if an investor wished to collapse a plan over five years, he would withdraw: 1/5 in year one, 1/4 in year two, 1/3 in year three, 1/2 in year four and 100% in the final year.

Table 18.6 shows an example of a fixed-period withdrawal plan.

TABLE 18.6 FIXED-PERIOD WITHDRAWAL PLAN

In this case, a specific fraction is withdrawn at the beginning of each year.

	Value at Beginning of Year				Value of Withdrawal					Value at End of Year
Year 1	$100,000	×	1/5	=	$20,000	($80,000	×	1.08	=	86,400)
Year 2	$86,400	×	1/4	=	$21,600	($64,800	×	1.08	=	69,984)
Year 3	$69,984	×	1/3	=	$23,328	($46,656	×	1.08	=	50,388)
Year 4	$50,388	×	1/2	=	$25,194	($25,194	×	1.08	=	27,209)
Year 5	$27,209	×	100%	=	$27,209					$0

The above assumes that the plan will be collapsed over five years.

LIFE EXPECTANCY–ADJUSTED WITHDRAWAL PLAN

This type of plan is a variation of a fixed-period withdrawal plan. Payments to the fund holder are designed to deplete the entire investment by the end of the plan, while providing as high an

© CSI GLOBAL EDUCATION INC. (2008)

income as possible during the fund holder's expected lifetime. However, to accomplish this, the amount withdrawn on each date is based on periods of time, which are continually readjusted to the changing life expectancy of the plan holder, taken from mortality tables. Thus, the amounts withdrawn vary in relation to the amount of capital remaining in the plan and the plan holder's revised life expectancy.

Table 18.7 shows an example of a life expectancy–adjusted withdrawal plan.

TABLE 18.7 LIFE EXPECTANCY–ADJUSTED WITHDRAWAL PLAN

Using actuarial tables it is assumed that the client is expected to live to age 85 and is currently age 75. Using the formula:

$$\frac{\text{Value of the Portfolio}}{\text{Life Expectancy} - \text{Current Age}}$$

	Value at Beginning of Year			Value of Withdrawal					Value at End of Year
Year 1	$100,000	$\frac{\$100{,}000}{85 - 75}$	=	$10,000	($90,000	×	1.08	=	$97,200)
Year 2	$97,200	$\frac{\$97{,}200}{85 - 76}$	=	$10,800	($86,400	×	1.08	=	$93,312)
Year 3	$93,312	$\frac{\$93{,}312}{85 - 77}$	=	$11,664	($81,648	×	1.08	=	$88,180)
Etc.									

Suspension of Redemptions

As with all rules, there are exceptions. Securities commissions require all Canadian mutual funds to make payment on redemptions within a specified time; however, redemption suspensions can be permitted. Almost all funds reserve the right to suspend or defer a shareholder's privilege to redeem shares under certain highly unusual or emergency conditions. For example, a suspension might be invoked if normal trading is suspended on securities that represent more than 50% of securities owned by the fund. Obviously, if the fund cannot determine the net asset value per share, it cannot determine the redemption price of a unit or share.

Historically, Canadian mutual funds have rarely implemented such suspensions. However, due to the events in New York City on September 11, 2001, stock exchanges throughout North America halted trading for several days. In Canada, a suspension in trading was placed on mutual funds until the markets reopened two days later. The Canadian Securities Administrators (CSA) also issued orders permitting Canadian mutual funds with significant exposure to U.S. securities to suspend redemptions until the U.S. markets resumed normal business operations.

© CSI GLOBAL EDUCATION INC. (2008)

COMPARING MUTUAL FUND PERFORMANCE

Once a mutual fund has been selected, the investor must be able to measure and evaluate the fund's performance, particularly over a certain time period. By doing so, the investor can evaluate how well the mutual fund manager has done over the evaluation period relative to the cost of management.

Performance measures include tools and techniques used to judge the historical performance of mutual funds, either in isolation or in comparison to other mutual funds. Although past performance is never a guarantee of future performance, performance measures can reveal certain historical trends or attributes that offer some insight into future performance.

Performance data is available from the mutual fund companies themselves, the websites of popular independent research firms such as Morningstar and Globe Fund, and special monthly mutual fund sections in the *National Post* and *The Globe and Mail*. In addition to their free services, Morningstar, Globe Fund and others offer more in-depth research and analysis for a fee.

Reading Mutual Fund Quotes

There are many financial sources that report the current net asset values of mutual funds on either a daily or weekly basis. *The Globe and Mail*, for example, publishes a weekly listing indicating whether the fund is load or no-load, whether it is RRSP eligible, and how it is distributed, as well as its NAVPS and the change in NAVPS. The financial press sometimes includes simple and compound rates of return, the variability (or degree of volatility) of each fund, the expense ratio, and the maximum sales or redemption charge of each fund.

A typical quotation for a mutual fund that traded in the last 52-week period would be presented as follows:

EXHIBIT 18.2 READING MUTUAL FUND QUOTATIONS

				– Friday data –			– Rate of Return –				– Weekly Data –				
High	Low	Fund	Vty	Cls	$chg	%chg	1mo	1yr	3yr	5yr	High	Low	Cls	$chg	%chg
16.63	14.50	ABC	4	16.62	-.06	-.36	4.0	6.3	10.0	7.9	16.73	16.62	16.62	.01	.06

This quotation is complex but very useful and may vary in format among financial newspaper quotation sections. This quotation shows that:

- The NAVPS of ABC Growth has traded as high as $16.73 per share and as low as $14.50 during the last 52 weeks.
- Vty is a measure of fund volatility (i.e., the variability in returns over the previous three-year period compared with other funds in this asset class). The scale is from 1 to 10. Funds with a Vty of 1 have the lowest variability in returns and funds with a Vty of 10 have the highest variability in returns.
- During the day under review, ABC closed at a NAVPS of $16.62. The fund closed down $0.06 from the previous trading day, representing a -0.36% fall over the previous day.

© CSI GLOBAL EDUCATION INC. (2008)

- ABC had a 1-month rate of return of 4%, a 1-year return of 6.3%, a 3-year return of 10% and a 5-year return of 7.9%. The rate of return assumes that all dividends have been reinvested in the fund.
- Over the previous week, ABC traded at a high of $16.73 and at a low of $16.62, finally closing at a NAVPS of $16.62 for a dollar increase of $0.01 and a percentage increase of 0.06% from the previous week.

The performance of money market funds is presented somewhat differently. Because of the relatively fixed NAVPS that these funds maintain, newspapers do not bother to report the NAVPS, but rather report each fund's current and effective yield. The current yield reports the rate of return on the fund over the most recent seven-day period expressed as an annualized percentage. The effective yield is the rate of return that would result if the current yield were compounded over a year, thereby allowing comparison with other types of compounding investments.

Investors who follow the performance of their funds in the daily paper should realize that dividends and interest earned by a fund's investments are distributed periodically. Many investors use these distributions to automatically purchase additional units in the fund. When distributions are made, the NAVPS is decreased by the amount of the distribution. This can be disconcerting to investors, but they should recognize that under automatic reinvestment plans, the distributions are used to purchase additional shares, with the net effect that they are just as well off as they were before the distribution decreased the NAVPS.

Measuring Mutual Fund Performance

Performance measurement involves the calculation of the return realized by a portfolio manager over a specified time interval called the evaluation period.

The most frequently used measure of mutual fund performance is to compare NAVPS at the beginning and end of a period. Usually this method is based on several assumptions, including the reinvestment of all dividends. The increase or decrease at the end of the period is then expressed as a percentage of the initial value. Consider the following example:

Beginning NAVPS	$19.50
Ending NAVPS	$21.50
Gain:	[($21.50 – $19.50)/ $19.50] × 100 = 10.26%

This calculation assumes that the investor made no additions to or withdrawals from the portfolio during the measurement period. If funds were added or withdrawn, then the portfolio return as calculated using this equation may be inaccurate.

When measuring the return on a mutual fund, it is important to minimize the effect of contributions and withdrawals by the investor, because they are beyond the control of the portfolio manager. This is best accomplished by using a time-weighted rate of return, which measures the actual rate of return earned by the portfolio manager.

TIME-WEIGHTED RATE OF RETURN

A **time-weighted rate of return** (**TWRR**) is calculated by averaging the return for each sub-period in which a cash flow occurs to create a return for the reporting period. Therefore, unlike a total return, it does account for cash flows such as deposits, withdrawals and reinvestments.

© CSI GLOBAL EDUCATION INC. (2008)

Methods of calculating a time-weighted return include the daily valuation method and the Modified Diez method.

Daily valuation method: With the daily valuation method, the incremental change in value from day to day is expressed as an index from which the return can be calculated. This is beneficial for mutual funds, which generally calculate NAVPS daily, so their return calculation at the end of the month is greatly simplified. The main drawback is the need to value the portfolio every day, which can become difficult when trying to price the market value of real estate, mortgage-backed securities, illiquid issues, etc.

Modified Dietz method: The Modified Dietz method reduces the extensive calculations of the daily valuation method by providing a good approximation. It assumes a constant rate of return through the period, eliminating the need to value the portfolio on the date of each cash flow.

The Modified Dietz method weights each cash flow by the amount of time it is held in the portfolio. The Modified Dietz formula is:

$$\frac{MVE - MVB - F}{MVB + FW}$$

Where:

MVE = the market value at the end of the period, including accrued income for the period

MVB = the market value at the beginning of the period, including accrued income from the previous period

F = the sum of the cash flows within the period (contributions to the portfolio are positive flows, and withdrawals or distributions are negative flows)

FW = the sum of each cash flow multiplied by its weight

Interim cash flows are included in the calculated return, generally from the start of the day after they take place. Because the formula is not influenced by client contributions, it measures the performance of the manager much better than other return measures. The Modified Dietz measure is used by the Association of Canadian Pension Management, is recommended by the CFA Institute, and is used by several major brokerage firms introducing or already producing performance measurement reports.

STANDARD PERFORMANCE DATA

To ensure that that mutual fund returns are comparable across different funds and fund companies, Canadian regulators have instituted standard performance data that specify which return measures, at a minimum, mutual fund companies must include, and how they are to be calculated. If these measures are presented in sales communications, they must be printed as prominently as any other performance data the mutual fund company provides.

For mutual funds other than money market funds, standard performance data includes compounded annual returns for one-, three-, five- and ten-year periods, as well as the total period since inception of the fund. For money market funds, the standard performance data include the current yield and the effective yield.

Mutual fund advisors should look at periods of three to five years or more as well as individual years. Periods of less than one year are not very meaningful. Nor is a one-year return conclusive, although it is reasonable to ask questions if the fund is falling well short of the average in its category. Always keep in mind, however, that past performance is not indicative of future performance.

© CSI GLOBAL EDUCATION INC. (2008)

COMPARATIVE PERFORMANCE

Return data is useful in telling us how much a particular fund earned over a given period. However, its usefulness is limited because it does not indicate whether the fund was performing well or poorly, especially relative to other funds in its group.

To determine the quality of fund performance, it is necessary to compare the return against some standard. For mutual funds, there are two general standards of comparison: the return on a fund's benchmark index and the average return on the fund's peer group of funds.

BENCHMARK COMPARISON

All mutual funds have a benchmark index against which their return can be measured, for example, the S&P/TSX Composite Index for broad-based Canadian equity funds or the DEX Universe Bond Index for bond funds. The benchmark indexes are used in the following ways:

- If a fund reports a return that is higher than the return on the index, we can say that the fund has outperformed its benchmark.
- If a fund reports a return that was lower than the return on the index, we can say that the fund has underperformed its benchmark.

Morningstar Canada has developed a series of mutual fund benchmarks that summarize average rates of return for Canadian bond, Canadian equity, U.S. equity, global bond and international equity funds. These indexes are available on their website at www.morningstar.ca. They provide a benchmark that investors may use to measure the relative performance of various funds.

PEER GROUP COMPARISONS

A **peer group** is made up of mutual funds with a similar investment mandate. To measure the performance of a fund, its return is compared to the average return of the peer group. So if a fund posted a one-year return of 12% while the average return of its peer group over the same period was 9%, we can say that the fund outperformed its peer group over the evaluation period.

Issues that Complicate Mutual Fund Performance

When comparing mutual fund performance, one must avoid comparing the performance of two funds that are dissimilar (e.g., a fixed-income fund versus a growth equity fund) or comparing funds that have differing investment objectives or degrees of risk acceptance.

One complicating factor occurs when the name or class of fund does not accurately reflect the actual asset base of the fund. For example, a study in the Winter 2004 edition of the *Canadian Investment Review* looked at the assets of 200 funds classified as Canadian equity funds and found that three-quarters of them had less than 85% of their assets in Canadian stocks. This is not to suggest that the fund manager is doing something wrong. Each manager must consider market trends and adjust the timing of the fund's investments. It does, however, suggest that the published results are often comparing apples with oranges.

This discrepancy between a fund's formal classification and its actual asset composition can impair attempts to create a portfolio. For example, an investor who wished to allocate 10% of a portfolio to gold stocks might be surprised to find that, at some points, gold mutual funds are holding 50% of their assets in cash. This results in an actual asset allocation of 5% in gold rather than the desired 10%.

© CSI GLOBAL EDUCATION INC. (2008)

In mid-1999, the Investment Funds Standards Committee (IFSC), representing all major third party disseminators of fund data, established standard basic categories for the classification of investment funds in Canada. These classifications include mutual funds and segregated funds, as well as asset allocation services with investment funds as the underlying components, and labour sponsored venture capital corporations.

The drive by the private sector IFSC to standardize categories was aimed at eliminating confusion on the part of individual investors. A consensus on how each fund should be classified also eliminates the possibility of unfair presentations of fund rankings that, in the past, stemmed from discrepancies in how funds were classified. For instance, a fund with a mediocre performance history could be advertised as a top performer if it were compared with funds in a different, often erroneous, category. The standard categories established by the IFSC are based primarily on fund holdings.

RISK

Another factor that complicates comparisons between funds is that there is often no attempt to consider the relative risk of funds of the same type. One equity fund may be conservatively managed, while another might be willing to invest in much riskier stocks in an attempt to achieve higher returns.

Any assessment of fund performance should consider the volatility of a fund's returns. There are a number of different measures of volatility, but each attempts to quantify the extent to which returns will fluctuate. From an investor's standpoint, a fund that exhibits significant volatility in returns will be riskier than those with less volatility. Measures used to quantify volatility include:

- the standard deviation of the fund's returns
- beta
- the number of calendar years it has lost money
- the fund's best and worst 12-month periods
- the fund's worst annual, quarterly or monthly losses

Standard deviation measures how volatile a fund has been over a past period to give an indication of how it might behave in the future. If a fund has consistently earned a 5% return per year over the past 20 years, although there is no guarantee, it would be reasonable to expect that the fund will earn 5% in the future. If, however, a fund's annual return fluctuated from a negative 20% to a positive 20% over a period of 20 years, it is much less likely that the fund will earn a return of 5% in the coming year. Standard deviation is a common measure of the consistency of a fund's return. The higher the standard deviation, the more volatile or unpredictable the return may be.

Other methods, which look at different time periods, can be used to calculate best-case and worstcase scenarios. Ratings systems based on multiple periods avoid placing too much emphasis on how well or poorly the fund did during a particular short-term period.

An advisor who deals with mutual funds should be aware of how the fund tends to perform relative to the stock market cycle. Some will outperform others in rising markets, but do worse than average in bear markets. The beta, available on most fund performance software, measures the extent to which a fund is more or less volatile than the underlying market in which it invests. The greater the variation in the fund's returns, the riskier it tends to be. Particular attention should be paid to periods during which the fund lost money.

© CSI GLOBAL EDUCATION INC. (2008)

PITFALLS TO AVOID IN JUDGING MUTUAL FUND PERFORMANCE

There are a number of pitfalls to avoid in judging a mutual fund's performance.

- Past performance is not indicative of future performance and there is no guarantee that any fund will be able to maintain or improve upon past performance, especially in a general market downturn. Mutual fund advisors scrutinize the past and attempt to predict future performances, although they are not correlated. Software products that permit advisors to review performance and sort funds according to various criteria include: Globe HySales and PALTrak.
- Some observers argue that the performance of a fund is a direct reflection of the skill of the portfolio manager. These observers suggest that historical performance must be discounted when there is a change in portfolio manager.
- While average returns for a peer group of funds are useful measures, averages may be artificially high because of "survivorship bias." This means there is a tendency for poorly performing funds to be discontinued or merged. Because of survivorship bias, the average returns of surviving funds do not fully reflect the past performance of the entire spectrum of funds.
- Mutual fund performance evaluations should take into account both the type of fund and its investment objectives. Bond funds cannot be compared with equity funds, and even equity funds with different investment objectives cannot be compared.
- Beta relates the change in the price of a security to the change of the market as a whole. Mutual funds with high betas are considered riskier than comparable funds with lower betas.
- Standard deviation is a statistical test that measures the dispersion of historic prices of a specific stock, or class of investments, around the historic average of that particular stock or class. A larger standard deviation is indicative of greater volatility.
- There is no single appropriate time horizon for rating risks and returns, and the practices of industry analysts vary considerably. For long-term funds, a three-year period is generally regarded as a bare minimum. More weight can be attached to longer periods of five to ten years, or at least two market cycles.
- Advisors should be wary of selective reporting of performance periods, or periods for which there are no comparable numbers for the performance of a market benchmark or a peer group of competing funds.

Review the on-line summary or checklist associated with this section.

© CSI GLOBAL EDUCATION INC. (2008)

SUMMARY

After reading this chapter, you should be able to:

1. Describe the types of mutual funds and discuss the risk-return trade-off of investing in each type.
   - Canadian mutual funds fall into four categories: cash and equivalent, fixed-income, balanced and equity funds.
     - *Cash and equivalent* funds invest in near-cash securities or money market instruments. They generally have a constant share or unit value. The net income of the fund is calculated daily and credited to unitholders, then paid out as cash or reinvested in additional shares on a regular basis.
     - *Fixed-income* funds are designed to provide a steady stream of income rather than capital appreciation. Interest rate volatility is the main risk associated with this type of fund. Interest income is the primary source of return.
     - *Balanced* funds invest in both stocks and bonds to provide a mix of income and capital growth.
     - *Equity* funds are invested primarily in the common shares of publicly traded companies with an investment objective of long-term capital growth. Funds vary greatly in degree of risk and growth potential, and are all subject to market risk.
   - An index fund is a passive investment strategy designed to match the performance of a specific market index through direct investment in the securities that make up the specified index.
   - Risk and return can be seen as a scale with the lowest risk/lowest return funds being cash and cash equivalent funds and the highest risk/highest return funds generally being specialty funds. Within that range there are (lower to higher risk) mortgage funds, bond funds, balanced funds, dividend funds, equity funds and real estate funds, among many others.
2. Evaluate mutual fund management styles.
   - The two broad categories of management style are passive and active. Passive management generally involves some form of indexing to a market or customized benchmark. Active managers try to outperform market benchmarks using active asset allocation and selection.
   - Other styles include closet indexing, where the portfolio fairly closely follows the market weightings of the benchmark, and multi-manager, where the portfolio is divided into two or more portions that are managed separately. Refer to Chapter 16 for the discussion on the other equity and fixed-income manager styles.
3. Calculate the redemption or selling price of a mutual fund, explain the tax consequences of redemptions, and describe the four types of withdrawal plans and the appropriate use of each plan for an investor.
   - Mutual funds are redeemed at a price equal to a fund's net asset value per share (NAVPS). Mutual funds redeemed while held in registered funds do not have any immediate tax consequences.

© CSI GLOBAL EDUCATION INC. (2008)

- Investors holding mutual funds in non-registered accounts are subject to tax on capital gains realized when the fund is sold and on annual distributions of income and capital gains earned within the fund.
- Many funds offer one or more systematic withdrawal plans: based on investor instructions, a partial payout of capital invested plus distributions reinvested are made at a specific time and/or interval.
  - In a *ratio withdrawal* plan, the investor receives annual income from the fund by redeeming a specified percentage of fund holdings on each withdrawal date.
  - In a *fixed-dollar withdrawal* plan, the investor receives a specified dollar amount on each withdrawal date.
  - In a *fixed-period withdrawal* plan, a specified amount is withdrawn over a pre-determined period of time with the intent that all capital be exhausted when the plan ends.
  - In a *life expectancy–adjusted withdrawal* plan, the goal is to deplete the entire investment by withdrawing amounts adjusted to reflect the portfolio's current value and the changing life expectancy of the plan holder.

4. Describe how mutual fund performance is measured and how the comparative performance of mutual funds are determined.
   - Performance is measured by calculating the return realized by a portfolio manager over a specified time interval called the evaluation period.
   - One approach is to calculate the percentage change in the NAVPS from the beginning to the end of a period, using specific assumptions including reinvestment of all dividends and no cash withdrawals or deposits.
   - A time-weighted rate of return better measures the actual rate of return earned by a portfolio manager because it minimizes the effect of contributions and withdrawal by investors.
   - The daily valuation method measures the incremental change in fund value from day to day and this is expressed as an index from which the return can be calculated.
   - The Modified Dietz method is a more accurate way to measure the return on a portfolio because it identifies and accounts for the timing of all interim cash flow while a simple geometric return does not.
   - Canadian regulations require standardized performance data, including which return measures are to be calculated, how often they must be calculated, and the way they must be calculated.
   - Quality of fund performance is determined by comparison against a relevant standard, which is either a fund's benchmark index or the average return on the fund's peer group of funds.

Now that you've completed this chapter and the on-line activities, complete this post-test.

© CSI GLOBAL EDUCATION INC. (2008)

Chapter 19

Segregated Funds

© CSI GLOBAL EDUCATION INC. (2008)

19

Segregated Funds

CHAPTER OUTLINE

© CSI GLOBAL EDUCATION INC. (2008)

Innovations in Segregated Funds

- Guaranteed Investment Funds
- Portfolio Funds
- Protected Funds

Summary

LEARNING OBJECTIVES

By the end of this chapter, you should be able to:

1. Evaluate the features of segregated funds, including participant roles, maturity guarantees, death benefits, creditor protection, bypassing probate and cost of guarantees, and compare and contrast segregated funds with mutual funds.
2. Describe the tax considerations of investing in segregated funds.
3. Describe the structure of segregated funds.
4. Discuss the regulation of segregated funds, including the role played by OSFI, Assuris and other regulatory agencies.
5. Identify and interpret trends and innovations in segregated funds.

ROLE OF SEGREGATED FUNDS

Segregated funds are unique in that they are insurance-based investment products with special features and benefits. Although they share many similarities with mutual funds, the insurance features make them quite different.

In the previous chapter we learned about the features and risks of investing in mutual funds. Investors must realize that the value of their investment can certainly increase when markets do well, but if markets do poorly or if the fund is poorly managed, there is also the opportunity for loss. Segregated funds give you the upside potential of market gains, but also in certain circumstances protect you from the loss of your investment.

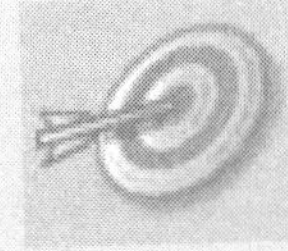

In the on-line Learning Guide for this module, complete the Getting Started activity.

Because of the different benefits, restrictions and costs involved with the purchase of segregated and mutual funds, sometimes one is more appropriate than the other. Which investment is appropriate in which circumstances?

This chapter first looks at the features and benefits of an investment in a segregated fund, which helps differentiate this product from mutual funds. The chapter also provides the background needed to assess the tax and regulatory aspects of investing in segregated funds. There are literally thousands of funds to choose from. Understanding the risk and return characteristics of the different types of funds is important and necessary to make an intelligent, well-informed and effective decision on the type of mutual fund to invest in.

© CSI GLOBAL EDUCATION INC. (2008)

KEY TERMS

- Allocation
- Annuitant
- Assuris
- Beneficiary
- Canadian Life and Health Insurance Association Incorporated (CLHIA)
- Contract holder
- Creditor protection
- Death benefit
- FundServ
- Guaranteed investment fund (GIF)
- Insurable interest
- Irrevocable beneficiary
- Maturity guarantee
- Notional units
- Portfolio funds
- Probate
- Protected funds
- Reset
- Revocable beneficiary
- Segregated fund

© CSI GLOBAL EDUCATION INC. (2008)

FEATURES OF SEGREGATED FUNDS

Segregated fund contracts and other widely held investment funds offer professional investment management and advice, the ability to invest in small amounts, regular client statements, and other services. They combine investments and related services in an integrated package. In the case of segregated fund contracts, investments and certain elements of insurance contracts are combined.

Segregated funds, however, also have unique features that enable them to meet special client needs, such as maturity protection, death benefits and creditor protection. Unlike other types of investment funds, segregated funds are regulated by provincial insurance regulators because they are insurance contracts. Contract holders who buy a segregated fund do not actually own the fund's underlying assets. Their rights are based solely on the provisions of the contract itself.

Because of the insurance benefits they offer, segregated funds are more expensive than uninsured funds, particularly in the form of higher MERs. In recommending a segregated fund to a client, the financial advisor should weigh the benefits of segregated funds against their added costs.

Since it is a insurance contract, the rights and benefits associated with holding a segregated fund are more complex than those of the owner of a security. Essentially, the contract covers the following three parties:

1. The person who bought the contract – the **contract holder** or owner of the contract.
2. The person on whose life the insurance benefits are based – the **annuitant**.
3. The person who will receive the benefits payable under the contract upon death of the annuitant – the **beneficiary**. (A contract may have more than one beneficiary.)

Owners and Annuitants

When the contract is held outside a registered plan such as an RRSP, the contract holder, or owner of the contract, does not have to be the person whose life is insured by the contract. When the contract is held in a registered plan, the contract holder and the annuitant must be the same person.

There are restrictions on whose life a contract holder can base a contract. The general rule in most provinces is that the contract holder, at the time that the contract is signed, must have an "insurable interest" in the life or health of the annuitant. Otherwise, the proposed annuitant must consent in writing to have his or her life insured.

The concept of insurable interest is illustrated in the *Québec Civil Code*, Article 2419, which specifies the persons who are eligible to be designated as annuitants. The Code states that a person has an insurable interest in his or her own life and health, and that of his or her spouse, as well as any descendants or descendants of the spouse. Also eligible to be insured are other persons who contribute to the contract holder's life and health, including employees and other persons in whose life and health the contract holder has a financial or moral interest.

If the contract holder and the person whose life is being insured are different people, the contract holder may die before the annuitant. If that happens, the contract can be transferred to a successor contract holder. If no successor has been designated by the original contract holder, the contract becomes part of his or her estate.

© CSI GLOBAL EDUCATION INC. (2008)

A segregated fund contract can be held within registered plans such as RRSPs, RESPs and RRIFs.

Beneficiaries

The beneficiary is the entity or person entitled to receive any death benefits payable under the contract upon the death of the annuitant. The contract holder may designate one or more beneficiaries, or may designate his or her estate as the beneficiary. The beneficiary does not have to be a person. It could, for instance, be a charitable organization.

The designation of beneficiaries can be revocable or irrevocable. A **revocable designation** offers greater flexibility, because the contract holder can alter or revoke the beneficiary's status. In the case of an **irrevocable designation**, the contract holder cannot change the rights of a beneficiary without the beneficiary's consent.

The designation of an irrevocable beneficiary is normally made in the segregated fund contract itself, but it can also be made in the contract holder's will, or in some other written form.

A beneficiary designation made in a will becomes invalid if the will is revoked and another designation is made. If there is a conflict between the will and an earlier designation made in the contract, the contract prevails, unless the will specifically refers to the contract holder's intentions for the contract.

One advantage of designating an irrevocable beneficiary is the ability to control the timing of bequests to surviving children. This might apply, for instance, in the case of the terminally ill single parent of a minor child. Suppose a dying parent wants to leave money to the child, but to postpone the child's access to the funds until the child has reached 21. Using a segregated fund contract, the parent could designate a grandparent of the child as the irrevocable beneficiary of the contract, with the proviso that the contract would be reassigned when the child turns 21.

Maturity Guarantees

Segregated funds alter one of the conventional principles of portfolio selection, namely the notion that the older the client, the less exposure he or she should have to riskier long-term assets.

With the availability of **maturity guarantees** of up to 100% of the amount invested after a ten-year holding period (along with death benefits, discussed below) the risks associated with capital markets become less of an investment constraint. Segregated funds enable clients to invest in higher-risk asset classes, while being assured that the principal amount of their contributions is protected.

One of the fundamental contractual rights associated with segregated funds is the promise that the contract holder or the beneficiary will receive at least a partial guarantee of the money invested. Provincial legislation requires that the guarantee be at least 75% of the amount invested over a contract term of at least a ten-year holding period or upon the death of the annuitant.

To offer greater capital protection, many insurers have increased the minimum statutory 75% guarantee to 100%. The guarantee provisions are set out in the fund's information folder. A more recent trend is the design of families of segregated funds that give clients a choice between maturity guarantees of 100% or 75%. The 100% guaranteed funds feature higher management expense ratios than the 75% guaranteed funds, reflecting the higher risks of offering full maturity protection after ten years. Some companies offer a 100% maturity guarantee on only a few of their funds.

© CSI GLOBAL EDUCATION INC. (2008)

These guarantees – whether full or partial – appeal to people who want specific assurances about their potential capital loss.

Maturity guarantees, particularly those that offer full 100% capital protection after ten years, alter the normal risk-reward relationship. With a maturity guarantee, a client may participate in rising markets without setting a limit on potential returns. At the same time, subject to the ten-year holding period, the client's invested capital is protected from loss.

When a contract holder makes deposits over the course of several years, it complicates the calculation of guarantees and maturity values.

There are basically three types of guarantees:

- *Deposit-based guarantee*: When deposits under the segregated fund contract are made at different times, such as regular monthly deposits, each deposit may have its own guarantee amount and maturity date.
- *Yearly policy-based guarantee*: This type of guarantee makes record-keeping simpler by grouping all deposits made within a 12-month period and giving them the same maturity date. Insurers may group all deposits within a calendar year. The first maturity date is generally exactly ten years after the contract was first signed.
- *Policy-based guarantee*: Bases all maturity guarantees on the date that the policy was first issued. With this type of guarantee, there may be restrictions on the size of subsequent deposits to prevent clients from making minimal deposits at account opening, and much larger deposits several years later. Doing so would effectively shorten the holding period required for the maturity guarantee and increase the potential risk to the insurer.

WITHDRAWAL FROM SEGREGATED FUND CONTRACTS

Contract holders can redeem units from a segregated fund contract at any time during the life of the annuitant. These withdrawals reduce the guarantee in the same proportion that the withdrawal reduces the market value of the investment. For example, if an investor withdraws 30% of the market value of his segregated fund, the guaranteed amount is also reduced by 30%.

Table 19.1 illustrates the impact on the guaranteed amount of a $6,000 withdrawal from a segregated fund that has a market value of $20,000 and a guaranteed amount of $16,000 (based on a maturity guarantee of 80%). The calculation is based on the percentage of current market value that is redeemed, and the guaranteed amount is reduced by the same withdrawal percentage.

TABLE 19.1 IMPACT OF WITHDRAWALS ON GUARANTEED AMOUNT

Market value before redemption	Market value of units redeemed	Percentage of units sold from current market value	Market value after redemption
$20,000	$6,000	30%	$14,000
Guaranteed value before redemption		**Percentage of reduction of the guaranteed amount (same as above)**	**Guaranteed amount after redemption**
$16,000		30%	$11,200

© CSI GLOBAL EDUCATION INC. (2008)

Table 19.1 shows that the redemption of 30% of the investment at current market value reduces the guaranteed amount by 30%. If the redemption would have been $10,000, or 50% of the current market value, the new guaranteed amount would have been $8,000, or 50% of the initial guaranteed amount.

AGE RESTRICTIONS

Insurance companies offering ten-year maturity guarantees that exceed the statutory requirement of 75% impose restrictions on who qualifies for the enhanced guarantee. Depending on the age of the client, and his or her requirements for death benefits, these restrictions can be a crucial consideration in selecting a provider of segregated funds.

Normally, the restrictions are based on age. A client of a certain age might be excluded outright from buying a company's segregated funds. Some firms may require that the individual on whom the death benefits are based must be no older than 80 at the time that the policy is issued. Alternatively, the purchaser might receive a reduced level of protection under the policy once he or she reaches a certain age.

For the industry as a whole, provincial insurance legislation does not specify a maximum age limitation. However, registered segregated fund contracts are subject to age maximums. The Income Tax Act requires that contracts held in RRSPs or in locked-in retirement accounts be terminated at the end of the year in which the contract holder turns 71. For non-registered contracts, individual companies may set maximum ages for contract ownership, such as 100.

Provincial insurance legislation may also set minimum age requirements to purchase segregated funds. Generally, the statutes provide that a minor of 16 or over can enter into an enforceable insurance contract.

RESET DATES

Although segregated fund contracts have at least a ten-year term, they may be renewable when the term expires, depending on the annuitant's age. If renewed, the maturity guarantee on a ten-year contract would "reset" for another ten years. A **reset** allows contract holders to lock in the current market value of the fund and set a new ten-year maturity date.

Recently, many insurers issuing segregated funds have added greater flexibility in the form of more frequent reset dates. In some cases, holders of segregated fund contracts may lock in the accrued value before the original ten-year period has expired and, in doing so, extend the maturity date by ten years.

Depending on the insurance company, the reset provisions may be initiated by the policy owner or may be an automatic feature of the policy. The frequency of reset dates varies according to the insurance company and is specified in the information folder. Reset dates can be anywhere from daily to once a year. The daily reset feature benefits clients in rising or falling markets. In a rising market, when the net asset value of fund units is increasing, daily resets enable contract holders to continually lock in accumulated gains. In a falling market, when net asset values are falling, contract holders will also be protected, because the guarantee is based on the previous high.

Table 19.2 provides a simplified example of how the daily reset works when the market value of a fund's assets is either rising or falling:

© CSI GLOBAL EDUCATION INC. (2008)

TABLE 19.2 DAILY RESET VALUES

Date	Accumulated Value	Guaranteed Maturity Value	Impact of Reset	New Maturity Date
Aug. 4, 2008	$10,000	$10,000	None	Aug. 2, 2018
Aug. 5, 2008	$9,900	$10,000	Protects against $100 market loss	Aug. 5, 2018
Aug. 6, 2008	$10,125	$10,125	Locks in $125 market gain	Aug. 6, 2018

The daily reset feature is intended to simplify the administration of segregated fund accounts. For clients, daily resets remove the chore of trying to time the market by speculating on the most advantageous reset dates. Because the guaranteed amount is available only ten years after the last reset date, the investor must stop resetting the guarantee as of a certain date to benefit from the protection ten years later.

Death Benefits

The **death benefits** associated with segregated funds meet the needs of clients who want exposure to long-term asset classes while ensuring that their investments are protected in the event of death.

The principle behind the death benefits offered by a segregated fund is that the contract holder's beneficiary or estate is guaranteed to receive payouts amounting to at least the guaranteed amount, excluding sales commissions and certain other fees. The amount of the death benefit is equal to the difference, if any, between the guaranteed amount and the net asset value of the fund at death.

Table 19.3 illustrates the death benefits when the market value of the units held in the segregated fund is below, the same as, or higher than the original purchase price. To simplify the illustration, it is assumed that the fund has been held long enough that any deferred sales charges are no longer applicable.

TABLE 19.3 DEATH BENEFITS

Guaranteed Amount	Market Value at Death	Death Benefit
$10,000	$8,000	$2,000
$10,000	$9,000	$1,000
$10,000	$10,000	None
$10,000	$11,000	None

As the table shows, death benefits are paid only when the market value of the fund is below the guaranteed amount. For example, when the market value at death is $9,000, the beneficiary will receive a death benefit payment of $1,000. Therefore, in addition to the payment of the $9,000 market value of the fund, the total payment to the beneficiary is $10,000. When the market value

© CSI GLOBAL EDUCATION INC. (2008)

at death is above the guaranteed amount, there is no death benefit payable because the beneficiary receives the full market value of the investment which is higher than the guaranteed amount.

Death benefits can provide reassurance to clients who want the potential for higher returns offered by equities and long-term fixed-income funds, but are concerned about preserving the value of their investment for their heirs. The death benefit enables these clients to pursue a long-term investment strategy while protecting the policy against capital losses if the death occurs during a losing period for the fund.

For instance, without the protection afforded by segregated funds, the death of the contract holder would trigger a deemed disposition at a loss, if the fund's market value at the time of death were below the original amounts deposited. A **deemed disposition** is the transfer of property, even without purchase or sale, upon the contract holder's death or emigration from Canada.

For a 100% death benefit, holdings in the form of a segregated fund are generally protected from any shortfall between the market value of the fund and the original price of the units. In this respect, segregated funds can be compared with other guaranteed investments such as index-linked GICs or fund-linked notes.

Because of death benefits and flexibility regarding beneficiaries, segregated funds can be very useful in estate planning. For example, the provisions relating to irrevocable beneficiaries allow contract holders to control the timing of bequests to surviving children.

However, death benefits commonly have conditions or exclusions that may eliminate or reduce payouts to the beneficiary. For example:

- Once the insured person reaches a certain age, the beneficiary may no longer be eligible for death benefits, or may be required to accept a reduced percentage of guaranteed benefits.
- When deposits have been made over a period of time and benefits vary according to the client's age, the death benefit is calculated according to a formula that factors in the amount of deposits and the client's age when they were made.

It is important for advisors and clients to check the contract for details on exclusions and age limits.

A segregated fund can include any combination of maturity guarantee and death benefit, provided that the contract complies with the 75% minimum and the 10-year period for the maturity guarantee. For example, one segregated fund may offer a 75% maturity guarantee and a 75% death benefit, a second one may offer a 75% maturity guarantee and a 100% death benefit, and a third one may offer a 100% maturity guarantee and a 100% death benefit.

Creditor Protection

Segregated funds may offer protection from creditors in the event of bankruptcy. This protection is not available through other managed investment products such as mutual funds. Creditor protection is available because segregated funds are insurance policies. The fund's assets are owned by the insurance company rather than the contract holder. Insurance proceeds generally fall outside the provisions of bankruptcy legislation.

Creditor protection can be a valuable feature for clients whose personal or business circumstances make them vulnerable to court-ordered seizure of assets to recover debt. Business owners, entrepreneurs, professionals or other clients who have concerns about their personal liability are among those who might welcome the creditor protection offered by a segregated fund.

© CSI GLOBAL EDUCATION INC. (2008)

For example, suppose that a self-employed professional died and left a non-registered investment portfolio of $300,000 and business-related debts of $150,000. If the portfolio were made up of mutual funds, creditors would have a claim on half of the portfolio, leaving only $150,000 for the surviving family members. In most provinces, except Québec, the estate would also be subject to probate fees based on the size of the estate.

If the entire portfolio had been held in segregated funds, $300,000 would be payable directly to the deceased person's beneficiaries. Creditors could claim nothing, and the beneficiaries would receive their money promptly and without having to deduct a portion for probate fees.

Creditor protection can be a valuable feature for clients whose personal or business circumstances make them vulnerable to court-ordered seizure of assets to recover debt. Business owners, entrepreneurs, professionals or other clients who have concerns about their personal liability are among those who might welcome the creditor protection offered by a segregated fund.

If the named beneficiary is revocable, he or she must belong to a designated class of individual. In Québec, the contract holder's rights under the contract are protected from creditor seizure if the beneficiary is a spouse, child or parent of the contract holder. These beneficiaries must receive the full amount of any benefits to them under the contract, regardless of any claims by creditors against the contract holder. In other provinces, the designated class of individuals protected is based on the relationship to the annuitant, the person whose life is being insured.

If the beneficiary is irrevocable, all non-registered contracts are eligible for creditor protection. There are no restrictions on the classes of individuals who receive creditor protection if an irrevocable beneficiary is named. One reason for naming an irrevocable beneficiary is to obtain this protection, which would otherwise be unavailable. For instance, a contract naming a charitable organization as beneficiary would not qualify for creditor protection if the designation were revocable. However, some registered contracts cannot designate a beneficiary irrevocably.

Bypassing Probate

Segregated funds can help clients avoid the costly **probate** fees levied on assets held in investment funds. The ability to bypass probate is one of the key estate-planning advantages of segregated funds.

Since segregated fund contracts are insurance policies, and not deemed to be assets of the contract holder, they are not regarded as part of the deceased's estate. The proceeds of segregated funds pass directly into the hands of the beneficiaries.

One advantage of bypassing probate is the ease of transfer of funds to the beneficiary. Proceeds of a segregated fund are payable immediately. There is no waiting for probate to be completed. Nor can payment be delayed by a dispute over the settlement of the estate. Moreover, by passing assets directly to beneficiaries through a segregated fund, contract holders can ensure that their beneficiaries save on fees paid to executors, lawyers and accountants.

Probate fees are set by the province, therefore the potential savings on probate fees vary by province. In every province except Québec, the fees charged for letters of probate – the court document that permits the distribution of the assets of the deceased – vary according to the assets to be distributed to beneficiaries of the deceased's will.

Any income or property received by the segregated fund belongs to the fund, and is for the benefit of contract holders and their beneficiaries only. If an insurance company fails, creditors have no claim to assets held in segregated funds. However, if the relevant segregated fund cannot satisfy their claim, contract holders have a claim on the general assets of the insurance company.

© CSI GLOBAL EDUCATION INC. (2008)

Cost of the Guarantees

In addition to the costs incurred by mutual funds, such as sales fees, switching fees, trailer fees and management expense ratios, segregated funds have added costs related to death benefits and maturity guarantees.

The shorter the term of the maturity guarantees on investment funds – whether they are segregated funds or protected mutual funds – the higher the risk exposure of the insurer and the cost of the guarantees. This inverse relationship is based on the premise that there is a greater chance of market decline (and hence a greater chance of collecting on a guarantee) over shorter periods. A contract holder's use of reset provisions also contributes to costs, since resetting the guaranteed amount at a higher level means that the issuer will be liable for this higher amount.

Assessing the true value of the insurance in segregated funds is a difficult issue. Certainly the management expense ratios for segregated funds are higher than those of comparable mutual funds. The high cost of full guarantees is evident in a reversion to the trend of guaranteeing only 75% of invested capital.

With either level of maturity guarantee, segregated funds offer the same benefits such as creditor protection and the opportunity for an estate to bypass probate. The main argument for the lower guarantee is that the cost to the insurance component becomes less onerous.

Table 19.4 illustrates the difference in management fees when one company offers the same fund with different guarantees.

TABLE 19.4 EFFECT OF DIFFERENT GUARANTEES ON MANAGEMENT EXPENSE RATIOS (MER)

Fund	100% Minimum Benefit Option MER (guarantee)	75% Minimum Benefit Option MER (guarantee)	Underlying Fund MER (no guarantee)
ABC Advantage Segregated Fund I	5.41	4.23	2.72
ABC Advantage Segregated Fund II	5.27	4.41	2.76
ABC Global Advantage Segregated Fund	5.56	4.48	2.80
ABC Value Segregated Fund	5.25	4.11	2.52
ABC Diversified Segregated Fund	4.98	3.49	2.44
ABC American Fund	4.98	3.66	2.44
ABC Money Market Fund	1.91	1.38	1.06

© CSI GLOBAL EDUCATION INC. (2008)

Comparison to Mutual Funds

Table 19.5 highlights some of the key similarities and differences between segregated funds and mutual funds.

TABLE 19.5 SIMILARITIES AND DIFFERENCES BETWEEN SEGREGATED FUNDS AND MUTUAL FUNDS

Features	Segregated Funds	Mutual Funds
Legal status	Insurance contract	Security
Who owns assets of fund	Insurance company	Fund itself, which is a separate legal entity
Nature of fund units	Units have no legal status, and serve only to determine value of benefits payable	Units are legal property which carry voting rights and rights to receive distributions
Who regulates their sale	Provincial insurance regulators	Provincial securities regulators
Who issues them	Mainly insurance companies; also a small number of fraternal organizations	Mutual fund company
Main disclosure document	Information folder	Prospectus
How often valued	Usually daily, and at least monthly	Usually daily, and at least weekly
Redemption rights	Right to redeem is based on contract terms	Redeemed upon request
Required financial statements	Audited annual financial statement	Audited annual financial statement and semi-annual statement for which no audit required
Sellers' qualifications	Licensed life insurance agents; BC, Saskatchewan and PEI also require successful completion of a recognized investment course, such as those offered by the CSI, IFIC or potentially by CAIFA	Licensed mutual fund representatives or registered brokers
Maturity guarantees	Minimum of 75% of deposits after 10 years. Companies may offer guarantees up to 100%	None
Government guarantees	None	None

© CSI GLOBAL EDUCATION INC. (2008)

TABLE 19.5 SIMILARITIES AND DIFFERENCES BETWEEN SEGREGATED FUNDS AND MUTUAL FUNDS *(Cont'd)*

Features	Segregated Funds	Mutual Funds
Protection against issuer insolvency	Assuris, a not-for-profit organization, provides up to $60,000 per policyholder per institution in compensation against any shortfalls in policy benefits resulting from the insolvency of a member firm (restricted to death benefits and maturity guarantees)	The Mutual Fund Dealer Association (MFDA) Investor Protection Corporation (IPC), a not-for-profit corporation, provides protection up to $1,000,000 to eligible customers of MFDA members as a result of a member's insolvency
Death benefits	Yes, may be subject to age or other restrictions	None, with rare exceptions
Creditor protection	Yes, under certain circumstances	None
Probate bypass	Yes, proceeds of contract held by deceased contract holder may be passed directly to beneficiaries, avoiding probate process	None

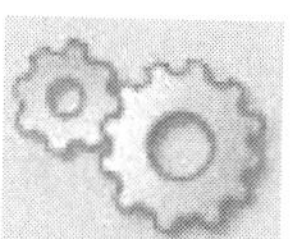

Complete the on-line activity associated with this section.

Review the on-line summary or checklist associated with this section.

TAXATION OF SEGREGATED FUNDS

Segregated funds are insurance contracts, but are taxed as if they were trusts. The Income Tax Act stipulates that the assets of segregated fund contracts are deemed to be trusts whose assets are separate from those of the insurance company sponsoring the funds. The insurance company itself, which is the legal owner of the assets of the segregated fund, does not pay taxes on income earned by the fund.

The fund's net income – whether in the form of dividends, capital gains or interest – is deemed to be the contract holder's income. In non-registered accounts, this income is taxable in the current year. The amount of income deemed to have been earned by each contract holder is calculated using a procedure known as **allocation**. A percentage of the fund's total income is allocated to each unit, according to the terms of the segregated fund contract.

Most funds allocate income to a contract holder based on the number of units held, and the proportion of the calendar year during which those units are held. For instance, a segregated fund contract held for six months of the year would receive half the per-unit allocations accorded to a contract held for the full year.

© CSI GLOBAL EDUCATION INC. (2008)

Time-weighted allocations allow segregated funds to treat contract holders more fairly in terms of tax liability than mutual fund buyers because mutual funds distribute all of the fund's income at the end of the calendar year to those who hold units at that date.

Impact of Allocations on Net Asset Values

The different ways in which mutual funds and segregated funds flow through income to unit holders is reflected in what happens to the net asset values (NAV) of the funds.

With a mutual fund, net asset values fall when a distribution is made, because income and capital gains may accumulate inside the fund and are then paid out. Periodically (usually annually or quarterly), the mutual fund makes distributions to existing unit holders, each time deducting the value of the distribution from the fund's assets. Net asset values decline by the amount of the distribution. Most distributions are reinvested in the fund, and the new units are issued to the unit holders. Therefore, although the NAV declines, the unit holder owns more units.

Most segregated funds do not suffer a decline in the NAV after an allocation of income. Instead, the segregated fund contract receives additional income, which is allocated to existing units. In most cases, these allocations are held in the policy, though they may also be redeemed by the contract holder and received as cash.

Table 19.6 illustrates the varying impact of distributions and allocations on the NAV of a mutual fund and a segregated fund. Assume that the funds had identical holdings and income for the year.

TABLE 19.6 EFFECT OF ALLOCATIONS ON SEGREGATED AND MUTUAL FUNDS

	I	II	III	IV	V
Type of fund	**Number of units and NAV, on Jan. 2**	**Income per unit earned during full year**	**Number of units and NAV at year end, before flow-through**	**Number of units and NAV after flow-through**	**Value of account after flow-through and reinvestment**
Mutual fund	100 @ $20 = $2,000	$1.20	100 @ $21.20 = $2,120	100 @ $20, plus 6 from reinvestment = 106 @ $20	$2,120
Segregated fund	100 @ $20 = $2,000	$1.20	100 @ $21.20 = $2,120	100 @ $21.20	$2,120

For the mutual fund investor, a payout of $1.20 per unit means that the investor has income of $120 for the year. Until the distribution is made, this income is reflected in an increase of the unit price from $20 to $21.20 (column III). Once this income is distributed to the investor, the unit price drops back to $20 (column IV). If the investor chooses to have this income reinvested in the fund, he or she would own six additional units of the fund. The total amount of the investment remains the same at $2,120. Alternatively, the investor could choose to receive the distribution in cash. In this case, the number of units remains unchanged but the price per unit

© CSI GLOBAL EDUCATION INC. (2008)

decreases. Note that the entire distribution of mutual fund income is equally distributed to existing unitholders at the date of distribution, regardless of whether the purchase was made on January 2 or on December 30.

This example assumes that the segregated fund contract holder held the fund for the entire year, from January 1 to December 31. Since a segregated fund accrues income throughout the year, the full $1.20 of income is allocated to the investor. If the investor held the fund for only part of the year, however, the income allocation would be less than the full $1.20. For example, holding the fund from July to December would entitle the investor to only half of the income distribution.

Continuing with the above example, assume that an investor purchases the segregated fund in September and holds it for the remainder of the year. Because the income allocation has accrued for eight months already, the NAV at the time of purchase would reflect the allocations since the beginning of the year. The calculation proceeds as follows:

- Per month distribution = $1.20 ÷ 12 months = $0.10 per month
- Distribution from January to September = 8 months × $0.10 = $0.80
- NAV at the end of August = $20.80
- December allocation on unit bought on September = $0.40 ($21.20 – $20.80)

The payout of $0.40 per unit means that the investor has income of $40 for the year (100 units × $0.40). At the end of the year, the NAV for the contract holder is also $21.20. The only difference is that the investor receives the allocations only for the months that the contract was owned. Segregated fund distributions can be received in cash. In this case, the price per unit increases as explained above, but units are redeemed, resulting in a smaller number of units after the distribution.

These examples illustrate four principles:

- Segregated fund NAVs are the same for all contract holders at any given point in time.
- The NAV at which an investor purchases a segregated fund varies depending on when during the year the fund is purchased.
- Income allocations do not reduce the NAV of a segregated fund.
- Segregated fund allocations per unit are paid throughout the year.

One of the advantages of segregated fund contracts over mutual funds is the fact that capital losses, as well as capital gains, can be passed on to the contract holder. This is not true of mutual funds, where capital losses cannot be flowed through to unit holders. They must be kept in the fund and used in future years to offset capital gains.

Tax Treatment of Guarantees

Payments from a segregated fund contract's maturity guarantees are taxable. If the proceeds of the contract (after commissions) are less than the adjusted cost base, income tax is payable on the guaranteed amount. However, the contract holder can use the difference between the market value of the segregated fund and the adjusted cost base as a capital loss.

The net effect is zero if the guarantee is considered to be a capital gain. If the guarantee paid is considered to be income, then the policyholder must pay tax on the full amount, but can use only 50% of any capital loss declared.

© CSI GLOBAL EDUCATION INC. (2008)

If the proceeds exceed the adjusted cost base, the contract holder is taxed on the difference.

The following examples illustrate the amount of tax payable under three different scenarios:

- Scenario I: The maturity value exceeds the original cost of the contract.
- Scenario II: The maturity value is less than the guaranteed amount.
- Scenario III: A reset provision has been used, making the maturity guarantee $30,000 higher than in the original contract. Resetting the maturity guarantee extends the policy over a new ten-year period. Even if the reset is used to lock in a capital gain, it does not constitute redemption and therefore does not trigger a taxable event.

Under each scenario, it is assumed that $100,000 was invested in a lump sum on a deferred sales charge basis, and that the policy was held long enough that there are no redemption fees applicable when the policy is surrendered. The calculations are based on a 100% maturity guarantee.

EXHIBIT 19.1

	Invested Amount	Maturity Guarantee	Market Value at Redemption	Maturity Guarantee Paid	Capital Gain	Taxable Capital Gain
Scenario I	$100,000	$100,000	$ 130,000	$0	$30,000	$15,000
Scenario II	$100,000	$100,000	$95,000	$5,000	$0	$0
Scenario III	$100,000	$130,000	$110,000	$20,000	$30,000	$15,000

Scenario I
Client redeems $100,000 deposit after ten years for proceeds of $130,000. The market value of the policy at maturity exceeds the adjusted cost base.

Tax consequences: 50% of the capital gain of $30,000 is taxable in the year of redemption.

Scenario II
Client redeems $100,000 deposit after ten years for proceeds of $95,000 in current market value. Since the net market value at maturity is less than the adjusted cost base, the client is paid $5,000 as the maturity guarantee.

Tax consequences: The maturity guarantee of $5,000 is taxable as a capital gain, but it is reduced to $0 by the $5,000 capital loss incurred because the client's $100,000 deposit is now worth only $95,000.

Scenario III
Client chooses to reset the maturity guarantee after five years, locking in the gain in market value to $130,000 and extending the policy. Ten years after the reset date, the policy matures at a market value of $110,000. The client receives a $20,000 maturity guarantee, for total proceeds of $130,000.

© CSI GLOBAL EDUCATION INC. (2008)

Tax consequences: No capital gains liability is triggered at the time of the reset. However, at the time of redemption (15 years after the original deposit), the capital gain of $30,000 ($10,000 from the increase in market value and $20,000 from the maturity guarantee) is taxable in the year in which it is paid out.

These are very simplified examples, as they assume there were no distributions paid by the issuing company over the period specified. In reality, distributions would likely be paid every year. Tax is paid on these distributions in the year that they were paid and cannot be taxed twice. Fortunately, the issuing company keeps track of these distributions and the adjusted cost base is reported on the recipient's T3 slip.

Tax Treatment of Death Benefits

When the insured person dies, the contract is terminated and the beneficiaries receive death benefits. If the contract holder is not the same person as the annuitant, the contract remains in force when the contract holder dies, but the deceased owner is deemed to have disposed of the contract at fair market value. This deemed disposition will normally trigger a capital gain or a capital loss. However, if the contract holder took advantage of the provision allowing his or her spouse to be named as the successor owner, the contract can be transferred to the spouse at its adjusted cost base, thereby deferring any capital gains liability. If the contract owner and annuitant is the same person, the gain or loss will be reflected on the owner's terminal tax return for the year of death.

EXAMPLE: A client purchases a segregated fund contract for $100,000. The contract provides for a 100% guarantee at death. Five years later, the client dies. At the time of the client's death, the market value of the segregated fund is $80,000. The death benefit payment would be $20,000. Assuming the fund was held in a non-registered plan, the client would report a $20,000 gain, but the client would also have an offsetting capital loss of $20,000. Because the fund declined from $100,000 to $80,000, there would be no tax impact as the two would cancel each other out.

Industry tax treatment of death benefits can be very complicated. It is recommended that the investor and the advisor clearly understand the tax implications of the contract by thoroughly reading the information folder provided with the purchase of a segregated fund.

Tax Reporting

Depending on the type of fund and the composition of its investment returns, the allocations will be in the form of:

- Capital gains
- Canadian dividends
- Other income
- Foreign-source income

These allocations are reported annually on a T3 slip and must be reported by the contract holder. The T3 slip indicates the income, dividend and capital gains earned during the year, based on the number of units and the length of time the units have been held by the contract holder. Since, for tax purposes, each type of income must be declared separately on a tax return, they appear separately on the tax slip.

© CSI GLOBAL EDUCATION INC. (2008)

Tax reporting on the T3 slip includes capital gains or losses both by the fund itself and by the individual contract holder as of the date of surrender (redemption) of the contract. As with any investment fund, a switch from one fund to another in the same fund family is a taxable event that will generally trigger a capital gain or loss. This type of gain or loss is also reported on the T3.

Because they enable contract holders to claim capital losses, segregated funds offer an advantage over mutual funds, which may use capital losses to reduce capital gains payable. For a segregated fund, if there are no capital gains from which to deduct losses, the contract holder can carry forward any capital losses to be applied against future gains.

Commission charges – whether front-end, deferred or switching fees – are reported separately on the T3 slip and can be claimed as a capital loss by the contract holder when the contract is surrendered. (This practice differs from that for mutual funds, where commission charges are added to the adjusted cost base or deducted from proceeds.)

STRUCTURE OF SEGREGATED FUNDS

As investment vehicles, segregated funds share many qualities with mutual funds, such as the fact that fund sponsors offer and maintain these managed products on behalf of their customers. However, segregated funds and mutual funds differ significantly in terms of their legal structure.

Most open-end mutual funds are structured as trusts, and the remainder as corporations. The structure of a mutual fund is either outlined in the declaration of trust at the time the fund is set up, or governed by the rules for business corporations. In both cases, the structure is one of ownership. In contrast, segregated funds are life insurance contracts, known as **individual variable insurance contracts** (**IVICs**), between a contract holder and an insurance company.

Unitholders do not own segregated fund assets, and are non-participating policyholders. In other words, segregated fund investors do not have the rights that usually belong to shareholders or unitholders. For instance, except in Québec, segregated fund contract holders cannot attend meetings and do not have voting rights.

This means that segregated funds do not require the approval of investors to change their management, investment objectives or auditor, or to decrease the frequency of calculation of net asset values. For open-end mutual funds, such changes would require a vote by unitholders.

However, the insurance company holds these assets apart from – or "segregated" from – other assets of the firm. Despite their legal structure, segregated funds are treated as trusts held on behalf of investors. If an insurance company fails financially and has insufficient assets to fulfill its guarantees, the assets of segregated fund holders would be dedicated solely to the contract holders and could not be claimed by other policyholders or by creditors.

Because of their legal structure, segregated funds do not issue actual units or shares to investors, since this would imply ownership. Instead, an investor is assigned **notional units** of the contract, a concept that measures a contract holder's participation and benefits in a fund. This concept also makes it possible to compare the investment performance of segregated funds with those of mutual funds.

© CSI GLOBAL EDUCATION INC. (2008)

Bankruptcy and Family Law

Under federal bankruptcy law, segregated funds are not normally included in the property divided among creditors. The *Bankruptcy and Insolvency Act* specifically excludes from bankruptcy proceedings any property that is deemed exempt from seizure under provincial law. For example, a bankruptcy trustee cannot change a beneficiary designation to make the proceeds of the contract payable to the contract holder's creditors.

However, the creditor-proofing features of segregated funds are subject to limitations. The purchase of the segregated fund must be made in good faith, and not with the intent of evading legal obligations such as those arising from bankruptcy.

Claims for creditor protection may be subject to a successful court challenge by the bankruptcy trustee if a segregated fund was purchased to wilfully or fraudulently evade a contract holder's debt obligations. Other types of challenges, involving statutes other than bankruptcy legislation, are available in the event of fraud.

Under the federal *Bankruptcy and Insolvency Act*, the proceeds of a segregated fund may be subject to seizure if it can be proven that the purchase was made within a certain period before the bankruptcy, normally within one year. But if the client was legally insolvent when the contract was purchased, the segregated fund purchases could be challenged as far as five years back.

It makes no difference, under bankruptcy law, if the beneficiary is a family member or an irrevocable beneficiary. The contract can still be revoked if bought within a year of the bankruptcy date, or within five years, if the contract holder was insolvent when the beneficiary was named.

Because segregated funds allow new contributions to be made over time, a portion of the segregated fund might be protected, while new contributions or reinvestment of fund distributions could be subject to seizure. The extent of the protected portion would depend on whether the contract holder's status changed during the life of the policy.

Family law also impacts segregated fund investors. A contract holder's matrimonial obligations may also affect a segregated fund. Although insurance contracts do not normally form part of the estate of the contract holder, they are subject to family law provisions designed to provide for the welfare of family members or other dependants.

Because there is a cash surrender value to a segregated fund contract – that is, the policy can be redeemed for cash at any time – the contract is considered matrimonial property. Outside Québec, the cash surrender value is included in total assets to be divided between two divorcing spouses.

In Québec, different rules apply. In addition to the cash surrender value of any contract acquired during a marriage, the income received from a segregated fund contract entered into before the marriage is subject to division. (The cash surrender value consists of both the contributions made to the contract and the income received by the contract holder as a result of the contributions.)

If a couple in Québec has a marriage contract that provides for separate ownership of property, the provisions regarding the division of segregated funds are more restrictive. Only the cash surrender value of the contract acquired during the marriage would be subject to division. Both the cash surrender value and any income earned from a contract that predated the marriage would be exempt.

© CSI GLOBAL EDUCATION INC. (2008)

Buying and Selling Segregated Funds

The purchaser's rights, including the rules governing purchases and withdrawals, are set out in each contract. Segregated fund contracts typically allow holders to withdraw or purchase at the most recent net asset value.

PURCHASES AND MINUMUM DEPOSITS

To purchase units – technically, to make a deposit or premium payment – in a segregated fund, an investor must first establish a contract with the insurer. The purchase price is valued the day the order is made. For segregated money market funds, trades settle the day after the trade date. For other types of segregated funds, settlement typically takes place three business days later, as it does for mutual funds.

Many segregated fund offerings are administered through **FundServ**, the industry organization that also provides clearing and settlement services to mutual funds.

In some cases, the minimum deposits to a segregated fund are the same as or similar to the minimum requirements for mutual funds. However, some companies require a bigger initial investment for segregated funds than for comparable mutual funds. Periodic investment plans are also available for some segregated funds.

WITHDRAWALS AND TRANSFERS

Except in the case of locked-in plans, which are governed by provincial pension laws, the owner of a segregated fund can withdraw or redeem some or all of the cash value of a segregated fund at any time while the annuitant is alive. In non-registered plans, most sponsors allow both systematic withdrawals and lump-sum withdrawals from segregated fund contracts. There may be a minimum for these scheduled payouts, or a minimum contract balance may have to be maintained. As discussed, any withdrawals may affect the value of the guarantees on a segregated fund.

The value of a withdrawal is based on the net asset value of the units at the close of business on the day the order is received. The settlement date is set by the contract and is usually a few days after the trade date.

Redemption requests may be affected by the liquidity of the fund. For instance, if normal trading on a relevant stock exchange is suspended, or a manager deems it impractical to close a position, the fund may not be able to meet redemption requests. Insurers generally reserve the right to suspend or delay requests for withdrawals.

Most insurers allow clients to transfer assets from one fund to another within the fund family without penalty. In many cases, the number of these transfers is limited in a calendar year. If the number is exceeded, a charge may be levied for further transfers. Transfers may affect the initial value and date of a policy, and maturity guarantees may be reset at varying levels or with different maturities.

Disclosure Documents

The offering documents for segregated funds must disclose all the important facts about the funds in concise and plain language. The key disclosure documents for a segregated fund contract consist of the acknowledgement of receipt card, application form, contract, information folder,

© CSI GLOBAL EDUCATION INC. (2008)

summary fact sheet, financial statements, and client statements. As well, as mentioned earlier, monthly performance tables for mutual funds in newspapers and on mutual fund software products incorporate segregated funds.

Acknowledgement of receipt card: Before a client signs an application for a segregated fund policy, the financial advisor must provide the client with a copy of the information folder. To prove that the information folder has been delivered by the advisor, the issuer must receive a signed "acknowledgement of receipt" card from the client.

Application form: The application form provides the insurance company with the information required to set up the insurance contract, including the names of the contract holder, annuitant, beneficiary and contributor (if, for instance, the plan is a spousal RRSP), as well as the maturity date for the policy.

Contract: A segregated fund contract must describe the benefits of the policy and identify the benefits that are guaranteed and those that vary according to the market value of the fund's assets. One element of a segregated fund contract is a warning to clients that the values of the policy's investments will fluctuate.

The contract also states how often and when the fund is valued, as well as outlining the fees and charges against the fund, and how they are determined.

Information folder: The information folder is the central document of segregated fund disclosure, comparable to the prospectus for open-end mutual funds. To avoid any confusion with other marketing materials, the information folder must be identified by the title "Information Folder" on its cover or the first right-hand page inside the cover.

The information folder includes the following key items of disclosure:

- The benefits guaranteed under the contract
- The benefits under the contract that fluctuate with the market value of the assets of the segregated fund supporting it
- The method used to determine benefits related to the market value of the segregated fund, if any
- Options for redemption, surrender and maturity
- Charges for withdrawals
- The method used to determine the price of units on acquisition or transfer, including any charges expressed in dollars and units or as a percentage of premiums
- Options for acquiring or transferring units and the minimum dollar amount to make a purchase, either lump sum or periodic
- The method used to determine unit values
- A statement of whether the insurer intends to market the segregated fund continuously or whether it is a limited-time offer
- A statement of the fund's investment policies
- An advisory that contract holders may request delivery of the complete investment policy of the segregated fund, and how to request this information
- The tax status of the fund and of contract holders
- Current management fees as a percentage of the fund's net assets, and all other expenses that may be charged against the fund's assets
- All other fees and charges that may be charged against the assets of the fund

© CSI GLOBAL EDUCATION INC. (2008)

- A one-page executive summary of the material facts about the fund

For segregated funds held in a registered plan, the information folder must also include statements such as:

- Segregated funds are one of a number of different vehicles for the accumulation of retirement income
- Certain regular contractual benefits may need to be modified
- Registered contracts may be more suitable for long-term holding periods than for the short term
- The prospective contract holder should discuss fully all aspects of registration with the insurer or agent before purchasing a registered segregated fund

For real estate funds, the information folder must also include information on the long-term nature of the fund's investments and the relatively illiquid nature of the fund. For instance, it must state that the contract may be redeemed only on specified dates and may be unsuitable for contract holders who require a high degree of liquidity.

Summary fact statement: A prospective contract holder must be given a copy of the summary fact statement when the information folder is delivered. This provides a snapshot of the fund, including the fund's historical performance, its investment policies and its three largest holdings. (Although guidelines call for the disclosure of the three largest holdings only, issuers usually go beyond this minimum requirement).

Financial statements: Audited financial statements, if available, must accompany the information folder, and must be provided annually to contract holders. These statements are similar to mutual fund financial statements.

Client statements: Confirmations of purchases, sales or transfers are sent to clients as they occur. Summary statements to policy owners are issued on a regular basis, usually semi-annually. This statement shows:

- Changes in the client's portfolio positions, including contributions and redemptions, since the previous statement
- The value of the contract holder's segregated fund holdings
- The unit value of each fund

Contract holders also receive an annual report that details the investment management and performance of the funds.

REGULATION OF SEGREGATED FUNDS

As of June 2007, according to the Canadian Life and Health Insurance Association Inc., of the 106 insurance companies in Canada 34 offer segregated funds. Most are federally registered insurance companies. Other issuers include fraternal organizations that are qualified to sell life insurance and provincially chartered insurance companies.

© CSI GLOBAL EDUCATION INC. (2008)

For the most part, segregated fund contracts are subject to the provincial legislation governing all life insurance contracts. Laws and regulations governing segregated funds are very similar in all provincial and territorial jurisdictions. Each province and territory has accepted the **Canadian Life and Health Insurance Association Inc. (CLHIA)** guidelines as the primary regulatory requirements. Ontario, for example, has adopted the CLHIA guidelines as regulations under the province's *Insurance Companies Act*. Other provinces and territories apply the CLHIA guidelines as industry standards.

There are, however, some differences between jurisdictions. Québec and Ontario, among others, have special rules governing the sale of segregated fund contracts. Provincial regulators in the four Western provinces have delegated some licensing and enforcement roles to provincial insurance councils made up of representatives of industry groups.

Federal insurance regulators do not regulate the sale of segregated funds. External money managers of the funds are subject to provincial securities legislation, if they are registered as portfolio managers.

Monitoring Solvency

The Office of the Superintendent of Financial Institutions (OSFI) is responsible for ensuring that federally regulated insurance companies are adequately capitalized under the requirements of the federal *Insurance Companies Act*.

Segregated fund contracts for equity-linked insurance and annuity contracts with guaranteed benefits are also subject to the OSFI guidelines on guarantee provisions.

OSFI's key requirements for segregated fund contracts include:

- The maturity guarantee payable at the end of the term of the policy cannot exceed 100% of the gross premiums paid by the contract holder. (This rule also applies to contracts carrying reset features, which allow the contract holder to lock in gains and set a new ten-year term to maturity.)
- The initial term of the segregated fund contract cannot be less than ten years.
- There can be no guarantee of any amounts payable on redemption of the contract before the annuitant's death or the contract maturity date.

When assets are not properly accounted for or liabilities are not paid, OSFI may take temporary control of an insurance company, including its segregated funds, and manage the company's affairs. Under the federal *Insurance Companies Act*, the appointed actuary of the insurance company must review and monitor liabilities created by the issuance of segregated fund contracts.

The Role Played by Assuris

Generally, the fact that the funds are segregated from the insurance company's general assets provides sufficient protection to contract holders against corporate insolvency. But there is also an additional layer of protection in the form of the Toronto-based, industry-financed Assuris.

Assuris, is the insurance industry's self-financing provider of protection against the loss of policy benefits in the event of the insolvency of a member company. Assuris is financed by assessments levied on its members, and is incorporated federally as a nonprofit organization.

The federal government, along with most provinces, requires life insurers to be members of Assuris and to pay its levies. There were 106 Assuris members as of July 2008.

© CSI GLOBAL EDUCATION INC. (2008)

Assuris' membership includes nearly all entities that sponsor segregated funds in Canada, including all life insurance companies that are licensed to sell life insurance or health insurance to the public.

Since 1990, when it first began providing coverage of segregated fund guarantees, Assuris has never had to make restitution to segregated fund contract holders. Assuris, guarantee covers only the death benefits and maturity guarantees in a segregated fund contract. The assets of the funds themselves are not eligible for Assuris protection, because they are segregated from the general assets of the insurance company. Segregated fund holders therefore enjoy a built-in form of protection against an insurance company's insolvency. Assuris' role is to "top up" any payments made by a liquidator to fulfill the insurance obligations under a segregated fund contract.

The maximum compensation that can be awarded under an individual segregated fund policy is up to $60,000 or 85% of the promised guaranteed amounts, whichever is higher. These limits apply both to amounts held by individuals in registered plans, such as RRSPs, RRIFs and life income funds, and to contracts held outside registered plans.

Exhibit 19.2 shows an example of the amount paid by Assuris on a segregated fund contract of $500,000, with a 75% guaranteed amount and bankruptcy of the insurance company.

EXHIBIT 19.2 EXAMPLES OF INDIVIDUAL SEGREGATED FUND POLICY

Step 1: Original Amounts

Policy amount when the insurance company fails	Policy guarantee when the company fails (75%)	Fund value at the bankruptcy date
$500,000	$375,000	$300,000

Step 2: Protection Amounts

Policy guarantee when the company fails (75%)	Amount of protection from Assuris	Assuris protected amount	Explanation	The amount paid out by Assuris
$375,000	Assuris applies 85% protection to the guaranteed amount because the amount exceeds $60,000. ($375,000 × 85% = $318,750	$318,750	The client receives $318,750 from the value of the fund. Assuris ensures that the client receives the difference between the Assuris protection and the value of the fund. ($318,750 – $300,000 = $18,750)	$18,750

Source: Assuris website.

© CSI GLOBAL EDUCATION INC. (2008)

Advertisements and Marketing

All communications are considered advertisements governed by the CLHIA guidelines. These guidelines have been approved by the Canadian Council of Insurance Regulators, which represents regulatory agencies in provincial and territorial jurisdictions across Canada. In addition to insurance companies, individual financial advisors are subject to CLHIA guidelines that limit what they are allowed to communicate to their clients.

CLHIA guidelines are intended to bring advertising, disclosure and financial reporting guidelines for segregated funds into line with those applied by securities regulators to mutual funds.

INNOVATIONS IN SEGREGATED FUNDS

In the past, segregated funds were the domain of insurance companies. Recently, the entry of mutual fund companies and the growing popularity of segregated funds for investors have led to significant product expansion in segregated funds. The result has been variations of and enhancements to the basic structure of the traditional segregated fund contract.

Segregated funds date back to 1961. At first, insurance companies used them to manage money for pension plans. In the mid-1960s, provincial regulatory authorities began to permit insurance companies to issue segregated funds. Now individual contracts account for 52% of insurance company assets.

At December 31, 2006, about $ $151.8 billion were held in segregated fund contracts compared to $115 billion in 2004. Premiums from segregated funds represented $24 billion, compared with $18.8 billion in 2004 This represents 36% of the total insurance premiums paid by Canadians in 2006, compared to 32% in 2004. This represents a huge leap from the end of 1995, when the industry held segregated fund assets of $30.3 billion.

Most assets of segregated funds are held in group plans. But there has been an increasing trend toward selling segregated funds to individual clients. In the late 1990s, mutual fund companies began to act as providers of investment management services to insurance company funds, and as sponsors of their own segregated fund families in co-operation with insurance companies.

The competitive environment for insured investment funds was fundamentally altered by industry developments in the late 1990s. Innovative products created by both the insurance and mutual fund industries, along with new marketing alliances between the two, created a convergence between segregated funds and mutual funds.

Today, segregated funds often have brand-name mutual funds as their underlying assets. Mutual funds with capital protection features, similar to the maturity guarantees offered by segregated funds, have also been introduced. And more and more financial advisors are obtaining dual licensing so that they can sell insurance products along with securities.

Guaranteed Investment Funds

A **guaranteed investment fund** (**GIF**) is a type of segregated fund whose underlying asset is a mutual fund. The first company to offer segregated funds that use brand-name mutual funds as their underlying investments was Manulife Financial, which launched its guaranteed investment

© CSI GLOBAL EDUCATION INC. (2008)

funds in January 1997. Manulife teamed up with a number of mutual fund companies to create a product that wraps well-known mutual funds within the features of segregated funds. The result is a product that combines known investment management from mutual fund companies with the guarantees that have traditionally been offered by insurance companies issuing segregated funds. As well as being popular with mutual fund companies, which gain an avenue for marketing their products, this "fund-on-fund" structure has proved attractive to investors because of the combination of investment and insurance.

Portfolio Funds

Portfolio funds, which invest in other funds instead of buying securities directly, allow investors to hold a diversified portfolio of segregated funds through a single investment. The responsibility for choosing or rebalancing the asset mix usually rests with the fund company.

For example:

- Empire Life used its own family of funds to create five portfolio funds, each aimed at fulfilling a specific investment objective.
- Desjardins Financial Security teamed up with a number of portfolio managers like AIM Trimark Investments and Jarislowsky Fraser to launch "Millenia III," a family of segregated portfolio funds that uses funds from both the chosen portfolio managers and Desjardins Financial families to create so-called "seg fund wraps."

Management expenses for portfolio funds are generally higher than for stand-alone segregated funds and guaranteed investment funds, because the investor pays for the asset allocation service, on top of the management costs for the underlying funds.

Protected Funds

The emergence of **protected funds** marks one way in which the mutual fund industry has responded to the popularity of insurance company segregated funds. Unlike segregated funds, protected funds are legally structured as mutual fund trusts and are not governed by insurance legislation. An important advantage of this structure for the mutual fund industry is that they can be sold by registered mutual fund salespeople at bank branches and by independent financial advisors who do not have life insurance licences. Also, investors and sellers of protected funds generally bypass the more complicated administrative processes required for insurance purchases. The disadvantage is that non-insurance products do not offer protection from creditors.

For example:

National Bank of Canada offers several protected funds, including a Protected Canadian Bond Fund and a Protected Canadian Equity Fund. The capital invested by unitholders in these funds is guaranteed by National Bank Life Insurance Company.

Review the on-line summary or checklist associated with this section.

Protected funds provide many of the same benefits as segregated funds. They typically have a maturity guarantee (usually ten years) and allow unitholders to reset the maturity value without triggering an income tax liability. However, unlike all segregated funds, some protected funds do not offer traditional death benefits. Instead of paying out the original investment to a designated beneficiary or the investor's estate on the death of the owner, the company may allow the five-year guarantee to be transferable.

© CSI GLOBAL EDUCATION INC. (2008)

SUMMARY

1. Evaluate the features of segregated funds, including participant roles, maturity guarantees, death benefits, creditor protection, bypassing probate and cost of guarantees, and compare and contrast segregated funds with mutual funds.

   - A *segregated fund* is a life insurance product that shares many similarities with mutual funds. The insurance component offers such features as maturity protection, death benefits and creditor protection.
   - The *contract holder* is the person who bought the segregated fund contract. The *annuitant* is the person on whose life the insurance benefits are based. The *beneficiary* is the person or persons who will receive the benefits payable under the contract on the death of the annuitant.
   - In registered plans only, the contract holder and the annuitant must be the same person.
   - Provincial regulations require that beneficiaries receive a guarantee of at least 75% to a maximum 100% of the return of the money invested over a contract term of at least a tenyear holding period.
   - Deposit-based guarantees are deposits made on a contract at different times, and each deposit may have its own guarantee amount and maturity date.
   - Yearly policy-based guarantees are made within a 12-month period and are grouped and given the same maturity date.
   - Policy-based guarantees are based on the date that the policy is first issued and, subject to some restrictions, apply to all deposits made throughout the contract.
   - Depending on the annuitant's age, the contract may be renewable when the term expires. If renewed, the maturity guarantee on a ten-year contract would reset for another ten years.
   - If a contract holder dies, the holdings in the fund bypass probate and pass directly to the beneficiaries.
   - Creditor protection is available because segregated funds are insurance policies. The fund's assets are owned by the insurance company rather than the contract holder, and insurance proceeds generally fall outside the provisions of bankruptcy legislation.
   - The management expense ratio (MER) on a segregated fund is typically higher than that on a comparable mutual fund because of the insurance components.

2. Describe the tax considerations of investing in segregated funds.

   - Net income earned from a segregated fund is deemed to be the contract holder's income and is taxable in the current year.

     The appropriate percentage of the income is allocated to the contract holder, generally based on the number of units held and the proportion of the calendar year in which the units were held.
   - The allocations are reported annually on a T3 slip, although they are made throughout the year.

© CSI GLOBAL EDUCATION INC. (2008)

- Payments from maturity guarantees are taxable. The amount taxed is the proceeds, less sales charges, minus the cost of the contract (which is the original amount deposited plus any allocations).
- The treatment of death benefits varies based on whether the contract holder is the annuitant and on the provisions of the specific contract.

3. Describe the structure of segregated funds.
    - Segregated funds are life insurance contracts between a contract holder and an insurance company. Purchasing units requires that an investor first establish a contract with the insurer.
    - Unitholders do not own segregated fund assets and do not have shareholder rights (for example, outside of Québec there are no voting rights attached to the units).
    - Purchasing units requires that an investor first establish a contract with the insurer.
    - Funds can be withdrawn for some or all of the cash value of the segregated fund as long as the annuitant is alive.
4. Discuss the regulation of segregated funds, including the role played by OSFI, Assuris and other regulatory agencies.
    - The offering documents for segregated funds must include all of the following: acknowledgement of receipt card, application form, contract, information folder, summary fact statement and audited financial statements.
    - Generally, segregated fund contracts are subject to the provincial legislation governing life insurance contracts, but there are some differences between jurisdictions.
    - The contracts are subject to the guidelines on guarantee provisions of The Office of the Superintendent of Financial Institutions (OSFI).
    - In the case of insolvency of a fund, Assuris guarantees cover the death benefits and maturity guarantees of the fund contract and will top up any payments made by a liquidator to fulfill these insurance obligations.
    - All communications considered advertisements are governed by Canadian Life and Health Insurance Association (CLHIA) guidelines.
5. Identify and interpret trends and innovations in segregated funds.
    - The increasing popularity of segregated funds means that there are many more distributors and a growing variety of products. The funds now often have a brand-name mutual fund as their underlying asset (a fund-on fund structure).
    - Portfolio funds invest in other funds instead of buying securities, thus allowing investors to hold a diversified portfolio of segregated funds through a single investment.
    - Protected funds, a new product similar to segregated funds, have been developed by the mutual fund industry and offer comparable benefits in a vehicle not based on insurance.

Now that you've completed this chapter and the on-line activities, complete this post-test.

© CSI GLOBAL EDUCATION INC. (2008)

Chapter 20

Hedge Funds

© CSI GLOBAL EDUCATION INC. (2008)

20

Hedge Funds

CHAPTER OUTLINE

Overview of Hedge Funds
- Comparisons to Mutual Funds
- Who Can Invest in Hedge Funds?
- History of Hedge Funds
- Size of the Hedge Fund Market
- Tracking Hedge Fund Performance

Benefits and Risks of Hedge Funds
- Benefits
- Risks
- Due Diligence

Hedge Fund Strategies
- Relative Value Strategies
- Event-Driven Strategies
- Directional Funds

Funds of Hedge Funds
- Advantages
- Disadvantages

Principal-Protected Notes
- Costs and Risks of PPNs
- Selecting a PPN

Summary

© CSI GLOBAL EDUCATION INC. (2008)

LEARNING OBJECTIVES

By the end of this chapter, you should be able to:

1. Define hedge fund, compare and contrast hedge funds with mutual funds and institutional investors with retail investors in hedge funds, summarize the history and growth of the hedge fund market and discuss how hedge fund performance is tracked.
2. Evaluate the benefits, risks and due diligence requirements of investing in hedge funds.
3. Identify the three categories of hedge fund strategies and describe how the specific strategies within each category work.
4. Describe the advantages and disadvantages of investing in a fund of hedge funds (FoHF) structure versus individual hedge funds.
5. Define principal-protected notes (PPNs) and describe the costs and risks of investing in PPNs.

ROLE OF HEDGE FUNDS

For many investors, hedge funds are a relatively new investment product. Popular awareness of hedge funds in Canada is recent and has grown markedly since 2001. Even though several high-profile hedge funds have failed over the years, bringing negative attention to the industry, hedge fund assets continue to grow.

Investors should realize, however, that hedge funds are not for everyone. They are commonly described as lightly regulated pools of investment capital that have greater flexibility in their investment strategies. Some hedge funds are conservative, others are more aggressive. Despite the popular name, some funds do not hedge their positions at all. Therefore, it is best to think of a hedge fund as a type of fund structure rather than a particular investment strategy.

These investments are less regulated, less controlled and less standardized than the majority of investments, but they also offer opportunities that cannot be ignored.

Part of the attraction of investing in hedge funds lies in the flexibility that allows them to pursue investment opportunities not available to mutual funds or segregated funds because of regulatory restrictions. Individual investors could also find it difficult to replicate the strategies because they may be prohibitively expensive or simply logistically impossible.

Because hedge fund managers have tremendous flexibility in the types of strategies they can employ, the manager's skill is more important in hedge funds than in almost any other managed product. This makes the amount of due diligence performed before recommending or investing in a hedge fund of significant importance. Thus, understanding the particular strategy the manager is employing and the manager's track record is critical to the success of the investment decision.

© CSI GLOBAL EDUCATION INC. (2008)

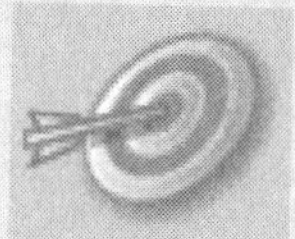

The chapter begins with an overview and history of hedge funds in Canada and then reviews the various hedge fund strategies. The chapter ends with a discussion of how to track hedge fund performance and the different types of hedge fund structures that have evolved recently.

In the on-line Learning Guide for this module, complete the Getting Started activity.

KEY TERMS

- Accredited investor
- Commodity pool
- Convertible arbitrage
- Directional hedge fund
- Event-driven hedge fund
- Expected return
- Fund of hedge funds (FoHFs)
- Hedge fund
- High-water mark
- Incentive fee
- Limited partnership
- Lockup
- Offering memorandum
- Principal-protected notes (PPNs)
- Relative value hedge fund

© CSI GLOBAL EDUCATION INC. (2008)

OVERVIEW OF HEDGE FUNDS

Hedge funds are lightly regulated pools of capital whose managers have great flexibility in their investment strategies. These strategies are often referred to as alternative investment strategies, although this term may also be used to describe investments in private equity, real estate and commodities/managed futures. Hedge fund managers are not constrained by the rules that apply to mutual funds or commodity pools. The managers can take short positions, use derivatives for leverage and speculation, perform arbitrage transactions, and invest in almost any situation in any market where they see an opportunity to achieve positive returns.

Because hedge fund managers have tremendous flexibility in the types of strategies they can employ, the manager's skill (his or her ability to select superior investments within the targeted strategy and within relevant markets) is more important for hedge funds than for almost any other managed product.

Some hedge funds are conservative; others are more aggressive. Despite the name, some funds do not hedge their positions at all. Therefore, it is best to think of a hedge fund as a type of **fund structure** rather than a particular investment strategy.

Comparisons to Mutual Funds

Like mutual funds, hedge funds:

- are pooled investments that may have front-end or back-end sales commissions
- charge management fees
- can be bought and sold through an investment dealer

Despite these similarities, there are many differences, summarized in Table 20.1.

TABLE 20.1 COMPARING MUTUAL FUNDS TO HEDGE FUNDS

Mutual Funds	Hedge Funds
• Can take limited short positions when regulatory authority has been granted	• No restrictions on short positions
• Can use derivatives only in a limited way	• Can use derivatives in any way
• Are usually liquid	• May have liquidity restrictions
• Are sold by prospectus to the general public	• Are generally sold by offering memorandums to sophisticated or accredited investors only
• Are subject to considerable regulatory oversight	• As private offerings are subject to less regulation
• Charge management fees but usually have no performance fees	• Charge management fees and in most cases performance fees
• "Relative" return objective; performance is usually measured against a particular benchmark	• "Absolute" return objective; fund is expected to make a profit under all market conditions
• Most are valued daily	• Most are valued monthly
• Quarterly or annual disclosure to unitholders	• Annual disclosure to unitholders
• Cannot take concentrated positions in the securities of a single issuer	• Can take concentrated positions

© CSI GLOBAL EDUCATION INC. (2008)

Who Can Invest in Hedge Funds?

The market for hedge funds can be split into (a) funds targeted toward high-net-worth and institutional investors, and (b) funds and other hedge fund-related products targeted toward the broader individual investor, or "retail" market.

Hedge funds targeted toward high-net-worth and institutional investors are usually structured as **limited partnerships** or trusts, and are issued by way of private placement. Instead of issuing a prospectus, these hedge funds usually issue an **offering memorandum**, which is a legal document stating the objectives, risks and terms of investment involved with a private placement.

To invest in these funds, investors must be considered either **sophisticated** or **accredited**. Sophisticated and accredited investors must meet certain minimum requirements for income, net worth, or investment knowledge. For example, to be considered an accredited investor in any province, a person must own, alone or with a spouse, net financial assets having an aggregate realizable value exceeding $1,000,000 or have had net income before taxes exceeding $200,000 (or $300,000, if combined with a spouse) in each of the two most recent years, and a reasonable expectation of exceeding the same net income level in the current year.

For the broader individual investor, alternative investment strategies are increasingly being used in hedge funds and hedge-fund products structured as something other than a limited partnership. These structures include commodity pools, closed-end funds and principal-protected notes.

1. *Commodity pools*: **Commodity pools** are a special type of mutual fund that can employ leverage and engage in short selling using derivatives. Unlike conventional mutual funds, commodity pools must be sold under a long-form prospectus. Also, special requirements are imposed on mutual fund salespersons who sell them. Commodity pools are one way that retail investors can gain access to some hedge fund strategies.
2. *Closed-end funds*: In order to avoid the mutual fund investment restrictions, a hedge fund may be structured as a closed-end fund (which means that redemptions by the fund, if any, occur only once a year or even less frequently). Closed-end funds can be offered to retail investors by prospectus, but are not subject to the investment restrictions that apply to mutual funds. To provide liquidity to fund investors, closed-end funds are often listed on the TSX, which allows retail investors to gain access to the fund through the secondary market.
3. *Principal-protected notes (PPNs)*: **Principal-protected notes** provide investors with exposure to the returns of one or more hedge funds and a return of principal on maturity that is guaranteed by a bank or other highly rated issuer of debt securities (the Canadian Wheat Board and Business Development Bank are two examples). These products are not defined as "securities" and therefore are not subject to the rules and restrictions of securities law. As a result, this a popular structure for providing retail investors access to hedge fund strategies. There is more on PPNs later in this chapter.

The trend toward broader access to investments that utilize alternative investment strategies is generally referred to as the *retailization* of hedge funds, or the retailization of alternative investment strategies.

© CSI GLOBAL EDUCATION INC. (2008)

History of Hedge Funds

Alfred Jones is recognized as the father of hedge funds. In 1949, he created a fund with a goal to offer protection from a declining equity market while achieving superior returns. He did this by taking two speculative tools, short selling and leverage, and merging them into a conservative investing strategy.

Jones's model was based on the premise that performance depends more on stock selection than market direction. He believed that in a rising market a successful manager should:

- Buy or go long securities that will rise more than the market; and
- Sell or go short securities that will rise less than the market.

Conversely, in a falling market a successful manager should:

- Sell or go short securities that will decline more than the market; and
- Buy or go long securities will fall less than the market.

Based on this premise, Jones believed that his fund could produce a net profit in both up and down markets.

In addition to using short sales, Jones also used a small amount of leverage and, in a revolutionary move, set up the fund as a general partnership with performance-based fee compensation. Jones also invested most of his own money in the fund, since he did not expect investors to take risks with their money that he was not comfortable assuming himself.

Jones was very successful with his hedge fund and outperformed the best mutual funds consistently through most of the 1950s and 1960s. His success led to the entry of many new hedge funds into the marketplace. Initially, these new hedge funds followed Jones's long/short strategy, but innovations in derivatives and technology, together with new liquid markets abroad, allowed for the creation of new hedge fund styles, such as arbitrage funds, event-driven funds and macro funds.

Size of the Hedge Fund Market

Hedge funds have experienced tremendous growth in assets over the last several years. By some estimates, there are about 10,000 hedge funds trading worldwide with combined assets in excess of US$1.76 trillion, up from $400 billion in 2001. For comparison purposes, there were only about 600 hedge funds in 1990 (source: Hedge Fund Research Inc. [HFR]).

In Canada, the Canadian chapter of the Alternative Investment Management Association (AIMA Canada), including hedge fund managers, institutional investors, pension fund managers and consultants, estimated total assets under management of about US$40 billion in 2005. An AIMA Canada study found that the number of Canadian hedge funds serving individual investors grew from less than 50 in December 1999 to 190 in June 2004, and assets under management grew from $2.5 billion to $26.6 billion over this same period (the latest year for available data).

The hedge fund landscape has changed dramatically over the past 15 years, particularly in terms of the distribution of assets under management across strategies. According to Hedge Funds Research Inc., in 1990, global macro funds accounted for 71% of hedge fund strategies, but in 2004 represented 11.5% of hedge fund strategies. Conversely, equity hedged strategies accounted for 5% of all hedge fund strategies in 1990, but in 2004 were the dominant strategy, representing 30% of all hedge fund strategies.

© CSI GLOBAL EDUCATION INC. (2008)

Tracking Hedge Fund Performance

There are many different hedge fund indexes, each of which tracks different groups of hedge funds. None of the indexes is exhaustive, since hedge funds are not required to report any information or even to disclose their existence. Any given hedge fund index does not, therefore, give a complete picture of the hedge fund industry.

That being said, hedge fund indexes are a valuable source of information, because most investors are interested in the performance of larger, more well-known funds that are tracked by indexes.

One of the best-known hedge fund indexes is the Credit Suisse/Tremont Hedge Fund Index. The index draws upon the Tremont TASS database, which tracks 2,600 funds and managers. TASS tracks only those funds that have $10 million or more under management and that have current audited financial statements. This index includes most of the major hedge funds in the U.S. and provides a good picture of the mainstream hedge fund market. It is interesting to note that historically the Credit Suisse/Tremont Hedge Fund Index has had a low correlation with major U.S. stock market indexes, including the Dow Jones Industrial Average, the NASDAQ Composite Index and the S&P 500 Index.

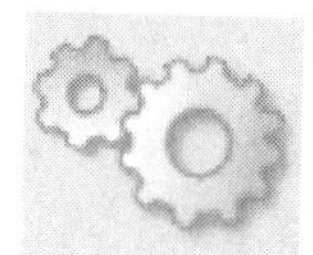

Complete the on-line activity associated with this section.

The Credit Suisse/Tremont Hedge Fund Index is also broken down into nine strategy sub-indexes, including the Credit Suisse/Tremont Long/Short Equity Index, the Credit Suisse/Tremont Equity Market Neutral Index and others. All told, Credit Suisse/Tremont claims to track more than 5,500 hedge funds. More information can be found online at www.hedgeindex.com.

BENEFITS AND RISKS OF HEDGE FUNDS

Benefits

Correlation with traditional asset classes: Although correlations can change over time, hedge fund returns usually have a low correlation to the returns on traditional asset classes, such as equity and debt securities. If these low correlations are maintained over time, hedge funds can provide diversification benefits and help lower overall portfolio risk. The extent to which a hedge fund provides diversification benefits depends on the type of hedge fund and on market conditions.

Risk minimization: Many hedge funds attempt to minimize risk. As shown in Table 20.2, the Credit Suisse/Tremont Hedge Fund Index had a low standard deviation relative to equities, as measured by the Dow Jones World Index and S&P 500.

© CSI GLOBAL EDUCATION INC. (2008)

TABLE 20.2 PERFORMANCE OF THE CREDIT SUISSE/TREMONT HEDGE FUND INDEX COMPARED TO THE S&P 500 AND THE DOW JONES WORLD INDEX

	Annual Returns (%)					
Year	**2007**	**2006**	**2005**	**2004**	**2003**	**5-Year Average**
Credit Suisse/Tremont Hedge Fund Index	12.56	13.86	7.61	9.64	15.44	11.82
S&P 500	5.49	15.79	4.91	10.88	28.68	13.15
Dow Jones World Index	8.43	18.52	9.41	14.47	33.02	16.77

Performance Statistics

	Annualized Standard Deviation	**Sharpe Ratio**	**Correlation with Credit Suisse/ Tremont Index**
Credit Suisse/Tremont Hedge Fund Index	7.46%	0.91	1.00
S&P 500	13.98%	0.43	0.49
Dow Jones World Index	13.51%	0.21	0.54

Source: Credit Suisse/Tremont website.

Absolute returns: Many investors underestimate the impact of negative years on overall wealth creation. Hedge fund managers seek to achieve positive or absolute returns in any market condition (up, down or trendless), not just returns that beat a market index, which is the goal of most mutual funds. Table 20.2 shows the returns of the Credit Suisse/Tremont Hedge Fund Index relative to the Dow Jones World Index and the S&P 500 over the most recent five-year period.

Potentially lower volatility and higher returns: With their potential for higher returns and generally lower standard deviations, hedge funds as a group usually outperform other asset classes on a riskadjusted basis. Note that the Sharpe ratio of the Credit Suisse/Tremont Hedge Fund Index is higher than the Sharpe ratio for both the Dow Jones World Index and S&P 500.

That being said, investors should not expect all hedge funds to have the same or even a similar return. Expected returns depend significantly on the type of hedge fund strategy.

Also, since hedge funds generally have a low correlation with stocks and bonds, including hedge funds in a portfolio with these traditional asset classes may improve returns while reducing overall risk. When hedge funds perform well, the benefit to the portfolio's overall risk-adjusted return can be substantial.

Risks

Light regulatory oversight: As hedge funds are generally offered as private placements, they are not required by securities laws to provide the comprehensive initial and ongoing information associated with securities offered through a prospectus. This lack of transparency may create a situation in which hedge fund investors may not always know how their money is being invested.

© CSI GLOBAL EDUCATION INC. (2008)

For example, it is possible that an unscrupulous hedge fund manager could be covering up losses by reporting inflated earnings. This type of fraud may not be identified until it is too late. Also, hedge fund managers may stray from the fund's stated investment strategy, engaging in a practice known as style drift. Once again, because of the lack of an ongoing reporting requirement, investors may not find out that this has happened until long after the fact.

To avoid these types of situations, the onus is on investors and their advisors to conduct thorough due diligence on hedge fund managers and their funds prior to investing in them. Advisors may also refer to due diligence performed by their in-house hedge fund specialists. Due diligence checks should include a review of audited financial statements to support representations of historical performance and a detailed review of a fund's offering memorandum. There is more on due diligence later in this chapter.

Manager and market risk: The management of mutual funds has evolved to the point where the investor's performance expectation is usually defined by the benchmark against which the manager is measured. In other words, the manager's performance is measured against a particular index. Hedge funds do not seek to produce returns "relative" to a particular index, but strive to generate positive returns regardless of market direction. Investors must therefore understand the risk/return characteristics of the strategies used by the hedge fund manager and whether they are focused on "hedging" strategies or strategies exposed to significant market risks.

A mutual fund manager's performance is more likely to reflect the general performance of the markets where they are trading, whereas a hedge fund manager's performance largely depends on the manager. In light of this, investors and their advisors should clearly understand the manager's targets, including the expected return, expected risk (as measured by the standard deviation), Sharpe ratio, overall percentage of positive months, etc. This way, investors and their advisors can measure the manager's performance against their stated targets instead of an index that is not related to the underlying strategies used by the hedge fund manager.

Investment strategies: Even if hedge fund managers try to mitigate risk, the methods they use may be difficult to understand. As a result, there is a risk that investors may not fully understand the techniques being used. It is the responsibility of investors and advisors to understand the strategies and investment products used by the hedge fund manager, as well as the fund's risk profile.

Liquidity constraints: Unlike mutual funds, hedge funds are typically not able to liquidate their portfolios on short notice. Holding less liquid investments often produces some of the excess returns generated by hedge funds. This liquidity premium is part of the trade-off against traditional investments. In light of this, there are often various forms of liquidity constraints imposed on hedge fund investors.

A **lockup** refers to the time period that initial investments cannot be redeemed from a hedge fund. Some hedge funds require lockups of three years or more! While lockups of this duration are not common for hedge funds offered on a continuous basis in Canada, some funds do have initial lockup periods or charge an early redemption fee if the initial investment is redeemed within the first three months to one year. Once the lockup period is over, the investor is free to redeem shares on any liquidity date specified in the offering memorandum.

Liquidity dates refer to pre-specified times of the year when investors may be allowed to redeem units in a hedge fund. Some hedge funds can be liquidated only on a quarterly or annual basis. Investors often need to give hedge funds advance notice of their desire to redeem their units, such as 30 days or more in advance of the actual redemption. Similar to traditional mutual funds, a

© CSI GLOBAL EDUCATION INC. (2008)

hedge fund manager can refuse redemptions if there is an occurrence in the markets that prevents the orderly liquidation of the hedge fund's investments.

The length of the lockup period represents a cushion to the hedge fund manager, especially a new one. If the hedge fund experiences a sharp drawdown (a sharp reduction in net asset value, defined as the peak to trough decline in the fund's net asset value) after the launch of the fund, the lockup period forces investors to stay in the fund rather than bail out. The ability of a hedge fund to demand a long lockup period and still raise a significant amount of money depends on the quality and reputation of the hedge fund manager and the market savvy of the fund's marketers.

Hedge funds offered through structured products such as bank notes have a specified maturity date at which time the fund is wound up and the investor is returned a pre-determined amount. Some bank notes have principal protection guarantees, which if backed by reputable banks, will ensure that investors are returned their original capital plus a specified portion of any returns generated in the hedge fund portfolio linked to the notes. In some cases, there are opportunities for liquidity through pre-established redemption notice periods that permit investors to redeem their units at the fair market value, less any early redemption penalties detailed in the offering document.

Incentive fees: In addition to management and administration fees, hedge fund managers often charge an incentive fee based on performance. Incentive fees are usually calculated after the deduction of management fees and expenses and not on the gross return earned by the manager. This detail can make a significant difference in the net return earned by investors.

The calculation of incentive fees can be subject to a high-water mark, a hurdle rate or both.

A **high-water mark** ensures that a fund manager is paid an incentive fee only on net new profits. In essence, a high-water mark sets the bar (based on the fund's previous high value) above which the manager earns incentive fees. It prevents the manager from "double dipping" on incentive fees following periods of poor performance.

For example, a new hedge fund is launched with a net asset value per unit of $10. At the end of the first year, the fund's net asset value per unit rises to $12. For the first year, the manager is paid an incentive fee based on this 20% performance. By the end of the second year, the fund's net asset value per unit has fallen to $11. The fund manager is paid no incentive fee for the second year and will not be eligible to receive an incentive fee until the fund's net asset value per unit rises above $12.

A hurdle rate is the rate that a hedge fund must earn before its manager is paid an incentive fee. For example, if a fund has a hurdle rate of 5%, and the fund earns 20% for the year, incentive fees will be based only on the 15% return above the hurdle rate, subject to any high-water mark. Hurdle rates are usually based on short-term interest rates.

It is important to determine whether the high-water mark is perpetual over the fund's life, or whether the manager has the authority to reset the level annually. If a fund has both a hurdle rate and a perpetual high-water mark, then incentive fees are paid only on the portion of the fund's return above the return needed to reach the perpetual high-water mark plus the hurdle rate.

For example, a hedge fund needs to earn a 10% return this year to reach its perpetual high-water mark. The fund also has a 5% hurdle rate. In this case, incentive fees will be paid only on the portion of the fund's return in excess of 15% (10% + 5%).

When the manager has the authority to reset the high-water mark, and does so, the calculation of incentive fees in the presence of a hurdle rate is more complicated.

© CSI GLOBAL EDUCATION INC. (2008)

Before buying a hedge fund, investors should confirm that there is a high-water mark, and ensure they understand how it is calculated and whether the hedge fund manager has the power to reset it. Note that management fees and expenses are paid regardless of the fund's performance.

Tax implications: The taxation of hedge funds is as varied as the structures used to offer them. Some hedge funds, such as limited partnerships and domestic trusts, are subject to full taxation annually. Others offer full tax deferral by using offshore structures to defer tax until disposition. In addition, some parts of the return may be taxed as income, while others are considered capital gains for tax purposes.

The tax structure is an important factor when selecting hedge funds, and investors and their advisors should ensure they understand the tax implications of the specific hedge fund structure.

Investors must assess whether the fund's investment strategies will generate primarily income or capital gains, or a combination of the two, and how the fund's investment and trading policies might affect their own tax obligations. Investors should seek the assistance of tax professionals to clarify the tax implications of a hedge fund.

Short selling and leverage: Unlike most mutual funds, hedge funds can both short sell and use leverage. Since security prices can, in theory, rise without limitation and since it may be difficult to buy back certain securities, hedge funds that use unhedged short-selling techniques to make directional bets may be risky.

Hedge funds may borrow several times the fund's invested capital. Although leverage can accentuate profits, it can also magnify losses.

Business risk: One of the biggest, and most overlooked, risks to investors is the business risk associated with hedge fund investing. Unlike large, well-capitalized mutual fund organizations, hedge fund companies are often start-up businesses. Investors assess the capitalization of the company and whether the manager has any experience running a business. A hedge fund manager may be a competent investment manager, but lack the skill or ability to run a business.

Due Diligence

Since most hedge funds provide investors with limited information, advisors and investors should fully research hedge funds before investing in them. Hedge funds are complex financial vehicles, and it is the advisors' responsibility to evaluate different hedge funds and select those suitable for each individual client.

Advisors have access to information about the hedge fund industry that clients do not. For example, they can participate in conference calls with hedge fund managers, and attend seminars and conferences featuring presentations by hedge fund managers. Most hedge fund managers allow advisors to phone and ask them questions about their funds.

Advisors should contact hedge fund managers, not only before buying into a fund, but routinely as part of an ongoing due diligence process. Hedge funds can change over time, and it is the advisor's responsibility to keep on top of these changes.

Advisors could develop a scoring system to assess a hedge fund's "risk profile" (like a "risk profile" for the client). The following questions should be addressed when assessing a hedge fund's risk profile (this list is not exhaustive):

© CSI GLOBAL EDUCATION INC. (2008)

MANAGER'S INVESTMENT PROCESS AND STRATEGY

- What is the hedge fund's investment process, philosophy and style?
- Is leverage used, and if so, how much? How is it employed?
- Does the fund use hedging strategies? Are derivatives used to hedge or to speculate?
- What hedging strategies are used and why?
- What risk controls does the hedge fund have in place?
- Have profits been made evenly across investments/strategies, or by a few more concentrated "home run" positions?
- Have losses come from a high number of trades, high expenses, from a small number of bad trades or positions, and/or for other market reasons?
- Does the fund have foreign exchange risk?
- Are there capacity constraints for the hedge fund's strategy?
- At the initiation of a position, does the manager have a maximum loss tolerance, and if so, does the manager use a stop-loss rule?
- What type of market environment is required for the manager's investment strategy to work? Is there something happening in the markets right now that makes this investment strategy more or less attractive?
- What is the worst type of market environment that could negatively affect the manager's trading strategy?

FUND DETAILS

- Are audited financial statements available for the fund?
- Are the fund's historical returns actual returns or pro-forma returns?
- What is the fund's lockup period?
- What is the fund's liquidity risk?
- How does the high-water mark for this fund work?
- What are the hedge fund's subscription and redemption policies?

INVESTORS' LEGAL AND TAXATION ISSUES

- What are the legal/taxation issues for fund investors?
- Where is the fund domiciled and how is its income treated for tax purposes?
- Is the hedge fund registered with or subject to regulation by any securities authority?
- What is the fund's legal structure and does it create any risk of personal liability to investors?

BUSINESS ISSUES

- Does the current manager have a long-term track record for the fund's strategies?
- How much capital has the manager personally invested in the fund?
- Is the hedge fund company profitable at their current level of assets under administration?
- How stable and well financed is the hedge fund company?

Advisors can also use hypothetical questions to assess how a particular set of circumstances could affect a hedge fund. Advisors can ask:

- How changes in market factors, such as prices, volatilities, and correlations, would affect the fund.

© CSI GLOBAL EDUCATION INC. (2008)

- About the fund's "credit risk," and how declines in the creditworthiness of entities in which the fund invests would affect the fund.
- About the fund's "liquidity risk," and how a decline in market liquidity could affect the value of the fund's investments.

HEDGE FUND STRATEGIES

While there are many different hedge fund strategies, there is no standardized industry classification for hedge funds. However, hedge funds can generally be broken down into three major categories based on the strategies they use – relative value, event-driven and directional, listed in order of increasing expected return and risk.

- **Relative value strategies** attempt to profit by exploiting inefficiencies or arbitrage opportunities in the pricing of related stocks, bonds or derivatives. Hedge funds using these strategies generally have low or no exposure to the underlying market direction.
- **Event-driven strategies** seek to profit from unique events such as mergers, acquisitions, stock splits, and buybacks. Hedge funds using event-drive strategies have medium exposure to the underlying market direction.
- **Directional strategies** bet on anticipated movements in the market prices of equity securities, debt securities, foreign currencies and commodities. Hedge funds using these strategies have high exposure to trends in the underlying market.

Table 20.3 shows the three major categories and the specific hedge fund strategies that fall within each one of these categories.

TABLE 20.3 MAJOR HEDGE FUND CATEGORIES

Relative Value Strategies (low exposure to market direction)	Event-Driven Strategies (medium exposure to market direction)	Directional Strategies (high exposure to market direction)
Equity market-neutral	Merger or risk arbitrage	Long/short equity
Convertible arbitrage	Distressed securities	Global macro
Fixed-income arbitrage	High-yield bond	Emerging markets
		Managed futures
		Dedicated short bias

Relative Value Strategies

EQUITY MARKET-NEUTRAL

An equity market-neutral strategy is designed to exploit equity market inefficiencies and opportunities by creating simultaneously long and short matched equity portfolios of approximately the same size. The goal of equity market-neutral investing is to generate returns

© CSI GLOBAL EDUCATION INC. (2008)

that do not depend on the direction of the stock market. Well-designed equity market-neutral portfolios hedge out the risks related to industry, sector, market capitalization, currency and other exposures. Leverage is applied to enhance returns.

The reasoning behind this strategy is that long positions will rise more in price than short position in rising markets and short positions will fall more in price than long positions in declining markets, resulting in a net positive outcome, no matter the market direction.

CONVERTIBLE ARBITRAGE

A convertible arbitrage strategy is designed to identify and exploit mis-pricings between convertible securities (convertible bonds or preferred shares) and the underlying stock.

Convertible securities have a theoretical value that is based on a number of factors, including the value of the underlying stock. When the trading price of a convertible bond moves away from its theoretical value, an arbitrage opportunity exists.

This strategy typically involves buying undervalued convertible securities and hedging some or all of the underlying equity risk by selling short an appropriate amount of the issuer's common shares. Properly executed, this strategy creates a net position with an attractive yield that can be almost completely unaffected by broader equity market movements. Interest income on the convertible bond added to the interest on the short sale proceeds contributes a relatively steady return. Given the low-risk nature of convertible bond arbitrage, leverage is used to enhance results.

FIXED-INCOME ARBITRAGE

A fixed-income arbitrage strategy attempts to profit from price anomalies between related interestrate securities and derivatives, including government and non-government bonds, mortgage-backed securities, repos, options, swaps and forward rate agreements. High leverage is normally used to help generate returns well beyond transaction costs. Leverage for this type of fund can range from 10 times to up to 30 times the capital employed.

EXHIBIT 20.1

Probably the most famous (or infamous) example of fixed-income arbitrage was the hedge fund run by Long Term Capital Management (LTCM). The managers engaged in fixed-income arbitrage strategies that often involved buying and selling bonds of different sovereign nations. Part of LTCM's downfall was that they began to trade in markets in which they had limited knowledge or experience. As well, they began using excessive leverage to enhance returns.

LTCM's strategy is best explained by Paul Krugman, a professor of economics at MIT, in his 1998 article "Rashomon in Connecticut. What Really Happened to Long-Term Capital Management?" (www.slate.com).

Imagine two assets – say, Italian and German government bonds – whose prices usually move together. But Italian bonds pay higher interest. So someone who "shorts" German bonds – receives money now, in return for a promise to deliver those bonds at a later date – then invests the proceeds in Italian bonds, can earn money for nothing. Of course, it's not that simple. The people who provide money now in return for future bonds are aware that if the prices of Italian and German bonds happen not to move in sync, you might not be able to deliver on your promise. So they will demand evidence that you have enough capital to make up any likely losses, plus extra compensation for the remaining risk. But if the required compensation and the capital you need to put up aren't too large, there may still be an opportunity for an exceptionally favorable trade-off between risk and return.

© CSI GLOBAL EDUCATION INC. (2008)

EXHIBIT 20.1 *(Cont'd)*

In fact, it's still more complicated than that. Any opportunity that straightforward would probably have been snapped up already. What LTCM did, or at least claimed to do, was find less obvious opportunities along the same lines, by engaging in complicated transactions involving many assets. For example, suppose that, historically, increases in the spread between the price of Italian compared with German bonds were correlated with declines in the Milan stock market. Then the riskiness of the bet on the Italian-German interest differential could be reduced by taking out a side bet, shorting Italian stocks – and so on. In principle, at least, LTCM's computers, programmed by Nobel laureates, allowed the firm to search for complex trading strategies that took advantage of even subtle market mispricing, providing high returns with very little risk.

As an example of one of its trades, LTCM, based on its computer models, went long Russian bonds against U.K. and U.S. bonds. In August 1998, the ruble was devalued, while U.K. and U.S. interest rates fell, meaning that LTCM lost on both ends of the trade. Since a considerable amount of leverage was used for this strategy, LTCM lost billions of dollars. Given the systemic risk to the global financial system, in August 1998, the Federal Reserve Board summoned 14 banks to set up emergency loans to meet margin calls while LTCM unwound their positions.

The moral of the story is that no matter how sophisticated the computer model or how smart the manager(s), volatile and unpredictable markets, combined with heavy leverage, can be a dangerous combination. It should be noted, however, that LTCM was not a typical hedge fund, given its sheer size. Today, most fixed-income arbitrage funds use leverage in the range of 20 to 30 times their capital.

Event-Driven Strategies

MERGER OR RISK ARBITRAGE

A merger or risk arbitrage strategy invests simultaneously in long and short positions in the common stock of companies involved in a proposed merger or acquisition. The strategy generally involves taking a long position in the company being acquired and a short position in the acquiring company. The hedge fund manager attempts to take advantage of the differential between the target company's share price and the offering price. Typically, the share price of the target company rises and the share price of the acquiring company drops after a takeover or merger announcement.

The returns on merger arbitrage are largely uncorrelated to the overall stock market. In general, equity risk is managed because the hedge fund manager is dealing with the probable outcomes of specific transactions rather than predicting the overall market.

DISTRESSED SECURITIES

A distressed securities strategy invests in the equity or debt securities of companies that are in financial difficulty and face bankruptcy or reorganization. Distressed securities generally sell at deep discounts, reflecting their issuers' weak credit quality. Many institutional investors are not permitted to own securities that are rated less than investment grade. Therefore, downgrading the credit rating of an issuer or security below the permissible minimum can precipitate a wave of forced selling that depresses the security's value below fair market value. Hedge fund managers attempt to profit from the market's lack of understanding of the true value of deeply discounted securities or the inability of institutional and other investors to hold these securities.

© CSI GLOBAL EDUCATION INC. (2008)

HIGH-YIELD BONDS

A high-yield bond strategy invests in high-yield debt securities (also known as junk bonds) of a company the manager feels may get a credit upgrade or is a potential takeover target. In general, these funds use little or no leverage.

Directional Funds

LONG/SHORT EQUITY

The long/short equity strategy is the most popular type of hedge fund strategy, constituting more than 75% of the hedge fund activity in Canada. These funds are classified as directional funds, because the manager has either a net long or net short exposure to the stock market. The manager is not trying to eliminate market effects or market trends completely, as would be the case with an equity market-neutral strategy; rather, he or she takes both long and short positions simultaneously, depending on the outlook of specific securities.

With a long/short equity strategy, managers try to buy stocks they feel will rise more in a bull market than the overall market, and short stocks that will rise less. In a down market, good short selections are expected to decline more than the market and good long selections will fall less.

In a long/short equity strategy, the fund is exposed to market risk based on the extent of the net exposure – either long or short. Compared to a long-only fund, this type of fund is often better able to profit in a declining market, as it can short stocks and manage the fund's net exposure to the market.

The amount of leverage used is usually modest, and is rarely more than three or four times capital. Most of these types of funds use smaller amounts.

A long/short equity fund's net exposure is calculated as follows:

$$\frac{\text{Long exposure} - \text{Short exposure}}{\text{Capital}}$$

For example, suppose a hedge fund manager feels that the shares of General Motors are underpriced relative to the shares of Ford Motor Company. The manager, with $1,000 in capital, buys shares in General Motors worth $1,000 and, at the same time, goes short shares in Ford worth $600.

This position can be viewed as having two components: a $600 "hedged" component and a $400 "unhedged" component.

In the "hedged" component, the manager has an equal dollar amount ($600) of long General Motors shares and short Ford shares, theoretically eliminating the market risk on this portion of the fund. The only risk that the hedged component is exposed to is stock selection risk, which is the risk that Ford's shares will outperform GM's shares.

The "unhedged" component consists of a directional bet on the likelihood that shares of General Motors will rise, since the fund is exposed to market risk on 40% of the portfolio.

With the additional bet made on General Motors, the fund's net market exposure is calculated as follows:

$$\text{Net exposure} = \frac{\$1{,}000 - \$600}{\$1{,}000}$$

$$= 40\%$$

© CSI GLOBAL EDUCATION INC. (2008)

If the stock market declines by 20%, the long/short equity fund's net exposure to this decline is only 40% of the market decline, or 8% (20% × 40%).

Of course, there is no free lunch: the price of protection from downside market movements is that the performance in rising markets will be lower than if the fund had not had a short Ford position. If the stock market rises by 20%, the fund's net exposure (or participation) to this increase will be only 40%. The portfolio of two stocks (GM and Ford) will rise by only 8%, or 40% of the 20% market increase.

Many long/short funds use some leverage. One method of calculating the fund's leverage is to add the fund's short market value to the long market value (this sum is called the fund's gross exposure) and then divide by the net capital invested. In this example, the fund's leverage is 1.6 times its capital.

$$\text{Leverage} = \frac{\$1{,}000 - \$600}{\$1{,}000}$$

$$= \frac{\$1{,}600}{\$1{,}000}$$

$$= 1.6 \text{ times}$$

As leverage can amplify both risk and return, hedge fund investors must understand the degree of leverage that the fund manager is using, as part of their due diligence before investing in a fund.

GLOBAL MACRO

The global macro strategy is one of the most highly publicized hedge fund strategies, although it constitutes only a small percentage of the strategies used by today's hedge funds. Its popularity is due to high-profile managers, such as George Soros and Julian Robertson who in the past have earned spectacular returns on well-publicized macro events.

Rather than make investments on events that affect only specific companies, funds using a global macro strategy make bets on major events affecting entire economies, such as shifts in government policy that alter interest rates, thereby affecting currency, stock and bond markets.

Global macro funds participate in all major markets including equities, bonds, currencies and commodities. They use leverage, often through derivatives, to accentuate the impact of market moves.

EXHIBIT 20.2

Examples of global macro hedge fund success stories include George Soros's Quantum Fund, which in 1992 bet – successfully as it turned out – US$10 billion, much of it leveraged, on the British pound being devalued, and David Gerstenhaber's Argonaut Fund, which in 1996 bet that interest rates in Italy and Spain would converge downward with the expected European Monetary Union. Both funds made spectacular returns.

Examples of global macro hedge fund disasters include the Niederhoffer Investments Fund, which was wiped out following some bad bets against the Thai baht and stock index futures in 1997.

© CSI GLOBAL EDUCATION INC. (2008)

EMERGING MARKETS

Emerging markets hedge funds invest in equity and debt securities of companies based in emerging markets. The primary difference between an emerging markets hedge fund and an emerging markets mutual fund is the hedge fund's ability to use derivatives, short selling and other complex investment strategies. However, since some emerging markets do not allow short selling and do not have viable derivative markets, these funds may not be able to hedge. As a result, performance can be very volatile.

DEDICATED SHORT BIAS

Up to 1997 this strategy was known as "dedicated short selling." However, the bull run of the late 1990s reduced the number of these funds and led the rest to change their strategy to a "short bias." To be classified as short bias, the fund's net position must always be short. In other words, the fund may have long positions, but on a net basis, the fund must constantly be short.

EXHIBIT 20.3

One of the better-known short-bias funds, which was closed out because of a continued increase in stock prices, was run by Julian Robertson of Tiger Management. Throughout most of the late 1990s, his fund was short several billion dollars' worth of technology stocks. He finally pulled the plug in early 2000 following the continued run-up in the NASDAQ Composite Index. Unfortunately, his timing could not have been worse. Shortly after closing out his fund, the NASDAQ Composite Index began a descent where it lost 60% of its value in the following nine months.

MANAGED FUTURES FUNDS

A managed futures fund invests in listed financial and commodity futures markets and currency markets around the world. Fund managers are usually called Commodity Trading Advisors (CTAs).

Most managed futures fund managers apply a systematic approach to trading, using technical and statistical analysis of price and volume information to determine investment decisions. Once the manager has developed the system, trading decisions are largely mechanical, and little or no discretion is involved. Other fund managers make discretionary decisions according to current economic and political fundamentals.

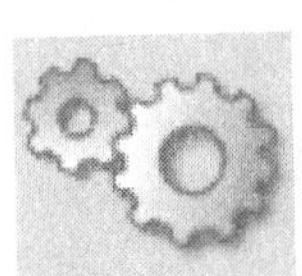

In Canada, managed futures funds are often established as commodity pools. Following a November 2002 Canadian Securities Administrators ruling (NI 81-104), these commodity pools can be sold as mutual funds to the general investor (not only accredited or sophisticated investors), and use derivatives in a leveraged manner for speculation. However, regulators require greater disclosure from and higher proficiency in the mutual fund companies and the agents who sell these products, compared to what is required of conventional mutual funds.

© CSI GLOBAL EDUCATION INC. (2008)

FUNDS OF HEDGE FUNDS

A fund of hedge funds (FoHF) is a portfolio of hedge funds, overseen by a manager who determines which hedge funds to invest in and how much to invest in each. There are two main types of FoHF:

- Single-strategy, multi-manager funds invest in several funds that employ a similar strategy, such as long/short equity funds or convertible arbitrage funds.
- Multi-strategy, multi-manager funds invest in several funds that employ different strategies.

Advantages

Funds of hedge funds have the following advantages:

- *Due diligence.* The task of selecting and monitoring hedge fund managers is time-consuming and requires specialized analytical skills and tools. Most individual and institutional investors do not have the time or the expertise to conduct thorough due diligence and ongoing risk monitoring for hedge funds. FoHFs constitute an effective way to outsource this function.
- *Reduced volatility.* By investing in a number of different hedge funds, a FoHF should provide more consistent returns with lower volatility or risk than any of its underlying funds.
- *Professional management.* An experienced portfolio manager and his or her team evaluates the strategies employed by the various fund managers and establishes the appropriate mix of strategies for the fund. Selecting funds that make up a low- or non-correlated portfolio requires detailed analysis and substantial due diligence. Ongoing monitoring is also required on each underlying fund to ensure performance objectives continue to be met.
- *Access to hedge funds.* Most hedge funds do not advertise and many are not sold through traditional distribution channels. Information on some hedge funds is closely held and hard to get hold of. Many successful hedge funds have reached their capacity limitations and either do not accept new money or only accept money from existing investors. Using their experience and contacts within the industry, reputable FoHF managers will know how to get hold of a hedge fund manager, or obtain information on a particular fund, and even reserve capacity with a fund. These are important qualities that a fund of funds manager brings to the table.
- *Ability to diversify with a smaller investment.* FoHFs increase access by smaller investors to hedge funds. While there are many Canadian hedge funds that accept as little as $25,000 from accredited investors, some funds have a minimum investment threshold of US$1 million, with some as high as US$5 million or more. An investor would need to commit significant funds to achieve the equivalent diversification offered by a fund of funds.
- *Manager and business risk control.* As hedge funds are less regulated than more mainstream investments, many investors believe that some hedge fund management firms may terminate their activities for business or other reasons at any time. This risk is based on the fact that hedge fund management firms tend to be relatively small business concerns, the success of which often rests upon one or a small number of managers and partners. Moreover, some hedge funds pursue riskier investment strategies, and may be more likely to experience problems, with some likelihood of having to terminate the fund. This "blowup risk" can be diversified away through a FoHF, as any individual fund likely represents only a relatively small fraction of the total assets invested. Additionally, the FoHF manager's duty is to continuously monitor and manage underlying funds in order to mitigate business risk.

© CSI GLOBAL EDUCATION INC. (2008)

For these reasons, funds of funds are increasingly the preferred hedge fund investment of choice for both institutional and retail investors.

Disadvantages

Funds of hedge funds do, however, have certain disadvantages and risks:

- *Additional costs.* Competent FoHF managers can be expensive to retain. Additional fees cover the management and operating expenses of the FoHF organization as well as its margins. Most FoHFs charge a base fee and an incentive fee, in addition to the fees (both base and incentive) charged for the underlying hedge funds. A typical FoHF charges a 1% management fee and a 10% incentive fee, plus fund expenses.
- *No guarantees of positive returns.* FoHFs do not constitute guaranteed investments and cannot be assured of meeting their investment objectives. In fact, during certain periods, FoHF asset values will probably decline. Investors and advisors need to understand that the FoHF is simply the sum of its component hedge fund investments. Despite the claims of some hedge fund marketers, investors should not, and cannot, expect positive returns in every reporting period.

Low or no strategy diversification. Some FoHFs are strategy-specific and invest only in one type of hedge fund, such as long/short equity or convertible arbitrage. Such FoHFs fill a specific role in the portfolio, and may contribute less diversification than multi-strategy, multi-manager FoHF.

- *Insufficient or excessive diversification.* The number of hedge funds in a FoHF can vary dramatically, from 5 to more than 100 hedge funds. Some may not provide adequate diversification, depending on the objectives sought by the investor. Others may dilute returns and provide more diversification than the investor needs.
- *Additional sources of leverage.* Some FoHFs add a second layer of leverage to enhance the FoHF's return potential (above leverage used by the underlying hedge fund managers). This adds to the costs and risk of the FoHF and needs to be understood and agreed upon by the investor.

PRINCIPAL-PROTECTED NOTES

Principal-protected notes (PPNs) and other structured products have gained increasing popularity with investors in the past five years. According to UBS, approximately US$80 to 100 billion were invested in hedge fund-based structured products globally in June 2004, while in Canada, Investor Economics estimates that at the end of June 2006, $13.8 billion was invested in hedge fund based PPNs.

Structured products bring together several components from financial markets into a product designed to offer attractive features to their investors. In this section we discuss only PPNs that are linked to hedge funds or funds of hedge funds, rather than the full range of structured products.

A PPN is an investment that combines access to the returns of one or more hedge funds (or funds of hedge funds) and a mechanism to protect the principal. The structure involves three separate roles: the guarantor or issuer, the hedge fund or FoHF manager and the distributor. These three roles may not necessarily be played by separate entities; for example, a guarantor may be both the manager and the distributor as well.

© CSI GLOBAL EDUCATION INC. (2008)

PPNs have particular importance for hedge funds. First, they give hedge funds a principal protection component, a highly desirable feature. Second, they offer significant regulatory benefits. Since the note is issued by a Schedule I or II Canadian bank or a Government of Canada crown corporation, it is considered a bank instrument, supported by the credit rating of the issuer. Moreover, the product extends a capital guarantee at maturity. For these reasons, no regulatory minimum is imposed on investing in these products, and no specific licensing requirements apply to the sale of these investment vehicles. Small-scale investors can gain access to hedge fund investing through PPNs, without being accredited or otherwise qualified investors. In this sense, PPNs make hedge funds accessible to an investing public that could not otherwise invest in hedge funds.

Costs and Risks of PPNs

Many costs are associated with PPNs. These products are not mutual funds and, in several provinces, are not even considered investment products; as a result, they are not held to the transparency standards of mutual funds or prospectus-based financial products. In fact, the lack of transparency in these products prevents investors from clearly understanding all the costs involved. It is particularly important, then, for advisors and investors to conduct due diligence on PPNs to determine their suitability for a specific investor.

In particular, they need to know the following costs:

- trailer fees and broker compensation
- marketing costs
- initial expenses
- fund of funds fees
- financing fees, including costs associated with leverage
- financing set-up fees

Although investors need to know what fees they are paying, and why, the lack of transparency in offering and marketing documents may make this hard to do. A good rule of thumb is to remember that nothing is free, and that ensuring the protection of capital entails many separate fees. The investor must decide whether capital protection is really needed, and if so, how much it is worth, keeping in mind that capital protection may entail a long holding period, that redeeming the note before maturity may incur costs (since a market maker must act as the counterparty to an investor wishing to redeem), and that any gains redeemed at maturity will be treated as ordinary income.

While there are several risks applicable to PPNs, we discuss only two of the most important ones here: performance risk and liquidity risk.

Performance risk: The performance of a PPN will probably not resemble the performance of the underlying hedge fund assets. This is particularly likely in the early years following the issue of the PPN.

Given the number of factors involved in valuing a PPN, including interest rates, various fees, and the actual performance of the underlying hedge fund assets, investors should realize that they are not purchasing a hedge fund's returns with a principal protection feature tacked on. Principal protection costs money, and the return from a PPN is unlikely to match the returns of the underlying hedge fund assets.

© CSI GLOBAL EDUCATION INC. (2008)

Liquidity risk: In some cases, no secondary market exists for PPNs unless the issuer chooses to make a secondary market. Typically, purchases in the secondary market will occur at a significant discount to the PPN's net asset value. Moreover, in certain situations (e.g., a high proportion of investors elect to redeem at the same time), the market maker is under no obligation to effect trades and investors may have to hold the PPN to maturity.

Selecting a PPN

Advisors and investors need to consider the following factors before investing in a structured product:

DUE DILIGENCE

- Does a qualified individual or team perform due diligence on hedge fund-related PPNs?
- What is reviewed in the due diligence? What is the depth of the review and how long does it take for one product? How often is it reviewed?

LIQUIDITY

- How often can investors redeem their investments? Is there a secondary market?
- Are there any restrictions on redeeming the note (lock-up periods, notice periods, redemption penalties)?
- Can investors redeem if the note goes into principal protection mode?

TAXES

- What are the tax consequences of selling before maturity?
- How is the note taxed if it is held to maturity?
- Are there any distributions? How are these taxed?

FEES, COSTS AND COMMISSIONS

- Is the cost structure clear, including all the fees being charged?
- What is the cost for the principal protection? Is it clearly disclosed?
- How much is the advisor being paid? Is this consistent with other similar products?
- Is it clear who receives which fees?

STRATEGY AND STRUCTURE

- Is the note based on a single hedge fund strategy or a fund of hedge funds?
- If it is a FoHF, is it diversified or concentrated in a particular strategy?
- How does the strategy work and how does the manager generate returns?
- •What are the risks associated with the investment (volatility of returns, leverage, concentration risk, liquidity risk, etc.)?
- Is leverage employed? How much?

Review the on-line summary or checklist associated with this section.

This is not an exhaustive list. However, it highlights many of the factors that investors need to understand before investing in a PPN. The offering document is the official source of information for any fund product.

© CSI GLOBAL EDUCATION INC. (2008)

SUMMARY

After reading this chapter, you should be able to:

1. Define hedge fund, compare and contrast hedge funds with mutual funds and institutional investors with retail investors in hedge funds, summarize the history and growth of the hedge fund market and discuss how hedge fund performance is tracked.
    - Hedge funds are lightly regulated pools of capital whose managers have great flexibility in their investment strategies, including using derivatives for leverage and speculation, arbitrage, and investing in almost any situation in any market.
    - Mutual funds are far more regulated and restricted in terms of permitted investments, valuation and reporting practices.
    - Institutional and high-net-worth investors are generally targeted by funds structured as limited partnerships or trusts that are issued as private placements.
    - Alternative ways of providing access to hedge fund opportunities, including commodity pools, closed-end hedge funds and principal-protected notes, are targeted at retail investors.
    - In 1949, Alfred Jones created a fund that used short selling and leverage to offer protection from a declining equity market while achieving superior returns.
    - Hedge fund performance is tracked against market indexes, although finding exactly correlated indexes is problematic because of variance among funds and the lack of regulatory requirements for funds to publicly report performance figures.
2. Evaluate the benefits, risks and due diligence requirements of investing in hedge funds.
    - The benefits of investing in hedge funds include low correlation to traditional asset classes, low standard deviation in relation to equities, a management theory in which managers seek to achieve positive or absolute returns in all market conditions, higher returns and generally lower standard deviations that equate to higher performance than other asset classes on a risk-adjusted basis.
    - The risks of investing in hedge funds include light regulatory oversight, manager and market risk, complex investment strategies that may not be fully visible to potential investors, liquidity constraints, incentive fees, tax implications, capital risk as a result of short selling and leverage, and business risk.
    - As most hedge funds provide investors with limited information, advisors recommending these funds as investments must perform thorough research to fulfill requirements of due diligence.
3. Identify the three categories of hedge fund strategies and describe how the specific strategies within each category work.
    - Relative value strategies (equity market-neutral, convertible arbitrage, fixed-income arbitrage): exploiting inefficiencies or arbitrage opportunities in the pricing of related stocks, bonds or derivatives.

© CSI GLOBAL EDUCATION INC. (2008)

- Event-driven strategies (merger or risk arbitrage, distressed securities, high-yield bonds): profiting from unique events such as mergers, acquisitions, stock splits and buybacks.
- Directional strategies (long/short equity, global macro, emerging markets, dedicated short bias, managed futures funds): investing based on anticipated movements in the market prices of equity securities, debt securities, foreign currencies and commodities.

4. Describe the advantages and disadvantages of investing in a fund of hedge funds (FoHFs) structure versus individual hedge funds.
   - A fund of hedge funds is a portfolio of hedge funds overseen by a manager.
   - Single-strategy, multi-manager funds invest in several funds that employ a similar strategy.
   - Multi-strategy, multi-manager funds invest in several funds that employ different strategies.
   - FoHFs have certain advantages: reduced need for due diligence, reduced volatility, professional management, ease of access, diversification with smaller amounts of capital, and lower manager and business risk.
   - FoHFs can also have certain disadvantages: additional costs, no guarantees of positive returns, low or no strategy diversification, insufficient or excessive diversification, and increased risk because of additional layers of leverage.
5. Define principal-protected notes (PPNs) and describe the costs and risks of investing in PPNs.
   - A PPN combines access to the returns of one or more hedge funds, or funds of hedge funds, with a principal protection feature (i.e., reduced risk of losing your invested capital).
   - Costs associated with PPNs include trailer fees and broker compensation, marketing costs, initial expenses, fund of funds fees, financing fees and financing set-up fees. These may not be easily determined because of the lack of regulatory oversight in reporting and documentation for these products.
   - The two most important risks for PPNs are performance risk (that the performance of the PPN will not replicate the performance of the underlying hedge fund assets) and liquidity risk (that no secondary market will exist for a PPN).

Now that you've completed this chapter and the on-line activities, complete this post-test.

© CSI GLOBAL EDUCATION INC. (2008)

Chapter 21

Analysis of Other Managed Products

© CSI GLOBAL EDUCATION INC. (2008)

21

Analysis of Other Managed Products

CHAPTER OUTLINE

© CSI GLOBAL EDUCATION INC. (2008)

- Scholarship Trusts
- Investment Contracts

Summary

LEARNING OBJECTIVES

By the end of this chapter, you should be able to:

1. Define closed-end funds and discuss the advantages and disadvantages of investing in closed-end funds.
2. Define income trust, differentiate among the types of income trusts, and describe their features.
3. Evaluate the advantages, disadvantages, and features of exchange-traded funds (ETFs).
4. Define labour-sponsored venture capital corporation (LSVCC), and discuss the advantages and disadvantages of LSVCCs.
5. Evaluate the features, advantages, and disadvantages of wrap accounts and other managed accounts.
6. Evaluate the features of index-linked guaranteed investment certificates (GICs), universal life insurance, mortgage-backed securities, scholarship trusts, and investment contracts.

OTHER MANAGED PRODUCTS

Since the early 1990s, managed products have become popular investment vehicles for many investors, particularly those who consider direct investing in bonds or equities too complex or risky. Managed products are often appropriate for investors who have a limited amount of money to invest but want the benefits of diversification and professional investment management.

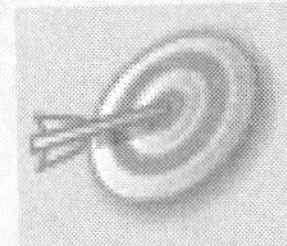

In the on-line Learning Guide for this module, complete the Getting Started activity.

As we learned in the previous chapter on segregated funds, managed products include more than just mutual funds. The one constant in the investment industry is change. Continual innovation in financial markets, products, and the wealth management industry in general has resulted in an overwhelming number and variety of managed products, which makes the process of making investment decisions all the more challenging. With more choice, investors have more homework to do before investing. Advisors are responsible for understanding the characteristics and features of these investment options to assess their suitability for clients.

© CSI GLOBAL EDUCATION INC. (2008)

This chapter continues to demonstrate one of the consistent themes we have presented in this course – investors are not limited to simply stocks and bonds for their investment choices. This chapter provides an overview, a discussion of the advantages and disadvantages, and the suitability of the many different types of managed products.

KEY TERMS

- Closed-end fund
- Income trust
- Replacement risk
- Discretionary account
- Guaranteed Investment Certificate (GIC)
- Universal life insurance
- Scholarship trust
- Labour-sponsored venture capital corporation (LSVCC)
- Real Estate Income Trust (REIT)
- Exchange-traded fund (ETF)
- Managed account
- Wrap account
- Mortgage-backed security (MBS)
- Reserve

© CSI GLOBAL EDUCATION INC. (2008)

CLOSED-END FUNDS

Closed-end funds are pooled investment funds that issue a limited or fixed number of shares. The number of shares or units in closed-end funds remains fixed, except in rare cases of an additional share offering, share dividend or share buy-back.

The prices of closed-end funds are based on market demand, as well as underlying asset value. Closed-end funds can trade at a discount, at par or at a premium relative to the combined net asset value of their underlying holdings. Most Canadian closed-end funds trade at a discount. An increase or decrease in the discount can indicate market sentiment. The greater the relative discount, all other things being equal, the more attractively priced the fund. However, it is important to find out whether the discount at which a fund is trading is below historical norms. A widening discount could indicate underlying problems in the fund, such as disappointing results from an investment strategy, a change in managers, poor performance by the existing managers, increased management fees or expenses, or extraordinary costs such as a lawsuit.

Funds that have the flexibility to buy back their outstanding shares periodically are known as **interval funds** or **closed-end discretionary funds**. They are more popular in the United States. In Canada, closed-end funds may also be structured with buyback or termination provisions. For example, a fund could be structured to terminate on June 30, 2012, at which time the proceeds will be distributed to unitholders. However, the fund manager could propose to continue the fund in 2011, subject to unitholder approval.

Because these funds trade on an exchange, the investor buys the fund just as he or she would purchase a stock and pays commission on the transaction rather than a front-end load or back-end load.

Advantages of Closed-End Funds

Diversification can reduce the risks associated with the varying discounts of closed-end funds. A portfolio of closed-end funds that have a low degree of correlation with each other will smooth out the adverse effects of closed-end discounts.

Closed-end funds offer certain opportunities for investment returns not available to investors in open-end investment funds, such as short selling. Thus closed-end funds can provide a boost to an investor's total returns. Typically a closed-end fund is more fully invested than an open-end fund. Open-end funds must keep a certain percentage of their funds liquid, in case of redemptions. Closed-end funds do not have this constraint. For instance, in addition to capital appreciation of the underlying assets, the trading discount to net asset value may shrink or the fund may trade at a premium.

In working with a closed-end structure, money managers have the flexibility to concentrate on long-term investment strategies without having to reserve liquid assets to cover redemptions.

Because the number of units of a closed-end fund is generally fixed, capital gains, dividends and interest distributions are paid directly to investors rather than reinvested in additional units. Therefore, tracking the adjusted cost base of these funds may be easier than for open-end mutual funds. Moreover, because there is only a fixed number of units to be administered, investors in closed-end funds may benefit from lower management expense ratios (MERs) than open-end funds with similar objectives.

© CSI GLOBAL EDUCATION INC. (2008)

Disadvantages of Closed-End Funds

Like stocks and unlike open-end funds, closed-end funds do not necessarily trade at net asset value. In bear markets, closed-end unitholders or shareholders may suffer as the value of the underlying assets declines, and the gap between the discount and the net asset value widens. Furthermore, since closed-end funds are not widely used in Canada, they may trade for extended periods at prices that do not reflect their intrinsic or true value.

Partly because of the divergence of trading prices from net asset value, closed-end funds are less liquid than open-end funds. Buyers and sellers must be found in the open market. The fund itself does not usually issue or redeem units. Commissions are paid at the time of purchase and at the time of sale.

Unlike the deferred sales charge option available on many open-end funds, there is no schedule of declining redemption fees. In fact, if closed-end shares appreciate, the commission payable on sale could be higher than it was at the time of purchase, since it would be based on the share's ending value.

Since many closed-end funds do not provide for automatic reinvestment of distributions (a feature of most open-end funds), the unitholder is responsible for reinvesting cash that may build up in his or her account.

For closed-end funds that trade on foreign exchanges, any dividend income earned is considered foreign income and is not eligible for the federal dividend tax credit.

INCOME TRUSTS

An income trust is similar in some ways to a closed-end fund. Investors purchase ownership interests in the trust, which holds interests in the operating assets of a company. These securities are exchange-traded and trade on the Toronto Stock Exchange.

Income trusts are investment trusts that have been created to purchase and hold interests in the operating assets of a company. Typically, there will be some sort of operating entity between the operating assets and the income trust. Income from these operating assets flows through to the trust, which in turn passes on the income to the trust unitholders. The income maintains its characteristics intact; that is, the income flows through to the unitholder as interest, dividends, capital gains or return of capital.

The trust itself avoids paying income tax because it pays out its pre-tax profits. Most pay out 85% to 95% of their cash flow.

Distributions from income trusts often include some return of capital. Although payment of tax on this income can be postponed, it reduces the adjusted cost base of the investment, ultimately increasing the taxable capital gain from the investment when it is sold.

An investor should be wary of an income trust that has a high payout of capital. It may be a sign that the company is generating income from a depleting asset, which may eventually become worthless. For example, an oil and gas royalty trust generates cash by depleting its oil and gas reserves. If the trust is to continue, it must acquire new oil and gas reserves at a reasonable price in order to extend its life.

© CSI GLOBAL EDUCATION INC. (2008)

Generally speaking, income trusts are divided into three primary categories (although these categories are not used consistently across the industry, which can make comparisons difficult):

- *Real Estate Investment Trusts (REITs)* purchase real estate properties and pass the rental incomes through to investors.
- *Royalty or resource trusts* purchase the right to royalties on the production and sale of a natural resource company. Usually the royalties are based on oil and gas production, but some trusts invest in power generation, mining, natural gas or propane. Some analysts put governmentregulated companies such as utilities into a unique category, as they tend to have more stable cash flows.
- *Business income trusts* purchase the assets of an underlying company, usually in the manufacturing, retail or service industry, in such diverse areas as peat moss extraction, restaurants, industrial appliances, canning and distribution.

Defined as a type of **asset-backed security**, they are also referred to as **equitized income products** or **high-yield securities**. The disparity in names highlights the controversy as to whether these securities are equities or fixed-income. They are most often compared to bonds because of the income they generate, but they do not have guaranteed payouts. Income trusts react to changing interest rates, similar to fixed-income securities, but trade on an exchange, like equities. Some industry experts feel that income trusts should be classified as a separate asset class.

Because they are backed by the specific revenue-generating properties or assets held in the trust, they face the same risks as common equities. The underlying business is affected by market conditions and economic cycles, as well as management performance. Depending on their structure, the priority and security of trusts typically rank below those of subordinated debentures.

The federal government changed the taxation of income trust distributions in late 2006. Beginning in 2007, a new tax became applicable to distributions from publicly traded income trusts established after October 31, 2006. Trusts already in existence on that date are not subject to the new tax until their 2011 taxation year. For income trust investors, the tax treatment will be more like that of corporations – investors will be taxed on their distributions as though the distributions were dividends.

For investors, distributions from an income trust will now be taxed in the same way as dividends received from taxable Canadian corporations.

Real Estate Investment Trusts (REITs)

Real Estate Investment Trusts (REITs) consolidate the capital of a large number of investors to invest in and manage a diversified real estate portfolio. Investors participate by buying "units" in the trust. REITs allow small investors to invest in commercial real estate previously available only to corporate or more affluent and sophisticated investors.

Canadian tax laws offer REITs significant tax deductions. For this reason, REITs pay out a high percentage of their income, typically 95%, to their unitholders.

REITs may be structured as either open-end or closed-end funds. If they meet the stringent standards set out under the *Income Tax Act*, REITs may qualify as registered investments for RRSPs and RRIFs.

© CSI GLOBAL EDUCATION INC. (2008)

REITs face many of the risks typical of real estate investments related to the quality of properties, rental markets, tenant leases, debt financing, natural disasters and liquidity. REIT managers generally minimize risk by avoiding real estate development and investing primarily in established income-producing properties. To reduce the danger of incurring too much debt, most REITs limit the extent of leverage to 50% to 60%. Leverage ratios tend to be significantly higher in the real estate industry.

Liquidity is a major benefit of REIT ownership. REIT units are much more liquid than real estate. However, investors should determine the liquidity of any particular REIT before investing, since some, especially the more specialized REITs, have thin trading volumes, despite being exchangetraded. As publicly traded instruments, REITs are also subject to full disclosure rules giving the investor access to more complete information for decision-making purposes.

When interest rates rise, REIT trading values may fall. On the other hand, REITs represent a good hedge against inflation since, in an inflationary environment; the value of the underlying real estate owned by REITs may appreciate.

Because rental income is fairly stable, REITs generally yield high levels of income but usually lack the potential for large capital gains or losses possible with equities. As with any investment, it may be necessary to accept lower yields to ensure a high-quality portfolio underlying the yield.

Buying REITs gives investors access to professional management. REITs, however, are just as susceptible to ineptitude on the part of management as any other company. The keys to minimizing risk lie in sound research before purchase and in diversification.

Royalty or Resource Trusts

Royalty trusts, also known as **resource trusts**, own royalties on natural resource assets. The owners of the assets must pay royalties on any income generated by these properties. Royalty trusts provide regular monthly income and, in the case of commodity price movements, the potential for capital gains or losses.

Income from royalty trusts may be eligible for federal or provincial tax credits. These trusts may act as a hedge against inflation if the underlying commodity price rises with inflation. The resource sector is considered volatile. By packaging revenue-producing properties into a trust format, royalty trusts tend to be less risky than investing in individual and unproven explorations. The most attractive royalty trusts are those that generate a regular cash flow while depleting investor capital to the smallest extent possible. The longer the reserve life of the property, the longer the royalty trust can maintain its payouts. Because of the proliferation of royalty trusts in recent years, the availability of suitable properties has become an issue.

Since the assets of royalty trusts are depleted over time, they must constantly find new asset bases. This is known as the "replacement risk" of royalty trusts. As with other income trusts, there is also liquidity risk, since royalty trusts tend to be illiquid.

Royalty trusts are suitable for investors who want some exposure to underlying commodity prices without the risk of investing directly in commodities or individual commodity stocks and for those who want regular income from their investments and can accept some risk. They are also eligible investments for RRSPs, RRIFs and other registered plans.

© CSI GLOBAL EDUCATION INC. (2008)

Business Trusts

Business trusts are as varied as the types of companies listed on a stock exchange. It is in this category that you see many examples of companies with strong, stable earnings, but little growth potential. Management uses the income trust structure to make an offering more attractive, since the company would be less attractive as a common share IPO.

Income trusts work best in markets where new competitors are unlikely to spring up – ideally a monopoly or a quasi-monopoly or a company operating in a protected niche.

The types of businesses held by business trusts are diverse. They include forest products, storage facilities, natural gas processing, propane, distribution terminals, restaurants, fish processing, fast food, sardine canning, dog food, aircraft parts, mattresses, school transportation, generators, cheque printing, peat moss, industrial washing machines, health care, biotechnology and food distributors.

Business trusts have provided the most growth in the income trust market in recent years. Analysts predict that this sector of income trusts will show continued growth in the future.

It is difficult to make generalizations about the risks of business trusts because of the diversity of the underlying businesses. Business income trusts are subject to the same interest rate risk as fixedincome securities. They are, however, also subject to the same risks as equity securities. Although they tend to be more stable than the equity market because the underlying business assets provide regular, stable income, they are still subject to market and economic risk.

EXCHANGE-TRADED FUNDS

Exchange-traded funds (ETFs) are open-ended mutual fund trusts that hold the same stocks in the same proportion as those included in a specific stock index. ETFs trade on recognized exchanges, such as the Toronto Stock Exchange in Canada and the American Stock Exchange in the United States. While most investors buy ETFs through the facilities of a stock exchange, new ETF units can be purchased from the distributor of the trust, although the minimum purchase amount is usually quite high.

Most investors use ETFs in one of two ways. Some investors use ETFs as a core passive investment in an index, and they typically intend to hold the ETF for a long time. Others, particularly active investors, use ETFs to implement their short-term forecast for a particular index. These investors sometimes trade ETFs frequently, and they may intend to maintain a position for only a short amount of time.

An investment in an ETF combines attributes of both index mutual funds and individual stocks. Like an index mutual fund, an ETF represents a passive style of investing which attempts to match the performance of an index such as the S&P/TSX 60 Index, the S&P/TSX Composite Index or the S&P 500 Index. Since ETF performance mirrors the index it tracks, if the index falls, so will the ETF.

© CSI GLOBAL EDUCATION INC. (2008)

Like stocks, and unlike index mutual funds, ETFs are traded on an exchange and can be bought and sold throughout the trading day. In this way, ETFs provide investors with a flexible way to participate in the performance of the underlying index. ETFs trade at or very near their net asset value, because investors who hold a specific quantity of an ETF can always exchange their holdings for an equivalent basket of the underlying stocks in the index. Variations in the supply and demand for a particular ETF at any time may cause the price of an ETF to be slightly higher or lower than its net asset value.

Table 21.1 illustrates the differences between ETFs and conventional mutual funds.

TABLE 21.1 COMPARING ETFS AND INDEX MUTUAL FUNDS

	ETFs	Traditional Index Mutual Fund
Pricing	Close to net asset value at any time during the day	Once per day using the closing price of the fund's net asset value
Cost	Low management fees Commissions to buy and sell	Low management fees May have front or rear loads
Portfolio Turnover	Low – lower taxable capital gains distributions lead to greater tax efficiency	Low – lower taxable capital gains distributions lead to greater tax efficiency
Short Selling	Yes	No

Canadian Market for ETFs

All Canadian ETFs are 100% eligible for inclusion in registered accounts such as RRSPs.

The ETF market has grown significantly in Canada over the last few years. There are now 62 ETFs listed on the TSX compared to 28 in 2006. With hundreds of ETFs to choose from in the U.S., it is expected that the Canadian ETF market will continue to grow. Three companies currently offer ETFs in the Canadian marketplace: Barclays Global Investors Canada Ltd., Claymore Investments Inc., and BetaPro Management Inc.

Table 21.2 lists a sample of some of the larger ETFs that trade on the TSX as of March 31, 2008 in terms of market capitalization.

© CSI GLOBAL EDUCATION INC. (2008)

TABLE 21.2 CANADIAN MARKET ETFS, BY MARKET CAPITALIZATION, MARCH 2008

Name	Fund Family	Market Value (C$)
iShares CDN S&P/TSX 60 Index Fund	Barclays	8,286,937,280
iShares COMEX Gold Trust	Barclays	1,813,110,000
iShares CDN Scotia Capital Universe Bond Index Fund	Barclays	852,849,030
iShares CDN MSCI EAFE 100% Hedged to CAD Dollars Index Fund	Barclays	786,621,546
iShares CDN S&P/TSX Capped Financials Index Fund	Barclays	493,904,346
Horizons BetaPro S&P/TSX 60 Bear Plus ETF	BetaPro	315,782,820
Claymore BRIC ETF	Claymore	161,628,147
Claymore Global Agriculture ETF	Claymore	146,992,500
Horizons BetaPro S&P/TSX Global Gold Bull Plus ETF	BetaPro	142,644,125
Claymore Canadian Financial Monthly Income ETF	Claymore	138,540,961

Source: Toronto Stock Exchange website.

As Table 21.2 shows, the most popular ETF in Canada, as of March 2008, was the iShares CDN S&P/TSX 60 Index Fund with a quoted market value of $8.3 billion. The fund holds a basket of stocks that represents the S&P/TSX 60 Index and trades under the symbol XIU on the Toronto Stock Exchange. The S&P/TSX 60 Index consists of 60 of the largest and most liquid stocks traded on the Toronto Stock Exchange in ten market sectors: consumer discretionary, consumer staples, energy, financials, health care, industrials, information technology, materials, telecommunication services and utilities.

The net asset value of each iShares S&P TSX 60 unit is approximately one-tenth of the level of the S&P/TSX 60 Index. The exact net asset value may be slightly more or less, depending on the fund's other assets and liabilities. Other assets include a cash balance that represents primarily accrued dividends from the underlying companies. Liabilities are typically related to management fees and other fund expenses.

The market price of iShares S&P TSX 60 fluctuates directly with changes in the level of the S&P/TSX 60 Index. For example, if the value of the S&P/TSX 60 Index is 700, each iShares S&P TSX60 unit would have a net asset value close to of $70 ($700 ÷ 10). The actual price at which the iShares S&P TSX 60 will trade may deviate slightly from the net asset value due to market fluctuations. Prices are quoted daily in the financial press in the same manner as other equities, and listed in the mutual fund section of newspapers under Barclays Canada.

Complete the on-line activity associated with this section.

The iShares S&P TSX 60 fund also provides dividend income for unitholders. Dividends are paid quarterly and consist primarily of dividends received from the companies held by the fund, interest on cash balances, and securities lending income, minus fund expenses.

© CSI GLOBAL EDUCATION INC. (2008)

U.S. Market for ETFs

The U.S. market is, by far, the largest market for ETFs. Most U.S. ETFs trade on the American Stock Exchange, and can therefore be bought and sold by Canadian investors in the same way that U.S. stocks can be bought and sold by Canadian investors. ETFs listed on the American Stock Exchange include:

- S&P Depositary Receipts (SPDRs, pronounced "spiders"), based on the S&P 500 Index
- Sector SPDRs, based on major sectors such as consumer staples, energy, technology and many more
- Dow Jones DIAMONDS, based on the Dow Jones Industrial Average
- NASDAQ-100 Index Tracking Stock (also referred to as Cubes or Qubes based on their trading symbol QQQ), based on the NASDAQ 100 Index
- iShares, based on a number of U.S. indexes as well as several Morgan Stanley Capital International country-specific indexes

LABOUR-SPONSORED VENTURE CAPITAL CORPORATIONS

Labour-sponsored venture capital corporations (LSVCCs) or **Labour-Sponsored Investment Funds (LSIFs)** are investment funds sponsored by labour organizations to provide capital for small to medium-sized and emerging companies. LSVCCs vary greatly in terms of size, risks and management style. Most are provincially based, although some are national. They can be divided into two broad categories:

- Funds that invest in a diverse range of industries
- Funds that concentrate on specific sectors

LSVCCs encourage individuals to invest in corporations that pool capital and invest it in eligible businesses in the province in which the LSVCC is created (for provincial funds) or across Canada (for national funds). Sales of labour funds are restricted by residency requirements.

Advantages of Labour-Sponsored Funds

The main attractions of LSVCCs are the generous federal and provincial tax credits that individuals receive for investing in them. Tax credits include a 15% federal credit on an annual investment up to and including $5,000, as well as an additional 15% provincial tax credit in some provinces. Therefore, depending on the type of fund and the residency requirements, LSVCCs generate a tax credit ranging from 15% to 30%. (Investors should note that the Ontario government has proposed to eliminate the 15% tax credit available on labour funds by the end of 2010. In Alberta, only the 15% federal credit is available.)

EXAMPLE: : Pierre invests $5,000 in an LSVCC in Québec, his province of residence. The fund is eligible for both federal and provincial tax credits. Pierre will receive a $750 federal tax credit (15% × $5,000) and a $750 provincial tax credit (15% × $5,000), for a combined tax credit of $1,500.

Although there is no maximum amount an investor may invest in an LSVCC, both the provincial and the federal tax credits are subject to annual maximum amounts. As mentioned, the federal

© CSI GLOBAL EDUCATION INC. (2008)

tax credit is available on a maximum of $5,000 invested in any one year. A province may have a lifetime limit applicable to provincial tax credits. The unused portion of the federal tax credits are not refundable and cannot be carried forward or back for application in subsequent or prior taxation years. Like the rules for RRSPs, an investor purchasing an LSVCC in the first 60 days of the calendar year can apply the tax credits either to the previous year's taxes or the current year's taxes.

Most LSVCC shares are eligible for RRSPs and RRIFs. In fact, buying an LSVCC investment within an RRSP, as most investors do, offers further tax savings. Shares can be purchased directly by an RRSP trust or may be purchased and then transferred to an RRSP or RRIF.

When LSVCC shares are purchased with money contributed to an RRSP, the contributor to the RRSP will receive the RRSP tax deduction as well as the LSVCC tax credits. The deduction of a sum equal to the purchase price in the case of a direct purchase, or a sum equal to the fair market value of the shares at the time of transfer, will be permitted, within the limits prescribed for contributions to an RRSP.

EXAMPLE: Pierre decides to invest $5,000 in an LSVCC for his RRSP. Assuming a 50% marginal tax rate, Pierre will realize additional tax savings of $2,500 ($5,000 × 50%) in addition to the $1,500 in LSVCC tax credits received on the purchase of the fund. Therefore, the effective after tax cost of his investment will be reduced to $1,000 ($5,000 – [$2,500 + $1,500]).

Disadvantages of Labour-Sponsored Funds

Because of the nature of the companies in which they invest, LSVCCs are considered a high-risk or speculative investment suitable only for investors who have a high risk tolerance. It is estimated that 80% of all new companies dissolve within five years of start-up.

The redemption of LSVCC shares is more complicated than the redemption of conventional mutual fund shares, since rules governing LSVCC redemptions differ from province to province and between provinces and the federal government. The *Income Tax Act* requires that the shares be held for eight years to avoid the recapture of federal tax credits. If redeemed before this minimum holding time, the investor must repay the tax credits received on the LSVCC when the fund was originally purchased.

EXAMPLE: If Pierre decides to redeem his LSVCC shares after holding the investment for only five years, he will have to repay the $750 federal tax credit and the $750 provincial credit he received.

Provincial requirements range from the right to redeem the shares immediately after purchase, to restrictions until a mandatory holding period has elapsed, to a ban on all redemptions.

An investor can avoid the recapture of tax credits in many circumstances. Here is a partial list of where the recapture does not apply:

- If the redemption request was made within 60 days of the acquisition, the form that would have been used to claim tax credits is returned to the LSVCC, and the share is not held for investment in an RRSP (i.e., the investor has not yet claimed the tax credits). Note that the redemption price is the original price paid for the shares, not the market price at the moment of the redemption.

© CSI GLOBAL EDUCATION INC. (2008)

- If the original purchaser reaches the age of 65, retires from the work force, or ceases to be a resident in Canada, and has held the shares for a minimum of two years (in some provinces only), he or she is exempt from tax credit recapture.
- If, after having acquired the fund, the original purchaser becomes disabled and permanently unfit for work or becomes terminally ill, he or she is exempt.
- If, as a consequence of the death of the original purchaser or the death of the original annuitant under a trust governing an RRSP or RRIF that was a holder of the share.

Since venture capital investing is more labour-intensive than investing in liquid stocks, the costs of administering these funds, as reflected in management expense ratios, tend to be much higher than for conventional equity funds. In addition, these funds must maintain a large cash reserve to finance redemptions. This cash position can drag down fund performance in rising markets.

Investing in an LSVCC

LSVCC shares are generally considered to be long-term investments for two reasons.

1. The nature of the underlying investments is such that time is required to allow the companies to grow and produce capital gains (and there is no guarantee that they will). The companies do not normally produce short-term income.
2. The tax credit system is designed to benefit those who hold their investment for the long term.

The illiquidity of the securities and the speculative nature of LSVCCs should be considered carefully when determining their suitability for an investor. The soundness of the investment, not the tax credit, should be the main motive for investing in a labour fund. A potential investor in these funds should examine the track record of the fund manager in venture capital and assess his or her ability to invest in successful companies.

MANAGED ACCOUNTS

Wrap Accounts

Wrap accounts or **wrap fee programs** are wealth management services that combine investment management and securities selection with order execution and custodial services. In these programs, the client assigns day-to-day management of an account to a qualified, licensed stockbroker, and gets professional money management and related services.

In **pooled wraps**, the investor's money is pooled with the money from other investors.

Investment dealers, financial planners and investment counsellors who are licensed to sell individual securities can offer wrap programs. They may invest in individual securities or in managed products such as mutual funds, pooled funds or segregated funds. Some managers offer several model portfolios from which to choose; others customize to a much greater extent. Some wrap accounts rely entirely on proprietary products as their underlying investments. (Proprietary products are those owned exclusively by the investment dealer.) Others, such as some mutual fund programs, use a wide range of non-proprietary products.

© CSI GLOBAL EDUCATION INC. (2008)

Although wrap accounts have traditionally targeted higher-net-worth individuals with minimum accounts between $75,000 and $150,000, these services are now available to account holders with amounts of $50,000 or even less, in the case of mutual fund wrap programs. This kind of account has increased steadily in popularity in recent years.

Wrap accounts generally charge the client an annual fee based on the assets under management. The larger the amount invested, the lower the percentage fee tends to be. Some programs have a flat fee, others have lower fees but charge for order executions and other transactions. In some cases, a flat fee is charged for a certain number of transactions, and a commission applies to trades above this maximum number. Fees for multi-manager wrap programs tend to be higher than those for a single management firm.

ADVANTAGES OF WRAP ACCOUNTS

The main advantages of wrap programs include:

- More individualized asset allocation than a fund of funds
- The structuring of efficient portfolios to achieve an optimal return for a given level of risk tolerance
- Enhanced reporting services

Many of these programs allow advisors to develop optimal asset mixes for clients, using computerdriven asset allocation programs in combination with client questionnaires to come up with an efficient portfolio that maximizes the expected return for a given risk. These asset allocation programs take into account assets and investments held outside the wrap program. In some cases, these programs also provide access to managers who might otherwise be available only to much larger accounts.

Because of the comprehensive nature of these accounts, the advisor is in a good position to get to know the client well. Long-term professional relationships are encouraged and the client's interests are kept at the forefront. Depending on the size of the account, the fees may be lower than those for mutual funds. Large accounts benefit even more from a tiered management fee structure: by eliminating sales charges and switching fees that apply to transactions within an account, managers have greater flexibility to adjust the portfolio without triggering costly sales charges.

Annual fees for traditional wrap programs generally depend on the amount of assets in the portfolio. Management fees are normally charged separately to the clients' account, rather than built into the management expense ratios of the underlying funds, as is the case with mutual funds. If clients have earned capital gains, a tax advantage is obtained if the fees are charged separately from the funds.

Separate fee arrangements enable clients to make payments to their registered plans such as RRSPs or RRIFs without using up part of their allowable contribution amount. Wrap fees are not taxdeductible inside an RRSP. Charging management fees directly to clients is also a clearer form of disclosure, as the fees charged appear separately in periodic client statements.

In some wrap accounts, the investment process is simplified through the use of a limited selection of managed funds for the underlying assets. Reporting on wrap accounts is generally more detailed than the client statements issued to regular mutual fund investors.

© CSI GLOBAL EDUCATION INC. (2008)

DISADVANTAGES OF WRAP ACCOUNTS

A possible drawback is the limited range of investment management alternatives available to the client through these programs. Proprietary programs usually tie the client more to the "house" than to the broker. Since wrap accounts are not readily portable between firms, this reduces flexibility for clients or advisors who want to change firms.

Other features that may make wrap accounts unsuitable for some investors include their inaccessibility, due to minimum investment restrictions, which are usually higher than for investments in mutual funds. There is usually an investment minimum of at least $50,000.

Management fees and expenses may not necessarily be lower than for regular retail mutual funds. Used within a wrap program, mutual funds create a layer of fees on top of the management expense ratios of the underlying funds.

USING A WRAP ACCOUNT

Wrap programs allow clients to work with an investment advisor to develop an integrated investment strategy. They are suitable for clients who want professional money management of their assets within a customized framework. They do not involve active trading, nor are they suitable for investors who want to play an active role in making trades or selecting individual stocks or bonds. Wrap accounts generally provide a vehicle for strategic asset allocation and, in some cases, act as a form of personal pension plan. In mutual fund wraps, the service may entail dividing money among asset classes according to a model portfolio that best suits the client's objectives.

For affluent individuals who want an enhanced level of service, wrap accounts provide an alternative to mass-market managed funds. By asking detailed questions, an advisor can ensure that a client's objectives are articulated, understood and met. The advisor can then customize an account according to the client's needs without being restricted to model portfolios.

Discretionary and Managed Accounts

Individuals who deal with investment dealers have another alternative to mutual funds. These investors may choose to have **managed accounts** or **discretionary accounts**.

- Managed accounts are accounts in which clients' investment portfolios are managed on a continuing basis by the investment dealer, usually for a management fee.
- Simple discretionary accounts are usually opened for a short period of time, as a matter of convenience for clients who are unwilling or unable to attend to their own accounts, for example, through illness or absence from the country.

The exchanges and the Investment Industry Regulatory Organization of Canada (IIROC) have adopted rules for discretionary and managed accounts. For example:

- Discretionary authority with respect to a managed account must be given by the client in writing and accepted in writing by a partner or director. The authorization must specify the client's investment objectives.
- Discretionary authority for these accounts may not be solicited, whereas managed accounts may be solicited.
- IAs other than partners or directors may not accept authorization for a simple discretionary account.

© CSI GLOBAL EDUCATION INC. (2008)

According to TSX procedures, IAs may make investment recommendations for simple discretionary accounts, provided that the decision to implement the recommendation rests with a partner or director and the IA receives written approval from the partner or director prior to carrying out the recommendation.

In managed accounts, discretionary authority may not be exercised by a member or any person on a member's behalf unless the person responsible for the management of the account is designated and approved as a portfolio manager.

The New Account Application Form provides for the identification of discretionary authority over an account. This form should be used to indicate the category of the account (i.e., simple discretionary account or managed discretionary account).

Fee-Based Accounts

The increasingly popular **fee-based accounts** are full-service brokerage accounts that entitle an investor to a fixed or unlimited number of trades for a fee. Commission is not charged on these trades. The client usually has access to professional advice.

Fees for a fee-based brokerage account range from 0.50% to 2.5% of the assets under management. In most cases, the annual fee is paid quarterly out of cash or money market funds held in the account. The fee depends on the following criteria:

- Dollar size of account
- Number of trades allowed
- Full-service or on-line
- Research availability
- Type of investment (equity, bond, money market)

Some large investment dealers offer two levels of fee-based accounts. The higher level typically offers more or unlimited free trading.

ADVANTAGES OF FEE-BASED ACCOUNTS

For a client who is an active trader, fee-based brokerage accounts can result in a substantial reduction in trading costs. Fee-based accounts enable brokers to continue recommending directly held securities and third-party mutual funds, but without regard for the commissions they normally carry. Brokers need no longer shun passive investment vehicles such as low-cost index funds and the fast-growing array of exchange-traded funds. The client has complete confidence that the advisor is recommending securities that are in the best interests of the client. Under a commission-based structure, the client might wonder if the advisor is suggesting investments because the product carries a higher commission. The fees charged are tax-deductible for nonregistered accounts.

DISADVANTAGES OF FEE-BASED ACCOUNTS

Not everyone in the industry feels that this move to fee-based brokerage accounts is necessarily positive. Opponents of fee-based brokerage accounts cite the following possible disadvantages:

- *Potentially more expensive*: It may not be less expensive for a client who is not an active trader. Nor is it necessarily cheaper for a client who is a very active trader. Some fee-based accounts have a limit to the number of trades in the account. The maximum ranges from 10 to 350,

© CSI GLOBAL EDUCATION INC. (2008)

depending on the firm, the size and the type of account. Some firms do have unlimited trading; however, one firm offers a fee-based account where trades are still paid for separately.

- *Long-term investments*: Some advisors feel that it is inappropriate to begin charging fees on investments if clients are likely to hold those investments for a long time.
- *Neglect by IA*: There is a chance that the IA could become "lazy," as he or she can count on a continuing stream of income regardless of how much time and effort is put into the account. The client could become neglected.
- *Losing sight of investment goals*: The client may begin to trade much more frequently than is necessary or advisable, because there is no cost. The client could begin to lose sight of the goals of the account.
- *Extra fees charged*: In some circumstances, the client is charged two fees. In addition to the fee charged on the account, the client may be charged extra fees from investments that have fees or commissions buried in their price, such as bonds or mutual funds.
- *Fees in a bear market*: Some clients may become upset when they realize that the broker receives a fee whether the portfolio goes up or down in value.

OTHER UNIQUE MANAGED PRODUCTS

Index-Linked Guaranteed Investment Certificates (GICs)

Indexed-linked GICs are hybrid investment products that combine the safety of a deposit instrument with some of the growth potential of an equity investment. Most financial institutions offer these securities. They have grown in popularity, particularly among conservative investors who are concerned with safety of capital but want yields greater than the interest on standard interestbearing GICs or other term deposits.

The yields of these products are a blend of guaranteed interest payments and a percentage of market index returns. The returns of some GICs are tied to domestic markets, while others are tied to global market indexes. For example, TD Canada Trust's Global GIC Plus tracks the S&P/TSX 60 (Toronto), S&P 500 (New York), FTSE 100 (London), Nikkei 225 (Tokyo) and DJ EUROSTOXX 50 (Frankfurt) indices.

Performance comparisons are difficult, but some features can and should be compared in determining whether to invest in index-linked GICs. Along with having different underlying benchmarks, the terms of these securities vary. Some tie returns to the level of the index on a particular date. Some base the return on the average return for a number of periods during the GIC's term. Others allow investors to lock in returns as of a given period. Still others allow early redemptions at specific dates, such as a one-year anniversary. Although averaging provisions reduce the effect of a sharp market plunge just before maturity, they also reduce the investor's returns in a gradually rising market.

The Canada Deposit Insurance Corporation (CDIC) insures index-linked certificates against issuer default, just as it does conventional fixed-rate GICs. However, this insurance underlines the fact that returns on index-linked GICs are considered interest income and are fully taxable. In addition, payouts on index-linked GICs are often based solely on movements in the index and ignore dividends paid by companies to direct shareholders.

© CSI GLOBAL EDUCATION INC. (2008)

Although the only risk to holders of these securities in a market downturn is the forgone interest that would have been earned by a conventional GIC, limited risk implies limited potential for gain. Holders of these instruments do not necessarily participate fully in the returns earned by equity markets. Issuers often cap the return of an index-linked GIC at a level below the potential return of the index.

Mortgage-Backed Securities (MBSs)

Mortgage-backed securities are pools of residential mortgages that have been securitized – that is, grouped together and resold to institutional and private investors. These securities trade in the secondary market. Introduced in 1986, MBS issues have become a routine part of the mortgage industry.

Canada Mortgage and Housing Corporation (CMHC) is the main creator of mortgage-backed securities in Canada, although private companies may issue them, too. CMHC guarantees the payment of interest and repayment of principal on its issues. Similar to the underlying mortgages, these pools can be closed (which means that no prepayments, or the opportunity to pay off the mortgage before maturity, are allowed) or open (prepayments are allowed, which increases the risk to the investor).

Most common are the five-year pools that are denominated in multiples of $5,000. MBSs earn returns that are comparable to GICs and are typically higher than Treasury bills or other Government of Canada bonds with similar terms.

With consistently low mortgage rates over the last five years, variable-rate mortgages and adjustable-rate mortgages have gained considerable popularity with home buyers. This has led to an increase in the demand for products offering variable-rate and adjustable-rate mortgages.

Mortgage-backed securities are attractive to income-oriented investors since investors receive a cheque every month. Although they are low risk, since most are guaranteed by CMHC, investors should be aware that liquidity in the secondary market for certain issues can be poor.

Universal Life Insurance

Universal life insurance is a form of permanent life insurance in which the investment component of the policy is separated from the insurance component. A universal life plan typically consists of insurance coverage in the form of a term life policy and a reserve account that represents the investment component of the policy. Annual premiums cover the insurance and the investment, and a portion is designated for administration and mortality charges (the death benefit).

Once these deductions have been made, any remaining cash is credited to a reserve account. This reserve account is essentially an investment account, controlled by the policyholder, that may be used to accumulate funds. Some options include a daily interest savings account, a term deposit account, or domestic and foreign equity market index accounts.

As a strategy for estate planning and tax deferral, paying more than the minimum premium into a universal life plan can provide considerable tax savings. Payments to the plan (including funds in excess of the premium requirements) continue to grow, presumably for future payment to one's estate. The returns are untaxed as long as they remain in the plan.

© CSI GLOBAL EDUCATION INC. (2008)

As with any leveraging strategy, the enhanced investment component of a universal life policy entails increased investment risk. The death benefits and the cash value of universal life policies are not always guaranteed but are tied to the movement of the investment account.

Because of the flexibility of the policies, universal life plans are useful for investors who have maximized their RRSP and have no contribution room left. Growth in the reserve account of a universal life policy is not taxable unless the funds are removed from the policy, just as tax is deferred on holdings in a registered plan. (To maintain its tax-exempt status, the plan must maintain a certain level of investments in relation to the amount of insurance protection.)

Scholarship Trusts

Scholarship trusts are available through several non-profit companies. They were created to help parents save for their children's post-secondary education and have been in existence since the early 1960s.

The subscribers (parents or grandparents) make contributions to the plan in the form of a lump sum payment, annual or monthly payments, or payments for a prescribed number of years. The contributions are used to purchase units in the scholarship trust. Like many insurance products, the earlier the plan is started, the lower the payments will be. The fees for opening a plan are deducted from the initial deposits. These plans are all eligible for the Canada Education Savings Grant (CESG) from the government, as they are registered as Registered Education Savings Plans (RESP). (These topics are discussed in more detail in Chapter 22)

Investment Contracts

Review the on-line summary or checklist associated with this section.

Some investment opportunities do not fall into any other category of security (such as equities, options or mutual funds), if the opportunity is customized for a specific situation, such as creating and selling innovative software.

A venture is considered by the securities commissions to be an Investment Contract (IC) if the investor supplying the capital, having been promised a share of the profits, has no pertinent knowledge of the business nor the power to participate in the decision-making process of the venture. The investor must be provided with a prospectus. The IC salesperson must be specifically registered with a provincial Securities Commission to sell this type of security.

© CSI GLOBAL EDUCATION INC. (2008)

SUMMARY

After reading this chapter, you should be able to:

1. Define closed-end funds and discuss the advantages and disadvantages of investing in closed-end funds.
   - Closed-end funds are pooled investment funds that issue a limited or fixed number of shares and trade on an exchange.
   - Fund prices are based on market demand and underlying asset value.
   - Funds can trade at a discount, at par or at a premium relative to the combined net asset value of their underlying holdings.
   - Advantages of closed-end funds include:
     - Diversification
     - Ability to short-sell
     - Increased investment flexibility for managers
     - Ease in tracking an adjusted cost base
     - Potentially lower management expense ratios than for open-ended funds
   - Disadvantages of closed-end funds include:
     - Lack of liquidity
     - Possibility of trading below net asset value
     - Paying regular commissions
     - Possibility of lack of availability of income reinvestment plans
     - Highly taxed income from funds that trade on foreign exchanges
2. Define income trust, differentiate among the types of income trusts, and describe their features.
   - Income trusts are asset-back securities that have been created to purchase and hold interests in the operating assets of a company.
   - Real estate investment trusts (REITs), which can be open or closed-end funds, consolidate the capital of a large number of investors to invest in and manage a diversified real estate portfolio. Rental incomes (as much as 95% of that generated) are passed through to investors who buy units in the trust. The units are more liquid than buying real estate directly.
   - Royalty or resource trusts purchase the right to royalties on the production and sale of a natural resource company and provide regular monthly income. Capital gains or losses may result from commodity price movements.

© CSI GLOBAL EDUCATION INC. (2008)

- Business income trusts purchase the assets of an underlying company, usually in the manufacturing, retail or service industry.

3. Evaluate the advantages, disadvantages and features of exchange-traded funds (ETFs).

   - Exchange-traded funds are quasi-open-ended mutual fund trusts trading on recognized exchanges that hold the same stocks in the same proportion as those included in a specific stock index.
   - ETFs offer the opportunity for short selling, continual valuation, marketability through exchange facilities, low management fees, and an easy-to-understand commission structure.

4. Define labour-sponsored venture capital corporations (LSVCCs), and discuss the advantages and disadvantages of LSVCCs.

   - Labour-sponsored venture capital corporations are investment funds sponsored by labour organizations to provide capital for small to medium-sized and emerging companies.
   - LSVCCs can be divided into two broad categories: funds that invest in a diverse range of industries and those that concentrate on specific sectors.
   - Advantages of LSVCCs can include:
     - Generous federal and provincial tax credits
     - RRSP and RRIF eligibility
   - Disadvantages of LSVCCs can include:
     - A high level of risk
     - Complicated redemption rules
     - Possible recapture of tax credits on early redemption
     - Comparatively high management expense ratios
     - A reduction in performance in cases where managers need to maintain high levels of cash to fund potential redemptions

5. Evaluate the features, advantages and disadvantages of wrap accounts and other managed accounts.

   - Wrap accounts assign account management to a qualified, licensed investment advisor and combine investment management and securities selection with order execution and custodial services.
   - In pooled wraps, the investor's money is pooled with money from other investors.
   - A percentage-based annual fee is charged based on assets under management, usually on a declining scale related to asset size.
   - Advantages of wrap accounts can include more individualized asset allocation than a fund of funds, more personalized investment management, and usually enhanced reporting.

© CSI GLOBAL EDUCATION INC. (2008)

- Disadvantages of wrap accounts can include lack of flexibility, lack of portability, high minimum investment amounts, and an additional layer of fees.
- Managed accounts are managed on a continuing basis by an investment dealer and are usually fee-based.
- Discretionary accounts, generally short-term in nature, are for clients unwilling or unable to manage their accounts.
- Fee-based accounts are full-service brokerage accounts that charge a flat fee and give a client entitlement to a fixed or unlimited number of trades without additional commission.
- Advantages of fee-based accounts can include a possible reduction in trading costs for active traders, elimination of commission considerations for investment advisors making investment recommendations, and possible tax-deductibility of fee charged.
- Disadvantages of fee-based accounts can include higher costs for non-active traders, fees charged regardless of activity level, lack of incentive for investment advisors to work with clients, over-trading as a result of the elimination of trading costs, an additional layer of fees, and fees charged regardless of investment performance.

6. Evaluate the features of index-linked guaranteed investment certificates (GICs), universal life insurance, mortgage-backed securities, scholarship trusts and investment contracts.
   - Index-linked GICs are CDIC-insured hybrid investment products in which the fully taxed yield is a blend of guaranteed interest payments and a percentage of market index returns.
   - Mortgage-backed securities are securitized pools of residential mortgages.
   - Universal life insurance is a form of permanent life insurance in which the investment component of the policy is separated from the insurance (usually term life) component.
   - Scholarship trusts, eligible for CESG grants, are pooled plans in which parents or grandparents make lump-sum payment(s) for a specific number of years. At maturity, principal and income are proportionately distributed to participants.
   - Investment contracts are prospectus-based, non-standardized, but regulated, security arrangements generally used for venture-capital situations.

Now that you've completed this chapter and the on-line activities, complete this post-test.

© CSI GLOBAL EDUCATION INC. (2008)

SECTION EIGHT

Working With the Client

© CSI GLOBAL EDUCATION INC. (2008)

Chapter 22

Canadian Taxation

© CSI GLOBAL EDUCATION INC. (2008)

22

Canadian Taxation

CHAPTER OUTLINE

Taxation

- The Income Tax System in Canada
- Types of Income
- Calculating Income Tax Payable
- Taxation of Investment Income
- Tax-Deductible Items Related to Investment Income

Calculating Investment Gains and Losses

- Disposition of Shares
- Disposition of Debt Securities
- Capital Losses
- Tax Loss Selling
- Minimum Tax

Tax Deferral Plans

- Registered Pension Plans (RPPs)
- Registered Retirement Savings Plans (RRSPs)
- Registered Retirement Income Funds (RRIFs)
- Deferred Annuities
- Registered Educations Savings Plans (RESPs)

Tax Planning Strategies

- Transferring Income
- Other Planning Opportunities

Summary

© CSI GLOBAL EDUCATION INC. (2008)

LEARNING OBJECTIVES

By the end of this chapter, you should be able to:

1. Describe the features of the Canadian income tax system, calculate income tax payable, and differentiate the tax treatment of interest, dividends and capital gains (and losses).
2. Calculate capital gains and capital losses and assess strategies for minimizing tax liability.
3. Describe and differentiate the different tax deferral plans and their uses.
4. Identify basic tax planning strategies and discuss their advantages.

TAXES AND INVESTMENTS

It is often said that there are only two certainties in life: death and taxes. Taxes are a reality of life for Canadians and they affect many personal and investment decisions. Complicating matters is the differential tax rates for income, dividends, and capital gains, not to mention continually changing legislation announced each year in the Federal Budget. The taxation of investment income also affects retirement planning through tax-favoured investments such as registered retirement savings plans (RRSPs).

In the on-line Learning Guide for this module, complete the Getting Started activity.

Investors and advisors must have a working knowledge of the taxation of investment income. Does this mean you need to become a tax expert? No. Most advisors rely on the professional input of accountants and tax experts when a decision on a specific tax matter is needed.

So why is there a section on taxation in this course? Because understanding the basic principles and practices of taxation, and some of the key strategies and opportunities, is necessary. Ignoring this area when making investment decisions could mean more tax is paid than necessary, or that a tax planning strategy is missed. This chapter also highlights when to contact a tax expert for more specific advice. Making mistakes related to the taxation of investments can be costly and can even result in an unexpected visit to a court of law!

© CSI GLOBAL EDUCATION INC. (2008)

KEY TERMS

Alternative Minimum Tax (AMT)

Annuity

Attribution rules

Canada Education Savings Grant (CESG)

Capital loss

Carrying charge

Contribution in kind

Deemed disposition

Deferred annuity

Defined Benefit Plans (DBP)

Defined Contribution Plan (DCP)

Fiscal year

Income splitting

Marginal tax rate

Money Purchase Plans (MPP)

Past Service Pension Adjustment (PSPA)

Pension Adjustment (PA)

Registered Education Savings Plan (RESP)

Registered Pension Plan (RPP)

Registered Retirement Income Fund (RRIF)

Registered Retirement Savings Plan (RRSP)

Self-directed RRSP

Spousal RRSP

Stock savings plan (SSP)

Superficial loss

Tax loss selling

© CSI GLOBAL EDUCATION INC. (2008)

TAXATION

This section discusses the fundamentals of taxation in Canada and deals with current issues only. Individuals seeking advice or information on prior taxation years should seek assistance from the Canada Revenue Agency (CRA).

Proper tax planning should be a part of every investor's overall financial strategy. The minimization of tax, however, must not become the sole objective nor can it be allowed to overwhelm the other elements of proper financial management. The investor must keep in mind that it is the after-tax income or return that is important. Choosing an investment based solely on a low tax status does not make sense if the end result is a lower after-tax rate of return than the after-tax rate of return of another investment that is more heavily taxed.

While all investors wish to lighten their individual tax burden, the time and effort spent on tax planning must not outweigh the rewards reaped. Tax planning is an ongoing process with many matters being addressed throughout the year. The best tax advantages are usually gained by planning early and planning often, allowing reasonable time for the plan to work and to produce the desired results.

While the tax authorities do not condone tax evasion, *tax avoidance* by one or more of the following means is completely legitimate:

- Full utilization of allowable deductions;
- Conversion of non-deductible expenses into tax-deductible expenditures;
- Postponing the receipt of income;
- Splitting income with other family members, when handled properly; and
- Selecting investments that provide a better after-tax rate of return.

Although this discussion will highlight some of the taxation issues that affect taxpayers, none of the suggestions made here should be considered specific recommendations.

As tax plays a significant part in the overall financial plan and can affect the choice of investments greatly, every attempt should be made to keep abreast of the ever-changing rules and interpretations. CRA can provide significant material to the investor by way of regulations and rulings upon request. Contact the local CRA offices (or their website at www.cra-arc.gc.ca) for further information. If the client is a U.S. citizen, green card holder or U.S. resident, U.S. tax laws will also have to be taken into account.

The Income Tax System in Canada

The federal government imposes income taxes by federal statute (the *Income Tax Act*, often referred to as the *ITA*). All Canadian provinces have separate statutes which impose a provincial income tax on residents of the province and on non-residents who conduct business or have a permanent establishment in that province. The federal government collects provincial income taxes for all provinces except two:

- Quebec, which administers its own income tax on both individuals and corporations; and
- Alberta, which administer their own income tax on corporations.

© CSI GLOBAL EDUCATION INC. (2008)

Canada imposes an income tax on world income of its residents as well as certain types of Canadian source income on non-residents. Companies incorporated in Canada under federal or provincial law are usually considered resident of Canada. Also, foreign companies with management and control in Canada are considered resident in Canada and are subject to Canadian taxes.

TAXATION YEAR

All taxpayers must calculate their income and tax on a yearly basis. Individuals use the calendar year while corporations may choose any **fiscal year**, as long as this time period is consistent year over year. No corporate taxation year may be longer than 53 weeks. A change of fiscal year end may be made only with the approval of the Minister of Finance.

Professionals and personal service corporations now must use a year end of December.

CALCULATION OF INCOME TAX

Calculating income tax involves four steps:

- Calculating all sources of income from employment, business and investments
- Making allowable deductions to arrive at taxable income
- Calculating the gross or basic tax payable on taxable income
- Claiming various tax credits, if any, and calculating the net tax payable

Once total income has been determined, there are a number of allowable deductions and exemptions that may be made in calculating taxable income. For individuals, these deductions and exemptions may include registered pension plan contributions and registered retirement savings plan contributions, childcare expenses, certain net capital and non-capital losses of other years and other items. In the case of corporations, deductions in arriving at taxable income include charitable donations, certain net capital and non-capital losses of other years and dividends received from other taxable Canadian companies and foreign affiliates.

Types of Income

There are four general types of income. Each is treated differently under Canadian tax laws. *Employment income*: Employment income is taxed on a *gross receipt basis*. This means that the taxpayer cannot deduct for tax purposes all the related costs incurred in earning income as a business does. However, employees are permitted to deduct a few employment-related expenses such as pension contributions, union dues, child care expenses and other minor items.

Business income: Business income arises from the profit earned from producing and selling goods or rendering services. Self-employment income falls in this category. In contrast to property income, business income requires activity on the part of the recipient. It is taxed on a *net-income basis*, calculated using GAAP. To encourage Canadian-controlled private corporations to expand, some companies are allowed a Small Business deduction, which can reduce the overall tax rate.

Capital property income: Dividend and interest income is considered income from capital property. Any income derived from pension plans, RRIFs, Old Age Security (OAS) or Canada Pension Plan (CPP) is also included in this category. This type of income is passive in nature since the property owner rarely does anything other than own the income-producing property. Individuals may deduct reasonable expenses such as property taxes, repairs and maintenance and,

© CSI GLOBAL EDUCATION INC. (2008)

possibly, financing costs on the acquisition of the property (such as interest paid on a margin loan). Only net income is subject to tax.

Capital gains and losses: Both corporations and individuals are subject to taxes on capital gains. A capital gain (loss) results when a capital property is disposed of at a sale price greater (lower) than its cost. Costs of disposition are also included in arriving at a capital gain or capital loss.

Calculating Income Tax Payable

Basic tax rates are applied to taxable income. Rates of federal tax applicable to individuals in 2008 (excluding tax credits) are as follows:

TABLE 22.1 FEDERAL INCOME TAX RATES FOR 2008

Taxable Income	Tax
• up to $37,885	15%
• between $37,885 and $75,769	$5,683 + 22% on the next $37,884
• between $75,769 and $123,184	$14,017 + 26% on the next $47,415
• above $123,184	$26,345 + 29% on the remainder

Source: Canada Revenue Agency website: www.cra.gc.ca.

Currently, all provinces levy their own tax on taxable income. Provincial amounts are calculated in essentially the same way as federal tax.

Adding the provincial rate to the federal rate gives the taxpayer's combined marginal tax rate. (The **marginal tax rate** is the tax rate that would have to be paid on any additional dollars of taxable income earned.)

EXAMPLE: Manitoba resident with taxable income of $50,000 would be subject to a 22% federal tax rate and a provincial tax rate of 12.75% giving him a combined marginal tax rate of 34.75%.

Given an investor's marginal tax rate, the tax consequences of certain investment decisions can be estimated. In this way an advisor can respond to a client's need to minimize taxes and select securities for the portfolio that offer the investor a higher after-tax rate of return. In addition to incorporating marginal tax rates into the decision-making process, the tax planning concepts outlined in this chapter should also be considered.

Employers are required to withhold income tax on salaries and wages and remit this amount on their employees' behalf to the government. Some individuals, and all corporations, pay their taxes by instalments:

- *Individuals* who receive more than 25% of their income from sources that do not withhold tax are required to pay quarterly instalments on March, June, September and December 15 unless federal taxes payable for that year or for the prior two years are $2,000 or less. These instalments are based on either the tax reported for the preceding year, the tax reported for the preceding and second preceding year or an estimate of the tax for the current year,

© CSI GLOBAL EDUCATION INC. (2008)

whichever is least. Interest is charged on deficient instalments. Adjustment for over- or underpayment is made at the year end through the annual tax return.

- *Corporations* must pay federal and provincial tax instalments at each month end, using the methodology outlined above.

Taxation of Investment Income

INTEREST INCOME

For investment contracts acquired after 1989, taxpayers are required to report interest income (from such investments as CSBs, GICs and bonds) on an annual accrual basis, regardless of whether or not the cash is actually received. An "investment contract" is specifically defined and includes virtually all debt obligations, as well as certain annuity and insurance contracts.

DIVIDENDS FROM TAXABLE CANADIAN CORPORATIONS

Individual taxpayers receive preferential tax treatment on dividends received from taxable Canadian corporations. The preferential treatment reflects the fact that corporations pay dividends from after-tax income—i.e., from their profits. The amount included in a taxpayer's income is 'grossed-up' to equal approximately what the corporation would have earned before tax. The taxpayer then receives a tax credit that offsets the amount of tax the corporation paid.

Eligible Canadian dividends are grossed-up by 45% and then the taxpayer receives a federal dividend tax credit in the amount of 19%. Dividend tax credits are also available at varying provincial levels.

For example, an individual receives a $300 eligible dividend from a Canadian corporation. The individual would report $435 ($300 × 45% plus $300 *or* 145% of $300) in net income for tax purposes. The additional $135 is referred to as the *gross up* and the $435 is known as the *taxable amount of the dividend.*

The taxpayer calculates net income using the $435 amount, and can then claim a federal dividend tax credit in the amount of 19% of the taxable amount of the dividend, which is $82.65 in this example (19% × $435). Again, provincial dividend tax credits are also available.

The dividend gross-up and federal tax credit are shown on the T5 form sent annually to shareholders. The source of the T5, i.e. who issues it, depends on how the shares are held. Registered shareholders receive the T5 from the dividend-paying corporation itself; investment dealers holding shares in street name issue the T5 to the beneficial owners. Quite often the investment dealer will combine all dividends paid to the investor during the year and issue just one T5 for all of them.

Stock dividends and dividends that are reinvested in shares are treated in the same manner as cash dividends.

DIVIDENDS FROM FOREIGN CORPORATIONS

Foreign dividends are generally taxed as regular income, in much the same way as interest income. Individuals who receive dividends from non-Canadian sources usually receive a net amount from these sources, as non-resident withholding taxes are applied by the foreign dividend source. Such investors may be able to use foreign tax credits to offset the Canadian income tax otherwise payable. The allowable credit is essentially the lesser of the foreign tax paid or the

© CSI GLOBAL EDUCATION INC. (2008)

Canadian tax payable on the foreign income, subject to certain adjustments. Details on what foreign tax is allowed as a deduction are available from the CRA.

INCOME EARNED FROM STRIP BONDS AND TREASURY BILLS (T-BILLS)

Strip bonds and T-bills are purchased at a discount and mature at par. The income earned, while not received until maturity, must be reported on an annual accrual basis. For the purposes of CRA, the income earned is considered to be interest income.

CAPITAL DIVIDENDS

A private corporation may elect to pay a dividend out of its capital dividend account, which is the non-taxable portion of the net capital gains realized by the corporation since 1971. The dividend is not included in the income of the investor at the time of receipt and has no effect on the adjusted cost base of the shares on which the dividend was paid.

MINIMIZING TAXABLE INVESTMENT INCOME

Dividends from taxable Canadian corporations (but not foreign corporations) are subject to less tax than interest. Accordingly, a shift from interest bearing investments into dividend-paying Canadian stocks may reduce taxes and improve after-tax yield.

Depending on the tax rate, the tax on Canadian dividends can be significantly lower than the tax payable on capital gains. This is illustrated in Tables 22.2 and 22.3. At a marginal federal tax rate of 29%, there is no difference in federal taxes owed on capital gains and Canadian dividends. But at a marginal tax rate of 22%, the taxes owed on dividends is $66.50 less than taxes owing on the same gross amount of capital gains. In both cases, there is a substantial difference between the tax owed on interest and the tax owed on capital gains and dividends.

TABLE 22.2 COMPARISON OF TAX CONSEQUENCES OF INVESTMENT INCOME IN A 29% MARGINAL TAX BRACKET

	Interest Income	Canadian Dividend Income	Capital Gains Income
Income Received	$1,000.00	$1,000.00	$1,000.00
Taxable Income	$1,000.00	$1,450.00 (Grossed up by 45%)	$500.00 (50% of $1,000)
Federal Tax (29%)	$290.00	$420.50	$145.00
Less Dividend Tax Credit (19%)	–	$275.50	–
Federal Tax Owed	**$290.00**	**$145.00**	**$145.00**

TABLE 22.3 COMPARISON OF TAX CONSEQUENCES OF INVESTMENT INCOME IN A 22% MARGINAL TAX BRACKET

	Interest Income	Canadian Dividend Income	Capital Gains Income
Income Received	$1,000.00	$1,000.00	$1,000.00
Taxable Income	$1,000.00	$1,450.00 (Grossed up by 45%)	$500.00 (50% of $1,000)
Federal Tax (22%)	$220.00	$319.00	$110.00
Less Dividend Tax Credit (19%)	–	$275.50	–
Federal Tax Owed	**$220.00**	**$43.50**	**$110.00**

Tax-Deductible Items Related to Investment Income

CARRYING CHARGES

Tax rules permit individuals to deduct certain carrying charges for tax purposes. Acceptable carrying charge deductions include:

- Interest paid on funds borrowed to earn investment income unless the funds are used for a rental property that is under construction or is vacant while being renovated.
- Investment counseling fees (other than a commission paid to registered investment counselors). Counseling fees for RRSPs and RRIFs are not deductible.
- Fees paid for administration or safe custody of investments. Administration and trustee fees for self-directed RRSPs and RRIFs are not deductible.
- Safety deposit box charges.
- Accounting fees paid for the recording of investment income.

BORROWED FUNDS

A taxpayer may deduct the interest paid on funds borrowed to purchase securities if:

- The taxpayer has a legal obligation to pay the interest
- The purpose of borrowing the funds is to earn income
- The income produced from the securities purchased with the borrowed funds is not tax exempt

The interest is deductible whether the transaction is or is not at arm's length. (Arm's length is an expression used to describe a transaction between persons whereby each acts in their own interests. In general, unrelated persons usually deal with each other at arm's length, while transactions with related persons are considered a non-arm's-length transaction.)

If the interest paid to borrow funds exceeds the amount of interest earned on a debt security, the loss or difference between the two amounts is not tax deductible. However, in the case of convertible debentures, normally all carrying charges are deductible since the debentures may be converted into common shares which could theoretically pay unlimited dividends.

© CSI GLOBAL EDUCATION INC. (2008)

Complete the on-line activity associated with this section.

CARRYING COSTS ON EQUITY INVESTMENTS

Part of the carrying costs of preferred shares with a fixed dividend rate may be disallowed as a tax deduction if the carrying costs exceed the grossed-up amount of the preferred dividend.

Carrying charges on common shares are, for the most part, tax deductible even for non-dividendpaying growth securities since earnings may later rise and dividends may be paid in future.

Thus, carrying cost deductibility is based on the income potential of the investment made.

CALCULATING INVESTMENT GAINS AND LOSSES

Investors and their advisors should have a general understanding of the concepts of capital gains and losses when developing an investment strategy.

A capital gain arises from the disposition of a capital property for more than its cost (i.e., the selling price is higher than the cost price). For tax purposes, however, the calculation may not be so simple because:

- Additional costs are often involved in the purchase and sale of property other than the cost price, e.g., commissions paid on the purchase and sale of listed securities.
- The past value of certain properties on which capital gains are calculated is difficult to determine, e.g., real estate held for many years.

For these and other reasons, the CRA applies complex rules for calculating capital gains. Although capital gains result in an additional tax burden to the taxpayer, only part of a capital gain is taxed.

Generally, the CRA treats share dispositions as being capital in nature. However, an exception may occur if the taxpayer's actions, indicated by intention, show that the taxpayer is in the business of trading securities to realize a speculative profit from the shares. In this case, the CRA may argue that gains realized are fully taxable as ordinary income (and losses fully deductible). Factors which the CRA would review in assessing whether trading is speculative (their definition) in nature include:

- Short periods of ownership
- A history of extensive buying and selling of shares or quick turnover of securities
- Special knowledge of, or experience in, securities markets
- Substantial investment of time spent studying the market and investigating potential purchases
- Financing share purchases primarily on margin or some other form of debt
- The nature of the shares (i.e., speculative, non-dividend type)

Although none of these individual factors alone may be sufficient for the CRA to characterize the taxpayer's trading activities as a business, a number of these factors in combination may be sufficient to do so. In every instance, the particular circumstances of the disposition would need to be evaluated before a determination can be made.

Taxpayers may elect that *all* gains and losses on the sale of Canadian securities be treated as capital gains or losses during their lifetime, provided they are neither a trader nor a dealer in securities nor a non-resident. CRA interprets a *dealer or trader* in securities to be a taxpayer who participates in the promotion or underwriting of a particular issue of shares or who, to the public, is a dealer in shares. In general, an employee of a corporation engaged in these activities is not a dealer. If, however, as a result of employment, an employee engages in insider trading to realize a quick gain, the taxpayer will be considered to be a *trader* of those particular shares.

© CSI GLOBAL EDUCATION INC. (2008)

Disposition of Shares

The general rules of capital gains (i.e., the proceeds of disposition minus the adjusted cost base plus any costs of disposing of the property) apply to the sale of shares.

EXAMPLE: An investor buys 100 ABC common shares at $6, and sells the 100 shares at $10 two years later. In the year of sale, the investor's taxable capital gain, would be as follows:

Gross proceeds from sale (100 × $10)		$	1,000.00
Less:	Adjusted cost base – Cost of shares (100 × $6) including commission	$	617.00
		$	383.00
Less:	Commission on Sale		25.00
	Capital Gain	$	358.00
	Taxable Capital Gain (50% of $358)	$	179.00

Investors who receive stock dividends or who subscribe to dividend reinvestment plans must declare these as income in the year the dividend is paid. Investors should keep a record of stock dividends and reinvestments as they increase the adjusted cost base of the investment. When the stock is sold, the higher adjusted cost base will reduce any capital gain and increase any capital loss.

ADJUSTED COST BASE – IDENTICAL SHARES

The adjusted cost base of shares sold is generally composed of the purchase price plus commission expense. However, investors often own a number of the same class of shares that were bought at different prices. When a taxpayer owns identical shares in a company, the method used to calculate the adjusted cost base of such shares is known as the *average cost method.* An average cost per share is calculated by adding together the cost base of all such stock and dividing by the number of shares held.

EXAMPLE: An investor buys 200 ABC common at $6 in January Year I, and 100 ABC common at $9 in June of Year II. Thus, when the investor sells any of these ABC common shares, the cost base used will be the average cost, or $7 per share, calculated as follows:

200 × $6	=	$	1,200.00
100 × $9	=	$	900.00
Total cost	=	$	2,100.00
$2,100 ÷ 300	=	$	7.00 per share

ADJUSTED COST BASE OF CONVERTIBLE SECURITIES

When an investor exercises the conversion right attached to a security, the conversion is deemed not to be a disposition of property, and therefore no capital gain or loss arises at the time of the conversion. Instead, the adjusted cost base of the new shares acquired will be deemed to be that of the original convertible securities.

© CSI GLOBAL EDUCATION INC. (2008)

EXAMPLE: An investor buys 100 ABC preferred shares at a total cost of $6,000. Each preferred share is convertible into 5 ABC common shares. These securities are later converted into the common and the investor now holds 500 ABC common shares. For tax purposes, the adjusted cost base of each ABC common share is $12, calculated as follows:

- Adjusted cost base of each preferred share (composed of original cost plus commission): $60
- Number of common shares acquired through conversion of one preferred share: 5 shares
- Adjusted cost base of one common share ($60 ÷ 5): $12 per share

ADJUSTED COST BASE OF DUAL SECURITIES

Units of securities (two or more securities offered as a package) are sold at a unit price. Since each security can be sold separately by the purchaser, a cost base for each security must be determined to calculate a capital gain (or loss) when either security is sold.

The owner of a unit calculates the cost base of each component by assigning the cost of the unit on a proportionate basis using the market values at the date of acquisition.

EXAMPLE: ABC Company sells a new issue of units comprised of one ABC preferred share and one ABC common share at a price of $60. At the time the new issue is formally cleared for sale, the market price of ABC preferred is $48 and ABC common is $13. Thus, on a proportionate basis, the cost base of each security is as follows:

- ABC Preferred: $48 ÷ ($48 + $13) × $60 = $47.21
- ABC Common: $13 ÷ ($48 + $13) × $60 = $12.79

Since a unit is sold as a new issue, the buyer pays no commission and so no adjustment for commission is necessary. However, when the securities are subsequently sold, the applicable commission(s) becomes a cost of disposition and reduces any potential capital gain.

ADJUSTED COST BASE OF SHARES WITH WARRANTS OR RIGHTS

Investors acquire warrants and rights in one of three ways:

- Through direct purchase in the market
- By owning shares on which a rights offering is made
- By purchasing a unit of securities (e.g., a bond with warrants attached)

The method by which warrants and rights are acquired is important because there is a different tax treatment for the shares acquired when the warrants or rights are exercised.

Direct purchase of warrants and rights: In this case, the tax treatment is the same as that discussed above under convertible securities.

Rights received from direct share ownership: The cost base of the original shares purchased must be adjusted in this case.

When the warrants or rights are not exercised: Warrants and rights are not always exercised. Instead, the investor may sell them in the open market or allow them to expire. If the warrants and rights were directly purchased, the capital loss would equal the purchase cost plus commission. If the warrants and rights were acquired at zero cost, there is neither a capital gain nor loss.

© CSI GLOBAL EDUCATION INC. (2008)

If the warrants and rights were received at zero cost and then sold in the open market, their cost would be considered to be zero and all the profits realized would be taxed as capital gains.

Disposition of Debt Securities

For tax purposes, *debt securities* include bonds, debentures, bills, notes, mortgages, hypothec and similar obligations. (A Canada Savings Bond or a provincial Savings Bond cannot generate a capital gain or loss because such bonds do not fluctuate in value and either mature or are redeemed at par.)

If the seller of a debt security is in the business of trading securities, proceeds from the sale must be included in business income, which is taxed as income. However, the sale or redemption of a debt security by an ordinary taxpayer often produces a capital gain or capital loss.

Capital gains and losses on debt securities are determined in the usual manner (i.e. proceeds of disposition less adjusted cost base and expenses of disposition). At the time of disposition, a debt security may have accrued interest owing. Accrued interest is not included in the capital gains calculation. Rather, interest at the date of sale is income to the vendor and may be deducted from interest subsequently received by the purchaser when reporting income on an income tax return.

EXAMPLE: An investor buys $1,000 principal amount of a 10% bond at par and has to pay accrued interest of $80 at the time of purchase.

$1,000 principal amount of 10% bonds @ $100	$	1,000
Plus: Accrued interest		80
Total cost	$	1,080

The buyer includes, as investment income for the year of purchase, net interest income of $20 from the bond ($100 interest for the year less $80 accrued interest paid to the seller). When the buyer later sells the bond, the adjusted cost base is $1,000 – not $1,080.

The seller of the bond includes for the year of sale investment income of $80 accrued interest that was received from the sale and any other interest received from owning the bond during the year. On the same return, the proceeds of disposition of $1,000 are used to calculate a capital gain or loss.

Capital Losses

A **capital loss** is the result of selling a security for less than its purchase price. Capital losses are calculated in the same manner as capital gains. They can only be deducted from capital gains in most circumstances. However, two additional factors involved in capital losses are important.

WORTHLESS SECURITIES

When a security becomes worthless, the security holder must fill out a form (from the CRA) electing to declare the security worthless, so that a capital loss can be realized for tax purposes. Of course, the tax rule does not apply to instruments that have an expiry date such as warrants, rights or options. Capital losses for such securities, which have expired, may be claimed without any declaration being signed.

© CSI GLOBAL EDUCATION INC. (2008)

One exception to the rule above occurs when a security becomes worthless due to bankrupcy (or under certain conditions, insolvency) of the underlying company. In this situation the *Income Tax Act* deems the taxpayer to have disposed of the security for nil proceeds and reacquired it at a cost of nil.

SUPERFICIAL LOSSES

A **superficial loss** occurs when securities sold at a loss are repurchased within 30 calendar days before or after the sale and are still held at the end of 30 days after the sale. Superficial losses are *not* tax deductible as a capital loss. The tax advantage may not be totally lost but, in most cases, is simply deferred.

The superficial loss rules are intended to make it more difficult for taxpayers to sell and re-purchase assets solely for the purpose of creating deductible capital losses. The rules are designed to avoid situations where taxpayers do not have the full intent of selling a stock and are only doing so temporarily to obtain a capital loss.

EXAMPLE: An investor buys 100 XYZ shares at $30 in mid April and later sells the shares at $25 on May 1. He incurs a $500 capital loss ($3,000 - $2,500). Normally an allowable capital loss of $250 (50% of $500) would be deductible against taxable capital gains. However, the superficial loss rules would apply in the following two scenarios:

- On May 15, the investor decides to repurchase 100 XYZ shares at a price close to the $25 sale price and hold the shares until July. Because the transaction takes place within 30 days after the sale on May 1 and the shares are held 30 days after the original sale, the loss is considered a superficial loss, not a capital loss and is not deductible against taxable capital gains.
- On April 29, the investor decides to purchase an additional 100 shares of XYZ near the initial $30 purchase price and hold the shares until July. He then carries out the sale of the 100 XYZ shares on May 1 at $25. Since the same shares were purchased less than 30 days before the sale on May 1 and owned for at least 30 days after the original sale, this loss is also considered a superficial loss.

Tax rules for superficial losses apply not only to trades made by the investor but also a person affiliated with the investor including:

- The investor's spouse or common-law spouse; or
- Corporations controlled by the investor and/or spouse.
- Trust in which the investor is a majority interest beneficiary

Although superficial losses are non-deductible for tax purposes, in most cases the taxpayer eventually receives the tax benefit of the superficial loss when the investment is sold. The amount of the superficial loss is added to the cost of the repurchased shares, thereby reducing the ultimate capital gain.

EXAMPLE: (using the previous example) If the investor's $500 capital loss had been a superficial loss and the shares were repurchased at $25 before May 31, the loss of $5 per share would be added to the cost of each XYZ share (100 in this example) owned on May 31. By so doing, the potential future amount of the capital gain is reduced.

If, later, 100 XYZ is sold at $40 per share, the capital gain is calculated as follows:

© CSI GLOBAL EDUCATION INC. (2008)

Proceeds from disposition (100 × $40)			$ 4,000.00
Less:	Cost of repurchasing shares (100 × $25)	$ 2,500.00	
	Commission on purchases	45.00	
	Superficial loss (100 × $5)	500.00	3,045.00
			$ 955.00
Less:	Commission on sale		60.00
	Capital gain		$ 895.00
	Taxable capital gain (50% of $895)		$ 447.50

Superficial losses do not apply, however, to losses which result from leaving Canada (emigration), death of a taxpayer, the expiry of an option, or a deemed disposition of securities by a trust or a disposition of securities to a controlled corporation.

Tax Loss Selling

A decision to hold or sell a security should be based on the investor's expectations for that security. However, in some circumstances, taxes may also be a consideration. For example, an investor may own shares whose market price has declined and the forecast is limited with no potential for appreciation in the immediate future. By selling the shares at this time, the investor creates a capital loss which can be used to reduce capital gains from other securities. Proceeds from the sale can then be re-invested in more attractive securities.

When a tax loss sale looks advantageous without breaching investment principles, a taxpayer should consider the following factors:

- If subsequent repurchase is planned, the timing of the sale and repurchase must be carefully scheduled to avoid a superficial loss.
- For tax purposes, the settlement date (usually three business days after the transaction date) is the date on which transfer of ownership takes place. This is an important tax rule for investors to remember when making securities sales near the end of a calendar year. For example, an investor who sells a stock on the last day of December does not incur a capital loss for the taxation year in which the sale occurred. The loss would apply to the next taxation year, since the settlement date would be in early January.

Minimum Tax

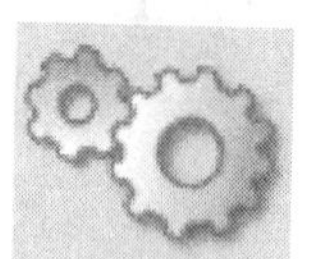

High-income investors must keep in mind special tax rules known as **Alternate Minimum Tax (AMT)**. The minimum tax is an alternative tax calculation that can be triggered by taxpayers who significantly reduce their income taxes by claiming legitimate deductions or earning large amounts of tax-preferred income (such as capital gains or dividends). Tax-payers falling in these categories must calculate tax the usual way and also under the minimum tax rules. They are required to pay the higher of the two amounts calculated.

© CSI GLOBAL EDUCATION INC. (2008)

TAX DEFERRAL PLANS

The principle of tax deferral plans is to encourage Canadians to save for retirement by enabling them to reduce taxes paid during high earning (and high taxpaying) years. Tax payment is deferred until retirement years when income and tax rates are normally lower.

Tax-assisted retirement savings plans, regardless of the timing of the contributions, or the contributor (employee or employer), use a uniform contribution level of 18% of earned income as the amount that can be contributed towards retirement to a maximum dollar amount per year, depending on the type of plan. It is necessary for the taxpayer to determine the contributions made to, or the value of the benefit accruing to an employee from **registered pension plans (RPPs)** and deferred profit sharing plans (DPSPs). The amount determined is called the **Pension Adjustment (PA)**. The PA reduces the amount an individual can contribute to a registered retirement savings plan (RRSP) so that the annual contribution limit, on all plans combined, is not exceeded. Employers, or administrators of pension plans, report a plan member's PA on the employee's T4.

Employers may upgrade employee pension plans within certain limits by making changes to existing pension plans or by introducing new plans. When an upgrade occurs, an employer may make additional contributions to an employee plan due to the increased benefits. This amount, calculated as the difference between the old plan PA and the new plan PA, is called the **Past Service Pension Adjustment (PSPA)**. The PSPA also reduces the amount an employee can contribute to an RRSP.

Investors do not have to contribute the maximum contribution allowed on all plans combined in any given year. If an investor does not contribute the maximum allowed carry-forward provisions will permit the individual to make up the deficient contributions, called " RRSP Carry Forward Room", in future years.

The most common tax deferral vehicles are explained below.

Registered Pension Plans (RPPs)

A registered pension plan is a trust, registered with CRA or the appropriate provincial agency, which is established by a company to provide pension benefits for its employees when they retire. Both employer and employee contributions to the plan are tax-deductible.

In general terms, there are two types of RPPs – **money purchase plans (MPP)** and **defined benefit plans (DBP)**. In a MPP (also known as a **defined contribution plan (DCP)**) the contributions to the plan are predetermined and the benefits, at retirement, will depend on how the contributions were invested. In a DBP the benefits are predetermined based on a formula including years of service, income level and other variables, and the contributions will be those necessary to fund the predetermined plan benefits. The maximum tax-deductible employee and employer contributions are as follows:

© CSI GLOBAL EDUCATION INC. (2008)

MONEY PURCHASE PLANS

The combined employer/employee contributions cannot exceed the lesser of:

- 18% of the employee's current year compensation; and
- The MPP contribution limit for the year, which is $21,000 for 2008, and $22,000 in 2009, after which it will be indexed annually to inflation.

DEFINED BENEFIT PLANS

The combined employer/employee contributions will be deductible up to the amount recommended by a qualified actuary so that the plan is adequately funded. The current DBP limits are designed to provide an employee a maximum pension of 2% of pre-retirement earnings per year of service. The current limit is $2,333.33 for 2008, and $2,444.44 for 2009, after which the limit will be indexed to inflation. The actual benefits an employee receives depends on the terms of the pension plan.

In addition, the employee current service contributions are restricted to the lesser of:

- 9% of the employee's compensation for the year; and
- $1,000 plus 70% of the employee's PA for the year.

Registered Retirement Savings Plans (RRSPs)

Registered Retirement Savings Plans (RRSPs) are one of the most popular vehicles available to individuals to defer tax and save for retirement years. Annual contributions are tax-deductible up to allowable limits. Income earned in the plan accumulates tax-free as long as it remains in the plan.

Essentially there are two types of RRSPs: Single Vendor RRSPs and Self-Directed RRSPs. There are no limits as to the number of plans a person can hold. Funds can be transferred tax-free from plan to plan if the taxpayer/investor so desires. This is accomplished by completing a transfer document with the trustee of the new plan. The documents are then forwarded to the original plan's trustee.

There are special features that the investor should understand about an RRSP account. First, an RRSP is a trust account designed to benefit the owner at retirement. Withdrawals from an RRSP are subject to a graduated withholding tax and such withdrawals must be included in income in the year withdrawn. More tax may be payable at year-end, depending on the income level of the taxpayer. Second, an RRSP cannot be used as collateral for loan purposes.

Single Vendor Plans: In these plans, the holder invests in one or more of a variety of GICs, segregated pooled funds or mutual funds. The investments are held in trust under the plan by a particular issuer, bank, insurance company, credit union or trust company. To qualify as acceptable investments for an RRSP (either Single Vendor or Self-Directed), pooled funds must be registered with the CRA. In Single Vendor RRSPs, no day-to-day investment decisions are required to be made by the holder. There may be a trustee fee charged for this type of plan in addition to any costs incurred for purchasing the investments themselves. Single Vendor RRSPs are very popular and a suitable vehicle for many investors.

Self-Directed Plans: In these, holders invest funds or contribute certain acceptable assets such as securities directly into a registered plan. The plans are usually administered for a fee by a Canadian financial services company. One advantage of Self-Directed RRSPs is that investors can make all investment decisions. Another advantage is that, while there are rules with respect to

© CSI GLOBAL EDUCATION INC. (2008)

allowable content, a full range of securities may be held in these plans, including GICs, money market instruments, bonds, equities and mutual funds. Investors may also hold direct foreign investments in these RRSPs.

The size of the proposed Self-Directed RRSP should be considered, in relation to the annual fee charged to administer the trust account, to determine if the plan is large enough to justify the fee. Single-vendor RRSPs may be more suitable for those who have a smaller amount to invest.

CONTRIBUTIONS TO AN RRSP

There is no limit to the number of RRSPs an individual may own. However, there is a restriction on the amount that may be contributed to RRSPs on a per-year basis. The maximum annual taxdeductible contributions to RRSPs an individual can make is the lesser of:

- 18% of the previous year's earned income; and
- The RRSP dollar limit for the year.

From the lesser of the above two amounts:

- Deduct the previous year's PA and the current year's PSPA.
- Add the taxpayer's unused RRSP contribution room at the end of the immediately preceding taxation year.

The RRSP dollar contribution limit is $20,000 for the 2008 taxation year. This limit is scheduled to increase to $21,000 in 2009,, $22,000 in 2010, after which the limit will be indexed to inflation. The contributions must be made in the taxation year or within 60 days after the end of that year to be deductible in that year.

For 1991 and subsequent years, an individual's unused RRSP contribution limit for a year may be carried forward and made use of in later years. Individuals can carry forward unused contribution limits indefinitely.

Earned income for the purpose of RRSP contributions may be simply defined as the total of:

- Total employment income (less any union or professional dues)
- Net rental income
- Net income from self-employment
- Royalties from a published work or invention
- Research grants
- Some alimony or maintenance payments ordered by a court
- Disability payments from CPP or QPP
- Supplementary Employment Insurance Benefits (SEIB), such as top-up payments made by the employer to an employee who is temporarily unable to work (for parental or adoption leave, for example), but not the Employment Insurance (EI) benefits paid by Human Resources and Social Development Canada

Planholders who make contributions to RRSPs in excess of the amount permitted by legislation may be subject to a penalty tax. Over-contributions of up to $2,000 may be made without penalty. A penalty tax of 1% per month is imposed on any portion of over-contribution that exceeds $2,000.

A planholder may contribute securities already owned to an RRSP. According to the CRA, this contribution is considered to be a **deemed disposition** at the time the contribution is made. Consequently, in order to calculate the capital gain or loss, the planholder must use the fair market value of the securities at the time of contribution as the proceeds from disposition. Any

© CSI GLOBAL EDUCATION INC. (2008)

resulting capital gain is included in income tax for the year of contribution. Any capital loss is deemed to be nil for tax purposes. This type of contribution is called a **contribution in kind**.

SPOUSAL RRSPs

A taxpayer may contribute to an RRSP registered in the name of a spouse or common-law spouse and still claim a tax deduction. If the taxpayer is also a planholder, he or she may contribute to the spouse's plan only to the extent that the contributor does not use the maximum contribution available for his or her own plan. For example, a wife who has a maximum contribution limit of $11,500 for her own RRSP, but contributes only $10,000 to her RRSP, may contribute $1,500 to her husband's spousal RRSP. The husband's RRSP contribution limits are not affected by the spousal RRSP, which is a separate plan. (Therefore, the husband, in this example, would have two plans: one for personal contributions and one for contributions made by his wife *on his behalf*.)

Unless converted to a Registered Retirement Income Fund (RRIF) or used to purchase certain acceptable annuities, the withdrawal from a spousal plan is taxable income to the spouse – not the contributor – since the spousal RRSP belongs to the spouse in whose name it is registered. However, any withdrawals of contributions to a spousal plan claimed as a tax deduction by a contributing spouse made:

In the year the contribution is made, or
In the two calendar years prior to the year of withdrawal,

are taxable to the contributor in the year of withdrawal rather than to the planholder.

EXAMPLE: In each of six consecutive years, a husband contributes $1,000 to his wife's RRSP, which he claims as tax deductions. In the seventh year there are no contributions, and the wife de-registers the plan. Thus, for the seventh taxation year:

- The husband includes as taxable income in his tax return the sum of $2,000 (contributions: 7th year – nil; 6th year – $1,000; 5th year – $1,000); and
- The wife includes as taxable income in her tax return the sum of $4,000 (i.e., contributions to the plan made in years 1, 2, 3 and 4) plus all earnings that accumulated on the total contributions of $6,000 in the plan.

OTHER TYPES OF CONTRIBUTIONS

Some pension income can be transferred directly to RRSPs. The following transfers can be contributed without affecting the regular tax-deductible contribution limits outlined elsewhere:

- Lump sum transfers from RPPs and other RRSPs, if transferred to the individual's RRSP on a direct basis, are not included in income and no deduction arises.
- Allowances for long service upon retirement often known as retiring allowances, for each year of service, under very specific guidelines.

TERMINATION OF RRSPs

An RRSP holder may make withdrawals or de-register the plan at any time but mandatory de-registration of an RRSP is required *during the calendar year when an RRSP plan holder reaches age 71.*

The following maturity options are available to the plan holder in the year he or she turns 71:

- Withdraw the proceeds as a lump sum payment which is fully taxable in the year of receipt;

© CSI GLOBAL EDUCATION INC. (2008)

- Use the proceeds to purchase a life annuity.
- Use the proceeds to purchase a fixed term annuity which provides benefits to a specified age;
- Transfer the proceeds to a Registered Retirement Income Fund (RRIF) which provides an annual income; or
- A combination of the above.

RRIFs, fixed-term annuities and life annuities, available from financial institutions which offer RRSPs, permit the taxpayer to defer taxation of the proceeds from de-registered RRSPs. Tax is paid only on the annual income received each year.

Should the annuitant die, benefits can be transferred to the annuitant's spouse. Otherwise, the value of any remaining benefits must be included in the deceased's income in the year of death. Under certain conditions, the remaining benefits may be taxed in the hands of a financially dependent child or grandchild, if named as beneficiary. The child or grandchild may be entitled to transfer the benefits received to an eligible annuity, an RRSP or an RRIF.

If a person dies before de-registration of an RRSP, the surviving spouse may transfer the plan proceeds tax-free into his or her own RRSP as long as the spouse is the beneficiary of the plan. If there is no surviving spouse or dependent child, the proceeds from the plan are taxed in the deceased's income in the year of death.

ADVANTAGES OF RRSPs

The following are some of the advantages provided by RRSPs:

- A reduction in annual taxable income during high taxation years through annual tax-deductible contributions;
- Shelter of certain lump sum types of income from taxation through tax-free transfer into an RRSP;
- Accumulation of funds for retirement, or some future time, with the funds compounding earnings on a tax-free basis until withdrawal;
- Deferral of income taxes until later years when the holder is presumably in a lower tax bracket;
- Opportunity to split retirement income (using spousal RRSPs) which could result in a lower taxation of the combined income and the opportunity to claim two, $2,000 pension tax credits.

DISADVANTAGES OF RRSPs

The following are some of the disadvantages provided by RRSPs:

- If funds are withdrawn from an RRSP, the planholder pays income tax (not capital gains tax) on the proceeds withdrawn;
- The RRSP holder cannot take advantage of the dividend tax credit on eligible shares that are part of an RRSP;
- If the plan holder dies, all payments out of the RRSP to the planholder's estate are subject to tax as income of the deceased, unless they are to be received by the spouse or, under certain circumstances, a dependent child or grandchild;
- The assets of an RRSP cannot be used as collateral for a loan.

© CSI GLOBAL EDUCATION INC. (2008)

Registered Retirement Income Funds (RRIFs)

As explained previously, a RRIF is one of the tax deferral vehicles available to RRSP holders who wish to continue the tax sheltering of their plans. The planholder transfers the RRSP funds into a RRIF. Each year (beginning with the year following acquisition of the RRIF) the planholder must withdraw and pay income tax on a fraction of the total assets in the fund, the "annual minimum amount". The assets are composed of capital plus accumulated earnings. The annual amount is determined by a table designed to provide benefits to the holder until death. The term of the RRIF may be based on the age of the holder's spouse (if younger) instead of the planholder's own age to extend the term, and reduce the amount of the required withdrawal.

While there is a minimum amount that must be withdrawn each year, there is no maximum amount.

A taxpayer can own more than one RRIF. Like a RRSP, a RRIF may be self-directed by the holder through instructions to the financial institution holding the RRIF, or it may be managed. A wide variety of qualified investment vehicles within the Canadian content framework are available for self-directed plans including stocks, bonds, investment certificates, mutual funds and mortgages.

RRIFs started prior to 1993 are paid out according to a prescribed schedule, which differs from the schedule for those started after 1992. Contact the Canada Revenue Agency for further information.

Deferred Annuities

An **annuity** is an investment contract through which the holder deposits money to be invested in an interest-bearing vehicle that will return not only interest but also a portion of the capital originally invested. With **immediate annuities**, payments to the holder start immediately. With **deferred annuities**, payments start at a date specified by the investor in the contract. Both types of annuities can be paid for in full at the beginning of the contract. The deferred annuity can also be paid for in monthly instalments until the date the annuity will begin payment.

Contributions to a deferred annuity, unlike those to an RRSP, do not reduce current taxable income since contributions are not tax deductible. What deferred annuities do provide is the opportunity of deferring the tax payable on investment income until a later time.

The annuitant is taxed only on the interest element of the annuity payments and not on the capital portion. This is because the annuity is purchased with after-tax income. This contrasts with annuities bought with money from RRSPs. In this case, the full annuity payment is taxable because the principal cost of the annuity was not taxed when deposited to the RRSP.

However, some deferred annuities may be registered as RRSPs. Investments in such annuities, within RRSP contribution limits, are deductible from income for tax purposes in the year deposited. The proceeds are fully taxable.

Deferred annuities are available only through life insurance companies.

© CSI GLOBAL EDUCATION INC. (2008)

Registered Education Savings Plans (RESPs)

Registered Education Savings Plans (RESPs) are tax-deferred savings plans intended to help pay for the post-secondary education of a beneficiary. Although contributions to a plan are not tax-deductible, there is a tax-deferral opportunity since the income accumulates tax-deferred within the plan. On withdrawal, the portion of the payments that were not original capital will be taxable in the hands of the beneficiary or beneficiaries, provided that they are enrolled in qualifying or specified educational programs. The assumption is that, at the time of withdrawal, the beneficiaries or beneficiary would be in a lower tax bracket than the contributor. Consequently, withdrawals from the plan should be taxed at a lower rate. In effect, RESPs allow for some income splitting within a family.

There is no maximum amount that can be contributed in a single calendar year for each beneficiary. There is a lifetime maximum of $50,000 per beneficiary. Contributions can be made for up to 21 years but the plan must be collapsed within 25 years of its starting date. This time limitation requires contributors to decide when would be the best time to start the plan.

There are two types of RESPs, pooled plans and individual plans. As their name suggests, pooled or group plans are plans to which a number of subscribers make contributions for their beneficiaries. The pooled funds are managed, usually conservatively, by the plan administrators. Annual contributions are generally pre-set. Under group plans, the administrator determines the amount paid out to beneficiaries.

Individual, or self-directed plans, are administered by a number of institutions including banks, mutual fund companies, and investment brokers. Contributions tend to be more flexible and contributors can participate in both the investment and distribution decisions.

More than one beneficiary can be named in any particular plan. These "family" plans are often used by families with more than one child. If one of the named beneficiaries does not pursue post-secondary education, all of the income can be directed to the beneficiaries who do attend.

There has always been a concern with RESPs since it has not been possible under the income tax laws to claim the income generated tax-free under the plan if the beneficiary did not attend a qualifying program. It has only been possible to reclaim the invested capital. Since 1998, the contributor (versus the beneficiary) now is allowed to withdraw the income from an RESP provided that the plan has been in existence more than 10 years and that none of the named beneficiaries has started qualified post-secondary programs by age 21 or all of the named beneficiaries have died.

As well, contributors are allowed to transfer a maximum of $50,000 of this income to their RRSPs if the beneficiaries do not attend qualifying programs. This is dependent on there being sufficient contribution room remaining in the RRSP. Any withdrawals of tax-deferred income in excess of amounts that can be transferred to an RRSP will be subject to a penalty tax of 20% in addition to regular income tax.

If the contributor (as opposed to the beneficiary) starts to withdraw income from the RESP, the plan must be terminated by the end of February of the following year.

© CSI GLOBAL EDUCATION INC. (2008)

CANADA EDUCATION SAVINGS GRANTS (CESGS)

Canada Education Savings Grants (CESGs) provide further incentive to invest in RESPs. Under this program, the federal government makes a matching grant of 20% of the first $2,500 contributed each year to the RESP of a child under 18. Worth between $500 and $600 per year (enhancements have been made to the program—see below), this grant is forwarded directly to the RESP firm and does not count towards the contributor's lifetime contribution limit. The lifetime grant a beneficiary can receive is $7,200. However, CESGs must be repaid if the child does not go on to a qualifying post-secondary institution.

There have been several enhancements to the CESG program since inception of the grants. Currently, the grant is 40% on the first $500 invested in the program by a family earning under $37,885; 30% on the first $500 invested by a family earning between $37,885 and $75,769; and 20% for any additional investment up to the remaining $2,500 per year maximum. These amounts are indexed to inflation.

Table 22.4 provides an example of the enhanced CESG program.

TABLE 22.4 CANADA EDUCATION SAVINGS GRANTS PROGRAM

Families earning*:	Grant on the first $500 invested		Grant on the remaining $2,000		Total Potential Grant	
	%	$	%	$	%	$
Under $37,885	40%	$200	20%	$400	24%	$600
Between $37,885 and $75,769	30%	$150	20%	$400	22%	$550
Over $75,769	20%	$100	20%	$400	20%	$500

*For 2008.

Source: Human Resources and Social Development Canada website

Thus, a lower income family that contributes $2,500 per beneficiary in a year will receive a maximum government contribution of $600 a year per beneficiary — 40% on the first $500 and 20% on the remaining $2,000 ($500 × 40% + $2,000 × 20%).

TAX PLANNING STRATEGIES

Income splitting is a tax savings strategy that involves transferring income from a family member in a higher tax bracket to a spouse, to children or to parents in a lower tax bracket so that the same income is taxed at a lower rate. However, as a result of tax law changes, the ability to split income in this manner now has limited applicability.

© CSI GLOBAL EDUCATION INC. (2008)

Transferring Income

Transferring income to family members can trigger what are called **attribution rules**. If property or income-producing assets are transferred from the taxpayer to other family members, the tax consequences may be passed back to the taxpayer. There is one exception to these rules and that occurs in the event of a marriage breakdown. If the married couple is living apart, the attribution rules relating to income and capital gains do not apply.

Both income and capital gains received by an individual from property transferred from or loaned by his or her spouse are attributed to the transferor unless the transfer is made for fair market value. If the transfer is made by way of a loan, the loan must bear interest. This rate cannot be less than the prescribed rates published by CRA. In addition, the interest must actually be paid within 30 days after the particular year to which the interest relates. It should be noted that a property substituted for the original property transferred will not avoid attribution.

Income, but not capital gains, received by minor children from transferred or loaned property is attributed to the taxpayer. This holds unless the property is sold at fair market value, or interest bearing loans at rates and conditions as noted above, apply.

Income, but not capital gains, received by an individual from property loaned by another individual with whom he or she was not dealing at arm's length, is attributed to the taxpayer. This holds true unless the transfer was made as a result of a sale at fair market value, or was evidenced by an interest-bearing loan at the prescribed interest rate or greater. Attribution does not apply if it can be shown that none of the main reasons for the transfer are to reduce or avoid tax on income from the property.

Income that is classified as business income, rather than income from property, is not subject to attribution, although rules exist which may deem income to be income from property in some cases.

Other Planning Opportunities

As noted earlier, the use of spousal RRSPs is an effective method of income splitting. Other methods of income splitting include the use of family trusts, partnerships, small business corporations and investment holding companies. As there are many technicalities involved in establishing these structures, professional advice should be sought. These techniques are covered in more advanced courses offered by CSI, such as the *Wealth Management Techniques* or the *Wealth Management Essentials Course*.

The following strategies offer other planning opportunities in addition to income splitting and transferring income.

Paying expenses: When both spouses have earnings, non-deductible expenses are not always paid in a tax effective manner. Instead of using funds for investment purposes, the higher-income spouse should first pay all family expenses while the lower-income spouse invests as much of his/her income as practical. Thus the lower-income spouse should be able to maintain a larger investment portfolio for earning income. Presumably this income will be taxed at a lower rate than if earned by the other spouse.

© CSI GLOBAL EDUCATION INC. (2008)

Making loans: As discussed above, the attribution rules do not apply when money is loaned and interest is charged at a rate prescribed by CRA and paid within 30 days after the year-end. When an investment can be expected to generate earnings in excess of this interest, it is often worthwhile for the higher-income family member to loan funds, at the appropriate interest rate, to the lower-income family member. The lower-income individual would then purchase the investment. This would result in the excess of the investment earnings, over the interest charged, to be effectively transferred to the lower-income individual. The interest charged must, of course, be added to the income of the higher income family member.

Discharging debts: The attribution rules do not apply if a taxpayer discharges directly the debt of his or her spouse, a designated minor or non-arm's length individual. These persons would borrow money from another third party and the taxpayer would then repay the original debt directly to the third party. For example, a wife might borrow money to pay off her husband's car loan. The wife assumes the debt and pays it off from her income. The husband, who no longer has to make the loan payments can use this freed up income to invest.

Review the on-line summary or checklist associated with this section.

Canada Pension Plan Sharing: The **Canada Pension Plan (CPP)** legislation permits spouses to share their CPP benefits. If both parties agree, the portion of the retirement pension being received can be split based on the ratio of time that the couple was living together to the period of time during which contributions were made. If both parties are eligible for a pension, both of these pensions must be shared.

Gifting to children or parents: It is possible for an individual to transfer investments to adult children or parents by way of a gift. Such a gift results in a deemed disposition at fair market value by the individual making the gift. Before making such a gift, it is important for the individual to consider the effect of any resulting capital gains or losses in the year the gift is made.

© CSI GLOBAL EDUCATION INC. (2008)

SUMMARY

After reading this chapter, you should be able to:

1. Describe the features of the Canadian income tax system, calculate income tax payable, and differentiate the tax treatment of interest, dividends, and capital gains (and losses).

   - Canada taxes the world income of its residents (including companies incorporated in Canada and foreign companies with management and control in Canada) and the Canadian source income of non-residents.
   - All taxpayers must calculate their taxable income on a yearly basis.
   - Net income tax payable is calculated by taking the gross tax applied to all sources of income from employment, business, or investments less allowable deductions and exemptions, and then reducing the result by any permissible tax credits.
   - There are four general types of income:
     - Employment income (taxed on a gross receipt basis);
     - Business income, including income from self-employment (the profit earned from producing and selling goods or rendering services);
     - Capital property income (dividend and interest income);
     - Capital gains and losses (profit or loss from disposition of property).
   - Combining the provincial tax rate and the federal tax rate on the next dollar of income earned gives the taxpayer's combined marginal tax rate.
   - Employers are required to withhold income tax on salaries and wages and remit this amount on their employees' behalf to the government. Some individuals, and all corporations, pay their taxes by instalments.
   - Interest income is reported annually regardless of whether the cash is received (for all investment contracts acquired after 1989).
   - Dividend income received from a taxable Canadian corporation is grossed up by a specified factor and then the taxpayer receives a tax credit.
   - Foreign dividend income is generally taxed as regular income.
   - Income earned on strip bonds and T-bills must be reported annually.
   - Certain items related to the earning of investment income are eligible for deduction against investment income.

© CSI GLOBAL EDUCATION INC. (2008)

2. Calculate capital gains and capital losses and assess strategies for minimizing tax liability.
   - A capital gain arises from selling a capital property for more than the adjusted cost base plus any costs of disposing of the property.
   - A capital loss arises from selling a capital property for less than the adjusted cost base plus any costs of disposing of the property.
   - The adjusted cost base for dual securities requires determination of proportionate cost.
   - The effect on the adjusted cost base of warrants and rights, as well as shares acquired through the exercise of warrants and rights, differs depending on the method of acquisition.
   - Disposition of worthless securities can result in an allowable capital gain.
   - Superficial losses are not eligible as capital losses.
   - Investors reducing their tax payable by a significant amount may be subject to an alternative minimum tax (AMT).
3. Describe and differentiate tax deferral plans and their uses.
   - Contributions to the plans are limited by legislation and are generally based on taxable income; taxpayers are usually able to carry forward unused contributions.
   - A registered pension plan is a registered trust established by a company to provide pension benefits for its employees when they retire. Both employer and employee contributions to the plan are tax deductible.
   - The two primary types of pension plans are defined benefit (benefits at retirement are based on a formula that is specific and defined) and defined contribution or money purchase (contributions to the plan are specified, and the eventual retirement benefit depends on money accumulated during the contribution period).
   - Registered retirement savings plans are vehicles for individuals to save for retirement. Contributions are tax deductible up to allowable limits, and income accumulates tax deferred while it remains in the plan.
   - RRSP contribution limits are based on earned income, which differs from taxable income.
   - A variety of RRSPs (including single vendor, self-directed, and spousal) are available, allowing individuals to customize their plan to their specific circumstances.
   - An RRSP holder may make withdrawals or de-register the plan at any time, but mandatory de-registration of an RRSP occurs during the calendar year when an RRSP plan holder reaches a specified age.
   - Advantages of RRSPs include reduction in annual taxable income during high-taxation years as a result of tax-deductible contributions, the ability to shelter certain lump-sum types of income, accumulation of funds on a tax-deferred basis, deferral of income taxes to lower-taxed times, and the opportunity to split retirement income.

© CSI GLOBAL EDUCATION INC. (2008)

- Disadvanatages of RRSPs include the inability to use the funds now, assets cannot be used as collateral for a loan, and foregoing the benefits of favoured tax treatment of investments that produce dividends and capital gains. All income is taxed as regular income when withdrawn.
- A registered retirement income fund (RRIF) is a tax-deferral vehicle available to RRSP holders who transfer some or all RRSP fund to a RRIF.
- A RRIF holder must make minimum, annual taxable withdrawals based on a formula related to age; there is no maximum withdrawal.
- An annuity is an investment contract in which a holder deposits money to be invested in an interest-bearing vehicle. Payments are composed of interest and a portion of original capital. Deferred annuities start payments at a date in the future chosen by the investor, while immediate annuities begin payments immediately.
- Registered education savings plans (RESPs) are tax-deferred savings plans intended to help pay for the post-secondary education of a beneficiary. Contributions are not deductible but income accumulates in the plan on a tax-deferred basis.
- Contribution amounts to RESPs are subject to legislated maximums. The government matches a certain portion of eligible contributions (the Canada Education Savings Grant [CESG]).

Now that you've completed this chapter and the on-line activities, complete this post-test.

4. Identify basic tax planning strategies and discuss their advantages.
   - Income splitting involves transferring income from a highly taxed family member to a spouse, child, or parent who is in a lower tax bracket. Attribution rules may be triggered.
   - Other tax-planning strategies include the higher-taxed spouse claiming tax-deductible investment expenses, making loans to family members, sharing government pension benefits, making gifts to children or parents, and spousal RRSPs.

© CSI GLOBAL EDUCATION INC. (2008)

Chapter 23

Working with the Client

© CSI GLOBAL EDUCATION INC. (2008)

23

Working with the Client

CHAPTER OUTLINE

© CSI GLOBAL EDUCATION INC. (2008)

LEARNING OBJECTIVES

By the end of this chapter, you should be able to:

1. Evaluate the importance of gathering information about, communicating with, and educating the client as part of the financial planning process.
2. Summarize the steps in the financial planning process.
3. Describe how life cycle analysis and the financial planning pyramid are used to understand a client's investment needs.
4. Summarize the five values on which the code of ethics is based and the five standards of conduct that advisors should apply in their relationships with clients..

ADVISING THE CLIENT

We have travelled a long road through this course, covering many topics. In this final chapter, we move our focus to the role the advisor plays in dealing with clients. In financial planning, clients and advisors move beyond looking narrowly at investing as buying, selling and trading securities, and focus on the purpose behind these activities.

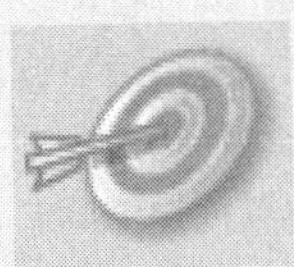

In the on-line Learning Guide for this module, complete the Getting Started activity.

Retail investing should be done with a reasoned approach to meeting needs, goals and objectives. Otherwise, clients will not likely succeed in achieving what they want, or simply not have realistic expectations of what they can expect to succeed. Financial planning provides a structure and framework that allows advisors to clearly understand their clients and formulate investment recommendations that fit a particular client today.

Tied into this approach is the important role ethics play in the process of making investment and financial planning decisions. When dealing with the public, financial advisors have a duty to act ethically, most importantly placing the needs and interests of the client above all else. Behaving ethically is the cornerstone of maintaining and enhancing the integrity of the capital markets.

This chapter brings together much of the learning in the course and looks at what else is necessary to help ensure that advisors are meeting the needs and reaching the goals of their clients.

KEY TERMS

- Code of Ethics
- Duty of care
- Ethics
- Financial planning pyramid
- Know your client
- Life Cycle Theory
- Standards of Conduct
- Suitability

© CSI GLOBAL EDUCATION INC. (2008)

FINANCIAL PLANNING

Although clients seek out financial advisors who are technically competent in the investment and financial planning area, it is not enough for advisors to "know their stuff." Advisors must be able to deal effectively with clients through the stages of information gathering, ongoing communication and education. As well, dealings with clients must be carried out in a way that is compliant with industry rules and regulations and that adheres to ethical standards.

The financial planning approach to managing wealth has benefits for both clients and investment advisors. Financial planning involves analysis of clients' age, wealth, career, marital status, taxation status, estate considerations, risk tolerance, investment objectives, legal concerns and other matters. Accordingly, a very comprehensive view of present circumstances can be formed and future goals better defined. In addition, the very discipline and self-analysis required to flesh out a plan causes clients to have a clearer understanding of themselves and their goals, making success in achieving those objectives far more realistic and likely.

Implicit in this arrangement is that there is a financial planner at the centre of the plan who co-ordinates the advice solicited from experts in various fields. An investment advisor will give advice on investments or, if registered as a portfolio manager, on portfolio management, but will not give advice in areas where he or she is not an expert. For example, an investment advisor will not give advice on the legal aspects of an estate plan; a lawyer is best suited to set up such documents as Wills. Accountants may be engaged to give tax advice, and other experts will provide advice as well, but all within their own fields of expertise. The financial planner then creates a plan that takes all of these inputs into account. The financial planner benefits as well, forming professional relationships with experts in these other disciplines, and receiving advice and information from this networking activity.

The need for individuals and families to plan clearly how financial goals are to be achieved has become more and more important as job security, general economic conditions and the viability of various social programs have become commonplace worries. While previous generations have relied on a more simplistic planning tool, the budget, today's complicated economic environment means that we must conscientiously plan for our financial future.

Before that plan is prepared, there are four objectives that must be considered. The plan to be created:

- Must be achievable
- Must accommodate changes in lifestyle and income level
- Should not be intimidating
- Should provide for not only the necessities but also some luxuries or rewards

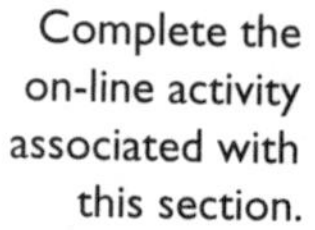

Complete the on-line activity associated with this section.

Each person or family will have a unique financial plan with which to reach goals. However, there are some basic procedures that can be followed to begin a simple financial plan. These steps are common to all.

© CSI GLOBAL EDUCATION INC. (2008)

THE FINANCIAL PLANNING PROCESS

The financial planning process should include the following steps in order for the advisor to best serve client needs

1. Interview the Client – Establish the Client-Advisor Engagement.
2. Data Gathering and Determining Goals and Objectives.
3. Identify financial problems and constraints.
4. Develop a written financial plan.
5. Implement or co-ordinate the implementation of the recommendations.
6. Periodically review and revise the plan and make new recommendations.

Interview the Client- Establish the Client Advisor Engagement

Interviewing the client provides an opportunity to determine what issues and problems the client has identified and whether development of a financial plan will deal with them. It also helps both the advisor and the client to determine whether they feel that a long-term relationship can exist. During the interview, the advisor should discuss the financial planning approach and how it will help the client meet his or her objectives. The advisor should communicate to the client that there will be choices and decisions to be made regarding alternative strategies for dealing with planning issues. Likewise, there will be alternatives in choice of product which should be dealt with by specialists in each area. The advisor should also disclose any areas where a conflict of interest may arise.

If the initial interview is successful from both the advisor's and the client's viewpoint, the advisor should formalize the relationship with either a letter of engagement or a formal contract. This is to ensure that the client is fully aware of exactly what services the advisor will provide and what information the advisor will require in order to prepare a plan. The letter should also outline matters such as the method of compensation and the client's responsibility for the compensation of other professionals, such as lawyers and accountants.

Data Gathering and Determining Goals and Objectives

A financial advisor contributes to a client's well being by understanding the difference between the client's current status and future requirements and goals, and by helping to resolve these differences. To do this effectively, information must be gathered about the client. To acquire this information, an advisor has to follow intuition and instinct while applying some sound techniques for gathering data and assessing the client's requirements.

Financial advisors are required to know the essential details about each of their clients including:

- The client's current financial and personal status;
- The client's investment goals and preferences; and
- The client's risk tolerance.

© CSI GLOBAL EDUCATION INC. (2008)

Successful advisors go beyond just knowing the essential details of a client's situation. They understand the client's unique personal needs and goals including:

- The process the client uses to make important decisions;
- The way in which the client prefers to communicate with the advisor;
- The psychological profile of the client; and
- The needs, goals, and aspirations of the client's family, if applicable.

A financial advisor does far more than just manage the financial lives of clients and provide advice to help them achieve their financial goals. Clients must also be encouraged to assess and re-examine their goals in the context of their evolving business and personal lives. Clients' motivations must be understood. Sometimes the advisor has to dig deep to find them, because clients' motivations are not always readily apparent. The advisor must work with the clients to understand what makes them tick and how they can best build a financial strategy.

There are a number of methods to identify and define clients' motivations for pursuing a particular financial objective. Most of them involve actively listening to clients and interpreting their statements in the context of their unique personality, background, character and context. As this process continues, the advisor will most likely come face to face with a client's most intense emotions, for which money, itself, is merely a symbol.

If a person's money was presented as a spectrum of emotions, it would range from red to blue to yellow and many combinations in between. In money, we find anxiety, security, pride, satisfaction, fear, anger, loss, guilt, joy, hope, greed, lust, and sorrow. These emotions are present in the wealthy individual who inherits money from his father and they are present in the self-made woman who earned every penny from her own hard work, independence and tolerance for risk. It is the advisor's job to help the client articulate those emotions and build a financial strategy to keep them under control.

COMMUNICATING WITH AND EDUCATING THE CLIENT

The job of gathering information about the client is really just the start of the client communication process. This process also includes regular contact and education. Clients rely on a financial advisor for a number of reasons, but almost all of them share one characteristic. They all want someone to understand and attend to the details of their financial lives. Clients may feel too busy or disinclined to attend to these details themselves, preferring to let a financial advisor do the job for them.

Calling clients on a regular basis reassures them that their financial advisor has their interests in mind. It also enables the advisor to keep current with the client's financial and personal characteristics that may influence investment decisions.

A financial advisor should call the client with news about their investments, whether it is good news or bad. In fact, by telling them bad news before they hear it from some other source, the client relationship can be strengthened. Clients want to know they have an advisor who is watching out for their interests, one who is thinking about them and is prepared to take the time and effort to call them, even when the news is not favourable.

© CSI GLOBAL EDUCATION INC. (2008)

Clients aim to achieve specific financial goals and they rely on their financial advisor's advice to help them be successful. The advisor's job will be easier if clients understand why specific decisions about the plan have been made. The advisor can explain in simple terms the technical nature of the plan's individual elements. ("A global equity fund invests in stocks on markets around the world." etc.)

The greater challenge is to earn clients' full co-operation and trust in making these decisions. In fact, without a client's co-operation, advisors cannot do their job. To gain this trust, advisors have to explain how specific investments will help clients achieve their goals.

A key job of the financial advisor is to determine clients' tolerance for risk. Before that is done, however, it is essential that clients understand the various types of risk above and beyond market risk. Quite often, this involves educating clients about the various types of risk, including:

- The risk of not investing or of investing too conservatively;
- The risk of not diversifying;
- Purchasing power risk;
- Default risk; and
- Currency risk.

The advisor should have the client gather the information necessary to complete the plan. This includes tax information (past and current tax returns) bank statements, pay slips, investment statements, insurance policies and other documents such as Wills and Powers of Attorney.

Personal data: There is a broad range of personal factors that should be considered before making investment recommendations. These include age, marital status, number of dependants, risk tolerance and health and employment status. An analysis of these factors may reveal special portfolio restrictions or investment objectives and thus help define an acceptable level of risk and appropriate investment goals.

Net worth and family budget: The advisor can obtain a precise financial profile by showing the client how to prepare a Statement of Net Worth and a Family Budget if the client does not already have these documents available. Appendix A of this chapter shows how this information may be presented. It is important to determine the exact composition of the client's assets and liabilities, the amount and nature of current income and the potential for future investable capital or savings. This information will be invaluable in determining the amount of income a portfolio will have to generate and the level of risk that may be assumed to achieve the client's financial goals.

Record keeping: Part of any financial plan includes advice or perhaps instructions for the client on keeping and maintaining adequate and complete records. It is important for family members to be aware of where records are kept so that they can access this information in an emergency. A document should be prepared which gives the location and details of wills, insurance policies, bank accounts, investment accounts as well as any other financial information. There should also be a list of the professional advisors used by the client, such as the name and contact information of any lawyers, accountants, financial planners, IAs or doctors consulted by the client.

© CSI GLOBAL EDUCATION INC. (2008)

Identify Financial Problems and Constraints

Setting personal investment objectives is a difficult task. The individual must objectively assess personal strengths and weaknesses as well as realistically review career potential and earnings potential. While to some, this in-depth review can be considered tedious and perhaps unnecessary, it should be noted that it is not possible to set realistic financial goals without one considering how to reach that goal. While many clients dream of striking it rich in the financial markets, those who actually reach that goal have done so by design, not by chance.

Since investments are selected to suit individual needs, it is essential to develop a clear client profile. Only by studying all factors that potentially affect a financial plan can suitable recommendations be made or an individual's investment strategy be designed.

EXAMPLES: Billy H. is a commissioned salesperson. His income is very high but it is very erratic. Billy is very risk tolerant and invests in more speculative vehicles. Ronnie W. is a geologist who works in the mining industry. Income is steady from the unionized plant. Ronnie is a risk-averse individual and invests mostly in GICs.

Despite the proclamations of both clients, the planner must consider the personal circumstances of each individual. A person such as Billy H., whose income source is uncertain, may be better off having his money placed in relatively conservative investments, with a portion of the portfolio in liquid securities. The planner may suggest that the client creates a small portion of the portfolio for speculative investments to address this need but should consider the broader picture – that income may be uncertain. If Billy were in real estate sales, investments in the real estate sector of the market may not be a good idea. Investing in the real estate sector would increase the risk of the portfolio, as a downturn in real estate would hurt both his income and his investments.

The other client, Ronnie W., is risk-averse by nature, but could be limiting investment choices because of an unrealistic fear. This fear should be addressed to ensure that it does not limit future decisions. Ronnie W. could invest in blue chip issues because of their relatively high quality and moderate risk.

Unless the advisor delves into personal circumstances such as job security, investment experience and possibly marital circumstances, important issues can be overlooked.

An individual's investment objectives are determined by a thorough analysis of his or her current financial position and future requirements. The New Account Application Form (NAAF) (Exhibit 23.1) requires that investment objectives be clearly stated and that they govern investment actions. Investment objectives generally can be described as a desire for income, growth of capital, preservation of capital, tax minimization or liquidity. These investment objectives were described more fully in Chapter 15.

© CSI GLOBAL EDUCATION INC. (2008)

EXHIBIT 23.1 NEW ACCOUNT APPLICATION FORM

Account Supervision

Office	Account		I.A.

New Account Application Form

(to be completed by Advisor)

(1) (a) Name Mr.________ Phones: Home ________

Mrs.________ Business________

Miss ________ Other ________

(Please Print)

Home ________ (Street) Fax________

Address ________ (City) (Province) (Postal Code)

Date of Birth________ Client's Social Insurance Number______ Client's Citizenship ______

Type of Account Requested

(b) Is Advisor registered in the Province or Country in which the client resides? Yes______ No______

Cash ______ RRSP/RRI____ U.S. Funds ____

Margin ______ Other ______

D.A.P ______ Pro______ CDN Funds____

---

(2) Special Instructions:________ Hold in Account __ Register and Deliver ______ DAP______

Duplicate Confirmation ________ And/Or Statement

Name: ________ Name________

Address ________ Address:________

________ Postal Code: ____ ________ Postal Code: ________

---

(3) Client's Employer: Name________ Type of Business ________

Address ________ Client's Occupation________

---

(4) Family Information:

Spouse's Name ________ No. of Dependants ________

Occupation ________ Employer ________

Type of Business ________

---

(5) How long have you known client? Advertising Lead __ Phone In ______ Have you met the client face to face?

Personal Contact__ Walk In ______ Yes______ No______

Referral by: ________ (name) (if customer, give account no.) ________

© CSI GLOBAL EDUCATION INC. (2008)

EXHIBIT 23.1 NEW ACCOUNT APPLICATION FORM *(Cont'd)*

(6) If yes for Questions 1, 2, or 3, provide details in (11).

1. Will any other person or persons: (a) Have trading authorization in this account? No___ Yes___
   (b) Guarantee this account? No___ Yes___
   (c) Have a financial interest in such accounts? No___ Yes___
2.. Do any of the signatories have any other accounts or control the trading in such accounts? No___ Yes___
3. Does client have accounts with other brokerage firms? (Type__________) No___ Yes___
4. Is this account (a) discretionary or (b) managed (a) ___ (b) ___

Insider Information

5. Is client a senior officer or director of a company whose shares are traded on an change or in the OTC markets? No___ Yes___
6. Does the client, as an individual or as part of a group, hold or control such a company? (______________) No___ Yes___

(7) (a) General Documents

	Attached	Obtaining
– Client's Agreement	______	
– Margin Agreement	______	
– Cash Agreement	______	
– Guarantee	______	
– Other	______	

(b) Trading Authorization Documents:

	Attached	Obtaining
– For an Individual's Account	______	______
– For a Corporation, Partnership, Trust, etc.	______	______
– Discretionary Authority	______	______
– Managed Account Agreement	______	______

(8) INVESTMENT KNOWLEDGE

Sophisticated__________
Good__________
Limited __________
Poor/Nil__________

EST. NET LIQUID ASSETS (Cash and securities less loans outstanding against securities) A ______

ACCOUNT OBJECTIVES
Income __________%
Capital Gains
 Short Term ________%
 Medium Term ________%
 Long Term ________%
 100%

ACCOUNT RISK FACTORS
Low __________
Medium __________
High__________
100%

EST. NET FIXED ASSETS (Fixed assets less liabilities outstanding against fixed assets) B ______

EST.TOTAL NET WORTH (A + B = C) C ______

APPROXIMATE ANNUAL INCOME FROM ALL SOURCES D ______

EST. SPOUSE'S INCOME E______

(9) Bank Reference: Name________ Branch________ Refer to________ Accounts________

Bank credit check acceptable? Yes___ No___
Or Credit Bureau check acceptable? Yes___ No___
Above credit checks considered unnecessary
Explain in (11)

(10) Deposit and/or Security Received ______________________________

Initial __________ Buy__________ Solicited__________ Amount__________
Order __________ Sell__________ Unsolicited __________ Description__________

(11) Advisor's Signature ____________________ Designated Officer, Director or Branch Manager's Approval____________________

Date____________________ Date of Approval____________________

Comments: ____

____

Client Signature____ Date______________

© CSI GLOBAL EDUCATION INC. (2008)

The client's tolerance for risk, investment knowledge and time horizon all impose constraints on the recommendations to be put forth in the financial plan. Constraints provide some discipline in the fulfilment of a client's objectives. Constraints, which may loosely be defined as those items that may hinder or prevent the advisor from satisfying the client's objectives, are often not given the importance they deserve in the policy formation process. This may result from the fact that objectives are a more comforting concept to dwell on than the discipline of constraints.

Develop a Written Financial Plan and Implement the Recommendations

After reviewing and assessing the information, a plan of action must be developed for the client to follow. This plan of action may require the input of other professionals. If this is the case, the advisor should prepare a list of instructions for these professionals as well. Clearly defined goals and tasks, as well as a schedule for achievement can be of enormous benefit to the client. The financial plan should be simple, easy to implement and easy to maintain.

It is important to implement a financial plan in a timely manner. Once the preparatory work of analyzing, determining and calculating is finished, it is up to the client to decide to put all the carefully thought-out ideas and strategies in motion.

At this point the client should review the plan, the goals, the objectives and the risk tolerance levels. The client should be in agreement with them before any products are purchased or deals are struck. The investment advisor must ensure that the client understands each product chosen and is aware of the potential risks as well as the potential rewards

Periodically Review and Revise the Plan and Make New Recommendations

The last step in this whole process is the review. A financial plan should never remain static. Just as investments rise and fall in market value, a person's financial situation can change. As well, economic changes, tax increases and health issues all can threaten even the "best-laid plans." While there is no set time frame for such a review, an annual review is the minimum required. Minireviews may be necessary depending on the circumstances (i.e., changing tax, economic or employment status). In extreme circumstances, such as a job loss, it may be necessary to devise a completely new financial plan.

Revisions can include reviewing a will, changing beneficiaries and ensuring that the client is continuing to take advantage of all tax savings techniques. Recommendations can be simple – no changes are necessary – or could entail a great number of changes. It is important that the advisor follow up with the client to ensure that suggestions are carried out

This overview of the financial planning process provides the client with the structure of a basic financial plan but does not deal with specialized issues such as trusts, estate freezes, the need for insurance, etc. To complete a thorough analysis of needs and requirements, these areas must be addressed as well; however, it is beyond the scope of this text to do so. A more thorough discussion of these topics is provided in more advanced courses offered by CSI.

© CSI GLOBAL EDUCATION INC. (2008)

FINANCIAL PLANNING AIDS

Life Cycle Analysis

To add perspective to the process of setting objectives, it can be helpful to think in terms of the life cycle. **Life Cycle Theory** states that the risk-return relationship of a portfolio changes because clients have different needs at different points in their lives. On this basis, it is assumed that younger clients can assume more risk in the pursuit of higher returns and that the risk-return relationship reverses itself as the client ages. In general, there are four definable stages in a person's adult life.

- *Early Earning Years – to age 35*: At this time the client is starting a career, building net worth and assuming family and home ownership responsibilities. The most common priorities are to have a savings plan and near-cash investments for emergencies. However, when funds are available for investing, growth is usually the primary objective because of the magnitude and duration of expected future earnings.
- *Mid-Earning Years – to age 55*: In this stage an individual's expenses usually decline and income and savings usually increase. As a result, savings continue to be a very important factor in the growth of an client's investment capital. Because such clients have more discretionary income, investment objectives tend to focus on growth and tax minimization.
- *Peak Earning Years – to retirement*: As an client approaches retirement, preservation of capital becomes an increasingly important objective. During this period, the average term of maturity of fixed-income investments should be shortened and the quantity of higher-risk common shares reduced.
- *Retirement Years*: During this period clients most frequently have fixed incomes and only limited opportunities for employment. Therefore the primary investment objectives of retired clients are preservation of capital and income, with the relative importance of each being determined by comparing the level of retirement income to budget requirements. When income is adequate, preservation of capital is more important. There must be enough growth in the portfolio so that the client does not run out of money.

While convenient, the life cycle approach to financial planning is to be considered a mere guideline in developing any plan. It is true that some clients might easily conform to this life cycle model, but many individuals' financial or other circumstances simply do not fit into the convenient fourstage approach outlined here. Special circumstances require an individualized approach.

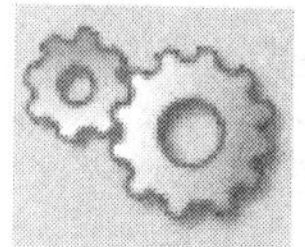

Although life cycle analysis can be helpful, it is far more important to consider the client's personal situation, financial position and responsibilities, tolerance for risk and investment knowledge. Only by assessing these factors in depth and relating them to the expressed needs of the client can the planner help an individual develop specific investment objectives.

The Financial Planning Pyramid

One tool to help the client and planner to both clarify the client's current situation and identify planning needs is the **financial planning pyramid**. Although the financial planning pyramid may appear simplistic, it often helps for the planner to use visual aids in dealing with clients. The financial planning pyramid helps the planner and the client alike visualize goals and objectives and review investment strategy.

© CSI GLOBAL EDUCATION INC. (2008)

EXHIBIT 23.2 THE FINANCIAL PLANNING PYRAMID

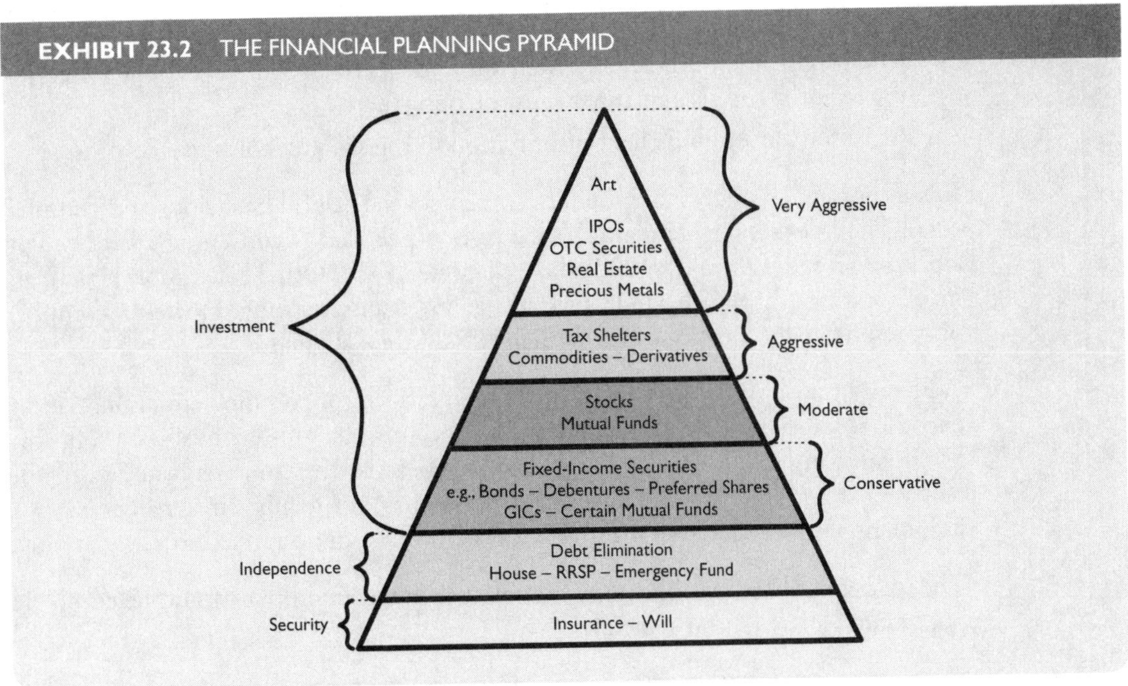

If the client is interested in IPOs for example, but lacks a Will and the proper insurance coverage, it is obvious that, by starting at the top with an IPO, the groundwork has not been done and the plan will be unstable. The client must have a good strong base from which to work to successfully reach the goals and objectives set.

ETHICS AND THE FINANCIAL ADVISOR

A critical element in building a solid trusting relationship with a client is behaving in an ethical manner. Ethics can be defined as a set of moral values that guide behaviour. Moral values are enduring beliefs that reflect standards of what is right and what is wrong.

The Code of Ethics

The securities industry has a Code of Ethics that establishes norms based upon the principles of trust, integrity, justice, fairness, honesty, responsibility and reliability. People registered to sell securities and mutual funds (registrants) must adhere to this code. The code encompasses the following five primary ethical values:

- Registrants must use proper care and exercise independent professional judgment.
- Registrants must conduct themselves with trustworthiness and integrity, and act in an honest and fair manner in all dealings with the public, clients, employers and colleagues.
- Registrants must, and should encourage others to, conduct business in a professional manner that will reflect positively on themselves, their firms and their profession. Registrants should also strive to maintain and improve their professional knowledge and that of others in the profession.

© CSI GLOBAL EDUCATION INC. (2008)

- Registrants must act in accordance with the securities act(s) of the province or provinces in which registration is held, and the requirements of all Self-Regulatory Organizations (SROs) of which the firm is a member must be observed.
- Registrants must hold client information in the strictest confidence.

It is important to understand the difference between ethical behaviour and compliance with rules. The rules set out standards. Some rules purely codify consensus practices. For example, stock trades settle three days after the trade date (T+3). Other rules approximate ethics by incorporating ethical behaviour, such as the law against stealing. However, compliance with rules only results in conformity with externally established standards.

While there are rules to deal with the most significant or common situations, rules cannot encompass every possible situation that may occur in day-to-day business. Following rules does not involve any judgment. People follow rules because they must, not necessarily because they believe it is morally correct. However, ethical behaviour requires internally established moral judgments. Ethical decision making is a system that can be applied to any situation.

The following short case illustrates an example of an action that would be compliant with rules but would violate ethical standards.

CASE #1 HANDLING AN ETHICAL ISSUE

A financial advisor, Betty Cho, is considering recommending that a client, Henry King, invest in a small but promising Internet company, NetTrack Enterprises. Betty's brother-in-law, Fred Wong, is NetTrack's main shareholder and CEO.

While there may not be a clear violation of industry rules or regulations, if Ms. Cho recommends NetTrack to her client, there is certainly an ethical issue that she is facing.

If she is acting in an ethically sound manner, Betty needs to:

1. Recognize that she faces a moral issue if she makes an investment recommendation in a situation in which she has a potential or actual conflict of interest.
2. Assess her options in terms of moral criteria and develop a morally appropriate strategy for managing conflict-of-interest situations. For instance, she should disclose to Henry that one of her relations has a major interest in NetTrack. She must consider whether her professional objectivity regarding NetTrack's promise might be compromised, or appear to be compromised, by her relationship to Fred.
3. Make a commitment to a morally appropriate strategy such as disclosure.
4. Have the courage to carry out the moral strategy by letting Henry know that Fred Wong is her brother-in-law.

This Code of Ethics establishes norms that incorporate, but are not limited to, strict compliance with "the letter of the law" but also foster compliance with the "spirit of the law." These norms are based upon ethical principles of trust, integrity, justice, fairness and honesty. The Code distills industry rules and regulations into five primary values.

© CSI GLOBAL EDUCATION INC. (2008)

Standards of Conduct

The securities industry has established Standards of Conduct, which expand on the Code of Ethics shown above and set out certain requirements for behaviour. These requirements are based in large part on the provincial securities acts and SRO rules. A brief summary of some of the key standards is discussed next.

EXHIBIT 23.3 CANADIAN SECURITIES INDUSTRY STANDARDS OF CONDUCT (SUMMARY)

Standard A – Duty of Care

- Know Your Client
- Due Diligence
- Unsolicited Orders

Standard B – Trustworthiness, Honesty and Fairness

- Priority of Client Interests
- Protection of Client Assets
- Complete and Accurate Information
- Disclosure

Standard C – Professionalism

- Client Business
  - Client Orders
  - Trades by Registered and Approved Individuals
  - Approved Securities
- Personal Business
  - Personal Financial Dealing with Clients
  - Personal Trading Activity
  - Other Personal Endeavours
- Continuous Education

Standard D – Conduct in Accordance with Securities Acts

- Compliance with Securities Acts and SRO Rules
  - Inside Information

Standard E – Confidentiality

- Client Information
- Use of Confidential Information

Standard A – Duty of Care

While duty of care encompasses a wide number of obligations towards parties, the obligation to know the client is of paramount importance in order to ensure the priority of clients' interests. Including this, the three major components of duty of care are:

- *Know Your Client*: The Know Your Client (KYC) rule is paramount for the industry. All registrants must make a diligent and business-like effort to learn the essential financial and personal circumstances and the investment objectives of each client. Client account documentation should reflect all material information about the client's current status, and

© CSI GLOBAL EDUCATION INC. (2008)

should be updated to reflect any material changes to the client's status in order to assure suitability of investment recommendations.

- *Due Diligence*: Registrants must make all recommendations based on a careful analysis of both information about the client and information related to the particular transaction.
- *Unsolicited Orders*: Registrants who give advice to clients must provide appropriate cautionary advice with respect to unsolicited orders that appear unsuitable based on client information. The registrant must be aware of the objectives and strategies behind each order accepted on behalf of his or her clients, whether it is solicited or not. Registrants should take appropriate safeguarding measures when clients insist on proceeding with unsolicited, unsuitable orders.

As discussed earlier, an advisor must make a concerted effort to know the client – to understand the financial and personal status and aspirations of the client. Thus, the advisor will make recommendations for the client to invest funds in securities that reflect, to the best knowledge of the advisor, these considerations. The advisor, having provided sound advice, will therefore be above reproach for potentially unsuitable purchases and sales of securities for a client if the client does not heed the advisor's advice.

The advisor must make a diligent and business-like effort to learn the essential financial and personal circumstances and the investment objectives of each client. Client account documentation should reflect all material information about the client's current status, and should be updated to reflect any material changes to the client's status in order to assure suitability of investment recommendations.

According to IIROC, full-service brokers now have the opportunity to accept non-recommended trades without a suitability obligation. To meet regulatory requirements in this matter, clients are required to sign a disclosure agreement document that gives their consent that non-recommended trades will not be subject to a suitability review.

Standard B – Trustworthiness, Honesty and Fairness

Registrants must display absolute trustworthiness since the client's interests must be the foremost consideration in all business dealings. This requires that registrants observe the following:

- *Priority of Client's Interest*: The client's interest must be the foremost consideration in all business dealings. In situations where the registrant may have an interest that competes with that of the client, the client's interest must be given priority.
- *Respect for Client's Assets*: The client's assets are solely the property of the client and are to be used only for the client's purposes. Registrants shall not utilize client's funds or securities in any way.
- *Complete and Accurate Information Relayed to Client*: Registrants must take reasonable steps to ensure that all information given to the client regarding his or her existing portfolio is complete and accurate. While the onus is on the investment firm to provide each client with written confirmations of all purchases and sales, as well as monthly account statements, the individual registrant must accurately represent the details of each client's investments to the client. The registrant must be familiar with the clients' investment holdings and must not misrepresent the facts to the client in order to create a more favourable view of the portfolio.
- *Disclosure*: Registrants must disclose all real and potential conflicts of interest in order to ensure fair, objective dealings with clients.

Advisors help clients think through their financial goals. In this role, clients need to know that the advisor is working to promote their best interests.

© CSI GLOBAL EDUCATION INC. (2008)

When clients trust their advisor, they do not personally have to verify everything that the advisor tells them. For example, they do not have to check the tax and estate implications of every investment recommendation or ask for details about its risk or volatility. They certainly do not waste time wondering if the advisor has made a recommendation that serves the advisor's interest rather than the client's own interest.

There are two parts to a trust relationship: trust in an advisor's *competence* and *integrity*. Both are essential. Competence, without integrity, leaves clients at the mercy of a self-serving professional. Integrity, without competence, puts clients in the hands of a well-meaning but inept professional.

In order to ensure that advisors and other registrants display absolute trustworthiness, the Standards of Conduct sets out that a client's interest must be the foremost consideration in all business dealings. In situations where the advisor may have an interest that competes with that of the client, the client's interest must be given priority. Furthermore, advisors must disclose all real and potential conflicts of interest in order to ensure fair, objective dealings with clients. This is why Betty Cho, in Case #1, should disclose her relationship with NetTrack's main shareholder, her brother-in-law.

In order to ensure that advisors are competent, they must meet proficiency requirements for their registration category. As well, the Canadian investment industry has a mandatory continuing education program, which helps ensure that investment industry professionals have the information and skills they need to serve their clients with the utmost professionalism.

CASE #2 GAINING A CLIENT'S TRUST

When Ottawa financial advisor Jo-Ann Carter assumed the account of 75-year-old Ena Beyer, she knew she had a challenge on her hands.

Mrs. Beyer, a widow, held more than $350,000 in a non-registered mutual fund account – and the entire amount was invested in a combination of GICs and a mortgage mutual fund. After the first meeting with her client, it was evident that her investment knowledge was very limited and that she relied almost entirely on her son for financial advice.

Therein lay the problem. Her son, a systems-services professional employed by a high-tech firm, had been generating great returns for his own portfolio by investing in various Canadian and U.S. technology stocks.

When Mrs. Beyer passed over a sheet of paper listing some of her son's recommendations, Carter immediately shook her head. The proposed list of holdings included an excessive amount in equities, especially aggressive high-growth situations, and not nearly enough in dividend-paying blue-chip names and fixed-income securities.

Convinced that the son's proposed strategy was overly aggressive for someone with Mrs. Beyer's client profile, Carter recommended to her a much more conservative approach. Mrs. Beyer balked at the suggestions for change, siding with her son over someone she was meeting only for the first time.

The easy way out for Carter would have been to go along with what the son suggested and Mrs. Beyer wanted. Carter could easily have rationalized the choices, since one of Mrs. Beyer's objectives was to pass on an inheritance to her son. By questioning the son's judgment, Carter risked losing an attractive account, and one that would generate a good chunk of commission income right away.

But in good conscience, Carter could not go along with Mrs. Beyer's requests without making further inquiries to determine what in fact was in Mrs. Beyer's best interests. Carter asked her to set up a meeting with her son so that the three of them could discuss her situation together.

© CSI GLOBAL EDUCATION INC. (2008)

CASE #2 GAINING A CLIENT'S TRUST *(Cont'd)*

A few weeks later, the agreed-on meeting started poorly. Mrs. Beyer's son, Roy, seemed skeptical of Carter's abilities and was a little suspicious about her intentions. Undeterred, Carter patiently explained her responsibility as an advisor, her concerns about his mother's account and the reasons for her recommendations.

After the first meeting, Roy said he was not yet convinced, but would think about it. His mother concurred. "It took some time, but after a couple more meetings, her son was impressed with my recommendations," says Carter. "In the end, we had totally revamped the asset mix to ensure prudent allocation of his mother's investments."

With Mrs. Beyer more comfortable knowing her son was involved, Carter also felt more assured that she would be able to get better results for her client. "We now meet regularly and the trust that has developed between the three of us is very strong." More recently, this trust went even farther, and Mrs. Beyer's account became a discretionary managed account, since Roy has found himself increasingly too busy to oversee his mother's investments.

Standard C – Professionalism

It is generally accepted that professionals, by having specialized knowledge, need to protect their clients, who usually do not have the same degree of specialized knowledge, and must continually strive to put the interests of their clients ahead of their own. Registrants must also make a continuous effort to maintain a high standard of professional knowledge.

- *Client business*: All methods of soliciting and conducting business must be such as to merit public respect and confidence.
- *Client Orders*: Every client order must be entered only at the client's direction unless the account has been properly constituted as a discretionary or managed account pursuant to the applicable regulatory requirements.
- *Trades by registered and approved individuals*: All trades and all acts in furtherance of trades, whether with existing or potential clients, must be effected only by individuals who are registered and approved in accordance with applicable legislation and the rules of the SROs.
- *Approved securities*: Only securities approved for distribution by the appropriate regulatory authority and partner, director or officer of the firm should be distributed, and all such transactions should be recorded in the normal way on the books and records of the firm.
- *Personal business*: All personal business affairs must be conducted in a professional and responsible manner, so as to reflect credit on the individual registrant, the securities firm and the profession.
- *Personal financial dealings with clients*: Registrants should avoid personal financial dealings with clients, including the lending of money to or the borrowing of money from them, paying clients' losses out of personal funds, and sharing a financial interest in an account with a client. Any personal financial or business dealings with any clients must be conducted in such a way as to avoid any real or apparent conflict of interest and be disclosed to the firm, in order that the firm may monitor the situation.

© CSI GLOBAL EDUCATION INC. (2008)

- *Personal trading activity*: Personal trading activity should be kept to reasonable levels. If a registrant is trading in his or her own account very actively on a daily basis, it is doubtful that the registrant will have enough time to properly service his or her clients. Excessive trading losses by a registrant will also present a negative image of the registrant as a responsible financial professional.
- *Other personal endeavours*: Each registrant must take care to ensure that any other publicly visible activity in which he or she participates (such as politics, social organizations or public speaking) is conducted responsibly and moderately so as not to present an unfavorable public image.
- *Continuous education*: It is the responsibility of each registrant to have an understanding of factors that influence the investment industry in order to maintain a level of competence in dealing with his or her clientele. A registrant must continually upgrade his or her levels of technical and general knowledge to ensure the accuracy and responsibility of his or her recommendations and advice.

When trust relationships are open-ended and involve "caring for" or "looking after" a client's interests, there is a *fiduciary relationship* between advisors and their clients. Fiduciary or trust relations in ethics and law are needed where there is an imbalance of knowledge or control between two morally related parties, such as a parent and a child, a physician and a patient, or a lawyer and a client. Fiduciary relationships are agent-principal relationships in which the principal has a certain vulnerability and the agent has greater expertise or authority.

In order to ensure that investment advisors and other registrants display the utmost in professionalism, the Standards of Conduct set a number of requirements. These requirements include that all methods of soliciting and conducting business must be such as to merit public respect and confidence, and that all personal business affairs be conducted in a professional and responsible manner.

CASE #3 BEING AWARE OF A CLIENT'S VULNERABILITY

There are times when Ron Springfield must advise a surviving spouse about what to do with inherited assets. But the time immediately following the death of a loved one is a time for grieving, not decision making, says Springfield, who over the years has guided many surviving spouses through this vulnerable period.

His widowed clients include Martina, whose retirement life in a peaceful small town in the B.C. interior was shattered by the sudden death, at age 67, of Ivan, her husband of 35 years. Amid the flurry of contacting friends and relatives and making funeral arrangements, Martina also worried about what she had to do about her deceased husband's RRSP and his other investment accounts. It was all overwhelming, particularly since it was Ivan, and not her, who had been the main overseer of the family's finances.

Martina felt some relief when she contacted Springfield by phone at the brokerage office. He assured her that no immediate action was required on her part. "The perception that most people in your situation have is, that things need to be done very quickly," Springfield told Martina. "The reality is that as long as you have enough cash on hand to pay the bills, there is really no great rush. When you're ready to sit down and talk, give me a call."

Though the timing of Ivan's passing was unexpected, such eventualities had been provided for in the financial plan crafted for the couple. Ivan's death triggered the payment of a life insurance policy that had been designed to cover any of his tax liabilities at death. The two largest tax payouts had to do with the deemed disposition of rental property owned by Ivan, and the deemed disposition of a portfolio of stocks, most of which had been held for at least ten years and had built up considerable capital gains.

© CSI GLOBAL EDUCATION INC. (2008)

CASE #3 BEING AWARE OF A CLIENT'S VULNERABILITY *(Cont'd)*

Additionally, the life insurance policy had been over-funded so as to ensure that Martina, the beneficiary, would have a cash reserve to cover all of the one-time expenses associated with a death. For her, these included the costs of plane fare to enable her son and his young family to make the trip to the West Coast from their home in New Brunswick.

While mourners gathered to comfort the grieving widow, Springfield was quietly taking care of business. Shortly after the death, his assistant produced an estate-evaluation report listing the market value of Ivan's investment and RRSP assets as of the date of his death, and the maturity dates of his bond and GIC holdings.

The report laid out clearly the information needed by Martina's executor, lawyer or accountant in order to do their jobs. "This is a lot easier to do right after the death than several weeks later," says Springfield.

Meanwhile, Springfield reviewed Martina's own investment account, which he has been looking after for many years. He saw that a five-year GIC was just about to expire, and that some stocks and mutual funds had recently paid quarterly dividends into her account.

In the weeks and months to come, the probate process would play out, and Martina would seek advice from Springfield on how to invest her existing and inherited assets. But now was hardly the time for reinvestment decisions. Springfield knew from his conversation with Martina that she would need the money for short-term expenses like visitation, funeral, catering and other related expenses. After consulting with Martina, he transferred the available cash from Martina's investment account to her daily chequing account at her bank.

Less may be more, when it comes to helping clients who are bereaved or otherwise going through a period when they are feeling very vulnerable. "A death in the family immediately changes a client's profile," says Springfield. "People have a lot more need for liquidity. You try to get everything accumulated and make it easier for them."

Standard D – Conduct in Accordance with Securities Acts

Registrants must ensure that their conduct is in accordance with the securities acts and the applicable SRO rules and regulations.

- *Compliance with securities acts and SRO rules*: Registrants must ensure that their conduct is in accordance with the securities acts of the province or provinces in which registration is held. The requirements of all SROs of which a registrant's firm is a member must be observed by the registrant. The registrant shall not knowingly participate in, nor assist in, any act in violation of any applicable law, rule or regulation of any government, governmental agency or regulatory organization governing his or her professional, financial or business activities, nor any act which would violate any provision of the industry Code of Ethics and Standards of Conduct.
- *Inside information*: If a registrant acquires non-public, material information, the information must neither be communicated (outside of the relationship) nor acted upon. Employees of a firm's trading, corporate finance or research departments must be aware of the need to safeguard non-public, confidential, material information received in the normal course of business.

© CSI GLOBAL EDUCATION INC. (2008)

Standard E – Confidentiality

All information concerning the client's transactions and his or her accounts must be considered confidential and must not be disclosed except with the client's permission, for supervisory purposes or by order of the proper authority.

- *Client information*: Registrants must maintain the confidentiality of identities and the personal and financial circumstances of their clients. Registrants must refrain from discussing this information with anyone outside their firm, and must also ensure that the firm's client lists and other confidential records are not left out where they can be taken or observed by visitors to the office.
- *Use of confidential information*: Information regarding clients' personal and financial circumstances and trading activity must be kept confidential and may not be used in any way to effect trades in personal and/or proprietary accounts or in the accounts of other clients. Not only must registrants refrain from trading in their own accounts based on knowledge of clients' pending orders, but they must also refrain from using it as a basis for recommendations to other clients or passing this information along to any other parties.

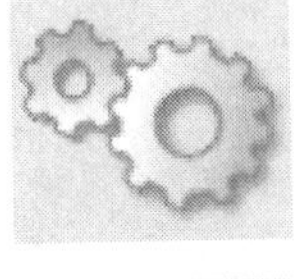

In addition to being skilled in the areas of investment and financial management, financial advisors must be able to deal effectively with clients through the stages of data gathering, ongoing communication and education. As well, as the investment industry is built on trust and confidence, advisors must adhere to strict rules and regulations with respect to dealing with clients, and abide by the industry Code of Ethics that establishes trust, integrity, justice, fairness, honesty, responsibility and reliability.

Review the on-line summary or checklist associated with this section.

In the Chapter Appendix B, two case studies are used to illustrate the integration of the portfolio management principles outlined earlier with the skill set required in building a relationship with the client. The situation in the first example – the Casuso family – contains many of the variables that an investment advisor has to assess in order to make suitable investment recommendations. While the family is fictitious and the ultimate selections are only one person's view, the case study is a useful summary of the process. The second example - Johanna Von Rosen – presents a client that recently retired and highlights the important elements a financial advisor must take into consideration when recommending an asset mix given the client's unique situation.

© CSI GLOBAL EDUCATION INC. (2008)

SUMMARY

After reading this chapter, you should be able to:

1. Evaluate the importance of gathering information about, communicating with, and educating clients as part of the financial planning process, and summarize the six steps in the financial planning process.
   - Gathering information properly fulfills legal requirements and allows an advisor to plan effectively for the client.
   - Effective communication establishes a relationship, builds trust, and allows an advisor to stay current with the client's situation.
   - Educating a client helps to establish clear objectives, expectations, and understanding of the client's investment situation and risk tolerance.
2. Summarize the six steps in the financial planning process.
   - The six steps in the financial planning process are:
     - Interview the Client- Establish the Client Planner Engagement
     - Data Gathering and Determining Goals and Objectives ;
     - Identify financial problems and constraints;
     - Develop a written financial plan;
     - Implement or co-ordinate the implementation of recommendations;
     - Periodically review and revise the plan with appropriate new recommendations.
3. Describe how life cycle analysis and the financial planning pyramid are used to understand a client's investment needs.
   - Life Cycle Theory states that the risk-return relationship of a portfolio changes because clients have different needs at different points in their lives.
   - It is assumed that younger clients can take on more risk in the pursuit of higher returns and that the risk-return relationship reverses as clients age.
   - In general, there are four definable stages in a person's adult life: early earning years (to age 35); mid-earnings years (to age 55); peak earning years (age 55 to retirement); and retirement years (after retirement from the work force).
   - Reviewing a client's personal circumstances against the stages on the financial planning pyramid can help identify whether a client is appropriately or inappropriately invested against her risk tolerance and portfolio asset allocation.
4. Summarize the five values on which the code of ethics is based and the five standards of conduct that advisors should apply in their relationships with clients.
   - There are five primary ethical values on which the code of ethics is based:
     - Registrants must use proper care and exercise independent professional judgment;

© CSI GLOBAL EDUCATION INC. (2008)

- Registrants must conduct themselves with trustworthiness and integrity, and act in an honest and fair manner in all dealings with the public, clients, employers and colleagues;
- Registrants must, and should encourage others to, conduct business in a professional manner that will reflect positively on themselves, their firms and their profession, and registrants should strive to maintain and improve their professional knowledge and that of others in the profession;
- Registrants must act in accordance with the securities act(s) of the province(s) in which registration is held and must observe the requirements of all self-regulatory organizations (SROs) of which the firm is a member;
- Registrants must hold client information in the strictest confidence.

• The standards of conduct build on the code of ethics:

Now that you've completed this chapter and the on-line activities, complete this post-test.

- Duty of care (know your client, due diligence, unsolicited orders);
- Trustworthiness, honesty and fairness (priority of client interests, protection of client assets, complete and accurate information, disclosure);
- Professionalism (client business, personal business, continuous education);
- Conduct in accordance with securities acts (compliance with securities acts and SRO rules, inside information);
- Confidentiality (client information, use of confidential information).

© CSI GLOBAL EDUCATION INC. (2008)

APPENDIX A

TABLE 23A.1 STATEMENT OF NET WORTH

ASSETS	
Readily Marketable Assets	
Cash (bank accounts, Canada Savings Bonds, etc.)	$
Guaranteed investment certificates and term deposits	
Bonds – at market value	
Stocks – at market value	
Mutual funds – at redemption value	
Cash surrender value of life insurance	
Other	
Non-liquid Financial Assets	
Pensions – at vested value	
RRSPs	
Tax shelters – at cost or estimated value	
Annuities	
Other	
Other Assets	
Home – at market value	
Recreational properties – at market value	
Business interests – at market value	
Antiques, art, jewellery, collectibles, gold and silver	
Cars, boats, etc.	
Other real estate interests	
Other	
Total Assets	$
LIABILITIES	
Personal Debt	
Mortgage on home	$
Mortgage on recreational property	
Credit card balances	
Investment loans	
Consumer loans	
Other loans	
Other	
Business Debt	
Investment loans	
Loans for other business-related debt	
Contingent Liabilities	
Loan guarantees for others	
Total Liabilities	$
ASSETS	
Minus LIABILITIES	
NET WORTH	$

© CSI GLOBAL EDUCATION INC. (2008)

TABLE 23A.2 FAMILY BUDGET AND EARNINGS AVAILABLE FOR INVESTMENT

	Monthly	Total Monthly	Total Annual
NET EARNINGS			
Self	$ ______		
Spouse	$ ______		
Net Investment Income	$ ______	$ ______	$ ______
EXPENSES & SAVINGS			
Maintaining Your Home			
Rent or mortgage payments	$ ______		
Property taxes	$ ______		
Insurance	$ ______		
Light, water and heat	$ ______		
Telephone, cable	$ ______		
Maintenance and repairs	$ ______		
Other	$ ______		
Total Monthly		$ ______	
Total Annual			$ ______
Maintaining Your Family			
Food	$ ______		
Clothing	______		
Laundry	______		
Auto expenses	______		
Education	______		
Childcare	______		
Medical, dental, drugs	______		
Accident and sickness insurance	______		
Other	______		
Total Monthly		$ ______	
Total Annual			$ ______
Maintaining Your Lifestyle			
Religious, charitable donations	$ ______		
Membership fees	______		
Sports and entertainment	______		
Gifts and contributions	______		
Vacations	______		
Personal expenses	______		
Total Monthly		$ ______	
Total Annual			$ ______
Maintaining Your Future			
Life insurance premiums	$ ______		
RRSP and pension plan contributions	______	______	______
Total Monthly Expenses and Savings		$ ______	
Total Annual Expenses and Savings		$ ______	
Available for Investment		$ ______	$ ______

© CSI GLOBAL EDUCATION INC. (2008)

APPENDIX B: CLIENT SCENARIOS

Juan Casuso

Juan Casuso, 50, and his wife Emily, 44, have been married for 22 years. Their only child, Jim, who joined the armed forces plans a career as a naval officer.

Over the last nine years, Juan has been promoted three times as a manager at The National Retail Com¬pany. Juan enjoys his present responsibilities and plans to continue his career with his current employer. In addition to his $52,000 annual salary, Juan has company benefits that include both disability and life insurance and a limited cover¬age dental plan. However, he has not yet joined his company's money purchase pension plan. Emily is an executive secretary with a small engineering firm. She receives a $27,500 annual income and does not participate in a benefits package.

The Casusos have a fairly modest lifestyle, their home being the focal point of many of their social activities. As a result, they can live comfortably on $3,000 per month and could save approximately $20,000 per year if they choose to.

The Casusos' house is located in an older part of an Ontario city, and Juan believes it to be worth $160,000. In addi¬tion to the house they have two newer cars ($20,000 each), Emily's jewellery worth $7,000, and $5,000 each in savings accounts. Their liabilities are com¬prised of a $38,000 7% mortgage due on March 1st of next year, car loans of $7,000 and credit card debt of $1,800. Of great significance is the fact that Juan is the main beneficiary of his uncle's estate and has just received a bequest of approximately $200,000. This has caused him to decide to retire in 15 years' time.

PERSONAL EVALUATION

The Casusos are a two-income family with total annual earnings of $79,500. Their employment seems secure, their son is self-sufficient and there is no evidence of additional responsibilities that should be reflected in their portfolio. Their net worth and family budget indicate that their overall financial position is sound and that they could contribute $20,000 to their portfolio each year if they choose to.

Because Juan's income will be higher with the addition of the investment income, the tax consequences of different investments must be considered when making individual selections. His marginal tax bracket may potentially increase, depending on the amount and type of investment income he receives.

While the risk factor can only be assessed accurately in discussions with the Casusos, two factors indicate that risk should be kept low. First, their investment knowl¬edge may be minimal because the majority of their assets are in deposits and the family home. Second, the Casusos wish to retire in 15 years but have only government pensions to generate retirement income. Therefore, they may have to rely heavily on their investments for income at retire¬ment and cannot assume a high level of risk in their portfolio although equities are likely required. Finally, other than Juan's desire to retire in 15 years, there are no time constraints on their capital.

© CSI GLOBAL EDUCATION INC. (2008)

INVESTMENT OBJECTIVES

Juan Casuso's situation calls for a portfolio with a primary investment objective of growth and secondary ob¬jectives of tax minimization and safety. Growth is primary because of the need to generate capital to provide for retire¬ment and because the family currently has excess income. Juan's potentially higher marginal tax rate suggests that investments that provide higher after-tax returns should be favoured in the port¬folio. The importance of the portfolio to their retirement income suggests that speculative securities should be minimized although equity investments are still a very viable option.

TAX PLANNING FOR JUAN CASUSO

Tax planning can be an integral part of investment planning. Based on the tax-planning concepts outlined in Chapter 22, Juan Casuso should consider the following points.

- Juan must ensure that he is not overlooking allowable deductions such as investment counseling fees. If Juan is not confident that he can find all allowable deductions, he should have his tax return prepared by an expert.
- By postponing the receipt of income, Juan can delay income until he is in a lower tax bracket. In his current situation, he should seriously consider RRSP contributions and investing in growth securities. In his current situation, he should seriously consider RRSP contributions and investing in growth securities. In the latter case, since Juan has the flexibility to take gains when he chooses, he can postpone some income indefinitely. Juan should also consider investing some of the portfolio into an RRSP, up to his contribution limit.
- Juan can utilize a tax-planning strategy that will ensure that some of his potential future income will be taxed in Emily's hands. Specifically, Juan can establish a spousal RRSP which, upon deregistration, will be taxed at a lower rate as part of Emily's income. In conjunction with a spousal RRSP, Juan may consider joining the company's pension plan so that both he and Emily will have independent pensions at retirement.
- Juan can select investments that will provide a better after-tax yield. For example, Juan can select discount bonds, if available instead of comparable bonds selling at par, dividend-paying preferred shares instead of bonds, and growth stocks instead of short-term fixed-income securities. In each case taxes will be minimized.

ASSET MIX

For the Casusos' situation, the asset mix could justifiably be cash 5%, fixed-income securities 15% and equities 80% (with a range of -5% +5% of the target in each asset class). Because Juan's primary investment objective is growth, it is appropriate to com¬mit a high amount to equities; his income and other circumstances indicate a minimum need for liquidity of 5% in cash; and the balance of 15% to fixed-income securities for diversification.

RECOMMENDED PORTFOLIO

In constructing the portfolio, Juan's primary investment objectives determine the final asset weightings and the secondary objectives determine which specific types of securities should be selected within each group. Juan Casuso's secondary objectives of safety and tax minimization direct the portfolio manager into certain risk groups and specific securities within those groups.

Specifically, Juan's situation suggests that government Treasury bills would be most suitable in the cash component, that a 15-year average term to maturity be structured into the fixed-income section, and that equities be concentrated in the growth categories. Juan's tax minimization objective also helps to determine which specific securities would be appropriate. Here the

© CSI GLOBAL EDUCATION INC. (2008)

portfolio manager would be directed to bonds trading at a discount and preferred shares in the fixed-income section, and common shares whose total return would be more the result of capital gains than dividends.

To facilitate the final step in the selection process, the portfolio manager can make percentage and dollar allocations to each of the basic risk groups. The results of this process are shown in Table 23B.1. Once completed, the portfolio manager would recommend those individual securities believed to be the most attractive in each area. When the choices have been made, a recommended portfolio is presented in the format shown in Table 23B.2 – Portfolio Valuation. This sample portfolio is only an example of what a real portfolio should look like.

TABLE 23B.1 RISK GROUP WEIGHTINGS

Juan Casuso – $280,000 Portfolio	**% of Total**	**$ Amount**
Cash (5%):		
Government Quality	3.77%	$10,497
Corporate Quality	-	-
Fixed-Income (15%):		
Short-Term	3.64%	10,132
Mid-Term	3.84%	10,678
Long-Term	4,26%	11,852
Equities (80%):		
Conservative	24.83%	69,044
Growth	56.36%	156,696
Venture	3.29%	9,140
Speculative		
Total Portfolio	100%	$278,039

© CSI GLOBAL EDUCATION INC. (2008)

TABLE 23B.2 PORTFOLIO VALUATION

Holdings	Security	Current Price $	Approx. Market Value $	Per Cent of Total Value %	Indicated Int. Rate or Div. % or $	Indicated Annual Income $	Current Yield %
10,000	Gov. of Canada T-bill, 6 months	98.78	9,878.10	3.55	1.26	121.90	1.23
619	Cash		619.00	0.22	1.25	7.74	1.25
	TOTAL Cash Equivalents		**10,497.10**	**3.78**		**129.64**	
Bonds and Debentures							
10,000	Prov. of BC, 5.25%, December 1, 2 years to maturity	101.32	10,132.00	3.64	5.25	525.00	5.18
10,000	Bell Canada, 6.25%, January 18, 3 years to maturity	106.78	10,678.00	3.84	6.25	625.00	5.85
10,000	Canada, 5.75%, June 1, 2 years to maturity	118.52	11,852.00	4.26	11.25	1,125.00	9.49
	TOTAL Bonds & Debentures		**32,662.00**	**11.75**		**2,275.00**	**6.97**
Preferred Shares							
600	Bank of Nova Scotia	26.29	15,774.00	5.67	0.98	590.40	3.74
	TOTAL Preferred Shares		**15,774.00**	**5.27**		**590.40**	**3.74**
Common Shares							
1,200	Bombardier	2.50	3,000.00	1.08	–	–	0.00
1,200	Noranda	22.40	26,880.00	9.67	0.80	960.00	3.57
1,500	Telus	41.42	62,130.00	22.35	0.70	1,050.00	1.69
1,500	BCE	28.86	43,290.00	15.57	1.23	1,845.00	4.26
1,000	Leitch Technology	9.14	9,140.00	3.29	–	–	0.00
700	Royal Bank	76.10	53,270.00	19.16	2.14	1,498.00	2.81
400	iShares S&P/TSX 60	53.49	21,396.00	7.70	0.844	337.60	1.58
	Total Common Shares		**219,106.00**	**78.80**		**5,690.60**	**2.60**
	TOTAL Portfolio		**278,039.10**	**100.00**		**8,685.64**	**3.12**

© CSI GLOBAL EDUCATION INC. (2008)

Johanna Von Rosen

Johanna Von Rosen has just retired at age 65. She had been a bookkeeper with a large number of small companies in her career and was unemployed for long periods of time on several occasions. In 1981, Johanna started her own bookkeeping service, but the venture did not succeed and left her with debts that took three years to pay off.

Johanna is a quiet, independent person who is single. In addition, she never joined a pension plan and did not seem to have excess cash or adequate qualifying income on those few occasions when she considered an RRSP. Her financial situation includes the large house that she purchased in 1975 and the $30,000 she has in a savings account. Johanna currently has no debts.

Johanna plans to sell her house (market value $120,000) and use the proceeds and her savings to generate income. Because she did not make maximum contributions to the Canada Pension Plan, she will only receive about $700 per month in Old Age Security and Canada Pension Plan benefits. Fortunately, these amounts will increase with inflation. Johanna has already found an apartment and feels that she requires $2,000 per month to live comfortably.

PERSONAL EVALUATION

In retirement, Johanna has only a modest lifestyle to maintain and no dependants to provide for. However, her position is complicated by the fact that she has a very small guaranteed income and a fixed amount of investment capital. Because her annual income will barely satisfy her needs, minimizing risk becomes a very important factor in her portfolio and tax minimization only a minor consideration.

INVESTMENT OBJECTIVES

Because approximately two-thirds of Johanna's income will be derived from her portfolio, her primary investment objective is income and her secondary objective is safety. To meet these objectives, Johanna requires a portfolio that is heavily invested in fixed-income securities.

THE RECOMMENDED PORTFOLIO

Johanna Von Rosen's dependence on the portfolio for income demands that the portfolio manager weight the fixed-income section heavily. The average term to maturity within the class would be shorter than the average term indicated by the outlook for interest rates. In addition, individual selections should be concentrated in government issues to further reduce risk. Since Johanna is only 65 years old, a small allocation to conservative equities may be considered.

Table 23B.3 indicates weightings that would be appropriate for Johanna Von Rosen and Table 23B.4 a recommended portfolio.

© CSI GLOBAL EDUCATION INC. (2008)

TABLE 23B.3 RISK GROUP WEIGHTINGS

Johanna Von Rosen – $150,000 Portfolio	% of Total	$ Amount
Cash (10%):		
Government Quality	10%	$15,000
Corporate Quality	–	–
Fixed-Income (80%):		
Short-Term	53%	80,000
Mid-Term	17%	25,000
Long-Term	10%	15,000
Equities (10%):		
Conservative	10%	15,000
Growth	–	–
Venture	–	–
Speculative	–	–
Total Portfolio	100%	$150,000

© CSI GLOBAL EDUCATION INC. (2008)

TABLE 23B.4 PORTFOLIO VALUATION

Holdings	Security	Current Price $	Approx. Market Value $	Per Cent of Total Value %	Indicated Int. Rate or Div. % or $	Indicated Annual Income $	Current Yield %
15,000	GOC T-bill, 9 months	98.78	14,817.00	9.81	1.26	183.00	1.24
754	Cash		754.00	0.50	1.25	9.43	1.25
	TOTAL Cash Equivalents		**15,571.00**	**10.31**		**192.43**	**1.24**
Bonds and Debentures							
20,000	Prov.of B.C. 9.50% January 23, 7 years to maturity	132.34	26,468.00	17.52	9.50	1,900.00	7.18
15,000	Bell Canada 6.15% June 15, 4 years to maturity	94.03	14,104.50	9.34	6.15	922.50	6.54
15,000	Prov.of Ontario 7.75% July 24, 1 year to maturity	105.48	15,822.50	10.47	7.75	1,162.50	7.35
20,000	Gov of Canada 7.25% June 1, 2 years to maturity	108.20	21,640.00	14.33	7.25	1,450.00	6.70
15,000	Prov of Nfld 6.15% April 17, 23 years to maturity	91.17	13,675.50	9.05	6.15	922.50	6.75
20,000	Gov of Canada 10% June 1, 3 years to maturity	122.06	24,412.00	16.16	10.00	2,000.00	8.19
	TOTAL Bonds & Debentures		**116,122.00**	**76.88**		**8,357.50**	**7.20**
Preferred Shares							
200	Bank of Nova Scotia	26.29	5,258.00	3.48	0.98	196.00	3.73
	TOTAL Preferred Shares		**5,258.00**			**196.00**	**3.73**
Common Shares							
200	Bank of Montreal	56.06	11,212.00	7.42	1.74	348.00	3.10
100	BCE Inc.	28.86	2,886.00	1.91	1.23	123.00	4.26
	Total Common Shares		**14,098.00**	**9.33**		**471.00**	**3.34**
	TOTAL Portfolio		**151,049.00**	**100.00**		**9,216.93**	**6.10**

© CSI GLOBAL EDUCATION INC. (2008)

Glossary

The following is a glossary of investment terms that will help you study for the CSC examination and increase your overall knowledge of the investment industry. Some of the terms also have a general meaning, but only their specialized investment industry meaning is given here. Words in **bold face** type within definitions have their own glossary definitions. Note that this list is not complete: it should be used in conjunction with your own definitions of terms compiled during your studies and with the Index.

© CSI GLOBAL EDUCATION INC. (2008)

Accounts Payable
Money owed by a company for goods or services purchased, payable within one year. A current liability on the balance sheet.

Accounts Receivable
Money owed to a company for goods or services it has sold, for which payment is expected within one year. A current asset on the balance sheet.

Accredited Investor
An individual or institutional investor who meets certain minimum requirement relating to income, net worth, or investment knowledge. Also referred to as a sophisticated investor.

Accrued Interest
Interest accumulated on a bond or debenture since the last interest payment date.

Adjusted Cost Base
The deemed cost of an asset representing the sum of the amount originally paid plus any additional costs, such as brokerage fees and commissions.

Advance-Decline Line
A tool used in technical analysis to measure the breadth of the market. The analyst takes difference between the number of stocks that increased in value each day less the number that have decreased.

Affiliated Company
A company with less than 50% of its shares owned by another corporation, or one whose stock, with that of another corporation, is owned by the same controlling interests.

After Acquired Clause
A protective clause found in a **bond's indenture** or **contract** that binds the **bond** issuer to pledging all subsequently purchased assets as part of the collateral for a bond issue.

After Market
See **Secondary Market**.

Agent
An investment dealer operates as an agent when it acts on behalf of a buyer or a seller of a security and does not itself own title to the securities at any time during the transactions. See also **Principal**.

All or None Order (AON)
An order that must be executed in its entirety – partial fills will not be accepted.

Allocation
The administrative procedure by which income generated by the **segregated fund's** investment portfolio is flowed through to the individual contract holders of the fund.

Alpha
A statistical measure of the value a fund manager adds to the performance of the fund managed. If alpha is positive, the manager has added value to the portfolio. If the alpha is negative, the manager has underperformed the market.

Alternative Trading Systems (ATS)
Privately-owned computerized networks that match orders for securities outside of recognized exchange facilities. Also referred to as Proprietary Electronic Trading Systems (PETS) or Non-SRO Operated Trading Systems (NETS).

American Option
An option that can be exercised at any time during the option's lifetime. See also **European Option**.

Amortization
Gradually writing off the value of an **intangible asset** over a period of time. Commonly applied to items such as **goodwill**, improvements to leased premises, or expenses of a new stock or bond issue. See also **Depreciation**.

Annual Information Form (AIF)
A document in which an issuer is required to disclose information about presently known trends, commitments, events or uncertainties that are reasonably expected to have a material impact on the issuer's business, financial condition or results of operations. Although investors are typically not provided with the AIF, the prospectus must state that it is available on request.

Annual Report
The formal financial statements and report on operations issued by a company to its shareholders after its fiscal year-end.

Annuitant
Person on whose life the **maturity** and **death benefit** guarantees are based. It can be the contract holder or someone else designated by the contract holder. In registered plans, the **annuitant** and contract holder must be the same person.

Annuity
A contract usually sold by life insurance companies that guarantees an income to the beneficiary or annuitant at some time in the future. The income stream can be very flexible. The original purchase price may be either a lump sum or a stream of payments. See **Deferred Annuity** and **Immediate Annuity**.

Any Part Order
A type of order in which the client will accept all stock in odd, broken or standard trading units up to the full amount of the order.

Approved Participants
See **Participating Organization**.

Arbitrage
The simultaneous purchase of a security on one stock exchange and the sale of the same security on another exchange at prices which yield a profit to the arbitrageur.

Arbitration
A method of dispute resolution in which an independent arbitrator is chosen to assist aggrieved parties recover damages.

Arrears
Interest or dividends that were not paid when due but are still owed. For example, **dividends** owed but not paid to **cumulative preferred** shareholders accumulate in a separate account (arrears). When payments resume, dividends in arrears must be paid to the preferred shareholders before the **common** shareholders.

Ask
The lowest price a seller will accept for the financial instrument being quoted. See also **Bid**.

Asset
Everything a company or a person owns or has owed to it. A balance sheet category.

Asset Allocation
Apportioning investment funds among different categories of assets, such as cash, fixed income securities and equities. The allocation of assets is built around an investor's risk tolerance.

Asset Mix
The percentage distribution of assets in a portfolio among the three major asset classes: cash and equivalents, fixed income and equities.

© CSI GLOBAL EDUCATION INC. (2008)

Assignment
The random process by which the clearing corporation allocates the exercise of an option to a member firm. A client of that member firm is then chosen to fulfil the obligation taken on when the option was written, by: in the case of a put, purchasing the underlying security from the put holder; or, in the case of a call, delivering the underlying security to the call holder. See also **Exercise**.

Assuris
A not for profit company whose member firms are issuers of life-insurance contracts and whose mandate is to provide protection to contract holders against the insolvency of a member company,

At-the-Money
An **option** with a strike price equal to (or almost equal to) the market price of the underlying security. See also **Out-of-the-money** and **In-the-money.**

Attribution Rules
A Canada Revenue Agency rule stating that an investor cannot avoid paying taxes at their marginal rate by transferring assets to other family members who have lower personal tax rates.

Auction Market
Market in which securities are bought and sold by brokers acting as **agents** for their clients, in contrast to a **dealer** market where trades are conducted **over-the-counter**. For example, the Toronto Stock Exchange is an auction market.

Auction Preferred Shares
A type of preferred share that offers a dividend rate determined by an auction between the holder and the issuer.

Audit
A professional review and examination of a company's financial statements required under corporate law for the purpose of ensuring that the statements are fair, consistent and conform with **Generally Accepted Accounting Principles (GAAP)**.

Authorized Shares
The maximum number of **common** (or **preferred**) shares that a corporation may issue under the terms of its charter.

Automatic Stabilizers
Elements in the economy which mitigate the extremes of the **business cycle** by running counter to it. Example: government payouts for unemployment insurance in recessionary periods.

Autorité des marchés financiers (Financial Services Authority) (AMF)
The body that administers the regulatory framework surrounding Québec's financial sector: securities sector, the distribution of financial products and services sector, the financial institutions sector and the compensation sector.

Averages
A statistical tool used to measure the direction of the market. The most common average is the **Dow Jones Industrial Average**.

Back-End Load
A sales charge applied on the redemption of a **mutual fund**.

Balance of Payments
Canada's interactions with the rest of the world which are captured here in the current account and capital account.

Balance Sheet
A financial statement showing a company's **assets**, **liabilities** and **shareholders' equity** on a given date.

Balloon
In some serial bond issues or mortgages an extra-large amount may mature in the final year of the series – the "balloon" payment.

Bank of Canada
Canada's central bank which exercises its influence on the economy by raising and lowering short-term interest rates.

Bank Rate
The minimum rate at which the Bank of Canada makes short-term advances to the chartered banks, other members of the **Canadian Payments Association** and investment dealers who trade in the money market.

Bankers' Acceptance
A commercial draft (i.e., a written instruction to make payment) drawn by a borrower for payment on a specified date. A BA is guaranteed at maturity by the borrower's bank. As with T-bills, BAs are sold at a discount and mature at their face value, with the difference representing the return to the investor. BAs may be sold before maturity at prevailing market rates, generally offering a higher yield than Canada T-bills.

Banking Group
A group of investment firms, each of which individually assumes financial responsibility for part of an **underwriting.**

Bankrupt
The legal status of an individual or company that is unable to pay its creditors and whose **assets** are therefore administered for its creditors by a Trustee in Bankruptcy.

Basis Point
One-hundredth of a percentage point of bond yields. Thus, 1% represents 100 basis points.

Bear
One who expects that the market generally, or the market price of a particular security, will decline. See also **Bull.**

Bear Market
A sustained decline in equity prices. Bear markets are usually associated with a downturn (recession or contraction) in the business cycle.

Bearer Security
A security (stock or bond) which does not have the owner's name recorded in the books of the issuing company nor on the security itself and which is payable to the holder, i.e., the holder is the deemed owner of the security. See also **Registered Security**.

Beneficial Owner
The real (underlying) owner of an account, securities or other assets. An investor may own shares which are registered in the name of an investment dealer, trustee or bank to facilitate transfer or to preserve anonymity, but the investor would be the beneficial owner.

Beneficiary
The individual or individuals who have been designated to receive the **death benefit**. Beneficiaries may be either revocable or irrevocable.

Best Efforts Underwriting
The attempt by an investment dealer (underwriter) to fulfill a customer's order or to sell an issue of securities, to the best of their abilities, but does not guarantee that any or all of the issue will be sold. The investment dealer is not held liable to fulfill the order or to sell all of the securities. The underwriter acts as an **agent** for the issuer in distributing the issue.

© CSI GLOBAL EDUCATION INC. (2008)

Beta
A measure of the sensitivity (i.e., volatility) of a stock or a mutual fund to movements in the overall stock market. The beta for the market is considered to be 1. A fund that mirrors the market, such as an index fund, would also have a beta of 1. Funds or stocks with a beta greater than 1 are more volatile than the market and are therefore riskier. A beta less than 1 is not as volatile and can be expected to rise and fall by less than the overall market.

Bid
The highest price a buyer is willing to pay for the financial instrument being quoted. See also **Ask**.

Blue Chip
An active, leading, nationally known common stock with a record of continuous dividend payments and other strong investment qualities. The implication is that the company is of "good" investment value.

Blue Sky
A slang term for laws that various Canadian provinces and American states have enacted to protect the public against securities frauds. The term blue skyed is used to indicate that a new issue has been cleared by a securities commission and may be distributed.

Bond
A certificate evidencing a **debt** on which the issuer promises to pay the holder a specified amount of interest based on the **coupon** rate, for a specified length of time, and to repay the loan on its maturity. Strictly speaking, assets are pledged as security for a bond issue, except in the case of government "bonds", but the term is often loosely used to describe any funded debt issue.

Bond Contract
The actual legal agreement between the issuer and the bondholder. The contract outlines the terms and conditions – the **coupon** rate, timing of coupon payments, **maturity** date and any other terms. The bond contract is usually administered by a trust company on behalf of all the bondholders. Also called a **Bond Indenture** or **Trust Deed**.

Bond Indenture
See **Bond Contract**.

Bond Switches
An investment strategy whereby the investor may sell one bond and replace it with another, to capture some advantage such as yield improvement.

Book Value
The amount of net assets belonging to the owners of a business (or shareholders of a company) based on **balance sheet** values. It represents the total value of the company's assets that shareholders would theoretically receive if a company were liquidated. Also represents the original cost of the units allocated to a **segregated fund** contract.

Bottom-Up Investment Approach
An investment approach that seeks out undervalued companies. A fund manager may find companies whose low share prices are not justified. They would buy these securities and when the market finally realizes that they are undervalued, the share price rises giving the astute bottom up manager a profit. See also **Top-Down Investment Approach**.

Bought Deal
A new issue of stocks or bonds bought from the issuer by an investment dealer, frequently acting alone, for resale to its clients, usually by way of a **private placement** or short form prospectus. The dealer risks its own capital in the bought deal. In the event that the price has to be lowered to sell out the issue, the dealer absorbs the loss.

Bourse de Montréal
A stock exchange (also referred to as the Montréal Exchange) that deals exclusively with non-agricultural options and futures in Canada, including all options that previously traded on the **Toronto Stock Exchange** and all futures products that previously traded on the Toronto Futures Exchange.

Broker
An investment dealer or a duly registered individual that is registered to trade in securities in the capacity of an agent or principal and is a member of a **Self-Regulatory Organization**.

Broker of Record
The broker named as the official advisor to a corporation on financial matters; has the right of first refusal on any new issues.

Bucketing
Confirming a transaction where no trade has been executed.

Budget Deficit
Occurs when total spending by the government for the year is higher than revenue collected.

Budget Surplus
Occurs when government revenue for the year exceeds expenditures.

Bull
One who expects that the market generally or the market price of a particular security will rise. See also **Bear**.

Bull Market
A general and prolonged rising trend in security prices. Bull markets are usually associated with an expansionary phase of the **business cycle**. As a memory aid, it is said that a bull walks with his head up while a **bear** walks with his head down.

Business Cycle
The recurrence of periods of **expansion** and **recession** in economic activity. Each cycle is expected to move through five phases – the **trough, recovery, expansion, peak, contraction (recession)**. Given an understanding of the relationship between the business cycle and security prices an investor or fund manager would select an **asset mix** to maximize returns.

Business Risk
The risk inherent in a company's operations, reflected in the variability in earnings. A weakening in consumer interest or technological obsolescence usually causes the decline. Examples include manufacturers of vinyl records, eight track recording tapes and beta video machines.

Buy-Back
A company's purchase of its common shares either by tender or in the open market for cancellation, subsequent resale or for **dividend reinvestment plans**.

Buy-Ins
If a client or a broker fails to deliver securities sold to another broker within a specified number of days after the value (settlement) date, the receiving broker may buy-in the securities in the open market and charge the client or the delivering broker the cost of such purchases.

Call Feature
A clause in a bond or preferred share agreement that allows the issuer the right to "call back" the securities prior to maturity. The company would usually do this if they

© CSI GLOBAL EDUCATION INC. (2008)

could refinance the **debt** at a lower rate (similar to refinancing a mortgage at a lower rate). Calling back a security prior to maturity may involve the payment of a penalty known as a **call premium**.

Call Option

The right to buy a specific number of shares at a specified price (the **strike price**) by a fixed date. The buyer pays a **premium** to the seller of the call option contract. An investor would buy a call option if the underlying stock's price is expected to rise. See also **Put Option**.

Call Price

The price at which a bond or preferred share with a **call feature** is redeemed by the issuer. This is the amount the holder of the security would receive if the security was redeemed prior to maturity. The call price is equal to par (or a stated value for preferred shares) plus any **call premium**. See also **Redemption Price**.

Call Protection

For callable bonds, the period before the first possible call date.

Callable

May be redeemed (called in) upon due notice by the security's issuer.

Canada Deposit Insurance Corporation (CDIC)

A federal Crown Corporation providing deposit insurance against loss (up to $100,000 per depositor) when a member institution fails.

Canada Education Savings Grant (CESG)

An incentive program for those investing in a **Registered Education Savings Plan (RESP)** whereby the federal government will make a matching grant of a maximum of $500 to $600 per year of the first $2,500 contributed each year to the RESP of a child under age 18.

Canada Pension Plan (CPP)

A mandatory contributory pension plan designed to provide monthly retirement, disability and survivor benefits for all Canadians. Employers and employees make equal contributions. Québec has its own parallel pension plan Québec Pension Plan (QPP).

Canada Premium Bonds (CPBs)

A relatively new type of savings product that offers a higher interest rate compared to the Canada Savings Bond and is redeemable once a year on the anniversary of the issue date or during the 30 days thereafter without penalty.

Canada Savings Bonds (CSBs)

A type of savings product that pays a competitive rate of interest and that is guaranteed for one or more years. They may be cashed at any time and, after the first three months, pay interest up to the end of the month prior to being cashed.

Canada Yield Call

A callable bond with a call price based on the greater of (a) par or (b) the price based on the yield of an equivalent-term Government of Canada bond plus a specified yield spread. Also known as a Doomsday call. See also **Call Price** and **Callable Bond**.

Canadian Council of Insurance Regulators

The association of insurance regulators in jurisdictions across Canada.

Canadian Derivatives Clearing Corporation (CDCC)

The CDCC is a service organization that clears, issues, settles, and guarantees options, futures, and futures options traded on the Bourse de Montréal (the Bourse).

Canadian Investor Protection Fund (CIPF)

A fund that protects investors against the insolvency of any member firm. It is financed by IIROC and the exchanges (except ICE Futures Canada) who are collectively referred to as **Sponsoring Self-Regulatory Organizations** (**SSROs**).

Canadian Life and Health Insurance Association Incorporated (CLHIA)

The national trade group of the life insurance industry, which is actively involved in overseeing applications and setting industry standards.

Canadian Originated Preferred Securities (COPrS)

Introduced to the Canadian market in March 1999, as long-term junior subordinated debt instruments. This type of security offers features that resemble both long-term corporate bonds and preferred shares.

Canadian Payments Association

Established in the 1980 revision of the *Bank Act*, this association operates a highly automated national clearing system for interbank payments. Members include chartered banks, trust and loan companies and some credit unions and caisses.

Canadian Securities Administrators (CSA)

The CSA is a forum for the 13 securities regulators of Canada's provinces and territories to co-ordinate and harmonize the regulation of the Canadian capital markets.

Canadian Trading and Quotation System Inc. (CNQ)

Launched in 2003 as an alternative marketplace for trading equity securities and emerging companies.

Canadian Unlisted Board (CUB)

An Internet web-based system for investment dealers to report completed trades in unlisted and unquoted equity securities in Ontario.

CanDeal

Provides institutional investors with electronic access to federal bond bid and offer prices and yields from its six bank-owned dealers.

CanPx

A joint venture of several IIROC member firms and operates as an electronic trading system for fixed income securities providing investors with real-time bid and offer prices and hourly trade data.

Capital

Has two distinct but related meanings. To an economist, it means machinery, factories and inventory required to produce other products. To an investor, it may mean the total of financial **assets** invested in securities, a home and other fixed assets, plus cash.

Capital Asset Pricing Model (CAPM)

A model that looks at the relationship between risk and return. In simple terms, the CAPM says that the return on an asset or security is equal to the **risk-free return** plus a **risk premium**.

Capital Cost Allowance (CCA)

An amount allowed under the *Income Tax Act* to be deducted from the value of certain assets and treated as an expense in computing an individual's or company's income for a taxation year. It may differ

© CSI GLOBAL EDUCATION INC. (2008)

from the amount charged for the period in depreciation accounting.

Capital and Financial Account
Account which reflects the transactions occurring between Canada and foreign countries with respect to the acquisition of assets, such as land or currency. Along with the **current account** a component of the **balance of payments**.

Capital Gain
Selling a security for more than its purchase price. For non-registered securities, 50% of the gain would be added to income and taxed at the investor's marginal rate.

Capital Leases or Capitalized Leases
An expenditure recorded on the balance sheet as an asset rather than as an expense.

Capital Loss
Selling a security for less than its purchase price. Capital losses can only be applied against capital gains. Surplus losses can be carried forward indefinitely and used against future capital gains. Only 50% of the loss can be used to offset any taxable capital loss.

Capital Market
Financial markets where **debt** and **equity** securities trade. Capital markets include organized exchanges as well as private placement sources of debt and equity.

Capital Stock
All shares representing ownership of a company, including preferred as well as common. Also referred to as **equity capital**.

Capitalization or Capital Structure
Total dollar amount of all **debt**, **preferred** and **common** stock, **contributed surplus** and **retained earnings** of a company. Can also be expressed in percentage terms.

Capitalize
Recording an expenditure initially as an **asset** on the **balance sheet** rather than as an earnings statement expense, and then writing it off or **amortizing** it (as an earnings statement expense) over a period of years. Examples include capitalized leases, interest, and research and development.

Carry Forward
The amount of RRSP contributions that can be carried forward from previous years. For example, if a client was entitled to place $13,500 in an RRSP and only contributed $10,000, the difference of $3,500 would be the unused contribution room and can be carried forward indefinitely.

Cash Account
A type of brokerage account where the investor is expected to have either cash in the account to cover their purchases or where an investor will deliver the required amount of cash before the settlement date of the purchase.

Cash Flow
A company's net income for a stated period plus any deductions that are not paid out in actual cash, such as **depreciation** and **amortization**, **deferred income taxes**, and **minority interest**. For an investor, any source of income from an investment including **dividends**, interest income, rental income, etc.

Cash-Secured Put Write
Involves writing a **put option** and setting aside an amount of cash equal to the strike price. If the cash-secured put writer is assigned, the cash is used to buy the stock from the exercising put buyer.

Cash Value
The current market value of a **segregated fund** contract, less any applicable deferred sales charges or other withdrawal fees

CBID
An electronic trading system for fixed-income securities operating in both retail and institutional markets.

CDS Clearing and Depository Services Inc. (CDS)
CDS provides customers with physical and electronic facilities to deposit and withdraw depository-eligible securities and manage their related ledger positions (securities accounts). CDS also provides electronic clearing services both domestically and internationally, allowing customers to report, confirm and settle securities trade transactions.

Central Bank
A body established by a national Government to regulate currency and **monetary policy** on a nationalinternational level. In Canada, it is the Bank of Canada; in the United States, the Federal Reserve Board; in the U.K., the Bank of England.

Charting
The use of charts and patterns to forecast buy and sell decisions. See also **Technical Analysis**.

Chinese Walls
Policies implemented to separate and isolate persons within a firm who make investment decisions from persons within a firm who are privy to undisclosed material information which may influence those decisions. For example, there should be separate fax machines for research departments and sales departments.

Class A and B Stock
Shares that have different classes sometimes have different rights. Some may have superior claims over other classes or may have different voting rights. Class A stock is often similar to a participating preferred share with a prior claim over Class B for a stated amount of dividends or assets or both, but without voting rights; the Class B may have voting rights but no priority as to dividends or assets. Note that these distinctions do not always apply.

Clearing Corporations
A not-for-profit service organization owned by the exchanges and their members for the clearance, settlement and issuance of **options** and **futures**. A clearing corporation provides a guarantee for all options and futures contracts it clears, by becoming the buyer to every seller and the seller to every buyer.

Clone Fund
Generally a fund that tries to mimic the performance and/or the objectives of a successful existing fund within a family of funds. A common example of a clone fund is when a fund company issues an RRSP version of a foreign equity fund, consisting of derivatives managed in a way that duplicates the returns of the underlying fund.

Closed-End Fund
See **Investment Company**.

Closet Indexing
A portfolio strategy whereby the fund manager does not replicate the market exactly but sticks fairly close to the market weightings by industry sector, country or region or by the average market capitalization.

Coincident Indicators
Statistical data that, on average, change at approximately the same time and in the same direction as the economy as a whole.

© CSI GLOBAL EDUCATION INC. (2008)

Collateral Trust Bond
A bond secured by stocks or bonds of companies controlled by the issuing company, or other securities, which are deposited with a **trustee**.

Commercial Paper
An unsecured promissory note issued by a corporation or an asset-backed security backed by a pool of underlying financial assets. Issue terms range from less than three months to one year. Most corporate paper trades in $1,000 multiples, with a minimum initial investment of $25,000. Commercial paper may be bought and sold in a secondary market before maturity at prevailing market rates.

Commission
The fee charged by a stockbroker for buying or selling securities as agent on behalf of a client.

Commodity
A product used for commerce that is traded on an organized exchange. A commodity could be an agricultural product such as canola or wheat, or a natural resource such as oil or gold. A commodity can be the basis for a **futures** contract.

Common Stock
Securities representing ownership in a company. They carry voting privileges and are entitled to the receipt of dividends, if declared. Also called common shares.

Competitive Tender
A distribution method used in particular by the Bank of Canada in distributing new issues of government marketable bonds. Bids are requested from primary **distributors** and the higher bids are awarded the securities for distribution. See also **Non-Competitive Tender**.

Compound Interest
Interest earned on an investment at periodic intervals and added to the amount of the investment; future interest payments are then calculated and paid at the original rate but on the increased total of the investment. In simple terms, interest paid on interest.

Confirmation
A printed acknowledgement giving details of a purchase or sale of a security which is normally mailed to a client by the broker or investment dealer within 24 hours of an order being executed. Also called a contract.

Conglomerate
A company directly or indirectly operating in a variety of industries, usually unrelated to each other. Conglomerates often acquire outside companies through the exchange of their own shares for the shares of the majority owners of the outside companies.

Consolidated Financial Statements
A combination of the financial statements of a parent company and its subsidiaries, presenting the financial position of the group as a whole.

Consolidation
See **Reverse Split**.

Constrained Share Companies
Include Canadian banks, trust, insurance, broadcasting and communication companies having constraints on the transfer of shares to persons who are not Canadian citizens or not Canadian residents.

Consumer Price Index (CPI)
Price index which measures the cost of living by measuring the prices of a given basket of goods. The CPI is often used as an indicator of **inflation**.

Continuation Pattern
A chart formation indicating that the current trend will continue.

Continuous Disclosure
In Ontario, a reporting issuer must issue a press release as soon as a material change occurs in its affairs and, in any event, within ten days. See also **Timely Disclosure**.

Contract Holder
The owner of a **segregated fund** contract.

Contraction
Represents a downturn in the economy and can lead to a recession if prolonged.

Contributed Surplus
A component of **shareholders' equity** which originates from sources other than earnings, such as the initial sale of stock above par value.

Contributions in Kind
Transferring securities into an **RRSP**. The general rules are that when an asset is transferred there is a **deemed disposition**. Any **capital gain** would be reported and taxes paid. Any **capital losses** that result cannot be claimed.

Conversion Price
The dollar value at which a **convertible** bond or security can be converted into common stock.

Conversion Privilege
The right to exchange a bond for common shares on specifically determined terms.

Conversion Ratio
The number of **common shares** for which a **convertible** security can be exchanged. Convertible preferreds and debentures would have a stated number outlined in their **prospectus** or indenture as to the exchange rate. For example, the conversion ratio on a bond may be 25. This means that the bond could be exchanged for 25 common shares. If the conversion ratio is divided into par value, the result is called the conversion price.

Convertible
A **bond**, **debenture** or **preferred** share which may be exchanged by the owner, usually for the **common stock** of the same company, in accordance with the terms of the conversion privilege. A company can force conversion by calling in such shares for redemption if the **redemption price** is below the market price.

Convertible Arbitrage
A strategy that looks for mispricing between a convertible security and the underlying stock. A typical convertible arbitrage position is to be long the convertible bond and short the common stock of the same company.

Convexity
A measure of the rate of change in duration over changes in yields. Typically, a bond will rise in price more if the yield change is negative than it will fall in price if the yield change is positive.

Corporate Note
An unsecured promise made by the borrower to pay interest and repay the principal at a specific date.

Corporation or Company
A form of business organization created under provincial or federal statutes which has a legal identity separate from its owners. The corporation's owners (shareholders) have no personal liability for its debts. See also **Limited Liability**.

© CSI GLOBAL EDUCATION INC. (2008)

Correlation
A measure of the relationship between two or more securities. If two securities mirror each other's movements perfectly, they are said to have a positive one (+1) correlation. Combining securities with high positive correlations does not reduce the risk of a portfolio. Combining securities that move in the exact opposite direction from each other are said to have perfect negative one (-1) correlation. Combining two securities with perfect negative correlation reduces risk. Very few, if any, securities have a perfect negative correlation. However, risk in a portfolio can be reduced if the combined securities have low positive correlations.

Correlation Coefficient
A measure of the relationship between the returns of two securities or two classes of securities.

Cost Accounting Method
Used when a company owns less than 20% of a subsidiary.

Cost of Goods Sold
An **earnings statement** account representing the cost of buying raw materials that go directly into producing finished goods.

Cost-Push Inflation
A type of inflation that develops due to an increase in the costs of production. For example, an increase in the price of oil may contribute to higher input costs for a company and could lead to higher inflation.

Country Banks
A colloquial term for non-bank lenders who provide short-term sources of credit for investment dealers; e.g., corporations, insurance companies and other institutional short-term investors, none of whom is under the jurisdiction of the Bank Act. See also **Purchase and Resale Agreement**.

Coupon Rate
The rate of interest that appears on the certificate of a **bond**. Multiplying the coupon rate times the **principal** tells the holder the dollar amount of interest to be paid by the issuer until **maturity**. For example, a bond with a **principal** of $1,000 and a coupon of 10% would pay $100 in interest each year. Coupon rates remain fixed throughout the term of the bond. See also **Yield**.

Covenant
A pledge in a **bond indenture** indicating the fulfilment of a promise or agreement by the company issuing the debt. An example of a covenant may include the promise not to issue any more debt.

Cover
Buying a security previously sold short. See also **Short Sale**.

Covered Writer
The writer of an option who also holds a position that is equivalent to, but on the opposite side of the market from the short option position. In some circumstances, the equivalent position may be in cash, a convertible security or the underlying security itself. See also **Naked Writer**.

Cross on the Board
Also called a put-through or contra order. When a broker has both an order to sell and an order to buy the same stock at the same price, a cross is allowed on the exchange floor without interfering with the limits of the prevailing market.

Cub
Canadian Unlisted Board – a web-based trade reporting system for unlisted securities.

Cum Dividend
With **dividend**. If you buy shares quoted cum dividend, i.e., before the ex dividend date, you will receive an upcoming already-declared dividend. If shares are quoted **ex-dividend** (without dividend) you are not entitled to the declared dividend.

Cum Rights
With rights. Buyers of shares quoted cum rights, i.e., before the **ex-rights** date, are entitled to forthcoming already-declared rights. If shares are quoted ex rights (without rights) the buyer is not entitled to receive the declared rights.

Cumulative Preferred
A **preferred** stock having a provision that if one or more of its **dividends** are not paid, the unpaid dividends accumulate in **arrears** and must be paid before any dividends may be paid on the company's **common shares**.

Current Account
Account that reflects all payments between Canadians and foreigners for goods, services, interest and dividends. Along with the **capital account** it is a component of the **balance of payments**.

Current Assets
Cash and assets which in the normal course of business would be converted into cash, usually within a year, e.g. accounts receivable, inventories. A **balance sheet** category.

Current Liabilities
Money owed and due to be paid within a year, e.g. accounts payable. A **balance sheet** category.

Current Ratio
A **liquidity ratio** that shows a company's ability to pay its current obligations from **current assets**. A current ratio of 2:1 is the generally accepted standard. See also **Quick Ratio**.

Current Yield
The annual income from an investment expressed as a percentage of the investment's current value. On stock, calculated by dividing yearly **dividend** by market price; on bonds, by dividing the **coupon** by market price. See also **Yield**.

CUSIP
Committee on Uniform Security Identification Procedures is the trademark for a standard system of securities identification (i.e., CUSIP numbering system) and securities description (i.e., CUSIP descriptive system) that is used in processing and recording securities transactions in North America.

Custodian
A firm that holds the securities belonging to a **mutual fund** or a **segregated fund** for safekeeping. The custodian can be either the insurance company itself, or a qualified outside firm based in Canada.

Cyclical Stock
A stock in an industry that is particularly sensitive to swings in economic conditions. Cyclical Stocks tend to rise quickly when the economy does well and fall quickly when the economy contracts. In this way, cyclicals move in conjunction with the **business cycle**. For example, during periods of **expansion** auto stocks do well as individuals replace their older vehicles. During **recessions**, auto sales and auto company share values decline.

© CSI GLOBAL EDUCATION INC. (2008)

Cyclical Unemployment
The amount of unemployment that rises when the economy softens, firms' demand for labour moderates, and some firms lay off workers in response to lower sales. It drops when the economy strengthens again.

Day Order
A buy or sell order that automatically expires if it is not executed on the day it is entered. All orders are day orders unless otherwise specified.

Dealer Market
A market in which securities are bought and sold **over-the-counter** in which dealers acts as **principals** when buying and selling securities for clients. Also referred to as the **unlisted market**.

Dealer's Spread
The difference between the **bid** and **ask** prices on a security.

Death Benefit
The amount that a segregated fund policy pays to the beneficiary or the estate when the market value of the segregated fund is lower than the guaranteed amount on the death of the **annuitant**.

Debenture
A certificate of indebtedness of a government or company backed only by the general credit of the issuer and unsecured by mortgage or lien on any specific asset. In other words, no specific assets have been pledged as collateral.

Debt
Money borrowed from lenders for a variety of purposes. The borrower typically pays interest for the use of the money and is obligated to repay it at a set date.

Debt/Equity Ratio
A **ratio** that shows whether a company's borrowing is excessive. The higher the ratio, the higher the **financial risk**.

Debt Ratios
Financial ratios that show how well the company can deal with its debt obligations.

Declining Industry
An industry moving from the **maturity** stage. It tends to grow at rates slower than the overall economy, or the growth rate actually begins to decline.

Deemed Disposition
Under certain circumstances, taxation rules state that a transfer of property has occurred, even without a purchase or sale, e.g., there is a deemed disposition on death or emigration from Canada.

Default
A **bond** is in default when the borrower has failed to live up to its obligations under the **trust deed** with regard to interest, **sinking fund** payments or has failed to redeem the bonds at maturity.

Default Risk
The risk that a debt security issuer will be unable to pay interest on the prescribed date or the **principal** at **maturity**. Default risk applies to debt securities not equities since equity **dividend** payments are not contractual.

Defensive Stock
A stock of a company with a record of stable earnings and continuous **dividend** payments and which has demonstrated relative stability in poor economic conditions. For example, utility stock values do not usually change from periods of **expansion** to periods of **recession** since most individuals use a constant amount of electricity.

Deferred Annuity
This type of contract, usually sold by life insurance companies, pays a regular stream of income to the **beneficiary** or annuitant at some agreed-upon start date in the future. The original payment is usually a stream of payments made over time, ending prior to the beginning of the annuity payments. See also **Annuity**.

Deferred Charges
An **asset** shown on a **balance sheet** representing payments made by the company for which the benefit will extend to the company over a period of years. Similar to a **prepaid expense** except that the benefit period is for a longer period. Deferred charges may include expenses incurred in issuing bonds, organizational expenses or research expenses.

Deferred Preferred Shares
A type of preferred share that pays no dividend until a future maturity date.

Deferred Profit Sharing Plan (DPSP)
A trust arrangement whereby an employer distributes a certain percentage of company profits to his/her employees. It must be an arms length transaction, and employees are not eligible to make a contribution.

Deferred Revenue
The revenue recorded when a company receives payment for goods or services that it has not yet provided. For example, a prepaid subscription to a magazine.

Deferred Sales Charge
The fee charged by a **mutual fund** or insurance company for redeeming units. It is otherwise known as a **redemption fee** or **back-end load**. These fees decline over time and are eventually reduced to zero if the fund is held long enough.

Defined Benefit Plan
A type of registered pension plan in which the annual payout is based on a formula. The plan pays a specific dollar amount at retirement using a predetermined formula.

Defined Contribution Plan
A type of registered pension plan where the amount contributed is known but the dollar amount of the pension to be received is unknown. Also known as a **money purchase plan**.

Delayed Floater
A type of **variable rate preferred share** that entitles the holder to a fixed dividend for a predetermined period of time after which the dividend becomes variable. Also known as a **fixed-reset** or **fixed floater**.

Delayed Opening
Postponement in the opening of trading of a security the result of a heavy influx of buy and/or sell orders.

Delist
Removal of a security's listing on a **stock exchange**.

Delivery
Delayed Delivery – A transaction in which there is a clear understanding that delivery of the securities involved will be delayed beyond the normal settlement period. **Good Delivery** – When a security that has been sold is in proper form to transfer title by delivery to the buyer. **Regular Delivery** – Unless otherwise stipulated, sellers of stock must deliver it on or before the third business day after the sale.

© CSI GLOBAL EDUCATION INC. (2008)

Demand Pull Inflation
A type of inflation that develops when continued consumer demand pushes prices higher.

Demutualization
The process by which insurance companies, owned by policy holders, reorganize into companies owned by shareholders. Policy holders become shareholders in an insurance company.

Depletion
Refers to consumption of natural resources that are part of a company's assets. Producing oil, mining and gas companies deal in products that cannot be replenished and as such are known as wasting assets. The recording of depletion is a bookkeeping entry similar to **depreciation** and does not involve the expenditure of cash.

Deposit-Based Guarantee
A **maturity guarantee** consisting of separate guarantees and guarantee dates for each of the deposits made in a segregated fund policy over time.

Depreciation
Systematic charges against earnings to write off the cost of an **asset** over its estimated useful life because of wear and tear through use, action of the elements, or obsolescence. It is a bookkeeping entry and does not involve the expenditure of cash.

Derivative
A type of financial instrument whose value is based on the performance of an underlying financial asset, commodity, or other investment. Derivatives are available on interest rates, currency, stock indexes. For example, a **call option** on IBM is a derivative because the value of the call varies in relation to the performance of IBM stock. See also **Options**.

Direct Bonds
This term is used to describe bonds issued by governments that are firsthand obligations of the government itself. See also **Guaranteed Bonds**.

Directional Hedge Funds
A type of **hedge fund** that places a bet on the anticipated movements in the market prices of equities, fixed-income securities, foreign currencies and commodities.

Director
Person elected by voting **common** shareholders at the annual meeting to direct company policies.

Directors' Circular
Information sent to shareholders by the **directors** of a company that are the target of a takeover bid. A recommendation to accept or reject the bid, and reasons for this recommendation, must be included.

Disclosure
One of the principles of securities regulation in Canada. This principle entails full, true and plain disclosure of all material facts necessary to make reasoned investment decisions.

Discount
The amount by which a **preferred** stock or **bond** sells below its **par value**.

Discount Brokers
Brokerage house that buys and sells securities for clients at a greater commission discount than full-service firms.

Discount Rate
In computing the value of a bond, the discount rate is the interest rate used in calculating the present value of future cash flows.

Discouraged Workers
Individuals that are available and willing to work but cannot find jobs and have not made specific efforts to find a job within the previous month.

Discretionary Account
A securities account where the client has given specific written authorization to a partner, director or qualified portfolio manager to select securities and execute trades for him. See also **Managed Account** and **Wrap Account**.

Disinflation
A decline in the rate at which prices rise – i.e., a decrease in the rate of inflation. Prices are still rising, but at a slower rate.

Disposable Income
Personal income minus income taxes and any other transfers to government.

Diversification
Spreading investment risk by buying different types of securities in different companies in different kinds of businesses and/or locations.

Dividend
An amount distributed out of a company's profits to its shareholders in proportion to the number of shares they hold. Over the years a **preferred** dividend will remain at a fixed annual amount. The amount of **common** dividends may fluctuate with the company's profits. A company is under no legal obligation to pay preferred or common dividends.

Dividend Discount Model
The relationship between a stock's current price and the present value of all future dividend payments. It is used to determine the price at which a stock should be selling based on projected future dividend payments.

Dividend Payout Ratio
A ratio that measures the amount or percentage of the company's net earnings that are paid out to shareholders in the form of dividends.

Dividend Reinvestment Plan
The automatic reinvestment of shareholder dividends in more shares of the company's stock.

Dividend Tax Credit
A procedure to encourage Canadians to invest in **preferred** and **common shares** of taxable, dividend-paying Canadian corporations. The taxpayer pays tax based on grossing up (i.e., adding 4 5% to the amount of dividends actually received) and obtains a credit against federal and provincial tax based on the grossed up amount in the amount of 19%.

Dividend Yield
A value ratio that shows the annual dividend rate expressed as a percentage of the current market price of a stock. Dividend yield represents the investor's percentage return on investment at its prevailing market price.

Dollar Cost Averaging
Investing a fixed amount of dollars in a specific security at regular set intervals over a period of time, thereby reducing the average cost paid per unit.

Domestic Bonds
Bonds issued in the currency and country of the issuer. For example, a Canadian dollar-denominated bond, issued by a Canadian company, in the Canadian market would be considered a domestic bond.

© CSI GLOBAL EDUCATION INC. (2008)

Dow Jones Industrial Average (DJIA)
A price-weighted **average** that uses 30 actively traded **blue chip** companies as a measure of the direction of the New York Stock Exchange.

Drawdown
A cash management open-market operation pursued by the Bank of Canada to influence interest rates. A drawdown refers to the transfer of deposits to the Bank of Canada from the direct clearers, effectively draining the supply of available cash balances. See also **Redeposit**.

Due Diligence Report
When negotiations for a new issue of securities begin between a dealer and corporate issuer, the dealer normally prepares a due diligence report examining the financial structure of the company.

Duration
A measure of bond price volatility. The approximate percentage change in the price or value of a bond or bond portfolio for a 1% point change in interest rates. The higher the duration of a bond the greater its risk.

Dynamic Asset Allocation
An **asset allocation** strategy that refers to the systematic rebalancing, either by time period or weight, of the securities in the portfolio, so that they match the long-term benchmark asset mix among the various asset classes.

Earned Income
Income that is designated by Canada Revenue Agency for **RRSP** calculations. Most types of revenues are included with the exception of any form of investment income and pension income.

Earnings or Income Statement
A financial statement which shows a company's revenues and expenditures resulting in either a profit or a loss during a financial period.

Earnings Per Share (EPS)
A **value ratio** that shows the portion of net income for a period attributable to a single **common share** of a company. For example, a company with $100 million in earnings and with 100 million common shareholders would report an EPS of $1 per share.

Economic Indicators
Statistics or data series that are used to analyze business conditions and current economic activity. See also **leading**, **lagging**, and **coincident indicators**.

Economies of Scale
An economic principle whereby the per unit cost of producing each unit of output falls as the volume of production increases. Typically, a company that achieves economies of scale lowers the average cost per unit through increased production since fixed costs are shared over an increased number of goods.

Efficient Market Hypothesis
The theory that a stock's price reflects all available information and reflects its true value.

Election Period
When an investor purchases an **extendible** or **retractable bond**, they have a time period in which to notify the company if they want to exercise the option.

Elliot Wave Theory
A theory used in **technical analysis** based on the rhythms found in nature. The theory states that there are repetitive, predictable sequences of numbers and cycles found in nature similar to patterns of stock movements.

Embedded Option
A term used to describe the **convertible**, **retractable** or **extendible** features of some securities. These features can often be valued using the same techniques used to value options.

Emerging Industries
Brand new industries in the early stages of growth. Often considered as speculative because they are introducing new products that may or may not be accepted and may face strong competition from other new entrants.

Enterprise Multiple (EM)
A ratio used to measure a company's overall value by comparing its enterprise value to its earnings before interest, taxes and amortization or EBITDA.

Enterprise Value (EV)
Reflects what it would cost to purchase a company as a whole. EV is calculated as the market value of the company's common equity, preferred equity and debt less any cash or investments that it records on its balance sheet.

Equilibrium Price
The price at which the quantity demanded equals the quantity supplied.

Equipment Trust Certificate
A type of debt security that was historically used to finance "rolling stock" or railway boxcars. The cars were the collateral behind the issue and when the issue was paid down the cars reverted to the issuer. In recent times, equipment trusts are used as a method of financing containers for the offshore industry. A security, more common in the U.S. than in Canada.

Equity
Ownership interest in a corporation's stock that represents a claim on its earnings and assets. See also **Stock**.

Equity Dividend Shares
Shares that trade like **bonds** and **preferred shares**, but can benefit from increases in dividends paid on the underlying **common shares**. Also known as **structured preferreds**. See also **Split Shares**.

Equity Income
A company's share of an unconsolidated subsidiary's earnings. The equity accounting method is used when a company owns 20% to 50% of a subsidiary.

Equity Method
An accounting method used to determine income derived from a company's investment in another company over which it exerts significant influence.

Escrowed or Pooled Shares
Outstanding shares of a company which, while entitled to vote and receive **dividends**, may not be bought or sold unless special approval is obtained. Mining and oil companies commonly use this technique when **treasury shares** are issued for new properties. Shares can be released from escrow (i.e., freed to be bought and sold) only with the permission of applicable authorities such as a stock exchange and/or securities commission.

Eurobonds
Bonds that are issued and sold outside a domestic market and typically denominated in a currency other than that of the domestic market. For example, a **bond** denominated in Canadian dollars and issued in Germany would be classified as a Eurobond.

© CSI GLOBAL EDUCATION INC. (2008)

European Option
An **option** that can only be exercised on a specified date – normally the business day prior to expiration.

Event-Driven Hedge Funds
A type of **hedge fund** that seeks to profit from unique events such as mergers, acquisitions, stock splits or buybacks.

Ex-Ante
A projection of expected returns – what investors expect to realize as a return.

Exchange Fund Account
A special federal government account operated by the Bank of Canada to hold and conduct transactions in Canada's foreign exchange reserves on instructions from the Minister of Finance.

Exchange Rate
The price at which one currency exchanges for another.

Exchange-Traded Funds (ETFs)
Open-ended mutual fund trusts that hold the same stocks in the same proportion as those included in a specific stock index. Shares of an exchange-traded fund trade on major stock exchanges. Like index mutual funds, ETFs are designed to mimic the performance of a specified index by investing in the constituent companies included in that index. Like the stocks in which they invest, shares can be traded throughout the trading day.

Ex-Dividend
A term that denotes that when a person purchases a **common** or **preferred share**, they are not entitled to the **dividend** payment. Shares go ex-dividend two business days prior to the shareholder record date. See also **Cum Dividend**.

Exempt List
Large professional buyers of securities, mostly financial institutions, that are offered a portion of a new issue by one member of the banking group on behalf of the whole syndicate. The term exempt indicates that this group of investors is exempt from receiving a **prospectus** on a new issue as they are considered to be sophisticated and knowledgeable.

Exempt Market
An unregulated market for sophisticated participants in government **bonds**, corporate issues and **commercial paper**. A **prospectus** has not been required to raise money privately from private investors (largely institutions, but also individuals) and registration with a securities commission for those so dealing has not been needed.

Exercise
The process of invoking the **rights** of the option or **warrant** contract. It is the holder of the option who exercises his or her rights. See also **Assignment**.

Exercise Notice
The instructions tendered by the option holder, through the investment dealer, which states the holder's decision to activate the rights given in the option contract. Once tendered, it is irrevocable. The holder of a **call** will buy the underlying security while the holder of a **put** will sell the underlying security.

Exercise Price
The price at which a **derivative** can be exchanged for a share of the underlying security (also known as **subscription price**). For an **option**, it is the price at which the underlying security can be purchased, in the case of a **call**, or sold, in the case of a **put**, by the option holder. Synonymous with **strike price**.

Expansion
A phase of the **business cycle** characterized by increasing corporate profits and hence increasing share prices, an increase in the demand for capital for business expansion, and hence an increase in interest rates.

Expectations Theory
A theory stating that the **yield curve** is shaped by a market consensus about future interest rates.

Expiration Date
The date on which certain rights or option contracts cease to exist. For equity options, this date is usually the Saturday following the third Friday of the month listed in the contract. This term can also be used to describe the day on which warrants and rights cease to exist.

Ex-Post
The **rate of return** that was actually received. This historic data is used to measure actual performance.

Ex-Rights
A term that denotes that the purchaser of a **common share** would not be entitled to a rights offering. Common shares go ex-rights two business days prior to the shareholder of **record date**.

Extendible Bond or Debenture
A **bond** or **debenture** with terms granting the holder the option to extend the maturity date by a specified number of years.

Extension Date
For extendible bonds the maturity date of the bond can be extended so that the bond changes from a short-term bond to a long-term bond.

Extraordinary Items
An event not typical of normal business activity and do not occur on a regular basis. For example, a company may write off an underperforming division or it may sell a large amount of real estate in a given fiscal year. The results of these special gains or losses are included as an extraordinary item on the **earnings statement**.

Face Value
The value of a bond or debenture that appears on the face of the certificate. Face value is ordinarily the amount the issuer will pay at maturity. Face value is no indication of market value.

Factors of Production
The resources that consumers, firms, and governments use to produce goods and services and include labour, natural resources, entrepreneurship and capital.

Fiduciary Responsibility
The responsibility of an investment advisor, mutual fund salesperson or financial planner to always put the client's interests first. The fiduciary is in a position of trust and must act accordingly.

Final Good
A finished product, one that is purchased by the ultimate end user.

Final Prospectus
The prospectus which supersedes the **preliminary prospectus** and is accepted for filing by applicable provincial securities commissions. The final prospectus shows all required information pertinent to the new issue and a copy must be given to each first-time buyer of the new issue.

Finance or Acceptance Company Paper
Short-term negotiable debt securities similar to **commercial paper**, but issued by finance companies.

© CSI GLOBAL EDUCATION INC. (2008)

Financial Intermediary
An institution such as a bank, life insurance company, credit union or mutual fund which receives cash, which it invests, from suppliers of capital.

Financial Risk
The additional risk placed on the common shareholders from a company's decision to use debt to finance its operations.

Financing
The purchase for resale of a security issue by one or more investment dealers. The formal agreement between the investment dealer and the corporation issuing the securities is called the **underwriting** agreement. A term synonymous with underwriting.

Firm Bid – Firm Offer
An undertaking to buy (firm bid) or sell (firm offer) a specified amount of securities at a specified price for a specified period of time, unless released from this obligation by the seller in the case of a firm bid or the buyer in the case of a firm offer.

First-In-First-Out (FIFO)
Inventory items acquired earliest are sold first.

First Mortgage Bonds
The senior securities of a company as they constitute a first charge on the company's assets, earnings and undertakings before unsecured current liabilities are paid.

Fiscal Agent
An investment dealer appointed by a company or government to advise it in financial matters and to manage the underwriting of its securities.

Fiscal Policy
The policy pursued by the federal government to influence economic growth through the use of taxation and government spending to smooth out the fluctuations of the **business cycle**.

Fiscal Year
A company's accounting year. Due to the nature of particular businesses, some companies do not use the calendar year for their bookkeeping. A typical example is the department store that finds December 31 too early a date to close its books after the Christmas rush and so ends its fiscal year on January 31.

Fixed Asset
A tangible long-term asset such as land, building or machinery, held for use rather than for processing or resale. A **balance sheet** category.

Fixed Exchange Rate Regime
A country whose central bank maintains the domestic currency at a fixed level against another currency or a composite of other currencies.

Fixed-Floater Preferred
See **Delayed Floater**.

Fixed-Income Securities
Securities that generate a predictable stream of interest or **dividend** income, such as **bonds**, **debentures** and **preferred shares**

Fixed-Reset Preferred
See **Delayed Floater.**

Flat
Means that the quoted market price of a **bond** or **debenture** is its total cost (as opposed to an accrued interest transaction). Bonds and debentures in default of interest trade flat.

Floating Exchange Rate
A country whose central bank allows market forces alone to determine the value of its currency, but will intervene if it thinks the move in the exchange rate is excessive or disorderly.

Floating Rate
A term used to describe the interest payments negotiated in a particular contract. In this case, a floating rate is one that is based on an administered rate, such as the **Prime Rate**. For example, the rate for a particular note may be 2% over Prime. See also **Fixed Rate**.

Floating-Rate Debentures
A type of **debenture** that offers protection to investors during periods of very volatile interest rates. For example, when interest rates are rising, the interest paid on floating rate debentures is adjusted upwards every six months.

Floor Trader
Employee of a member of a stock exchange, who executes buy and sell orders on the floor (trading area) of the exchange for the firm and its clients.

Forced Conversion
When a company's stock rises in value above the **conversion price** a company may force the **convertible** security holder to exchange the security for stock by calling back the security. Faced with receiving a lower **call price** (par plus a call premium) or higher valued shares the investor is forced to convert into **common shares**.

Foreign Bonds
If a Canadian company issues **debt** securities in another country, denominated in that foreign country's currency, the bond is known as a foreign **bond**. A bond issued in the U.S. payable in U.S. dollars is known as a foreign bond or a "Yankee Bond." See also **Eurobond**.

Foreign Exchange Rate Risk
The risk associated with an investment in a foreign security or any investment that pays in a denomination other than Canadian dollars, the investor is subject to the risk that the foreign currency may depreciate in value.

Foreign Pay
A Canadian debt security issued in Canada but pays interest and principle in a foreign currency is known as a foreign pay **bond**. This type of security allows Canadians to take advantage of possible shifts in currency values.

Forward
A forward contract is similar to a **futures** contract but trades on an OTC basis. The seller agrees to deliver a specified commodity or financial instrument at a specified price sometime in the future. The terms of a forward contract are not standardized but are negotiated at the time of the trade. There may be no secondary market.

Frictional Unemployment
Unemployment that results from normal labour turnover, from people entering and leaving the workforce and from the ongoing creation and destruction of jobs.

Front-End Load
A sales charge applied to the purchase price of a **mutual fund** when the fund is originally purchased.

Front Running
Making a practice, directly or indirectly, of taking the opposite side of the market to clients, or effecting a trade for the advisor's own account prior to effecting a trade for a client.

© CSI GLOBAL EDUCATION INC. (2008)

Full Employment
The level of unemployment due solely to both frictional and structural factors, or when cyclical unemployment is zero.

Fully Diluted Earnings Per Share
Earnings per common share calculated on the assumption that all **convertible** securities are converted into **common** shares and all outstanding **rights**, **warrants**, **options** and contingent issues are exercised.

Fundamental Analysis
Security analysis based on fundamental facts about a company as revealed through its financial statements and an analysis of economic conditions that affect the company's business. See also **Technical Analysis**.

Funded Debt
All outstanding bonds, debentures, notes and similar debt instruments of a company not due for at least one year.

FundServ
An industry organization that administers segregated fund offerings as well as provides clearing and settlement services to mutual funds.

Future Income Taxes
Income tax that would otherwise be payable currently, but which is deferred by using larger allowable deductions in calculating taxable income than those used in calculating net income in the financial statements. An acceptable practice, it is usually the result of timing differences and represents differences in accounting reporting guidelines and tax reporting guidelines.

Futures
A contract in which the seller agrees to deliver a specified commodity or financial instrument at a specified price sometime in the future. A futures contract is traded on a recognized exchange. Unlike a forward contract, the terms of the futures contract are standardized by the exchange and there is a **secondary market**. See also **Forwards**.

GAAP
Acronym for Generally Accepted Accounting Principles which are conventions, procedures and guidelines for accounting practices.

Good Delivery Form
When a security is sold it must be delivered to the broker properly endorsed, not mutilated and with (if any) coupons attached. To avoid these difficulties and as a general practice most securities are held in street form with the broker.

Good Faith Money
A deposit of money by the buyer or seller of a futures product which acts as a financial guarantee as to the fulfilment of the contractual obligations of the futures contract. Also called a performance bond or **margin**.

Good Through Order
An order to buy or sell that is good for a specified number of days and then is automatically cancelled if it has not been filled.

Good Till Cancelled Order
An order that is valid from the date entered until the close of business on the date specified in the order. If the order has not been filled by the close of the market on that date, it is cancelled. This type of order can be cancelled or changed at any time.

Goodwill
Generally understood to represent the value of a well-respected business – its name, customer relations, employee relations, among others. Considered an **intangible asset** on the **balance sheet**.

Government Securities Distributors
Typically an investment dealer or bank that is authorized to bid at Government of Canada debt auctions.

Greensheet
Highlights for the firm's sales representatives the salient features of a new issue, both pro and con in order to successfully solicit interest to the general public. Dealers prepare this information circular for in-house use only.

Grey Market
A colloquialism used to describe the unlisted if, as, and when market for newly issued but as of yet, unlisted securities. It is an **over-the-counter market**.

Gross Domestic Product (GDP)
The value of all goods and services produced in a country in a year.

Gross Profit Margin
A **profitability ratio** that shows the company's rate of profit after allowing for cost of goods sold.

Growth Stock
Common stock of a company with excellent prospects for above-average growth; a company which over a period of time seems destined for above-average expansion.

Guaranteed Amount
The minimum amount payable under **death benefits** or **maturity guarantees** provided for under the terms of the **segregate fund** contract.

Guaranteed Bonds
Bonds issued by a crown corporation but guaranteed by the applicable government as to interest and principal payments.

Guaranteed Income Supplement (GIS)
A pension payable to **OAS** recipients with no other or limited income.

Guaranteed Investment Certificate (GIC)
A deposit instrument most commonly available from trust companies, requiring a minimum investment at a predetermined rate of **interest** for a stated term. Generally nonredeemable prior to maturity but there can be exceptions.

Guaranteed Investment Fund (GIF)
A type of **segregated fund** whose underlying asset is a **mutual fund**. GIFs are often described as consisting of mutual funds with segregated fund "wrappers".

Halt in Trading
A temporary halt in the trading of a security to allow significant news to be reported and widely disseminated. Usually the result of a pending merger or a substantial change in dividends or earnings.

Hedge Funds
Lightly regulated pools of capital in which the hedge fund manager invests a significant amount of his or her own capital into the fund and whose offering memorandum allows for the fund to execute aggressive strategies that are unavailable to mutual funds such as short selling.

Hedging
A protective manoeuvre; a transaction intended to reduce the risk of loss from price fluctuations.

High Saling
Deliberately causing the last sale for the day in a security to be higher than warranted by

© CSI GLOBAL EDUCATION INC. (2008)

the prevailing market conditions (also referred to as window dressing).

High Water Mark
Used in the context of how a hedge fund manager is compensated. The high water mark sets the bar above which the fund manager is paid a portion of the profits earned for the fund.

Holding Period Return
A transactional **rate of return** measure that takes into account all **cash flows** and increases or decreases in a security's value for any time frame. Time frames can be greater or less than a year.

Hypothecate
To pledge securities as collateral for a loan. Referred to as collateral assignment or hypotec in Québec for **segregated funds**.

ICE Futures Canada (formerly the Winnipeg Commodity Exchange)
An exchange that trades agricultural futures and options exclusively.

Income Bond
Generally, an income bond promises to repay principal but to pay interest only when earned. In some cases, unpaid interest on an income bond may accumulate as a claim against the company when the bond matures.

Income Splitting
A tax planning strategy whereby the higher-earning spouse transfers income to the lower-earning spouse to reduce taxable income.

Income Statement
See **Earnings Statement**.

Income Tax Act (ITA)
The legislation dictating the process and collection of federal tax in Canada, administered by Canada Revenue Agency.

Income Trusts
A type of **investment trust** that holds investments in the operating assets of a company. Income from these operating assets flows through to the trust, which in turn passes on the income to the trust unitholders.

Index
A measure of the market as measured by a basket of securities. An example would be the S&P/TSX Composite Index or the S&P 500. Fund managers and investors use a stock index to measure the overall direction and performance of the market.

Indexing
A portfolio management style that involves buying and holding a portfolio of securities that matches, closely or exactly, the composition of a benchmark **index**.

Individual variable insurance contract (IVIC)
The term used in the IVIC Guidelines to describe a **segregated fund** contract.

Inflation
A generalized, sustained trend of rising prices.

Inflation Rate
The rate of change in prices. See also **Consumer Price Index**.

Inflation Rate Risk
The risk that the value of financial assets and the purchasing power of income will decline due to the impact of **inflation** on the real returns produced by those financial assets.

Information Circular
Document sent to shareholders with a **proxy**, providing details of matters to come before a shareholders' meeting.

Initial Public Offering (IPO)
A new issue of securities offered to the public for investment for the very first time. IPOs must adhere to strict government regulations as to how the investments are sold to the public.

Initial Sales Charge
A commission paid to the financial adviser at the time that the policy is purchased. This type of sales charge is also known as an acquisition fee or a **front-end load**.

Insider
All directors and senior officers of a corporation and those who may also be presumed to have access to nonpublic or inside information concerning the company; also anyone owning more than 10% of the voting shares in a corporation. Insiders are prohibited from trading on this information.

Insider Report
A report of all transactions in the shares of a company by those considered to be insiders of the company and submitted each month to securities commissions.

Instalment Debentures
A bond or **debenture** issue in which a predetermined amount of principal matures each year.

Instalment Receipts
A new issue of stock sold with the obligation that buyers will pay the issue price in a specified series of instalment payments instead of one lump sum payment. Also known as Partially Paid Shares.

Institutional Investor
Organizations, such as a pension fund or mutual fund company, that trade large volumes of securities and typically have a steady flow of money to invest.

Insured Asset Allocation
An **asset allocation** strategy whereby there is a base portfolio value below which the portfolio is not allowed to drop.

Intangible Asset
An **asset** having no physical substance (e.g., **goodwill**, patents, franchises, copyrights).

Integrated Asset Allocation
An **asset allocation** strategy that refers to an all-encompassing strategy that includes consideration of capital market expectations and client risk tolerance.

Interest
Money charged by a lender to a borrower for the use of his or her money.

Interest Coverage Ratio
A **debt ratio** that tests the ability of a company to pay the interest charges on its debt and indicates how many times these charges are covered based upon earnings available to pay them.

Interest Rate Risk
The risk that changes in interest rates will adversely affect the value of an investor's portfolio. For example, a portfolio with a large holding of long-term bonds is vulnerable to significant loss from changes in interest rates.

International Monetary Fund (IMF)
Entity whose purpose is to promote cooperation and collaboration on international monetary and trade issues.

Interval Funds
A type of **mutual fund** that has the flexibility to buy back its outstanding shares periodically. Also known as closed-end discretionary funds.

© CSI GLOBAL EDUCATION INC. (2008)

In-the-Money
A call option is in-the-money if its strike price is below the current market price of the underlying security. A **put option** is in-the-money if its strike price is above the current market price of the underlying security. The in-the-money amount is the option's **intrinsic value**.

Intrinsic Value
That portion of a **warrant** or **call** option's price that represents the amount by which the market price of a security exceeds the price at which the warrant or call option may be exercised (exercise price). Considered the theoretical value of a security (i.e., what a security should be worth or priced at in the market).

Inventory
The goods and supplies that a company keeps in stock. A **balance sheet** item.

Inventory Turnover Ratio
Cost of goods sold divided by **inventory**. The ratio may also be expressed as the number of days required to sell current inventory by dividing the ratio into 365.

Investment
The use of money to make more money, to gain income or increase capital or both.

Investment Advisor (IA)
An individual licensed to transact in the full range of securities. IAs must be registered in by the securities commission of the province in which he or she works. The term refers to employees of **SRO** member firms only. Also known as a Registrant or Registered Representative (RR).

Investment Company, or Fund
A company which uses its capital to invest in other companies. There are two principal types: **closed-end** and **open-end** or **mutual fund**. Shares in closed-end investment companies are readily transferable in the open market and are bought and sold like other shares. Capitalization is fixed. Open-end funds sell their own new shares to investors, buy back their old shares, and are not listed. Open-end funds are so-called because their capitalization is not fixed; they normally issue more shares or units as people want them.

Investment Counsellor
A professional engaged to give investment advice on securities for a fee.

Investment Dealer
A person or company that engages in the business of trading in securities in the capacity of an agent or principal and is a member of IIROC.

Investment Industry Association of Canada (IIAC)
A member-based professional association that represents the interests of market participants.

Investment Industry Regulatory Organization of Canada (IIROC)
The Canadian investment industry's national self-regulatory organization. IIROC carries out its regulatory responsibilities through setting and enforcing rules regarding the proficiency, business and financial conduct of dealer firms and their registered employees and through setting and enforcing market integrity rules regarding trading activity on Canadian equity marketplaces.

Investment Policy Statement
The agreement between a portfolio manager and a client that provides the guidelines for the manager.

Investor
One whose principal concern is the minimization of risk, in contrast to the **speculator**, who is prepared to accept calculated risk in the hope of making better-than-average profits, or the gambler, who is prepared to take even greater risks.

Irrevocable Beneficiary
A beneficiary whose entitlements under the **segregated fund** contract cannot be terminated or changed without his or her consent.

Issue
Any of a company's securities; the act of distributing such securities.

Issued Shares
That part of **authorized shares** that have been sold by the corporation and held by the shareholders of the company.

Issuer Bid
An offer by an issuer to security holders to buy back any of its own shares or other securities convertible into its shares.

Jitney
The execution and clearing of orders by one member of a stock exchange for the account of another member. Example: Broker A is a small firm whose volume of business is not sufficient to maintain a trader on the floor of the exchange. Instead it gives its orders to Broker B for execution and clearing and pays a reduced percentage of the normal commission.

Junior Bond Issue
A corporate bond issue, the collateral for which has been pledged as security for other more senior debt issues and is therefore subject to these prior claims.

Junior Debt
One or more **junior bond issues**.

Keynesian Economics
Economic policy developed by British economist John Maynard Keynes who proposed that active government intervention in the market was the only method of ensuring economic growth and prosperity. See also **Monetarism**.

Know Your Client Rule (KYC)
The cardinal rule in making investment recommendations. All relevant information about a client must be known in order to ensure that the registrant's recommendations are suitable.

Labour Force
The sum of the population aged 15 years and over who are either employed or unemployed.

Labour Sponsored Venture Capital Corporations (LSVCC)
LSVCCs are investment funds, sponsored by labour organizations, that have a specific mandate to invest in small to medium-sized businesses. To encourage this mandate, governments offer generous tax credits to investors in LSVCCs.

Lagging Indicators
A selection of statistical data, that on average, indicate highs and lows in the business cycle behind the economy as a whole. These relate to business expenditures for new plant and equipment, consumers' instalment credit, short-term business loans, the overall value of manufacturing and trade inventories.

Large Value Transfer System (LVTS)
A Canadian Payments Association electronic system for the transfer of large value payments between participating financial institution.

© CSI GLOBAL EDUCATION INC. (2008)

Leading Indicators
A selection of statistical data that, on average, indicate highs and lows in the business cycle ahead of the economy as a whole. These relate to employment, capital investment, business starts and failures, profits, stock prices, inventory adjustment, housing starts and certain commodity prices.

LEAPS
Long Term Equity Anticipation Securities are long-term (2-3 year) option contracts.

Leverage
The effect of fixed charges (i.e., debt interest or preferred dividends, or both) on per-share earnings of **common** stock. Increases or decreases in income before fixed charges result in magnified percentage increases or decreases in **earnings per common share**. Leverage also refers to seeking magnified percentage returns on an investment by using borrowed funds, **margin accounts** or securities which require payment of only a fraction of the underlying security's value (such as rights, warrants or options).

Liabilities
Debts or obligations of a company, usually divided into **current liabilities** – those due and payable within one year – and long-term liabilities – those payable after one year. A **balance sheet** category.

Life Cycle
A model used in financial planning that tries to link age with investing. The underlying theory is that an individual's asset mix will change, as they grow older. However the life cycle is not a substitute for the "know your client rule".

Limit Order
A client's order to buy or sell securities at a specific price or better. The order will only be executed if the market reaches or betters that price.

Limited Liability
The word limited at the end of a Canadian company's name implies that liability of the company's shareholders is limited to the money they paid to buy the shares. By contrast, ownership by a **sole proprietor** or **partnership** carries unlimited personal legal responsibility for debts incurred by the business.

Limited Partnership
A type of partnership whereby a limited partner cannot participate in the daily business activity and liability is limited to the partner's investment.

Liquidity
1. The ability of the market in a particular security to absorb a reasonable amount of buying or selling at reasonable price changes. 2. A corporation's current assets relative to its current liabilities; its cash position.

Liquidity Preference Theory
A theory that tries to explain the shape of the **yield curve**. It postulates that investors want to invest for the short-term because they are risk averse. Borrowers, however, want long-term money. In order to entice investors to invest long-term, borrowers must offer higher rates for longer-term money. This being the case, the yield curve should slope upwards reflecting the higher rates for longer borrowing periods.

Liquidity Ratios
Financial ratios that are used to judge the company's ability to meet its short-term commitments. See **Current Ratio**.

Liquidity Risk
The risk that an investor will not be able to buy or sell a security quickly enough because buying or selling opportunities are limited.

Listed Stock
The stock of a company which is traded on a stock exchange.

Listing Agreement
A stock exchange document published when a company's shares are accepted for listing. It provides basic information on the company, its business, management, assets, capitalization and financial status.

Load
The portion of the offering price of shares of most open-end investment companies (**mutual funds**) which covers sales commissions and all other costs of distribution.

London InterBank Offered Rate (LIBOR)
The rate of interest charged by large international banks dealing in Eurodollars to other large international banks.

Long Position
Signifies ownership of securities. "I am long 100 BCE common" means that the speaker owns 100 **common shares** of BCE Inc.

Long-Term Bond
A bond or debenture maturing in more than ten years.

Macroeconomics
Macroeconomics focuses on the performance of the economy as a whole. It looks at the broader picture and to the challenges facing society as a result of the limited amounts of natural resources, human effort and skills, and technology.

Major Trend
Underlying price trend prevailing in a market despite temporary declines or rallies.

Managed Account
Similar to a **discretionary account** but more long-term in nature. May be solicited.

Management Expense Ratio
The total expense of operating a **mutual fund** expressed as a percentage of the fund's **net asset value**. It includes the **management fee** as well as other expenses charged directly to the fund such as administrative, audit, legal fees etc., but excludes brokerage fees. Published rates of return are calculated after the management expense ratio has been deducted.

Management Fee
The fee that the manager of a **mutual fund** or a **segregated fund** charges the fund for managing the portfolio and operating the fund. The fee is usually set as fixed percentage of the fund's net asset value.

Managers' Discussion and Analysis (MD&A)
A document that requires management of an issuer to discuss the dynamics of its business and to analyze its financial statements with the focus being on information about the issuer's financial condition and operations with emphasis on liquidity and capital resources.

Margin
The amount of money paid by a client when he or she uses credit to buy a security. It is the difference between the market value of a security and the amount loaned by an investment dealer.

Margin Agreement
A contract that must be completed and signed by a client and approved by the firm in order to open a margin account. This sets out the terms and conditions of the account.

© CSI GLOBAL EDUCATION INC. (2008)

Margin Call
When an investor purchases an account on margin in the expectation that the share value will rise, or shorts a security on the expectation that share price will decline, and share prices go against the investor, the brokerage firm will send out a margin call requiring that the investor add additional funds or marketable securities to the account to protect the broker's loan.

Marginal Tax Rate
The tax rate that would have to be paid on any additional dollars of taxable income earned

Market
Any arrangement whereby products and services are bought and sold, either directly or through intermediaries.

Market Capitalization
The dollar value of a company based on the market price of its issued and outstanding common shares. It is calculated by multiplying the number of outstanding shares by the current market price of a share.

Market Correction
A price reversal that typically occurs when a security has been overbought or oversold in the market.

Market Maker
A trader employed by a securities firm who is authorized and required, by applicable self-regulatory organizations (SROs), to maintain reasonable liquidity in securities markets by making firm bids or offers for one or more designated securities.

Market Order
An order placed to buy or sell a security immediately at the best current price.

Market-Out Clause
A clause that allows a dealer to cancel the issue if market conditions changed to the point where the issue becomes un-saleable.

Market Risk
The non-controllable or systematic risk associated with equities.

Market Segmentation Theory
A theory on the structure of the **yield** curve. It is believed that large institutions shape the yield curve. The banks prefer to borrow short term while the insurance industry, with a longer horizon, prefers long-term money. The supply and demand of the large institutions shapes the curve.

Market Timing
Decisions on when to buy or sell securities based on economic factors, such as the strength of the economy and the direction of interest rates, or based on stock price movements and the volume of trading through the use of **technical analysis**.

Marketability
A measure of the ability to buy and sell a security. A security has good marketability if there is an active secondary market in which it can be easily bought and sold at a fair price.

Marketable Bonds
Bonds for which there is a ready market (i.e., clients will buy them because the prices and features are attractive).

Marking-to-Market
The process in the futures market in which the daily price changes are paid by the parties incurring losses to the parties earning profits.

Married Put or a Put Hedge
The purchase of an underlying asset and the purchase of a put option on that underlying asset.

Material Change
A change in the affairs of a company that is expected to have a significant effect on the market value of its securities.

Mature Industry
An industry that experiences slower, more stable growth rates in earnings and sales than growth or emerging industries, for example.

Maturity
The date on which a loan or a **bond** or **debenture** comes due and is to be paid off.

Maturity Date
The date at which the contract expires, and the time at which any **maturity guarantees** are based. Segregated fund contracts normally mature in 10 years, although companies are allowed to set longer periods. Maturities of less than 10 years are permitted only for funds such as protected mutual funds, which are regulated as securities and are not segregated funds.

Maturity Guarantee
The minimum dollar value of the contract after the guarantee period, usually 10 years. This amount is also known as the annuity benefit.

Medium-Term Bond
A bond or debenture maturing in over three but less than ten years.

Member Firm
A stock brokerage firm or investment dealer which is a member of a stock exchange or the **Investment Industry Regulatory Organization of Canada.**

Microeconomics
Analyzes the market behaviour of individual consumers and firms, how prices are determined, and how prices determine the production, distribution, and use of goods and services.

Monetarists
School of economic theory which states that the level of prices as well as economic output is determined by an economy's money supply. This school of thought believes that control of the money supply is more vital to economic prosperity than the level of government spending, for example. See also **Keynesian Policy**.

Monetary Aggregates
An aggregate that measures the quantity of money held by a country's households, firms and governments. It includes various forms of money or payment instruments grouped according to their degree of liquidity, such as M1, M2 or M3.

Monetary Policy
Economic policy designed to improve the performance of the economy by regulating money supply and credit. The Bank of Canada achieves this through its influence over short-term interest rates.

Money Market
That part of the **capital** market in which short-term financial obligations are bought and sold. These include **treasury bills** and other federal government securities maturing in three years or less and **commercial paper, bankers' acceptances**, trust company **guaranteed investment certificates** and other instruments with a year or less left to maturity. Longer term securities, when their term shortens to the limits mentioned, are also traded in the money market.

Money Purchase Plan (MPP)
A type of **Registered Pension Plan**; also called a **Defined Contribution Plan**. In this type of plan, the annual payout is based

© CSI GLOBAL EDUCATION INC. (2008)

on the contributions to the plan and the amounts those contributions have earned over the years preceding retirement. In other words, the benefits are not known but the contributions are.

Montréal Exchange (ME)
See **Bourse de Montréal**.

Mortgage
A contract specifying that certain property is pledged as security for a loan.

Mortgage-Backed Securities
Similar to bonds, the current $5,000 units with five-year terms are backed by a share in a pool of home mortgages insured under the National Housing Act. Units pay interest and a part of principal each month and, if homeowners prepay their mortgages, may pay out additional amounts of principal before normal maturity. They trade in the bond market at prices reflecting current interest rates.

Mortgage Bond
A bond issue secured by a **mortgage** on the issuer's property.

Moving Average
The average of security or commodity prices calculated by adding the closing prices for the underlying security over a pre-determined period and dividing the total by the time period selected.

Moving Average Convergence-Divergence (MACD)
A technical analysis tool that takes the difference between two moving averages and then generates a smoothed **moving average** on the difference (the divergence) between the two moving averages.

Multiple
A colloquial term for the **Price/Earnings** ratio of a company's common shares.

Mutual Fund
An **investment fund** operated by a company that uses the proceeds from shares and units sold to investors to invest in stocks, bonds, derivatives and other financial securities. Mutual funds offer investors the advantages of diversification and professional management and are sold on a load or no load basis. Mutual fund shares/units are redeemable on demand at the fund's current **net asset value per share** (NAVPS).

Mutual Fund Dealers Association (MFDA)
The Self-Regulatory Organization (SRO) that regulates the distribution (dealer) side of the mutual fund industry in Canada.

Naked Writer
A seller of an **option** contract who does not own an offsetting position in the underlying security or a suitable alternative.

NASDAQ
An acronym for the National Association of Securities Dealers Automated Quotation System. NASDAQ is a computerized system that provides brokers and dealers with price quotations for securities traded OTC.

National Debt
The accumulation of total government borrowing over time .It is the sum of past deficits minus the sum of past surpluses.

National Policies
The Canadian Securities Administrators have developed a number of policies that are applicable across Canada. These coordinated efforts by the CSA are an attempt to create a national securities regulatory framework. Copies of policies are available from each provincial regulator.

National Registration Database (NRD)
A web-based system that permits mutual fund salespersons and investment advisors to file applications for registration electronically.

Natural Unemployment Rate
Also called the full employment unemployment rate or the nonaccelerating inflation rate of **unemployment** (NAIRU). At this level of unemployment, the economy is thought to be operating at close to its full potential or capacity.

Near Banks
See **Country Banks**.

Negative Pledge Provision
A protective provision written into the trust indenture of a company's debenture issue providing that no subsequent mortgage bond issue may be secured by all or part of the company's assets, unless at the same time the company's debentures are similarly secured.

Negotiable
A certificate that is transferable by delivery and which, in the case of a registered certificate, has been duly endorsed and guaranteed.

Negotiated Offer
A term describing a particular type of financing in which the investment dealer negotiates with the corporation on the issuance of securities. The details would include the type of security to be issued, the price, coupon or dividend rate, special features and protective provisions.

Net Asset Value
For a **mutual fund**, net asset value represents the market value of the fund's share and is calculated as total assets of a corporation less its liabilities. Net asset value is typically calculated at the close of each trading day. Also referred to as the **book value** of a company's different classes of securities.

Net Carrying Amount (Net Book Value of the Assets)
The value of capital assets recorded on the balance sheet less accumulated depreciation or amortization.

Net Change
The change in the price of a security from the closing price on one day to the closing price on the following trading day. In the case of a stock which is entitled to a **dividend** one day, but is traded ex-dividend the next, the dividend is not considered in computing the change. The same applies to **stock splits**. A stock selling at $100 the day before a two-for-one split and trading the next day at $50 would be considered unchanged. The net change is ordinarily the last figure in a stock price list. The mark +1.10 means up $1.10 a share from the last sale on the previous day the stock traded.

Net Earnings
That part of a company's profits remaining after all expenses and taxes have been paid and out of which dividends may be paid.

Net Profit Margin
A **profitability ratio** that indicates how efficiently the company is managed after taking into account both expenses and taxes.

New Account Application Form (NAAF)
A form that is filled out by the client and the IA at the opening of an account. It gives

© CSI GLOBAL EDUCATION INC. (2008)

relevant information to make suitable investment recommendations. The NAAF must be completed and approved before any trades are put through on an account.

New Issue
An offering of stocks or bonds sold by a company for the first time. Proceeds may be used to retire outstanding securities of the company, to purchase fixed assets or for additional working capital. New debt issues are also offered by government bodies.

New York Stock Exchange (NYSE)
Oldest and largest stock exchange in North America with more than 1,600 companies listed on the exchange.

NEX
A new and separate board of the TSX Venture Exchange that provides a trading forum for companies that have fallen below the Venture Exchange's listing standards. Companies that have low levels of business activity or who do not carry on active business will trade on the NEX board, while companies that are actively carrying on business will remain with the main TSX Venture Exchange stock list.

No Par Value (n.p.v.)
Indicates a common stock has no stated face value.

Nominal GDP
Gross domestic product based on prices prevailing in the same year not corrected for inflation. Also referred to as current dollar or chained dollar GDP.

Nominal Rate
The quoted or stated rate on an investment or a loan. This rate allows for comparisons but does not take into account the effects of inflation.

Nominee
A person or firm (bank, investment dealer, CDS) in whose name securities are registered. The shareholder, however, retains the true ownership of the securities.

Non-Client and Professional Orders
A type of order for the account of partners, directors, officers, major shareholders, IAs and employees of member firms that must be marked "PRO" , "N-C" or "Emp", in order to ensure that client orders are given priority for the same securities.

Non-Competitive Tender
A method of distribution used in particular by the Bank of Canada for Government of Canada marketable bonds. **Primary** distributors are allowed to request **bonds** at the average price of the accepted **competitive tenders**. There is no guarantee as to the amount, if any, received in response to this request.

Non-Controlling Interest
1. The equity of the shareholders who do not hold controlling interest in a controlled company; 2. In **consolidated financial statements** (i) the item in the **balance sheet** of the parent company representing that portion of the **assets** of a consolidated subsidiary considered as accruing to the shares of the subsidiary not owned by the parent; and (ii) the item deducted in the **earnings statement** of the parent and representing that portion of the subsidiary's earnings considered as accruing to the subsidiary's shares not owned by the parent. Also referred to as minority interest.

Non-Cumulative
A preferred dividend that does not accrue or accumulate if unpaid.

Non-Trading Employees
Employees of securities firms who are not primarily engaged in sales may occasional accept orders from the public. Such employees are designated as Non-Trading Employees and may be exempt from registration by the administrator.

Odd Lot
A number of shares which is less than a **standard trading unit**. Usually refers to a securities trade for less than 100 shares, sometimes called a broken lot. Trading in less than 100 shares typically incurs a higher per share commission.

Of Record
On the company's books or records. If, for example, a company announces that it will pay a **dividend** on January 15 to shareholders of record, every shareholder whose name appears on the company's books on that date will be sent a dividend cheque from the company.

Offer
The lowest price at which a person is willing to sell; as opposed to bid which is the highest price at which one is willing to buy.

Offering Memorandum
This document is prepared by the dealer involved in a new issue outlining some of the salient features of the new issue, but not the price or other issue-specific details. It is used as a pre-marketing tool in assessing the market for the issue as well as for obtaining expressions of interest.

Offering Price
The price that an investor pays to purchase shares in a **mutual fund**. The offering price includes the charge or load that is levied when the purchase is made.

Offsetting Transaction
A futures or option transaction that is the exact opposite of a previously established long or short position.

Off-the-Board
This term may refer to transactions **over-the-counter** in unlisted securities, or, in a special situation, to a transaction involving a block of listed shares which is not executed on a recognized stock exchange.

Office of the Superintendent of Financial Institutions (OSFI)
The federal regulatory agency whose main responsibilities regarding insurance companies and **segregated funds** are to ensure that the companies issuing the funds are financially solvent.

Officers
Corporate employees responsible for the day-to-day operation of the business.

Old Age Security (OAS)
A government pension plan payable at age 65 to all Canadian citizens and legal residents.

Ombudsman for Banking Services and Investments (OBSI)
An independent organization that investigates customer complaints against financial services providers.

Open-End Fund
See **Mutual Fund**.

Open Interest
The total number of outstanding option contracts for a particular **option** series. An opening transaction would increase open interest, while a closing transaction would decrease open interest. It is used as one measure of an option class's liquidity.

© CSI GLOBAL EDUCATION INC. (2008)

Open Market Operations
Method through which the Bank of Canada influences interest rates by trading securities with participants in the money market.

Open Order
An order usually entered at a specified price (perhaps at the market) to buy or sell a security that is held open until executed or cancelled.

Opening Transaction
An option transaction that is considered the initial or primary transaction. An opening transaction creates new rights for the buyer of an **option**, or new obligations for a seller. See also **Closing Transaction**.

Operating Band
The Bank of Canada's 50-basis-point range for the overnight lending rate. The top of the band, the **Bank Rate**, is the rate charged by the Bank on **LVTS** advances to financial institutions. The bottom of the band is the rate paid by the Bank on any **LVTS** balances held overnight by those institutions. The middle of the operating band is the target for the overnight rate.

Operating Cash Flow Ratio
A liquidity ratio that shows how well liabilities to be paid within one year are covered by the cash flow generated by the company's operating activities.

Operating Income
The income that a company records from its main ongoing operations.

Operating Performance Ratios
A type of ratio that illustrates how well management is making use of company resources.

Operating Profit Margin
A **profitability ratio** that is a stringent measure of a company's ability to manage its resources effectively.

Option
A right to buy or sell specific securities or properties at a specified price within a specified time. See **Put Options** and **Call Options**.

Option Premium
The amount paid to enter into an option contract, paid by the buyer to the seller or writer of the contract.

Option Writer
The seller of the option who may be obligated to buy (put writer) or sell (call writer) the underlying interest if assigned by the option buyer.

Oscillator
A **technical analysis** indicator used when a stock's chart is not showing a definite trend in either direction. When the oscillator reading reaches an extreme value in either the upper or lower band, this suggest that the current price move has gone too far. This may indicate that the price move is overextended and vulnerable.

Out-of-the-Money
A **call option** is out-of-the-money if the market price of the underlying security is below its **strike price**. A **put option** is out-of-the-money if the market price of the underlying security is above the strike price.

Output Gap
The difference between the actual level of output and the potential level of output when the economy is using all available resources of capital and labour.

Outstanding Shares
That part of **issued shares** which remains outstanding in the hands of investors.

Over-Allotment Option
An activity used to stabilize the aftermarket price of a recently issued security. If the price increases above the offer price, dealers can cover their short position by exercising an overallotment option (also referred to as a **green shoe** option) by either increasing demand in the case of covering a short position or increasing supply in the case of over-allotment option exercise.

Overcontribution
An amount made in excess to the annual limit made to an **RRSP**. An overcontribution in excess of$2,000 is penalized at a rate of 1% per month.

Override
In an **underwriting**, the additional payment the **Financing Group** receives over and above their original entitlement for their services as financial advisors and syndicate managers or leads.

Over-the-Counter (OTC)
A market for securities made up of securities dealers who may or may not be members of a recognized stock exchange. Over-the-counter is mainly a market conducted over the telephone. Also called the **unlisted**, inter-dealer or street market. NASDAQ is an example of an over-the-counter market.

Paper Profit
An unrealized profit on a security still held. Paper profits become realized profits only when the security is sold. A paper loss is the opposite to this.

Par Value
The stated **face value** of a **bond** or stock (as assigned by the company's charter) expressed as a dollar amount per share. Par value of a common stock usually has little relationship to the current market value and so no par value stock is now more common. Par value of a **preferred** stock is significant as it indicates the dollar amount of assets each preferred share would be entitled to should the company be liquidated.

Pari Passu
A legal term meaning that all securities within a series have equal rank or claim on earnings and assets. Usually refers to equally ranking issues of a company's **preferred** shares.

Participating Feature
Preferred shares which, in addition to their fixed rate of prior dividend, share with the **common** in further **dividend** distributions and in capital distributions above their par value in liquidation.

Participating Organizations
A firm entitled to trade through the **Toronto Stock Exchange** or **TSX Venture Exchange**. The equivalent term on the **Bourse de Montréal** is Approved Participant.

Participation Rate
The share of the working-age population (15 to 65) that is in the labour market, either working or looking for work.

Partnership
A form of business organization that involves two or more people contributing to the business and legislated under the federal Partnership Act.

Past Service Pension Adjusted (PSPA)
An employer may increase a member's pension by the granting of additional past service benefits to an employee in a **defined benefit plan**. Plan members who incur a PSPA will have their **RRSP** contribution room reduced by the amount of this adjustment.

© CSI GLOBAL EDUCATION INC. (2008)

Payback Period
The time that it takes for a convertible security to recoup its premium through its higher yield, compared with the dividend that is paid on the stock.

Peer Group
A group of managed products (particularly mutual funds) with a similar investment mandate.

Penny Stocks
Low-priced speculative issues selling at less than $1 a share. Frequently used as a term of disparagement, although some penny stocks have developed into investment calibre issues.

Pension Adjustment (PA)
The amount of contributions made or the value of benefits accrued to a member of an employer-sponsored retirement plan for a calendar year. The PA enables the individual to determine the amount that may be contributed to an **RRSP** that would be in addition to contributions into a **Registered Pension Plan**.

Performance Bonds
What is often required upon entry into a futures contract giving the parties to a contract a higher level of assurance that the terms of the contract will eventually be honoured. The performance bond is often referred to as margin.

Perpetual Bonds
A unique type of **debt** security that has no maturity date.

Personal Disposable Income
The amount of personal income an individual has after taxes. The income that can be spent on necessities, nonessential goods and services, or that can be saved.

Phillips Curve
A graph showing the relationship between inflation and unemployment. The theory states that unemployment can be reduced in the short run by increasing the price level (inflation) at a faster rate. Conversely, inflation can be lowered at the cost of possibly increased unemployment and slower economic growth.

Piggyback Warrants
A second series of **warrants** acquired upon exercise of primary warrants sold as part of a unit.

Point
Refers to security prices. In the case of shares, it means $1 per share. In the case of **bonds** and **debentures**, it means 1% of the issue's **par value**, which is almost universally 100. On a $1,000 bond, one point represents 1% of the face value of the bond or $10. See **Basic point**

Policy-Based Guarantee
A **maturity guarantee** based on the date when the policy was first issued. This type of guarantee may involve restrictions on the size of and date of subsequent deposits.

Political Risk
The risk associated with a government introducing unfavourable policies making investment in the country less attractive. Political risk also refers to the general instability associated with investing in a particular country.

Pooled Shares
See **Escrowed Shares**.

Pooling of Interest
Occurs when a company issues **treasury shares** for the assets of another company so that the latter becomes a division or subsidiary of the acquiring company. Subsequent accounts of the parent company are set up to include the **retained earnings** and assets at book value (subject to certain adjustments) of the acquired company.

Portfolio
Holdings of securities by an individual or institution. A portfolio may contain debt securities, preferred and common stocks of various types of enterprises and other types of securities.

Potential Output
The maximum amount of output the economy is capable of producing during a given period when all of its available resources are employed to their most efficient use.

Preemptive Rights Clause
A term in a company's charter that states that if a company wishes to issue additional new shares they must give the "right of first refusal" to the existing shareholders. This allows the existing shareholders to maintain their proportionate interest.

Preferred Dividend Coverage Ratio
A type of profitability ratio that measures the amount of money a firm has available to pay dividends to their preferred shareholders.

Preferred Shares
A class of share capital that entitles the owners to a fixed **dividend** ahead of the company's common shares and to a stated dollar value per share in the event of liquidation. Usually do not have **voting rights** unless a stated number of dividends have been omitted. Also referred to as preference shares.

Preliminary Prospectus
The initial document released by an underwriter of a new securities issue to prospective investors.

Premium
The amount by which a **preferred** stock or **debt** security may sell above its **par value**. In the case of a new issue of **bonds** or stocks, the amount the market price rises over the original selling price. Also refers to that part of the **redemption** price of a bond or preferred share in excess of face value, par value or market price. In the case of **options**, the price paid by the buyer of an option contract to the seller.

Prepaid Expenses
Payments made by the company for services to be received in the near future. For example, rents, insurance premiums and taxes are sometimes paid in advance. A **balance sheet** item.

Prescribed Rate
A quarterly interest rate set out, or prescribed by Canada Revenue Agency under **attribution** rules. The rate is based on the Bank of Canada rate.

Present Value
The current worth of a sum of money that will be received sometime in the future.

Price-Earnings (P/E) Ratio
A **value ratio** that gives investors an idea of how much they are paying for a company's earnings. Calculated as the current price of the stock divided current **earnings per share**.

Primary Distribution or Primary Offering of a New Issue
The original sale of any issue of a company's securities.

© CSI GLOBAL EDUCATION INC. (2008)

Primary Market
The market for new issues of securities. The proceeds of the sale of securities in a primary market go directly to the company issuing the securities. See also **Secondary Market.**

Prime Rate
The interest rate chartered banks charge to their most credit-worthy borrowers.

Principal
The person for whom a broker executes an order, or a **dealer** buying or selling for its own account. The term may also refer to a person's capital or to the face amount of a **bond**.

Private Placement
The underwriting of a security and its sale to a few buyers, usually institutional, in large amounts.

Pro Forma
A term applied to a document drawn up after giving effect to certain assumptions or contractual commitments not yet completed. For example, an issuer of new securities is required to include in the **prospectus** a statement of its **capitalization** on a pro forma basis after giving effect to the new financing.

Pro Rata
In proportion to. For example, a **dividend** is a pro rata payment because the amount of dividend each shareholder receives is in proportion to the number of shares he or she owns.

Probate
A provincial fee charged for authenticating a **will**. The fee charged is usually based on the value of the assets in an estate rather than the effort to process the will.

Productivity
The amount of output per worker used as a measure of efficiency with which people and capital are combined in the output of the economy. Productivity gains lead to improvements in the standard of living, because as labour, capital, etc. produce more, they generate greater income.

Profitability Ratios
Financial ratios that illustrate how well management has made use of the company's resources.

Program Trading
A sophisticated computerized trading strategy whereby a portfolio manager attempts to earn a profit from the price spreads between a portfolio of equities similar or identical to those underlying a designated stock index, e.g., the Standard & Poor 500 Index, and the price at which **futures** contracts (or their options) on the index trade in financial futures markets. Also refers to switching or trading blocks of securities in order to change the asset mix of a portfolio.

Prospectus
A legal document that describes securities being offered for sale to the public. Must be prepared in conformity with requirements of applicable securities commissions. See also **Red Herring** and **Final Prospectus**.

Protected Funds
A fund legally structured as a mutual fund trust and not governed by insurance legislation. This type of segregated fund can be sold by registered mutual fund salespeople at bank branches and by individual financial advisors who lack life insurance licenses.

Proxy
Written authorization given by a shareholder to someone else, who need not be a shareholder, to represent him or her and vote his or her shares at a shareholders' meeting.

Prudent Man Rule
An investment standard. In some provinces, the law requires that a fiduciary, such as a trustee, may invest funds only in a list of securities designated by the province or the federal government. In other provinces, the trustee may invest in a security if it is one that an ordinary prudent person would buy if he were investing for the benefit of other people for whom he felt morally bound to provide. Most provinces apply the two standards.

Public Float
That part of the issued shares that are outstanding and available for trading by the public, and not held by company officers, directors, or investors who hold a controlling interest in the company. A company's public float is different from its **outstanding shares** as it also excludes those shares owned in large blocks by institutions.

Purchase Fund
A fund set up by a company to retire through purchases in the market a specified amount of its outstanding **preferred** shares or debt if purchases can be made at or below a stipulated price. See also **Sinking Fund**.

Pure Insurance
See **Term Insurance**.

Put Option
A right to sell the stock at a stated price within a given time period. Those who think a stock may go down generally purchase puts. See also **Call Option**.

Quantitative Analysis
The study of economic and stock valuation patterns in order to identify and profit from any anomalies.

Quick Ratio
A more stringent measure of liquidity compared with the **current ratio**. Calculated as **current assets** less inventory divided by **current liabilities**. By excluding inventory, the ratio focuses on the company's more liquid assets.

Quotation or Quote
The highest bid to buy and the lowest offer to sell a security at a given time. Example: A quote of 45.40–45.50 means that 45.40 is the highest price a buyer will pay and 45.50 the lowest price a seller will accept.

Quotation and Trade Reporting Systems (QTRS)
Recognized stock markets that operate in a similar manner to exchanges and provide facilities to users to post quotations and report trades.

Rally
A brisk rise in the general price level of the market or in an individual stock.

Random Walk Theory
The theory that stock price movements are random and bear no relationship to past movements.

Rate of Return
See **Yield**.

Rational Expectations
School of economic theory which argues that investors are rational thinkers and can make intelligent economic decisions after evaluating all available information.

© CSI GLOBAL EDUCATION INC. (2008)

Real Estate Investment Trust (REIT)
An investment trust that specializes in real estate related investments including mortgages, construction loans, land and real estate securities in varying combinations. A REIT invests in and manages a diversified portfolio of real estate.

Real GDP
Gross Domestic Product adjusted for changes in the price level. Also referred to as constant dollar GDP.

Real Interest Rate
The **nominal rate** of interest minus the percentage change in the **Consumer Price Index** (i.e., the rate of inflation).

Record Date
The date on which a shareholder must officially own shares in a company to be entitled to a declared **dividend**. Also referred to as the date of record.

Red Herring Prospectus
A preliminary **prospectus** so called because certain information is printed in red ink around the border of the front page. It does not contain all the information found in the **final prospectus**. Its purpose: to ascertain the extent of public interest in an issue while it is being reviewed by a securities commission.

Redemption
The purchase of securities by the issuer at a time and price stipulated in the terms of the securities. See also **Call Feature**.

Redemption Price
The price at which **debt** securities or **preferred** shares may be redeemed, at the option of the issuing company.

Redeposit
An open-market cash management policy pursued by the Bank of Canada. A redeposit refers to the transfer of funds from the Bank to the direct clearers (an injection of balances) that will increase available funds. See also **Drawdown**.

Registered Education Savings Plans (RESPs)
A type of government sponsored savings plan used to finance a child's post secondary education.

Registered Pension Plan (RPP)
A trust registered with Canada Revenue Agency and established by an employer to provide pension benefits for employees when they retire. Both employer and employee may contribute to the plan and contributions are tax-deductible. See also **Defined Contribution Plan** and **Defined Benefit Plan**.

Registered Retirement Income Fund (RRIF)
A tax deferral vehicle available to **RRSP** holders. The planholder invests the funds in the RRIF and must withdraw a certain amount each year. Income tax would be due on the funds when withdrawn.

Registered Retirement Savings Plan (RRSP)
An investment vehicle available to individuals to defer tax on a specified amount of money to be used for retirement. The holder invests money in one or more of a variety of investment vehicles which are held in trust under the plan. Income tax on contributions and earnings within the plan is deferred until the money is withdrawn at retirement. RRSPs can be transferred into Registered **Retirement Income Funds** upon retirement.

Registered Security
A security recorded on the books of a company in the name of the owner. It can be transferred only when the certificate is endorsed by the registered owner. Registered debt securities may be registered as to principal only or fully registered. In the latter case, interest is paid by cheque rather than by coupons attached to the certificate. See also **Bearer Security**.

Registrar
Usually a trust company appointed by a company to monitor the issuing of **common** or **preferred** shares. When a transaction occurs, the registrar receives both the old cancelled certificate and the new certificate from the transfer agent and records and signs the new certificate. The registrar is, in effect, an auditor checking on the accuracy of the work of the transfer agent, although in most cases the registrar and transfer agent are the same trust company.

Regular Delivery
The date a securities trade settles – i.e., the date the seller must deliver the securities. See also **Settlement Date**.

Regular Dividends
A term that indicates the amount a company usually pays on an annual basis.

Reinvestment Risk
The risk that interest rates will fall causing the cash flows on an investment, assuming that the **cash flows** are reinvested, to earn less than the original investment. For example, **yield to maturity** assumes that all interest payments received can be reinvested at the yield to maturity rate. This is not necessarily true. If interest rates in the market fall the interest would be reinvested at a lower rate. Reinvestment risk recognizes this risk.

Relative Strength Graph
Shows the relative strength of a stock compared to the action of the market as a whole. The price of the stock is calculated as a ratio of some market performance series such as the Dow Jones Industrial Average.

Relative Value Hedge Funds
A type of hedge fund that attempts to profit by exploiting irregularities or discrepancies in the pricing of related stocks, bonds or derivatives.

Reporting Issuer
Usually, a corporation that has issued or has outstanding securities that are held by the public and is subject to continuous disclosure requirements of securities administrators.

Reserve
An amount set aside from retained earnings to provide for the payment of contingencies, retirement of preferred stock, or other necessary payouts.

Reset
A contract provision which allows the **segregated fund** contract holder to lock in the current market value of the fund and set a new maturity date 10 years after the reset date. Depending on the contract, the reset dates may be chosen by the contract holder or be triggered automatically.

Resistance Level
The opposite of a **support level**. A price level at which the security begins to fall as the number of sellers exceeds the number of buyers of the security.

Restricted Shares
Shares that participate in a company's earnings and assets (in liquidation), as **common** shares do, but generally have

© CSI GLOBAL EDUCATION INC. (2008)

restrictions on **voting rights** or else no voting rights.

Retail Investor
Individual investors who buy and sell securities for their own personal accounts, and not for another company or organization. They generally buy in smaller quantities than larger **institutional investors**.

Retained Earnings
The cumulative total of annual earnings retained by a company after payment of all expenses and **dividends**. The earnings retained each year are reinvested in the business.

Retained Earnings Statement
A financial statement that shows the profit or loss in a company's most recent year.

Retractable
A feature which can be included in a new **debt** or **preferred** issue, granting the holder the option under specified conditions to redeem the **security** on a stated date – prior to maturity in the case of a bond.

Return Forecasting
The prediction of rates of return for each of the three major asset classes as part of the asset allocation process.

Return on Equity
A **profitability ratio** expressed as a percentage representing the amount earned on a company's **common shares**. Return on equity tells the investor how effectively their money is being put to use.

Return on Invested Capital
A **profitability ratio** that shows the amount earned on a company's total capital – the sum of its **common** and **preferred** shares and long-term debt. It is a useful measure of management efficiency.

Reversal Patterns
Formations that usually precede a sizeable advance or decline in stock prices.

Reverse Split
A process of retiring old shares with fewer shares. For example, an investor owns 1,000 shares of ABC Inc. pre split. A 10 for 1 reverse split or **consolidation** reduces the number held to 100. Results in a higher share price and fewer shares outstanding.

Revocable Beneficiary
A beneficiary whose entitlements under the **segregated fund** contract can be terminated or changed without his or her consent.

Right
A short-term privilege granted to a company's **common** shareholders to purchase additional common shares, usually at a discount, from the company itself, at a stated price and within a specified time period. Rights of listed companies trade on stock exchanges from the **ex-rights** date until their expiry.

Right of Action for Damages
Most securities legislation provides that those who sign a prospectus may be liable for damages if the prospectus contains a misrepresentation. This right extends to experts e.g., lawyers, auditors, geologists, etc., who report or give opinions within the text of the document.

Right of Redemption
A mutual fund's shareholders have a continuing right to withdraw their investment in the fund simply by submitting their shares to the fund itself and receiving in return the dollar amount of their **net asset value**. This characteristic is the hallmark of mutual funds. Payment for the securities that have been redeemed must be made by the fund within three business days from the determination of the net asset value.

Right of Rescission
The right of a purchaser of a new issue to rescind the purchase contract within the applicable time limits if the **prospectus** contained an untrue statement or omitted a material fact.

Right of Withdrawal
The right of a purchaser of a new issue to withdraw from the purchase agreement within two business days after receiving the prospectus.

Risk-Averse
Descriptive term used for an investor unable or unwilling to accept the probability or chance of losing capital. See also **Risk-Tolerant**.

Risk-Free Rate
The rate of return an investor would receive if he or she invested in a risk free investment, such as a **treasury bill**.

Risk Premium
A rate that has to be paid in addition to the **risk free rate** (T-bill rate) to compensate investors for choosing securities that have more risk than T-Bills.

Risk-Return Trade-off
A graph that shows the relationship between the risk associated with an investment and the expected return on that investment. Investors hope to get higher returns when investing in higher-risk securities.

Risk-Tolerant
Descriptive term used for an investor willing and able to accept the probability of losing capital. See also **Risk-Averse**.

Sacrifice Ratio
Describes the extent to which **Gross Domestic Product** must be reduced with increased unemployment to achieve a 1% decrease in the inflation rate.

Sale and Repurchase Agreements (SRAs)
An open-market operation by the Bank of Canada to offset undesired downward pressure on overnight financing costs.

Scholarship Trusts
A type of managed product created to help parents save for their children's post-secondary education. The subscribers (parents or grandparents) make contributions that are used to purchase units in a scholarship trust.

Seat
A traditional term for membership on a **stock exchange**.

SEC
The Securities and Exchange Commission, a federal body established by the United States Congress, to protect investors in the U.S. In Canada there is no national regulatory authority; instead, securities legislation is provincially administered.

Secondary Issue
Refers to the redistribution or resale of previously issued securities to the public by a dealer or investment dealer syndicate. Usually a large block of shares is involved (e.g., from the settlement of an estate) and these are offered to the public at a fixed price, set in relationship to the stock's market price.

© CSI GLOBAL EDUCATION INC. (2008)

Secondary Market
The market where securities are traded through an exchange or **over-the-counter** subsequent to a **primary offering**. The proceeds from trades in a secondary market go to the selling dealers and investors, rather than to the companies that originally issued the shares in the **primary market**.

Securities
Paper certificates or electronic records that evidence ownership of **equity** (**stocks**) or debt obligations (**bonds**).

Securities Acts
Provincial Acts administered by the securities commission in each province, which set down the rules under which securities may be issued and traded.

Securities Administrator
A general term referring to the provincial regulatory authority (e.g., Securities Commission or Provincial Registrar) responsible for administering a provincial Securities Act.

Securities Eligible for Reduced Margin
Securities which demonstrate sufficiently high liquidity and low price volatility based on meeting specific price risk and liquidity risk measures.

Securitization
Refers in a narrow sense to the process of converting loans of various sorts into marketable securities by packaging the loans into pools. In a broader sense, refers to the development of markets for a variety of **debt** instruments that permit the ultimate borrower to bypass the banks and other deposit-taking institutions and to borrow directly from lenders.

Security Market Line
A formula that depicts the **risk-return trade-off** for securities. The formula can be used to calculate the expected return on a stock or an equity fund.

Segregated Funds
Insurance companies sell these funds as an alternative to conventional **mutual funds**. Like mutual funds, segregated funds offer a range of investment objectives and categories of securities e.g. equity funds, bond funds, balanced funds etc. These funds have the unique feature of guaranteeing that, regardless of how poorly the fund performs, at least a minimum percentage (usually 75% or more) of the investor's payments into the fund will be returned when the fund matures.

Self-Directed RRSP
A type of RRSP whereby the holder invests funds or contributes certain acceptable assets such as securities directly into a registered plan which is usually administered for a fee by a Canadian financial services company.

Self-Regulatory Organization (SRO)
An organization recognized by the Securities Administrators as having powers to establish and enforce industry regulations to protect investors and to maintain fair, equitable, and ethical practices in the industry and ensure conformity with securities legislation. Canadian SROs include the **Investment Industry Regulatory Organization of Canada**, the **Mutual Fund Dealers Association**, the **Montréal Exchange**, the **Toronto Stock Exchange**, the **TSX Venture Exchange** and **ICE Futures Canada**.

Selling Group
Investment dealers or others who assist a **banking group** in marketing a new issue of securities without assuming financial liability if the issue is not entirely sold. The use of a selling group widens the distribution of a new issue.

Sentiment Indicators
Measure investor expectations or the mood of the market. These indicators measure how bullish or bearish investors are.

Serial Bond or Debenture
See **Instalment Debenture**.

Settlement Date
The date on which a securities buyer must pay for a purchase or a seller must deliver the securities sold. For most securities, settlement must be made on or before the third business day following the transaction date.

Shareholders' Equity
A **balance sheet** item that represents the excess of the company's assets over its **liabilities** and shows shareholder's interest in the company. Also referred to as net worth as it represents the ownership interest of **common** and **preferred** shareholders in a company.

Short-Form Prospectus Distribution System
This system allows reporting issuers to issue a short-form **prospectus** that contains only information not previously disclosed to regulators. The short form prospectus contains by reference the material filed by the corporation in the **Annual Information Form**.

Short Position
Created when an investor sells a security that he or she does not own. See also **short sale**.

Short Sale
The sale of a security which the seller does not own. This is a speculative practice done in the belief that the price of a stock is going to fall and the seller will then be able to cover the sale by buying it back later at a lower price, thereby making a profit on the transactions. It is illegal for a seller not to declare a short sale at the time of placing the order. See also **Margin**.

Short-Term Bond
A bond or debenture maturing within three years.

Short-Term Debt
Company borrowings repayable within one year that appear in the current liabilities section of the balance sheet. The most common short-term debt items are: bank advances or loans, notes payable and the portion of funded debt due within one year.

Simplified Prospectus
A condensed prospectus distributed by mutual fund companies to purchasers and potential purchasers of fund units or shares.

Sinking Fund
A fund set up to retire most or all of a debt or preferred share issue over a period of time. See also **Purchase Fund**.

Small Cap
Reference to smaller growth companies. Small cap refers to the size of the **capitalization** or investments made in the company. A small cap company has been defined as a company with an outstanding stock value of under $500 million. Small cap companies are considered more volatile than large cap companies.

Soft Landing
Describes a business cycle phase when economic growth slows sharply but does

© CSI GLOBAL EDUCATION INC. (2008)

not turn negative, while inflation falls or remains low.

Soft Retractable Preferred Shares
A type of retractable preferred share where the redemption value may be paid in cash or in common shares, generally at the election of the issuer.

Sole Proprietorship
A form of business organization that involves one person running a business whereby the individual is taxed on earnings at their personal income tax rate.

SPDRs
An acronym for the Standard & Poor Depository Receipts (a type of derivative). These mirror the S&P 500 Index. They are referred to as "Spiders".

Special Purchase and Resale Agreements (SPRAs)
An open-market operation used by the Bank of Canada to relieve undesired upward pressure on overnight financing rates.

Speculator
One who is prepared to accept calculated risks in the marketplace. Objectives are usually short to medium-term capital gain, as opposed to regular income and safety of principal, the prime objectives of the conservative investor.

S&P/TSX Composite Index
A benchmark used to measure the performance of the broad Canadian equity market.

Split Shares
A type of **common share** that has been split into two components. The **dividend** payments are directed to the equity dividend share, while the capital gain potential is assigned to the capital share. Also known as **structured preferreds** and **equity dividend shares**.

Sponsoring Self-Regulatory Organization (SSRO)
An SRO that sponsors the **Canadian Investor Protection Fund**. The SSROs are IIROC, the TSX Group of Companies, and the Bourse de Montréal.

Spot Price
The market price of a commodity or financial instrument that is available for immediate delivery.

Spousal RRSP
A special type of RRSP to which one spouse contributes to a plan registered in the beneficiary spouse's name. The contributed funds belong to the beneficiary but the contributor receives the tax deduction. If the beneficiary removes funds from the spousal plan in the year of the contribution or in the subsequent two calendar years, the contributor must pay taxes on the withdrawn amount.

Spread
The gap between **bid** and **ask** prices in the quotation for a security. Also a term used in option trading.

SRO
Short for self regulatory organization such as the **Investment Industry Regulatory Organization of Canada** and the principal stock exchanges.

Standard Deviation
A statistical measure of risk. The larger the standard deviation, the greater the volatility of returns and therefore the greater the risk.

Standard Trading Unit
A regular trading unit which has uniformly been decided upon by the stock exchanges, in most cases it is 100 shares, but this can vary depending on the price of the stock.

Statement of Cash Flow
A financial statement which provides information as to how a company generated and spent its cash during the year. Assists users of financial statements in evaluating the company's ability to generate cash internally, repay debts, reinvest and pay dividends to shareholders.

Statement of Material Facts
A document presenting the relevant facts about a company and compiled in connection with an underwriting or secondary distribution of its shares. It is used only when the shares underwritten or distributed are listed on a recognized stock exchange and takes the place of a prospectus in such cases.

Stock
Ownership interest in a corporation's that represents a claim on its earnings and assets.

Stock Dividend
A pro rata payment to common shareholders of additional common stock. Such payment increases the number of shares each holder owns but does not alter a shareholder's proportional ownership of the company.

Stock Exchange
A marketplace where buyers and sellers of securities meet to trade with each other and where prices are established according to laws of supply and demand.

Stock Savings Plan
Some provinces allow individual residents of the particular province a deduction or tax credit for provincial income tax purposes on investments made in certain prescribed vehicles. The credit or deduction is a percentage figure based on the value of investment.

Stock Split
An increase in a corporation's number of shares outstanding without any change in the shareholders' equity or market value. When a stock reaches a high price making it illiquid or difficult to trade, management may split the stock to get the price into a more marketable trading range. For example, an investor owns one **standard trading unit** of a stock that now trades at $70 each (portfolio value is $7,000). Management splits the stock 2:1. The investor would now own 200 new shares at a market value, all things being equal, of $35 each, for a portfolio value of $7,000.

Stop Buy Orders
An order to buy a security only after it has reached a certain price. This may be used to protect a short position or to ensure that a stock is purchased while its price is rising. According to TSX rules these orders become **limit orders** when the stop price is reached.

Stop Loss Orders
The opposite of a **stop buy order**. An order to sell a security after its price falls to a certain amount, thus limiting the loss or protecting a paper profit. According to TSX rules these orders become **limit orders** when the stop price is reached.

Stop Orders
Orders that are used to buy or sell after a stock has reached a certain price. See **Stop Buy Orders**, **Stop Loss Orders**.

Strategic Asset Allocation
An asset allocation strategy that rebalances investment portfolios regularly to maintain a consistent long-term mix.

© CSI GLOBAL EDUCATION INC. (2008)

Street Name
Securities registered in the name of an investment dealer or its nominee, instead of the name of the real or beneficial owner, are said to be "in street name." Certificates so registered are known as street certificates.

Strike Price
The price, as specified in an option contract, at which the underlying security will be purchased in the case of a **call** or sold in the case of a **put**. See also **Exercise Price**.

Strip Bonds or Zero Coupon Bonds
Usually high quality federal or provincial government bonds originally issued in **bearer** form, where some or all of the interest **coupons** have been detached. The bond principal and any remaining coupons (the residue) then trade separately from the strip of detached coupons, both at substantial discounts from par.

Structural Unemployment
Amount of unemployment that remains in an economy even when the economy is strong. Also known as the natural **unemployment rate**, the full employment unemployment rate, or the non-accelerating inflation rate of unemployment (NAIRU).

Structured Preferreds
See **Equity Dividend Shares**.

Subordinate Debenture
A type of junior **debenture**. Subordinate indicates that another debenture ranks ahead in terms of a claim on assets and profits.

Subscription or Exercise Price
The price at which a right or **warrant** holder would pay for a new share from the company. With options the equivalent would be the **strike** price.

Subsidiary
Company which is controlled by another company usually through its ownership of the majority of shares.

Suitability
A registrant's major concern in making investment recommendations. All information about a client and a security must be analyzed to determine if an investment is suitable for the client in accounts where a suitability exemption does not apply.

Superficial Losses
Occur when an investment is sold and then repurchased at any time in a period that is 30 days before or after the sale.

Supply-Side Economics
An economic theory whereby changes in tax rates exert important effects over supply and spending decisions in the economy. According to this theory, reducing both government spending and taxes provides the stimulus for economic expansion.

Support Level
A price level at which a security stops falling because the number of investors willing to buy the security is greater than the number of investors wishing to sell the security.

Surrender Value
The cash value of an insurance contract as of the date that the policy is being redeemed. This amount is equal to the market value of the **segregated fund**, less any applicable sales charges or administrative fees.

Suspension of Trading
An interruption in trading imposed on a company if their financial condition does not meet an exchange's requirements for continued trading or if the company fails to comply with the terms of its listing agreement.

Swap
An over-the-counter forward agreement involving a series of cash flows exchanged between two parties on specified future dates.

Sweetener
A feature included in the terms of a new issue of **debt** or **preferred** shares to make the issue more attractive to initial investors. Examples include **warrants** and/or **common** shares sold with the issue as a unit or a **convertible** or **extendible** or **retractable** feature.

Syndicate
A group of investment dealers who together underwrite and distribute a new issue of securities or a large block of an outstanding issue.

System for Electronic Disclosure by Insiders (SEDI)
SEDI facilitates the filing and public dissemination of insider reports in electronic format via the Internet.

System for Electronic Document Analysis and Retrieval (SEDAR)
SEDAR facilitates the electronic filing of securities information as required by the securities regulatory agencies in Canada and allows for the public dissemination of information collected in the filing process

Systematic Risk
A non-controllable, non-diversifiable risk that is common to all investments within a given asset class. With equities it is called **market** risk, with fixed income securities it would be **interest rate** risk.

Systematic Withdrawal Plan
A plan that enables set amounts to be withdrawn from a **mutual fund** or a segregated fund on a regular basis.

T3 Form
Referred to as a Statement of Trust Income Allocations and Designations. When a mutual fund is held outside a registered plan, unitholders of an unincorporated fund is sent a T3 form by the respective fund.

T4 Form
Referred to as a Statement of Remuneration Paid. A T4 form is issued annually by employers to employees reporting total compensation for the calendar year. Employers have until the end of February to submit T4 forms to employees for the previous calendar year.

T5 Form
Referred to as a Statement of Investment Income. When a mutual fund is held outside a registered plan, shareholders are sent a T3 form by the respective fund.

Tactical Asset Allocation
An **asset allocation** strategy that involves adjusting a portfolio to take advantage of perceived inefficiencies in the prices of securities in different asset classes or within sectors.

Takeover Bid
An offer made to security holders of a company to purchase voting securities of the company which, with the offeror's already owned securities, will in total exceed 20% of the outstanding voting securities of the company. For federally incorporated companies, the equivalent requirement is more than 10% of the outstanding voting shares of the target company.

© CSI GLOBAL EDUCATION INC. (2008)

Tax Loss Selling
Selling a security for the sole purpose of generating a loss for tax purposes. There may be times when this strategy is advantageous but investment principles should not be ignored.

T-Bills
See **Treasury bills.**

Technical Analysis
A method of market and security analysis that studies investor attitudes and psychology as revealed in charts of stock price movements and trading volumes to predict future price action.

Term Insurance
A type of insurance policy that pays a death benefit if the insured dies within the given contracted period. It is sometimes called **pure insurance** as it does not have a savings component and is put in place strictly for insurance purposes.

Term to Maturity
The length of time that a **segregated fund** policy must be held in order to be eligible for the **maturity guarantee.** Normally, except in the event of the death of the **annuitant**, the term to maturity of a segregated-fund policy is 10 years.

Thin Market
A market in which there are comparatively few bids to buy or offers to sell or both. The phrase may apply to a single security or to the entire stock market. In a thin market, price fluctuations between transactions are usually larger than when the market is liquid. A thin market in a particular stock may reflect lack of interest in that issue, or a limited supply of the stock.

Tilting Yield Curve
The yield curve that results from a decline in long-term bond yields while short-term rates are rising.

Time to Expiry
The number of days or months or years until expiry of an option or other derivative instrument.

Time Value
The amount, if any, by which the current market price of a **right, warrant** or **option** exceeds its **intrinsic value.**

Time-Weighted Rate of Return (TWRR)
A measure of return calculated by averaging the return for each subperiod in which a cash flow occurs into a return for a reporting period.

Timely Disclosure
An obligation imposed by securities administrators on companies, their officers and directors to release promptly to the news media any favourable or unfavourable corporate information which is of a material nature. Broad dissemination of this news allows non-insiders to trade the company's securities with the same knowledge about the company as insiders themselves. See also **Continuous Disclosure.**

Tombstone Advertisements
A written advertisement placed by the investment bankers in a public offering of securities as a matter of record once the deal has been completed.

Top-Down Approach
A type of fundamental analysis. First, general trends in the economy are analyzed. This information is then combined with industries and companies within those industries that should benefit from the general trends identified.

Toronto Stock Exchange (TSX)
The largest stock exchange in Canada with over 1,700 companies listed on the exchange.

Trade-Weighted Exchange Rate
Rate produced by the Bank of Canada that measures the Canadian dollar's movements against ten major currencies.

Trading Unit
Describes the size or the amount of the underlying asset represented by one option contract. In North America, all exchange-traded options have a trading unit of 100 shares.

Trailer Fee
Fee that a **mutual fund** manager may pay to the individual or organization that sold the fund for providing services such as investment advice, tax guidance and financial statements to investors. The fee is paid annually and continues for as long as the investor holds shares in the fund.

Transaction Date
The date on which the purchase or sale of a security takes place.

Transfer Agent
An agent, usually a trust company, appointed by a corporation to maintain shareholder records, including purchases, sales, and account balances. The transfer agent may also be responsible for distributing dividend cheques.

Treasury Bills
Short-term government debt issued in denominations ranging from $1,000 to $1,000,000. Treasury bills do not pay interest, but are sold at a discount and mature at par (100% of **face value**). The difference between the purchase price and par at maturity represents the lender's (purchaser's) income in lieu of interest. In Canada, such gain is taxed as interest income in the purchaser's hands.

Treasury Shares
Authorized but unissued stock of a company or previously issued shares that have been re-acquired by the corporation. The amount still represents part of those issued but is not included in the number of shares outstanding. These shares may be resold or used as part of the option package for management. Treasury shares do not have voting rights nor are they entitled to dividends.

Trend
Shows the general movement or direction of securities prices. The long-term price or trading volume of a particular security is either up, down or sideways.

Trust Deed (Bond Contract)
This is the formal document that outlines the agreement between the **bond** issuer and the bondholders. It outlines such things as the **coupon** rate, if interest is paid semi-annually and when, and any other terms and conditions between both parties.

Trustee
For bondholders, usually a trust company appointed by the company to protect the security behind the bonds and to make certain that all covenants of the trust deed relating to the bonds are honoured. For a **segregated fund**, the trustee administers the assets of a **mutual fund** on behalf of the investors.

© CSI GLOBAL EDUCATION INC. (2008)

TSX Venture Exchange
Canada's public venture marketplace, the result of the merger of the Vancouver and Alberta Stock Exchanges in 1999.

Two-Way Security
A security, usually a **debenture** or **preferred** share, which is **convertible** into or exchangeable for another security (usually common shares) of the same company. Also indirectly refers to the possibility of profiting in the future from upward movements in the underlying common shares as well as receiving in the interim interest or dividend payments.

Underlying Security
The security upon which a derivative contract, such as an option, is based. For example, the ABC June 35 call options are based on the underlying security ABC.

Underwriting
The purchase for resale of a security issue by one or more investment dealers or underwriters. The formal agreements pertaining to such a transaction are called underwriting agreements.

Unemployment Rate
The percentage of the work force that is looking for work but unable to find jobs.

Unit
Two or more corporate securities (such as **preferred** shares and **warrants**) offered for sale to the public at a single, combined price.

Unit Value
The value of one unit of a **segregated fund**. The units have no legal status, and are simply an administrative convenience used to determine the income attributable to contract holders and the level of benefits payable to beneficiaries.

Universal Market Integrity Rules (UMIR)
A common set of trading rules that are applied in all markets in Canada. UMIR are designed to promote fair and orderly markets.

Unlisted
A security not listed on a stock exchange but traded on the **over-the-counter** market.

Unlisted Market
See also **dealer market**.

Valuation Day
The day on which the assets of a **segregated fund** are valued, based on its total assets less liabilities. Most funds are valued at the end of every business day.

Value Manager
A manager that takes a research intensive approach to finding undervalued securities.

Value Ratios
Financial ratios that show the investor the worth of the company's shares or the return on owning them.

Variable Rate Preferreds
A type of preferred share that pays dividends in amounts that fluctuate to reflect changes in interest rates. If interest rates rise, so will dividend payments, and vice versa.

Variance
Another measure of **risk** often used interchangeably with volatility. The greater the variance of possible outcomes the greater the risk.

Vested
The employee's right to the employer contributions made on his or her behalf during the employee's period of enrollment.

Volatility
A measure of the amount of change in the daily price of a security over a specified period of time. Usually given as the standard deviation of the daily price changes of that security on an annual basis.

Voting Right
The stockholder's right to vote in the affairs of the company. Most **common** shares have one vote each. **Preferred** stock usually has the right to vote only when its **dividends** are in **arrears**. The right to vote may be delegated by the shareholder to another person. See also **Proxy**.

Voting Trust
An arrangement to place the control of a company in the hands of certain managers for a given period of time, or until certain results have been achieved, by shareholders surrendering their voting rights to a trustee for a specified period of time.

Waiting Period
The period of time between the issuance of a receipt for a preliminary prospectus and receipt for a final prospectus from the securities administrators.

Warrant
A certificate giving the holder the right to purchase securities at a stipulated price within a specified time limit. Warrants are usually issued with a new issue of securities as an inducement or sweetener to investors to buy the new issue.

Working Capital
Current assets minus **current liabilities**. This figure is an indication of the company's ability to meet its short-term debts.

Working Capital Ratio
Current assets of a company divided by its **current liabilities**.

Wrap Account
Also known as a wrap fee program. A type of fully discretionary account where a single annual fee, based on the account's total assets, is charged, instead of commissions and advice and service charges being levied separately for each transaction. The account is then managed separately from all other wrap accounts, but is kept consistent with a model portfolio suitable to clients with similar objectives.

Writer
The seller of either a **call** or **put option**. The option writer receives payment, called a premium. The writer in then obligated to buy (in the case of a put) or sell (in the case of a call) the underlying security at a specified price, within a certain period of time, if called upon to do so.

Yield – Bond & Stock
Return on an investment. A stock yield is calculated by expressing the annual dividend as a percentage of the stock's current market price. A bond yield is more complicated, involving annual interest payments plus amortizing the difference between its current market price and par value over the bond's life. See also **Current Yield**.

Yield Curve
A graph showing the relationship between yields of bonds of the same quality but different **maturities**. A normal yield curve is upward sloping depicting the fact that short-term money usually has a lower yield than longer-term funds. When short-term funds are more expensive than longer term funds the yield curve is said to be inverted.

© CSI GLOBAL EDUCATION INC. (2008)

Yield to Maturity

The rate of return investors would receive if they purchased a **bond** today and held it to **maturity**. Yield to maturity is considered a long term bond yield expressed as an annual rate.

Yield Spread

The difference between the yields on two debt securities, normally expressed in basis points. In general, the greater the difference in the risk of the two securities, the larger the spread.

Zero Coupon Bonds

See **Strip Bonds**.

© CSI GLOBAL EDUCATION INC. (2008)

Selected Web Sites

If you are connected to the Internet, you have access to all kinds of financial information. This list is far from complete. Many of these sites will have links to other related sites. Remember to type the site "address" exactly as listed. Some sites track usage by asking you for a password. Do not confuse the need to register and provide a password with the necessity to become a subscriber. Some sites offer a limited amount of information for free and require you to register and pay a fee before you can access more detailed information.

© CSI GLOBAL EDUCATION INC. (2008)

BANKING

Canadian Bankers Association: www.cba.ca

GOVERNMENT SOURCES

Bank of Canada: www.bankofcanada.ca or www.banqueducanada.ca

Canada Customs and Revenue Agency: www.ccra-adrc.gc.ca

Canadian Investment and Savings: www.cis-pec.gc.ca

Financial Industry Regulatory Authority: www.finra.org

Industry Canada: www.ic.gc.ca

Office of the Superintendent of Financial Institutions: www.osfi-bsif.gc.ca

Statistics Canada: www.statcan.ca

U.S. Securities and Exchange Commission: www.sec.gov

HEDGE FUNDS

Canadian Hedge Fund Watch: www.canadianhedgewatch.com/

Credit Suisse Tremont Hedge Index: www.hedgeindex.com

EHedge.com: www.e-hedge.com

Greenwich Alternative Investments: www.greenwichai.com/

Hedge Fund Association: www.thehfa.org/

Hedge Fund Centre: www.hedgefundcenter.com/

HedgeFund Intelligence: www.hedgefundintelligence.com/

INSURANCE

Financial Advisors Association of Canada (ADVOCIS): www.advocis.com

Insurance Canada: www.insurance-canada.ca

© CSI GLOBAL EDUCATION INC. (2008)

INVESTMENT ORGANIZATIONS

Canadian Deposit Insurance Corporation: www.cdic.ca

Canadian Derivatives Clearing Corporation: www.cdcc.ca

Canadian Investor Protection Fund (CIPF): www.cipf.ca

Canadian Society of Technical Analysts: www.csta.org

CDS Clearing and Depository Services Inc: www.cds.ca

CSI Global Education inc.: www.csi.ca

EDGAR: www.edgar-online.com

International Organization of Securities Commissions: www.iosco.org

Investment Industry Regulatory Organization of Canada: www.iiroc.ca

Mutual Fund Dealers Association of Canada: www.mfda.ca

North American Securities Administrators Association: www.nasaa.org

System for Electronic Document Analysis and Retrieval: www.sedar.com

World Federation of Exchanges: www.world-exchanges.org

INVESTOR SERVICES

Advice for Investors: www.adviceforinvestors.com

BigCharts: www.bigcharts.com

Canadian Financial Network: www.canadianfinance.com

Globeinvestor: www.globeinvestor.com

Investorwords: www.investorwords.com

Investopedia: www.investopedia.com

iShares: ca.ishares.com

Quicken Financial Network: www.quicken.ca

Stockhouse: www.stockhouse.ca

Yahoo Finance: www.ca.finance.yahoo.com

© CSI GLOBAL EDUCATION INC. (2008)

MUTUAL FUNDS

Fund Library: www.fundlibrary.com

Globefund: www.globefund.com

Investment Counsel: www.investment.com

Investment Funds Institute of Canada: www.ific.ca

NEWS ORGANIZATIONS AND PUBLICATIONS

Canada Newswire: www.newswire.ca

Canoe (Canadian Online Explorer): www.canoe.ca

Financial Post: www.nationalpost.com

Globe and Mail: www.theglobeandmail.com

Moneysense: www.moneysense.ca

PROVINCIAL SECURITIES ADMINISTRATORS

Alberta: www.albertasecurities.com

British Columbia: www.bcsc.bc.ca

Manitoba: www.msc.gov.mb.ca

Ontario: www.osc.gov.on.ca

Québec: www.lautorite.qc.ca

New Brunswick: www.nbsc-cvmnb.ca/nbsc

Newfoundland and Labrador: www.gs.gov.nl.ca

Northwest Territories: www.justice.gov.nt.ca/securitiesregistry

Nova Scotia: www.gov.ns.ca/nssc

Prince Edward Island: www.gov.pe.ca/securities

Saskatchewan: www.sfsc.gov.sk.ca

Territory of Nunavut: www.gov.nu.ca

Yukon: www.community.gov.yk.ca/corp/secureinvest.html

© CSI GLOBAL EDUCATION INC. (2008)

STOCK EXCHANGES

The American Stock Exchange: www.amex.com

CBOE: www.cboe.com

CNQ: www.cnq.ca

Bourse de Montréal: www.m-x.ca

Ice Futures Canada: www.theice.com/wce

Nasdaq: www.nasdaq.com

New York Stock Exchange: www.nyse.com

Toronto Stock Exchange: www.tsx.ca

TSX Venture Exchange: www.tsx.ca

TAXATION

Canada Customs and Revenue Agency: www.ccra-adrc.gc.ca

Canadian Tax Foundation: www.ctf.ca

Ernst & Young (Canada): www.ey.com/global/content.nsf/Canada/Home

KPMG: www.kpmg.ca

PricewaterhouseCoopers: www.pwc.com

© CSI GLOBAL EDUCATION INC. (2008)

Index

© CSI GLOBAL EDUCATION INC. (2008)

Index

© CSI GLOBAL EDUCATION INC. (2008)

C

© CSI GLOBAL EDUCATION INC. (2008)

© CSI GLOBAL EDUCATION INC. (2008)

© CSI GLOBAL EDUCATION INC. (2008)

F

© CSI GLOBAL EDUCATION INC. (2008)

© CSI GLOBAL EDUCATION INC. (2008)

N

O

© CSI GLOBAL EDUCATION INC. (2008)

© CSI GLOBAL EDUCATION INC. (2008)

Q

R

S

© CSI GLOBAL EDUCATION INC. (2008)

© CSI GLOBAL EDUCATION INC. (2008)

© CSI GLOBAL EDUCATION INC. (2008)

Z

© CSI GLOBAL EDUCATION INC. (2008)